CHANGE OF HEART
A BANTAM BOOK : 0 553 40497 0

Originally published in Great Britain by Doubleday,
a division of Transworld Publishers Ltd

PRINTING HISTORY
Doubleday edition published 1994
Bantam edition published 1995

Set in 10pt Monotype Joanna by
Phoenix Typesetting, Ilkley, West Yorkshire.

Bantam Books are published by Transworld Publishers Ltd,
61–63 Uxbridge Road, Ealing, London W5 5SA,
in Australia by Transworld Publishers (Australia) Pty. Ltd,
15–25 Helles Avenue, Moorebank, NSW 2170,
and in New Zealand by Transworld Publishers (N.Z.) Ltd,
3 William Pickering Drive, Albany, Auckland.

Printed and bound in Great Britain by
Cox & Wyman Ltd, Reading, Berks

CHANGE OF HEART

Charlotte Bingham

BANTAM BOOKS
LONDON · NEW YORK · TORONTO · SYDNEY · AUCKLAND

For my beloved partner
without whom indeed . . . . .

There is more than one reality.

Buddhist belief

Some things that happen for the first time
Seem to be happening again
And so it seems that we have met before
And laughed before
And loved before
But who knows where or when?

Lorenz Hart

Prologue

They are all around her, silent figures gathered in the half darkness, watching and waiting. He knows that they're there even though he can only hear them, their footfalls cracking sticks in the bracken, their feet padding softly over beds of leaves. He thinks he can smell them, smell the mixture of sweat and tobacco and gunpowder that a breeze carries to him, a smell that grows stronger as now they pass right by him and begin to run, and he hears their breath hard and short as the chase begins in earnest.

They are in woods lit by the pale light of a summer's sun not yet risen, its radiant fingers only just beginning to spill over the edge of the world and in the half light he can see them closing on her. They run her up against a fence which is too high for her to jump but somehow she manages to escape and starts to run along the line of the fence, ahead for a moment of her pursuers.

Now she is maddened with terror and panic-struck as she plunges through brambles which tear her and thorns which paint ribbons of blood along her back and sides. The men raise their guns, he can see the sunlight glint on the barrels and tries to call out to warn her, but no sound comes as beside him he suddenly finds a gate just where the risen sun has now entered the woods in one huge beam of clear bright light.

He opens the gate and she runs through it, into the light and is gone, vanished from the shadowy huntsmen who fade silently back into the dark woods which have spawned them.

Turning to follow her he finds he is in a garden which is fresh with a summer dew. The air is pungent with the heady scent of old-fashioned roses, filled with larksong and the music of thrushes who sing like nightingales, while a whisper of wind stirs the leaves of the great beech trees and dapples the bright water of a carp pond.

On the far side of this beautiful place is a group of deer gathered around the foot of a flight of stone steps on which stands a girl who is feeding them. She has her head down so that he cannot yet see her face and he knows she hasn't yet seen him because she doesn't look up.

But he knows her. He has this feeling that when she does finally look up he will know exactly who she is.

FIRST MOVEMENT

Introduction and Allegro

1

3rd June 1994

Freddie was still trying to find out which button to press for recording from the radio when Mrs Davies came in to tell him he was wanted on the telephone.

'Hell,' he muttered, getting up from the floor with a tangle of hi-fi wires around one foot. 'Darn it, is it urgent?'

'It seems so, Mr Jourdan,' his new housekeeper replied. 'It's a Miss Smith-Werner calling from Washington.'

It would have to be, Freddie thought as he pulled the wires from round his foot. Diane only ever called him when he was in the middle of something, and knowing how she talked now not only wouldn't he be able to record the violin concerto to which he was listening, because he had tuned in late he wouldn't even know what the music was or who was playing it.

'Hell and darnation,' he muttered again as he padded barefoot into the stone-flagged hall. 'Hell and darnation, anyway.'

'Freddie?' said a voice as he picked up the telephone.

'Hi, Diane,' he said. 'Sorry, I was just busy.'

'I guess that makes a change from sleeping, sweetheart. Every time I ring, that quaint housekeeper of yours tells me you're *asleep*. How much sleep does a person *need*, darling?'

Freddie sat himself down in one of the pair of Chippendale carvers which stood either side of the telephone table, stretched his long legs out in front of him, and hooked his spectacles into the top of his grey tee shirt.

'I *said* – how much sleep does a person need, Freddie?'

'Yes I know you did, Diane,' Freddie replied, staring up at the ornate ceiling high above him, its plasterwork picked out in pale pink and white. 'But I just can't find an answer. You know, how long is a piece of string exactly?'

'Freddie,' his fiancée sighed in reprimand at the other end. 'I was simply worried about the amount of time you were spending sleeping, *that* was all.'

'Sure you were, Diane. But isn't that what I'm here for?'

'So what in fact were you doing?'

'I was trying to find out how to work this state-of-the-art hi-fi I've rented.'

'I should get an engineer in, Freddie,' Diane laughed. 'You're the man who can't even put batteries in a torch, remember? So. Tell me about the house instead. You haven't really told me *anything* about the house yet.'

Freddie privately sighed, regretting as always Diane's habit of overemphasizing parts of her speech and invariably the wrong parts, before describing to her in some detail the handsome Queen Anne house which he had rented for his sabbatical. Like all true WASPS few things interested Diane Smith-Werner more than other people's possessions, particularly their houses. This one was built in a red brick which had now paled to a warm pink with the passing of nearly three centuries. The main house stood on four floors, only three of which were visible since the kitchens and utility floor lay out of sight in a dry moat below ground level. It was approached up a long drive lined with fine horse-chestnut trees and flanked on either side by iron-railed paddocks which ended in a broad carriage sweep in front of the house, while at the back a flight of fine stone steps led down into formal gardens originally designed and laid out, so he had already been told, by a pupil of the enchantingly nicknamed 'Capability' Brown.

'How do the gardens look now?' Diane asked. 'Seeing the house hasn't been lived in for so long.'

'The whole place is just perfect,' Freddie replied, hearing what sounded like the concerto coming to an end and holding the receiver away from his ear in a futile attempt to catch the details of the recording, but from where he stood in the large echoing hallway the announcer's voice was no more than a barely audible murmur.

'It sounds *very* grand,' he heard Diane saying. 'I *can't* wait to see it.'

'No it's a fine house, but it really isn't what you'd call grand,' Freddie said, hoping thereby to put her off. The last thing he wanted was Diane coming over anywhere in the foreseeable future.

'I've been looking at my diary, sweetheart—' she began, only for Freddie to cut her off hastily.

'No, there's no point in looking at your diary *yet*, Diane,' he said. 'Heck I've only just got here and all I want to do at the moment is crash out, hang out, chill out, blank out – I'm going to do all the outs I can think of.'

'Good,' Diane purred approvingly. 'That is exactly what I was hoping to hear. Just remember the one thing that is most definitely *out* while we're talking outs. The one thing you are *not* to do is work. You're not *even* to think about it. Is there a piano there?'

'Sure there is. Why?'

'Because you're to keep it shut and locked, that's why. You know perfectly well what the doctors said.'

'They didn't say anything about not playing the piano, Diane. At least not for pleasure.'

'They said you were to have a complete rest from everything, Freddie.'

17

Freddie closed his eyes. He hadn't forgotten what the doctors had told him, he just didn't want to be reminded of it. He knew how vital it was that he took this six-month break, but even so the thought of living all that time without working was unbearable. His work was his second nature, like breathing out and breathing in. But there was no point in remonstrating because he knew full well that work to Diane was something that began at nine and ended at five.

So to distract her he told her more about the house, about its proximity to the Malvern Hills where the famous composer Edward Elgar was said to have found so much of his inspiration, about the ornamental lake and the trout stream that ran through its grounds both of which he intended to fish, about the horses which grazed in its paddocks, the courtyard stable block and the staff cottages, the staff themselves – Mrs Davies the cook-housekeeper, Thomas the lugubrious Welshman who managed the house and the grounds, and Enid the sharp-faced endomorph who cycled up every day from the village to clean. He even recounted how just before Diane had telephoned, on only his second day in the house, the very first piece of music he'd heard when he turned on the hi-fi equipment he'd just rented had been appropriately enough Edward Elgar's *Enigma Variations* which seemed to personify the woods and the countryside by which he was now surrounded.

As he finally put down the phone he realized he'd told Diane everything that had happened to him, and indeed everything he had learned so far about the place, with only one exception. For some reason and he didn't yet know why, he had told her nothing of the white house which stood in its own grounds on a hill to the north end of the park, a small white-painted Regency house with Gothic windows which, because it stood on higher ground and was completely surrounded by a ring of mature trees, was

18

almost hidden from sight at ground level. It was known, Mrs Davies had told him when asked, as The Folly.

He hadn't told Diane about it because even after only two days at Stoke Park, he found that for some unknown reason he was already intrigued by it, and he couldn't have borne hearing Diane make one of her inevitable remarks about it – the sort of remarks she invariably made when Freddie enthused about something and she wished to cut whatever it was back down to size. If he'd tried to describe the pretty little house in the woods which so far he had only seen from his bedroom, she'd have called it something like *cute* or *perfectly Disneyesque*, immediately removing some of its magic and its mystery. So he'd left the house on the hill out of the picture he had painted for his fiancée for that very reason, and because he was determined that for as long as possible it should remain his secret.

Later that day, when Freddie was exploring the big house more fully, he found himself up in the attics on the fourth floor. From the largest of the rooms, which judging from the way it was still half furnished must have been the day nursery and which looked out down the long drive and over the parkland, he found there was a perfect view to be had of the house on the hill which half hidden away behind its belt of trees and shimmering in the summer haze looked as if it were something out of a fairy tale. How long he stared at it he had no idea, but when he came out of his reverie he found he was sitting on the window seat with his knees pulled up under his chin and his arms wrapped around his legs, still staring dreamily out across the park. Moreover the sun, which had been at about three o'clock in a cloudless sky was now much nearer four o'clock, and sure enough when he checked his watch he found he must have been sitting there for the best part of an hour.

Sitting there asleep, he decided, yet he had no recollection of taking up the position in which he now found himself nor of waking up. He didn't feel he had been sleeping either because he had no sense of weariness and none whatsoever of that feeling of slight disorientation people admit to when they find themselves awakening from an unexpected sleep. Instead he felt as he had felt when he'd successfully undergone hypnotherapy to conquer his fear of flying, as if his bodily mechanism had simply been switched off for a given period and then switched back on. At the time his therapist had described it as like being in a spell, just as he imagined ancient enchantments to have been, namely a form of deep hypnosis.

Freddie would have preferred to put this unfathomable slumber down to delayed jet lag had he not remembered that before flying he had taken a recommended dose of melatonin to insure that the body's biorhythms remained undisturbed by the time change. Besides on the many occasions when he had previously been jet lagged he'd known it, and he'd certainly never before found himself just dropping off into an inexplicable sleep with no recollection of having done so. So something else had happened to him, something else must somehow have mesmerized him and induced a kind of trance. Maybe some unseen siren had sung to him, Freddie grinned to himself, in an effort to lure him on to her rocky island. Or perhaps it was that odd little house over there in the far woods. Perhaps it was enchanted, and while he had been sitting there looking at it, he had been caught up in its spell. In fact the more he looked at it the more he got a growing feeling that his lost hour was all to do with the house, however absurd he knew that seemed, because he felt it was a house he already knew which, of course, was impossible because he had never visited this part of England before in his entire life.

So why, he wondered, this feeling of *déjà vu*? Why this bewildering feeling of familiarity?

As if a closer sight of it might help, he suddenly found himself hurrying off to fetch a pair of powerful field glasses he'd seen hanging downstairs in a cloakroom and then running back up the two floors taking the stairs two at a time in his rush to see what was actually there.

There was no visible sign of life, although through the field glasses he could see the place was quite obviously immaculately maintained, with its lawns freshly mown and the earth in its full-flowering rose borders recently turned over. To one side he could quite clearly see a large ornamental pond decoratively set with shrubs and small trees, which he stared at hard and long because he again felt that he knew it – yet he didn't know from where. Even so he was certain that the path at the end of the two-tiered lawns led down towards a gate which itself opened onto a beech wood, although he couldn't see on account of the screen of trees which backed the property. But nowhere was there any other human being to be seen, neither at any of the windows nor anywhere in the gardens.

Then just as he went to put his field glasses down he saw something. Behind the shrubs which surrounded the pond he caught sight of a slowly moving shadowy form. Refocusing the glasses he trained them exactly on that spot, just where he could see the branches of a bush still moving quite vigorously as if someone was tugging at them.

Seconds later the culprit came into view, and the moment Freddie saw it the back of his neck prickled and his hands began to shake, for there standing looking out across the lawn chewing the leaves it had just plucked from the branches of the shrub it had been attacking was a deer.

But that wasn't what took his breath away. What made him look so hard and look again was the fact that the deer was white. Just as he remembered from somewhere before.

2

As Mrs Davies served Freddie his second unappetizing dinner in a row, this time one of cold ham, chicken and an undressed salad of lettuce, tomato, hard-boiled egg and beetroot, he asked her what she knew about the white house at the far end of the park.

'It belongs to this house, Mr Jourdan,' she explained, setting down a full bottle of Heinz mayonnaise beside him, 'as far as I understand it and I'm relatively new to these parts. Meant to have been built as some sort of music room. Somewhere where the family of the day could go and play and not disturb anybody. Only wish I could have afforded such a thing. You couldn't hear yourself think when our son was growing up, not once he started playing the electric guitar. You never heard such a noise.'

'Who lives there now?' Freddie wanted to know, putting a surreptitious finger in the salad and finding the lettuce to be warm. 'Is it still family owned?'

'Again I can't be too sure, Mr Jourdan, not knowing all the ins and outs, but as far as I hear, the family haven't used it since some time in the seventies. Not to live in, that is. It was let for a long time, but now it's rented out summer only. Now is everything all right, Mr Jourdan? I do hope the food's to your liking. Because if it isn't you just have to say.'

Freddie took off his glasses and frowned then put them back on again, pretending to take a closer look at the salad.

'I was wondering if you have any oil, Mrs Davies?' he said as quietly as he could, trying to make it sound like an afterthought rather than an absolute necessity.

'Oil, Mr Jourdan?' Mrs Davies repeated. 'Whatever would you be wanting oil for while you're eating?'

'No no, oil for the salad, Mrs Davies,' Freddie said, removing his glasses once more and scratching his mop of long dark brown hair with one sidepiece. 'Olive oil, you know? And wine vinegar and maybe some black pepper? I think maybe that's what this salad might need.'

Mrs Davies stared at Freddie as if he was speaking in a foreign tongue, which Freddie supposed now he came to consider what she had prepared for him so far, he undoubtedly was. He had heard plenty about old-fashioned English domestic cooking but this was his first experience of it and for an expert cook such as Freddie it was not a happy one.

'Come along, Mrs Davies,' he said getting up from the table. 'Let's go have a look in the pantry.'

A thorough search of the cupboards in the larder revealed some of the ingredients which Freddie required, and with the addition of some spring onions, green peppers, bottled olives and a tin of anchovies, Freddie remade the salad and then proceeded to demonstrate to the nonplussed Mrs Davies how to make a proper French dressing.

'You're obviously a bit of a cook then,' she observed finally, as he tossed the salad.

'It's my hobby,' Freddie replied.

'Lucky you,' Mrs Davies said with a sigh. 'I'd far rather cook as a hobby than a job.'

'I love cooking. Cooking is like love. You have to enter into it with abandon, Mrs Davies. Or not at all.'

Contrary to what he was expecting, Mrs Davies gave a great guffaw of laughter at this remark.

'Yes. Well – that puts a different complexion on it altogether, Mr Jourdan!' she said. 'Oh yes, I'll remember that all right next time I'm making a spotted dick!'

24

Freddie grinned and pinching the rest of the new potatoes Mrs Davies had cooked and all but ruined, he set about redeeming what was left of them with a parsley-and-butter dressing.

'Tell me more about the little white house,' he said, as he finished off his act of redemption.

'The Folly, Mr Jourdan. Least to give it its proper name.'

'I take it someone's staying there, yes? I mean the gardens look awful neat.'

'The gardens are always done come what may, Mr Jourdan. All the year round no matter what. The family have always insisted on that.'

'But I couldn't actually see any sign of life,' Freddie said, setting the freshly made dishes on a tray which Mrs Davies took from him, following him back to the dining room.

'You been up there already then. Pretty little place, isn't it?'

'Utterly charming. But it appears there's no-one there at present?'

His housekeeper set the tray down on the table without replying while Freddie retook his seat. As he helped himself to a glass of Chablis from the bottle he'd already opened, Mrs Davies wiped both her hands down the front of her floral apron, preparatory to leaving.

'Right,' she said, taking the wine bottle and placing it out of reach on the sideboard. 'Then if you've got everything you want, Mr Jourdan—'

'You still haven't told me whether or not anyone's living there, Mrs Davies,' he reminded her, pointing out of the window ahead of him. 'In The Folly. I think there has to be.'

'What makes you think there might be, Mr Jourdan? As I said, the gardens are always done on a regular basis, and—'

'Because I can see a plume of smoke from behind the trees. Look.'

Where Freddie was pointing, against the evening blue of the summer sky a faint curl of smoke could be seen rising up from the house on the distant hill.

'Most likely the gardener,' Mrs Davies remarked. 'Most likely the gardener lighting a bonfire.'

'I suppose so,' Freddie replied, sensing his housekeeper's evasion. 'I guess it has to be far too warm an evening for anyone to be lighting a fire in the house.'

When he had finished picking his way through his now almost palatable meal, instead of retiring to the drawing room and listening to music on the now fully operational hi-fi, Freddie sat on at the dinner table watching the column of smoke which was now rising steadily and more thickly from behind the ring of trees.

He knew it wasn't a bonfire because bonfire smoke billows in clouds and soon dies down, while this smoke had risen in a steady plume all evening, just like smoke which rises from a chimney. This suspicion was confirmed the moment Freddie went upstairs to the attics and, looking out once more across the parkland through his purloined binoculars, saw against the evening sky a line of fire-smoke curling clearly up from one chimney. He sat watching it in fascination, as if it might be a signal to him from the mysterious occupant of the house.

He carried on watching until the evening finally turned to night and the house disappeared into the darkness.

Unable to contain his curiosity any longer, the following morning he made his way across the parkland, out of the back gate and climbed up the road which he imagined would lead him to The Folly. At first he was unable to find a way in since the entrance was unmarked by either a sign or a gateway and thus was all but invisible. Finally he found a single track leading off the lane up which he had climbed from the back gate of the park, and which must have been built originally purely as a service road for the house. In fact so anonymous was the first part of the entrance to The Folly that anyone ignorant of the fact that there was a house there would think it was simply a path leading into beech woods.

Knowing better, Freddie sunk his hands deep in the back pockets of his chinos and trying to look as casual as he could, mooched up the unmade road for a good hundred yards until it divided into two. There were car tracks up both, and guessing wrong first time Freddie took the left-hand turn and a hundred or so yards further on came to a dead end where the path simply ran out. Turning back and trying the other route he finally arrived outside a pair of high ornamental iron gates. They were closed and when he tried them he found they were not only closed, they were also locked. On the right-hand stone pillar was a small dark green professionally painted sign which read:

PRIVATE
Visitors strictly by
appointment only.

Below the notice there was a brass grill, and underneath that a bell. After a moment's contemplation while he stared at the bell wondering who or what it was going to conjure up Freddie pressed it, then stood back and waited. Through the gates and just beyond the turn of the drive he could see part of the front of the house, the rest of it being half hidden by the shrubbery and trees. But above the trees the plume of smoke still rose from the chimney, even though it was now nearly eleven o'clock in the morning on a hot June day.

He tried the bell again, having waited fully two minutes for an answer. On this occasion after only half the time a voice suddenly spoke to him through the grill. It was a woman's voice, not young and definitely not welcoming.

'Yes?'

'Oh. Good morning. My name is Frederick Jourdan.'

'Yes?'

'Yes. I've – I've taken Stoke Park for six months. For a sabbatical. Maybe you heard?'

'And you obviously can't have read the notice, Mr Jourdan. The one right in front of you.'

'No, I read it all right. I read it as I was waiting. But then I thought since we were kind of neighbours—'

'You don't have an appointment.'

'No, that is correct.' Freddie took his glasses off, checked them for invisible dirt, and then put them back again as he spoke. 'That is perfectly correct I do not have an appointment. But as I was saying I thought that since we're neighbours I'd come up and introduce myself.'

'I'm sorry, Mr Jourdan, but admission is strictly by appointment only,' the voice said. 'Good day.'

'Now wait a minute! I'm only trying to be neighbourly! Are you there? I only wanted to call and say hello!'

But the voice behind the grill was now silent and stayed that way, despite Freddie trying the bell again in a vain attempt to call it back.

'Okay,' he muttered to himself as he made his way back down the driveway. 'Fine. You want to play hard to get whoever you are, then that's fine by me.'

He found Mrs Davies down in the kitchens when he arrived back, sitting at the long scrubbed wooden table sharing a pot of tea with Enid.

'Lunch made, Mrs Davies?' Freddie asked, still feeling faintly exasperated after his unsuccessful call. 'I like to eat not much later than one as a rule.'

'Lunch is all done, Mr Jourdan,' Mrs Davies replied. 'And you're all right for time, because it's still not gone five to.'

The women sipped their tea and watched in what seemed to him to be a critical silence as he unpacked the dozen or so bottles of wine he'd bought in Worcester where he'd gone to shop after his abortive call at The Folly.

'So what's on the menu today then?' he asked, putting two bottles of Pouilly-Fuissé in the large old-fashioned refrigerator.

'What's the recipe today, Raymondo?' Enid said for what seemed to Freddie no good reason at all.

'I've done you a nice tongue salad, and a gooseberry flan with custard,' Mrs Davies replied. 'And a nice shepherd's pie for tonight.'

'I don't like tongue, Mrs Davies,' Freddie said. 'I don't even much like the word, let alone the taste. And what in heaven's name is a shepherd's pie?'

After his housekeeper had described the dish she was intending to make him for dinner, Freddie told her kindly but firmly that they were going to have to discuss menus, explaining that he had very particular tastes.

'In fact if it's all the same to you,' he added, 'I'd like to help out with the cooking. I'll design the menus, you can help me prepare, and I'll cook.'

'Mr Jourdan is a bit of a cook, Enid,' Mrs Davies told the cleaner who was busy pouring herself yet another cup of tea. 'He likes to cook as a hobby.'

'It wouldn't be my idea of a hobby,' Enid said, eating the last of the cookies. 'My idea of a hobby's not doing nothing.'

To prevent himself from laughing out loud, Freddie busied himself with opening a bottle of good dry sherry and pouring a glass, held it up to the light to admire its amber glow.

'Now then,' he said, eyeing the two women through the glass of sherry. 'There is someone in The Folly. Because I called there before I went into the town. I know there's someone there because they spoke to me through the entryphone.'

As he sipped his drink he watched attentively as the pair of them first eyed each other in silence and then carefully eyed him.

'Yes. Well time I was going, Freda,' Enid said getting up from the table. 'Leonard won't get no dinner otherwise.'

'Come on, ladies!' Freddie laughed. 'Who precisely is the mysterious occupant? What's the big secret for heaven's sake?'

'I really must be off, Freda,' Enid repeated, stuffing her last bit of cookie into her mouth and hanging her housecoat on the back of the door. 'If I'm late again it'll be more than my life's worth.'

As the cleaner departed Mrs Davies tried her best to get Freddie to take his drink upstairs while she prepared his lunch, but he wasn't in the mood to be fobbed off. Far from deterring him, the fact that no-one would give him one straight answer about the occupant of The Folly only doubled his interest.

'Oh for goodness sake so what if there is someone up there now, Mr Jourdan?' Mrs Davies finally relented. 'I don't really see what concern it is of ours.'

'My concern is purely a neighbourly one, Mrs Davies,' Freddie replied, pretending that was the sum of his concern. 'That's the American way when we move into a new neighbourhood. We like calling on each other, and introducing ourselves.'

'Don't misunderstand me, Mr Jourdan,' Mrs Davies said as she ladled out onto his plate a portion of cold mashed potato. 'What I meant by it not needing concern you was because it won't, you see. It won't concern you because the person staying up there in The Folly won't concern herself with you. She don't with anyone, not ever. She comes down with her companion or housekeeper or what-have-you for the summer – in fact it was most likely her what spoke to you this morning, her housekeeper or whatever. Anyhow that's the way it is. She comes down here for the summer from June through August, no-one sees her, she don't see no-one, and then she goes back to wherever she come from again. And that's the way it is. That's how it's always been.'

'For how long is it "how it's always been", Mrs Davies?' Freddie asked, finding himself following her back upstairs once again to the dining room. 'And is this person young, or what? If young, how young? If old, how old?'

'I've only been here two years, Mr Jourdan,' his housekeeper told him as they made their way through the pass door. 'So all I can say is like that's the way it's been ever since I been here. I'm not from these parts, you see. After my husband died I come down from London when I got this job. So all I know is what I seen, Mr Jourdan. Which isn't much over two years, as you may imagine.'

'Someone must know who she is, Mrs Davies. Whoever is staying up there in The Folly can't be a total mystery to everyone.'

'I never heard the matter discussed, truth to tell,' his housekeeper replied. 'That's how people are round these parts. Not like in the city where everyone's after everyone else's business. No I never heard the matter ever really being discussed. Not as such. Now if there's anything else you'll be wanting, you just ring the bell.'

The next time Diane rang, Freddie told her nothing of the mystery in which he seemed bent on involving himself, and which were he to admit it was mostly of his own making since the occupant of The Folly appeared to be of no real interest to any of his staff. The reason Freddie chose not to tell his fiancée was that Diane was possessive enough at the best of times, and the very thought that there was a mysterious single woman living in a romantic white house within the boundaries of Stoke Park would undoubtedly have been enough to get her on the next plane over.

'God I hate the telephone,' she said, suddenly halfway through their conversation.

'Why's that, Diane? You've never hated using it.'

'I hate it when I'm talking to you because I can't see what you're doing. What you're thinking.'

And that was just as we. Freddie thought, since his thoughts were elsewhere, across the parkland and in a garden which lay circled by beech trees. He talked but he didn't have an idea what he was saying, but whatever it was was making Diane laugh which soon brought Freddie back to earth because the one thing Freddie really couldn't stand about Diane was her laugh. That and the way she was forever rearranging his unarrangeable hair. But her laugh was the really bad thing. She didn't laugh breathing out as did most people, laughed breathing in, sounding consequently as if she was in distress rather than having fun. As he listened to her still laughing away, Freddie really wasn't at all sure he could spend the rest of his life living with someone who made such a terrible sound every time she found something funny.

'I won't be able to call you this time tomorrow, Freddie darling,' she was saying now she'd stopped creaking. 'I'm in court defending this case I told you about. The molestation case? Which looks as if it'll run and run. But I promise I'll try and call you the moment I'm home.'

'Don't,' Freddie said, almost too quickly. 'What I mean is you don't have to call me every day, Diane. In the time I'm going to be here, that'd work out at around two hundred calls and you'd be bored stiff of me by the time I get home.'

'In your dreams. The day you ever bore me Freddie, you sweet man, it'll be in your dreams. Talking of which, how are your dreams?'

'Why should you ask that?' Freddie asked quickly,

without beginning to understand why he found himself suddenly on the defensive.

'Because I wanted to know, Freddie, that's why. Have you been having any more of those dreams? About—'

'No, I haven't,' he cut in. 'Since getting here I've been sleeping – and dreaming – like a baby. I haven't had one bad dream.'

'That's great. That's the whole idea of your – your sabbatical. Right? To catch up on some sleep. Unravel the famous sleeve of care. So keep on sleeping well, sweetheart. And pleasant dreams. I love you.'

'Okay. Me too, Diane.'

He couldn't lie. He couldn't tell her he loved her, he could only make it sound as if he did. He couldn't tell Diane he didn't love her any more when he knew he didn't, because he didn't yet know why.

That night as he lies in bed with the curtains wide open and the bright moon shining he thinks about dreaming. He thinks about the dreams he's had, most especially the recurrent one. It's always the same, at least as far as he can remember. It begins in exactly the same way, with him in a vast tunnel where there is no light at either end although voices shout to him from both directions to come their way because their direction is the only safe route out. And every time he turns the voices come from different directions and the shape of the tunnel changes. Then he is in a rowing boat which is moving downstream. He tries to steer it but although it has a rudder it's useless because the boat won't steer, no matter which way and how hard he turns the rudder. In the bottom of the boat is a jar of flour he has just bought and which he must deliver before the boat which is now leaking fills with water and ruins it. The boat moves slowly down the stream, and as it does his fear increases, until right above him a window suddenly appears in the roof of the tunnel through which he can see the night sky. With his hands he tries to paddle the boat back against the stream so that he remains under this window which is now getting smaller and smaller. It is absolutely vital that he stays under this window until the shooting star he's been waiting for crosses the sky, but the force of the water is getting too strong and the window is getting higher and higher and smaller and smaller. He tries to call for help because someone is coming through a door which is beginning to open very slowly in the wall beside him, but hard as he tries to shout no sound comes from his mouth. Instead he tries to grab the rudder but it isn't there any more, it's a rattlesnake which recoils from him, sitting up and hissing. Still trying to call for help but only managing a strange low moaning sound, he crawls down the boat and under the seats which are now endless and occupied by people in life jackets who although they are all sitting up he knows are dead, all of them drowned because of the water coming from their mouths and their ears. The door in the wall then bursts open and someone is coming through it although he can't see who, just as a light has appeared at the end of the tunnel but too late, because the door is opening beside him and it's dark beyond it, darker than anything he has ever seen while the light at the end of the tunnel is getting further away rather than nearer until it is just the merest pinprick which is when he wakes up, making this slow and terrible moan, just as he wakes up now with his arm bent in front of his tightly closed eyes still trying his best to make someone hear him before it's too late.

'No!' he shouts, at last managing to turn the terrible moan into an articulate cry for help, but in his panic he has sent one of his bedside lights flying and knocked his night-time glass of water clean off the table as he sits up in his bed in the pitch dark suddenly and all at once wide awake. The curtains are billowing at the windows while outside a sudden summer storm is bringing the rain down in torrents. For a moment he has no idea where he is. At first he imagines he's home in his apartment but he can't be because nothing is familiar. The windows are in the wrong place, he can see that straightaway as he wipes the streaming sweat off his brow. The ceiling is higher, the shape of the other lamp beside his bed is different, and even the bed isn't his, so where in hell is he?

With his heart still pumping as if it's a piston, Freddie reaches out to switch on the lamp which is still standing and as soon as he does he knows where he is and that he has been dreaming. He is in bed at Stoke Park, the house he has rented for six months and where he has come to rest, and since it is dark but his book is beside him he must have fallen asleep as he was reading. The clock beside his bed says it is just after three o'clock in the morning.

The bottom half of one of the windows is open and letting in some of the rain so he gets out of bed and goes to shut it. When he has pushed the sash down closed he stands and looks out across the park, trying to bury the nightmare that is still in his head, and as he stands there the summer storm suddenly stops in the way summer storms do, as if all at once it has been turned off at a tap. In a matter of seconds the sheets of heavy rain turn to a brief flurry of drizzle and then cease altogether.

Across the park everything comes back into view, the shadowy outlines of the huge chestnut trees, the long drive, the hill, the beech woods and finally the outline of the white house itself, and as he looks across at the house half hidden behind its girdle of trees, upstairs a light suddenly comes on and a moment later the silhouette of someone appears at the window.

Whoever it is could probably see him. At least they must be able to see the light in his window as clearly as he can see theirs. Or hers rather, for it has to be a woman. The person standing at the upstairs window in the house across the park has to be the tenant of that house.

By what coincidence, he wonders, has she been brought to her window at the very moment he has risen to stand at his? Since the house is a good distance away he can't see anything at all clearly without the aid of his field glasses, so he reaches for them. They are close to hand, still where he had left them earlier on the arm of the chair, right by the window. Carefully he puts a hand out for them, and puts them to his eyes and when he does he sees her outline now quite clearly, although because she is standing with the light behind her she is in silhouette and he cannot make out her features. In fact he can remark little else other than that the figure is definitely that of a woman.

Who is also watching him.

At least that is what he feels since she stands facing him and is looking directly back towards where he is standing. Intrigued, he drops his field glasses as if to let her see what he looks like in spite of the distance and the darkness outside. He even stands there for a moment at the window resting his forearms on top of the lowered half of the sash while the night breeze ruffles his long brown hair. He finds himself smiling, as he would if someone was taking his photograph and although without the aid of his field glasses he can't see exactly what the woman is doing, he feels sure she is watching his window as closely as he is watching hers.

Then when he picks up his glasses once more and is again about to focus them on the distant window, it suddenly goes dark. Because he was still watching with the naked eye he doesn't know whether the woman turned off the light or simply pulled close the curtains. All he knows is that she is no longer in sight.

The event becomes ever more enigmatic the more he contemplates it from his bed, and even though he knows he can't supply the answers to any of the questions, he still keeps posing them to himself as he lies there in the darkness. What brought her to her window at exactly the same moment as he was brought to his? If she was indeed watching him why was she watching him? Why did he keep getting this feeling that there was something he already knew about her and the place where she lived? Was it just exhaustion, or was it something else? Were the things he was thinking when he was awake coming from the dreams he dreamed?

Or were his dreams dreaming him?

3

Not knowing her name Freddie was unable to telephone, so he delivered his carefully worded invitation for her to come for drinks on the following Sunday by hand to The Folly, dropping it into the old-fashioned mailbox on one of the gateposts. She ignored it, even though he'd carefully included and ringed his telephone number. Undaunted, he delivered a reminder on the Friday but receiving no reply to that one either, he found he had no choice but to put himself at the mercy of Mrs Davies once again.

'I know that for the most part English society is a pretty closed book,' he said one morning as he was giving his cook yet another cookery lesson. 'But if the same person has been taking The Folly all summer for the last two or maybe three summers is it? Then heck – surely someone knows *something* about her?'

'I'm sure they might well do, Mr Jourdan,' Mrs Davies replied, chopping an onion in far too large chunks. 'But the way I see it is if a body wants to keep themselves to themselves then that's their affair.'

'Sure you do, Mrs Davies, right on,' Freddie said, tongue firmly in cheek. 'But then the way I see it, it's simply a question of manners. Excuse me.' Freddie removed the knife from her hand and started to chop the onion down to the right sized slices. 'The way I see it is if a person doesn't want to say "yes", then they don't have to. But what in tarnation is wrong with writing to say so? Lawdy-me, Mrs Davies, and I thought you English were sticklers for etiquette.'

'Perhaps whoever is staying there has gone away for a few days,' Mrs Davies replied, assuming what she considered to be a diplomatic expression. 'If so, that could explain it.'

'If she has, she's left the fire burning all week,' Freddie retorted.

'Not necessarily. She might have left her housekeeper or companion or whoever she is behind.'

'Okay. But why would anyone want to burn a fire in this weather, I wonder?' Freddie continued. 'Who would burn a fire in the middle of summer? Only the old, wouldn't you say? Or the sick.'

'She'd hardly be sick now, Mr Jourdan, would she? You'd hardly go away for the summer if you weren't very well.'

'That leaves old. And I don't get the feeling that she's old.'

'What sort of feeling do you get then, Mr Jourdan?'

'I don't know, Mrs Davies,' Freddie replied. 'I just – I just get this feeling.'

'Oh yes?' Mrs Davies said, wiping more onion tears from her eyes with the hem of her apron. 'I see.'

'The point is, I think she might have let me know, one way or the other,' Freddie continued hastily, anxious to move the conversation away from the metaphysical. He could see from his housekeeper's present expression and hear from the tone of her voice that his last remark had only gone to confirm what she and Enid had already suspected by virtue of his nationality alone, namely that he was half barking mad. 'It's not as if we've met and I've caused her some offence,' he added. 'Like I keep saying, all I'm doing is trying to be sociable.'

'And maybe whoever it is living up there isn't, Mr Jourdan. I'm quite sure it's nothing personal, mind, because like I said, apparently that's how she's always been. Standoffish, you might say.'

'You might say totally reclusive from the sound of her.'

'You might indeed, Mr Jourdan, since I don't know anyone who's ever as much as seen her out of the place.'

Even so, Freddie still got the distinct impression that Mrs Davies was giving away a lot less than she really knew, as indeed everyone he'd tried asking for information about The Folly and its mysterious tenant seemed bent on doing. He'd thought at first perhaps it was just the usual Yank-in-the-court-of-King-Arthur syndrome, the paranoid belief of the American Abroad that everyone was either laughing up their sleeves at them or trying to rip them off, but now he felt a growing certainty that there was in fact a conspiracy of silence surrounding The Folly and its tenant.

'I should put the whole matter out of your mind, Mr Jourdan, really I should,' Mrs Davies concluded as she finished clearing away the onion skin.

'I wish I could.'

'I don't see any reason why as not.'

'I'm sure you don't, Mrs Davies. But then,' he added with a boyish smile, 'you're not inside my head.'

Freddie decided to leave it at that. There seemed little point in trying to explain to someone who thought it eccentric to stand on your head in the morning why he felt a compulsion to meet a woman about whom he knew absolutely nothing, not even her age let alone what she looked like. Instead, since conventional approaches seemed to be getting him precisely nowhere, he decided to use the characteristic with which the British assume all Americans to be imbued, namely a brass neck, even though nothing could have been further from his real nature. Although most people who met Freddie considered him to be socially confident and a man who made friends easily, in reality he was the opposite, truly confident in only his work. Because of what was now his fame as a composer, he'd found that in advance of meeting him people supposed him to be the sum of their preconceptions so Freddie had been forced by those circumstances (in public anyway) to learn to be the character that was expected of him, rather than the rather private person he really was. It was just as well he had finally learned the trick, because as the only son of a large, closely knit family he had been so over-protected by his five older sisters that by the time he'd finished his studies and started to earn his living in the world of the commercial theatre, he'd found to his horror that he'd been totally unprepared for the real world.

Among the other survival techniques he'd come to learn was the ability to play the Yank Abroad, and now seemed as good a time as any to utilize one of this character's many imagined vices, in this instance the Yank Abroad's social impertinence, and beard the lion in its den. He knew from the couple of excursions he'd already made to The Folly that the main entrance afforded no 'accidental' way in, with its locked gates and eight-foot stone wall which ran right into the woods, so he made another recce to try and look for the property's Achilles' heel which he soon found, tucked away to the rear of the property at the bottom of the beech woods in the shape of a small half-hidden wicker-gate which opened onto a path leading up to the garden. This gate was also chained, padlocked and signposted with another warning notice for unsolicited visitors to keep out of the private grounds, but for someone as tall and as athletic as Freddie there would be no difficulty in simply vaulting over it and making his way on up to the house.

The only question was when. Freddie had to consider at which particular time of day he would be most likely to encounter his quarry. Having watched the house over the course of several days, despite the fine summer weather he had never once seen anyone outside other than an old gardener whom Thomas – Stoke Park's own groundsman – assured him would be of no use as a source of information since the old boy was absolutely stone deaf.

So if Miss Smith, as Freddie had now dubbed his anonymous obsession, never even ventured out into her beautiful garden, how best then to stage an encounter? Or indeed how possibly? The animals grazing at the foot of the copse where he was walking gave him the answer, the creatures who haunted his dreams, the herd of red deer. He suddenly could see them in his mind's eye standing early in the morning in the garden right above him, encircling a figure who was hidden from him, but who he knew was her – the woman at the window, the woman in the house.

Feeling suddenly light-headed and faint, Freddie held on to the padlocked gate in front of him and stared blankly into the half-darkness of the deep woods. More was coming back to him and the more it did the fainter he felt, as if he were slipping slowly under water and leaving reality behind. He could hear people moving through the woods snapping branches which lay underfoot, just as he could make out the sound of a creature running panic-struck before them; he could hear the animal's breath and the breath of the hunters and he knew where he was without knowing where he was at all, just that he was back somewhere he had been before at some other time.

And the deer were also there then, standing at the foot of some steps, and they were being fed. Someone was feeding them and that someone had to be her. So that was when they would meet. Just as he had dreamed it. Of course, they would meet at first light, in the garden of the white house on the hill high above him.

He straightened up from the gate feeling strong again and clear-headed now that he realized that this was what all this odd feeling of familiarity had been about. It wasn't a result of jet lag, exhaustion or overwork, it was simply something he had dreamed, a piecemeal picture which since his arrival at Stoke Park his subconscious mind had been busy putting together from single unconnected events and which all came together one night in a dream, a dream which like most had vanished out through the door before he'd been able to catch it. But even so, he told himself as he began his walk back across the park, the memory of it however faint and obscure had at least given him a way in, it had at least indicated the time of day he was most likely to meet his mysterious quarry. So for that he was most grateful to his psyche. Had his dream not surfaced he would never have known even that, and had he not known that, Freddie mused, who knows?

Who knows indeed? said another voice inside his head. Who knows what? Who knows for instance that what you have just remembered was in fact a dream?

Dismissing the thought as the sort of idle nonsense produced by an overtaxed and overtired brain, Freddie vaulted the iron railing into a paddock and went on his way singing to himself a song he hadn't sung for ages, *Where or When*. They would meet just as he had dreamed they would of course. They would meet at first light, in the garden of the white house on the hill high above him.

It was twenty-five after four and still dark as Freddie let himself out of the house and into the gardens to make his way across the park. The night had been so warm there was little or no dew on the grass and only the faintest of breezes stirred the magnificent beech trees which lined the drive. The hill where The Folly stood lay to the east of the main gates so just as he had done on his return the day before, Freddie vaulted over the same set of iron rails to take a short cut through one of the paddocks where he startled a sleeping foal which had been stretched out in the lush grasses. At first it followed him curiously, unafraid and sniffing at his jacket as he made his way towards his destination, but after a while it lost interest and Freddie heard it canter away behind him to rejoin its contentedly grazing mother.

There were no signs of any deer, but other things came back.

The woods, for instance. The woods he found himself climbing up through after he'd cleared the wicket-gate were exactly the woods he'd seen in his dream. He remembered that the moment he began the climb up the path, and so strong was the picture in his mind's eye that he stopped and literally pinched his arm good and hard to make sure he wasn't in fact still asleep. The only thing that was different was that the woods were silent and this didn't feel right, it felt different from the rest of the remembered fragments. Something was missing, and then he remembered what it was. It was the sound of the other people in the woodland, the huntsmen, the shadowy predators bent on the murder of the creature they were hunting, which he should have been able to hear crashing ahead of him through the undergrowth, but all around him the beech woods lay silent, their quiet as yet unbroken even by the dawn chorus.

To the right of him, in a sky still hidden by the thicket of trees, the sun was now rising, as he knew it would. There were the fingers of pale light feeling their way into the trees until as the earth spun another league or so the probing fingers became a sudden blaze of sunlight which thrust its way deep into the woodland, slanting past the magnificent beeches, lighting the path ahead with a dazzling brilliance and stopping Freddie dead in his tracks, exactly as he now remembered from his dream. For there, too, was the gate in the trees, exactly where the shaft of sunlight pierced the woods and there, too, miraculously appearing from out of the shadows was the snow-white deer.

It must have sensed him, yet it didn't turn and it didn't run. Instead it seemingly vaporized into the shimmering sunshine, into the gardens beyond where Freddie now went, as if in a dream.

Emerging from the beam of sun and standing to one side so that he could see where he was, he found himself by another gate, the same sort of wicket-gate over which he had climbed a moment ago except this one was open and caught back on an iron hasp. The fragrances from the roses in full summer bloom beside him made him catch his breath, their aroma so pungent it could have just been sprayed on the morning air while behind him and all around and above him the first of the dawn birds broke suddenly into song, and there on the other side of the two-tiered lawn stood a group of does. There must have been twelve or more, headed now by the white doe which had made its way through the middle to the foot of the steps where beyond the group of wild animals stood a pale-faced, dark-haired young woman, with a skin as snow white as the nightgown she wore beneath an old-fashioned dark velvet cloak.

Freddie held his breath before he realized the young woman couldn't have seen him because she was continuing to feed her deer without looking his way once. He looked at her however. He took a good, long look at her and as he did a hand suddenly clutched at his heart and squeezed it, forcing the breath up into his throat where he quickly put his own hand to hold it there, until the unseen fingers loosened their grip and the film of red mist cleared from his eyes.

Then it was she looked directly up at him, with large dark eyes and the morning breeze ruffling the long curls of her black hair. She said nothing as she stared at him, both of her pale slender hands empty now of food for her deer, both of them resting on two of the animals' heads.

'Hi,' he said, in a voice which seemed to come from somewhere other than himself. 'What a morning.'

Still she said nothing, but just went on looking at him while Freddie kept watching her. She wasn't tall, she wasn't old, in fact he guessed she couldn't have been more than around twenty years of age, and the most beautiful girl he'd ever seen.

'I'm Frederick Jourdan,' he said, deciding to start again from the top and trying to make it sound natural, as if people always met at early dawn. 'I don't know whether you know, but I've taken the house below – Stoke Park. I've taken it for the summer.'

'I'm sorry. You have no business here,' she replied, and taking her hands from the deer she wrapped her old-fashioned velvet cloak tightly around herself and began to hurry back towards the house.

'No – come on! Wait!' Freddie ran after her across the lawn, scattering the deer as he did so. 'Please!' he called again. 'No – don't go! Not yet!' She stopped by the half-open French doors and turned back to him for a moment. In spite of her hostility, as he looked at her Freddie became overwhelmed with the idea that at long last he was looking upon the other half of himself.

'What is it?' she said. 'Because I'm cold.'

'You have such a pretty voice,' Freddie said, gazing at her.

'I'm sorry,' she insisted, 'but I really am cold.'

'No.' Freddie's own insistence made her stop again in the doorway, even though she now had the door half open. 'This is going to sound ridiculous, but you can't go. Not now.'

'If it wasn't so early—' the young woman said, then stopped. 'You're not drunk, are you.'

It was a statement rather than a question so feeling only slightly more confident, Freddie put out an arm although not daring to touch her.

'No, I'm not drunk,' he said. 'Not in the slightest.'

'So what are you doing here?' she asked. 'I don't understand.'

'It's kind of difficult to explain,' Freddie said with a sudden frown. 'I don't know how to begin. Or quite where.'

'Could you be brief?' she asked. 'Because I really am getting rather cold. So why did you come up here exactly? And at this unearthly hour?'

'I really don't know how to say this. I mean you're going to think it sounds absurd. But I came up here because I – because I just felt I had to.'

She looked at him without expression, then beyond him at the deer which were back once again, grazing her lawn.

'No,' she said, almost to herself. 'I don't think that sounds absurd. Now I really must go. I'm sorry. I really am. Goodbye.'

'No!' Freddie found himself almost shouting in a vain effort to stop her going inside her house and shutting him out. But even as he ran towards the doors she was inside and closing them. 'No! I don't understand! What do you mean – you're sorry?' he shouted, banging on the window glass in one last attempt to make her stop and listen. But she didn't and she wouldn't. Instead he could see her walking away from him across the room. 'Won't you let me try and explain?' he called after her. 'Why I felt I had to come up here was— Look! This is crazy but it's all to do with what the Greeks believe. They thought the Gods created people in two halves, right? And so people could only find happiness when and if they found their other half. However long it took! Even if it took centuries! They believed we were all just two halves of one soul waiting

46

to be united with the other half. Which according to the Fates they inevitably will be. And that's what I'm trying to tell you! I think this is what's happened to us! At least to me it certainly has! I think you and I were meant to meet and that we finally have! It's the only thing that makes sense, goddamnit! Don't you see?'

Halfway across the room she had stopped by a grand piano and now looked back at him for what seemed to Freddie to be a lifetime while they both stood in silence. For a moment he thought she was going to say something to him, but then the look in her eyes changed, and turning away from him she disappeared into the all-enfolding darkness of the house.

4

Diane's current long stint in court on behalf of some luckless divorcee had been keeping her away from the telephone, but Freddie knew that sooner or later she must ring and when she finally did he was going to have to tell her. Somehow or other he was going to have to tell the woman to whom he was engaged to be married that as a couple they were now history. And if that wasn't bad enough he would have to convince her of his reasons which was going to be the very worst part of all. Diane Smith-Werner was not the sort of woman who believed in kismet.

The more Freddie thought about it the deeper he sank into the bath he was taking. Already he could hear Diane's scratchy laugh at the news that he Freddie hadn't merely suffered just a *coupe de foudre* but had found the missing fifty per cent of his cosmic self. *Don't Freddie!* he could hear Diane imploring. *God, when you start out on one of those fantasies of yours—*

Perhaps he should write to her. Yes. Perhaps he should just get Mrs Davies to field all the telephone calls, say he was in London or something, or that he'd gone off somewhere unreachable on a fishing trip – anything – just to give him the time to write Diane a Dear John, and maybe not bother to offer any explanation. A *Dear Diane, I'm sorry, but there you are these things happen* sort of one-pager. Better surely by far than hear her laugh her terrible laugh at him trying to tell her that he had met the person he had been destined to meet. *God Freddie when you start out on one of those fantasies of yours—*

*   *   *

Yes. A letter was the answer, Freddie decided. A plain straightforward dishonest-to-God Dear John. Imagine, Freddie sighed as he ran some more hot water into the bath. Imagine Diane's reaction to hearing him tell her that he'd first met the girl who was his destiny in his dreams. She'd be on the next plane over armed with a tranquillizing gun and straightjacket.

Freddie eased the hot tap off with his toes and lay back in the bath to think again.

First things first; was he crazy or wasn't he? No, he wasn't crazy, it was. That was the first thing he had to admit. The whole thing was crazy because that is what people call things they can't understand. They call them crazy, mad, off the map, as if abstractions could be certifiable. So he wasn't crazy/mad/off the map – it was what had happened to him that was crazy/mad, etc. – maybe. But as far as he went – no way. As he lived and breathed there in the large claw-footed bath in the house he had hired for the summer, he was as sane and sober as Moses.

The next step, Freddie instructed himself as he soaped his chest and arms, was to forget about Diane for the moment and concentrate on – on what was he to call her, he wondered? Miss X? That was just too ridiculous, like a spy or an assaulted woman in a court case. Her. He would call her Her with a capital 'H'. So. Given that he had suffered un coup de foudre with Her, the most beautiful young woman – or was she a girl? He stopped to wonder again. She looked so young. She looked almost childlike. She can't have been a day over nineteen? Twenty? So really she was still a girl, what Freddie would call a girl anyway, and to hell with political rectitude. She was a girl. And the loveliest girl he had ever seen, what was more. But. Did he have even the very slightest indication of how she felt about him? And when he thought about it, Freddie had to admit to himself the impression he had got was that she wasn't exactly knocked out.

But then when he reconsidered that particular opinion, Freddie decided that was only to be expected because any woman in her right mind would probably have resisted the approach he had just made. Turning up in someone's garden at the crack of dawn unannounced to declare a love predetermined by Fate? What would he have done if the positions had been reversed, he asked himself? Offered her a cup of coffee, perhaps, while suspecting his surprise visitor was either high or mad, and then sent her off home with some vague promise to stop by and see how things were going some time.

But would he have looked at her in that way?

Would he have looked at her in the way she had – just for one moment – looked at him?

No. No, he wouldn't have looked at any total stranger who had come to make some mad declaration of love unannounced in his garden at the crack of dawn with that sudden softness, that sudden wistfulness, that sudden sadness with which she had looked at him as she had stopped by the piano halfway across the room. There was surely no disguising that look, he assured himself. It was as if she too had been searching for hundreds or maybe even thousands of years until the three sisters of the Fates had at last decided the two of them could be united.

So what of her numbness, her peremptory behaviour, her curtness? So what? So everyone reacted differently to things. Some people meeting their destiny face to face might respond in the way he had done, flippantly at first and then almost absurdly truthfully, declaring with utter conviction and with head and heart as light as if drugged, that this was the Real Thing, while others might respond in the way that she had, as if struck almost dumb by this thunderbolt that had come and hit them right out of the blue, as if stunned to numbness by it all, with all emotions paralysed and all senses lost. You say potato and I say potarto.

Freddie pulled the plug out of the bath with a toe and sat in it still deep in thought until all the water had run out and he started to get cold. Then he got out, dried himself, dressed and went downstairs to consider things further, sitting out on the terrace in the evening sunshine with a bottle of cold white wine. Yet the more he considered matters the more senseless they became. For instance, who or what could explain his and Her coincidental appearances at their bedroom windows at the dead of the night before, he wondered. Had she too been dreaming? Had she even been dreaming a dream she, too, had dreamed before, like the one he himself had dreamed? Their joint appearances at their windows could perhaps be explained away by coincidence, he could see that, but what he couldn't see was how to explain away the dream he'd had, the dream in which he had seen the white deer, and Her, before he had ever seen or met either?

' "The lunatic, the lover, and the poet, Are of imagination all compact",' Freddie reminded himself as he walked through the park after dinner. 'So suppose I am mad? So what? Because what is madness anyway? Mark Twain said every one of us is mad, and the moment we remember that we are, then all the mysteries disappear and life stands explained.'

He stopped and leaned on the paddock railing, looking up at the white house on the knoll. And still the only sign that it was still there and that She was still there was the thin plume of smoke rising up into the evening sky.

'Okay, that's quite enough philosophizing,' he told a mare and her foal who were grazing a few yards from him. 'It's not getting me anywhere and it's sure as hell not going to help one whit when it comes to me giving Diane the news that I don't love her any more because I've fallen in love with someone else. With a person unknown.'

By the time he finally arrived back at the big house on a walk which had taken him all around the park Freddie had concluded that the lesser of the two evils had to be telling Diane that he wasn't going to marry her, rather than actually being married to her. He'd never been altogether certain that he really was in love with her, certainly not like he was now with the girl he'd just met that very morning. He'd never had one hundredth of the feelings he was feeling now for Diane. Not that there weren't a lot of things to love about Diane Smith-Werner. She was terrific-looking, athletic and very handsome, the sort of woman who'd be picked from thousands to be the face of some new French perfume or some such. Who wouldn't have been knocked out by her? Freddie reasoned. He had been, but had he ever been in love with her? Does a KO equal love? No, he decided. A punch in the emotional solar plexus was not the same as an arrow in the heart.

Diane Smith-Werner was the sort of woman men lived for, not the sort they'd die for, but then that was the sort of woman most men preferred. Her credentials were impeccable, Vassar and Yale and old money, a junior partner in an upwardly mobile firm of divorce lawyers, a good golfer and expert tennis player. And, as everyone said at the time of their engagement, the perfect match for Frederick Jourdan – only son of the late George Jourdan, Senator for New Hampshire, and of Mirielle Mireau, the famous French opera singer now retired – one of America's most illustrious young composers (six Broadway hit musicals so far in a twelve-year career, including Days of Night and Goodbye Song, and the winner of two Academy Awards as musical director and the title-song composer for The Spell), as well as being a highly rated jazz pianist and one of the best green-room poker players around.

But while it had all looked ideal on paper and in the papers, Freddie had always nursed a doubt that their match might not be quite as perfect as described. It wasn't because of Diane's laugh or her habit of doing his hair with her fingers, because he was sure there were things about him which irritated her just as much. That was just the way it was with couples. No, the doubt Freddie had nursed for some time was to do with something else altogether, and now that he had found real love Freddie knew he was right and that he could never ever really have been in love with Diane because he'd never felt this ill over her.

When he was with Diane what he felt was fine, and when he was without her what he felt was also fine. Even when he'd first seen her at the club he didn't feel much else. No hand had suddenly grabbed at his heart that day and started to squeeze the breath from him, not for one second did his vision cloud over when he saw her, nor did he find it even slightly difficult to breathe. He just thought that this was one heck of a beautiful girl with one heck of a pair of legs who played one heck of a game of tennis. Then when he took her for a drink in the club bar he thought this was going to be an okay thing because they seemed so very ideally matched, a perfect couple for a mixed doubles, and the more time they spent together the more he thought they suited each other because when he was with her he felt just fine.

Diane described it differently. She said that she felt very comfortable with him. That in fact was how Diane had deducted that she was in love and ready to marry. They'd been seeing each other for about six months when one evening she took hold of both of Freddie's hands, a gesture with which he was never very happy, and she told him she knew that they were right for each other because she'd never felt like this with any other man, she'd never felt this *comfortable*. How he had taken that straight on the chin without cracking up, Freddie really didn't know now. It made him grin insanely just to think of it. How he had ever taken seriously a woman whose declared reason for love and marriage was because she felt *comfortable* with someone made him sit and shake his head in amazement, and as for then going right ahead and proposing to her, which is what he had actually gone and done, was now totally beyond belief. He could only think that he'd gone and done it because he was bored, not bored with living alone because he wasn't but actually just bored at the moment he had chosen to propose, so bored that he couldn't think of anything better to do than propose marriage to a girl who had just bored him into proposing to her.

He leaned back in the old leather library chair where he'd sat himself once he'd poured his usual nightcap of whisky and realized what a disastrous union his and Diane's would be. As far as love went he was all for the union of opposites but not of the diametrically opposed.

Besides, what he felt or rather had felt for Diane Smith-Werner wasn't love. Love didn't enter into it. Comfort and feeling fine was where their relationship was at, and while Freddie knew an awful lot of people would buy that as a contract of marriage for him it fell way short of the game line. It certainly bore no comparison to what he was feeling now, to what had hit him in the plexus that very morning, this feeling which was affecting him so badly he felt literally suicidal at the thought of the girl he now loved rejecting him. Diane and he would have had a marriage of comfortable convenience, with a love they would have been able to measure, but the love he had for the marvellously beautiful dark-eyed girl on the hill could never be beggared in such a way.

5

As soon as the shops were open the next morning Freddie rang the main florists in Worcester and instructed them to send four dozen red roses to Whom It May Concern, c/o The Folly, Stoke Park. He instructed them to enclose a card which read:

> Love nothing but that which
> comes to you woven in the
> pattern of your destiny.

He then directed the shop to repeat the order for the subsequent five days, enclosing the same inscribed card with each delivery, and then on the seventh day he ordered them to send just one red rose with a card which he wished inscribed:

> Fate has terrible power
> You cannot escape it by wealth or war
> No fort will keep it out
> No ships outrun it
> So how about dinner?

Not expecting to hear anything in return until perhaps the final rose had been delivered, he spent the week fishing the trout stream. Even so all the time he fished, telling himself he was relaxing, he kept a weather eye on the house on the hill – most of which he found he could see from the top of the far bank of the stream which was where he subsequently sat for his picnic lunches and teas. All week, despite the fine, hot July weather, the plume of smoke curled up nonstop from the main chimney of the house, yet never once did he see any sign of life besides the old man who daily attended the garden from nine until one o'clock midday. He never caught one sight of Her, hard though he watched the house, nor did he ever see a light shine from any window on any evening. Upon close and careful inspection from the attic nursery through his field glasses, Freddie ascribed the lack of any lights to the fact that all the windows seemed to be heavily curtained, a fact which added to the mystery which to Freddie now surrounded the place, and most of all to the mystery of its incumbent.

He couldn't think who she could be. For once his famous imagination failed him. She was surely too young to be the heartbroken and inconsolable widow, too immature to be an agrophobic writer who took the summer months off to sit in a half-darkened house to recharge her imagination, and too beautiful to be abandoned to her own devices for such a long time. The obvious choice was that she was some sort of invalid, which would explain the constant fires and the hermit-like existence. Yet because of her still-tender age Freddie was inclined to dismiss that particular theory, since he felt that if a girl like that really was ill the last thing her family would do would be to allow her to spend the summer months unsupervised with only a housekeeper for company. The moment anyone in his family had fallen ill they were never let out of sight until they were completely recovered.

Or until they were convalescing.

That had to be it, Freddie decided as he fished, remembering how when Bette, his youngest and best-loved sister had fallen sick with a particularly severe bout of glandular fever *at about the very same age*, as soon as she was well enough to look after herself she'd been packed off to spend the summer with one of their maiden aunts in Virginia. Bette had in fact spent two summers with her aunt, because it had taken her over two years to recover her strength and health in full.

So that had to be the explanation. His Dulcinea had been sent away to the country in the company of some kind relative to recuperate from whatever illness had laid her low, rather than sent far from her home to wither away and die. The very thought of the latter thing happening was so preposterous that Freddie was able readily and happily to dismiss such a notion, while if she was indeed convalescing then a profusion of red roses must surely help raise her spirits as would an invitation to dinner.

So in growing confidence he fished for a week, and then on the evening of the seventh day after dining on a fine two-pound brown he had landed at tea time, he took a cut-glass tumbler and a bottle of malt whisky up to his bedroom where lifting the bottom half of the main sash window open to its full height, he pulled an armchair up and sat looking out at the distant house. As usual there was the thin plume of fire smoke at the chimney and no lights on anywhere, even once it had grown dark. Pouring himself a last whisky before turning in, Freddie raised the glass in a silent toast to the unseen inhabitant only to find that as he did so the curtains of an upstairs room suddenly parted and in a blaze of light she appeared, her silhouette framed in the window. Once again because the light was behind her Freddie could make no details out through his field glasses which he now kept permanently to hand, other than that she was wearing what looked like a long white nightgown and that her tousled hair cascaded down around her shoulders.

For a moment while Freddie stood watching her with the field glasses clamped to his eyes, she stood watching him back, standing quite motionless with her arms crucifixed out either side of her holding the curtains apart. Then as suddenly as she had appeared she was gone, the curtains closed and the window once more dark.

The next morning after he had bathed and dressed, when he looked across to the little white house Freddie saw for the first time since he had arrived that there was no smoke curling up from the chimney.

Even after breakfast there still wasn't a sign of any smoke.

'Why should that bother me I wonder, Mrs Davies?' Freddie asked, pushing his chair back and going to stand at the dining-room windows. 'Why should it bother me that today, on yet another beautiful summer's day, whoever it is living up there in The Folly has chosen not to light a fire?'

'It really is a beautiful day, Mr Jourdan, and that's for sure,' the housekeeper said ignoring the main content of what he'd just said as she began to clear away his breakfast. 'I take it you'll be off fishing again, and wanting another packed lunch?'

'Because she's gone, goddammit!' Freddie said as it came to him. 'Goddammit of course – she's upped sticks and gone!'

He was out of the dining room via the open French windows and halfway across the lawns before Mrs Davies could open her mouth to speak. Not that she would have said much. Certainly nothing that would have been of any help to him. She most certainly wouldn't have told him that the first thing she had learned from Enid when she'd arrived that morning was that the two people staying at The Folly had closed up the house and had been driven into Worcester by taxicab to catch the six-forty train to London.

Every shutter was shut, front and back. The only thing she had left open in her flight were the main gates.

Freddie entered The Folly at the back over the wicket-

60

gate, having run all the way from the house, but he knew it was too late all the while that he was running, running as fast as he could run. He knew in his heart she was gone. Just as he knew she had appeared at the window to show him she was going, to tell him goodbye.

There were no deer in the garden that morning, just a pair of large crows picking at something in one of the rosebeds. They flew off as he ran across the lawn, leaving their meal of a fallen sparrow unfinished as they flapped away awkwardly up into the blue sky. Freddie ran straight round to the front door to ring the bell and bang the old brass knocker, even bending down to peer through the letterbox, even though he knew it was in vain.

When no-one came, just as he knew they wouldn't, he went round to the back again, this time going to the end where the back door was. It was so clean and tidy it was as if no-one had ever been in the house. There were no empty milk bottles outside the kitchen door, no old cardboard grocery boxes from the weekly shopping, no bulging dustbin bags waiting to be collected. Everything must already have been disposed of or burned, because the only thing Freddie could find in the dustbin were seven message cards and six dozen beautiful and still-perfect red roses.

On his return to Stoke Park he ran into Thomas coming out of the estate office which was housed in part of the stable block. Directing him back inside Freddie followed him in and closed the door behind him.

'Okay, Thomas,' he said, leaning on the door and sinking his hands deep into his pockets. 'I really would appreciate some help here, because someone round here has to know something. For instance, you. You're in charge of the management of this place, so I reckon if you don't know who rents The Folly every year then no-one does.'

'Like I told you, sir,' Thomas replied with a sad shake of his head, 'I has nothing to do with The Folly, all except that is to see to its maintenance. Any other arrangements are made by the family. All the other arrangements are made by the family so you'd really best ask them, sir.'

'Ah, yes. Would you believe I don't even know who this famous "family" is, Thomas? My lawyers and their lawyers did the paperwork for the tenancy, and all I did was sign them. I know nothing whatsoever about "the family", so I wouldn't know where to look for them in the first place, let alone ask them anything.'

'I'm afraid I can be of little help to you, sir,' Thomas sighed. 'I only got this job once the family were gone, do you see. None of us who's here now were here when the family was. Her ladyship took her staff away, see, least that's how I heard it, she took her man and her personal maid, and God knows where all the other staff went because there were plenty of them, Mrs Davies said, grooms, lads, gardeners. Those were the days, eh?'

'You said her ladyship,' Freddie said, frowning intently at him. 'Lady what, do you know? What was the family name?'

'Again, sir, and odd though it seems, I don't have a single clue. I only ever heard her spoken of as her ladyship.'

'I see. And you've never tried to find out anything more? In the bars, when you go drinking down in the village for instance—'

'No I never do my drinking in the village, sir, not since I first started work here. They don't like Taffs much, see, and I likes to drink where I feel comfortable.'

'Taffs?'

'Us Welsh. Even though I was born not thirty miles from here as the crow flies. They think we come and take their jobs, see, so on my days off I goes back over the mountains home to Llanfaredd, where my mother's family come from. And your best bet, sir, if I may say so, if you have business with the family, is to do it through their solicitors.'

Thomas pulled open a drawer in his neatly ordered desk and from it produced a card which he handed to Freddie.

'For a start I could always make a few more enquiries round here,' Freddie said, as he read the name of a firm of lawyers and their address on the card. 'I mean all I want to know is who rents the goddamn house every year.'

'The lawyers will be by far your best bet, sir,' Thomas replied, reclosing the desk drawer. 'You can ask away round here but most like you'll only find yourself chasing a lot of wild geese.'

'You trying to tell me they don't like Americans round here as well as Taffs?'

'I gather an American gentleman bought another big house not far from here, sir. Pychard Court. And did things to it they didn't approve of. Least that's what I heard.'

'But I have no intentions of buying this place, Thomas.'

'No, sir,' Thomas agreed, suddenly looking Freddie in the eye. 'But you are an American.'

According to the woman in the offices of Markson and Co., who as it emerged wasn't in the offices at all but was manning the telephone line from home, the firm was in recess for three weeks while both Mr Markson senior and Mr Markson junior took their holidays, and much as she would like to help the woman on the other end of the telephone told him she was not empowered to give him any information concerning Stoke Park which was not directly related to his tenancy.

'Look. All I want to know is who rents The Folly, Miss,' Freddie repeated. 'Surely you can just give me the name of the tenant?'

'In line with the family's wishes I'm afraid all matters

63

concerning The Folly and its tenancy are completely confidential, Mr Jourdan,' the woman replied. 'I'm only sorry I can't be of more help.'

'Just the family name then,' Freddie suggested. 'That would be a little more help.'

'It really is outside my brief, Mr Jourdan. As I said, I can only help in matters directly relating to the tenancy of Stoke Park. Mr Markson will be back in the office on Monday week when I'm sure he'll give you all the help he can.'

There was nothing to help Freddie in Stoke Park either. All traces of the family had been removed or locked away. Where there should have been family portraits there were none. Freddie'd noticed this soon after he had taken up his residency. From the telltale marks of fresher paper or paint on the walls he could see where other smaller or larger paintings had recently hung in place of substitute paintings which to judge from their all-embracing mediocrity had been bought as job lots at auction. There were no family photographs either, that is none that were any use. The few mildewed and well-faded ones to be found in some of the downstairs cloakrooms were all extremely old and offered an outsider no clue as to the family's identity.

Everything else was locked away either in desks, military chests, or behind closed doors in the attics. Even the glass doors fronting the library shelves were secured, not only by bolt and key but also with small security padlocks. Even the considerable collection of long-playing records had been rendered unplayable by long steel bars which had been specially fixed and padlocked into place along the rows of shelves which housed them. Even the piano stool was locked.

Under more normal circumstances any tenant would have considered such precautions merely sensible, given the risks inherent in letting a family home. But to the now obsessed Freddie it looked as if a deliberate effort had been made by the owners to render the place as anonymous as possible before surrendering it to any paying guest. At the height of his impassioned search for clues around the house, Freddie had seriously contemplated breaking in somewhere or into something simply in order to give himself a starting point, and having spied a set of what looked like old tea chests through the keyhole of one of the attic doors, he was just about to force that particular door open and then in turn the chests, when on the landing immediately below him the telephone suddenly rang.

It wasn't that which stopped him, however. In fact he didn't even make an attempt to go and answer it but just left it ringing until somewhere in the house Mrs Davies picked up an extension. It simply brought him back to his senses. With a jolt he realized he had no right whatsoever to invade the privacy of his landlords by breaking into their personal property. Whoever these people were they hadn't locked everything away from him because they had known in advance that he was going to fall in love at first sight with another of their tenants and would then urgently need to know their own identity so that he could trace her when she fled. What on earth could he have been thinking? Freddie wondered as he sat down on an old nursing chair in order to refocus himself. These people had simply locked away their private papers and anything of real value because that is what people did when they let their family houses.

'There was a telephone call for you,' Mrs Davies told him when he appeared downstairs half an hour later. 'A Mr de Burgh? He said to tell you he and his wife are in the vicinity and was wondering if you could go to dinner with them. I left the name and number of their hotel by the phone in the hall.'

It was just the break Freddie had needed and until he remembered that Theo and Finty de Burgh, the very friends who had recommended Stoke Park to him, had for the past month been away somewhere far distant on holiday, he couldn't believe why he hadn't thought of enlisting their help earlier. Not only would they know the identity of the owning family, Freddie thought as he changed out of his tee shirt and chinos and into a blue shirt and his favourite old white linen suit to go out, they might also know the identity of The Folly's mysterious tenant.

He had deliberately said nothing of his dilemma on the telephone when he had called back to accept the invitation, preferring to save any such a conversation for dinner. The de Burghs were on their way back from Ireland and were breaking their return journey to London for Theo, who was a bloodstock agent, to look at a couple of likely horses in the neighbourhood. They were staying overnight at a hotel in a village called Chaddesley Corbett, about twenty miles to the north-east of Stoke Park, which on arrival Freddie found to be an elegant Georgian house standing in its own small park with sheep contentedly grazing at the front and geese and ducks swimming on a lake.

It was such a fine evening the three friends sat and drank champagne outside before going in to dine. Freddie heard a typically anecdotalized version of Theo and Finty's travels while he in turn regaled them with an American's eye view of life in deepest Worcestershire. It wasn't until they were halfway through the main course that the subject closest to Freddie's heart was broached.

'You're hardly eating, Freddie,' Finty remarked. 'You hardly touched your first course and now you're playing with your salmon as if you were fishing for it rather than eating.'

'Perhaps your man's in love,' Theo said, helping them all to some more excellent Château de Rozay. 'You know these hopelessly artistic people, Fin. They have to be in love all the time. Even when they're in love already.'

'As it happens I'm not in love.'

'Aaah,' said Finty, and it was long and drawn out.

'Oh,' said Theo, raising his eyebrows. 'Then what's with the big Sad Sam eyes?'

'What I mean is I'm not in love with Diane,' Freddie announced.

'All the more reason to marry the woman,' Theo replied quickly. 'Marrying for love is what keeps solicitors in business.'

'Here we go,' Finty sighed.

'Seriously,' Theo insisted. 'Anyway, love and marriage have absolutely nothing in common. Otherwise we'd get married every time we fall in love.'

'Come on,' said Finty, in mock encouragement. 'We might as well have the full bit. How Venus was the goddess of love and Juno the goddess of marriage—'

'They were and it's true,' Theo interrupted. 'And didn't they hate each other's guts? So if you've discovered you don't love the goddess Diane, Freddie me-lad, I raise my glass to you. Because you're guaranteed to have the perfect marriage. One free of any pain. *Slainte*.'

Theo raised his wine glass in salute while his pretty red-haired wife took good aim under the table and kicked him on the shins.

'See what I mean, Freddie?' Theo asked, picking up his napkin to wipe the wine he'd spilled from his chin. 'Marry for love and you divorce happiness.'

'Shut up, Theo,' Finty said affably, nodding sideways at Freddie. 'Our chum here wants to get serious.'

'*Get* is a little late,' Freddie said, putting down his knife and fork. 'I've already got.'

'You Americans are so advanced in everything,' Theo sighed. 'Over here we only have bits on the side *after* we're married.'

'Shut up, Theo,' Finty repeated, turning to Freddie. 'Something has happened, hasn't it, Fred? It's serious, isn't it?'

When Freddie had finished telling the de Burghs the story of his madness, of his mid-summer lunacy, his wasn't the only food that had gone cold.

'God,' Finty finally whispered after a long silence. 'Now that is what even I could call romantic.'

'Romantic my socks,' Theo snorted. 'This is Frederick Jourdan all over. Remember when we were staying with you in New York? We were all watching the tennis on TV, and you saw this woman sitting in the crowd. You kept seeing her because she was sitting near where the players change over, and by the end of the second set you were so deeply, madly and truly in love, you took a taxi out to where is it?'

'Flushing Meadows,' Freddie said.

'You took a taxi all the way out there to try and find her.'

'I thought that was desperately romantic too,' Finty sighed. 'But I think this is even more so. Just imagine. Love at first sight at first light.'

'Love at first sight indeed,' Theo snorted again, helping them all to some more wine. 'Hallucinosis. Otherwise known as Holiday Romance.'

'How in God's name can you be so prosaic, Theo?' his wife asked him. 'This comes well from the man who learned how to ride so he could dress up as a knight in armour and propose to me. Jesus, Theo, come on.'

This so disarmed her husband that he blushed and completely dropped his pose.

'I wish I could help you, old duck,' he said to Freddie good-naturedly, 'but I can't. At least not as far as this pash of yours goes. I can give you the dirt on the family, not that there is any and what I know ain't going to be much use, but at least I can tell you who they are and where most of them have gone. But as for the girl, you're going to have to gumshoe it. Truth to tell, I didn't even know there was someone at The Folly. At

68

'least not nowadays. When I used to stay at Stoke Park, this is nearly twenty years ago, mind—'

'You stayed there more recently than that. We stayed there together—'

'What I was going to say, Fin, was when I first used to stay at the house there was a family living in The Folly full time. I don't remember meeting them but then there were always an awful lot of bods all over the shop at Stoke Park most of the time, but I seem to remember they had kids because Cousin Luce used to ride with them. I think.'

'Cousin Luce?' Freddie enquired.

'The old lady's granddaughter, a distant cousin of mine. Terrific horsewoman. Married a New Zealander and's gone to live out there and breed thoroughbreds. Anyway – where was I? You wanted to know about the family.'

'The family that lived in The Folly first,' Freddie said, as the waiter cleared away their half-eaten dinner.

'Oh they're of no interest,' Theo declared. 'Whoever they were, they're history. You're after the present incumbent, that's who we've got to i.d. Pity the old lady's dead.'

'Just what I was thinking,' Finty glumly agreed.

'Which old lady are you talking about?' Freddie asked quickly. 'Not the owner of Stoke Park, please?'

'Well of course, who else?' Theo replied. 'She died at the beginning of the year. Mind you, she was a fair old age, isn't that right, Finty?'

'Where was she living?'

'South of France somewhere. She'd moved there six or seven years ago, when Stoke Park got too big for her. She was a great old bird, once she'd got to know you.'

'Emily Margaret Stourton,' Finty said. 'Or to give her her full title, the Lady Emily Margaret Stourton.'

'The Earl of Beauchamp's daughter,' Theo added. 'But like I said, not that any of this is going to be the slightest bit of use to you.'

                    *   *   *

Yet all the time they were talking, the girl Freddie now loved was there in the room with them. She had been with them throughout the whole of Freddie's account of her, yet so preoccupied had he been he had never once been aware of her presence.

Oddly enough, others in the same dining room had. One man when he realized who it was had stopped eating and drinking to listen, while another couple, an elderly couple sitting at the next-door table to him had fallen completely silent, the woman finally sitting with tears in her eyes, which moved the man with her so much he put down his things and held her hand in his.

Freddie however paid her no attention whatsoever, because he didn't know it was Her. He didn't even notice the sound of her soaring above the voices of his fellow diners, a sound so plaintive she could have been calling to him directly. But most ironically of all, had he noticed Her he would have been aggravated and wondered why he was being forced to listen. One thing the normally even-tempered Freddie Jourdan hated was being expected to be able to listen to two things at once.

So as he and Theo and Finty had talked on, the girl he sought so desperately went by unnoticed, and by the time he had stopped talking to think over what his friends had told him, she too had fallen silent.

Meanwhile on the other side of the room the woman with the tears in her eyes dabbed at them with her husband's handkerchief before calling the patron over.

'Excuse me,' she said. 'I'm so sorry to bother you, but that was Her, wasn't it? Just now? That was that wonderful little girl.'

6

For once all roads led not to Rome but back up the same old blind alley. Lady Stourton was dead, her husband long gone before her in the War, her grandchild somewhere in the Antipodes, her daughter a divorcée living in Provence, and her household staff disbanded, retired or deceased.

And her lawyers sworn it seemed to silence.

Once their office reopened Freddie made an immediate appointment with the senior partner and then on the appropriate day took the train up to London and met with the elder Mr Markson, a florid-faced gentleman whose mind seemed to be constantly elsewhere, to such an extent that Freddie had to keep redrawing his attention to the matter in hand. Even so, it seemed his journey had been in vain, since all Freddie learned was that the now late Lady Stourton had made it a legal stipulation that the anonymity and privacy of the particular person leasing The Folly was to be preserved absolutely.

'It's such an unusual move I'd have said she must have had a good reason for it,' Freddie supposed.

'You don't say,' Mr Markson senior replied, making a chain out of some paperclips. 'A reason for what, might I ask?'

'Sorry? Why for making such a stipulation.'

'Indeed. To which particular stipulation are you referring?'

'The one you were just referring to, the one binding you legally not to reveal the identity of the person renting The Folly.'

'That is indeed so. That is precisely the position in

which this firm finds itself. Which is somewhat unusual, I grant you that.'

'That's it. Just as I was saying.'

'You were?'

'I was indeed. I was saying that such a stipulation was surely a little out of the ordinary.'

'Forgive me, Mr – er . . .'

'That's okay. Jourdan.'

'Forgive me, Mr Jourdan, but exactly what is it you find so unusual?'

So the hour Freddie was wasting with Mr Markson senior dragged on in its Carrollian way, with the red-faced old man going all around the houses and finally unable to come to any point. That at least was how it had seemed as Freddie sat in the stifling unventilated office hoping to learn just one small thing to his advantage, until the thought occurred to him that the lawyer was deliberately prevaricating because he had nothing better to do.

'You know something? I seem to have made an awful long journey all to no avail,' Freddie said as he rose to leave. 'Am I mistaken or didn't you say on the telephone that you would be only too happy to help me?'

'Yes, yes, Mr um—'

'Try Jourdan again. I find I answer to that best.'

'Yes, yes, I would indeed have been only too happy to help, I do assure you, Mr Jourdan,' the old man agreed. 'If I had been able. But as you have seen, and as I have told you, alas it is not within my power to do so.'

'You could perhaps have told me that on the telephone, sir, and spared me the journey,' Freddie remarked, his hand on the door handle.

'I could indeed, my good sir,' the lawyer replied. 'But then I would not have had the pleasure of meeting you. My daughter is a great admirer. Good day.'

It wasn't until Freddie was halfway down the Strand

that he realized he had forgotten his umbrella. The fine spell of weather had been broken that morning by heavy rain so he'd grabbed an umbrella from the hall hatstand before leaving Stoke Park. However, being so unused to carrying one he would first of all have forgotten it on the train had it not been for the kindness of a fellow passenger, and now because it had long stopped raining he had left it where he'd put it on his arrival, propped up in a corner of the reception area of Marksons.

But as he later realized, far from being an accident, forgetting the umbrella had been an act of Fate, because when he returned to the lawyers' offices there was a different girl in Reception, a young and diminutive blonde who was idly buffing her nails while cupping a telephone receiver between shoulder and ear. Since it was midday, Freddie assumed that the woman who had dealt with him earlier had gone for her lunch, to be replaced by this youngster who most probably and very conveniently would have no idea of who he was.

'Can I help you?' she asked, still cupping the receiver between shoulder and ear. Freddie suppressed a grin. She was overdoing the performance, and the fact that it was one that he saw so many aspiring actresses overdoing when auditioning for one of his shows didn't make it less funny.

'Yes you can indeed help me,' Freddie said, spying his umbrella still propped up exactly where he'd left it. 'Or rather I can help myself. I was here earlier, and that's my umbrella.'

'I was wondering whose that was,' the blonde said, smiling up at him, still with the phone tucked under her right ear. 'I thought it must be a client's.'

He was about to leave, his umbrella safely recovered, when the girl spoke again but this time into the telephone. When she had finished Freddie felt as if his hair was standing up on end.

'Sorry to keep you waiting, Miss Smith,' the receptionist had said. 'I'm putting you through now. Mr Markson, it's Miss Smith for you. The lady what rents The Folly?'

For a moment Freddie stayed right where he was, standing facing the outer door away from the desk in order to try and regain his composure. This was why he had forgotten his umbrella, because just like their meeting, this moment had also been predestined.

'Excuse me,' Freddie said, turning back and doing his best to give an easy, matter-of-fact sort of smile. 'Forgive me if I'm mistaken, but the call you've just put through – did I hear you say Miss Smith who rents The Folly? Because The Folly is on the estate I'm renting and that's my Miss Smith. I suppose she's calling in here because she wonders where the hell I've got to.'

'Sorry?' Freddie could see the girl was outpaced from the way she was looking up at him from her open magazine, her pretty but over lipsticked mouth slightly open and her Minnie Mouse eyes screwed up in a frown. 'What was you saying?'

'It's just been one of those days, ever since I got up this morning,' Freddie sighed, looking at his watch. 'First thing I did was tread on the cat. And now forgetting my goddamn umbrella's going to make me later than ever. Miss Smith and I are meant to be having lunch.'

'Oh,' the girl said, frowning ever more deeply. 'Perhaps you'd like me to interrupt? I could cut in and tell her you're here. Mr Markson won't mind because knowing old Mr Markson he probably won't even notice.'

'No really,' Freddie said, just in time to prevent her from activating her suggestion. 'This is personal so I'll ring her from my mobile – except would you believe this?' He made a quick pantomime of searching his pockets and then his small shoulder bag. 'I've only left my address book behind. I told you it was one of those days.'

'I have them all the time,' the girl agreed. 'They're a nightmare, aren't they?'

'Too right,' Freddie agreed, too quickly. 'Look – if you'd be just kind enough to write her home telephone number down, I'll call her from my mobile soon as I grab a cab.'

Hardly able to believe his good fortune, Freddie watched as the receptionist happily copied out a telephone number from the page she'd called up on the computer screen in front of her which she then handed to him on a memo.

'Sure you wouldn't just like me to tell her you're on your way?' she asked as Freddie began to hurry towards the door.

'No no,' he urged. 'Really not. It's a lot more complicated than that, you see. A whole lot more complicated.'

He called the number from the nearest phone booth he could find, only a matter of minutes after he had left the office. To his delight the line was still busy which meant she was still there on the other end of it, still talking to old man Markson. Turning his back on the couple of people who were now forming a small queue beside the booth, Freddie faked another call, and then tried the number again. This time it rang, three times, and with every ring Freddie's heart beat the faster.

He heard the phone being answered the other end and then a silence.

'Hello?' he said, but that silence was unmistakeable. He had her answering machine.

'Hello,' she said to him, without knowing who he was. 'I'm sorry I can't speak to you but if you leave a message after the tone I'll call you back when I can.'

'Please listen,' he said after the signal to speak. 'I know you're there so please listen. It's me, Freddie Jourdan from the house. From Stoke Park. The man you met in your garden. I'm up in London and—'

'Yes I know you're up in London,' a quiet voice suddenly interrupted him. 'I've just been speaking to Mr Markson.'

'I can't believe that's really you,' Freddie asked quietly after a moment. 'Is it really? Is it really you?'

'How did you get my number?'

'Meet me and I'll tell you.'

'Please. Just tell me how you got my number.'

'I won't tell you how, I'll tell you why,' Freddie laughed. 'Because it was meant, that's why. I was meant to get your number. Just like our meeting was meant to happen, in exactly the way it did. Now. Where and when can we meet?'

'We can't.' Her soft pretty voice which Freddie could barely hear over the traffic faltered for a moment, then she continued. 'Sorry but I'm afraid we can't meet.'

'Why not?' Freddie knew he had to keep talking, he had to keep blustering if necessary. Anything to keep her on the line. 'It's okay, really,' he said. 'I'm not married, I'm not a monster, I don't have any really terrible habits, besides – so I'm told – besides sticking one arm up in the air when I'm sleeping. Otherwise I'm a perfectly normal, run of the mill sort of guy. Except as far as you're concerned. As far as you are concerned, Miss Smith, I am neither normal nor even the slightest bit run of the mill. So please. Just meet me for a drink. Or a coffee.'

There was a long silence before she replied.

'I can't,' she said, in a voice not much louder than a whisper. 'There isn't any point.'

The moment the phone went dead Freddie dialled her number again, ignoring the woman who had come round the other side of the booth and was knocking on the side before pointedly tapping the face of her watch. After three rings, the phone was answered.

'Hello,' her voice said. 'I'm sorry I can't speak to you

76

but if you leave a message after the tone I'll call you back when I can.'

When he called her the moment he got home the number rang directly into a central message agency. The operator verified this, telling him this was because the number was in the process of being changed. Freddie said he'd like the new number and asked when it would be possible to get it, only to be told in return that the new number would, like the previous number, be ex-directory.

'So?' he further enquired, as patiently as he could. 'Look, if I had the last number and that was ex-directory then surely by right I should have the new one.'

'I'm sorry, caller,' the operator informed him, 'but you will have to request that information from the subscriber personally.'

He was back in the blind alley and again could see no way out of it. Yet he refused even to consider the possibility that the woman he'd fallen in love with might not feel the same about him, that the reason she didn't want to meet him was because he was of little or no interest to her.

'That just can't be so!' he shouted at the night sky as he walked around the park at midnight. 'I saw the look in her eyes! You just don't get that look unless it's hit you, too! Oh God – oh Jesus what am I going to do?'

He was just below her house now, the place he had first seen her, the house high on the hill unseen above him, hiding away behind its dark trees, lying silent behind its beds of fragrant roses. Perhaps there was some clue to her identity there, he wondered, as he stood with his hands on the wicket-gate, looking up the dark path. In her hurry to leave that morning, perhaps inadvertently she left something behind, something with her address on it, or failing that some little clue as to where exactly she lived or what she did, and what was her real name.

It wouldn't be hard to find out, Freddie realized now that he was standing on the lawn looking up at the shuttered house, because it wouldn't be that hard to break in. No house was, so he'd been told, not if you seriously wanted to burgle it, and while all the downstairs windows were securely shuttered up from the inside, the upstairs ones were not, and if they were anything like the windows in Stoke Park Freddie bet his last dollar they would be fastened with those old-fashioned and ill-fitting window hasps, the sort of fixture which could be prised open in a moment with the blade of a knife.

Rather than stopping to consider precisely what sort of madness was gripping him, Freddie's only thought was how to reach the first floor of the house into which he now intended to break. With his natural athleticism he realized he would be able to climb the drainpipes without much difficulty, the only problem being not his climbing skill but whether or not the pipes were securely enough fixed. Preferring the possibilities afforded by a ladder, Freddie went to check the outbuildings which he found to be all locked up. The garage, however, for some reason had been left unbolted on the inside, and after a couple of good hard shoves the doors bounced back open towards him with the lock still shot. Inside hanging on the wall was a pair of double step-ladders.

The first bedroom window he tried opened as easily as he had predicted and in a second he was over the sill and inside the house. Since he knew that once the curtains were drawn any lights that were on couldn't be seen from without, he went into each room and closed every one of the heavy interlined drapes, then room by room, turning on one light only in whichever one he was in, he methodically searched the house for clues, starting downstairs in the kitchen.

There all he could find was a list of emergency numbers by the telephone, local police, plumber, electrician, doctor, and judging from the yellowing colour of the card on which the numbers had been written, it had hung there for some time. Nothing else was of any real help, a fridge empty of everything but a carton of long-life milk, food cupboards stocked with a few unexceptional tinned provisions, and a totally empty pedal wastebin. To judge from the embers in the wood-burning stove, in her flight the retreating Miss Smith had even remembered to burn any unwanted correspondence.

A search of the rest of the house was seemingly as unproductive as the kitchen, although the fact that he didn't know quite what he expected to find hindered Freddie rather than helped him. Old envelopes certainly, because they could well provide a lead, those that is which had been forwarded on to the occupant at The Folly from the tenant's London address, but all the waste baskets had been completely emptied and as he had already discovered their contents reduced to indecipherable ashes.

She seemed to have out-thought him from move one, because just as Stoke Park had been reduced to anonymity so too it seemed had The Folly. Perhaps some fictional detective could have found a clue by following through the forensic theory of displacement or by looking for things for which an amateur would never look, but lacking such professionalism all he was drawing was a set of blanks. The way the house was it could be let again to a new tenant the next day. Even the bed in the main bedroom had been stripped and left with the two pillows placed on top of the pile of neatly folded blankets.

Maybe she'd left a book somewhere, Freddie thought suddenly as he made his way back downstairs and as a small red light on a panel hidden under the stairs winked without cease on the second every second. Perhaps there was a book left behind with her name in it? Her proper name rather than the obviously bogus Miss Smith, a book with an Ex Libris sticker in it, announcing to whom the said book belonged, a book she'd been reading during her stay and that had slipped unnoticed down the back of a chair, or under one, or left out of sight up on a shelf. There should be books, because summer houses were always full of old and much read books left behind by previous tenants who'd finished with them, so the chances were she too might have forgotten something.

She had, and of all places he found what she had forgotten inside the grand piano. Oddly enough he hadn't even intended looking there because it had never occurred to him to be a place to find books. What had attracted him to the piano was simply the fact that he could never resist trying other people's pianos out, and this one, which was a fine and perfectly maintained old Broadwood in a beautiful rosewood case, he found irresistible, even though he was there to burgle, not to play.

But he saw no harm in playing it. He knew the sound would disturb no-one because no-one would hear him. Besides Stoke Park there was no other house within at least one mile of The Folly, so without giving it another thought and as the small red light beat on remorselessly out of sight under the stairs, Freddie opened the lid of the keyboard before lifting and propping up the top lid.

That was where he found it, lying face down in the space between the top end and the dampers, the one place she had forgotten to check, the one place anyone would have forgotten to check. She was probably reading it, he thought as he lifted it out, and then with it still in her hand had sat down at the keyboard, placing the book beside the music stand where perhaps it stayed for days until she lost sight of it, covered with books of the music she'd been playing, and then as she tidied everything up before leaving she must have lifted the music up without realizing the book was underneath and tipped it into the space under the main lid which she would have shut down before putting the music away in the locked piano stool.

He guessed what it was before he even read the title on the spine. How he knew he never knew, but his guess was right. *The Divine Comedy* by Dante Alighieri. Under the circumstances Freddie told himself it couldn't be anything else. It was an old copy, leather bound, and to judge from the cracks in the book's spine and the wear on the hide which bound it, it was a much read and treasured volume.

There were sheets of paper, slightly larger than the pages of the book itself, all the way through as if marking places, and the very first one he checked to see which particular passage it marked fell open at the very lines he had long ago made his motto:

> *If thou follow thy star, thou can'st not*
> *fail of glorious heaven.*

Feeling almost faint with excitement Freddie sat down on the piano stool and stared at the page. Then he stared at the sheet of paper which had marked the place and saw that it was covered with copious and closely written notes. He didn't read what they said but he checked all the other loose leaves and found that they too were entirely covered in jottings and notes. But the clue he wanted was to be found on the flyleaf of the book if anywhere, so at once he turned back to the front of the book and there it was. There was an inscription which read:

> *To dear Fleur, because our learning begin*
> *with each new day and with as much grow our*
> *understanding*
> *Isaac K. (1988)*

Fleur. Now she had a name, a real name albeit only part of her real name. But the rest would come. Freddie knew it now as he held the book in his hand, he knew this was the key to the truth he so desperately sought, this was something positive however preposterously small. She was called *Fleur* and she had been given a book by someone called Isaac whose surname began with a 'K' in 1988 and obviously, and coincidentally, *The Divine Comedy* was as special to her as it was to him, judging from the vast collection of personal notes and jottings it contained.

Overcoming the urge to sit down and sift through her notes to see what else he might learn, Freddie put the leather bound book carefully in his coat pocket and then shutting the piano back up he turned off the last of the lights, made his way quickly back upstairs and escaped from the house the same way he had come into it, out through the bedroom window, down the double ladder and straight into two blinding torchlights which snapped into life the moment his feet touched the ground.

7

When he understood of what he was to be accused, Freddie declined to say anything until he had spoken to his lawyer. Unfortunately it was now well past midnight and because the only lawyer in the country he knew was Mr Markson Senior whose office telephone number Freddie didn't have to hand let alone offhand, let alone his home telephone number, and since he was unable to call anyone else to stand bail for him without causing himself extreme embarrassment, Freddie was obliged to stay overnight in jail, banged up by himself in a small ceiling-to-floor white tiled cell with only a lavatory in one corner and a one-blanketed wooden bed for his comforts. He had been stripped of his shoelaces, his belt, his watch, rings and naturally the one thing he was alleged to have stolen, Her copy of *The Divine Comedy*, but even so Freddie fell immediately and happily asleep, because at last he had her name. She was called *Fleur*.

'Mr Markson?' he asked when he finally got through to the old lawyer the next morning. 'This is Frederick Jourdan speaking. I came to see you yesterday – that's right, you got me first time – and I'm afraid I guess I need your help again, but over an entirely different matter this time.'

He knew what the old man would say, even as he was explaining his predicament. But the old man didn't know what Freddie would say in return once he had delivered his predicted reply.

'Of course I would love to help you, Mr er—'

'Try Jourdan again. We found it worked before.'

'Mr Jourdan, of course, forgive me,' the old man said. 'But of course as you surely must realize I represent the person into whose property you stand accused of breaking and entering. So ethically I cannot possibly represent you as well, as you surely must have known.'

Freddie said nothing by way of reply. Of course he had known, and that really wasn't the object of his telephone call whatsoever.

'I can recommend someone if that is any help, Mr Jourdan. Or you could simply take pot luck with the Yellow Pages directory. Find some chappie in Worcester with the right credentials, you know – Law Society and all that sort of thing. The right sort of chappie would be only too happy to take on a chap like you. No problem at all.'

'That's good advice, sir,' Freddie replied, 'and I thank you for it. However there is something else you can do, something which is perfectly ethical. I'd be most grateful if you would kindly convey a message to your client for me.'

'And which particular client would that be, Mr—'

'Jourdan,' Freddie got in before the old man could forget yet again. 'It's a very simple message. I'm not going to ask you to reveal anything. I'd just like you to tell Fleur – right? Tell Fleur I agree with everything Isaac says. And that The Divine Comedy is my favourite book as well.'

There was a good long silence at the other end of the phone, which far from disconcerting him Freddie found he hugely enjoyed.

'Thank you, Mr Jourdan,' Mr Markson Senior finally replied in an altogether different tone of voice. 'I hope you manage to find yourself good representation.' Then the phone went dead.

While he was waiting to hear back from a local lawyer whom he had selected at gleeful random, Freddie was returned to his cell where he sat happily waiting for his unconditional release which he guessed was imminent.

Sure enough half an hour later the cell door was swung open and a policeman told him he was free to go.

'I imagine this is because Mr Markson called back?' Freddie said as he collected his personal belongings. 'I guess he must have verified what I told you.'

'Near enough,' the policeman behind the desk replied, weary already from a long shift. 'As if we haven't got enough to do trying to find boney-fider burglars. Breaking into a neighbour's property to rescue a book she'd left behind. Dear, dear, dear.'

'With some people it's cats, with some people it's their pet birds,' Freddie said, fixing his gold Rolex watch back on. 'With my neighbour it's her books.'

'Funny how she forgot to tell you about the alarm. Sir.'

'She forgot to tell me about the alarm — sorry, what do those stripes of yours denote?'

'That I'm a sergeant. Sir.'

'She forgot to tell me about the alarm. Sergeant. Because I guess she must have forgotten clean about the alarm. Much as she forgot clean about her book. May I go now, please? Sergeant?'

The moment he reached home Freddie fetched himself a cold beer and hurried to the study with Her copy of *The Divine Comedy*, intending to sort through the handwritten notes in search of further information. He hadn't even settled in his chair let alone opened the book when the telephone rang beside him.

'Hello?' he said. 'Freddie Jourdan speaking.'

'Hello,' a voice said back quietly, such a pretty voice but still a long way from being a friendly one. 'So now you know who I am.'

'Hello,' Freddie replied carefully putting the still-closed book down on his knee. 'Hello, Fleur.'

He wanted to try and make it sound as if she rang him all the time, rather than how he actually felt which was as if he had been hit in the stomach by a meteorite, but even so couldn't manage to keep the quiver out of his voice.

'We don't really know each other so I'd prefer it if you weren't quite so informal, Mr Jourdan,' the angelic voice said.

'Fine by me,' Freddie agreed. 'You mean you'd rather I called you—'

He waited, hoping for the break he'd played for.

'I'd rather you called me by my surname, Mr Jourdan,' the voice said, denying him entry. 'And you really had no right to break into my house.'

'It isn't really any more your house than Stoke Park is mine, wouldn't you say? And since Stoke Park owns The Folly—'

'That's not the point. You had no right to break in.'

'I agree. So why didn't you go ahead and bring charges?'

There was a short silence, during which Freddie tried to imagine how she was, what she was looking like, and what she was doing, but all he could see in front of him was how she had been in the dawn of the day they'd met.

'I didn't see any point,' she finally answered. 'Not once I knew it was you. Anyway. What did you want?'

'I've got what I want, thanks. Up to one point, that is. I know who you are.'

'I think this is where I say so what,' she said, very quietly, as if she was rehearsing the line rather than delivering it.

'Okay,' Freddie agreed, 'and in return I say so what about seeing you again? And not just again, but again and again and again.'

'There's no point. I already told you.'

'I'm sorry, I can hardly hear you.'

'I said – there's no point.'

'Why not? So what's the problem? Are you married? Is that it? Or is there somebody else – I mean what is it? You tell me.'

'There isn't a problem,' she said finally. 'At least – well. That's not the point.'

'So what is the point, Fleur? We have to meet – you know that—'

'No I do not!' she broke in, raising her voice from a near whisper for the first time. 'And please don't call me – don't call me by my Christian name.'

'Look – why are you upset? There's really nothing weird about this, you know. Nothing unusual in the desire of one perfectly sane and healthy man wanting to see the woman he's fallen in love with.'

'You're not.'

'I'm not what?'

'You're not in love with me.'

'How do you know? How do you know how I feel? You're not inside my head. You're not inside my heart—'

'You're not in love with me,' she said cutting in again. 'You can't be. It doesn't make sense and I have to go now.'

'No please don't.'

'I have to. Goodbye.'

'Okay,' Freddie said. 'But even if you do, don't worry. I'll find you.'

'Because you know who I am now.'

'You got it.'

'So who am I?'

There was yet another silence, this one caused by Freddie as he racked his brain to find a way out of this one.

'You don't know who I am, do you?' she asked suddenly.

'What makes you think that? Of course I do,' he replied, much too quickly for his own good. 'How else would

I know you're Fleur? How else would I know about Isaac?'

'Because you found something. You found something at The Folly. You found my Dante.'

'Your Dante? I don't know what you're talking about,' Freddie protested feebly. 'What's a Dante when it's washed and dried?'

'My copy of *The Divine Comedy*. I know where it was. The one place I didn't look. It was in the piano, wasn't it?'

'Yes,' Freddie said with a weary sigh. 'It had fallen inside the case.'

'Can you send it back to me, please?'

'Yes of course,' Freddie quickly agreed, seeing his opportunity. 'Just give me your address and I'll mail it to you straightaway.'

He thought he had her because she started to say it, she began to give him her address. 'It's number one hundred and—' Then she stopped as she realized and paused before going on while Freddie silently cursed his bad luck. 'If you don't mind sending it via Mr Markson, that'll be fine.'

'Sure,' Freddie reluctantly agreed. 'I'll put it in the mail soon as I can.'

'I want it now, please,' she said, still quietly but there was no mistaking her firmness, 'and I don't want you reading it.'

'I won't. As a matter of fact I have my own copy.'

'I meant please don't read my notes. You might have noticed there are a lot of notes in the book. And they're private.'

Freddie looked at the book, lying closed in his lap. When he hung up all he had to do was go through them and there was no saying what he would find. If she didn't want him to read her notes there was good reason. So all he had to do was to cross his fingers and agree then take his time going through the pages and pages of closely written notes to find out all about her. He would probably find out everything, more than he'd ever get to know in their initial conversations.

'I know what you're thinking,' her voice suddenly said in his ear. 'But if you want to see me again, I – I wouldn't advise it.'

'Of course I want to see you again,' Freddie replied.

'Then post the book straight back to Marksons without reading my notes,' she said. 'After all, they're private. Please promise that you won't.'

'Very well.' Freddie shrugged his shoulders, and although he was quite alone, he put his free hand on his heart. 'If that's what you want – I promise I won't read your notes. So now what about your side of the bargain?'

'As long as you keep your word, you'll see me again.'

'Yes that's all very well, but how will you know? If I keep my word that is? As it were you'll only have my word for it.'

'Not really. Not if you think about it. I'll know whether or not you've read them by what you say to me when we meet.'

Then the line went dead.

Freddie put the phone back and looked at the book lying on his knee. On the sheets of notes within the well-worn covers must lie everything he wanted to know about Fleur, all her innermost thoughts and secrets. All he had to do was open the book and start sorting through the pages to learn all about her character. It had to be so, otherwise she wouldn't have made him promise not to read them.

Of course she was bluffing, Freddie decided, still holding the unopened book in his hand. There was no way she could know from what he said to her when they next met that he had read her notes. All he had to do was take particular care not to refer to whatever any of the notes said when he saw her, it was as simple as that. He would talk of shoes and ships and sealing wax but never once about anything she had written in her precious and private notes. So how could she know? She really had to be bluffing. She was just trying to worry him out of it — and why? Because somewhere among those notes was the revelation not only of her full identity but even more probably the reason why she wouldn't see him.

But then just as he was about to open the volume and take out the first sheet of notes a voice inside his head told him not to, that he was wrong. She'd know he had read her book not because of anything he said (or didn't say), but because he would have found out who she was. It was really as simple as that. If he knew where and how to find her he could only have found out those things from her personal observations and jottings, the very things he had just promised her, hand on heart, not to read. At the moment all he knew and all she knew that he knew was that she rented The Folly, that her first name was Fleur and that she had been given a copy of Dante's *The Divine Comedy* by someone called Isaac in 1988. That was the extent of his knowledge, and the minute he revealed that he knew one thing more about her or where to find her she would know at once he had broken his word and he would never see her again.

So instead he closed the leather-bound book up, found a large enough envelope to contain it, and addressed it to Markson and Markson. Then having sealed the package securely with tape he drove to the village and posted it Recorded Delivery as recommended by the woman in the village Post Office when she discovered he needed a proof of posting.

'Could you please put the time on the counterfoil as well?' Freddie requested, going to choose a postcard from the adjacent display while the woman behind the counter amended the form.

There was only one postcard which caught his eye just as it must have been intended to do. It was a picture of a girl in an old-fashioned black velvet coat feeding deer in a winter garden, a painting. Freddie saw when he turned the card over with a now slightly trembling hand that it was called *The Orphans* by an artist named Samuel Edmund Waller. When he was sufficiently recovered, Freddie wrote on the back the following:

Please note time on enclosed counterfoil. You rang off at 12.08 p.m. Drive to village (as you know) takes 12 mins. Time of posting 12.32 p.m. Ergo: no time for reading. My word is my bond. How about yours? I now wait to hear back from you re our meeting.

Resisting the temptation to sign off with some reference to their first meeting and the apt nature of the painting, or with any kind of hint at love or affection or anything resembling it in case it might act as a deterrent, Freddie signed the card with just his name and then enclosed it and the counterfoil in a separate envelope which he also posted to reach her via Markson and Markson. After that he crossed the road to the King's Arms where he drank a lukewarm beer and discussed the continuing good weather in depth with the locals before returning to Stoke Park to spend the afternoon fishing and swimming in the lake.

After a silent ten days he gave in to temptation and sent her another postcard, exactly the same one, via her lawyers, which simply read: *Still waiting.*

A week later and still waiting he rang Markson and Markson.

'I wonder if you would mind passing another message on to your client, Mr Markson,' he enquired of the senior partner once he was put through. 'To Miss Smith.'

'To which Miss Smith are we referring, sir?'

'Miss Fleur Smith? The sometime tenant of The Folly, Stoke Park? I need to get in touch with her again, Mr Markson. Now.'

'Indeed, um – Mr—'

'Jourdan. You'll get it soon, Mr Markson, if this charade continues. This really is a matter of some urgency, you understand.'

'Of course, sir, I understand perfectly,' the lawyer returned, 'but alas such a thing will not be possible. I am led to understand that the Miss Smith to whom you refer has left the country.'

There had been no point in asking where or when or for how long. In fact after he had replaced the receiver Freddie had seriously wondered whether there was any point in anything any more. He'd kept his word and she'd broken hers. If he hadn't kept his word he could have found out who she was and where she lived, at least giving himself some semblance of an outside chance of winning her over if not of actually winning her heart. But now, with her disappearance, all chance would seem to have gone.

Worst of all, yet most fortunately for Freddie because he does not realize it, he knows who she is but has forgotten (had he known, imagine the torment). He has forgotten because when she was an overnight sensation he was just sixteen years old and attending High School in Lewiston, Maine, heavily into jazz, baseball and really nothing else, particularly if that anything else was happening way across the pond. Yet that is what is so extraordinary, he did know her then because two years later he actually bought something of hers to give to his then current girlfriend, a lion-maned redhead with the ridiculous name of Muffin who like him also played piano except her taste was Bach rather than Brubeck. Not only that, but he knew her both by her Christian name and her surname, because when he bought this thing of hers he asked for it using her full name, and then he actually remarked to his girlfriend when he saw her face properly for the very first time what a very beautiful face it was.

92

In fact what he said was that her face had to be the most beautiful face he'd ever seen and quite understandably Muffin got upset and very nearly ruined her birthday celebration with her sudden fit of jealousy, because such was the look in his eyes when he saw her face for the first time it was small wonder Muffin had been unnerved.

'I thought you were supposed to be in love with me!' she'd protested. 'Yet here you are obsessed with some picture of someone you don't even know! How do you think that makes me feel, Freddie?'

Even then, in those long-gone days when he'd seen her face for the first time, he'd thought that he knew her. Wasn't that odd?

She would have been bound to agree, particularly knowing her own thoughts, how she herself had felt when she had seen him for the very first time.

While the girl with the unlikely name of Muffin tugged his sleeve and cried in his ear, and before he teased her out of her pique, how Freddie had stared and stared at the extraordinary face which was staring back at him. Not only had he felt then that he already knew her, at that moment he'd also felt that he was somewhere else, as if he had gone back in time and more than that, he'd felt as if he were someone else, as if he were in a different body and mind altogether. It was as if the two of them were already one.

But of course all this is long forgotten. It might be hard to believe but now as he stands at the open windows in his hired English country house staring out across the quiet parkland he really has forgotten entirely how he fell in love with her then, how he looked into the secrets that were and still are in her dark eyes and how his heart stopped when he first heard her voice. Even though he knows her first name, even that doesn't ring any bells, certainly not the bell that will bring him to her, not yet but that's because it isn't yet meant. When it is, he will find her. He will find his way to her side and finally he will be with her, but not yet. Not yet because that time has been appointed and has still to come round.

8

Realizing he had been bested Freddie thought there to be no further point in any more pursuit or detection. He thought that had she felt just one per cent for him of what he felt for her it would have been enough for her to agree to their meeting, that was all she needed to feel, just one per cent of the love he felt for her. No more. All it needed to be was merely the idlest of curiosities, a need to know the merest scrap more about him, just enough interest to whet her appetite sufficiently, but no. She hadn't even that much care in her. So in that case, Freddie concluded, quite obviously she had absolutely no interest in him whatsoever which was why, as she said, she thought *there was no point*. It really was as simple as that.

A long way from being any sort of a hard drinker, even so Freddie reached for the bottle that night at Stoke Park and drank himself steadily insensible, finding he could stand the desolation no longer.

He didn't even remember going to bed. All he could remember when he woke an hour before dawn the next morning was that he had dreamed a piece of music, seemingly an entire composition. He didn't even notice the hangover which was already in place and about to materialize as an almighty temple-splitting headache because all he could feel was the music that still seemed to sound in his head, the music he had dreamed, and he knew that every note of it was still in place in his mind even though he was now sitting up and wide awake.

Afraid to move and reach out for the notebook he

always kept by him at night lest what he was hearing so clearly should vanish away through the door the way he knew dreams mostly did (mostly – but not it seemed this one), he remained sitting perfectly still in his bed while trying to get a hold of the sounds which now seemed to be growing fainter, slowly becoming echoes rather than the very real pulses that had just been reverberating through his subconscious. As he sat there motionless he became aware of two things. Firstly he knew with that odd certainty dreaming bestows on the dreamer that the music he had dreamed was in three movements and was therefore a concerto. Secondly, and this is what puzzled him even further, it wasn't a piano concerto which by rights it should have been since the piano was his instrument both for playing and composing; it was a concerto for the violin.

He had no idea of how long he sat like that in his bed. It must have been some time, because when he'd woken it had still been pitch dark, and now the early morning sun was flooding his room. The pain in his head brought him to full consciousness otherwise he might have sat there all morning in a state of stupefaction, a condition induced by the fact that far from forgetting his dream, the longer he had been awake the more the memory stayed with him. So much so that once he'd become aware of how much his head hurt, he then promptly forgot all about the pain in the excitement of realizing it seemed he could still actually remember the music he had dreamed. So, going for broke, he reached for his notebook to see what he could put down of the sublime music his imagination had just been sent.

At first when he started to put pen to paper and nothing came, in his panic he thought it had gone, that the throbbing pain in his head had drummed the music out of his head and he was nearly physically sick from the disappointment. But then as he composed himself he discovered that although the detail had gone, the main melodic theme had not. In fact so strong was the memory of it he found he could sing it out loud – which he did, over and over again, with the same sort of confidence with which most music lovers can sing their way through the entire first theme of Tchaikovsky's First Piano Concerto. So overjoyed that the memory of the theme was that intact, once again he started to write, only this time he didn't stop.

How long he sat there in bed writing he could never have said. He must have presented a ridiculous sight, sitting there unwashed and unshaven, singing out loud at the top of his voice while he wrote, but that was the last thing that concerned him. The point was he was getting it all down, note for note, while the sun rose and set in a cloudless sky and Mrs Davies came and went in summons to his constant calling on the house phone for trays of black coffee and toast, bottles of mineral water and plates of Marmite sandwiches (to which Freddie had become currently addicted). Further pots of black coffee and bars of dark plain chocolate helped perpetuate the creative energy that was positively humming around the composer's bedroom.

By dusk Freddie had sketched out the entire concerto, the opening *allegro*, the *andante cantabile*, and the concluding movement which he designed to be composed as another *allegro*, this one *andante grazioso – cadenza – allegro ma non troppo*. It was only as yet in abbreviated and annotated form, but the shape was there musically and thematically and there for good, not lost as it might well have been, as it had so often been for writers and composers who had also dreamed something up in their slumbers.

With the initial part of his work done, for the first time in twenty-four hours he felt quite ready to dress. He pulled on a tee shirt and an old pair of chinos, and took himself and his precious notebook down to the drawing room where, having asked Mrs Davies to bring him a light supper on a tray, he sat at the Steinway grand and began the task of transcribing his composition in full onto the eleven lines of the great stave. Had he been able to step outside his body and see himself, Freddie would never have recognized the person sitting at the keyboard as himself. Instead so fast and frantically was he working that he would most probably have been reminded of the way Hollywood had always preferred to portray composers and musicians at work, as if they were madmen possessed by some sort of demon.

Of course nowadays most likely they would depict him surrounded by all the very latest in computer technology, in fact all the stuff in which Diane was always trying to get him interested, gizmos which did everything for the modern composer from reproducing every sound of the orchestra to transcribing whole scores in whatever key and time signature the writer wanted, let alone small state-of-the-art portable keyboards with their own memory which enabled creative musicians to work when and where they liked instead of having to rely on the old system of pen, piano and manuscript. But Freddie had resisted the lure of the technological sirens, firstly because as far as computers went he was totally illiterate, just as he was mechanically illiterate. Freddie couldn't even work the remote control on his television set properly, let alone programme his video recorder, and Diane's remark about Freddie and torches hadn't been a joke. If and when a torch or flashlight failed Freddie always took it back to the shop to have its batteries changed. Secondly, however, and perhaps more to the point, Freddie was a purist. He worked in the way he did because he believed it was the best way, either straight onto the piano keyboard or paper. Freddie could hear the sounds of the orchestra in his head, just the way composers always had done long before the days of sequencers and transposers, and that was the way he preferred it. To Freddie, music was not matter for computers, something written and programmed by a silicon chip. Music was metaphysical and came from the spheres.

Even so, given the shortcomings of his preferred method, with his foot flat to the floor Freddie still managed to write the whole concerto in just under ten days, not just the violin part but the entire orchestral score, exactly so he believed as he had heard it in his dream. When he got up from the piano he had a ten-day-old beard and was still wearing the same clothes he had put on when he had begun. He'd slept a maximum of four hours a night, most nights no more than three, and towards the end perhaps no more than one or two, yet he didn't feel in the slightest bit exhausted. On the contrary he was so fresh he felt he could start out all over again.

It was early in the afternoon on the day he finished, when the last chord had been defined, structured, recorded and then allowed to die away, the sound of the imagined orchestra rolling out triumphantly through the open windows and away across the sunny meadows across to the very hills which had inspired Edward Elgar. As Freddie sat at the piano gazing out at the view before him, he could hear the sound of a violin floating and soaring up into the pale summer blue beyond, cast on the air the way an angler's line snakes out over the clear waters of the chalk stream, the way a lark hovers high above the May meadows.

That too was how Freddie felt, as if he were miles high and flying. He couldn't begin to comprehend what he had done, how he had done it, or why. What it felt like was as if it had all happened to someone else because Freddie didn't feel that he had achieved anything personally, in fact he had absolutely no feeling of any singular achievement whatsoever, just a sense of complete fulfilment. He had put himself into whatever hands had been guiding him and gone with the flow, knowing that if for one moment he'd tried to make sense of what was happening to him he would have lost it. At least these were his thoughts as he now sat dumbly trying to give the whole adventure some sort of perspective. Slowly but surely he found that the only way he could do this was to tell himself that he'd simply been given a job to do and he had done it. He had been required to try and remember the music he had heard in the night, and he had done so. He had remembered the music that had come to him in the darkness, in his sleep, in his dreams, he had written it all down as he had heard it and there it was in front of him. For a composer of stage musicals it was the most unlikely thing he could ever have thought to see: *Violin Concerto in E Minor by Frederick Jourdan*.

Perhaps the whole thing was a dream, he began to wonder as he came to from his reverie and poured himself some wine, then stopped as he watched the pale yellow liquid settle in the glass. Even that action could be an imaginary one, he realized. All this could still be the imaginings of his subconscious, not just the music that had come to him but the whole damned run, the entire sequence of him hearing the music, of *waking up and writing it down*, right up to this moment of him sitting out in a garden somewhere under slowly passing summer clouds listening to the song of birds hidden up in the ever-whispering beech trees. It all felt so unreal, it all seemed so unreal, more than anything it all seemed so completely and utterly preposterous that there could be no other explanation. He was still asleep and dreaming.

Unless as someone once said, in a saying which was now to haunt him constantly, unless instead of dreaming our dreams, our dreams dream us.

At this thought Freddie at once slapped himself hard

around the face. When he opened his smarting eyes everything was still there exactly as it had been, garden, sky, trees, birds, wine glass, and the manuscript. Everything was where it had been, except more so. He rubbed the ten-day growth of beard on his chin, saw the ink stains on his fingers, felt the aching muscles in his neck and writing hand and realized he was wrong, that this was reality after all.

He knew it also from the exhaustion which suddenly hit him, because that was something else dreamers didn't feel, they didn't feel as if they needed to sleep for a week. But before he did it seemed to him that the first thing he had to do was to take his precious manuscript down to the local library and make a couple of photocopies. Then he would crash out. He would come back to the house and crash out until the evening when he would get up and cook himself a good hot chilli *con carne* which was exactly the sort of food he needed to pull himself together.

It was getting dark when he awoke, and it was raining, a fine summer's drizzle which hardly sounded as it fell. While he bathed, shaved off his stubbled beard and washed his hair, he began to sing without realizing either that he was singing or what he was singing. He carried on all the way through drying himself and his hair and getting dressed in a dark blue crew-neck cashmere sweater and a clean pair of chinos, right up till the moment he checked himself in front of the cheval mirror, just as he was slipping his feet into a pair of nut-brown loafers, when he saw himself and finally heard himself. He'd been singing 'Where or When'.

He stopped and stared back at himself, wondering why of all the songs he knew he had chosen that one, before slowly starting to sing through it again, right from the top of the verse.

When you're awake the things you think come from the dreams
you dream.
Thought has wings and lots of things are seldom what they
seem.
Sometimes you think you've lived before all that you live today.
Things you do — come back to you, as though they knew the way.
Oh, the tricks your mind can play—

He wasn't in that sort of mood. Normally people sing the songs of the mood they're in, and he most certainly was not in a romantic frame of mind, not in the slightest, that is not any more, particularly as far as a certain person who had reneged on her word was concerned. If he was out of her hair, then, man — was she out of his, and not just his hair but his life. To show her just how far out she exactly was, Freddie determined to sing something else, something entirely unromantic. He knew plenty of other songs, songs much more appropriate to the mood he was in, the mood he was enforcing on himself, songs about plenty of other things besides love and dreams and people you think you've met before. Silly songs, songs like 'Lydia the Tattooed Lady'. 'Lydia' would suit the way he was feeling just fine, he decided as he brushed out his nearly dry hair and splashed on some Floris cologne.

He sang it all the way downstairs, loud and clear, like Groucho Marx had so memorably sung it, then when he reached the drawing room he sat down at the piano where he played and sang it all the way through again, from first note to last. But when he finished playing he found all that he really wanted to play was Lorenz Hart's wonderful love song, 'Where or When'.

'Nice to have you up and about again,' Mrs Davies said after she'd knocked on the drawing-room door. 'We'd just about given you up for dead.'

'I felt as if I was dead,' Freddie replied, still staring down at the keyboard. 'But now I feel fine. Relaxed, refreshed and not in the slightest bit tired.'

'And so you should, Mr Jourdan,' Mrs Davies said as she came in carrying the ice bucket and a salver of pistachios on a tray. 'You've been asleep for well over twenty-four hours.'

Freddie looked up and stared at his housekeeper's back as she set her tray down.

'You saying it's Thursday today?' he ventured.

'It's Thursday today and has been all day, Mr Jourdan,' Mrs Davies replied. 'I left you sleeping because after all that hard work I said to Enid it was the best thing for you. You should have seen yourself, really. We couldn't get a word of sense out of you these past ten days. I suppose it's something else we'll be hearing on the radio one day, yes? Another of those nice songs of yours, from one of your shows.'

'I haven't really been asleep since yesterday afternoon have I, Mrs Davies?'

'Out to the world, Mr Jourdan. I said to Enid and that's where you'll stay, I said. Much the best thing for you. Anyway, I'm glad you're quite yourself again, Mr Jourdan, because truth to tell as I said to Enid this last week truth to tell I was beginning to get more than a bit worried, the way you was going at it.'

After he had poured a good measure of whisky over several large clear cubes of ice and Mrs Davies had gone to see to the turbot she'd bought him for his dinner, Freddie took the original manuscript of the concerto off the top of the piano and sat by the fireplace with it on his lap while he drank his whisky. Now that he was properly awake he hardly dared to look at it in case what he found was a nonsense. The chances of it being such he knew to be far, far greater than the chances of finding he had written a master work, or even a half-respectable one. Although obviously when he'd studied music in New York at the Juillard he'd been taught classical form and composition, from the outset his ambitions had always been directed towards the theatre and not the concert hall, and although he loved classical music, when he listened to it he did so for pleasure and relaxation. He never took it apart and examined it critically the way he did the work of his theatrical rivals and so consequently he really didn't consider himself sufficiently well versed in the mechanics of classical composition to be able to sit down and write an entire concerto, particularly not for an instrument with which he was really not at all familiar.

So his delay in reviewing the product of his ten-day frenzy was wholly understandable. In fact it wasn't until he was halfway through his second whisky that he dared actually open the score and read it rather than just stare at the title page, and when he did he was astounded.

There it all was certainly, note for imagined note. There was the violin part, there its entry set in the instrument's lowest register, an entry defining the eight-note statement which was the summary of the concerto's theme. There, too, was the theme gaining ground, reinforced now by the violas an octave above and here the surprise — no reappearance of the opening march in either the development by the solo violin nor in the recapitulation, although hidden away among the oboes and the horns there was just a reminder here and there of its dotted rhythm.

Then the *andante*, music of simple eloquence scored even more lightly than the opening *allegro* and built on three melodies, a movement filled with caressing tenderness, a feeling of love and warmth which is carried through into the third and last movement which begins with rapid, dazzling ascending passages for the violin before the orchestra returns to the march-like main theme which, in turn, the soloist then elaborates over the orchestra so that it seems the climax must come at any moment – but no. Instead the key changes to the tonic minor, and the orchestra goes to silence, except for the plaintive voice of a solo oboe introducing the *cadenza* in which the violin muses on and then embellishes all the themes before returning to the opening statement, which with the orchestra triumphantly entering once again turns into the closing statement, thrillingly, expansively, conclusively, saying farewell to what has gone and opening up a future full of hope and joy.

'How?' Freddie said quietly aloud to himself. 'How in hell did I do it? Or did I do it? How in God's name did this ever come to pass?'

9

He was told not to put too much faith in musicians. They were rather too much like actors, his London agent told him when Freddie went up to town to see him, and actors were too much like jockeys. Never follow a jockey's tip, Marshall Williams advised, never listen to what actors have to say about a script, or musicians about a new composition. They will either praise it inordinately because they need something to bring them back into the public eye, or they will disparage it entirely because they are either too grand or too busy.

'History is littered with such anecdotes,' his agent told him. 'The great and the grand turning down Rachmaninoff, Tchaikovsky, let alone Mozart, and the has-beens lauding the non-existent talents of the non-entities. In theory a leading conductor should be your man, but with your track record he'll think you must be a lightweight and having to be careful with his time he'll only give your piece to some minion to assess, someone who is of course incapable of assessing anything until he has heard the audience's applause and read the critical notices which is why, of course, he is still a minion. At this point we have to stop to wonder how in hell anything ever gets put on in the first place which of course it never does, but only in the third or the fourth or the fifth place. So here's my final recommendation – namely that you let the man best qualified in the country study it. The only man I know who is capable of giving an objective, unprejudiced opinion on whatever is put before him, be it food or the food of love. Let me send your work to my dear old friend Izzy Kline.'

'Who he?' Freddie asked, for a moment unable to explain why the name rang a bell.

'Izzy Kline is one of the world's best violin teachers, and probably the very best reader of new music anywhere, so he's just the man for you,' his agent explained.

'I know why his name rings a bell,' Freddie suddenly said. 'One of my doctors, in fact Diane's doctor, he has the same name. The same last name that is.'

'Izzy will come a lot cheaper than any New York doctor, Freddie,' Marshall Williams replied. 'But I must say whatever it cost you, you're looking a whole lot better.'

'Just as well you can't see inside,' Freddie said, tapping his manuscript into shape on the desk.

'How so?'

'Nothing,' Freddie said, with the faintest of smiles. 'Let's just say this piece of work took a lot more out of me than I thought.'

Days passed, but they passed so slowly while Freddie waited to hear. He spent most of them lying out in the garden reading and sleeping, his sun bed turned away from the little white house high on the knoll behind him. At last Kline wrote to him rather than calling in person, because as Marshall Williams had explained the music teacher was in declining health and had been in fact for some years. His letter was long and detailed, and the grateful Freddie read it slowly and carefully.

Dear Mr Jourdan,
At least I write in better English than I still speak it, so you will be spared my shall we call them 'Kaplanisms'. Now for your concerto which I come to next. First let me say this although much good

may it do us all. I just must say that once I knew just the musician for this. In fact as I read your composition I could hear the performance and her playing this so beautifully. If ever a piece was written for this most brilliant of musicians this was it, but there we are. *C'est la vie, n'est ce pas?* That she no longer plays we all know what a pity. What a pity! Two, three year ago now? I would be able to say to you don't even think about who plays this because there is only this one violinist. You of course would have agreed – yes of course you would because I know from how you write this piece, and everyone say yes, this is a marriage indeed made in heaven, the marriage of true minds.

However, this is not to be because we no longer have this great talent for us all to love and enjoy and that is the sadness. The joy is that this is a beautiful work, one I myself would love to play if I still might but not with this infernal artharitis (is it spelt arthar or arthur I don't never know).

Yes, it is a fine, beautiful and so sensitive work I do not believe this is your first try at the classics, that you never write a concerto, sonata, even a bagatelle before in this tradition. That you only write what they describe as theatre music, which even you seem to pooh-pooh. But why? What about Walton? He wrote the film music also? Remember Erich Korngold? The man who writes the score for most famous Robin Hood of all, Errol Flynn, yes? Yet he also writes when he is just seventeen such an inventive string sextet so full of character. And some say even this Floyd Webber that writes musical shows as you do. Not me, but some do and so enough nonsense about what you say you worth. Your music say what you are worth and this concerto who knows? It might be of the highest worth.

There are flaws, sure there are, but such things would be mended with work. Instance, the development of the second theme in the first movement is haphazard (I think) and not enough definition between that and the next development. Perhaps too the climax of the last movement and so the piece as a whole is somewhat *too* determined, as much as you are saying to us what you feel rather than letting us feel it by showing it through the music. What I am trying to tell you here is let the music speak for itself but again, this is only a feeling. We would need to hear it played, which it must be and that is the next thing.

For this is fine work, lyrical, rhapsodic and so very full of emotion (I am imagining that you write it about someone, but then that is a presumption, forgive me), it really does have an almost Elgarian *noblimente* passion in its conception. I like too the way the orchestra seems to have big dramas of outbursts and not our usually predictable steady growing climaxes – this is exciting and what you intend, yes? Like I hear the opening statement of the violin, imagining if I may this remote, transparent thread of sound firstly (what contrast to those big orchestral colours!) and then the sound opening out into this big full throated tone! And so lacking my first choice, you must approach another ex-pupil of mine (for might I say I think this a *female* piece?) and if I have your blessing I will speak also with her. Send it to Marie-Anne Schiller (just as in the poet and indeed an ancestor) who I am convinced will be as interested in this work as I.

Failing her, for maybe you might not be so great an admirer, there is also your young fellow American Tamara Glasse who is rightfully making the big reputation now she has always merited. Alas, her I do not know but perhaps you may. Or perhaps you have someone yourself in your mind? Whatever, this must be your purpose, to find the right voice for your song. There is no doubt in this mind that your work being of the highest order is deserving of the best interpreters. I would be pleased to learn your choice, and hope some little of this what I have said will be of use. Of course we must communicate more (if that is your wish) when it is decided on your next step. Please do not hesitate to write to me more and please God I live to hear your lovely music played.

Well done!

Yours most sincerely,
I.A.L. Kline

10

He was very bad, very bad on violinists. Freddie could name all the very best pianists alive and most of those not long dead, but knew only those violinists who were household names.

This was the main cause of his present bewilderment since he kept asking himself why his unconscious should (apparently) have produced a work for an instrument which was not his instrument. Naturally he knew how to write for other instruments because that had been part of learning the art of composition, but as a professional composer he worked on and for the piano. When scoring a composition the violin never entered his head except as part of the orchestra. Yet the work he had found himself compelled to write was a piece for violin which this most renowned music teacher (how right Marshall had been to revere his former colleague, how brilliant to think of contacting him) had just identified as fine, lyrical and beautiful before one single note of it had even been played. And as far as the mechanics of writing had gone it was as if Freddie had always been writing for the violin instead of the piano. It simply didn't make any sense at all.

On receipt of Kline's letter Freddie at once took himself into Worcester where, at the best music shop in the city, with the help of a knowledgeable assistant, he bought the best examples of the top twelve living violinists who were still performing. They included four women and a collection that featured the two players Kline had recommended to him. These recordings he took back to Stoke Park where for the next two days he sat and listened to them over and over again, waiting for one of the soloists to speak to him.

But none did.

Each was exemplary and more often than not brilliant, but no one single voice spoke in the way he wanted. Not that he knew precisely what he was waiting to hear or for what he was searching, far from it. All he understood was that when he heard the right voice he would know it at once.

As far as Kline's recommendations went, his two nominees were far and away the most suitable out of all the unwitting applicants. Marie-Anne Schiller had a glorious tone and a blazing intensity, at least these were the qualities she demonstrated in the recording Freddie had just bought of her playing the Sibelius, while Tamara Glasse's rendition of the over-played and consequently undervalued Tchaikovsky was tenderly affecting and finally genuinely exhilarating without ever indulging in the usual sentimental histrionics, particularly in the central *canzonetta*.

Yet finally neither said enough to him, or at least what they said wasn't said in the utterly right way for which Freddie was waiting. It wasn't a question of him setting his sights too high or of losing his sense of proportion. In spite of the praise lavished on his unperformed work by Izzy Kline, Freddie had not allowed himself to indulge in any absurd delusions about the stature of his composition. His quest was for something quite other, and although he had no real conception of what this other might be, the part of himself to which he now listened assured him that when it was presented to him he would know it beyond any doubt.

So he waited. He put aside all the recordings he had bought on his first visit to the music shop and on the subsequent ones when he'd returned there to see what else they might have in stock which they could recommend. He put everything aside, the CDs, the tapes, his manuscript, the letter from Kline, his own and as yet unfinished reply, the books on the violin and the musical guides and magazines he had purchased; even the radio he turned off and left off, even the piano he left unplayed. Instead he tied some new flies onto his casts and went fishing for days on end. And waited.

While he was waiting Diane rang and told him she was planning to come over to see him the following week. Freddie who'd been deliberately avoiding her, now realized that it was pointless and as far as Diane was concerned hurtful for him to continue with the charade, so he began by telling her that there was no point in her coming all the way over to England to see him because it was all over between them. When after a long tense silence she finally asked him why, Freddie then told her.

She changed her tone completely when he'd finished. Freddie had anticipated fireworks or at the very least recriminations but what he got was the very opposite.

Obviously, she told him, it was imperative that she see him as soon as possible so she would clear her desk immediately and travel over at once. What had happened was her fault, not his. She should have taken her own counsel and not listened to the doctors. The doctors had been wrong, as usual. If she had taken her own counsel, she assured Freddie, this never would have happened.

'I was overworked, that's all, Diane. I just got a bit overtired. The new show needed a lot more work than we all realized. Out of town was tough, and I got exhausted, it's as simple as that. So how can you think any of this is down to you?'

Diane sidestepped this one for a moment and simply asked him in return if he was taking the pills he'd been prescribed. Freddie took a deep breath and counted up to three before he answered, thinking how like being grilled by a nurse this all was. Here he was trying to explain the seemingly inexplicable thing that had happened to him, turning his whole life upside down and here was his fiancée asking him in a special sort of nurse's voice if he was still taking his goddamn pills.

'No I'm not,' he said, as blithely as he could manage. 'I stopped taking any dope the moment I got here because this place does more for a guy than any medication you can name, Diane. Instead of tranquillizers I go fishing, and instead of sleepers I take long walks. I haven't popped a pill since I settled in here.'

This was greeted with another short silence but before Freddie could bring the conversation back to the subject he wanted to discuss with Diane, she cut in.

'You really shouldn't have stopped taking what you were so carefully prescribed, Freddie,' she said in an ominously calm way. 'They give you these things for a reason, you know? And this is not the sort of medication you can simply "come off", Freddie. Some of these drugs have pretty heavy withdrawal symptoms, such as hallucinosis?'

'Look. That stuff they gave me is for geriatrics,' Freddie reasoned, trying to stay as calm as he could. 'Those pills made me feel like the walking dead. No way was I going to spend my time letting down in a place like this, looking at it all through a haze of medication, unable to appreciate the beauty of it, unable to let myself mend myself. Sure – I guess it must have looked bad for a while, but I'm fine now, really. And I've done it all without pills. End of story.'

'You're fine now really? You should hear yourself,' Diane replied. 'Going on about things you've dreamed coming true? Falling in love at first sight with someone you don't even know but have seen in your dreams? And you don't think dreaming whole concertos in your sleep is ridiculous? Concertos which you then set about writing? For an instrument you know nothing about, yet which you are convinced is a great work of art and now you want to break off our engagement so that you can run off with someone whose name you don't even know and you say you're all right?'

'Look.' Freddie took a pull, trying to slow things up a bit. 'I know how this all must sound to you. You have a right to be angry, and hurt—'

'I am not hurt and angry,' she interrupted. 'I just want you to put everything on hold till I see you.'

'There's nothing you can do, Diane,' he said. 'This isn't in your emotional canon. It isn't in most people's come to that. What's happened here is obviously something that has just been waiting to happen. It's like two stars finally colliding and making another sun. It's called inevitability and if it's going to happen to you, you sure as hell can't get out of the way of it.'

'Yes I'm sure, Freddie dear,' Diane said, changing her tone. 'Now just promise you'll take things nice and easy until I get there. I shall be over as soon as I can, okay?'

'No it is not okay, Diane!' Freddie shouted, suddenly losing it, and immediately regretting that he had because it had made him sound desperate and in need of help. 'What I meant to say, Diane, was there's nothing you can do,' he began again, as calmly as he could manage. 'There's nothing you can do because I don't love you any more.'

'You only think that,' she replied as if he'd just told her he didn't like the dress she was wearing. 'You imagine you don't love me any more because you aren't yourself. Your imagination has obviously had more than it can take—'

'This isn't to do with my imagination, Diane.'

'What else is it to do with? All you've been going on about for the past half hour is what you've dreamed or what you haven't. So it seems to me to be perfectly obvious that what we're looking at is just another form of stress here. Stress suffered by an overactive imagination. However, I have every confidence in the doctors when they say that your condition is only a temporary one, and that the delusions you're still suffering from—'

'I'm not suffering from delusions, Diane! I'm not *suffering* from anything. What I have running around in my head are simply convictions, one of which is that I'm really not in love with you any more. I really didn't want to tell you like this, Diane. Not over the telephone, but there you go. You can't make what has happened unhappen.'

'Nothing – *has* happened, Freddie. Only in your mind.'

'The concerto isn't a phantasm, Diane, it's a fact,' he said. 'It's written, it's all down on paper.'

'Freddie,' she replied, with obviously growing impatience. 'People imagine they are Napoleon, right? Psychopathologically-wise, this is an old shoe.'

'Diane, I did not imagine the concerto. I have it right here in front of me, with a letter of assessment from one of the best musical brains in the country. This guy called Izzy Kline.'

'Who?' Diane asked carefully.

'Izzy Kline. This famous violin teacher I mentioned, remember?'

'Yes. Who apparently shares the same name as your doctor.'

'What are you talking about now?'

'The doctor I sent you to and whose full name is Dr Isaac Klein, Freddie. You surely can't have forgotten that.'

A cold hand gripped the guts of Freddie's stomach. 'So what?' he asked feebly, his confidence suddenly shaken for the first time. 'So what if it is?'

'You don't find it odd that the man who says your dreamed-up composition is a masterpiece and the man who is treating you for your anxiety crisis *have one and the same name*?'

'No – why should I!' Freddie returned, the whole of his insides now turning to ice. 'That is just sheer coincidence, damnit! Besides, if I remember it's spelt differently. Doctor

Klein spells his name "E-I-N" not "I-N-E", which is how my Isaac Kline spells his name. Not the same way at all as your Isaac Klein spells his.'

'As your Isaac Klein, Freddie. You're the one who's being treated here.'

'Freddie,' Diane added finally after a silence. 'I'll tell you what we're going to do, darling.'

Realizing that as far as convincing Diane had gone he had fought a losing battle, Freddie allowed the rest of what she had to say wash over him. He leaned back in his chair and let her expound her plans while he tried to concentrate on figuring out the precise state of his sanity.

He knew that there was a perfect possibility that Diane was right, that he was in fact temporarily insane. He certainly could well be in the middle of a full-scale hallucinosis, a *folie* not *de grandeur* but *d'amour*. These sort of things happened to people and most particularly to people like him. He knew how close to the brink you could get when you worked as hard as he'd been working, particularly if you were creative and had to pluck your substances from the thin air, and when you were there teetering on the brink it was all too easy to lose sight of reality.

So maybe it was all part of a gigantic delusion: the dream of the white deer, the dawn meeting in the garden, the last sight of Fleur at the window, finding the book, Fleur ringing him up, dreaming the concerto, getting a letter from someone with what sounded like the same name as the consultant Diane had taken him to see; perhaps none of this had actually happened at all, just as he himself had thought earlier. Even the house he was staying in, even Stoke Park might not be what it seemed. Stoke Park could just as easily be not a private home but a private nursing home staffed by Mrs Davies, Enid, and Thomas, while Markson and Markson might not be whom he thought them to be but doctors to whose joint care he had been committed.

He knew this was all perfectly and entirely possible because some time ago he'd had to study the case histories of certain mentally disturbed patients for a show he'd once started writing. He knew that people affected with this sort of hallucinosis often imagined they were undertaking long journeys when in fact all they were doing was walking down the corridor from their ward to the psychologist's consulting room. These poor people often lived in a world entirely of their own making, seeing their nurses and doctors as entirely different people – such as housekeepers, housemaids and gardeners – and the institutions in which they were confined as large country houses where they were taking a well-earned holiday, safe and beautiful places where they imagined they saw unicorns, or white deer, dreamed up masterworks in their sleep and imagined themselves falling in love with beautiful strangers who didn't even exist. Oh yes he well knew *the tricks your mind can play*—

And when someone said to you they were coming right over to see you and make sure you were all right, they weren't necessarily coming over the Atlantic to see you, they might be coming over from just a few blocks down, or maybe an hour's drive away, because the person in the institution and the person coming over to see if they were all right weren't separated by any great distances at all, only the distances between their mental states.

It was all perfectly possible and rather entirely so.

As if to underline what he was thinking, the door opened and Mrs Davies came in carrying supper on a tray which she began to set out at a table in the window. Judging from her appearance and by her manner Freddie knew she could just as easily be working in a nursing home as could Enid, as could Thomas who always gave

Freddie the distinct feeling he was trying to humour him.

Diane could well be right. All of this — everything that was happening to him and everything that had already happened to him — it could just be going on in his head. In the wrong part of his head.

That could also explain why nobody had been able to tell him anything, about the 'house', the 'family' and most of all about the mysterious girl in 'The Folly', perhaps because in fact there was no family, no such place as The Folly and no such beautiful girl living there.

'You're at the office I take it, Diane,' Freddie suddenly said back into the phone, and when she confirmed that she was he told her he'd call her right back then put down the phone.

'Hi there, Mrs Davies,' he said, getting up from his chair. 'And what have we got for supper tonight?'

'I've cooked you a nice fish pie,' Mrs Davies replied, 'but the way you like it. The way you showed me. With fresh parsley, not dried. After all, we don't want you tearing your hair out again, do we? Simply because it's not precisely the way you like it.'

Mrs Davies restraightened the knife and fork she had already straightened twice and then stood back a step to give the table one final inspection. Freddie walked round the other side of the table to face her.

'That was my fiancée on the phone, and you know something Mrs Davies?' he asked her with a smile. 'She thinks I'm nuts. What do you think? Do you reckon I'm nuts as well?'

'Come, come, Mr Jourdan,' Mrs Davies returned his smile, but nervously. 'That really isn't for the likes of me to comment on now, is it?'

'It's okay, I don't think she means nuts as in certifiably mad,' Freddie pretended to assure her. 'I think she just means — odd. Let's say she thinks that I'm a little *odd*.'

'Yes, well each to his own, that's what I've always said,' Mrs Davies replied. 'Ours not to reason why, if you know what I mean.'

'I know what you mean, Mrs Davies. What you mean is you think I'm a little "odd" as well, don't you? Don't worry, I won't be offended. And I won't turn into a werewolf, I promise.'

'Well.' The housekeeper yet again restraightened the knife and fork she'd just straightened and then cupped one hand under the back of her hair to make sure that too was tidily in place. 'Since you ask I'd have to say that when you was scribbling away at your music like, Mr Jourdan, and the way you went at it, all those days and all those nights, I'd have to say I did find that a little – well – odd, as you have it. I'd have to say the way you was going on I was more than a little bit concerned. And then when you said you was writing out all this music you'd heard in the night, I did wonder. A person would though, wouldn't they? Although of course bearing in mind what they said when you come here—'

She stopped, obviously seeing and reading the sudden look in Freddie's eyes.

'What who said, Mrs Davies?' he asked carefully, trying not to give in to the sense of panic that was rising up within him. 'Who said what to you when I came here?'

'Nobody really, Mr Jourdan,' Mrs Davies replied, eyeing the door. 'That is nothing of any account. Now if that will be all—'

Freddie reached out and took her by the arm as she tried to make a move for the door.

'Just tell me what you were told, Mrs Davies,' he said. 'Tell me about this place, about what you were told, and why you think I'm here.'

'Oh I'm sure you know the answers to those questions as well as I do, Mr Jourdan,' Mrs Davies replied, looking him in the eye. 'They sent you here because you'd been overdoing it and needed a good long time off. You were suffering from exhaustion, at least according to Mr Markson, and what better place for anyone to come to for a nice long rest? Now if that's everything, I really must be off now. If you don't mind.'

It was Mrs Davies' smile more than anything which gave Freddie the most cause for concern. As she eased her arm out of his grip he was convinced the smile she was giving him was the sort of calm but firm smile nurses are trained to use on difficult patients.

'Thank you,' she said as he released her. 'Enjoy your supper now, and I opened a nice half bottle of that wine you like. You just ring if you want anything else.'

He didn't touch his food or his wine. He just sat and looked at it, wondering what might have been put in it because since they weren't giving him any direct medication the obvious alternative would be to put it in his food or in his drink. So he would wait until just before the time when he should have finished his meal then get rid of it outside in the flowerbeds, wine and all, just in case, because for what he intended to do he needed a clear head.

While he sat silently waiting for the right moment the telephone suddenly rang. It was Diane again, wanting to know why he hadn't called her back.

'I couldn't get a line,' he lied. 'We're in the middle of a storm here and I guess it's affected the whatever. The connections.'

'You sound a little strange,' Diane said. 'Is everything all right? Maybe you ought to go see a doctor there because you really do not sound yourself, Freddie.'

'I really don't need to see any doctor, Diane,' Freddie replied. 'I'm as right as rain, believe me.'

'Okay.' He heard her agreeing, but he knew from the flat tone in her voice that she was just pretending. When she hung up no doubt she'd be back on the phone ringing

Mrs Davies, or Thomas or God alone knew who, to make sure he wasn't left too long to his own devices. 'You just hang on in there then, Freddie, and don't worry about a thing because I've managed to organize everything so I'll be with you Thursday evening, God willing.'

'Very well, Diane,' he said, making ready to kill the call. 'If I can't dissuade you, if that's what you want. All I can say is that it'll be a wasted journey because I won't be here.'

He put the receiver down immediately, then leaving his food and drink untouched, he hurried next door to the study where he took the phone off the hook, thereby leaving the number unobtainable, before shutting himself in for the next hour and a half until Mrs Davies had finished clearing away and locking up and the house was completely silent – all except for the whine coming from the uncradled telephone receiver on the desk beside him.

Still he waited, just to make sure, and then once he was completely convinced there was no-one about he stole silently upstairs to his bedroom where he quickly packed one small suitcase with a few clothes and his shoulder bag with his notebook, address book, passport and credit cards. Feeling rather as if he was a small boy escaping for the day to go fishing, he stuffed the bed with some pillows and rolled-up garments to make it look as if he was asleep, found his car keys, and tiptoed all the way out of the house carrying his shoes in one hand with his case in the other, and his shoulder bag slung around his neck.

By chance rather than foresight his rented Toyota was still parked at the opposite side of the house to the staff quarters, so he was able to start the car and drive slowly off down the side drive without attracting any attention. Even so, despite the fact that he knew the car couldn't be heard or seen he negotiated the service road without the help of either head or side lights, guided only by the full moon above him. It wasn't until he was well clear of the house, which in his driving mirror he saw was still in darkness, that he put on his lights and pulled the driver's door properly shut before accelerating away out of the park and heading for Worcester and the main road for London.

11

As Freddie drove through the night revelling in his freedom, the thought suddenly occurred to him that to think in the way he had been thinking, logically, deductively and analytically, must surely prove that he wasn't mad, in the same way he had proved to himself that he hadn't still been dreaming. If he really was still in the throes of some sort of anxiety crisis he wouldn't have been able to suppose the hypothesis which he had supposed. He'd simply have gone on the way he'd been going on, without questioning his situation, without imagining the existence of any other possibility. In his excitement at realizing this, he banged the steering-wheel with both hands and heard himself telling himself out loud that of *course* he wasn't mad! Until a few miles further on when he closed his eyes and very nearly crashed the car as he saw through what he had just thought to be a watertight argument.

Because of the way he was behaving, and thinking, and perceiving, it was even more possible that he was sick, for who else but someone in the throes of an anxiety crisis might imagine the place where he was resting and holidaying to be a nursing home for the mentally ill? For the ordinary people employed there as housekeepers and cleaning ladies to be nurses? For semi-senile lawyers and genially cooperative agents to be psychiatrists? Far from proving his sanity, the fact that he could imagine such an improbable scenario and then suppose it to be actuality, must prove the very opposite; for who else but someone with a mind out of balance could imagine such things?

The more he thought about his situation and the more he tried to fathom it out, the more confused and bewildered he became. Madness was the one disease which those suffering from it could not self-diagnose, he knew that as well as anyone. People who deludely thought other people were putting pins in their food didn't consider themselves mad, they considered the people putting the pins and needles in their food to be the ones in need of help.

He was wasting his time. The only person who could help him was someone detached from his plight, an expert in the field, namely a professional psychiatrist, which was why his instinct to flee Stoke Park was the right one after all. It had not been anything to do with Diane. It had all been to do with getting himself to London, finding a top psychiatrist, and submitting himself to analysis. That was the way to find out whether or not all that had happened to him was real or whether it was imagined. It was the only way.

When he realized this he stopped being afraid and his mind felt suddenly clean and refreshed, as if a window had been thrown open in his head and a fresh breeze had blown in off the sea. He put the radio on and suddenly the car was filled with the glorious sound of a violin in full flight that suffused him with a warm joyous feeling in which he indulged himself freely and without question, little realizing how the Fates were drawing in their net, and how close he was coming to finding that which he had thought forever lost.

'Yes,' he said aloud, as the sound of the strong and urgent yet tenderly poetic music filled the car. 'I know this. This is the Brahms Concerto in D. But who is this? Who is this *playing*?'

For the more he listened, particularly when the soloist reached the delectable, songful central *Andante*, the more he felt sure that he had found his voice. This was the voice for which he had been waiting and searching and now at last he had found it. But whose was it? Who was this wonderful musician with the voice of an angel?

But the Fates didn't want him to know quite yet, the Three Sisters still had one more trick to play before they produced their trump card. So as Freddie entered London, one of the Sisters (it really doesn't matter which, it could have been Clotho, Lachesis or Atropos) pointed a finger at the red Toyota as it dropped down off the Hammersmith flyover onto the Cromwell Road just as the recording of the concerto was coming to an end.

'That—' said the voice of the Radio Three announcer.

'Is quite enough,' said Clotho (or Lachesis or Atropos), and promptly interrupted the broadcast with a traffic warning.

Freddie cried aloud in anguished disbelief. He had no idea what had happened to the car radio since he had only previously used it to play cassettes, but having forgotten to pack any for this particular journey instead he'd relied on the radio for entertainment. The last thing he knew was that the set was programmed to interrupt broadcasts with traffic bulletins. In desperation he pressed every illuminated button he could see on the machine but, exactly as the Fates had decreed, by the time he had finally rediscovered the station the announcement was long over and an orchestra was playing Dvorak's Ninth Symphony 'From the New World'.

Once he'd stopped cursing and swearing he consoled himself with the thought that he would surely be able to find details of the programme he'd just heard in one of the broadcasting guides, so he switched the radio off and turned his attention to booking himself into a hotel.

Cunning was now replacing any kind of logic. If Diane really intended coming over, having found he'd fled Stoke Park she'd know where he would have gone, namely London, and the first place she'd look for him would be The Beaufort Hotel where he always stayed. So Freddie booked himself into The Hilton which was the last place Diane would come searching, knowing how he hated huge hotels.

Finding the right psychiatrist wasn't so easy. It wasn't exactly the sort of recommendation which the hotel reception could be expected to make, nor was it the sort of information which could be gleaned from the Yellow Pages. It was as Freddie well knew the sort of referral which only a doctor or someone familiar with your medical history could make, but having at present no such contact in England it seemed he was at an apparent impasse.

Until he remembered Stephen Noyes.

Besides looking after all the voices, chests and throats of the cast of the London production of Freddie's first hit musical *Just That*, Stephen Noyes had become a friend. Freddie and he would dine out together regularly, evenings to which the fashionable young composer always looked forward because besides being the best 'voice' man in London, Stephen was also one of the best raconteurs. Remembering, also, how well connected Stephen was in the medical profession, Freddie realized he had found his man and rang him at once, only to get his answering machine which assured the caller if he left a number he would be called back as soon as possible.

Freddie left a message to say where he was and for Noyes to ring him as soon as was conceivably possible, but that was all. Explanations as to what exactly Freddie wanted from his old friend could wait until they spoke to each other person to person. In the meantime he would lie low. At the moment he had little taste for wandering London in company with thousands of other tourists, but most of all and, absurd though it seemed to him afterwards, he was afraid that somehow he might bump into the incoming Diane. Or someone who knew them both, which was much more likely. So instead he would stay hidden away in his tenth-floor room in The Hilton until Stephen returned his call and then take it from there, starting with finding himself a good psychiatrist.

By the time he'd decided on his plan of action and settled into his hotel room, he had completely forgotten to look up in the broadcast guides exactly who had been playing the Brahms Violin Concerto on Radio Three the night before.

Of course it was one of the Three who made him forget to look it up. It was done quite deliberately. Normally for reference purposes Freddie always made a note of any singer, musician, dancer, actor, choreographer or lyricist whose work attracted him, yet somehow on this occasion he forgot, even though he had known as he had listened to the recording that he had found his voice. Moreover he forgot completely, not even suddenly remembering halfway through the weekend and setting about putting it to rights. The matter just went entirely out of his head.

It wasn't until very much later that he had time to wonder at this uncharacteristic lapse, only when the pieces of the puzzle had all fallen into shape to form a complete picture. And when he did consider it, he came to the conclusion that like everything else that had happened to him since he had first dreamed of the white deer, even his forgetfulness must have been preordained. He had not been meant to know until the right moment. A right moment which that particular Sunday evening when he returned from a long walk around Hyde Park, the one excursion he had allowed himself, was then but a matter of minutes away.

The time was nearly half past ten as he finished undressing and finally flopped down onto the bed, trying to decide whether to read or watch television. Because he was pleasantly tired after his walk he chose television and flicked it on with the remote control, channel-hopping to see what was on. On the first channel there was some old spy film which was so tired the print had lost its colour, on the next there was a news programme, the third was showing the concluding part of some cheapo mini-series about sex on the show-jumping circuit, and on the last some alternative comedians were demonstrating their alternative to comedy. Freddie settled for the news programme, and taking off his hotel-supplied bath robe slipped between the bedsheets to settle down and watch.

He very nearly missed it. By the time the presenter was reviewing the headlines of the following day's newspapers he had dropped off asleep in front of the set. Something woke him just as the credits were coming up, he didn't know what it was that woke him, but something did (or somebody), and remembering that he hadn't cleaned his teeth he got up and went to do so, leaving the television on only because somewhere in the bedding he had lost the remote control.

'*And now in place of the advertised edition of Delectus which due to legal technicalities we are unable to show,*' he heard the announcer saying, '*here's another chance to see one of the most often requested earlier editions of the programme. A film by Martyn Vaunte about the nature of musical prodigy and about one musical prodigy in particular. The film is simply entitled — Fleur.*'

He was there even before the opening shot, even before the music began. He couldn't remember getting from bathroom to bed, he couldn't remember being in the bathroom, he just knew he was there and that he couldn't miss a frame or a word because he knew it was Her.

And it was.

There she was. Even though as he first saw her she was just a child, he knew it was her. He knew it was Fleur, it *was* Fleur, it was his Fleur. It was Her.

The music. The music next, or was it at the same time? He didn't know as he knelt by the bed on the floor to watch, reaching behind him as he did so to turn off the bedside light so that he could see Her better. The music probably started at the same time as her face appeared, or maybe a moment after but it didn't matter at all because it was Her; most definitely definitely it was Her and he wasn't mad after all because there she was! She was there on the screen before him and she was called Fleur just as he had known she was.

The music. Of course it was the Brahms, just as he'd heard it the night before on the radio and the moment he heard it again he knew what it was and he knew she was playing it. No-one had said so yet, but Freddie knew it, just as he had always known Her and known about Her, just as she must have always known him and about him. Her face was changing now, melting through dissolves as she grew from a child of six through to a young oh-so-beautiful woman of seventeen? Eighteen? No-one says, at least not yet. The music plays, that's all, the luscious central *Andante*, and as it does Freddie feels the tears smart in his eyes and he doesn't give a damn. He just smiles and goes with it.

Now the film starts properly, the credits now over. The first sequence is a mid-shot of someone playing the violin in front of a symphony orchestra in a vast and packed auditorium. She is dressed formally in a long-sleeved, high-necked burgundy red silk evening dress but in contrast her mane of dark hair is not restrained and hangs loose, dressed in carefully arranged tangles which are covered with a multitude of small diamond-sewn bows that catch little flecks of light. She looks Pre-Raphaelite both in shape and countenance, a beautiful countenance almost heart shaped with perfectly proportioned features dominated by a pair of huge and darkly flashing eyes which are now half closed under a deeply furrowed brow as she, the soloist, reaches the climax of the concerto, the tempo suddenly slowing almost to a halt before the majestic last three chords, the bow coming off the violin with a sweeping flourish exactly as the orchestra finishes and then for a moment, one silent moment, she stands there violin in her left hand, bow in her right, looking high above her audience into the unseen roof of the great building before there is a spontaneous outbreak of simply tumultuous applause.

She plays the violin, Freddie whispers to himself in wonder, yes she is a solo violinist. Yet how, he wonders, how in heaven's name could he possibly have known it?

'Well,' says an astonished voice off-camera, 'there ends what has to be one of the most definitive performances ever of the Brahms Concerto in D, a simply astonishing tour de force by a young woman of seventeen whose talent seems to know no bounds, a performance full of daring yet also full of insight and lyrical eloquence. And just hear for yourself what the promenaders think of it—'

The commentator falls silent while the film cuts to shots of the packed floor of the Albert Hall where with the traditional foot stamping and shouting the informally dressed concert-goers are already demanding an encore as the soloist emerges, smiling, through the violin section of the orchestra. Summoned back by the tall elegant figure of the conductor and her quite obviously adoring fans, she stands by the podium bowing, and then as she stands upright again the film freeze-frames on the image of a beautiful young woman with her arms full of flowers and her eyes full of stars.

She plays the violin, Freddie whispers again. She is a virtuoso.

Now he sees her walking in what must be the grounds of The Folly. Exactly when this is isn't yet clear, but from her looks it has to be about the same time as the concert, Freddie reckons. Still on his hands and knees by the bed, he watches this beautiful girl with a wonderful easy swinging walk, dressed now in a loose tunic-type ribbed wool sweater, hands sunk deep in the pockets of a calf-length dark brown suede skirt and her hair still dressed in that marvellous wild way. As the camera moves in closer Freddie sees that she is younger than he first thought, and certainly younger than the day he

134

first met her. But only by two or perhaps three years at most.

He watches her walking across the very lawn where they'd met and towards the very woods from which he'd appeared, accompanied by a man wearing a loose dark blue suit and open-necked shirt.

The man was tallish, middle-aged, smooth haired with a heavy build and craggy permanently puzzled features, and the two of them were deep in conversation as they walked away from The Folly, back to camera, while a voice-over began the narration.

Fleur Fisher-Dilke—

Freddie missed the next bit as first he banged the bed in front of him with clenched fists before getting up and searching for a pad and pen to write her full name down. He had to in case he would never see or hear her name again.

Fleur Fisher-Dilke. He imagined that was how it was spelt but even if it wasn't, even if there was a hidden 'C' in Fisher, or a Y in Dilke, it would be more than enough to go on, enough surely to find her in the telephone directory, the record shops, the music catalogues, in the directories of the famous, enough to find her somewhere at long, long last.

When he looks up at the screen again, resuming his kneeling position with her name carefully written down on the memo pad which he puts in front of him on the bed, Freddie see that Fleur and her interviewer have stopped by the gate which leads to the woods and are talking on camera now, having turned to look at the house which had been behind them.

The man is saying that this is where it all began and Fleur agrees, yes, that everything all began in that room there. She points at the room Freddie knows is the drawing room of The Folly, and says that's where the whole thing started when she was six. It was the first year of the lease her parents had taken on the house. Rather than follow a straight narrative, the interviewer then asks Fleur if she was aware of being different, that is when she started playing, of being anything special at such a young age. And Fleur just shakes her head, eyes opening wide and smiling, says, 'No, no not really. People always ask this, they always want to know what it felt like, as if this sort of thing—'

'Prodigy?' the interviewer volunteers and Fleur shrugs. 'If that's what it is,' she allows, adding that people want to know if there's something they can relate to, because it all seems so wildly incomprehensible. Which she says she finds difficult for the simple reason that she's never been able to understand her gift herself. It's just always been something that was there in her, it's as simple as that.

'Well of course it isn't,' the interviewer laughs good-naturedly. 'It might seem like that to you,' he says, 'but for the vast majority of us who have tried to play some musical instrument and failed, your sort of gift is totally bewildering. To be able to sit down and just play – from a young age, as if someone is guiding you, as if you have arrived in this world already taught – it must be quite extraordinary.'

Fleur smiles and opens the gate to the woods. The two of them file through into the beech woods where long golden fingers of sunlight, just as in Freddie's dream, dance on and around and ahead of them.

'Of course there are some,' the man now says, 'there are some who don't accept the prodigy theory at all, as you probably realize.' 'No,' Fleur replies as if it's the first she's heard of it and also as if it's not of much interest. 'Yes,' her interviewer assures her. 'For instance there's this professor at the moment at Hull University who's just announced that there's simply no evidence to show that musicians are born and not made. He claims that apparently even Mozart wasn't at all "prodigious" but simply capable of playing "prodigiously" because he'd been force fed music from a very early age.'

'Yes, well,' Fleur replies laughing, 'For a long time, and not that long ago "professors" thought herons wintered on the moon.'

They're at the bottom of the flight of steps that finally leads through the other wicket-gate, the one over which Freddie vaulted, out on to Stoke Park. He leans forward, as if by some odd chance of the moment he might catch sight of himself in the lovely grounds of the quite beautiful house which can now be seen in the distance. He scans the wonderful eighteenth-century landscape with its paddocks and ornamental lake, its bridge and stone summer houses, its trout stream and its thickly wooded banks, but of course he is nowhere to be seen because this is then and not now.

Instead what he sees is Fleur and her interviewer sitting on a bench by the side of the still, dark brown waters of the lake which are reflecting the autumn reds, yellows and browns of the surrounding trees and shrubs. On the far bank a curlew calls and just off the near bank a fish rises to take a fly, dappling the satin waters with slowly expanding ripples.

'Of course,' the man says, pointing over the lake, 'A lot happened in that house as well, didn't it? Certain events that took place there also influenced the way you were going to go. Mostly due to the woman who owned it, Lady Margaret Stourton; quite a formidable woman, I gather, and also quite an accomplished amateur musician herself. But then I'm jumping the gun,' he says, smiling round at Fleur. 'We really should start your story, your extraordinary story, right from the beginning, don't you think?'

'Because it really is an extraordinary story,' the interviewer says, turning to camera in close up. 'One of the most extraordinary of all the stories concerning this mysterious, enigmatic, perhaps even worrying phenomenon we call *prodigy*, because Fleur Fisher-Dilke, not quite yet eighteen years of age but for many years hailed as one of the world's very best violinists, didn't discover her prodigality on the violin at all. In fact she very nearly didn't even become a musician and if you like you can say it was only by sheer chance – or indeed Fate if you prefer – that she did.'

Fate, Freddie said back to the screen. *It has to be Fate. Everything to do with her, with this, is all to do with Fate.*

'It all began here nearly eleven years ago,' the interviewer's voice continues off camera, 'when Fleur Fisher-Dilke was six years old.'

And there now, on screen, a house was emerging slowly through the trees, a pretty white-painted Regency house with large Gothic windows set perfectly on a grassy knoll and backed by fine tall trees. In front of it stand three people who are coming closer to Freddie all the time, two adults and a child who is holding something in her arms. The child is standing between the two figures: one must be her father, a short prematurely balding man with glasses, dressed in a sports coat, flannels, shirt and tie even though it's summer. And the other must be her mother, a tall woman with the figure of a fashion model, and a pretty but somewhat bland face. The mother has her arms draped over both shoulders of her daughter, who is holding up in her arms a pet rabbit which also has its head turned to the camera although both its ears are laid flat back.

Still the people in the photograph get closer and closer to Freddie until only the child's face fills the screen, a solemn-faced child with an unruly mop of dark hair and large dark round eyes already wide open on the world.

Over the face comes a caption which reads, '*Worcester. May. 1980.*'

SECOND MOVEMENT

Andante cantabile

12

Worcestershire. 1980.

It stood in the corner of the room which the spring sun was flooding; shining, silent and shut, a dustsheet half thrown over its rosewood case. Fleur felt drawn to it at once, like the sea to the moon, and when she thought no-one was looking she walked quietly over and lifted a corner of the sheet to get a proper look at what lay underneath. At once she felt a hand on her shoulder.

'No, dear,' her father said. 'No touching anything, thank you. I'm quite sure that Lady Stourton here does not want fingermarks all over her valuable furniture.'

'Fingermarks polish out, Mr Fisher,' Lady Stourton replied turning around to look down at Fleur who was still staring at the piano. 'Scratches are what one must look out for.'

'Even so.'

Fleur felt her mother's hand on her back this time as she was steered further from the grand piano.

'Do you play the piano, child?' Lady Stourton asked, but Fleur just blushed and stared down at the old lady's beautiful, buttoned leather shoes.

'She's still a little young,' her father replied, yet again answering for his daughter who so far hadn't said a word.

'Oh one is never too young for music, Mr Fisher. Particularly when one is young.' Lady Stourton cleared her throat and slowly widened her large cornflower-blue eyes at Fleur as the little girl finally plucked up the courage to look up. 'What do you think, child?'

Fleur wanted to agree with the old lady but all she could manage was a half smile and a small shrug in response.

'You must forgive her, Lady Stourton,' her mother said. 'Fleur is dreadfully shy.'

'Absurdly so,' her father said, turning round to survey the finely furnished room with his hands clasped behind his back. 'But she'll grow out of it.'

'My youngest brother John never grew out of it,' Lady Stourton said. 'Even when he was a grown man he'd get up and leave the room if a stranger came in. Only ever spoke to me, and then only if I didn't speak to him ... So you want to take this place just for the weekends, Mr Fisher. I understand that is the case?'

'No, no, Lady Stourton, not at all,' Richard Fisher said, as Fleur tried to wriggle out of the grip her mother now had on her shoulders. 'No, we intend to use it as our family home. It's just that my work is in London, which will mean that I myself will only be here for weekends and holidays, but my wife and daughter, and Deanie, my wife's old nurse – they would be living here permanently.'

'I see. Well, it's certainly a wonderful part of the country in which to raise a child. Just a pity you cannot all enjoy it *en famille*.'

'My work demands that I remain in London, Lady Stourton,' Richard Fisher said, taking off his spectacles, folding them carefully and putting them in the top pocket of his jacket. 'I am a surgeon, you see. Cardiovascular.'

'A heart surgeon?' said Lady Stourton, as if correcting him. 'It must be very strange, I imagine, to look into people's hearts.'

'Not really,' Richard replied. 'After all the heart is only another organ, Lady Stourton. It's no different to any other of our organs. No different from our kidneys, our livers, our spleens—'

'Richard—' Fleur's mother took her hands off Fleur's shoulders for a moment while she tried to attract her husband's attention.

'No that is something with which alas I cannot agree, Mr Fisher,' Lady Stourton said to Richard. 'The heart after all is the very centre of our feelings. After all sadness does not break our kidneys, does it? Our livers do not quicken with excitement when we see those whom we love. No I do not think for one moment that the heart is merely another organ, Mr Fisher. Not for one minute.'

While her father's attention was distracted from her, Fleur tugged at her mother's sleeve to indicate she wanted to whisper something to her. Her mother sighed but bent down nonetheless to hear what exactly Fleur wanted.

'Fleur—' her father said warningly, seeing the two of them whispering.

'She was only wondering if it would be all right to go out into the garden, Richard,' Amelia Fisher said, straightening up. 'She thought she could see some deer.'

'She can,' Lady Stourton replied. 'There are two herds, one red and one fallow, and I'm afraid they often stray up here into the garden because the rascals have a soft spot for roses. Who is that in the garden, I wonder?'

'Ah yes,' Richard said quickly, following Lady Stourton's surprised look. 'That is Deanie, my wife's old nurse.'

'If she's anything like my old nanny what she says goes, I imagine,' Lady Stourton said, going to open the French windows. 'For your sake I hope this place passes muster.'

Lady Stourton gave Fleur a slow, secret wink, which although Fleur didn't know why she did, made her smile shyly back all the same.

'Well?' Lady Stourton asked of the old woman standing out on the terrace as she threw open the doors. 'And what do you make of what is possibly to be your new home, Nanny?'

'It's all very nice, thank you,' Deanie replied, dressed from head to toe in macintosh despite the glorious spring weather. 'But I'd have to say it's a long old hike to the village when you've forgotten some'at.'

'One makes lists in the country, Nanny,' Lady Stourton replied. 'The secret of surviving in the country is always to make lists. Of everything.'

'That's as maybe,' Deanie sniffed. 'But it'll be a different story come winter.'

'Fleur wants to explore the gardens, Deanie,' Amelia said, putting Fleur's small hand in the old nurse's big red one. 'We have to sort out one or two things still with Lady Stourton.'

'So you'll be taking the place then, Miss Amelia?' Deanie asked.

'Oh I think it's lovely, don't you? Fleur likes it, don't you, sweetie?'

Fleur nodded, her eyes widening as she saw the park that lay below the hill on which The Folly stood.

'Fleur doesn't have to do the shopping, I say,' Deanie replied with yet another sniff. 'Just imagine running out of some'at here. You seen how far we are from village?'

'We shall make lists, Deanie,' Amelia said. 'Just as Lady Stourton here has suggested.'

While her parents went back inside the house with Lady Stourton, Fleur ran off across the lawn over to the large fishpond she had just noticed. Deanie followed after her, grumbling and muttering to herself nonstop.

'Lists,' she mumbled. 'Lists indeed. We all know who'll be up and down to the village every morning and afternoon because of some'at that's been forgot.'

'Come and look at these fish, Deanie!' Fleur exclaimed. 'They're really huge!'

'Them's carp,' Deanie said, as they stood staring into the crystal clear water of the pond, and as the huge fish swam slowly round staring back at them. 'Them's mirror carp. We used to catch them, when I was your age. Me brother and me. Then cook 'em over an open fire.'

'You didn't?' Fleur said, lying on her stomach to get a closer look at the fish. 'Did they taste nice?'

'Wonderful,' Deanie said. 'Particularly to those what usually only had bread and scrape. Now off the lawn, young lady, or we'll have your mother after us for grass stains.'

Together Fleur and her old nurse wandered round the beautiful garden which was obviously tended all year round, even though Fleur had heard her father and mother saying on the way down that no-one had lived in the actual house for years.

'It's been empty since the war,' her father had said, although Fleur had no idea which war he had meant. 'It's very beautiful, and it's in a lovely position. It overlooks Stoke Park, that is the parkland of the main house, where Lady Stourton lives, then beyond that are the Malverns.'

'It sounds deeply romantic,' her mother had replied. 'I know I'm going to love it.'

'Won't be what you've been used to, Amelia,' her father had continued, laughing in the way he did when he wasn't really amused. 'Not after the glamour of the catwalk, you know.'

'I left that all behind when I had Madam here,' her mother had said, nodding backwards in the direction of Fleur. 'You know that, Richard. Now tell me more about the house. Because it really does sound so lovely.'

'Apparently it was built by the family, by Lady Stourton's forbears, as a music room,' her father had explained. 'In about 1760 I understand. People literally would come up from the main house to play music there. It was built solely and specially for that purpose.'

'Imagine that,' her mother had exclaimed, turning round to Fleur. 'Think of that, sweetie. A special house of one's own just to go and play the piano.'

'We could do with some'at like that in London,' Deanie had muttered. 'Or rather them next door could. What with that dreadful electric guitar an' all.'

'Has nobody really lived here for years, Deanie?' Fleur asked her old nurse as they left the fishpond behind them and walked up a path towards a wooden building at the top.

'Not since the war,' Deanie confirmed. 'Though you could eat off the floors. So it's hardly not been looked after.'

'I think it's lovely,' Fleur said, looking all around her, and as they walked on all of a sudden Fleur knew that she would always remember this day, that it would always come back to her even when she was as old as Deanie. She would remember every flower, every wonderful tree, the paths lined with primroses, the woods which she could see full of bluebells, the vivid pink of a plant Deanie called 'swallow-wort', which she said opened with the arrival of the swallows and closed with their departure, the wild anenomes, the late daffodils. But most of all the deer.

She had never seen deer before, not in the flesh, not close to. But when she and Deanie came through the far side of the first woodland into which they ventured, a place carpeted with bluebells and planted with huge beech trees which had just burst into full leaf, they chanced upon a herd of red deer quietly grazing on the side of the hill right below them. Deanie was pulled to a standstill by one tug from Fleur and together they stood as still as statues watching the animals peacefully eating.

'How they can hunt such creatures is a long way beyond me, that's all I can say,' Deanie remarked when they finally walked on.

'They don't, do they?' Fleur asked. 'What for? Why?'

' 'Cos they can't defend themselves if you ask me, child,' Deanie replied. 'Or more like 'cos deer are a sight prettier than most folk.'

At the top of the hill they finally came to an old summer house which had been the building Deanie had spotted from below on the lawns.

'Aye,' she said as they went inside. 'This'll do us nicely, child.' She drew up one of the old steamer chairs that had been stacked at the back and sank into it with a grateful sigh, as Fleur rubbed one of the windowpanes free of dirt and stared outside. The musty smell of the summer house was very beguiling and the atmosphere so peaceful, that as Deanie appeared to nod off for a few minutes Fleur found herself wondering what it would be like to live in this little wooden house without ever having to see anyone except the deer and the other animals in the woods.

Eventually Deanie opened her eyes and gave a cough. Fleur turned and looked at her.

'Aye this'll do right nicely for us, child,' she said again, with a nod of approval. 'We can come up here and picnic, just thee and me. Would you like that?'

'Yes,' Fleur said, going to sit on Deanie's ample lap. 'Yes, please.'

'Course you would, child,' her old nurse said. ' 'Cos that's how we like it, in't it? Whatever. Just thee and me.'

Every day for a fortnight after the Fishers had moved into The Folly it rained. The downpour didn't bother Amelia and Deanie too much as they were far too busy setting the place in order, but for Fleur it meant nothing to do, at least nothing which she had been so looking forward to doing. Every night before they had moved she had lain in her bed dreaming of the wonderful garden and the parkland beyond, of the places she would explore, the tree she would climb, but most of all she had dreamed of the deer and how she would tame them by feeding them and making them her friends. Fleur loved being outside as much as she hated being indoors, but now as the early summer downpour continued remorselessly every day, she found herself trapped in her new home with only her books and jigsaws for amusement.

She tried hard not to make a nuisance of herself because she knew how her mother hated her following her around when she was busy, so she did her best to keep herself out of her mother's and Deanie's way by painting at the kitchen table or doing a jigsaw spread out on the polished old wood floor of the drawing room. But boredom finally won the day and her mother or Deanie kept finding her constantly standing at the window of whatever room they were busy in, fed up and staring out at the rain.

'There must be something she can do, Deanie,' Amelia sighed, as she began setting out all her husband's precious books on the shelves of the room which was to be his study. 'Do find something for her, will you? Because she drives me mad when she gets in one of her mooching moods.'

'I'm not in a mooching mood, Mummy,' Fleur replied. 'I'm just trying to make the rain stop.'

Since her father forbade Fleur to watch any television except the programmes he had nominated and since there was never anything suitable on the radio for children of her age, other than endless pop music which was also proscribed, and having not as yet had the chance to make any new friends locally, by now Fleur was at her childish wit's end, unable to think of anything else she could do to keep herself occupied.

'Here,' her mother said to her finally, with a tired sigh as she handed her a duster. 'Here, go and make yourself useful then. Go and dust the furniture in the drawing room now all the covers are off.'

It was the first time Fleur had seen the grand piano without its dust sheet. It was a magnificent instrument with a case made of a dark brown highly polished wood. Fleur did her best to ignore it as she made her way round the room carefully dusting all the other beautiful pieces of furniture which had been left in the house by Lady Stourton, but every now and then she found herself turning to have yet another look at the piano – not only because quite naturally it dominated the room, but also because Fleur felt as if it was calling to her, or rather calling her to it. Finally, unable to resist its siren's lure, Fleur tiptoed over to it and very cautiously lifted the lid of the keyboard.

'Blüthner,' she read to herself, fingering the delicate gold inlaid lettering on the inside of the lid before turning her attention to the milk-white and jet-black ivory keys which gleamed up at her like a set of perfect teeth. 'Hello, Mr Blüthner,' she whispered. 'My name is Fleur.'

Then after carefully running her fingertips up and down the satin smooth white notes she sat herself down on the piano stool, closed her eyes, and holding her hands high over the keyboard mimed playing the grand piano just as she had once seen someone on the television playing one in a concert her father and mother had been watching one Sunday.

'What do you think you're doing, Fleur?' her mother's voice suddenly said from behind her. 'I asked you to come in here and dust, not fool around, particularly on Lady Stourton's precious piano.'

Her mother came over and shut down the lid.

'Now get down from there at once, please,' she ordered. 'And do as I ask you.'

'I wasn't touching it,' Fleur said, looking at the floor and scratching the back of her head. 'I was only pretending.'

'And I can't see the harm,' Deanie said, coming into the room with a box of the Fishers' ornaments. 'It's only an old piano, and if the child wants to play it—' She finished her sentence with a shrug.

Amelia laughed. 'But she can't play it, Deanie! And whatever you may think and whatever Lady Stourton

149

might have said, it really isn't the sort of piano for children to bang about on. It's a very beautiful piece of furniture.'

'Oh nonsense, Miss Amelia,' Deanie rumbled. 'A piece of furniture indeed. If that's the case I'll eat me dinner off it.'

'Suppose she damages it, Deanie. My husband had to put down a sizeable deposit against everything Lady Stourton left here. He won't take kindly to being out of pocket if Fleur ends up damaging something like this grand piano, I assure you.'

'How can she damage it, I ask you? The child's hardly Desperate Dan, is she? She's got nowt to do cooped up inside here and no-one to play with, so I can't see as what harm she's going to do. Not if she's careful.'

'Oh very well,' Amelia sighed, turning Fleur back towards the piano. 'But as long as you really are careful, and try and play it, rather than play with it.'

While her mother and Deanie unpacked the ornaments and set them out on the side tables and the top of the desk, Fleur sat back at the piano and reopened the lid. Just looking at the keys again filled her with an intense excitement, for reasons she couldn't begin to comprehend. The only feeling to which she could compare it was being handed a parcel at Christmas time or on her birthday without having an idea as to what the contents might be.

But she didn't depress any of the keys, not yet. While her mother and Deanie were still busying themselves setting out the ornaments, Fleur only pretended to play, moving both her hands up and down the keyboard gracefully while only brushing the actual notes with her fingertips. It wasn't until the two grown-ups had left the room, having long stopped taking any real notice of what Fleur was doing, that she actually stopped pretending and sounded her first note for real.

Gently, but very deliberately and with sufficient weight behind it she pressed down the very top note of the piano, allowing the unseen hammer to rise, strike the string and sound a note which sung out like the note of a glass bell. Entranced by the purity of the sound, Fleur then played the note four times in succession, *one two three four*, rhythmically, evenly, but this time more firmly, allowing the sound of the note to ring out before next playing the top three notes in sequence, sitting back to listen round-eyed to the sweetness of the instrument's tone.

When the sound of Fleur's first triplet died away, she got down from the piano and quickly built herself a higher seat, made from music books she found inside the piano stool, so that she could reach the keyboard more easily. Then when she was once again seated she played a run of five notes, the octave above middle C, and once again sat entranced by the purity and the sheer magic of the sound the fine piano made. She played the five notes again and again, up and down, and down and up, before doing the same with her left hand, just five notes up and down and down and up, before stopping and staring transfixed at the keyboard.

What she saw wasn't what people normally see when they sit at the piano for the first time, a senseless assortment of keys some of which are inexplicably white and some black. What Fleur could see as she sat at the piano was music. She could see the very shape and form that music would make long before she even tried to play it, but of course being a child she saw nothing at all unusual about this. Naturally she imagined this was what happened to everyone when they decided to play the piano. They sat down in front of it and it all made perfect sense, in just the same way as she had been able to understand how to play draughts within minutes of her father explaining the game, and then likewise how to play chess.

Now she could see music and she understood how to play it. Of course what she saw wasn't graphic, far from it. She didn't see crochets and minims dancing in the air as in some animated cartoon, in fact it would probably be more accurate to say that Fleur sensed the music rather than visualized it. Even so, that was the way she liked to explain it later when asked how and what she felt at that moment, that she just saw music – and so be it. When she looked at the keyboard, music simply flooded into her head.

How long she experimented with the notes and the sounds, Fleur certainly had no idea and so there is no detailed record of exactly how Fleur's genius first took shape. Neither her mother nor her old nurse were aware of what was happening, because by now they were both locked away in the kitchen with the half-deaf Deanie's radio playing full blast on Radio Two while the two of them scrubbed out the larder and all the old wooden store-cupboards. All that Fleur knew was that one day, this particular one day when she was six years old, she sat down at the grand piano in the house her family had just rented and started to play. She never remembered working out such things as scales, or how and when to sharpen a note or flatten it, she would simply say that after a while, and not a very long while at that, having looked at the keyboard and tried out every note that constituted an octave (a form she recognized at the first time of hearing, that at least she would remember), she then sat down and began to play.

Even assuming that the first time she played she did so in the beginner's key of C major, it would still be a remarkable feat particularly since she used both hands. In fact by the time she felt ready to play for her mother and old nurse, those two hands were not playing some three or four note tune in unison but her left hand was accompanying the right with simple harmonic chords, while her right hand was playing a simple but perfectly conjoined melody.

There is no explanation for what happened because there cannot be. Whenever such a thing happened before it was deemed inexplicable, and when it happens again in the future as it is bound to, even then it will still remain out of the reach of rationalization. No-one has ever understood prodigy and no-one ever will. A child takes up an instrument and plays it and by doing so proves what was to be proved. *Quod erat demonstrandum*. Just as the facts of the matter subsequently prove what initially appears to be an unbelievable occurrence. Age six, Fleur Fisher sat at a piano for the very first time in her life and within no time at all was playing the way most novices would play only after long and regular tuition.

The melody Fleur had finally settled on playing was her favourite one, the German carol 'Silent Night'. By the time Deanie had finally arrived back to fetch her for her tea Fleur could play it the whole way through, carrying the tune in her right hand and playing basic two-note chords with her left.

'Do you want to hear what I can play, Deanie?' she asked.

'Not really,' Deanie replied, lifting her charge down off the piano stool. 'I'm that done in from all the scrubbing all I want is me tea and toast.'

'I can play a tune, Deanie,' Fleur said, frowning deeply as her nurse led her to the door. 'Would you like me to play it to you after?'

'Not a lot of point, child,' Deanie said. 'Even when I could hear I had a tin ear. Whatever you play'd sound like Beethoven to me.'

Halfway through tea, when her mother put down her copy of *House and Garden* for the first time, Fleur summoned up the courage to tell her mother what she could do.

'I can play a tune, Mummy,' she said, jiggling her legs nervously up and down under the table. 'I can play a whole tune.'

'Jolly good,' her mother said, flicking her magazine open at the back page again. 'I do hope you were careful.'

'Course she weren't,' Deanie rumbled. 'She chopped the bloomin' piano up for firewood.'

'That really isn't funny, Deanie, and you know it,' Amelia said, frowning at Fleur who was grinning down at her plate. 'It really isn't funny, Fleur,' she repeated.

'It's all right, I was careful,' Fleur assured her, before eating the last of her Marmite soldiers. 'Could I play you my tune after tea?'

'I suppose so,' her mother replied, ringing an advertisement in her magazine with a pencil. 'Just once, and then bed.'

'I can play it all the way through, Deanie.'

'Can you indeed? Now there's a thing.'

'It isn't very difficult.'

'You don't say.'

'I mean playing the piano.'

'Hark at you,' Deanie said, pouring herself more tea. 'It'll be the Albert Hall next stop then. Now off with you and run your bath. I'll be up soon as I've made me tea.'

'I've got to play you my tune first,' Fleur replied.

Reluctantly Amelia put her magazine down and got up to follow Fleur and Deanie through into the drawing room, but only after having had to be reminded by Deanie of her promise.

'So you're going to play us a tune, are you, sweetie?' she said, finding her cigarettes on the desk and lighting one. 'After just one go? Or have you been secretly practising?'

Her mother blew out a long plume of smoke and smiled at Fleur who was carefully reopening the piano.

'I haven't practised once,' she said, climbing on to her pile of books. 'You know I haven't.'

'Oh Lord,' Amelia sighed. 'I do hope you're not going to turn out like your grandfather.'

'You mean your father, Miss Amelia?' Deanie enquired, helping Fleur to get comfortable. 'He was a wonderful musician.'

'And a rotten father,' Amelia replied, sitting down in a button-back chair. 'And according to my mother a rotten husband as well.'

'Aye,' Deanie said, settling herself down in a chair as well. 'But then our Fleur's not going to be a father nor a husband, is she then? So I don't know why you're bothered.'

'It's the practice,' Amelia said. 'Among other things. Imagine living with someone who practises — that's not playing, mind. Practice is quite different from playing, and God knows that must be hard enough. But imagine living with someone practising the piano *eight hours a day*. Drove my mother mad.'

'Aye,' Deanie said. 'But then practice makes perfect, don't it. That's what they say. You just remember that, young lady!' she called, raising her voice to Fleur. 'Practice makes perfect!'

'Then I shall practise every day,' Fleur replied, getting ready to play. 'I shall practise every single day.'

'Not at the weekend you won't, sweetie,' her mother contradicted. 'Not once Daddy is home. The last thing poor Daddy will want is to have to listen to you banging around on the piano.'

'Can I play him my tune?'

'Once. You can play it once, but no "practising". Now come along if you're coming, because it's way past your bedtime.'

'So what you going to play us, child?'

' "Silent Night", Deanie,' Fleur said. ' "Silent Night" played by Fleur Fisher.'

She didn't get beyond the first four notes before disaster struck. At least that's what her mother thought as she saw

155

a large fragment of ivory break off a note and fall to the floor.

'What was that?' Amelia gasped at once, jumping up and hurrying to the piano. 'What on *earth* have you done, Fleur?'

'Nothing, Mummy,' Fleur said, frowning at the broken note in front of her. 'I was only playing.'

'Oh, but you have done something, look what you've done! You've broken an ivory, Fleur!' Amelia was on her hands and knees, holding up half of the broken key. 'I knew something like this would happen! I just knew it!'

All Fleur had done was play in just the same way as she had been doing all through her first session at the piano. She'd done nothing different, she hadn't banged that key particularly hard or lifted the edge with her finger accidentally. Besides, her young hands were too small and weak to do any real damage to a piano which had been built to withstand the rigours of the concert platform, but to her mother Fleur must be held responsible because after all it was she who had been playing it when the ivory had broken.

'What were you *doing*, Fleur?' Amelia asked, with more sadness in her voice than anger which always made Fleur feel worse than if she was being scolded. 'I *knew* one of us should have kept an eye on you, instead of leaving you to your own devices. I told you not to fool about, didn't I?'

'But I wasn't,' Fleur whispered, fighting back her tears. 'I wasn't fooling around.'

'Then how did this happen?' Amelia held up the broken ivory as evidence. 'Bits don't just fall off grand pianos, Fleur. Not unless someone abuses them. This was why my father never let us fool around on his piano. That's why he always kept *his* locked.'

'I wasn't fooling around!' Fleur cried, no longer able to control the tears she felt welling up. 'I was playing it, I wasn't fooling around!'

'Don't be silly, Fleur,' her mother replied, lifting her off the piano stool and closing the keyboard lid. 'How can you have been playing it when you can't play a note? You mean you were playing *around*. What on earth is Lady Stourton going to say? What's your father going to say? I knew something like this would happen.'

Fleur made a fist of one of her hands and stuck it in her mouth to stop herself from crying out loud, while her mother stood with her cigarette in one hand and the broken ivory in the other staring down at the damage.

'Most like we can fix it with some adhesive,' Deanie said, trying to come to the rescue.

'Oh Deanie, don't be so silly,' Amelia retorted. 'You don't know what you're talking about. You can't stick ivory back on with glue, not once one's broken. You have to replace the whole note, because otherwise it keeps coming off.'

'We could always try some of the super-glue stuff,' Deanie continued. 'The stuff what sticks anything.'

'You have to replace the whole note, Deanie. Believe me, I know what I'm saying, because my father told me. You have no idea the importance musicians attach to their instruments. They can't stand this sort of thing happening to them. It's as if the wretched things were alive, with a heart and soul of their own. You've no idea how they carry on. My father kept his piano locked ever since the day he caught my brother and me playing it, with our orange drinks perched either end of the keyboard. He gave us both a jolly good hiding, too, I can tell you.'

'Little wonder neither of you followed his footsteps then, is it?' Deanie said, putting her hands on Fleur's trembling shoulders. 'And if you'd only take my advice about the glue—'

'No that's quite enough, Deanie, thank you,' Amelia said, stubbing out her cigarette. 'Now take Fleur straight up to bed will you, please? And no story.'

'I don't reckon that's fair,' Deanie said.

'You can reckon what you like, Deanie,' Amelia replied. 'Those are my orders.'

In spite of what her employer had ordered, Deanie read Fleur a quick story as Fleur lay in bed staring up at the ceiling.

'Don't you worry about a thing, child,' the old woman said as she eased herself back up on to her feet. 'Least said soonest mended. I'll keep on at your mother about the glue, so don't you worry.'

Fleur didn't worry. She just lay in bed in despair. She had wanted so much to play her mother her tune, not to show off, but because she thought it was beautiful and she wanted her mother to love it as well. Instead she had ended up damaging the piano, which most probably she would never be allowed to play again. Somehow it all seemed so wrong, so desperately unfair.

Just as Fleur had thought, the following day – after a piano technician had been summoned from Worcester to repair the damage – the piano was placed out of bounds.

'When you go to proper school in the autumn you can learn it, if you still want to,' her mother told her. 'If you're still that keen and you prove to have any talent for it, then we might – but I only say *might* – we might then review the situation.'

'Couldn't we have a piano of our own?' Fleur asked, having summoned up all her courage.

'Oh don't be silly, Fleur,' Amelia replied. 'For a start we're only renting this house, and anyway where would we put it? We couldn't put some cheap and ugly old piano in that lovely drawing room, and there's certainly no room in Daddy's study.'

'We could put it in the kitchen,' Fleur tried, remembering a friend in London whose parents had a piano in their kitchen. 'The kitchen's quite big.'

158

'We are not having a piano in the kitchen, Fleur. The kitchen is for cooking and eating,' Amelia replied, hoping that would put paid to the argument. 'Besides, Daddy would not take kindly to paying out for something we don't even know you can play yet.'

'I can play it,' Fleur replied, staring at the floor where she was shuffling her feet. 'If only you'd let me show you.'

'Now you're being silly again, Fleur,' Amelia sighed, opening the doors to the garden. 'You can't possibly say you can play the piano when all you've done is just mess around on one for a few minutes. Now off you go. It's stopped raining at long last, so why don't you go out and play in the garden? It's what you've been waiting for. And what you'd really rather be doing, I'm sure.'

It wasn't, but then Fleur was too shy to argue with her mother and answer her back. Instead she did as she was told and went out to play horses in the lovely garden, only to find that the very game she had always loved playing now bored her, and that all she really wanted was to sneak back inside the house, climb up on the stool and play the piano she could see through the windows waiting for her in the empty drawing room.

However, strong though the temptation was, Fleur bided her time until at last it was the day of the week for her mother to go into Worcester to get her hair done, and she was left alone in the house with Deanie, who was preparing to tackle a mound of ironing in the kitchen.

'I'm going to do this in the drawing room, Deanie,' she told the old woman, showing her the jigsaw puzzle she'd just fetched from her toy chest.

'You can do it at the table here, child,' Deanie replied, turning her radio on full blast. 'You can do it where I may keep my eye on you.'

'I don't want to,' Fleur replied, heading for the door. 'Your radio's too loud.'

Knowing that Deanie trusted her and didn't really mean what she said, Fleur tucked the puzzle under her arm, took some cookies from the jar to keep her going and, easily avoiding Deanie's half-hearted attempt at a smacked hand, ran off into the drawing room. Slowly and carefully she eased the door almost shut before quickly laying out the jigsaw on the wood floor. As soon as she had it in some sort of order, she set about completing some of the outside as fast as she could, and then once she was satisfied she had enough for a plausible alibi and that Deanie couldn't see or hear her, Fleur ran to the piano stool, climbed up, and began to play at once.

Even so at first she only played *pianissimo*, just in case – as it often seemed – Deanie wasn't *quite* as deaf as she made out. But every time she tiptoed back to the door to check, she was relieved to see that her old nurse was still busy with her washing and ironing and paying her no attention whatsoever. As one last confidence booster Fleur banged out a double-fisted discord to see if that would bring about any reaction, then seeing that it didn't, finally she turned her full attention to the keyboard and to learning how to play some more of her favourite tunes.

By the time she saw her mother's car turning into the drive over an hour later Fleur had not only mastered two handed versions of 'London's Burning' and 'Three Blind Mice', but she had even made up a tune of her own which she had decided to call 'Running Deer' since it had been inspired by seeing the herd of red deer running distantly across the parkland. As her mother got out of the car, Fleur jumped down from the piano, and having closed the lid carefully and replaced the pile of music books in the stool, she returned to her jigsaw, lying down in front of it on the floor as if that was where she'd been all morning.

'Oh,' Amelia said as she came in and saw Fleur conspicuously putting away the bits of a jigsaw, 'I'd 'rather have liked to have seen that. You know I always like to see puzzles when they've been done.'

'You've seen it, Mummy,' Fleur said, trying to sound as bored as she could. 'It's that old one of that castle.'

'Ah,' Amelia said suspecting nothing, her mind on a cup of coffee and a cigarette. 'Anyway – come on, I've bought you some fish fingers for lunch. They're a new sort.'

That was Fleur's routine for the rest of the school holidays. Whenever her mother was out in the city and Deanie was distracted with household chores, Fleur would retire with a puzzle or a game to the drawing room to play the piano. No-one suspected, and she was never once caught in the act, at least not to her knowledge.

One person saw her, a fact of which Fleur wasn't aware. One rainy day early in September a week before Fleur started school, she was busy playing her latest composition while Deanie scrubbed and polished the kitchen floor to the sound of her favourite radio programme, both of them unaware they had a visitor. Having tried and failed to get through on the telephone, due to the volume at which Deanie was playing the radio, Lady Stourton had called at The Folly on her way past, and having tried the doorbell several times and heard the sound of a radio blaring somewhere in the house, she had then walked round to the garden to see if she could attract anyone's attention at the French windows. When she saw Fleur sitting at the piano she hesitated before knocking, to look a little closer, and to listen. Although she could still just hear the radio playing somewhere in the back of the house, the predominant sound was that of the piano, and what she heard made her hesitate even longer before announcing her presence – so extraordinary was the music being made by the child at the keyboard.

She had no notion what Fleur was playing but what it sounded like was Bach, formal and rhythmic, graceful and flowing: the linear melody in the right hand being

161

propelled by simple but strict bass figures in the left, although the music was confined to just the two middle octaves. The child sat bolt upright at the piano with her head still, apparently staring ahead of her rather than down at the notes she was playing. Only when Lady Stourton caught sight of Fleur's face in the mirror beyond the piano did she see that in fact the child had her eyes tight closed.

How long Lady Stourton stood there she had no idea. What she did know was that she was witnessing genius, the gift that people say has no country, the thing that is born from the unconscious and understood neither by those who own it nor by those who witness it, the miracle which enables a child to sit at a piano and play like an angel without having to understand one thing about it but just to play like an angel, without inhibition and straight from the heart.

Once she grasped the importance of what she was seeing, Lady Stourton decided against knocking on the glass and disturbing the child lest she might frighten her out of what seemed to be a trance. Instead she made her way round to the back door to rap sharply on the side window with the head of her cane in order to be heard above the radio.

'Oh lor,' Deanie groaned when she opened the door and saw who it was. 'You don't have to say. You been standing ringing the front door without ever me hearing you. What must you be thinking. Come in, ma'am, come in.'

The old woman stood aside, anxiously wiping her perfectly clean hands on her apron as Lady Stourton walked into the kitchen.

'One was just going to leave one's card,' Lady Stourton said, casting a doubtful eye on the improvements Amelia had already begun to make on the old kitchen, 'when one heard music.'

'That'll have been my radio, ma'am,' Deanie sighed,

having already switched it off when she realized she had a caller. 'It's a mite loud 'cos of my hearing. What can I do for you?'

'The child,' Lady Stourton said, placing both hands on the silver top of her cane. When she saw the child's old nurse was staring blankly back at her, she raised her voice and tried again. 'The child, Nanny. Do you know what she's doing?'

'She's playing in the sitting room, ma'am,' Deanie replied. 'Why's that?'

'Has one any idea what she is playing, Nanny?'

'Aye.' Deanie nodded. 'She said she were playing cards right enough. Patience or some such. Why? She's not up to something, is she? 'Cos if she is—'

Deanie made to leave the room but Lady Stourton stopped her by raising her cane in front of her.

'No no, Nanny, the child is not up to anything. At least not anything about which you need concern yourself. Can you not hear what she's doing?'

Deanie frowned, leaning her head slightly towards the door.

'She's not playing your piano, is she?' Deanie wondered. 'Because if she is, it's not as if she hasn't been told—'

Lady Stourton's cane was still in place.

'But why shouldn't she play my piano, Nanny? Heaven's above one gave one's express permission.'

'Her mother won't have it,' Deanie replied, regarding both Lady Stourton and her raised cane dubiously. 'Least not without the proper supervision.'

'The child plays under her mother's supervision, yes?'

Deanie paused, still wondering whether or not to hint at the truth before deciding against it.

'No,' she said, shaking her head. 'She only played the once, then her mother told her she was to wait till she went to school. To see if she had any real talent. That's why I was worried in case she were playing.

Her mother won't have her playing your piano, you see. Least not till she knows how.'

Lady Stourton eyed Deanie steadily before she too decided to keep Fleur's secret.

'Very well,' she announced, dropping her cane back down. 'Kindly tell your employers I called with an invitation for her and the child to come to tea on Friday.' Lady Stourton gave Deanie two visiting cards which she had taken from her handbag. 'Perhaps Mrs Fisher could telephone should it not prove convenient.'

After Lady Stourton had left, Deanie went at once through to the drawing room to see exactly what Fleur was doing, only to find Fleur sitting at the card table playing Racing Demon, exactly as she said she had been intending to do. Fleur looked up and smiled as she tapped out her cards and asked Deanie if she might have a drink, before returning to her game of Patience.

13

Three other women were invited to tea at Stoke Park on that Friday, all described by Lady Stourton as 'neighbours' although even the nearest lived over fifteen miles away. All of them had children approximate to Fleur's age, but there the similarities ended. It seemed clear from the nature of their conversation that the other three women all knew each other well. But after the initial polite interchanges even Fleur – sitting silently beside her mother on the old faded damask sofa – became aware of her mother's struggle to join in the conversation around her which seemed entirely about horses and hunting, before she fell into a silence as complete as Fleur's own.

Later Fleur experienced similar difficulties with the other children Lady Stourton had invited. They also all knew each other, and since all they also wanted to talk about was their ponies, like her mother Fleur found that she, too, had nothing in common with them. Only a tall, friendly, freckled-faced girl called Lucy who proved to be Lady Stourton's granddaughter appeared polite enough to try to make friends with her, but once she had found out that Fleur didn't ride, however good her intentions, she too soon ran out of conversation and she eventually turned away to talk to the children she already knew.

Even worse, as Fleur had been hoping that once they had finished tea they might at least go out into the garden and play, it began to rain heavily. So instead of being able to go and look at Lucy's pony, or walk across the parkland to see the sheep and the lambs grazing in a distant paddock, the children ended up in a large and obviously unused playroom with only a derelict model railway, the games box and an upright piano for their amusement.

Fleur didn't know how to play the board game in which the rest of the children immediately became absorbed, so she found herself left out and alone and wandered round the large, barely furnished room in search of something to amuse her. For a while she played with what was left of the derelict train set, pushing the few carriages which still had their wheels through a tunnel and over a bridge, and then finally boring of that she turned her attention to the upright piano.

She had seen it the moment she had come in, and try as she might to ignore its charms, her eyes kept coming back to it and her fingers itched to play it. She hadn't played the piano in The Folly now for almost a week, since her mother had insisted that Fleur accompany her into Worcester on the two occasions she had visited the city in that time, almost as if she had known what Fleur was doing when her back was turned. For a moment Fleur thought Deanie must have heard her and told her mother in confidence, but when the reasons for taking Fleur with her emerged – namely a visit to the dentist and to the stationer's to buy her what she would need for her new school – Fleur realized her secret was safe. And she felt it was safe to play this piano, the playroom being so far from where the adults were all gathered, most of all because playing it would go some of the way to relieving the suffocating shyness she was feeling.

Yet even so, for a moment she hesitated, as if she knew that once she began to play something would be over and gone for ever, which in fact it was, for when Fleur finally took a deep breath and sat down at the keyboard of the old upright playroom piano her youth was lost and forever gone.

It was Lucy who in her innocence gave the game away. Everyone was in the hall getting ready to leave, the children struggling into their raincoats while their parents said their goodbyes. Having been buttoned by her mother into her bright shiny pink mackintosh and prompted to go and thank Lady Stourton, Fleur did as she was told and crossed the flagstoned floor to where the old lady stood leaning on her cane. As she made her way over Lucy joined her, taking her hand.

'Can I have piano lessons, Grandmother?' Lucy asked, before Fleur had a chance to speak.

'And just why would you want piano lessons, Lucy?' Lady Stourton enquired.

'Because I want to play the piano like Fleur,' Lucy replied, just as Amelia walked up behind them.

Lady Stourton drew herself upright and, having given Amelia one of her most significant glances, returned her attentions to the two small girls in front of her.

'Have you been using the playroom piano, child?' she enquired of Fleur. 'It really is a perfectly dreadful instrument.'

'That would hardly matter to Fleur,' Amelia said with a little laugh. 'Seeing that she doesn't play the piano. Unless you've been telling your new friend Lucy here whoppers, Fleur.'

'No she can play,' Lucy said gravely. 'We've all just heard her. And she plays really well. Just like someone on a record.'

'Don't you just love children's imaginations, Lady Stourton?' Amelia asked her hostess, adjusting Fleur's rain hat while Fleur stood clutching one of her feet held up behind her.

'Yes, but in this instance I don't think they are imagining things, Mrs Fisher,' Lady Stourton replied. 'Are you, Lucy Lockett?'

'No, Grandmother. Fleur really can play. That's why I

want lessons. So please can I have piano lessons? *Please?* '

'It's no good asking me, child,' her grandmother said. 'You're going to have to ask your mother.'

'But she said I was to ask you. She said something about not affording it.'

'Oh heavens,' Amelia said with another laugh. 'If Fleur's as good as you say she is, Lucy, then perhaps she should teach you.'

'Even better,' Lady Stourton said, 'perhaps first of all Fleur should play for us.'

'But she can't, Lady Stourton,' Amelia replied, now beginning to worry in case the old lady insisted and Fleur made a fool of them both in front of not only Lady Stourton, but also the other mothers who were all gathering around. 'She's never had a lesson in her life, and she's not allowed to play the piano at The Folly. Your grand piano.'

'But why ever not?' asked Lady Stourton, and she gave Amelia a puzzled look. 'One gave one's permission.'

'In case something happened, I mean. It's such a lovely instrument.'

'Hmmm,' Lady Stourton said, extending a hand to Fleur. 'Then one could be in for something of a surprise. Come along, my dear.'

The four of them returned to the drawing room where Lady Stourton opened up a magnificent Steinway grand before winding the piano stool up to its full height.

As soon as she saw the instrument Fleur made to move forward.

'Whatever have you been up to, Fleur?' Amelia whispered, catching her by the shoulder and bending down.

'Nothing, Mummy.'

'Then what is all this about?' her mother hissed.

Fleur didn't have the chance to reply as Lucy came up to pull her by her other hand.

'Play everyone the last thing you played, Fleur,' she

said, as Fleur let go of Lady Stourton's hand and followed Lucy over to the piano. 'What was it called?'

'A Butterfly,' Fleur replied, eyeing the shining white keyboard. 'I called it A Butterfly.'

'Fleur is now going to play you a piece called "The Butterfly",' Lucy announced excitedly. 'And she made it up.'

'Ah,' said Lady Stourton nodding and sitting with her cane held in front of her. 'Not just a recital. A World Premiere. Excellent.'

They're taking a walk across the park, rather Lucy and Fleur are running ahead while Amelia walks slowly behind, trying to convince herself she's not in a dream. It's very difficult for her to do so, because ever since the first notes rang out from the grand piano, shimmering through the hush of the drawing room for all the world like a butterfly fluttering across the flowers in a summer garden, everything has seemed to be distant, as if in a life lived before. This is why Amelia imagines she is dreaming, because there is no feeling of reality. Reality isn't a child of seven who has had no musical education whatsoever sitting down at a piano and playing one of her own compositions, a piece of music which turned out to be no childish study but something of which an aspiring young composer might even be proud, a piece which seemed to capture the spirit of its subject so completely, white wings in the air, insects dancing in the summer breeze. No Amelia must be dreaming, she tells herself, dreaming of a child with long dark hair and her eyes closed sitting at a vast mahogany piano and playing music of her own, sounds which come from the child's own mind, a melody which springs from her soul. This is not her child, Amelia tells herself, smiling at the absurdity and picking a long stem of grass as she walks on, happy because she knows this is a dream, and that even picking the straw is part of the imagining. The child with the mop of long dark hair running ahead with the other little girl, the auburn-haired child, she isn't Amelia's child.

She is a child of Amelia's only in her mind. This makes sense to Amelia because she's what Amelia might have been, she's Amelia with her father's talent; she's what Amelia's father wanted her to be, what he'd hoped for in his daughter until he found his daughter couldn't play the piano even moderately well and what was worse wasn't even interested. The child is not Fleur. The child running ahead up the hill is going to stop and turn round and when she does Amelia will see that it's really herself, it's Amelia aged seven, not Fleur who has never learned a note of music. She will see herself as her father had wished her to be, then the dream will be over and Amelia will wake up and life will go back to normal. She'll wake up in her bed with Richard beside her and below in the garden she'll see Fleur out there, standing and feeding her deer from her flowered bowl, pretty little Fleur, good little Fleur, ordinary untalented little Fleur. Look — you see? She's turning round now and as she does Amelia hurries forward, closer, to make sure she can see the child's face properly and make sure it's not Fleur — and there she is now, close to the child who is smiling from beneath her pink rain hat, smiling and waving to her friend who's now running back down the hillside. Amelia can see her now quite clearly and to her horror she sees that it's Fleur.

14

Fleur could hear her parents quarrelling even though the doors of both the kitchen and her father's study were closed. It helped that for once Deanie's old Roberts radio was off as well and its owner well and truly fast asleep in the chair by the Aga, otherwise Fleur might have missed what her parents were saying. Not that she liked hearing her parents argue, but because she had already heard that she was the cause and centre of the argument it was only natural that she would want to hear its resolution.

It had begun with her father insisting that there must be some mistake. Fleur couldn't imagine what had been a mistake, but she heard her father going on over and over again that this was the case.

'It's a one-off experience!' he shouted. 'Some childish mischief to nonplus all of you who were there!'

'It wasn't, Richard!' her mother insisted. 'How could it possibly be? I saw and heard it with my own eyes!'

'Use your common sense, Amelia! It has to be a mischief because otherwise it just is not possible!'

'I knew I shouldn't have told you!'

'Don't be so stupid how could you not tell me! Anyway if you hadn't told me someone else would! Lady Stourton for instance! She'd have taken a great delight in telling me! With her highfaluting ways! Remember how she interviewed us about renting this place? When it should have been us interviewing her? We're paying for this place, Amelia – she's not letting us stay here out of charity! Oh yes, Lady Stourton would have taken great delight in telling me all about it!'

Fleur missed the next bit because for some reason her parents both dropped their voices to their normal levels while they discussed something over which they must have been in agreement, until suddenly she heard her father raise his voice once more, this time in a kind of despair.

'Are you seriously trying to tell me you think that any bright child with access to a piano – rather like the chimpanzee and the typewriter theory? That any child finally will end up playing Grieg's Piano Concerto? Don't be so utterly ridiculous, Amelia! You know as well as I do what this means – if not better than I do with your history! Good God, woman, a seven-year-old child sitting down and playing one of her own compositions two-handed at a piano is hardly any run-of-the-mill occurrence, is it!'

Their voices dropped again, almost to inaudibility, so that Fleur had to get up from the table and go and open the kitchen door to see if she could hear anything of what was now going on. But all she could hear was just the normal rumble of adult conversation until suddenly the door of her father's study opened and her father appeared.

Fleur darted back into the kitchen and was back at her place at the table just in time as her mother looked round the door.

'Fleur?' her mother said. 'Your father wants to see you.'

Fleur played for him just as she had played for Lady Stourton because not having understood the argument she had half overheard, she thought he would be angry with her if she didn't, rather than the other way round which was actually the case. She had misinterpreted his mood completely but then that was only to be expected because Fleur was only seven years old, and when her father demanded to know what was all this he'd just been told about her playing the piano like some sort of genius, she could hardly be blamed for thinking that she'd be in trouble if she didn't come up to scratch, if she didn't play her very best.

So she played 'A Butterfly' as well as she had ever played it, and when with a deep frown on his face her father leaned forward and asked for something more, something else, she played him 'Deer Running'. When she had finished, and after a brief silence, he then got up and poured himself and his wife a drink.

'Yes,' he said finally, having drunk half his glass of whisky and walked around the piano a couple of times as if the instrument itself might be partly responsible. 'You know I'm not at all sure I want a freak for a daughter.'

'Perhaps it's only to be expected,' Amelia replied, lighting a cigarette and earning a reproving glare from her husband. 'After all my father started playing the piano when he was three.'

Richard looked round at her sharply, almost accusingly.

'You never told me that. I'd always assumed your father had gone to the Royal College to study and come out as a solo pianist.'

'No. My grandmother used to take him to the theatre with her apparently, practically as soon as he could walk. She loved the music hall and musicals, and when they got home, because she couldn't play the piano she used to make my father play. She used to make him play all the tunes they'd just heard and by the time he was Fleur's age all he had to do was hear a tune or a song once, that's all, then he'd sit down and play it.'

'Thank you very much,' Richard asked, running a hand through his thinning hair. 'You might have told me.'

'I did tell you. I'm sure I told you.'

'And I'm sure you didn't. Well. Well that would explain it, wouldn't it Fleur?' Her father ruffled her hair as he walked past her where she was still sitting on the piano stool waiting to be allowed to get down. 'That would explain her prodigiousness. I suppose I must have forgotten, that is if you did tell me, Amelia. What with you not being musical, I mean I just never thought . . . Of course these things can miss a generation. Of course they can. Are you quite sure you told me?'

'Yes. Quite sure.'

'Knowing you I suppose you told me when I had something else on my mind. So it would go in one ear and out the other.'

'So what do you think we should do, Richard?' Amelia asked. 'I mean it's pretty damned obvious she's got *some* sort of gift.'

'I would think such a summation is a little premature, my dear,' Richard replied, clasping his hands together and cracking his knuckles. 'There still could be a perfectly rational explanation. She could have learned it somehow, off the radio, off the television. I don't know. Or it could be as I said, a one-off. It does not *necessarily* mean she's prodigous. Children often have these odd knacks which don't always develop into fully fledged talents. I could do logarithms when I was eight, at practically the same age, but I didn't turn into Einstein. It was just a knack. Like a lot of these things are. Here today, gone tomorrow. That's probably all it's going to be *avec notre fille.*'

'Lady Stourton thought we should have her professionally assessed.'

'Lady Stourton is a lonely old widow-woman living in the country where nothing very much happens unless you *make* it happen. Yes? Good. So Lady Stourton can keep her theories to herself and I thought you were giving up smoking?'

'I am,' Amelia replied. 'Rather I was. I shall. Once this has all blown over. So what are we going to do *avec notre chére fille?*'

'I have an idea,' her father said, smiling at Fleur before lapsing full time into French. '*A very, very good idea.*'

'I hope–' her mother replied, also in French, tapping the end of her cigarette nervously on the rim of a silver ashtray, 'because I don't want anything to come between us. But it is very difficult to know quite what to do.'

'I'll tell you what we're going to do, Amelia,' Richard replied after a long pause, coming to lift their daughter down from the piano stool. 'I don't think we're going to do anything, because it's not up to us to decide. It's really up to Fleur. What we have to do is wait and see what Fleur wants. Right – now off to bed with you, choufleur.' Richard lapsed back into English as he kissed Fleur on her forehead. 'Go and get old Deanie to take you upstairs and Mummy and Daddy will come and tuck you in when you're ready.'

As Fleur closed the drawing-room door behind her, her father said something more to her mother, but what it was was indistinct because he had dropped his voice to a murmur.

What she did hear quite clearly, however, was the genuinely surprised laugh her mother gave in return.

15

As she was allowed to do every Sunday evening when her father was home, Fleur sat in the button-back chair in the corner of the bedroom watching her father packing the items he needed to take with him back to London into a small suitcase.

Like everything her father did, he packed very precisely, just as when he picked up some ornament or something off the dining table he would always replace it in exactly the same place and position. Nor did he ever hesitate before making a choice, seeming to know exactly what he wanted and when he wanted it, not like Fleur's mother who was forever dithering over something, forever considering and then reconsidering and then considering once again. For that reason alone Fleur loved to watch him pack because he did it all so beautifully and deftly, picking up a shirt as he was doing now and folding it exactly in the right way before placing it in exactly the right amount of space he had made in the case.

Normally at such times they didn't talk much because Fleur never quite knew what to say to her father when he seemed more preoccupied with getting his suitcase perfectly packed. But tonight he seemed determined to talk and for a while chattered on to Fleur about their life together as a family and then more specifically about how much Fleur loved her home.

'You do love your home, don't you, my dear?' he asked, turning a pair of light fawn socks inside out and tucking them down the side of the case. 'Of course you love your home, you love it more than anything in the world don't you? So then what on earth would you think if I said you might have to leave it? I mean that would hardly bear thinking about surely? Being made to go away and leave Mummy and Daddy? It's such an unthinkable notion we mustn't even contemplate it, wouldn't you say?'

'Yes, Daddy,' Fleur agreed, frowning at her feet which were stuck straight out in front of her and trying not to feel sick at the thought that had just been put into her head. 'But why should I have to leave home?'

'Ah,' her father said with a smile. 'Ah.'

'You said I was going to be a day girl when I start school,' she continued. 'So why would I have to go away then, Daddy?'

'Yes, well that's just the point, my dear,' her father replied. 'That is the whole point if you'll allow me to explain. Not that I can imagine such a thing myself either, because it would mean I'd see even less of my precious daughter than I do now. But these things must be faced, I'm afraid.'

'But you said I didn't have to go away,' Fleur insisted, the tears beginning to well up in her eyes. 'Why are you saying this? I don't understand.'

'Ah, well I'm telling you this,' her father replied, glancing round at Fleur, 'because if you're not very careful, dear, that is what is going to happen, and there are no two ways about it. If you are not very careful they will take you away from here to wherever they all think best, and I'm sure that's the last thing you want to happen, right? Because as we've just said, you love your home, you love Mummy and your Daddy and Deanie – and what about all your animals? What about Fancy the cat and Pinky your Christmas rabbit? And all your new friends, all the wild animals in the garden? I can't see you being parted from them, Fleur, not for a moment.'

'No, Daddy, I couldn't,' Fleur whispered, the tears running down her face. She was frightened now, puzzled and frightened at a threat she couldn't even begin to understand. She wondered what she could possibly have done that could mean her being sent away somewhere, somewhere far from home?

'Now it isn't because you've done something wrong, you understand,' her father continued, checking the contents of his sponge bag. 'You're too good a little girl to do anything wrong, and nobody *wants* to have to send you away, but there again if we don't do something, or rather if you go on doing something – then we won't have any choice.'

'What, Daddy?' Fleur asked carefully, doing her best to keep calm because she felt that if she started to cry out loud, which was what she wanted to do, it might drive her father into making the decision which he was obviously trying not to make. 'If I go on doing what? Please tell me and I promise I won't go on doing it. I promise.'

'Yes?' her father asked, looking up from his packing. 'Cross your heart and hope to die, promise?'

'I promise,' Fleur insisted. 'Cross my heart and hope to die.'

'It's the piano, my dear,' her father sighed, pushing his two hairbrushes together. 'People your age who can play the piano as well as you can play, they have to go away to special schools. It's as simple as that.'

'Then I won't play it any more!' Fleur cried. 'I promise I won't!'

'That's what will happen if you do, darling,' her father continued, now carefully zipping up his case. 'They'll send you away to a special school far away from home, and from your parents, and think of what you'd miss. You'd miss all the fun of being an ordinary child, you'd miss your home and Mummy and me, and you'd miss all your animals because of course these special schools, they don't allow animals, you see, none at all.'

'Then I won't, Daddy, I promise,' Fleur whispered, her eyes as big as saucers. 'Look.' She crossed herself. 'Cross my heart and hope to die,' she said. 'I promise I won't ever play the piano ever again, ever.'

'It's something you have to choose, you understand,' her father said, picking his case up and putting it on the floor. 'It's not something Mummy or me can choose for you, because we're not the ones who can play the piano like you. But if that's what you want—' He looked at his watch and then smiled briefly at Fleur. 'Nearly time for me to go, my dear.'

'I don't want to go away to a special school, Daddy,' Fleur said, biting back her tears and getting down off her chair. 'Please don't make me, please.'

'No, no, dear, I wouldn't make you, that's what I've been trying to explain. The choice is entirely yours. But if you do choose not to, Fleur, then at least you'll know that no-one will ever take you or send you away because there won't be any reason, will there?'

'No, Daddy.'

'No of course there won't. So you can grow up here in this lovely part of the country with all your friends—' Her father stopped by the door and put his free hand out to her. Fleur ran over and took it, snuggling herself in as close as she dared to her father who stroked the top of her head the way Fleur stroked her pet rabbit. 'No if you don't go on with the piano you can do all your growing up here at home,' he said. 'With Mummy and Daddy, and best of all, and here's Daddy's big surprise – with your very own pony.'

Fleur couldn't believe what she had just heard as she hurried out of the room after her father.

'What did you say, Daddy?' she said. 'Did you say I could have a pony?'

'Isn't that what we moved to the country for after all,' he said as he started down the stairs. 'And it is what you want more than anything in the world, isn't it?'

'Oh yes, Daddy!' Fleur said, jumping down the stairs two at a time. 'Yes! And I promise I'll be good! I promise I'll do whatever you say!'

'I know you will, Fleur, because you always do, which is why you're going to have a pony,' her father replied. 'Just as long as you're sure it's the thing you want most. Because we can't have everything we want. Do you understand that?'

'Yes, Daddy.'

'Good. Now come and give me a hug because it's time for me to go back and earn the money to buy the wretched creature.'

Nothing more was said about a piano, least of all by Fleur, not until there was absolutely no alternative when it had ceased to matter anyway because the die had long been cast. In the meantime she put all thoughts of the piano far from her head, which wasn't a very difficult thing to do for a seven-year-old girl whose world was now about to be dominated by a ten-hand bay gelding so fond of polos that Fleur would unhesitatingly nickname it Minty.

Since Richard was away in London all week he left Amelia to make all the arrangements, and since she knew absolutely nothing about horses she hadn't the least idea even where to begin looking. When the matter had been briefly discussed before Richard had left for London that Sunday, Amelia had wondered now they had decided finally to buy a pony where exactly they were going to keep it. To which Richard had replied that they could put it in livery. Fleur had put in her tuppence worth at this point, reminding them of the riding stables that were just outside the village, so as he climbed into his car Richard told Amelia to start making enquiries both about riding lessons and the cost of keeping a pony there.

'You want to be careful,' Deanie advised her when Amelia was preparing to take Fleur off with her yet again to look at yet another pony. 'Horse folk are worst of 'em all. I should know because my granddad was a dealer and he used to say a fool and his money are soon parted, but even sooner over a horse. Like I keep saying, you'd be best talking to someone who knows.'

'We could ask Lady Stourton,' Fleur suggested, holding her left elbow behind her back with her right hand. 'Lady Stourton knows all about horses.'

'Fleur's right you know, Miss Amelia.'

'So you also keep saying, Deanie, but as I keep saying I really don't think we should trouble Lady Stourton. The poor woman. She's got quite enough on her plate without us bothering her about buying Fleur a pony.'

'That's not your reason,' Deanie muttered. 'You're frightened she'll ask you some'at. Some'at you don't rightly want to answer.'

'Lady Stourton, she loves horses,' Fleur insisted, not understanding either what Deanie had meant nor why her mother was glaring quite so angrily at her old nurse. 'Her house is full of all sorts of horsey things.'

Fleur knew that Lady Stourton had to know all about horses not only because of the horses and foals in the paddocks and the hunters she saw being ridden out from the stables, but also because, as she'd just said, Stoke Park was full of horsey things: paintings and photographs of Lady Stourton's best horses as well as herself and other members of the family riding them, and providing ornamentation throughout were all sorts of hunting memorabilia, masks, fox feet and even whole stuffed foxes. Yet it was obvious to Fleur that her mother had no intention of asking Lady Stourton, preferring instead to make fruitless visits to fields to see what turned out to be totally unsuitable mounts for a totally inexperienced child of Fleur's tender age. But it seemed that news travelled fast in the countryside, and never faster than when it concerned a potential buyer for a pony or horse.

'One hears one is looking for a pony,' an all too familiar voice said finally one day behind them in the Post Office, causing both Fleur and Amelia to start.

It had long been Fleur's habit, whenever they went shopping in the village, to keep an eye out for Lady Stourton's old damson-coloured Daimler in the hope of catching sight of Lucy in the back of it. That afternoon when she'd walked down the hill and into the main street she'd seen no sight of it, yet now as Fleur looked out of the Post Office window as the grown-ups began to talk, she could see the car parked opposite with the chauffeur sitting at the wheel and what looked like a riding hat belonging to Lucy on the back shelf, which must mean that Lucy was inside.

'Perhaps one'd care for a lift back, Mrs Fisher,' Lady Stourton continued, placing a small perfectly wrapped parcel on the scales. 'If so, then one could discuss the matter.'

'That's very kind, Lady Stourton, but I still have some shopping to do,' Amelia replied, hoping that would be sufficient an excuse.

'Perfectly all right,' Lady Stourton said, opening her purse. 'One's in absolutely no hurry.'

It took them almost as long to drive back to The Folly as it did for Fleur and Amelia to walk to it, so slowly did Collins the chauffeur drive.

'The colours at this time of year are so very lovely down here one cannot bear to see them flash past,' Lady Stourton said, as Fleur and Lucy whispered to each other, both dying to get back to Stoke Park where they could chatter away unconstrained by adults. 'Do you not find that to be the case? After the grime of London? Of course you must, otherwise you simply would not have moved here. Now about this pony you're after.'

Fleur and Lucy stopped talking at once now the all important subject had again been raised.

'Absolutely no point in buying one that one knows absolutely nothing about,' Lady Stourton announced, still surveying the autumnal landscape from her car window, 'not when one has the perfect animal standing at home doing nothing. One keeps him as a companion for Lucy's animal and he's a complete Christian. Far better than getting something one knows nothing about, and then standing it at livery and having other children on it. Far better.'

Lucy nudged Fleur and Fleur grinned back at her friend without her mother seeing.

'You'll love him,' Lucy whispered. 'He's the best pony in the world next to mine.'

'I said we'd pay of course,' Amelia explained to Richard on the telephone when he rang that evening from London, as Fleur practised her riding astride on the arm of the big library chair. 'But she wouldn't hear of it. She said she bred the pony and letting Fleur ride it isn't going to cost her any more than it does already. —No, no I don't think there's any catch and I don't think you have to be quite so cynical. Sometimes there is such a thing as a bargain. I think there is in this case. —No of course she's not going to do any such thing. She didn't even mention the dreaded subject once and even if she had a certain party did such a good brainwashing job I doubt if notre petite fille will ever go near a you-know-what again. —Absolutely. Yes of course we saw it. We were taken straight to the stables and the pony was produced, all groomed and gleaming, as if it had all been arranged beforehand, which of course it undoubtedly was.'

Fleur looked round from her imaginary mount and smiled at her mother when she picked up on what she and her father were talking about, remembering the afternoon in every detail, an afternoon which she would never forget as long as she lived. He was really such a lovely pony, just as her mother was saying now, so sweet-tempered and so handsome. She couldn't wait to ride him.

'Giddyup, Minty!' she urged the would-be pony under her. 'Go on, giddyup!'

'That's the other good thing,' her mother continued. 'Because frankly I don't really think we thought enough about how much this was all going to cost – no, darling, don't go off the deep end until you hear what I have to say. —Yes, that's the whole point. We don't have to pay for tack. "Tack" is what saddles and everything are called, darling, and they're very expensive if you have to buy them, believe me. So is keep. Yes, *keep*. Food, Richard. Horses have to eat and apparently they eat rather a lot. Then there's lessons. Riding is not a cheap sport, darling, and if we'd had to pay for all of what I've just said, let alone a pony – there would have been very little left over in the budget for certain other things. —No I'm not the only one who enjoys them, Richard. Think about it. No I was not talking about my hair and I do *not* have it done twice a week. But if you'd rather I didn't have it done at all? No, I thought you wouldn't.' Amelia laughed and glanced round at Fleur, but although Fleur looked round, she didn't see her mother. All Fleur could see were all the horses which she and Minty had left for dead behind them. 'That is what I was just about to tell you, Richard,' Amelia continued. 'Lady Stourton suggested that Welton who's her head groom, and apparently a first-class teacher, could train Fleur – no, *no*, for free, because as Lady Stourton said he's being paid anyway, and most of the time he's got nothing to do. He taught Lucy. You know who Lucy is? Lady Stourton's granddaughter. —Yes, I think it's wonderful too. It couldn't have worked out better. Economically and politically.'

* * *

Playing horses was one thing, as was being on the ground feeding them peppermints and sugar lumps and stroking their velvet soft muzzles, but sitting on their broad, strong backs with only two thin leather reins and a small metal bar to hold them was the opposite side of the coin. Try as she might, and despite Lady Stourton's initial assurance that there really was nothing to it and that girls her age learned to ride in no time, Fleur simply couldn't understand how someone as small as herself could possibly hope to control an animal at least twenty times her size just by pulling at the leather reins which led to the bit of steel in the creature's mouth.

'No, that's not how it's done, missie, ridin' t'ain't done through your hands, t'is done through your seat,' Mr Welton explained which only served to confuse Fleur more. It was even harder to understand how her seat, as Lady Stourton's groom had just referred to her backside, could possibly stop her pony from galloping away with her wherever and whenever he liked.

'Your seat and your legs make your horse do what you want it to, see,' Welton continued. 'The hands is just there for feel. The legs and the seat are the throttle and the brake, and the hands just rest on the steering wheel. You don't stop a car with a steering wheel, missie, do you? No, so you don't stop your horse with your hands.'

He was letting Fleur circle round him, with the pony safely anchored on a lunge rein. Fleur had never felt so uncomfortable in her life, but she was very relieved to find that far from wanting to run off, Minty was much more interested in trying to get his head down and eat grass. The only trouble was that whenever he did, he almost pulled Fleur out of the saddle.

'Your reins is too slack, missie!' Welton called when the pony persisted. 'You might not stop your car with the steering wheel but you got to keep hold of it when you're driving, ain't you? So keep a hold of your pony!'

The trouble was that just as Fleur had suspected, Minty had more strength in his neck than Fleur had in her entire body, and as soon as she tugged at the reins to pull the pony's head up the pony tugged back and Fleur fell off.

'Are you all right, sweetie?' Amelia called, running from the edge of the paddock where she'd been watching to pick Fleur up off the ground. 'You're not hurt, are you?'

But Welton had beaten Amelia to it, and had Fleur up on her feet and was busy straightening her riding hat by the time Amelia arrived by her side.

'No harm done, ma'am,' he said, lifting Fleur up with one arm and putting her back on the pony. 'She just needs to get her legs in the right place. She's not sitting in you see, ma'am. Once we get her sitting in deep, she'll be right as rain.'

Several times during her initial instruction none of them thought she would ever make the grade, least of all Fleur herself. She might have found that playing the piano came naturally to her, but riding most certainly didn't. The fact that she had grasped the sense of different tempos and rhythms instinctively didn't help her one bit when it came to understanding the rhythm of rising to the trot. Fleur simply couldn't find the cadence and spent hour after hour bumping up and down in great discomfort on Minty's back, much to the unspoken and well-concealed despair of her instructor.

By the end of the second week not even Fleur could pretend to herself that she wasn't utterly miserable and obviously not enjoying the experience at all. So far she wasn't showing the slightest aptitude for riding, and her lack of any real progress was duly reported at the weekend to her father.

'Look, it's like everything else,' Richard announced when the matter was brought up over lunch with all the authority of someone who has never even tried to sit on a horse. 'It's like riding a bicycle. It suddenly comes to you. All at once you realize no-one's holding on behind the saddle any more and that you've cycled all the way down the drive by yourself. Just wait and see. I'll bet you whatever you like by Christmas you won't be able to get off that pony.'

'No I won't,' Fleur said miserably, thinking nothing would or could be worth yet another set of sore legs and bruises.

'Very well — I'll bet you another rabbit,' her father said. 'I'll bet you a friend to go with whatever your other rabbit's called.'

'Mr Benjamin,' Fleur said, shifting in her seat in an effort to find a patch of her that wasn't saddlesore.

'Good. Then I'll buy you a Mrs Benjamin. You have to learn to ride, you know. Living in the country.'

But even the promise of a mate for her beloved flop-eared rabbit didn't appear to work the oracle. It was chance that taught Fleur how to ride, although none of the riding party ever let on. Lucy, Fleur and Mr Welton swore themselves to secrecy, allowing Richard, Amelia and Lady Stourton to believe Fleur had finally mastered the mystery of rising to the trot in the safety of the ménage.

It happened when they were hacking back down from the Malverns one Saturday afternoon in late October. As usual Fleur was on a leading rein in the charge of Mr Welton, and as usual the ride had been completely uneventful, until the moment when a cock pheasant rose with a loud *Korr-Kock!* right under Minty's nose. For some reason the normally bomb-proof pony took exception to this particular bird, perhaps because they were walking so slowly back down the steep and familiar path that Minty had half gone to sleep, so that the bird's sudden rise right in front of him startled the animal into bolting. Whatever the reason, so sudden and unexpected was the pony's frightened sidestep that Mr Welton was also caught napping and the leading rein flew right out of his hand. In fright Fleur leaned back as far as she could, tugging hard at her pony's bit, but the start and the sudden freedom were too much for Minty and laying his ears flat back on his head he took off at full speed down the steep and winding path.

All Fleur knew was that she had to stay on. If she came off at that speed, a speed which she was finding absolutely terrifying, she knew she was as good as dead. So as the browned bracken went whizzing past and the rain stung her eyes, she sat and gripped and held on for her life. Luckily the pony ran in a straight line along the narrow path and up over the small hillocks they met as they plunged on their way. Luckily, also, his flight was more for fun than from fright so Minty soon changed his pace from a mad dash to a steady gallop, and although running at full speed at least the pony didn't try to pull any tricks such as bucking or shying, so that when they reached the final stretch of track which flattened out into a long, fast stretch Fleur was still in place and firmly so, sitting well down on the saddle and crouching low over the reins. Her hard hat had all but slipped down over her eyes but even so through the now driving rain ahead she could see the blurred outlines of the five-bar gate which shut the ride off from the road beyond.

For a moment her heart seemed to stop as Fleur realized the alternatives. Either Minty would suddenly pull up short, throwing her over his head and over the gate, or else he'd jump it. So Fleur sat up and back and down, just as Welton had been trying to get her to do for weeks.

Without realizing what she was doing, the moment she sat up and back, Fleur dropped her hands for just long enough to stop the bit from continuing to jab the pony's mouth. As soon as the pain stopped Minty stopped, not in his tracks but in his flight, and slowing up, he decided very sensibly not to jump the gate. Instead he went from a flat-out gallop to a sensible canter, wheeling round in a long arc away from the gate and the road beyond, until finally coming down to a trot just as Lucy and Welton breasted the final rise and came into view.

What they saw in front of them was what they had by now decided was the impossible, namely Fleur trotting her pony round in circles, back straight, knees in, heels and hands down, in textbook fashion.

'Well, there you are,' Welton said as the three of them walked sedately down the road. 'They do say necessity is the mother of invention.'

Fleur had no idea what Welton meant by that, but smiled all the same because she knew it must somehow refer to her suddenly getting the knack, just as her father had predicted she would, and a few minutes later she even felt confident enough to copy Lucy who was riding back with only one hand on her reins.

'Only trouble is, young ladies,' Welton remarked as they turned down the road which led to Stoke Park, 'if and when her ladyship finds out the hows and wherefores of Miss Fleur's new-found ability, I fear I'll be getting my marching orders.'

Such a thought had never occurred to either of the girls who at once declared together that nothing would be said about what had happened out on the ride, not one word. As far as they were both concerned, Fleur had suddenly found the knack of rising to the trot on the way home, by a miracle, and on that very stretch of road they were on now.

'So look all excited, Fleur!' Lucy called as they began to trot up the long drive. 'Look as though it's only just happened!'

Both Fleur's parents had come to pick her up that day, and as soon as the children were seen approaching the house, Lady Stourton brought Richard and Amelia out on the front terrace to witness the sight.

'Just when one thought one was going to have to eat one's words,' Lady Stourton said. 'What a splendid sight!'

Fleur waved at her mother and father while demonstrating her newly found skill by trotting Minty round in a circle in front of them.

'When did the penny finally drop, Welton?' Lady Stourton called to her groom, only to be answered by two happily grinning little girls.

'On the road back!' they called as one. 'Just as we were coming home!'

'You're a very clever girl,' Richard said to his daughter as they walked home hand in hand, 'and I'm very proud of you. Do you know that? Daddy's very, very proud of you indeed.'

Fleur smiled up first at her father on one side of her, and then up at her mother on the other side, holding onto and swinging from both their hands. At that moment she felt nothing but love and thought she understood at last what it meant. Of course she didn't because in order to understand the true nature of Love, it is also necessary to understand Betrayal, which in this instance was already hard on Love's heels.

16

By Christmas Fleur and Minty were inseparable, just as her father had predicted. By then the late afternoons were too dark for riding what with lighting-up time now at a quarter to four, but the mornings were still light enough. So whatever the weather, Fleur would be out of the house every Wednesday and Friday before first light and across the park on her bicycle to meet Lucy at the stables — where the two friends would groom and tack up their ponies before going out on a short hack with the ever patient Welton. Following their early morning ride, the girls would return for breakfast either to Lucy's home on the far side of the estate if it was her mother's turn for the school run, or back to The Folly if Amelia was on duty.

The drama began towards the end of term when it became known that on the first Monday of the holidays, Lady Stourton was to host the Pony Club Meet at Stoke Park, and Fleur was expected to have her first day out hunting. For some reason whenever the matter was brought up at home Fleur changed the subject. She didn't quite know why she did, because really she knew very little about the ifs and buts of hunting, yet somehow she found just the word upsetting. Sometimes she thought it was perhaps because the sight of all the fox masks and pads frozen rigid in death always upset her so much whenever she wandered into the trophy room at Stoke Park. At other times she wondered whether she was frightened of making a fool of herself by doing one of the things Lucy had told her she mustn't do, such as overtaking the Master or galloping ahead of the hounds, or whether she was just simply frightened. But whatever the reason, it was a strong one. For on the night before the Meet when she and Deanie were putting the final touches to her kit, Fleur suddenly found herself putting down her boot brush and announcing to Deanie and her mother that she didn't think she wanted to go hunting after all.

'Don't be so silly, Fleur,' her mother said at once. 'After all the trouble everyone has been to? Of course you're going hunting.'

'I really don't want to,' Fleur said carefully, twisting her mouth sideways in her anxiety. 'I've been thinking about it, and I really don't want to.'

'You're just being childish,' Amelia said, handing her back her boot brush.

'Most likes because she is only a child,' Deanie said.

'Deanie, please.' Amelia glared at Deanie. 'I can handle this, thank you.'

'You best give us me cards then,' Deanie said with a wink to Fleur. 'If I'm not needed any more.'

Amelia gave her old nurse one last look and then turned her attentions back to her daughter.

'Lady Stourton assures me that you'll be well looked after, Fleur, so there's nothing to be frightened of. I gather there'll be plenty of parents on duty both on horseback and on foot, so there's really no need to be frightened.'

'I'm not frightened,' Fleur replied. 'It's just that I don't want to see a fox killed. That's all.'

Both women stared down at her but for different reasons.

'Quite right too,' Deanie said. 'Well said, child.'

'Deanie—' Amelia cut in, white with anger. 'Didn't you hear me? I said I can handle this.'

'The child's got a right to her opinions, Miss Amelia. After all, it's her that's going hunting, not us.'

'And I don't want to,' Fleur said with a shrug. 'Not now, anyway.'

'I have never *heard* such nonsense,' Amelia said, taking Fleur by the arm. 'When you think of the trouble we've all gone to, I really cannot believe my ears. Just wait till your father hears.'

'He'll only hear if you tell him,' Deanie said, but this time she was ignored.

'Look,' Amelia said, pretending to be patient. 'You don't have to see a fox killed, if that's the problem. Anyway the chances are they won't kill a fox. Lady Stourton said the Pony Club day is mostly just a fun day out.'

'Lucy said they killed at least two foxes at the Pony Club Meet last year,' Fleur replied, looking up at the ceiling rather than into her mother's determined eyes.

'Even so,' Amelia said. 'Even if they did. *You do not have to see the kill.* Understand? Lady Stourton said so.'

'I still don't want to go, Mummy,' Fleur replied, shaking from the effort of making such a decision. 'I'm sorry.'

At that moment her father came downstairs and into the kitchen, suitcase in hand, having finished his packing.

'Car keys,' he said. 'Car keys.'

He took his keys off a hook on the dresser which he had carefully labelled 'Keys: car/house', before staring at the now silent group round the table.

'I thought we were going hunting, not to a funeral,' he said.

'Fleur has now decided she doesn't want to go,' Amelia said, going to the dresser to fetch her cigarettes. 'After all this, Richard, she has just announced she doesn't want to go hunting tomorrow after all. Can you believe it?'

'No I cannot,' her father said, putting down his suitcase and looking at his watch. 'I've got five minutes still, so we'd better sort this out pretty quick. Sit down, Fleur. And someone tell me what all this is about.'

With sinking heart Fleur sat at the table with Deanie sitting down beside her. Out of sight under the table, the old woman took Fleur's hand.

'Remember, Richard,' Amelia said. 'That it is the Pony Club Meet. At Lady Stourton's.'

'I'm only too well aware of the facts, thank you, Amelia,' Richard said, waving her cigarette smoke away from his face as he leaned both his fists on the table. 'Now then, young lady.'

'She don't want to kill a fox, that's why,' Deanie said, squeezing Fleur's hand. 'You can't say that's unreasonable. Not coming from a child.'

'I've already told Deanie to keep out of this,' Amelia said.

'Is that what it's all about, Fleur?' Richard asked, smiling at his daughter. 'Because if it is, you won't be killing anything. That's the huntsmen's job. They do the hunting and you'll just be following.'

'It's not that, Daddy,' Fleur said, once again summoning her courage. 'If they catch a fox and kill it, it might be my fox.'

'What is this?' Richard glanced at Amelia, who raised her eyebrows and shook her head. 'You don't have a fox, Fleur. What on earth are you talking about?'

'Pity none of you listen, or bother to ask,' Deanie said. 'She has a fox all right. She feeds it at night, out by the dustbins—' Deanie stopped when she saw the look on Fleur's face but it was too late. In trying to defend the child, instead she had betrayed her.

'If you leave food out for foxes,' Fleur said, almost inaudibly, 'they don't eat your chickens.'

'We don't have any chickens, Fleur,' Amelia said, exhaling a cloud of smoke. 'Anyway, whoever gave you that idea?'

'Mrs Welton. Mr Welton's wife.'

'Now listen,' Richard said, taking another glance at his watch. 'I really don't have time for this, so we'd better get something sorted out here and now. Even if you have been feeding a fox and trying to tame it, that doesn't mean you can't go out with the Pony Club.'

'It does,' Fleur said, not daring to look at her father, but determined to make her point. 'Suppose they do catch a fox? How do you know it won't be mine?'

'Because,' her father said, standing up straight and taking a deep breath. 'Because if your fox is being fed here, and if you make sure to feed him tonight and tomorrow morning, my dear, then it stands to reason he won't be out looking for food when the hunt sets off. So he will not be the one being hunted.'

Fleur looked up at her father who after a moment managed a smile for her.

'And just think,' he continued. 'Think what it'll look like if you don't go. Think what it'll look like to Lady Stourton. It'll be so rude. And what about your friend Lucy?'

'Lucy will understand.'

Her parents exchanged a brief but mutually exasperated look.

'Will you please tell your daughter, Amelia, exactly what sort of creatures foxes really are? Because I am going to be late,' Richard said, once more picking his car keys off the hook where he had carefully replaced them. 'Will someone please get it into her head that foxes are not cuddly storybook animals, but hard-hearted killers? They kill things just for the fun of it, often not even eating their prey which means they can't always be killing things just because they're hungry. They bite the heads off chickens and then just leave them. And they do charming things like tearing the tongues out of lambs.'

'Not if you put out herbs and vegetables and bread for them,' Fleur persisted, egged on by another hand-squeeze from Deanie. 'And when they kill lots of things together, it's so that they can bury them and keep them for another day. Like we put our food in larders. That's what Mrs Welton says.'

'Mrs Welton is talking nonsense,' Richard said. 'Foxes are pests and have to be killed. They are killers, not creatures to be made pets of. Now I really have to go. I have a very important day tomorrow.'

'Cats kill birds,' Fleur said. 'Fancy used to kill birds, that's why Mummy put a bell on her.'

'That is nothing to do with what we're talking about,' Richard replied sharply.

'I'd say it's got everything to do with what you're talking about,' Deanie said. 'The child's made a perfectly good point.'

'This is nothing to do with you, Deanie!' Amelia almost shouted at the old woman. 'Will you for once just mind your own business!'

'Funny that,' Deanie said, quite unperturbed. 'I always thought it were the children that were my business.'

'This is my last word on the matter,' Richard said. 'You are to go hunting, Fleur, if only to see whether or not you really like it, which I assure you that you will. Hunting is part of country life. It's only by hunting that you can make your way in English Society, that is the case believe me, that is the way it has always been. Anyway, there is absolutely no point in you learning to ride and us going to all this expense if you're not going to hunt. All your friends will be out tomorrow and what are they going to think if you don't show up? And if you're worried you're going to see something you don't like, then you don't have to look. As far as I understand it there's no obligation to be in at the kill.'

The last two words were enough to strengthen Fleur's wavering resolve.

'I'm not going,' she said. 'And no-one can make me.'

There was a long silence before Richard pulled a chair out from under the table and much to everyone's surprise, seeing what a fuss he always made about being on the road by nine o'clock at the latest, sat down opposite his daughter.

'I think I could if I wanted to, Fleur,' he said quietly, but with a smile, 'except that's not the way I do things. That's not the way this family works at all. If we do something, then we all have to be happy doing it, that's the way it's always been.'

Fleur frowned at her father, wondering why he was being so nice and understanding all of a sudden when only a moment ago he had been telling her that she was to go hunting or take the consequences. But somehow she knew better than to say anything.

'So,' her father continued, reaching across and putting one finger under her chin to tilt her face up to him. 'If that's really how you feel, then I must respect it. You must always do whatever you think is right, that's an absolute rule in life, not what someone else tells you what is right. Just because I see nothing wrong in foxhunting doesn't mean that you must also see nothing wrong in it, and so you do what you think is right, my dear.'

'So it's all right if I don't go, you mean?' Fleur asked.

'If that is what you believe is right, yes,' her father replied. 'And now it's time for me to go, and time for you to go to bed. Mummy and Deanie will take you upstairs now and tuck you in, and when I've put my cases in the car, I'll come up and give you one last kiss good night.'

Again there was a silence as Amelia, Deanie and Fleur all tried to make sense of the change not only in Richard's fixed routine but also in his attitude. But seeing that she might have got her way, Fleur broke the silence by getting up and going round the table to kiss her father shyly.

'Thank you, Daddy,' she said. 'Thank you very much.'

'That's perfectly all right, my dear. I'm sorry if I was a little hard on you at first. I just didn't want you letting anyone down.'

Deanie took Fleur, who was already in her night things, out of the kitchen and up to bed, followed shortly by Amelia who had stayed behind to have a word with her husband. As Deanie was turning down Fleur's bed and her mother was hanging up her clothes, they all heard a door bang downstairs and Fleur looked out of her bedroom window expecting to see her father out in the drive packing up his car. Instead a moment later he appeared in her bedroom.

'Right,' he said, rubbing his hands together. 'Never let anyone say I'm not a man of his word. A good night kiss promised, one good night kiss delivered.'

Having kissed Fleur on both cheeks and hugged her briefly, Richard turned and went, promising Amelia he would as usual ring her the moment he got to London.

Fleur crawled across her bed to watch her father drive off. He didn't look back or up, but just opened the boot to put in both his overnight bag and his briefcase before settling into the front seat and driving off into the winter night.

17

It wasn't in Fleur's nature to scream. So far as she knew, until that moment she never had, but she just couldn't help herself. It was the blood, the blood on the ground and the entrails, the dark crimson blood staining the ground frost where the dead rabbit lay torn open, its throat ripped right out and half its face missing. There was no sign of the second rabbit anywhere, but even while Fleur was screaming and while her senses were still reeling she could see the cage door was open. It was wide open, the door she remembered she had locked so carefully the night before. As she became fully aware of what had happened, she ran to the bushes and vomited.

By the time her mother, still in her dressing gown, had rushed from the house to see whatever was the matter Fleur was standing pointing and jabbering at the cage, hopping from one leg to the other.

'Whatever's happened, Fleur? What on earth is all the screaming about?' Amelia asked, suddenly seeing exactly what the matter was. 'Oh, my God. Oh Christ! Oh God what on earth has *happened*!'

'The cage, Mummy!' Fleur sobbed, her screams having changed to hysterical tears. 'The door was open!'

'But it can't be. You always shut it.'

'But it *was* open, look!'

There was no need for Fleur to point and no need for Amelia to look. The door was wide open as it had to be for the fox to have got the rabbit.

'Then someone must have opened it,' Amelia said, plucking up the courage to walk past the dead and dismembered animal on the ground to go and inspect the door. 'Someone or something.'

'The fox couldn't have opened it,' Fleur sobbed. 'I shut both the bolts and foxes can't open bolts.'

'You can't have shut it properly, sweetie,' Amelia said. 'Because – look. Both the bolts are still shot. You must have only thought you'd locked it.'

'But I did, Mummy! I know I did!'

'You can't have done, darling. If you remember it was getting dark, and it was awfully cold, and it happened once before when you fed them one morning, remember? You came back from school and found Mr Benjamin running round the garden.'

At the mention of her dead pet's name Fleur turned to run inside the house, but found herself instead in the arms of Deanie who had also now arrived at the back door.

'Oh lord, child,' Deanie said, surveying the fox's work, and hugging the distraught child to her. 'In heaven's name how on earth did this happen?'

'Someone opened the cage. Deanie,' Fleur whispered. 'Someone opened the cage.'

'She forgot to close the cage properly, Deanie,' Amelia called over her shoulder, as she began to shovel up the dead rabbit's remains. 'It's the only explanation.'

'I didn't, Deanie,' Fleur whispered again. 'I know I closed it.'

'The only thing that can be said about it I suppose is that at least she knows what foxes really do now,' Amelia concluded as she emptied the load on her shovel into a dustbin. 'Just like her father was trying to tell her.'

'Aye,' said Deanie. 'You're right there any road. It's exactly as her father was saying.'

But Fleur didn't wait to hear any more. She wriggled out of Deanie's arms and wiping the tears away from her eyes with the sleeve of her dressing gown, ran into the house. Of course her father had been right, she realized as she charged up the stairs and into her bedroom. Foxes were cruel horrid animals that tore people's pet rabbits to death, and for that reason she hoped that when the hunt caught a fox today they would tear it to pieces in the same way that her beloved Mr Benjamin had been torn to bits.

'Of course I have to,' Fleur told her old nanny only minutes later when Deanie discovered what Fleur was doing. 'I have to and I want to.'

'If you want to, then it's a different thing, child,' Deanie said. 'As long as you really want to.'

'Daddy said foxes were cruel and he was right, Deanie,' Fleur continued, pulling on her string riding gloves.

'Aye, but happen it might not have been a fox, child,' Deanie said, bending down to button up her charge's jacket. 'It could always have been some other animal.'

'What sort of animal?'

'A weasel. A stoat maybe. Not only foxes that kill rabbits, you know.'

'I saw fox footmarks, Deanie.'

'Sure it weren't a dog?'

'No. I know it was a fox.' Fleur stared at her old nanny, her lips almost as pale as her face. 'I know it was.'

Then she was gone, off out of the house without saying another word, gone, leaving even her small saddlebag which Deanie had packed with sandwiches and Mars bars, left behind on the table because as she told herself she wouldn't need it since she'd be much too busy hunting Mr Fox.

Fleur had never known such excitement. By the time they moved off the frost was out of the ground and a weak sun shone out of a pale December sky. Away across Stoke Park they moved, hounds already at work up ahead, the huntsmen at their heels watching their every move, and the Master on his magnificent grey at the head of the followers. Because she already had some few years hunting experience, while all the other children were being marshalled into order, Lucy had contrived for Fleur and herself to manoeuvre their way to the top of the line so that they were nearest the Master and the Hunt members when the field moved off. And due to the handiness of their ponies, that was where they stayed all day.

Once the earth warmed and with no wind to speak of, it was a day of good scents, and within an hour of moving off from the meet hounds found at a covert known oddly as The Oiks. Hearing their baying as well as the thrilling sound of the huntsman blowing away for the very first time, Fleur's blood rose even higher and she kicked her pony on after the red-coated horsemen in front, her determination earning a quick and succinct reprimand from one of the Hunt members, lest she override hounds. Even when forced to rein back however, Fleur could still see the fox running ahead, tall and dark red against the stubbled corn and going so easily he could have been sailing in a wind. There seemed little chance of hounds catching him, so well was he running and so long was his head start. Perhaps the fox felt it too, for before disappearing completely from view over a small hill ahead of them, he stopped and looked back for a moment as much as if to check on the proximity of his pursuers.

'Cunning devil!' Fleur heard someone call behind her. 'He's crossed Mayber's Brook! You can say good night to that chap!'

Sure enough by the time they gathered on the banks of a small but fast-flowing river, the fox and his scent were gone. Another day they might have forded the river and tried to make a fresh find, but with so many young and inexperienced children out the huntsman turned his pack and swinging west sent them about their business in a huge field of kale. Fleur was hard on their heels, calling to Lucy to come and join her at the corner of the field so they could watch the hounds working and it was Fleur who cried *View Holloa!* as they'd all been instructed to do when they spotted another fox darting out from the crop not fifty yards from where they waited.

So the day went on. By two o'clock when the Master and his team of huntsmen took second horses they had enjoyed three good points, although they had been forced to give the fox best on each occasion.

'No matter!' the Master called to one of the following parents. 'It's a good day's sport which is just what we wanted for the young!'

The hounds all but mobbed a fox in the first covert they drew after the break. From the noise coming from within the woods it seemed to Fleur that the quarry was being killed on the spot, until out of the tangle of bramble and briar a fox ran out right under her pony's feet, blood pouring from where its ear had been, a bloodstained tongue lolling out of its mouth and a deep tear in its side.

Seeing Fleur and her pony made the fox hesitate. It stopped and looked up at Fleur and, as it did, for a second the terror seemed to leave its eyes as they met hers. This was the moment they realized that they knew each other. In the woods behind, hounds and huntsmen could be heard getting ever closer but this time Fleur didn't *holloa*, she just sat and watched as the wounded animal began what she knew would be a futile attempt at escape.

The fox made it to the first wall before the pack picked up the line and streamed out from the covert in pursuit. Somehow the badly wounded animal found the strength to jump up on the wall, where for a moment it stood poised, as if wondering where best to run. Meanwhile twelve pair of hounds streamed towards it homing in for the kill. Then it was gone from off the wall and away into the dead bracken and scrub beyond. The pack streamed after it, some jumping the wall clean, others scrambling it or diving through holes, the air full of wild high crying and the drum-like thunder of horse hooves. Figures flashed by Fleur, red coats and black, bay horses and grey, ponies and steeple-chasers. Over the wall some flew while others less resolute galloped through an open gate but all of them were racing to be in at the death, their blood up and mindless of any risks they might be taking as they put their horses blindly at the oncoming fences and hedges and walls.

'Come on, Fleur!' Lucy cried as she galloped by. 'Quickly! They're heading up Garr Hill to the Stones! They're bound to catch him there!'

Fleur tried to rein Minty back but her pony, too, had his blood well up by now, and seeing his stable companion racing by him he took hold and carried Fleur off. Soon they were threading through the field, leaving behind the shouts and admonishments of the trailing adults as they caught up with the Master and his huntsmen. Remembering their manners just in time, Lucy and Fleur sawed at their ponies' mouths, managing to rein back before they were sent back, tucking themselves in behind the huntsmen and the pack ahead.

Except for the thunder of the hooves and the rush of the wind in their ears, it was oddly silent as they raced on up the hill. Hounds were running mute now as is often the case when they run hard on a good scent, although as she scoured the land ahead and saw no sign of their quarry Fleur wondered how the wounded animal still held its lead. Then she saw the fox not a hundred yards ahead now, its brush no longer flying up in confidence behind it but dropped from weariness and the knowledge of impending death. It was just a matter of time, minutes perhaps, or maybe even just seconds, before the hounds caught and tore it to shreds. This time there was no escape, there was no giving best.

Up a hill they all ran finally, up a bank that abruptly steepened, causing both horses and hounds to slow almost to a walk until the climb levelled out into a track which swept in a long curve round a bend to lead into a circle of stones from which there was no escape. Into the clearing rode the huntsmen almost on top of their fast-tiring pack, into a place where the cold wind moaned and where turning to face them, its back to the sheer slope running up behind it, Fleur's fox stood awaiting its death.

It didn't have long to wait before its life ran out, a moment perhaps, a matter of seconds, a count perhaps as far as three or four at most before the hounds tore out its throat and its belly. But to Fleur the moment lasted a lifetime. Above the high cries of its killers she heard it scream and saw the look in its eyes just as a hound caught it by the neck, and what she saw she never forgot as she witnessed death for the first time. She'd seen things dead before of course, small animals or birds dead in the garden, and even that very morning her pet rabbit dead at her feet, and she had touched and felt the little corpses she had found to see what death felt like. But until that moment she had never seen anything actually die.

Now she had; now she had seen death close to and at first hand, and what she saw was like nothing she would ever see again, for the first death witnessed is the death that stays and marks all the others. This moment would stay with Fleur for ever and become a part of her very being so that whenever she wished to express a certain dreadful pain or an anguish, it was there ready inside her, instantly on call. The torment of that moment became a sound which in turn was to become her trademark.

'Who's to have the mask, Master?' the huntsman asked, holding up the bloody head which he'd hacked from the animal's body. 'He's not the one bit spoilt besides missing his ear.'

'Give the mask to Mrs Clifford here,' the Master replied, nodding to a veiled woman on his left, 'and the brush to this young lady, who's hardly left my side all day.'

The Master indicated Fleur who for a moment became frozen in horror as another huntsman bent down to amputate the fox's tail.

'This your first time out, young lady?' the Master asked her, as Fleur felt her gorge rising. All she could see were smiling faces, the same faces which had been looking in the same fixed way at her fox when he met his death, smiles and what-a-lark eyes watching her, while she tried not to look at the red and mutilated remains on the ground in front of her.

'I said is this your first time out, young lady?' the Master repeated. 'Because if that's so, if that's the case then we must blood you.'

The Master nodded again, this time to the huntsman who had decapitated the fox as if he was chopping up an onion, and who now advanced towards Fleur holding the bloody end of the fox's brush up to smear down her face. But before he could reach her, Fleur took hold of her reins and wheeling her pony round kicked him on to gallop full pelt out of the ring and the circle of hunters.

She could still hear their laughter in her head as she galloped back down the hill and across the fields for home. She could hear it as she skidded into Lady Stourton's stable yard and quickly unbuckled her pony's tack. She could still hear them laughing later in the dark as she lay safely in her bed. But above all their laughter she could hear the scream of the fox, even when she closed her eyes tightly. Only after she had finally fallen fast asleep did the real process of absorbing the terror and the pain begin, when the metamorphosis which was to turn such private griefs and torments into the sound Fleur was to make and then make known all around the world. And all the while, below in its hutch, sat a grey angora rabbit, the one which had survived the massacre, the one which had managed to escape and hide itself away from harm when the fox had quietly come into the garden not long

208

after the door of the rabbit hutch had been deliberately unbolted and left to swing wide open.

From Turning Point, 13th May 1989
Fleur Fisher-Dilke talking to Teresa Munro.

What I was meant to be was well educated and accomplished, but only up to a point that is. I wasn't really meant to be that good at something, at any one thing. The plan was for me to be a polished young woman with all the necessary domestic and social skills. Like so many other girls, I was brought up to be married really, hence the early concentration on riding which was intended to advance me in society, even at that tender age. Which, of course, it perhaps did in its own way through The Pony Club and all that went with it, although I have to say I didn't hunt. It just wasn't for me. The trouble was (and still is) that whatever I took up I did it 'for England', probably in an effort to overcome my intense shyness. But, then, inevitably I would become disillusioned when I found I wasn't going to be that good anyway. But that's all part of the process of growing up. Trying things, and then finding 'No, that's not for me.'

It all came down to my best friend Lucy, whose grandmother owned the house in Worcestershire where we were living. I was just approaching my ninth birthday, and I really hadn't thought about playing music at all since, I suppose, I was six? Anyway, Lucy and I got back from a ride and I stayed the night with her because my mother wasn't very well and Lucy and I were planning to go on a long picnic ride the following day. Then that evening as I lay asleep in bed I suddenly heard this heavenly sound. It was the usual thing at first — you now, thinking you'd died and gone to heaven? It really was that, well, cliché-ed. But it wasn't the music, it was the sound, this heart-stopping, thrilling, ethereal sound, a sound I'd never heard before. So, leaving Lucy to sleep, I stole downstairs to see who and what was making this utterly bewitching sound. And when I looked through the half-open drawing-room door I saw someone at the piano, but I didn't take any notice of him. The person I'd come to see was standing the other side of the piano, a beautiful dark-haired woman in a green silk dress and she was playing a violin. And in that moment I knew. That was the moment that I had heard the sound I wanted to make, that without realizing it I had always been searching for. In a way I realized that, shy as I was, I had, if you like, found my voice.

From The Food Of Love, *a selection of critical essays* by Lionel Cardew.

I have never heard the Elgar played so wondrously well. Never more sublimely, never more thought-fully, particularly the *Andante*. Each time I play her recording of the concerto with Sir Hadleigh Vernon and the Liverpool Philharmonic a feeling suffuses me which I cannot ever quite describe, try as I may and try as I have. There is melancholy, certainly, but then there is melancholy and there is melancholy and what this soloist brings is more than just a pensive sadness. It's as if she's seen something and that something is still there in her mind's eye, a moment of such spiritual affliction that listening to her you feel as martyrs must surely feel when they sacrifice their very lives for the things they love, a sublime torment, an agonizing ecstasy. The music she makes transports us to an emotional precipice where her plaintive mournfulness induces an ache of such depth that one can hardly bear to listen on. Whatever it is in her mind's eye, whatever it was she once saw, it must so have scorched her memory that it has affected her for ever. If this is so, although I pity her for what she witnessed, I also thank God that she did if as a result of her reliving this memory we are privileged enough to be allowed just a moment of a time and place which lies beyond us, and far out of our reach, as we make our common daily round.

18

On the top floor of Lady Mary's School for Girls in Malvern there were six small soundproofed rooms, each with a piano, where the girls could practise their chosen instruments. The music teacher's room was at the head of the corridor, a much larger room housing a baby grand piano and a large and well-cared for collection of violins, cellos, clarinets, flutes and oboes, as well as a smaller selection of the less popular musical instruments. When the eight-year-old Fleur had been enrolled at the school at the beginning of that year, riding, tennis tuition and extra French were the only extras her parents had nominated. Although Fleur and her mother had been shown the suite of practice rooms on their initial tour of the premises, Fleur never made that long climb up to the fourth floor of the school again – until the term after she'd witnessed Deliah Carlisle playing Debussy's Violin Sonata in G minor in Lady Stourton's drawing room late that summer night.

During the rest of that particular school holiday Fleur had said nothing about her moment of self-discovery. She was particularly careful not to give the slightest sign of any rekindled interest in music, because this time she really knew there was a difference, even though she couldn't begin to explain what that difference was. All she knew was that, quite by chance, she had found out not only what she wanted to do but also what she *had* to do, and such was the force of her conviction that she also knew no internal or external force was going to stop her from what Deanie had always called 'following her bliss'. So she tried her hardest to behave completely as normal, continuing with her usual activities right up until the moment she returned to Lady Mary's. Then, during Long Break on the very first day of the Christmas term, she ran up the stairs all the way up to the top floor where she made straight for the music teacher's room.

The violin she chose was not the best-looking one, the almost new highly polished Hendricks in a blue-lined, mock lizard-skin case, but an old and dull-looking apparent nonentity which was not even cased but lay out on a shelf among the metronomes, mouthpieces, reeds and resin blocks. In fact it was Mr Stayner the music teacher's own instrument which he had been playing during a class earlier, explaining why it was in tune and lying out of its case. But Fleur didn't choose it as a matter of convenience. She selected it because, having run a tightened bow across the strings of the others which had been tuned in readiness for the day's lessons, she found that Mr Stayner's old violin sounded far and away closest to the sound she could hear in her mind.

Tucking it almost under the point of her chin and holding it in place by weight rather than balance, she drew the bow carefully first across the open top string and then the other three. After the notes had died out she repeated the exercise, this time beginning with the bottom string and drawing the bow evenly back across to the top. Even the production of those four naked and unadorned notes, which she could feel vibrating through her chest and head, thrilled and inspired her, so much so that within the short space of time she was in the music room, a matter of no more than twenty minutes before the bell for the end of break sounded in the quadrangle far below, Fleur had already discovered how to finger and play a perfectly correct scale of G major. But most importantly of all, when Fleur picked the violin up and placed it under her chin she felt something she had never felt with the piano. She felt immediately that she and the violin were one.

If Fleur had been thought to be prodigious on the piano, then it is impossible to express what the same listeners would have made of the now nine-year-old girl's playing of the violin one month after she had picked up the instrument for the very first time. Still unable to read a note of music, she had to rely on her own compositions just as she had done when playing the piano, the only difference being that the music she now wrote in her head was altogether more adventurous and imaginative, precociously so in fact. She still held the violin all wrong, her bowing was totally unorthodox as was her fingering, but it didn't matter because the sound she made was already sweet and round. Had anyone ever entered the music teacher's room during Long Break over those first four weeks of Fleur's love affair with the violin, they would have sworn that the music they heard being produced was the result not of private experimentation but of the best tuition.

As it happened for a month no-one heard her, at least no-one that mattered. Only once were her secret sessions interrupted by another pupil arriving early for her music lesson, whereupon Fleur immediately started playing so appallingly that her schoolmate was quite easily convinced that she was just fooling around. After that Fleur shut herself in one of the soundproof practice rooms with her back to the window in the door, where, keeping a close eye on the time, she managed with complete success to play and practise unnoticed and without further interruption.

Fleur had no real understanding of her formidable talent. Certainly she knew she could play the violin in just the same way that she had known she could play the piano. The way she saw it was that she simply had a facility for music, just as some of her friends had for playing netball or tennis. But unlike her first efforts on piano, this time she knew there was no denying the

215

gift. What she would have done about it had Fate not intervened, however, must remain as speculation. No doubt she would have tried to keep it as her secret until she was both old enough and strong enough to resist the will of her father, whom she felt sure would again immediately impose a ban on her playing in precisely the same way, and for the very same reason, that he had done before. Probably she would have kept her new-found ability a secret for as long as possible, perhaps because she felt guilty about it, her guilt being fuelled by her father's previous warnings that gifts such as this were always rewarded by enforced separations. Exactly how long she could have kept her light hidden is anybody's guess. Although when Fleur was a grown woman, she was to say it would have been no time at all.

'It seemed there was no real problem then,' she would answer the journalists who frequently asked her the same question. 'When you're that age and you find something out as I did, that you can make music and that you like making music, quite honestly you think so-what? You don't really think ahead, not when you're only nine or ten. You don't make decisions like "This is what I want to do with the rest of my life." I mean I think I really did know that for the rest of my life I'd play violin, but when you're a child how you're going to set about doing things just doesn't occur to you. What I do remember consciously deciding was that I mustn't tell anyone, because I didn't want to leave home. When you're that age that equals leaving love behind. So as long as I could sneak up to the music floor at school whenever possible, and just play, I was happy. You see I was a day girl, I went home every night, so why rock the boat? Of course by the time I became a teenager, well, it would have become totally different, I don't doubt that. But then was then. And at that moment it was just me, Mr Stayner's violin, and nobody else. At least that's the way it was and the way I meant it to be, had it not been for Mr Stayner's tape recorder.'

Fleur had never taken much notice of any of the machinery lying around the music room. From the word go she had only had eyes for the violins and, finally, for ~the one violin she had chosen to play. Anything else in the music room was of precious little interest to her. As for the actual cassette recorder itself, she knew perfectly well what it was, but since none of the machines were ever running when she let herself into the teacher's room she soon forgot all about the tape decks, the cassette recorders, the amplifiers, and all the rest of the mechanical bits and pieces which lay out on the shelves.

On the day in question the cassette recorder was in a different place, but Fleur failed to notice the fact, nor did she notice that two of its buttons were depressed and that one of its lights was on – a small red light on the front of the deck itself.

There was another reason for Fleur's lack of interest in the detail of her surroundings. When she'd made her way up to the fourth floor that day she'd found all six practice rooms occupied by pupils rehearsing for the forthcoming concert but, still determined to play herself, she took the risk of using Mr Stayner's room. So she was in no mood to notice anything else different, because her concentration was already taken up with watching to see if anyone was coming down the corridor which, if she stood on a bench in the corner while she played, she could see through the room's upper windows.

No-one came near the practice room, or even passed it. No-one disturbed her, so she was able to play in a totally relaxed fashion for her usual twenty minutes, the only difference between this session and her usual ones being that she made sure she left early so that the other pupils wouldn't see her coming out of the teacher's room.

217

So it wasn't until she had put the violin back in its place and was preparing to leave that she saw for the first time that the cassette recorder was in a different position, that it was on and running, and that a long silvered lead led from the front of it up to a microphone on top of the piano.

She knew how the machine worked because her father had a smaller version which he used mainly for dictating notes. But although she knew how to turn it on and off, she had no idea how to do anything else to the machine, such as wiping anything which it might have recorded. Not only that, she didn't know why the machine was on. It could simply have been left running by mistake, which was the likeliest possibility and which didn't mean that it was actually recording anything. Even if it was, Fleur wondered as she stood staring down at it, what could she do? If she tried to undo whatever it was doing, she might break or damage it. Her only hope was to leave well alone and hope and pray that whatever function the machine was performing, it wasn't anything that might give her away.

Besides, she thought, as she tiptoed to the door and ran quietly down the corridor, no-one had seen her arrive and no-one had seen her leave, so even if the machine had been recording and Mr Stayner played it back, there was no possible way he could find out *who* was playing. It could be anybody, and Fleur wasn't even one of his pupils.

'I knew because I recognized your voice,' Mr Stayner told her when he had summoned Fleur up to his room after School Assembly the following day. 'I very nearly didn't play on to the end of the tape because I didn't think there was anything else on it. It rewinds automatically when it comes to the end, do you see? So by the time I'd come back here for my next lesson the tape was rewound and it just seemed I'd forgotten to turn it off.'

Fleur stared at the music teacher, trying to guess his mood, wondering what punishment he was going to think up for her trespass. He'd never had occasion to talk to her before, so she had no idea what sort of man he was. He looked kind enough in his baggy worn clothes, with his mop of unruly black and grey hair, and his large eyes made even larger by the lenses of his spectacles, and so far he had only spoken to Fleur slowly and kindly. Even so Fleur was wary and said nothing, because although she had done no harm she realized she might still have done some wrong.

'As I was saying,' the music teacher continued, taking off his tortoiseshell glasses and wiping each of the lenses carefully on the end of his red tweed tie. 'I thought all that was on the tape was the lesson I'd just recorded. A duet I'd been practising with Rachel Langton for the school concert. It was just by chance I let the tape run. Completely by chance.'

Mr Stayner stopped polishing his glasses for a moment and holding them at arm's length looked through them at Fleur. Then humming quietly to himself, he swung the spectacles slowly to and fro in his hand before putting them back on, carefully hooking each of the wires behind his ears. It was a habit of his Fleur was to get to know all too well.

'Then I heard your voice, do you see?' he continued, after inhaling deeply. 'Or rather I heard a voice because of course there would have been no way of knowing it was your voice. Had you not announced the fact.'

Mr Stayner looked up at Fleur, raising his eyebrows as much as to say to her didn't she want to know how? Fleur did of course, she was dying to ask him but afraid to do so because she still didn't know what sort of man the teacher was. So instead of wondering out loud, she dropped her eyes to stare at the floor, trying to remember what she might have inadvertently said to herself while the recorder was running and which had consequently identified her.

'Listen,' Mr Stayner said, switching on the machine by his side. 'Listen.'

Fleur listened. Over the background hum of the machine she could hear the sounds of someone moving, almost imperceptible footfalls, a recording of what had to be her own sandalled feet on the cork flooring as she'd walked across the room, but at what precise moment? Then she heard herself plucking the four strings of Mr Stayner's violin as she always did when she got ready to play, one two three four, then the sound of the bow drawn across all four strings together, and lastly a dextrous scale up and down the top string. She glanced up at Mr Stayner to see how he was looking but he was staring upwards at the ceiling with both hands clasped behind his neck, so she stared down at the machine instead, still wondering how she had given herself away.

As she did, she heard herself clearing her throat and then singing very quietly the melody of the tune she'd been about to play. But there was still nothing that could identify her precisely, Fleur thought frowning hard, unless it was that because Mr Stayner taught music, he was able to identify everyone by their singing voices, a fact which she doubted very much.

'Now,' said Mr Stayner, still staring up at the ceiling. 'This is it.'

' "Swallows Leaving a Garden",' Fleur heard her own voice announcing quite clearly. 'By Fleur Fisher.'

How stupid, she thought. She hadn't even known she was speaking as she'd prepared to play. It was just something she always did as a matter of routine to remind herself of the piece she was intending to play. The habit had started the day she'd made up her first tune on the piano and it had stuck ever since, so much so that by now Fleur did it automatically. She began to try and say something in explanation to Mr Stayner, but as soon as she spoke he simply held up one index finger and hushed her into silence.

'In a moment,' he intoned. 'I want you to listen.'

They both listened and while they did they both wondered, Fleur as to how she was going to escape from this dilemma, and the music teacher as to how and where this child had learned to play the violin so exquisitely. And most of all why she wasn't taking lessons.

Mr Stayner left the tape running after the melody had ended and while she waited Fleur could hear herself putting the violin back on the shelf, walking back across the room and then stopping, which had to be the moment she'd seen that the tape recorder was on. And the moment Mr Stayner now chose to lean forward and click it off.

' "Swallows Leaving a Garden",' he mused, frowning and putting both hands on the top of his head. 'I don't know the piece at all.'

'No,' Fleur replied. 'You wouldn't.'

'Why not, um – Fleur? *Why* wouldn't I?'

Fleur shrugged.

'Because I made it up, Mr Stayner.'

Keeping his hands still on top of his head, Mr Stayner made his mouth into a small 'O' and then blew out his cheeks.

'I don't understand,' he said after a puzzled moment, letting all the air out of his puffed-up mouth. 'You mean as well as playing what we've just heard, you wrote the piece as well?'

'No I made it up,' Fleur explained. 'I didn't write it, because I can't write music. Or read it.'

This piece of information so stunned Mr Stayner that all he could do was widen his large eyes to their limit and puff his cheeks up again, and deflate them after a long silent moment spent staring wildly at the child in front of him.

'Very well,' he said finally with a deep sigh, pulling a chair up for Fleur to sit on. 'I think we'd better start at the very beginning, don't you?'

*　　*　　*

The seemingly affable and straightforward Leo Stayner was a much more complex character than Fleur had assumed him to be initially. Not that it bothered her in the least at the outset because, as long as she was allowed to play the violin, Fleur would endure anything and everything – including Leo Stayner's compulsive desire to talk when she would rather he taught. But Fleur didn't mind for two good reasons. Firstly, being young, she immediately understood that the reason her teacher wanted to talk was because he was lonely. His wife had only recently left him for a younger man, according to school gossip. Secondly, while her teacher was rambling on, Fleur could study hard and fast how to read music.

This posed no great difficulties, despite Mr Stayner's forebodings. Because of her unique gift and the length of her teacher's reminiscences Fleur had learned to read music within a month, much to Leo Stayner's muted but utter astonishment.

'I used to dream about having a pupil like you, Fleur,' he said to her. 'But then of course what teacher doesn't? And what teacher does? Ever get a pupil like you, I mean? Precious few if any, I'm afraid. Which is why I'm afraid to go to sleep at night. In case when I wake up in the morning I find I've dreamed you, and that you're not real at all.'

'I won't be real if my parents ever find out,' Fleur warned him early on. 'I mean I don't think they'd allow me to go on having lessons.'

'But you're not having lessons, Fleur. I'm teaching you for nothing, and I'm teaching you in my spare time and yours . . . in our lunch breaks, and at elevenses, and so on and so forth. So how are they ever going to find out?'

'They will in the end, Mr Stayner. They're bound to. I mean – well – they're bound to.'

'Ah yes, Fleur. I agree,' Leo Stayner said, whipping off his glasses theatrically and swirling them round in one hand. 'But by then it will be too late!'

They had discussed Fleur's problem from early on, since Leo Stayner was naturally at a loss to understand why someone so brilliantly talented was not one of his star pupils. Fleur had explained all about her experience with the piano and why she had stopped playing while her new teacher listened to her with his eyes closed and hands clasped on the top of his head, nodding every now and then when he thought Fleur had made a point, before dismissing it when Fleur had finished as bunkum.

'Tut tut!' he said with two clicks of his tongue. 'It's so often the same old story. It's parents, I'm afraid. Either they think their children are brilliant when they most patently are not, and yet they push them as if they were prodigies until the child can take no more. In a way that was what happened to me. Or else they refuse to recognize talent when there is a talent, most usually because they are jealous of it.'

'I don't think that was the reason for me not playing the piano,' Fleur said. 'My father is a surgeon, you see. So he wouldn't be jealous.'

'Suppose he wants to be a GREAT surgeon?' Leo asked her, opening his eyes wide and rolling them to make her laugh. 'Maybe GREAT surgeons don't have the time for BRILLIANT daughters.'

'Daddy's not like that,' Fleur said. 'He's terribly kind. That's why he's a surgeon, you see. Because he wants to help people.'

'Hmmm,' said Leo, putting his glasses back on. 'My father was also terribly kind, and he ended up being just the opposite. He was a string player in the BBC Symphony Orchestra, but wanted me to be – no he *expected* me to be another Yehudi Menuhin. And I just wasn't up to it. I wasn't even up to being the leader of the orchestra, which became his alternative. I wasn't even up to being a member of an orchestra. I don't have the temperament suited to a career of slow advancement, you see. To rising gradually through the ranks of the orchestra until possibly you became the Leader, playing the same old repertoire over and over again, as well as playing the same old politics. So finally I ended up teaching, and my father ended up despairing of me. He believed what so many people believe. You know, those who can't do, teach.'

'But what would happen if we didn't have teachers?' Fleur asked. 'Somebody has to teach, don't they? Or there wouldn't be any schools.'

'You're right! Of course you're right!' Leo laughed, slapping both his knees while Fleur watched in fascination as his ruddy face turned an even deeper red. 'But then you're a genius so you should be right! Pity I didn't discover you when I was still married. You could have told my wife that I'm not a failure after all. And who knows? I might still be married.'

Fleur had no idea what to say to this, even though when she had her violin in her hand, or under her chin, all her feelings of shyness disappeared and she became both talkative and confident. But matters such as people's marital problems were still way beyond her so whenever the conversation between her teacher and herself began to get personal, Fleur would switch off and go over scales and keys in her head.

There really was only one overriding problem and that was the one of secrecy. At first Leo Stayner was obviously loath to believe what Fleur had told him about her parents' attitude, arguing that once they heard how brilliantly she played the violin they would have no option but to concede that she was destined for a glittering musical career. Fleur, however, knew otherwise and argued back, telling her new teacher that Lady Stourton had told her parents that she played the piano brilliantly, and although Fleur was too modest at first to describe Lady Stourton's actual words and Leo had to prise them out of her, she explained that nonetheless her father had warned her off the piano and her mother had joined in the discouragement by tacit agreement.

'It will be the same with the violin, Mr Stayner,' Fleur assured him. 'My father will only say I'll have to go away to a special school, I know he will.'

'So suppose he does, Fleur?'

'I don't want to go away. Not yet.'

'No. I don't want you to go away either.'

'I like it here. All my friends are here. And I like my home.'

'Very well,' Leo had finally agreed. 'We will keep it our secret for as long as we can, I promise.'

But later Leo Stayner turned his promise into a bargain. In return for teaching her and for keeping her secret, he said that she was to be his. Fleur didn't understand what he meant, so Leo explained exactly what he had in mind and Fleur could see by the sudden serious expression on his face that for once he was not fooling around. Leo was serious.

He began by explaining that after he had failed his father not only in the talent stakes, being a long way below the standard required to be a soloist, but also by demonstrating his inability to settle down in an orchestra, he had gone off round the world – 'bumming it' as he said, ending up in Australia where he nearly died of a rare tropical disease picked up on his travels. That was where he had met his wife, a bright green-eyed and red-haired Irish girl called Finnoulha Flynn who was nursing at the hospital to which he'd been admitted and with whom Leo had fallen so deeply in love that he said he felt himself literally pulling himself back from the jaws of death. They were married within two weeks of him being discharged from hospital with a clean bill of health.

Fleur had begun to fidget at this point in the story, uncertain what all this had to do with her and anxious to get on with her lesson, but noticing her impatience Leo told her that he had to tell her all this so that she would understand better what he was about to say.

'You see shortly after we got married we moved to Sydney where I began to teach music, and to my great surprise I found actually enjoyed teaching. In fact the job suited me down to the ground. Being able to improve the musicianship of others, by coaching and demonstration, I found very satisfying. I tried to teach by allowing my pupils their head, yet always being there by their side when they faltered. I found I had a bit of a knack for it, and in no time at all I was getting some good results and my success as a violin teacher was growing very nicely, thank you.'

Fleur took a deep breath and sighed quietly, shifting her weight from foot to foot, hoping the story would end soon because her precious lesson was in danger of being totally wasted. But this time her teacher failed to notice her disquiet and carried on regardlessly.

'But then I made a great mistake, you see, Fleur. I came back here when I should have stayed out there. I returned far too soon and despite the glowing references I brought with me, I just couldn't get any private pupils here. The fact of the matter was I'd returned to England uninvited. People who do that, you know, are thought to be people who had failed. While if only I'd waited another year, Constance Browne would have brought me over with her. She was my best pupil and I would have been the man who taught the best violinist ever to come out of Australia. But no. Impatient to return home, I left behind the greatest opportunity of my life, and until you came into my life, Fleur, I had put away any thoughts of success. Was it sheer chance that you recorded yourself on my tape? Or was it maybe Fate? Who knows? The point is now I can live in hope again, Fleur, because with you life has once again begun.'

Fleur looked awkwardly at the ground, and then up at Mr Stayner's anxious, expectant face and eventually she smiled, mainly because she hoped the story had come to an end and they could at least devote the final ten minutes of the session to some actual teaching. But Leo Stayner was nowhere near through.

'So now we come to my plan, Fleur, which I hope you will agree with. In fact I know you will, just as you know I will keep your secret for as long as is possible.' Leo Stayner leaned towards where Fleur was still standing and she could see that small beads of perspiration had broken out on his forehead. 'I discovered you, wouldn't you say? Isn't it true to say that although by the time I heard the tape you could play the violin a little – I am the person who is teaching you the instrument properly. So that when you come to play in public – which you will, Fleur, make no mistake about that – you are going to be a very big STAR!' Leo did a trick with his eyes, rolling them widely, but Fleur didn't laugh because she was too busy trying to understand the implications of what was being said.

'What I am saying, Fleur, is that when you come to play in public it will be because of me. I will be the person who has put you up there, because not only will I be the person who has taught you all you know, but I will have kept your SECRET! And if I don't keep your secret, you won't go on playing, will you? Not if what you say is true.'

'No I won't, Mr Stayner.' Fleur shook her head, a little afraid of the somewhat stern note that had crept into her teacher's usually jolly voice. 'So what do you want me to do?'

'It's quite simple.' Suddenly Leo Stayner relaxed again and sat back, much to Fleur's relief, mopping his forehead with a red handkerchief. 'I want to look after you, Fleur. Would you like that? You're going to need somebody to look after all your musical interests. So would you like that, yes? If I was that person?'

'Well – yes,' Fleur said, unable to see exactly what the problem was. 'Yes that would be fine, Mr Stayner.'

'Good,' Leo said, stuffing his handkerchief back in his pocket. 'Then let's shake on it, that'll be that, and we'll get on with the business of turning you into one of the very greatest violinists the world has ever heard.'

There were all sorts of things to arrange because there were all sorts of difficulties they hadn't foreseen. Fleur had thought it would simply be a case of carrying on at home exactly as she had done before, since she couldn't imagine how taking up the violin at school could ever alter the domestic status quo. To all intents and purposes she imagined her daily routine would be undisturbed. She'd go to school, attend all her usual classes, have her violin lessons, and then come home. To her young and innocent mind nothing could have been simpler.

But Mr Stayner knew better and soon realized that in order to teach Fleur properly without anyone suspecting anything, he would have to find a way around her timetable, to try and find times when he could teach her without interrupting the normal flow of her studies.

Her usual periods of playtime, Short Break mid-morning and Long Break after lunch, were out of the question because as he told her sooner or later someone would notice her absence. Otherwise the normal school day yielded no other opportunities since Fleur was too young to have any free study periods where Mr Stayner could organize a private class. Last of all, being a day girl she had to catch the bus home at a preordained time.

'To be perfectly frank, Fleur, we're going to need help,' Mr Stayner told her when he had explained the difficulties facing them. 'We're going to need allies, people we can allow in on our secret, people we can trust, because otherwise I don't see how we're going to be able to manage.'

'But who, Mr Stayner?' Fleur asked, her heart sinking at the prospect of entrusting any of her friends, since she knew exactly how long anything stayed secret in the playground. 'I can't get to school any earlier, and there's no class I can exactly skip without being noticed.'

'Would your parents let you be in the school play?' Mr Stayner wondered, pushing his glasses on top of his head where they got lost in the tangles of his hair. 'They're doing *A Midsummer Night's Dream* this term and although all the principals have been cast, Miss Fenton tells me she's still going to need lots of extras to play fairies and so on.'

'But if I do the school play, Mr Stayner, I won't have time for lessons,' Fleur said, pointing out what she considered to be an obvious flaw.

'No, no, Fleur,' her teacher interrupted. 'All we need to establish is whether or not your parents would have any objection to your being in the play, that's all. They rehearse after school, you see. Three days a week, more when it gets nearer the actual production. Which would give us a lot of time together. It would be a start, at least.'

The idea was that Fleur would ask permission to do the play and if that was granted, then all possible rehearsal time would be spent in the music rooms rather than in the school hall. Mr Stayner assured Fleur that Miss Fenton was a good friend of his who could be trusted, and that she would organize rehearsals in such a way that Fleur would not be needed until the last half hour of any day, right up until the week before the play's three performances.

'It's all going to be worth it,' Leo Stayner said once he had outlined his plan. 'It's all going to be well worth it, just you wait and see. Once your parents have heard you play, there will be no difficulty at all about getting them to agree to you having formal lessons and it will also put a stop to any more nonsense about sending you away. There will be no point in sending you away when they realize how BRILLIANTLY you are being taught here!'

This time when Leo Stayner did his rolling-the-eyes trick Fleur laughed, not so much because she found the face he was pulling funny but out of relief. What he said seemed to make perfect sense.

It was a Friday when Leo Stayner gave Fleur the go-ahead to tell her mother that Miss Fenton had asked her to be in the school play, and when she hurried up the drive of The Folly to break the so-called news she was surprised to see her father's car in the drive. Since they had moved to the country the earliest he ever arrived down for the weekends was late Friday night, when Fleur was invariably asleep.

When she got in the house she could see both her parents sitting at the kitchen table with Deanie at the sink peeling the potatoes for dinner. None of them was talking and Fleur's greeting as she hung up her coat and satchel was barely acknowledged.

'Hello, Daddy,' she said as she came to the kitchen door. 'You're home early.'

'That is what is called stating the obvious, Fleur dear,' her father sighed. 'Yes I am home early and with good reason.'

As her mother told her to go and wash her hands then come and sit down at the table, Fleur noticed that while her mother had a cup of tea in front of her, her father had a drink.

'Is it all right if I ask you something?' Fleur asked as she dried her hands.

'Them that asks don't get,' Deanie said, tidying Fleur's hair at the back before bending over to whisper to her. 'If it's something you're after you'd do best to wait.'

'No it's not, Deanie,' Fleur replied. 'It's telling rather than asking really.'

'Even so,' Deanie said, again in a whisper. 'Even so just hold your horses.'

As she sat down at the table between her parents her father shook his head and gave another sigh. 'It's absolutely ridiculous,' he said. 'Totally and utterly without any sense.'

'I know, Richard,' her mother said, pouring herself some more tea. 'But even so—'

'Yes, Amelia?' her father asked. 'Even so what?'

Amelia glanced at Fleur and then went on pouring her tea.

'Nothing,' she said. 'I just think perhaps – well, what I mean is you've got the whole weekend to consider it.'

'Amelia dear,' Richard replied with unconcealed exasperation. 'You don't have the slightest conception as to what I am talking about. As to what this means. There is nothing in this instance to which you can relate. The world of fashion modelling is in another universe compared to the world of medicine.'

'I know that, Richard,' Amelia replied nervously. 'I know exactly how important your work is and how important it is to you—'

'Of course you don't.'

'I do, Richard. Because you tell me about how important it is, constantly, and I'm very sympathetic. But other people get passed over too, you know—'

'I am not other people, Amelia. I am me. Me, Richard Fisher, one of the best cardiologists they've got and they had no right to pass me over! Particularly for a—' Richard stopped and looked at Fleur as if noticing her presence for the first time. 'It's a token appointment, Amelia, and you know it,' he continued. 'It's a purely political one, one that takes no account as to who is best qualified for the consultancy.'

'I know, Richard. But all I'm saying is you do have the weekend to think about it. Then on Sunday evening, if you still feel the same—'

'Oh I shall, Amelia, don't you worry, I shall!' Richard assured her, getting up from the table and draining his glass. 'I shall feel exactly the same on Sunday night, and on Monday morning I shall tell the hospital board what they can do with their rotten job! Now if you'll excuse me, I'm going to get myself another drink.'

As he left the room Deanie placed Fleur's supper in front of her and ruffled her hair before returning to the sink, while her mother just lit another cigarette and stared moodily into space.

'What's the matter?' Fleur asked. 'Why's Daddy so cross?'

'Your father isn't cross, sweetie,' Amelia replied, tapping the end of her cigarette rhythmically on the rim of the ashtray even though she had only just lit it. 'Your father's just a bit upset.'

'He's not usually home this early.'

'He hasn't lost his job if that's what's worrying you.'

'I didn't think he had. It's just that I thought – well, I thought something might be wrong. When I saw his car.'

'You're not to say anything,' her mother said, giving Fleur a sudden look as she pulled on her cigarette. 'Promise.'

'Yes. I won't say anything. Promise,' Fleur replied, thinking it must be the week for promises.

'Your father was in line for this top job at the hospital, consultant cardiologist it's called, and he'd set his heart on it,' Amelia explained, keeping her eye on the kitchen door. 'It would have meant a lot to him, and to us as it happens, because it's a big step up. And your father should have got it because he's the best qualified. I mean it's ridiculous.'

Amelia took another nervous pull at her cigarette while Fleur ate her supper and waited for her mother to continue.

'Anyway,' Amelia said at last, having carefully removed a piece of tobacco from the end of her tongue. 'The fact of the matter is they didn't give your father the job, they gave it to a—' She stopped and took a deep breath, exactly as Richard had done at the thought of the doctor who had been given the post instead. 'They gave it to someone who isn't half as qualified as your father and naturally your father is bitterly disappointed.'

'Why did they give it to this other person then? If he isn't as good as Daddy?'

'It's what your father calls a cosmetic appointment, one that makes the hospital look good rather than one that does it any good. Oh it's all terribly complicated, Fleur, and it's way, way above your head.'

'It wouldn't be if you explained it,' Fleur argued.

'Yes it would, Fleur, because it's all to do with politics. Daddy was absolutely the right man for the post and everyone was sure he was going to get it. Now all we've got to hope is that he doesn't go through with his threat to resign. Anyway, that's enough of that,' Amelia said, stubbing out her half-smoked cigarette. 'And you're not to say a word, remember. Not a word.'

'I won't. I promised.'

'Good. So now tell me all about your day. What sort of time have you had?'

Fleur put her knife and fork down together and pushed her plate away, seeing her opportunity.

'And don't push your plate away,' her mother sighed. 'I've told you about that.'

'I've been offered a part in the school play,' Fleur said, all in one breath. 'It's only a small part but Miss Fenton wants me to be one of the fairies.'

'That sounds fun,' her mother said without much enthusiasm. 'I don't see why not. Anyhow, as your father's always saying, the more strings you have to your bow the better.'

For a moment Fleur's heart stopped at the mention of the word bow, until she realized with relief that the reference was only accidental and turned her expression from a worried frown into a private smile.

'It means I shall be coming home later,' Fleur continued, telling it as it had been rehearsed. 'But Miss Fenton who's producing the play said she'll give me a lift because she only lives down the road.'

'Yes, well that's fine,' her mother agreed. 'I can't see any great difficulties there. What did you say the play was again?'

'I didn't,' Fleur replied. 'It's *A Midsummer Night's Dream*.'

19

By the time the weekend was over her father's equilibrium had been restored and common sense prevailed. That at least is how Fleur heard it explained by her mother to Deanie after her father's car had driven off. It seemed he had decided to stay on at the hospital as assistant to the new consultant while keeping his eyes open for another consultancy elsewhere.

'It would be ridiculous to walk out of the hospital where he's done so much good work,' Amelia said. 'It's only common sense after all.'

'Yes, well if you ask me common sense in't so common,' Deanie replied. 'Proper common sense is a sixth sense, and Mr Richard's doing right by staying. And it can't have been easy, 'cos we know this weren't first time it's happened.'

Fleur noticed her mother's surprised look but since nothing more was said that evening she gave the matter no more thought. Her head was too full of what awaited her at school, a series of properly organized violin lessons held in secret after hours. She was so excited that night she could hardly sleep.

Her excitement was perfectly justified because Leo Stayner was as good a teacher as he had promised. Once he began to instruct Fleur in earnest for two hours every day she very soon realized that what she was doing was going to turn out to be something of which her parents would be very proud. Not that any such thing ever was said precisely or even hinted at, rather it was something that just existed between teacher and pupil in the privacy of the music room, and which lingered in Fleur's mind afterwards. Finally, and much to Fleur's relief, even the need to tell lies stopped as her mother lost the slight interest she'd initially shown in the progress of the school play. From what Fleur had told her it was obvious her daughter would have very little to do and within a matter of a week, the only question she was asking her as she packed Fleur off to the bus stop in the morning with Deanie was what time she should expect her back in the evening. Soon she stopped asking even that since the answer was always the same.

As for Fleur, she asked nothing of anybody, least of all her teacher into whose hands she was prepared to commit herself completely. Seeing how quickly and with what ease Fleur was learning how to read music, wisely Leo saw there was no need to devote whole lessons to this side of her craft. He could see that all Fleur really wanted to do was to play. So from the outset he allowed each lesson to start with Fleur playing the piece of her choice, then they would work on it together with Leo accompanying Fleur on the piano, after which, and only then, for the last quarter of the lesson they would turn to the theoretical side of their music making.

As they had both already discovered, Fleur found little difficulty with theory. She would simply stare at a page of music as if she was visualizing the melody, before picking up her violin and playing it straight through in the very same way she had previously stared at the piano keyboard before confidently and fluently picking out a tune. As far as the academic side of her studies went, her teacher merely had to identify and interpret the music's symbols and markings, explanations he only needed to make once in order for Fleur to understand and commit them to memory, such was her unique and precocious talent.

As for teaching the violin itself, Leo Stayner followed the path he had always taken, which was to concentrate on the individuality of the pupil and try to channel his or her character into the music. Having been taught by his own father who believed in the old tradition of following a rigidly constructed set of rules in order for music to be properly produced, and having found this way of learning a struggle, Leo had abandoned any such method as a teacher himself. This was why, like so many before her, Fleur enjoyed his classes so much and why Leo was able to produce such exceptionally good results.

'You see what I believe, Fleur,' he told her, 'is that by concentrating on your individuality, and encouraging you to express what is unique inside you I too can learn, which is as I've always believed that teaching should be, a two-way traffic. But then I've never experienced anything which can even remotely compare with what is happening here, in our classes together. Every time you pick up your violin and play, I feel as if I am being born again. My only problem is, which is a huge one, and one I'm going to have to face quite soon if you ask me, is what will there be left to teach you.'

'I don't understand, Mr Stayner,' Fleur said, suddenly worried that for some reason she hadn't foreseen her lessons were going to come to an end. 'You've only been teaching me a few weeks.'

'I know I have, my dear child,' Leo replied with a deep sigh. 'But it's as if you have been playing for centuries. What you do is really quite incredible.'

'Why?' Fleur wondered. 'I mean it's just something I love to do. Like a lot of my friends are good at doing something, like riding, or tennis or whatever, I just like playing the violin. Because it's − it's me.'

'Ah − but whereas your friends are very good at what they do, Fleur, they are not prodigious. Prodigy's a very different kettle of fish. Most of us can learn how to play tennis, and possibly we can learn to play very well. But we can't be taught how to play brilliantly. Genius is something else altogether. People have tried to explain it in all sorts of ways but they've never come up with the answer, and because they can't understand it that upsets them. People can live with talent but not with genius. Genius says things never heard before. Which is what you do on the violin, and which is why you must take great care of the gift that has been entrusted to you. Believe me I know. And what you have you owe us all.'

For once Fleur listened to her teacher all the way through without regretting the time she was spending not playing. She had never before thought deeply about what she could do, because as she had explained to her teacher she thought it was just a simple knack, like putting spin on a tennis serve or making pastry as light as Deanie's. But now she began to realize that perhaps what she could do was something more than just a knack, most of all because when she played she felt so strange. It was as if the violin and herself were welded together and that the music which flowed effortlessly from her came from somewhere else, from another source altogether, a place perhaps a whole universe away which could only ever be reached when she picked up her violin and bow.

'You have gone very quiet, Fleur, even for you,' Leo said out of the silence. 'I think perhaps you're beginning to understand.'

'Yes, I think I am,' Fleur agreed. 'At least a little bit.'

'Good,' Leo said, taking his glasses off and staring at them at arm's length. 'Now here is your first sacrifice, because whereas we have only talked of the light side, there is also a dark side to genius. Much as we would want you to lead a normal life, it isn't possible. You just cannot do all the normal, mad, ridiculous, crazy and sometimes *dangerous* things kids do.'

'I know what you're going to say, Mr Stayner,' Fleur said. 'I know exactly.'

'Of course you do,' Leo agreed. 'Because you know what could happen if you had an accident. At best it would set you back at the most crucial time of your life, and at worst — it could mean you might never play again.'

'So what do I do?'

'Here's exactly what you do.'

'Your father won't hear of it,' her mother said at once. 'You must be mad even to suggest it.'

'But Daddy says we must always only ever do what we want to do, you've heard him,' Fleur replied. 'And I don't want to ride any more.'

'I can't believe what I'm hearing *now*,' her mother said. 'After all the trouble everyone's gone to. I just cannot believe it.'

Amelia breathed in and out slowly, turning to look at Deanie who was slowly and carefully folding up the ironing.

'Deanie?' she asked. 'What are we going to do?'

'It's not us who's riding, Miss Amelia, is it?' Deanie replied, placing another of her employer's shirts on top of the pile. 'The child must have her reasons.'

'Don't be ridiculous, Deanie. She's too young to have her reasons. I wasn't allowed to have reasons at her age!'

'You were too. Or have you forgotten why you wanted to give up your dancing classes?'

Amelia glared at the old woman and then turned her attention back to Fleur.

'Very well,' she hissed. 'But they'd better be good.'

'What?' Fleur enquired.

'The reasons why you want to give up riding. Even so, I'm telling you, your father won't have it. You do know that, don't you?'

Fleur did. She knew exactly that, and she had told her teacher the very same thing in more or less the very same words, which is how Mr Stayner had come to devise his plan.

'If you'd been at the Pony Club Hunter Trials the other

239

day you'd understand, Mummy,' Fleur replied carefully. 'This girl's pony who was jumping immediately in front of me—'

'Which was jumping in front of you, Fleur. Ponies aren't human beings.'

'Sorry. I meant the girl, not her pony. Anyway her pony slipped and crashed into the railway sleepers and turned a whole somersault as it fell, and the girl was only just thrown clear.'

'Yes? These things happen all the time when you're riding, Fleur. You knew that when you insisted on having a pony.'

'Is that right?' Deanie wondered from her ironing board. 'Somehow I thought it were Mr Richard what insisted on the pony.'

'Go on, Fleur,' Amelia said, doing her best to ignore the interruption. 'I still don't see what this has to do with you.'

'This girl's pony trampled on her,' Fleur said. 'It broke two of her ribs apparently and kicked her right in the face. I saw it all.'

'That doesn't mean the same thing will happen to you, does it? Anyway, the girl's pony was probably nowhere near as good as Minty. Lady Stourton said that pony has never fallen once in its whole life.'

Fleur fell silent for a moment, finding this the hardest part. It was all right as long as Minty's name was not mentioned, but as soon as it was Fleur could see him and everything about him, his big ears, his cheeky bright eyes, and his beautiful gleaming coat. Mr Stayner had warned her this would be the hardest part, and told her if and when the pony's name was mentioned to think as hard as she could about playing the violin. So Fleur took his advice and imagined playing the piece which was her current favourite, Tchaikovsky's Melody in E Flat.

'It wasn't the rider's fault and it wasn't her pony's

either,' Fleur replied. 'The approach was all wrong, everyone said so. Even Mrs Ferguson.'

'Look, if it's a simple case of you losing your nerve—' Amelia began, only to be stopped by a derisive snort from Deanie.

'I haven't lost my nerve,' Fleur replied. 'I just don't want to get kicked in the face, that's all.'

Of course her face wasn't Fleur's concern at all. It was her hands. She'd realized that without Mr Stayner even having to point it out, just as she'd realized that she would have to give up riding. A girl at the Pony Club had once had one of her hands kicked as she'd been loading her pony into a trailer and Fleur had seen the result, her right hand left with two middle fingers permanently damaged.

'And what about Minty?' her mother asked. 'And what about all the trouble everyone has been to in order that you could ride one of the best ponies in the whole county? Of course these things don't matter to you, do they? To spoiled little kids like you a pony is just a pony, any old pony!'

Again Fleur heard the Tchaikovsky soaring through her head as she tried to obliterate the sight of her beloved Minty from her mind for ever.

'Lady Stourton won't mind, Mummy,' she somehow managed to get out. 'She always says she can put Minty to run out at grass if ever I change my mind. So Minty will be fine.'

'Then if that's all that lovely pony means to you, fine,' Amelia said. 'Fine. But God knows what your father is going to say.'

Her father woke her up at midnight that Friday when he got home.

'What is all this nonsense?' he demanded to know, standing over Fleur's bed while she rubbed the sleep from her eyes. 'Your mother says something about you having lost your nerve.'

'Is this about Minty?' Fleur asked blearily.

'I think you know perfectly well what this is about, young lady. Now sit up, please, and tell me exactly what is going on. I understand you wish to give up your riding. And if this is so I'm here to tell you that you are making a mistake.'

'No, I haven't made a mistake.' Fleur replied, having sat up as instructed. 'At least I don't think so.'

'Now is the time to make sure, young lady, because if you have, let me tell you there will be no going back. Surely this can't be because some girl or other fell off and got a few bruises, surely?'

'No,' Fleur assured him, reminding herself of the speech she'd rehearsed. 'I made up my mind to give up riding for another reason.'

'I'm waiting,' her father said. 'I am all ears.'

'You wanted me to learn to ride and I have, haven't I?'

'That part is true at least, yes.'

'But you don't want me to ride for a job, do you? Because you said so.'

'Of course I don't want you to ride for a job. Now you're just being silly.'

'I'm not. You said you wanted me to learn to ride, like you want me to do well at school, and then get married to someone nice.'

'If you want it in a nutshell, my dear, then that is the size of it,' her father nodded in reply. 'But I still don't see what all this is in aid of.'

'The thing is, Daddy, suppose I did have an accident?'

'That would depend on what sort of accident.'

'The sort of accident like Jane Burrows did.'

'Jane Burrows?' Her father frowned and as he did, he sat down on Fleur's bed. Fleur instinctively knew this was a good move for her, because for a start it made him less threatening.

'She was a girl at school,' Fleur replied carefully, pulling her sheet up under her chin. 'She left last term. She got kicked while out hunting, right in the face. In the eye actually, and besides being blinded the kick smashed her cheekbone in so her face was all sort of hollow on one side. Like this.'

Fleur picked up one of her dolls which was lying on her bed and pushed in the plastic on one side, so that the doll's face caved in with a snap.

'And besides her cheek being broken, she had stitches in her forehead from here,' Fleur continued, indicating the area on the doll's face, 'right down across her blind eye down to here. Just by her mouth. Everyone at school says because of what happened to her nobody will ever want to marry her.'

'I see,' her father said, seeing all too well. 'I think I'm beginning to understand.'

'You see now I *can* ride, which was what you wanted, I can take up riding again any time, Daddy,' Fleur said, restoring her doll's face to normal before putting it in bed beside her. 'Mrs Ferguson at the Pony Club said once you've really learned to ride you never forget it, so if I ever have to ride again, or want to, I can.'

'Very good,' her father said after a moment. 'I think that's very sensible.' He patted Fleur on her hands and smiled.

'Is this what you told Mummy?'

'Mummy thought it was because I'd lost my nerve.'

'Then I'd say it's Mummy who's being silly, not you, my dear. Good night. We'll make the necessary arrangements with Lady Stourton tomorrow.'

Nothing more was said about her decision, because Fleur had utterly convinced her father. So she should have, since Leo Stayner and she had been rehearsing all week what to say and how to say it, during which time they'd also concocted the story about a mythical girl Jane Burrows and her equally mythical hunting accident.

The hardest part had been saying goodbye to Minty, which Fleur had done early the following morning. Her pony had never looked more beautiful. He'd lost his winter coat and Welton had groomed and strapped him, bringing up such a sheen on his new coat that Fleur could almost see her face in it.

'Goodbye, Minty,' she said as she gave the pony some peppermints. 'I shall miss riding you dreadfully but I shall always love you.'

With that Fleur turned and quickly walked off rather than let the girl who was sweeping out the yard see her cry. She tried to summon up the Tchaikovsky but for once all she could see was Lucy on her pony and herself on Minty, cantering down the drive at dawn as the mist swirled up from the paddocks around them, walking back down the hills on long summer afternoons through long grasses full of humming insects, splashing through the edge of the lake and out into its depths with their ponies happily swimming under them. And the long walks back home on winter evenings with the steam still rising from Buttons and Minty, while the cold started to nip her own and Lucy's cheeks.

She made it safely out of the yard without giving into her tears, then feeling them welling up inside her she began to run, and as she did her tears began to fall until she couldn't see where she was running any more and she fell over on the circle of grass which lay in the middle of the carriageway at the front of the house.

'Fleur?' a voice called from somewhere near. 'Why – what ever is the matter, child? Come over here at once, and tell me what the matter is!'

When she cleared the tears from her eyes, Fleur could see the upright figure of Lady Stourton who had just come down the steps of her house to get into her car, the door of which her chauffeur still held open.

By the time they had reached the end of the drive, down which Collins the chauffeur had driven at no more than two miles an hour, Fleur had told Lady Stourton everything, and in return Lady Stourton had promised to keep it all a secret.

20

'We are now fast approaching the point I told you we should reach, Fleur, where I will not be able to teach you anything more,' Leo Stayner announced a week before the school play. 'Already in the few weeks we have had together, you are playing better with your eyes shut and the bow in your wrong hand than most people ever play in their entire life.'

It was of course something of an exaggeration, but Leo Stayner was so amazed by his pupil's growing excellence that he felt the hyperbole to be perfectly justifiable.

'There are lots of things you can teach me, Mr Stayner,' Fleur replied, standing before him with her violin in her hand. 'I want to learn this for instance.'

She arched her left hand back over the neck of the violin and, taking her bow, played the opening dozen bars of the Brahms Violin Concerto.

'It was being played on television the other night,' she explained, 'but that was all I heard, because Deanie came in and turned it over to some quiz programme.'

'One day,' Leo Stayner replied very slowly as he stared up at the ceiling, barely able to believe what he had just heard, 'one day, young lady, it will be my pleasure not to teach you that, but to hear you play it. However in the meantime we must stick to the job in hand, namely to perfect your balance.'

He had never tried to teach Fleur how to stand or how to hold either the bow or the violin, he had simply taught her balance. Remembering how restricted he had felt when he had been forced into adopting what was apparently the correct way to bow the violin and where exactly to place it on his collarbone, he had always been determined not to impose any similar constraints on the pupils who came to him.

'This is why we're talking about balance, Fleur,' he said, taking the violin from her and resting it under his chin. 'I'm not going to show you how. Teaching isn't about showing, it's about finding the way together. All I want to do is explain how I feel when I play. Or rather how I want to feel. I want to feel perfectly balanced. I want to achieve perfect balance. Because playing the violin is all about weight and energy, not strength or brute force. Energy and balance, and we cannot produce that energy, not the way we want to produce it, and control it, do you see? Unless first we achieve perfect balance. Balance in motion.'

He demonstrated what he meant, swaying slightly on the balls of his feet the way a tightrope walker might do in order to confirm his stability, before drawing the bow lightly across the strings, producing a full round note.

'Never think of *holding* your violin, Fleur,' he said, removing both his hands from the instrument under his chin. 'You don't hold it here, between your shoulder and your chin. Balance it. You must feel that if you lift your chin – the violin will stay in place, because it is *perfectly balanced.*'

Within days, not weeks or months, but within just days of receiving this instruction, young and small and still weak as she was, Fleur was standing or walking around the music room with her violin balanced between chin and collarbone at the same time being able to gesture freely with both hands. For a while Leo Stayner said nothing, pretending he hadn't noted her achievement, until one class he suddenly stopped what he was saying and pointed to the instrument.

'What is that?' he asked.

'What?' Fleur returned, staring behind her in genuine wonder, thinking her teacher must have seen something unusual.

'No no, no what is that *there*, Fleur? Under your pretty little chin? There on the duster on your shoulder?'

'You mean my violin?'

'You know what your trouble is,' Stayner said with a beaming smile. 'You're such a slow learner.'

Next he taught her what he described as 'absolute tune', and what he meant by 'middle of the note'.

'Think of each note like a sphere,' he suggested. 'A perfect transparent globe. If you play it anywhere, anywhere on its roundness, you will play the note. At least it will sound like the note but it won't be the middle of the note. To do that you must hit the sphere right in the centre, *bang*.' He pointed with one index finger to the middle of an unseen circle. 'That is what we mean by middle of the note,' he said. 'Not round the edges of the note, not a fraction this side of centre, nor a fraction the other side, but slap bang in the middle of it.'

He leaned over to his piano and struck middle C.

'It's different on the piano,' he continued. 'The note is already there, you see. The pianist doesn't create it. He has to search for the sound he wants, but only in its tone quality. But the violinist makes his note. He has to find and *make* the note in order to play it, which is why learning the violin is more painful than learning how to play a keyboard. The music of the violin doesn't come from a hammer striking a string. It comes from the violinist drawing the bow over a string, with the result that the sound you create is your voice. It comes from inside you.'

'I think that's why I love playing the violin,' Fleur replied.

Then one day, when Leo was trying to demonstrate a point on his own violin, a beautiful Guarnerius which as he told Fleur had been left to him by an adoring great uncle, Fleur found herself getting irritated. This had become an increasing problem with her, and because she was ashamed of herself it was a problem she had tried to brush under the mat, but try as she did it wouldn't go away. Every time her teacher picked up his violin Fleur found herself becoming impatient.

She was impatient not because he was 'showing' her, but because of the way he played. He played everything so very differently from the way Fleur would have played the same piece or in fact did play the same piece although what her teacher was trying to demonstrate at these moments was not interpretation but technique. Nonetheless it irked Fleur and the more it irked her the more ashamed she became.

'Ah yes,' he said finally with a theatrical sigh, 'Of course I knew this day would come, and I should have foreseen it. And spared you the *embarrassment*.'

'Sorry?' Fleur said, pretending to retune her violin. 'What do you mean exactly?'

'Oh you know exactly what I mean, Fleur,' Leo replied. 'If only you weren't so ultra polite and so shy, you would have said so ages ago and spared a silly man his blushes. I wasn't trying to *show* you—'

'I know that, Mr Stayner.'

'I wasn't trying to show you how to play the Bach,' he repeated. 'It's just that I think it would help your double-stopping were you to—'

'If I had my wrist like this,' Fleur completed.

'Oh my,' Leo sighed again. 'A mind reader, too.'

'It's not that, Mr Stayner,' Fleur tried to explain. 'I didn't mean to be rude but I was working on that last night—'

'At home?' Leo asked in mock wonder.

'I use a frying pan,' Fleur grinned. 'It's perfect for your wrist exercises.'

'I will never show you another thing,' Leo swore, but now he was smiling too. 'I know it is the worst thing for a teacher to do and as I said I always try not to do it. But a little bit of the player will keep popping out. Now tell me, while we have stopped, tell me if you are or if you were a lonely child.'

'Yes,' Fleur agreed as they sat eating a chocolate bar Leo had brought in for them to share as usual. 'I suppose so, but then I would be, not having a brother or a sister.'

'Hmmm,' Leo nodded in agreement. 'Just as they say. They say violinists are always lonely children, while pianists aren't. Don't ask me why. It's all to do with inner voices, I believe. Children who deliberately choose the violin as their instrument are either only children or lonely children. Or, at the very least, highly individualistic children who are inquisitive and who usually require the many questions they ask to be answered as seriously as they have been posed.'

'It's funny though, because I've never actually felt lonely, never,' she said. 'Particularly, which is even funnier, since we moved to the country.'

'No, perhaps you haven't felt it, but whether you like it or not you are a solitary person. You actually like being on your own, and that I suppose − or they suppose − is why children such as you are attracted to the violin.'

'Do you know why I love the violin?' Fleur asked as she carefully folded up the empty chocolate wrapper. 'I love it because it takes me out into space.'

By the time the school play came and went, Fleur was playing Schubert's Violin Sonatina in D and Bach's unaccompanied Partita No 2. So well was she playing them that Leo was tempted to spring his surprise earlier than intended at the end-of-term recital, the plan being to force her parents' hand by presenting a *fait accompli*.

'Really it was Miss Fenton's idea,' Leo told Fleur when he outlined his plan. 'She and I thought we could surprise your parents by disguising you as a fairy musician and have you playing on stage while the fairies do their dance or whatever, and then reveal you – lights up! To take your bow. You can play the Mendelssohn in your sleep as it is, so there's no problem there. Then having heard what you can do, and even more importantly having seen you doing it and in front of everyone else, voilà! Your parents will understand that they have given birth to a young genius.'

Fleur listened quietly until Mr Stayner finished, then she slowly shook her head.

'Not really, Mr Stayner,' she said. 'They'd both go through the roof at the thought of me playing the violin without them knowing, never mind lying about being in the play.'

'But you will be in the play, Fleur! Just as you said!'

'I didn't say I'd be playing the violin, Mr Stayner.'

'You are going to have to tell them some time, Fleur, we both are,' her teacher reminded her. 'So I would say this time is as good as any.'

'I wouldn't, Mr Stayner, honestly,' Fleur argued. 'It's just that too many things have been happening at home recently. I'm not sure my parents could cope.'

As it happened the matter was taken out of their hands, because the day before the school play and a week before term ended Fleur was taken ill with a very severe bout of influenza.

'My husband said to ask you if you're quite sure it is just influenza, Dr Peters,' Amelia asked their GP as he straightened up from examining Fleur.

'Yes, Mrs Fisher, I'm quite sure,' the doctor said. 'There's an epidemic apparently. Half of this young lady's school is away sick with it.'

'She says she has a lot of aches in her joints.'

'That would be typical flu pains, Mrs Fisher. Aches in the joints, in the arms and legs. And back. Nothing to worry about.'

'My husband wanted to know if there was any inflammation anywhere? Any swelling of any particular joints. He wanted to make sure I asked you that.'

'No, there's no apparent swelling, not as far as I can see. Your husband is a doctor as well, is he not?'

'He's a surgeon, Dr Peters, a heart surgeon.'

'But he's also a parent and obviously wants reassurance.' The doctor pulled off his stethoscope and stuffed it in his pocket. 'No, this is just a very nasty dose of flu, tell him. All being well the patient should be up and about by the end of the week. Now I must be on my way, I'm afraid. I have about twenty more house calls to make yet.'

Amelia followed the doctor downstairs leaving Deanie to settle the feverish Fleur back down in her bed.

'I remember now, your husband is a heart man,' Dr Peters said, collecting his old tweed hat and coat from the bottom of the stairs. 'He's at one of the big London hospitals I seem to recall?'

'Not for much longer he doesn't think, Dr Peters,' Amelia said. 'He's just applied for an assistant consultancy in Harley Street. With a heart practice who've just lost a consultant. And he has high hopes. He got on very well at his initial interview.'

'I'll keep my fingers crossed for him,' Dr Peters said, opening the front door. 'Cardiology's certainly the place to be these days. Good night, Mrs Fisher. I'll call back in a couple of days.'

Half an hour later Fleur's bedside bell rang, so Amelia and Deanie dropped everything and hurried back up to the bedroom where they found the child sitting up in bed crying and holding her elbows.

'What on earth's the matter, Fleur?' Amelia asked, taking the thermometer from the glass of antiseptic on the chest of drawers. 'You look as if you've got a fever again.'

'There were rats all over my bed,' Fleur said, shivering and holding her elbows even more tightly. 'I woke up and there were all these rats everywhere.'

Amelia stroked the child's hair which was soaking wet with sweat, while popping the thermometer under her tongue with the other hand.

'Get me a towel, Deanie,' she said when she saw the sweat Fleur was in. 'I need a towel, a clean nightdress and some fresh sheets,' she said. 'God knows what this child's temperature is.'

She eased Fleur back down under her bedclothes and sat on the edge of the bed, taking one of her daughter's hands in hers. A little white face looked back at her over the top of the sheet, and every now and then the bed suddenly shook with what Amelia took to be her daughter trembling.

'Am I going to die, Mummy?' Fleur asked, so bad were the pains wracking her body. 'Please I don't want to die, not yet. Not till you've heard me play.'

'It's all right, sweetie, of course you're not going to die,' Amelia said, mishearing her. 'And you mustn't worry about the play because you've missed that now.'

'But you didn't hear me, Mummy,' Fleur moaned. 'You haven't heard me yet.'

'I'll hear you as soon as you're better,' Amelia assured her. 'You can do the whole thing for me. All right?'

'I'll do you the Sarasate, Mummy,' Fleur whispered. 'It's my new favourite. I do want you to hear me so much. And please don't be angry. Because I'm doing it all for you and Daddy.'

'Of course you are,' her mother agreed, thinking Fleur to be delirious which indeed she was.

'I don't want to die until you and Daddy have seen what I can do,' she whispered.

Amelia reassured her daughter that while she certainly had a very nasty dose of flu she wasn't in any mortal danger, although had she known the extent and severity of the pains which were present in most of Fleur's joints she might have dramatically revised her opinion. By now, however, Fleur was too delirious to make real sense of what was happening to her. Even before her fever worsened she'd made no special mention of the acuteness of the pains in her joints, putting them down to her influenza, although in the back of her mind she wondered whether the real cause of the pains in her arms, neck, hands and shoulders might not be due to the hours spent playing the violin.

'Mmmmm,' her mother muttered, having removed the thermometer and seen Fleur's temperature to have risen to over 101 degrees. 'Pass me the aspirins and some water please, Deanie. Then go and wring me out a couple of cold flannels.'

'I'm not sure about this at all,' Deanie grumbled on her way to the door. 'For an attack like this I'd have thought the least the doc should have prescribed was some penicillin.'

'It's only a dose of flu, Deanie,' Amelia sighed, shaking the thermometer down in the way she'd always seen her own mother do it. 'It's hardly double pneumonia.'

But by three o'clock in the morning with the thermometer now indicating a fever of 102 degrees and with Fleur in a convulsive delirium, Amelia was forced to call the doctor back. Without a word of complaint the sixty-four-year-old Dr Peters, who had spent most of the night getting up from his bed to answer his patients' calls, arrived back in Fleur's bedroom with his pyjama bottoms sticking out from under the legs of his trousers.

'You're right to call me back out, Mrs Fisher,' he said, once he had noted the severity of Fleur's fever and the apparent tenderness of whichever of her joints he touched or tried to manipulate. 'This young'un's got the worst case so far, and I should have spotted it earlier. Trouble is you get a bit punch drunk when there's an epidemic. I'm going to give her an intramuscular injection straight away, because I don't like the sound of her chest or the look of those tonsils come to that, so I'm going to give her a shot of penicillin – benzyl-penicillin to give it its proper name – and I bet you can't spell that, young lady,' he said to Fleur who was frowning up at him through grossly reddened eyes.

'No I can't,' she croaked. 'But I can play Wieniawski with my eyes shut.'

'More than I can,' Dr Peters smiled, preparing the injection. 'I couldn't even spell that, let alone phenoxymethylpenicillin. This isn't going to hurt.'

He injected her as carefully as he could but it did hurt. Fleur just screwed up her eyes and bit her bottom lip hard, while she played the Sarasate Fantasy through in her head.

'Good girl,' said the white-haired doctor, taking out his prescription pad. 'Wish they were all as brave as you. Now then. I'm going to put her on a course of 250mg of the same antibiotic drug to be taken by mouth every six hours on an empty stomach, so take this in first thing in the morning if you would. And in the meantime, keep up with the aspirin every four hours.' He then addressed his patient again, 'You can pop this in your mouth, young lady, because it'll help settle you down. Help you with the "fidgets".'

He gave Fleur a grey-and-white lozenge to swallow with some water, telling Amelia in an aside that it was a mild but effective sedative he always used to help deal with the sort of feverish restlessness Fleur was experiencing.

'Do you still think it's flu?' Amelia asked as Dr Peters began to pack up once again. 'I'm sorry, but my husband will want to know when he rings again.'

'I'd say so, although anything that runs up a fever of 102 we can't just think of as flu, Mrs Fisher,' Dr Peters replied. 'I don't like the amount of pain your daughter appears to be in. It's hard to tell at this stage quite how bad that pain is or isn't, since the child is delirious, but I think we've got to keep an eye on this, a good close eye. It's all too easy to miss any complications when one's in the middle of an epidemic.'

'What sort of complications?' Amelia asked anxiously.

'There's no need to be alarmed, Mrs Fisher, I'm sorry – that wasn't my intention. I mean in cases such as this, one must take influenza very seriously, but thank God nowadays we have the drugs to deal with these things pretty quickly and effectively, so rest assured your daughter is in no immediate danger. But as I said, when a patient starts to run a high fever and if it doesn't start to subside when it should, we can't just call it flu and treat it like a heavy cold. So what's the time now? Half past three. Good. Then I'll call back before morning surgery, at about a quarter to eight, and if all's still well which I'm sure it will be now we've got a good shot of penicillin in her, I'll be back again at lunchtime to keep an eye on her progress. That's what we have to do. We just have to keep our eye on the ball. Naturally any change for the worse, which is please God unlikely—'

'What sort of change, Doctor?'

'If the temperature rises any more, if the fever doesn't respond to the medication, then I'd have to think of moving her straight to hospital, just to be on the safe side. But like I said, I should be very surprised if this proved to be the case. I'll see you in the morning.'

Fleur remembered nothing of her illness until the fever abated, which it did quite suddenly. One night she was still seeing the rats on her bed, and the next morning she felt well enough by lunchtime to sit up and watch the birds feeding on the seed Deanie was throwing out for them on the frost-covered lawn.

'How do you feel now, sweetie?' her mother asked when she brought up some thin soup and Marmite toast for Fleur's lunch as requested. 'You look as if you've lost a lot of weight.'

'I feel all right really,' Fleur replied. 'A bit weedy, and my elbows and wrists still hurt. But I mean compared to when I went to bed—'

Fleur smiled at her mother, remembering how suddenly the flu had hit her. One minute she'd been sitting doing her homework in the kitchen and the next thing she was huddled up against the Aga trying to stop shivering.

'It was quite a bout,' Amelia said, sitting on her bed. 'You had us all worried. What with the rats, and wanting to do your play for us—'

'I wanted what?' Fleur frowned.

'Because you missed the school play, all you could keep saying was that you must do it for us. I have to do the play for you, you kept saying. And something about Sarasate? Was that the name of the fairy you were going to be? Oh yes, and who on *earth* is Mr Stayner?'

'Oh,' Fleur said, feeling herself turning bright red. 'He's just one of our teachers.'

'One you've got a pash on, obviously, seeing the colour you've gone.' Her mother laughed. 'Mr Stayner this, Mr Stayner that. Anyway. The main thing is you're better. Or rather getting better.'

'What's the date?' Fleur asked suddenly, as she realized she had no idea of how long she'd been in bed.

'December the twenty-first,' her mother replied. 'So you'd better sleep a lot and eat a lot if you're going to be up and about for Christmas.'

21

It wasn't until the Spring term had started that Fleur was finally deemed recovered enough to return to school. She had spent Christmas in bed as well as the New Year, although according to Deanie she hadn't missed much. Deanie had kept Fleur company through most of her long convalescence, somehow even managing to persuade Fleur's father to let Fleur have a hired portable television in her bedroom to help relieve the monotony of such a long illness. Also according to Deanie, Christmas had more or less been blighted by the fact that her father had once again been passed over for a job, this time for the assistant consultancy in Harley Street upon which he had set his heart.

Besides the company of her old nurse and the luxury of her own television, the only other thing that had kept Fleur going throughout her convalescence was the increasing tameness of her pet deer, who by now were feeding out of her hand. Every morning once she was allowed to get up again, Fleur would wrap up well against the January weather and go out to offer them a bowlful of bread softened with milk. The once timid creatures had lost all their shyness and used to wait for her in a circle by the steps where, full of confidence, they would take the bread from her hands, pushing their shiny wet noses against Fleur's outstretched fingers as they jostled to get their daily treat. All except the white deer who waited until last as if she knew she was special. Only when all the other deer had eaten their fill would she walk out of the shadow of the trees to collect the special portion of bread and milk which she knew awaited her.

Back at school Leo Stayner decided that this term Fleur's alibi was to be the school choir, and because it came directly under his own authority as Head of Music it was even easier to arrange. As their Easter offering the Senior and Junior school were jointly to present Handel's *Messiah*, so the reasons for Fleur being late home were fully understandable and accepted at once by her mother, particularly since Miss Fenton was to continue to act as Fleur's personal chauffeur. It was an even more satisfactory arrangement than the previous one, since one of the assistant music teachers and not Leo Stayner was in charge of the choir, leaving the Head of Music to continue with his clandestine violin lessons. As far as her part in the singing of the *Messiah* went, such was Fleur's ability to learn that initially she hardly had to attend rehearsals at all. The complicity of the choir master also helped.

The arrangement was almost too good to be true, but their luck lasted through the term, up to the week before the recital when Fleur joined the choir full time and then right through the two highly successful performances of Handel's great oratorio itself. Before that there were only two bad moments. The first one came the weekend immediately after the two recitals when Fleur and her parents were taking their Sunday morning walk across Stoke Park, which was now a mass of golden daffodils.

On the way back to The Folly, after feeding Lady Stourton's pregnant mares their ration of peppermints, Fleur had taken her father's hand which he allowed her to hold until they reached the gate at the bottom of the woods. At this point he had turned to Fleur, holding her hand palm upwards.

'What's this?' he asked, pointing to her fingers. 'What are all these calluses on your fingers?'

Luckily Fleur was ready for this, having long ago

realized that sooner or later either her father or mother were bound to notice the patches of thickened skin on the ends of her four left fingers.

'Oh, a friend has this guitar,' she said easily but with perfect truth. 'Celia Braithwaite. She got given it for her birthday and everyone's been playing it. We've all been learning these Donovan songs. And the latest Beatles.'

This time there was no lie told, because by now Fleur had honed her skills in deception. What she said was indeed a perfect truth. All she did was omit the fact that she had not been one of those who had actually been playing her friend's new guitar, which to her mind was an altogether different thing from saying that she had been.

'The Beatles,' her father sighed, letting go of her hand and swinging open the gate. 'There's good music, there's bad music, and there's The Beatles.'

After that for a while it was plain sailing, helped along by the fact that Richard Fisher at long last had got a new position in a smaller hospital in a south London suburb, away from the hospital which he had been trying vainly to leave since he was first passed over.

'It may not sound much,' he told the family over a celebratory lunch in Worcester, 'and although I am not as yet the consultant there, I'm told that due to the present incumbent's age it will not be long before I am. In the meantime I shall be consultant in all but name.'

Fleur was very pleased for her father, more than anything because he visibly cheered up. She also hoped that a side effect of his new job and his happier outlook would be that when her secret was revealed at the school concert he would be in a better frame of mind to accept it.

Leo Stayner had no such worries. As he kept telling Fleur, once an audience heard her play, the die would be cast and her future would be assured. In return Fleur reminded him that he didn't know her father, how strong-minded and determined he was, but Leo paid little attention to her warnings.

'Dear child,' he would laugh. 'Even if they call the police and have me arrested for impertinence, at least everyone else will have had the chance to hear you play. The appeal court will quash the sentence Daddy will have passed on me and the world will have custody of your talent!'

'Supposing I'm not as good as you say, Mr Stayner?' Fleur asked, and this was where the second bad moment came, because of a sudden doubt that had been sown in her mind by one of her classmates who had told her tales of 'Patch' Stayner's drinking bouts and rumoured wild behaviour. *Some of us in the choir think he's dotty, besides being a boozer,* her classmate had told her. *He's always going on about seeing things and hearing things that nobody else can, and Amanda Fielding whose father's a psychiatrist says that really is a sign of madness.*

'I mean supposing this is just what you feel but nobody else does?' she enquired.

'Are you quite mad, Fleur?' her teacher asked her back, rolling his eyes side to side and slapping both his knees at once. 'Can't you hear yourself? Have you no idea of the music you are making?'

'Not really, Mr Stayner,' Fleur replied perfectly truthfully. 'So far you're the only person who's heard me play.'

'Very well,' Leo Stayner replied. 'Then we will have an independent judgement. But it will have to be made by someone we can both trust.'

'I have someone I can trust,' Fleur said.

'Good,' her teacher replied. 'And so do I.'

Which was how early one evening while the choir was rehearsing the *Messiah*, Lady Stourton and Miss Fenton found themselves sitting together in camera to pass judgement on Leo Stayner's prodigy.

Fleur and Leo played them the whole of Mozart's Sonata for Piano and Violin in C Major and, when they had finished, both witnesses were first sent out of the room and then invited back independently. Each confessed that they had never seen or heard anything so extraordinary in their entire lives.

'One has only ever heard, speaking for oneself, one so young playing on record, which is staggering enough,' Lady Stourton told Leo. 'But to see this child play with such authority and confidence, let alone such ability, I confess is simply breathtaking.'

'Sometimes you forget – as I just did – quite how beautiful the violin can be,' Miss Fenton said. 'Particularly teaching music at school when you get so used to hearing it scraped and scratched all the time. But listening to Fleur playing just now, now I know why they say it's the voice of angels. And for it to be played like that by a child! By *a child*. How old is she, Leo?'

'Nine,' Leo said, putting his hands on top of his head and beaming at his two witnesses who were now in the room together while Fleur waited outside. 'Nine, nine and half. So now may I call her in so that you can *both* tell her that I am not mad?'

'One moment, please,' Lady Stourton requested. 'I seem to have something in my eye.'

'Yes, me too,' Miss Fenton agreed as both women searched their bags for handkerchiefs.

'Yes indeed,' Leo said. 'It really is quite remarkable, isn't it? You have this feeling she's been playing the violin for ever. Right the way down, ever since time begun.'

'So what is she going to play at the concert, might one ask?' Lady Stourton enquired, having dried her eyes. 'Fleur mentioned the last movement of *The Kreutzer Sonata*.'

'That was my idea,' Leo agreed, 'but Fleur prefers the Sarasate. The Concert Fantasy on *Carmen*. Do you know it?'

'Indeed,' Lady Stourton replied. 'It's rather fun. Not at all easy, but fun.'

'Did she think the *Kreutzer* too much for her then?' Miss Fenton asked.

'On the contrary,' Leo replied, grinning. 'We thought it might be too much for the audience. Too much to take in first time round. No, no, she's fully capable of playing it I assure you, but in a way it would be *too* incredible.'

'I agree,' Lady Stourton said. 'I think the first time anyone else hears this child playing, you're right, it should be something that sounds less daunting. It has to be something that is astounding technically of course, something most of us couldn't imagine a child of nine being able to play, yet something the sort of audience one is going to get at a school concert can grasp and marvel at. So you are absolutely right, Mr Stayner. The Sarasate will be perfect.'

Once Fleur learned the verdicts of the witnesses, verdicts which the two women told her verbally and independently, her confidence in herself was fully restored as was her belief in her teacher. But then as quickly as her confidence had returned it deserted her, as the reality of what she was about to try and do dawned on her. For the whole of the week before the concert, she hardly ate a thing nor slept a wink, so much so that because of her pallor both Deanie and her mother thought she was sickening for something and summoned Dr Peters.

'There's nothing wrong with her physically, nothing at all as far as I can see,' he reported. 'But mentally is another matter altogether. She's got herself into a high state of anxiety. Has she exams or anything like that coming up?'

'She has exams at the end of term, Doctor,' Amelia replied, 'but they're still weeks away, and it certainly isn't like Fleur to worry about examinations. Fleur isn't a worrier, and she's right on top of her schoolwork. Anyway, if she was worried about them, she'd say so.'

'There's nothing else you can think of?' Dr Peters wondered. 'Nothing else that might be troubling her. If you don't mind me asking, I mean there's nothing worrying her here at home?'

Amelia laughed, putting both hands up to her face as if she couldn't imagine such a thing, before assuring their doctor that as far as their home life went they were one big happy family.

'Well perhaps a little less of the big,' she corrected herself. 'But certainly still plenty of the happy.'

'Then maybe it's just another part of the growing-up process,' Dr Peters said. 'Children this age are often very prone to strange moods. I'm sure it's nothing to worry about. Although funnily enough, if she wasn't so young, I'd say she's showing all the symptoms of being in love.'

Then with only two days to go before the concert and at the start of her very last lesson with her teacher, Fleur announced that she wasn't going to play. But Leo Stayner had been expecting this, so he was ready. He knew that as a general rule when the good things in life happened they were invariably *too* good to be true, and ever since he'd made that discovery he'd always had a second line of defence ready. So instead of arguing with the child and possibly frightening her into total and unmitigated defiance, he very simply and quickly agreed with her.

'I quite understand,' he said. 'Too much all too soon and you're just not ready for it.'

'No, Mr Stayner, that's not the reason at all,' Fleur replied.

'Look if you're frightened, if you're very nervous, then that's perfectly understandable,' Leo Stayner assured her, doing his old trick of removing his spectacles and looking at her through them held at arm's length. 'So please don't worry, Fleur, you have all the time in the world. The last thing anyone wants to do is to rush you.'

'No,' Fleur said again, this time with considerably less patience. 'It really isn't that at all. It's just that I know what will happen. It'll be exactly as my father said it would be. They will take me away from here and send me somewhere else and I don't want them to. I don't want to be sent away from home, and most of all I don't want to be sent away from here. From all my friends. And from – from you.'

Fleur shrugged hopelessly and stared down at the violin and bow in her two hands.

'We've been over this, Fleur. You think it's going to be like when you played the piano, and I assure you it's not.'

'How do you know? You can't say. I don't mean to be rude, but you can't.'

'Uh-huh,' Leo Stayner said, as if agreeing with her, while carefully replacing his spectacles. 'Then let's go over the facts for one last time. You have no need for any anxiety, Fleur, none whatsoever. Whereas before, when you began to play the piano all by yourself, you weren't at school. You hadn't a teacher. So naturally when your parents heard how clever you were, and at that age, they were bound to think that the only course open to them was to send you away. Do you follow what I'm saying?'

'Sort of. Yes, I think so,' Fleur replied, still staring down at her violin.

'Now it is a totally different proposition. You are at a school, and you do have a teacher. You're at a school famous for its music, and a teacher who whatever else his failings at least knows how to teach. Otherwise we wouldn't have got as far as we have now, would we?'

'No.'

'No. So now when your parents hear you play—'

He stopped to draw a deep breath, realizing that this was the make or break point. If he lost her now by an ill choice of words, then Fleur Fisher might be lost not just to him but to posterity forever more.

'Now when they hear you play, Fleur, they'll realize that there is no *need* to send you away anywhere,' he continued, happy to see that at last Fleur was looking back up at him. 'As I've told you, in order to play as well as you're playing you must have been taught properly already. So therefore what possible reason could there be to send you away? Only a complete fool would want to interfere with the status quo, and I'm altogether sure neither of your parents are that, Fleur. Aren't you?'

'Yes,' Fleur answered slowly. 'Nobody could have taught me better than you, Mr Stayner, so they can't really have any reason to change things.'

'No, of course they can't!' Leo Stayner laughed, leaning back in his chair. 'And if they do, I'll kidnap you myself and take you off to a desert island until you are ready for your concert debut!'

Fleur looked at him but said nothing, at least not in words. Instead she tucked her violin back under her pretty little chin and handing him a music sheet together they played Kreisler's *Liebesleid*.

22

The programme for the school concert read as follows:

Fingal's Cave. Overture from The Hebrides. Mendelssohn.
Le Tic-Toc-choc. Pieces de clavecin, book 3. Couperin. Anne
Widdicombe (Harpsichord).
Divertimento for strings No. 2 in B flat. K. 137. Mozart. Lady
Mary's Octet. (Orch).
Concert Fantasy on Carmen Op. 25 Sarasate.
Allegro Moderato
Moderato
Lento Assai
Allegro Moderato
Moderato Violin. (TBA)
The Lady Mary's School Orchestra
Serenade No. 1 in D Op. 11 Brahms. The Lady Mary's School
Orchestra.
CONDUCTOR. Leo Stayner. FRCM.

Fleur had brought an preview copy home for her parents
to see along with their tickets which had to be reserved
well in advance, such was the popularity of St Mary's
annual orchestral concert.

The production of the programme and the tickets was all
part of Leo Stayner's strategy. Afraid that since to all intents
and purposes their child was not playing in the concert
Fleur's parents would not bother to show up, Leo had
procured two tickets for them and pretended that he had
arranged for Fleur to play the triangle in the last piece in
the concert, the Brahms Serenade. It was a fail-safe routine,

at least that was what Leo hoped. Having gathered from the common-room gossip that Fleur's parents were socially ambitious, he felt they would be only too happy to put on their glad rags and attend one of the most notable dates in the school's entire calendar. As it happened, it wasn't as straightforward as he and Fleur had hoped.

Her father simply didn't want to attend. He had agreed the weekend before when Fleur had produced the tickets and the programme, and told them of her sudden promotion to triangle in the orchestra. But on the night before the actual concert, an accident trapped him on the M4 motorway for the best part of two and a half hours and Amelia told Fleur at breakfast the next morning that it seemed her father was neither in the mood nor a sufficiently fit state to attend the concert that evening. In a way Fleur was greatly relieved because it seemed to mean postponing the moment she was dreading, but nonetheless she began to argue the case for her father attending because she knew if she didn't her teacher would, which given Richard Fisher's propensity for taking against any outside interference where his family was concerned, could very well ruin everything.

So Fleur told her mother what Leo Stayner had instructed her to say in case of any last-minute crisis such as this. She mentioned exactly who was going to be at the concert, all the dignitaries from Worcester as well as the parents of the richest children at the school, and how the cream of them had been invited by the Headmistress to a reception afterwards with Sir Miles Brewster, the local MP. Her mother argued that such a thing was all very well but that her father and she hadn't been invited, whereupon Fleur produced Leo Stayner's trump card by handing her mother an envelope containing an invitation which she pretended she had forgotten to give her earlier.

At once her mother galvanized herself into action, first of all berating Fleur for forgetting the invitation then wondering aloud and in desperation how and where she was possibly going to get her hair done in time, and what on earth she was going to wear, before rushing upstairs to wake her husband and tell him he was going to have to go to the concert after all. By the time Fleur had packed all the things she would need for that evening, she had gathered from her parents' nonstop dialogue that they would both be in attendance.

The Great Hall of the Senior School, where the concert was always held, was packed to its linen-panelled walls as usual, not only with pupils and their parents but also with many music lovers from the town of Malvern and its environs. Altogether the concert-goers made up an enthusiastic but by no means uncritical audience, for such was the school's high musical standards that the event was taken as seriously as any other in Malvern's rightly famous musical calendar.

Fleur showed her mother and father to their seats in the sixth row, amongst those reserved for important guests and parents with children participating in the concert, before excusing herself and hurrying off to prepare for her part in the proceedings. As she hastened along the balcony that ran outside and along the whole of one side of the Great Hall, she passed her teacher and headmistress who were deep in conversation about the contents of the programme.

'I've been so busy with examinations, I'm afraid, Leo, that I've hardly even had the time to see what's on offer this year,' Fleur heard her headmistress saying as she approached. 'Let's see. Oh good, I shall look forward to the Mozart, and the Couperin, and the Sarasate. That is interesting. Except there isn't anyone actually down to play it. What are you doing? Drawing the name out of a hat?'

'No, no, Headmistress,' Leo replied with a nervous laugh. 'Far from it. It's just that when the programme went to the printers it hadn't been finally decided exactly who was going to play what, you see.'

'No I don't, Leo,' the headmistress returned with a smile. 'You mean you have more than one pupil capable of playing the Sarasate?'

'No, Headmistress, that isn't what I mean at all,' Leo confessed, trying to tidy his wild head of hair with his fingers. 'But all will be revealed I promise you, when you hear this particular pupil play.'

'Good, Leo. I shall look forward to it,' the headmistress replied, little realizing that the little girl quietly squeezing by her was indeed the performer in question.

'Come on, into the Green Room with you,' Leo instructed Fleur after the headmistress had gone into the Hall. 'Everything's ready. Miss Fenton's laid out all your clothes.'

The orchestra were nearly in place and beginning their final tuning up as Leo and Fleur hurried up the flight of stone steps at the end of the balcony, which led to an anteroom on one side of the stage where the soloists waited their turn to go on stage and perform. This year besides Fleur there was only one other girl playing, Anne Widdicombe the sixth former who was to perform the Couperin on the harpsichord. The eighteen-year-old girl who had the infinitely easier task was in a terrible state of nerves, as white as frost and walking up and down the length of the small room biting what was left of her fingernails, when Fleur arrived and got ready to change.

'I think I'm going to be sick,' Anne Widdicombe said. 'I really do, Mr Stayner, I actually think I'm going to be sick.'

'No, of course you're not,' Leo Stayner replied quickly. 'Or if you are, Anne, if you really are then I suggest you go and get it out of the way now.'

'Yes, I think I will,' the girl replied, dashing out of the room and into the washroom off it. 'Sorry!'

'Oh lord,' Leo said, looking back at Fleur. 'You're not going to throw up as well, I hope?'

'No I'm fine, Mr Stayner,' Fleur assured him as she went behind a screen to change. 'I did all that last night.'

'So how are you now?' Leo called. 'Do you want anything? A drink of water? Or I don't know — some chocolate or something?'

'I'm fine,' Fleur repeated, putting her head round the edge of the screen. 'Really I am. I just wish it would start, that's all.'

'Well I could do with something, I tell you,' Leo said, mainly to himself, as he straightened his tail coat. 'I don't think I've ever been more nervous in my entire life.'

'Ssshhh,' Miss Fenton warned him good-humouredly as she went to help Fleur zip up her dress. 'You have no reason to be nervous. All you've got to do is wave your silly baton.'

Another pupil arrived at the door of the room to tell Leo the orchestra was ready.

'I have to go, Fleur!' he called. 'Good luck!'

'Thank you, Mr Stayner!' Fleur called back. 'I'll try not to let you down!'

Just before he let himself out of the room his other soloist arrived back from the washroom with watery eyes and a worried face. Somehow the sight of the poor frightened girl made Leo forget his own fears as he comforted her and made sure she was well enough to go on.

'It's okay, Mr Stayner,' the girl reassured him. 'I'll be fine once I'm on and playing. I promise.'

Then with one last wish of good luck to both his soloists, and after one last and futile attempt to smooth his recently washed hair down with his hands, Leo straightened his bow tie and went out to face the packed auditorium which was buzzing with anticipation.

By the time the orchestra was halfway through the

overture, Fleur was dressed and ready. She wore her best dark red velvet party dress with a big sash at the waist and her long hair pulled back in a pony tail tied with a matching bow. With her violin and bow in hand, she looked like something out of an Edwardian painting. Miss Fenton asked her if she needed to warm up, to which Fleur replied that all she needed was to play her scales and warming-up exercises once during the Mozart since she had spent two hours practising at tea time. In the meantime she settled down in a corner and began to read a copy of *Girl*, which another pupil had left on a chair, while the audience acclaimed the school orchestra's immaculate performance of the Mendelssohn.

'Good luck,' Fleur said to her senior, as Anne Widdicombe adjusted the hem of her dress and checked her hair in the mirror.

'Thanks,' the girl replied. 'I just wish I was somewhere else miles away.'

There was no need for her to wish so because the eighteen-year-old played the Couperin brilliantly, with so much verve and clarity that she had the audience calling for an encore, a request which she answered by playing Bach's Prelude No 1 from *The Well-Tempered Clavier*. Eight string players forming the Lady Mary Octet then played Mozart's second Divertimento for strings in B flat with great charm and elegance. As they did so, Fleur shut herself in another room further away from the stage where she played through her exercises ritualistically – emptying her mind of everything except the thought of what she was about to play, until Miss Fenton knocked on the door and told her to stand by.

'Mr Stayner's saying something,' Miss Fenton whispered, as Fleur prepared to make her entrance. 'He's just saying something about you to the audience, so not quite yet – I'll tell you when.'

Fleur stood patiently by the half-open door through

which she could see her teacher at the head of the waiting orchestra, addressing the audience.

'Ladies and Gentlemen,' he began. 'As I said, generally I make a rule not to say anything during these concerts, not unless something goes amiss which I am very glad to report is not the case. I just want to tell you about the next item because it is worth remarking on, particularly since as you may well have noticed the soloist is unnamed in your programmes. First, the piece she is to play. Those of you familiar with music for the violin will know that the chosen piece, Pablo de Sarasate's Concert Fantasy on the opera *Carmen*, a piece often played as an encore or used as a show stopper, is technically fiendish. Sarasate himself, a nineteenth-century Spaniard, was considered to be one of the greatest violinists of the day and Bruch, Dvorak and Saint-Saens all wrote pieces for him – such was his reputation. But he also wrote a lot for himself, over fifty pieces in fact, and composed the ingenious piece you are about to hear in 1883 when Bizet's great opera had at last achieved the recognition it deserved. But as I said, Sarasate's own composition is a formidable challenge even for the professional musician. Yet today you are going to hear it played by a pupil of this school. Of course you must reserve judgement on what you are about to hear until the soloist has played – but in advance I can confidently predict that you will be astonished. Not because the child in question is only nine years old—'

At which not unexpectedly the audience immediately broke into expectant and excited whispers.

'But because—' Leo Stayner continued, holding up his hands, 'because, ladies and gentlemen, in my opinion this child is truly blessed with genius. Ladies and gentlemen and children – Fleur Fisher.'

Leo Stayner turned and nodded to Miss Fenton at the door of the anteroom and Miss Fenton now fully opened the door to allow Fleur to make her entrance. Keeping her eyes firmly on Leo Stayner as he had instructed her to do Fleur made her way down the flight of stairs, carrying her teacher's precious Guarnerius which he had lent her for her debut, until she was in her place by her teacher's side and at the head of the orchestra.

Out there she knew were her parents, but that was all she thought. She allowed herself no imagining as to what they must be feeling or thinking as they realized the identity of the secret soloist. Instead, again just as her teacher had instructed her, she concentrated only on checking the tune of her violin and then finding her balance. Once she had done these two things, she turned to Leo Stayner and nodded once that she was ready.

For a silent moment the world hung fire before in response to Leo's cue all at once the orchestra struck up the Spanish rhythm of the introductory bars, with tympani and tambourine underlining the flamenco before the violin entered on a downward sweep and incredulity set in. As Fleur played, it seemed the entire audience held their breath as if cast in a spell which might be broken were they to move or breathe out and once again find themselves back in stern reality – a reality where there would be no beautiful dark-haired angel-child thrilling them with the sound of her playing, but just some schoolgirl battling her way through a piece of music far beyond her present capabilities.

So the hundreds of people gathered in the school hall sat motionless as the music coursed and flowed around them, music played with such maturity, such emotion and technical brilliance it would have been impossible to believe a child was playing had those privileged to be there not witnessed it for themselves. Fleur never faltered once, never missed the shape of a phrase, never forgot the flow of the music. She played seamlessly and without nerves, confident not in her own ability but in the brilliance of the sublime music, and as she played

276

she lifted the orchestra with her to heights it had never previously scaled. The only thing she forgot was where she was, both in time and place, so that when she finished playing and the tumult of applause engulfed her, she had to stare long and hard at her surroundings before she finally remembered her location.

Almost as one, the audience in the Great Hall rose to its feet, children and parents, strangers and friends. Fleur bowed and looked round to her teacher to find he was smiling back at her like the Cheshire Cat, although it seemed he was a cat with tears in his eyes. Still the hundreds applauded, as one of the senior girls came on to the platform and presented Fleur with a bouquet of bright flowers wrapped in crinkly cellophane which Fleur received as gracefully as if she'd been receiving such presentations all her young life. She then took her music teacher's hand quite unselfconsciously and, bowing deeply once more, walked off to the wings of the stage.

Still her audience applauded, now calling for more. Fleur stood in the wings and looked back at her teacher who was now holding up his hands again for silence.

'Thank you,' he said when at last the audience finally fell quiet. 'Now you know what I meant when I introduced Fleur to you. Now you have heard for yourself what a truly wonderful talent she possesses.'

A voice from the back of the hall suddenly called again for an encore, to be joined at once by several more, only for Leo Stayner to hold up his hands to say no. But the audience simply ignored him and called for more until Leo had no option but to turn to the anteroom and beckon Fleur back down to the platform.

'Very well,' he said with a smile as the audience quietened down now they realized they were going to get their way. 'We hadn't really prepared for this eventuality, but I can't foresee any great difficulty.'

He then bent down to have a whispered conference with

Fleur before standing back up and announcing what they were going to play.

'Thank you,' he said. 'What we are going to play for you now is something Fleur composed herself. Something she calls "Summer's End".'

With that he sat himself down at the piano and total silence finally fell, followed by one chord from the piano, A flat minor, loud and soft pedalled at the same time so that it hung like fading summer sunshine on the air before two full octaves above it the violin entered, becoming a skylark high in the pale blue skies above the Malvern Hills singing its ode to the last of that year's summer.

Fleur saw the head girl escorting her parents into the library where the reception was being held, but hung back, uncertain whether or not to join them since she hadn't yet had a chance to speak to them and so judge their mood in the mêlée that had followed her performance. The headmistress, however, shared none of her pupil's doubts and signalled for Fleur to come over the moment her parents were introduced to her.

'You too?' her headmistress was saying as Fleur slowly made her way over. 'I had no idea. I thought you surely must have been party to the conspiracy.'

'Not a bit of it, Miss James,' Richard said, turning to look at Fleur as she joined them. 'No, her mother and I were kept completely in the dark.'

'Silly, isn't it?' Amelia laughed, seeing the expression on her husband's face. 'But obviously it was meant to be a surprise.'

'A surprise?' the headmistress laughed. 'I think perhaps revelation might be a more appropriate term. I have never heard such exquisite playing from someone so young, ever. Not ever. You must be very proud of your daughter. And well done, you,' she said, bending down to Fleur. 'Words fail me, I'm afraid, Fleur. What you did was beyond comprehension.'

'Yes. I'd agree with that,' Richard said, taking a glass of wine from a tray being offered around. 'I think what Fleur did was quite beyond comprehension.'

'You must have had some idea of her prodigy,' Miss James remarked. 'From hearing her practise alone. Or are neither of you particularly musical, because of course this often happens, I believe—'

'No, no—' Richard said, cutting in with a smile. 'You see we never heard Fleur practise. She hasn't played at home at all. At least not the violin.'

Fleur saw her headmistress looking bewildered as her father then remained silent, obviously determined not to make Miss James' life any easier.

'That's not quite true, Richard,' Amelia offered, only for Richard to contradict her immediately.

'It's perfectly true, Amelia and you know it. Fleur has never once played the violin at home.'

'She did play the piano, if you remember, Richard. For which she showed a great talent—'

'The piano is not the violin, Amelia. And if you remember, that was a few years ago now.'

'Well,' Miss James said after an uncomfortable silence. 'Perhaps we should call Mr Stayner over.'

'Mr Stayner?' Amelia picked up at once, looking at Fleur at the same time.

'He's Fleur's music teacher,' Miss James said. 'Perhaps he can explain all the mystery. Leo?'

Leo Stayner excused himself from the group of people who were surrounding him, all busy questioning him about Fleur, to answer his headmistress' summons.

'Yes, Headmistress?' he said, changing his empty glass for a full one as another tray passed him by. 'Ah, and you must be Fleur's mother and father. How do you, how do you do.'

Leo shook hands with Richard and Amelia, then widened his eyes at Fleur, as much as to say how's-it-all-going? Only for Fleur to look glumly back at him.

'Leo,' Miss James began.

'You must be very proud,' Leo said, still addressing Richard and Amelia while brushing some pastry flakes off his satin lapels. 'And excited. Stunned even. You may well have produced the finest young home-grown violinist in living memory.'

'Leo,' Helen James insisted. 'Leo it would seem that Mr and Mrs Fisher didn't know anything about their daughter playing the violin, which I find a little difficult to believe. Not that I doubt Mr and Mrs Fisher's word, but as to why you thought it necessary to conceal such a thing from them . . .'

'That is perfectly easy to explain, Miss James,' Leo answered happily. 'Particularly now you have heard Fleur play. For a start we decided it would be best to say nothing just in case. In case it didn't work out that is. These things all too often can turn out to be flashes in the pan, as is well known. But then when it became apparent that this was no morning glory, but fully fledged genius . . . well, from what Fleur had told me of her previous history, I was more than a little afraid that if I blew the whistle too early her parents here wouldn't allow her to continue.'

23

'I have never been so embarrassed in all my life,' Richard said on the drive home. 'I have never been so embarrassed or humiliated. Not in all my life. And I have my daughter to thank for that.'

'I'm sorry,' Fleur said from the back seat. 'I didn't mean to embarrass you.'

'But you succeeded.'

'I don't know what you can have been thinking,' her mother said, redoing her hair in the illuminated vanity mirror on the back of her sun visor. 'After everything your father has done for you. I don't know what you can have been thinking.'

'I thought if I told you—' Fleur began.

'Yes?' her father said forcefully, glancing up at her in his driving mirror. 'Yes?'

'I thought if you knew you'd say I'd only be sent away again.'

'When did your father ever say such a thing, Fleur?'

'When I was playing the piano.'

Fleur saw her mother look sharply at her father, who in return shook his head and sighed.

'This is all water under the bridge, Amelia. This is neither here nor there.'

'You said—'

'Did you want us to be separated, Amelia, is that it?' Richard interrupted. 'Because that is what it would have meant and you know it. It would have meant you being in one place with our infant prodigy and me being in another – and what sort of bloody marriage do you think that would have been?'

'But I'm in one place now anyway as it happens, Richard, and you're in another, and we only see each other at weekends and not always then nowadays—'

'*Pas devant*, Amelia. *Pas devant*,' Richard said, with another glance in his mirror at Fleur. Except by now Fleur had been learning French for over two years and, more often than not, knew what her parents meant when they thought they were talking in secret.

'Well,' Amelia said tightly, 'I just don't see the point of your argument. If that is your argument. And you certainly can't apply it this time round because it won't wash.'

'We'll see, Amelia. We'll soon see.'

'I'm afraid things are a little bit too far advanced now, Richard. The facts of the matter have been made public. Very public indeed. You're not going to be able to shoo this one away so easily.'

'So,' Richard said to Fleur once she was safely tucked up in bed, 'you must be feeling very proud of yourself.'

Fleur said nothing. She just sat brushing out her hair and watching her father as he stood looking out of her window on to the darkening garden.

'I said – you must be feeling very proud of yourself.'

'I know you did.'

'Now don't you be impertinent.'

'I'm not. I just don't know what else I'm meant to say.'

'You do know what you've done, don't you?'

'No I don't. Other than learn how to play the violin.'

'Then let me put it another way. Do you want to go away to a special school? Is that what you want?'

'I don't mind,' Fleur replied, answering exactly as Leo Stayner had told her to answer. 'If that's what's necessary.'

'You mean playing the fiddle's that important to you? That you'd leave home because of it? And cause your mother and father all sorts of miseries and difficulties?'

'Playing the violin is very important to me, that's all I mean.'

'And you really wouldn't mind being sent away from home?'

'No. Not if it was necessary.'

'I see. Good. Well that's all I wanted to know, thank you very much.'

Her father went, turning off her light and shutting tight her door. Fleur put her hairbrush down on her bedside table and got out of bed to pull her curtains back so that she could see the night sky from her bed, then she got back into bed and shut her eyes as firmly as she could. This was meant to be the best day of her life, so far, and she was determined not to spoil it by crying.

The next day, Sunday, they were all invited for drinks at Lady Stourton's. The date had been fixed well in advance of the concert, as had Amelia's acceptance, although as Lady Stourton was later to tell Fleur, she'd made sure to issue the invitation immediately after she'd heard Fleur play that evening in Leo Stayner's music room.

'One just got the feeling,' she explained, 'that one might need a little bit of moral support.'

There was a good crowd of people gathered in the drawing room of Stoke Park, as there invariably was when Lady Stourton entertained. Just as invariably few of those gathered had much interest in the Fishers, certainly initially, all except the half dozen or so guests who had also attended the school concert the night before. They'd mostly gone at Lady Stourton's behest, and had been as bedazzled by Fleur's playing as everyone present.

At first Fleur thought her father seemed resentful of the adulation and praise she was receiving from her admirers, and she did her best to avoid the company of those determined to compliment her. But then as word spread

283

around the party that there was a prodigy in their midst, Richard's attitude changed and Fleur was relieved to see that he appeared to mellow and actually begin to enjoy himself. Just as her mother, who had started the day by arguing that it was probably Fleur's ability to play a difficult piece at such a young age that the audience had applauded rather than her musicianship, was now only too happy to take as much of the credit as she could for having such a brilliant daughter.

Amelia excused the mystery of her child's prodigy as being because she and Richard had always wanted Fleur to have a normal childhood, particularly since she herself had come from a musical family and therefore knew all too well the stresses and strains. She then proceeded to declare in front of her now captive audience that while they still had no desire for their daughter to be some sort of freak show, her husband had indicated to her only last night how impossible it was to try and contain a volcano with a saucer. This was why with proper guidance from her talented music teacher Leo Stayner, and the benefaction of Lady Stourton who had already very generously offered whatever help she could, they hoped to shape their daughter's career responsibly and wisely.

But since all those who were now gathered around Fleur and her parents were really interested in was hearing the prodigy play, Lady Stourton lent Fleur her violin and accompanied her on the piano as Fleur played Milstein's exquisite arrangement of Liszt Consolation No 3 in D Flat.

'Excellent,' was Richard's verdict as they walked homewards across the park. 'We have been invited to the de Rotherhams and the Bryce-Lamberts. I said I'd leave it to you to make the arrangements, Amelia.'

'What about my arrangements, Daddy?' Fleur wondered, falling into step alongside her parents. 'Have you decided what's going to happen to me?'

'Nothing is going to happen to you, cuckoo,' her father replied, tousling her hair. 'It just came as a bit of a shock to me, that's all. Caught me a little off balance. Nothing's going to happen to you, cuckoo, don't you worry.'

'*Eh bien!*' her mother laughed as Fleur began to run happily ahead. '*Expliques-moi cette volte-face hein?*'

'*Ah ha!*' she only just heard father replying. '*C'est comme je dis tous le temps, il vaut mieux gagner la bataille sinon la guerre!*'

But this time Fleur had no idea what they were talking about nor did she care. Even if she had understood that her father's innate belief was that if you can't beat them, you should join them, it wouldn't have interested her in the least, because ahead of her she'd just seen Minty being turned out in one of the paddocks.

24

As far as Fleur was concerned the next year was the happiest one of her life so far. Once the initial and inevitable furore had died down after her public debut, and it was decided that she should stay on at Lady Mary's both as an ordinary and as a musical pupil rather than give in to the temptation to groom her up for an immediate but precocious stardom, life finally settled back once again into a routine, the difference being that now her violin tuition was an accepted part of Fleur's daily procedure. So far from being sent to study away from home as she had feared, Fleur now had the best of both worlds, the attention and devotion of her dedicated teacher and the security of her home life. It was hardly surprising therefore that under these circumstances her wonderful talent burgeoned. Her father even relented and authorized Leo Stayner to find and buy Fleur a good second-hand half-size violin.

Best of all as far as Fleur was concerned was that her parents and her teacher became the best of friends. Leo was a regular guest at The Folly, often bringing his friend the fair-haired and somewhat over-earnest Miss Fenton with him. During these visits Fleur's future would be discussed and planned in detail.

The declared but informal arrangement was that Leo Stayner should continue to teach his star pupil until it was jointly considered that the time was ripe for Fleur to perform in public professionally, then if all went according to this plan of things and Fleur became as successful as they all believed, Leo would take over the management of Fleur's career with the proviso that everything should always first be agreed with Richard and Amelia.

Most of these discussions went way above Fleur's head on the occasions she was present. To her the arrangements seemed ideal since they involved all the people in the world of whom she was fondest, and they meant that she would be able to go on playing her beloved violin. To her teacher as well the scheme seemed exemplary. In fact it seemed almost too good to be true, which was why Leo never asked for the formalization of any part of the agreement, since he saw no real need.

Occasionally the subject would crop up, as it did one hot August day which had turned into the perfect summer's evening, cloudless and without a breath of wind. While Fleur was attending the barbecue on the terrace, her father and her teacher sat nearby looking out over the paddocks beyond the end of the garden where the air was busy with swallows searching for insects, swooping and diving into the heat haze that hung above the browning grassland.

'Look at that,' said Leo. 'It's like a mirage. Extraordinary. Makes the birds look like flying fish.'

'House Martins, aren't they?' Richard said, reaching for the bottle of wine. 'Or are they swifts?'

'No no, no those are swallows, Daddy!' Fleur called. 'House Martins are smaller and they've got white rumps. And the bottom half of their head is white, not chestnut like swallows. Swallows' tails are longer as well. With deeper streamers, do you see? Miss Hart was telling us in Biology only the other day that not so long ago, when people didn't understand migration, they thought swallows spent the winters rolled up in mud balls at the bottom of streams. And that herons wintered on the moon!'

'Quite the chatterbox now, isn't she?' Fleur overheard Leo say as she turned the fire down under the sausages. 'Time was when you could hardly get her to say a word.

She's much more confident now, thanks I think to her music.'

Later, after they had all eaten and Fleur was collecting the left-over bread for her deer, her father called her over and asked her to run inside and fetch a pen and paper so that her teacher and himself could set down their agreement on paper, only for Leo to declare that he would have no such thing because to his way of thinking a gentleman's word was his bond, and what was Richard if he wasn't indeed a gentleman? This seemed to put paid to the matter amidst much bonhomie and laughter.

Certainly Richard was becoming very much the country gentleman, so much so that with her parents' increasing popularity Fleur sometimes hardly saw them at all at weekends so busy were they either being entertained or entertaining themselves. Not that Fleur worried because life couldn't have been better. She saw a lot of Lucy during the holidays, even though she didn't ride any more, and when she wasn't over at Stoke Park she would spend hours happily practising her violin, either out in the garden surrounded by her beloved deer or inside in the drawing room when the weather was wet or too cold.

Otherwise the only thing of note that long hot summer was the night Leo Stayner got drunk. Fleur had been out all day at Stoke Park playing tennis and swimming in the lake, and had been so tired when she finally got home that she'd gone straight up to bed and missed the dinner party. So when the noise awoke her, at first she couldn't think what had happened and it gave her a fright. Despite the rumours she had heard about her teacher being prone to sudden drinking bouts, she had never seen him have more than a couple of drinks whenever he came to dinner at The Folly, and he only ever smelt of peppermint during their lessons. So when she was disturbed by the sound of Leo shouting underneath her window, she thought something dreadful had happened. Pulling her curtain back, she looked down and saw her father trying to hold Leo up as they slowly made their way towards Miss Fenton's car. Thinking her teacher had fallen ill, Fleur was just about to jump out of bed and go downstairs when she saw both her mother and Miss Fenton doing their best to stop laughing.

Then as soon as Leo started up again, Fleur realized what had happened.

'You don't know what you all mean to me!' Leo Stayner was shouting, very slowly and deliberately as if the people he was addressing were a long way away. 'You simply have no idea! You simply just *don't know!*'

What her father said in return wasn't audible, nor what her mother said to the normally demure Miss Fenton who by now was leaning against the wall and shaking with silent laughter. Then, before Richard and Leo could reach the car, Leo's knees suddenly buckled and both he and Fleur's father fell over on the grass.

Somehow her father managed to get Leo upright again. Leaning up against Miss Fenton's car, whose roof he now clutched with both hands while his head hung down between his arms, Leo continued with his diatribe. Not shouting so much now, but talking loudly and very carefully as if choosing each word with great deliberation while her father stood alongside trying to open the car door and get his guest inside.

'Whatever happens, Richard,' Fleur's teacher said, suddenly jerking his head up and looking at the night sky above him. 'Nothing must ever happen between any of us. And nothing must ever happen to Fleur, swear. You're to swear it, do you hear? I want you to swear that on your life.'

'Yes, Leo, fine. I swear it,' Richard said, waving at Amelia and Miss Fenton to come over and help him. 'But what we have to do now is get you home.'

'You don't understand, Richard,' Leo said, still gripping

the roof of the car to resist the now combined effort to get him inside. 'You don't understand what this all means to me. What Fleur means to me.'

'Of course we do, Leo,' Fleur's father assured him, taking first one hand off the car roof and then the other, as Amelia and Miss Fenton tried to turn Leo sideways into the car. 'But it really is very late now, and you really do have to get home. Now come on, into the car.'

Just before he folded over, Leo suddenly looked up to Fleur's window. He must have seen her, Fleur thought before she dived back into the shadows, because his face suddenly went as sad as a clown before he collapsed in two like a jacknife. As he fell all three adults caught him and the next minute he was bundled into the back seat, the door was shut, and Miss Fenton after a hurried good night was in the driving seat and taking the drunken Leo Stayner back to his home.

Fleur heard the front door close below and her parents' voices as they finally shut up the house. Then hearing them come upstairs, she slid down in her bed as far as she could, pulling the sheets up nearly over her head in case by chance one of them should look in on her and feel it necessary to try and explain what had happened.

In fact her parents made no reference to the incident at all the next morning and neither did Fleur. They just exchanged a few generalizations about the sort of day they'd all had before getting on with preparing to go out for Sunday lunch. But as her parents were getting dressed, snatches of their conversation floated down to where Fleur was sitting learning a score hidden under the big sun umbrella on the terrace.

One swallow doesn't make a summer, her mother's voice floated down.

And a little drop can lead to a great fall, came her father's reply. *Taking responsibility, Amelia. Is what concerns . . .*

The next fragment she caught was her father, *wondering whether we're . . . thing for Fleur. Entrusting her . . . of hands? . . . abroad somewhere. Anywhere in the world.*

Exaggerating, her mother thought. *As I said, . . . one summer. Imagine . . . age fourteen, fifteen . . . tour somewhere far . . . Leo and he . . . only this time worse. A total blind that . . . disappearance . . . daughter . . . only child . . . behind . . . alone, aband . . . hotel . . . somewhere on . . . of the world.*

'She wouldn't be, Richard.' Her mother was by the window now right over Fleur's head. 'She wouldn't be by herself. I'd be with her. You don't think I'd let her travel the world alone with just Leo?'

Then there was a silence during with Fleur imagined her father coming to her mother's side and pursing his mouth to one side, the way he always did when he started to consider something.

'All right,' he finally agreed, apparently also at the window now. 'For the sake of argument, or rather to prevent an argument, let's suppose you're with her as well. But even so, Amelia, could you cope with it? Let's say you're in New York, with some big important concert to give the following day and there's no Leo. No Leo to take Fleur through her final practice, and guide her through rehearsals with the orchestra . . .'

She was losing him now, he was moving away from the window again. *. . . that responsibility? I'm not at all . . . light of what's happened I'm not any longer . . . best thing entrusting Leo . . . sibility . . . not sure at all.*

. . . kill him was all she caught her mother saying next.

. . . dramatic, Amelia, her father replied *. . .aying is we should reconsider the arrange . . . formalize anything. Not just yet. Not quite yet. That's all.*

That was the end of it, the end of what Fleur overheard. But it was enough to increase her growing concerns, not about her parents or herself, but about her teacher and mentor, Leo Stayner.

'Then you must ask him, Fleur, you must confront him with your concern. After all this is your life and your career, not his, not anyone else's. It won't affect anything he has done for you so far, but it might affect things he does in the future. And for once I have to say that your parents are quite right to be anxious, just as you are.'

Fleur had finally taken her worries where she always took them, to Lady Stourton who was willing to help in every way she could even if it meant making Fleur face up to what might be some of life's more unpalatable truths.

'But I don't see how I can do it, Lady Stourton,' Fleur said. 'At least not by myself.'

'One wouldn't expect you to, child,' the beautiful old woman answered. 'I shall invite him here, and we shall both confront him.'

Once the small talk had been dispensed with and Leo Stayner understood the reason he had been invited by Lady Stourton to tea at Stoke Park with his pupil in attendance, he expressed himself not only happy to discuss the matter but also apparently relieved that it had been brought up.

'I don't think anyone need have any worries on that score at all, not if and when it ever comes to that point which please God it will do,' he said. 'I have every confidence that I will be able to look after this young lady here, regardless of the incident to which you refer, the night of that particular dinner at her parents' house. I really hardly ever drink, Lady Stourton, and if I might explain the reason for my behaviour?'

'Please,' Lady Stourton agreed. 'One should be most interested.'

'Thank you,' Leo replied, 'and might I also take the opportunity of thanking you for your interest and concern in this matter? I realize—'

'It is not my interest, Mr Stayner,' Lady Stourton interrupted him, 'but in the interests of your pupil that you are here. It goes without saying that it is her future we have at heart, not either of our own.'

'Of course, Lady Stourton, I couldn't have put it better myself,' Leo replied, carefully wiping the palms of both hands on his cord trousers. 'Anyway. To return to the matter of my apparent misdemeanour at Fleur's parents' house. The point was, you see, I had been taking antibiotics. Dr Page, the school physic, had put me on a course of the wretched things to try and get me over some thing or other from which I was suffering, and I completely forgot that I shouldn't drink with them. It was as easy as that. In fact I have the bottle here with me, in my pocket. And it says quite clearly on the label, do not take with alcohol.'

Leo fished into his jacket pocket but Lady Stourton stopped him with a smile and a gesture.

'That will not be necessary, Mr Stayner, I take your word for it,' she said. 'One knows what these modern drugs are like all too well.'

'Thank you, Lady Stourton,' Leo said. 'I should have hated young Fleur here to have thought this was my habitual sort of behaviour when off duty, and of course I understand her and your own concern, Lady Stourton, as to whether or not I should be the best man to look after Fleur's future interests. But all I can assure you is that I am. That I promise you. I shall look after my pupil's interests as if they were my very own.'

'Which, indeed, in a way I feel sure they will be, Mr Stayner,' Lady Stourton replied. 'More tea?'

'Yes,' Leo stumbled, going slightly pink, Fleur noticed as she took his cup. 'Yes, I mean another cup would be lovely, thank you.'

As they drank their second cup of tea Lady Stourton got Leo to describe his plans for his pupil. She listened with interest and hardly any interruptions as he explained the career he proposed for Fleur while Fleur herself spent the time petting and playing with Lady Stourton's dogs on the floor. It seemed his idea was for Fleur to make her concert debut the very next year under his guidance and then, if all went well which he was fully confident it would do, he planned to show her talents off nationally at first, and then on the international stage with a series of short but key tours interposed with a programme of recordings which he was already in the process of planning. Leo got very excited as he explained his blueprint for the first part of Fleur's young career; so much so that by the time he had finished, Fleur could see his forehead was gleaming with perspiration and that his hands, which were still holding his teacup, had started to shake.

'Most interesting, Mr Stayner,' Lady Stourton said when her guest had finished his summary. 'But do you not think, perhaps, that your pupil will need further tuition before undertaking such an ambitious programme?'

'Ah no, no on the contrary,' Leo explained, wiping his forehead with yet another of his collection of motley handkerchieves. 'I really think that in cases such as this, where one finds such a pure and perfect talent, that instead of knocking the corners off, too much tuition more often than not knocks all the heart out, and ends up destroying the very thing it is trying to further.'

'Thank you, Mr Stayner, I see,' Lady Stourton said, rising and bringing the tea party to an end. 'One is so glad one has had this little talk.'

After Leo had driven off in his battered old Mini, Lady Stourton walked some of the way across the park with Fleur.

'He's a nice man, Fleur,' she said. 'You were a lucky girl to have had such a sensitive first teacher. So many young musicians are ruined by their first teachers, you know.'

'My first teacher, Lady Stourton? How do you mean?' Fleur asked. 'Mr Stayner is going to be my only teacher. I promised.'

'I'm sure you did, Fleur, but to be perfectly honest it was not your responsibility to make such a commitment,' Lady Stourton said, stopping by the gate to the home paddocks.

'I wasn't the only one, Lady Stourton,' Fleur said. 'I've heard my father saying more or less the same thing.'

'Alas, neither should this be your father's decision, my dear. Your father, fine surgeon though he may be, is not necessarily the best judge when it comes to your musical career. Personally one feels that this is something that should be left to the professionals.'

'Isn't Mr Stayner a professional, Lady Stourton? I mean he is a proper teacher.'

'And a very good one too,' Lady Stourton assured her, as she swung open the paddock gate. 'But you have a long journey to make, and Mr Stayner will only be able to take you some of the way, and I fear that you will all too soon exhaust his resources if you have not done so already, my dear.'

Lady Stourton smiled at Fleur, touched her cheek and then closing the gate walked back to her house, leaving Fleur to ponder on Lady Stourton's words as she walked back across the paddocks past the grazing mares and foals to wonder exactly what the future held in store.

25

The future arrived halfway through the Spring term one Saturday morning when they were all at breakfast and Amelia opened and read a letter that had arrived addressed to them all.

'It's an invitation from Lady Stourton,' she said.

'Oh, can I see?' Fleur said, taking the card from her mother.

'What for this time?' her father asked, referring to the invitation. 'If it's yet another charity bunfight—'

'It's not, it's for her birthday,' Fleur said, fingering the embossed lettering on the white card. 'Her seventieth.'

'I think we must go to that, Richard. I think we simply have to,' Amelia said, taking the card back from Fleur and shooting her husband a knowing glance. 'Don't you?'

'Of course,' Richard agreed. 'Absolutely. Black tie, I take it?'

The phone call came a few days later and it was Lucy for Fleur. As a surprise for her grandmother, she asked Fleur to bring her violin. It seemed several of Lady Stourton's musical friends and relatives wanted to pay a tribute by each playing something in a small informal recital after dinner, and Lucy knew how thrilled her grandmother would be if Fleur was amongst their number.

'It's really only going to be just a bit of fun, that's all,' Lucy said. 'What Harry apparently calls a jam session.'

'Who's Harry?' Fleur asked.

'Oh, just a cousin,' Lucy said before hanging up. 'You'll meet him there.'

*   *   *

It was the best party Fleur had ever been to in her life. It wasn't a large party and it wasn't very grand, although everyone was beautifully dressed and Lady Stourton had organized it to perfection. There were fifty, perhaps sixty guests, Fleur reckoned, mostly relatives or very close friends as Lucy had pointed out, a fact which had prompted Fleur's father to remark not once but several times to his hostess as to how honoured he and Amelia felt at being included in such a select number.

There were not many children of Fleur and Lucy's age, only about half a dozen and most of whom Fleur knew from previous parties at Stoke Park, all except an older and very tall ginger-haired boy with an extraordinarily long thin face and a Norman nose who turned out to be Lucy's cousin Harry Grevil. He also turned out to be a talented jazz pianist, as he demonstrated in the impromptu recital after dinner when he played a number called 'Wolverine Blues' at breakneck speed, in the process earning himself a tumult of delighted applause. Because it was a celebration rather than a concert, Fleur also chose a pyrotechnical piece, Rimsky-Korsakov's glittering miniature 'The Flight of the Bumble Bee' which she played with such brilliance and bravura that it was greeted, first by an astonished silence, and then by a universal demand for an encore.

Fleur asked Lady Stourton, who was sitting in the place of honour in the front row, if there was anything particular that she would like to hear for her birthday. Her hostess replied without hesitation that she would love to hear 'On Wings of Song' by Mendelssohn. Fleur then played it for her accompanied, as she had been before, by a very tall and thin gentleman with a large beaked nose and slicked-back brilliantined hair who was dressed in a plum-coloured velvet smoking jacket and large, floppy matching bow tie.

Again her performance was greeted with wonder and

rapturous applause and since she had been the last guest to perform, she was surrounded immediately by people wishing to congratulate her and marvel at her prodigy. When she finally managed to slip away in the hope of rejoining Lucy and her cousin Harry, Lady Stourton called her over to talk to the man who had acted as her accompanist.

'I want your parents to meet him as well,' Lady Stourton told Fleur after she had intercepted her, and began to head for where Richard and Amelia were standing. 'This will be of interest to them as much as to you I imagine, my dear. So perhaps if we all went into the library?'

Fleur's accompanist was already awaiting them, attended by a young fair-haired man who was busy lighting the musician's cigar when Lady Stourton came in with her three guests.

'Fleur dear, no doubt you will have heard the name of your accompanist when I tell you, although obviously you did not recognize him,' Lady Stourton smiled. 'While I'm perfectly sure, with her background, your mother knows who he is. Iain, allow me to introduce Fleur's parents Mr and Mrs Fisher. Mr and Mrs Fisher – Sir Iain Walcott.'

Fleur knew the name at once now she took it in properly, because so many of the recordings Leo Stayner had played her during their lessons together had been conducted by the very tall, distinguished man who was standing shaking her parents' hands, but she had rarely ever given his likeness more than a glance on the various record sleeves, because she was always only interested in the violinist and even more importantly in the recordings themselves. Her mother, however, was agreeing that she had indeed thought it might be Sir Iain when she had caught a fleeting glance of him earlier on in the evening, but wasn't altogether sure when he sat down to play, since being a friend of the family he had only been introduced by his Christian name.

'Yes of course, Lucy only introduced you as Uncle Iain, did she not?' Lady Stourton laughed. 'And like most uncles, Iain is no such thing. Although he and I are indeed related as third cousins.'

'And your father and I played a concert together but only once, alas,' Sir Iain said to Amelia. 'Before you were born, I should imagine, when we were both just starting out. We played the Schumann, at Watford Town Hall, I seem to remember.'

'I think it was, Sir Iain,' Amelia agreed. 'In fact I think I still have the programme somewhere. I must look it out.'

'Do,' the conductor agreed. 'It would be most interesting.'

Lady Stourton introduced the young man hovering attentively around Sir Iain as Mr Rogers, the conductor's personal assistant. Then, telling Richard to help himself and his wife to anything they would like from the drinks tray, she settled herself down in a chair by the fireside.

'Besides being our foremost orchestral conductor, as of course you well know,' Lady Stourton said to Richard and Amelia who were both now sitting on the old chesterfield, 'Sir Iain originated the annual Birmingham Violin Competition, which he also helps adjudicate. So the violin is something of a speciality.'

'It was in fact my chosen instrument, until I decided to take up conducting,' Sir Iain continued, tapping the ash of his cigar. 'So not unnaturally I was very interested to hear your daughter playing, and as far as she goes I should imagine like all fond parents you think she's a little bit different. Well she isn't.'

Fleur didn't flinch or move the smallest of muscles, because somehow she knew Sir Iain had only just started rather than finished. She couldn't help noticing, however, that a slight smile had flitted briefly across her father's face.

'If I may explain,' Sir Iain continued. 'I see many such children, as you can appreciate. In the course of a long life I have had countless so-called talented children wheeled in front of me, invariably with such high expectations. The next so and so, the new so-and-so. You can imagine. I have simply lost count of how many budding virtuosi I have seen and heard. As soon as a child picks up an instrument and plays it – which many children do with far, far greater ease than we adults because they have no prejudices or inhibitions – the poor child is somehow considered to be an aspiring genius. Parents hearing and seeing their beloved children playing what they themselves consider to be impossibly difficult instruments assume their little ones to be something out of the ordinary. Such, in my very long experience, is very rarely if indeed ever the case. In fact as far as real prodigy goes, in terms of what has been presented to me personally sad though it is to say it has never once proved to be the case.'

'Never once?' Richard enquired.

Sir Iain stared at Richard for a moment, the way Richard himself often liked to stare at people, only this time it was Richard who began to feel uncomfortable and disconcerted.

'Never once, Mr Fisher,' the great man repeated. 'I have heard the purely terrible, the adequate, the good, the excellent and the brilliant. But I have never witnessed prodigy, not once.'

'I see, Sir Iain,' Richard replied carefully. 'Then how would you assess our daughter? Whom people down here have already hailed as brilliant. Having heard her play yourself, and with more experience in these matters than everyone who has heard Fleur play so far put together, how exactly would you rate her? Would you rate her as brilliant?'

'Hmmm.' Sir Iain said, regarding the end of his cigar thoughtfully. 'No Mr Fisher, since you ask, no that is not the word I would choose to describe your daughter.'

'What word would you use then, if I might ask?'

'I'm not altogether sure, Mr Fisher, to be perfectly frank with you. You seem to be a little agitated by this, so please – if you have something to say I would be most interested to hear what it is.'

Richard took a drink of his whisky then put it to one side before getting up from the sofa.

'This is, I feel, a very happy encounter, Sir Iain, if I may say so,' Richard began. 'Listening to what you have had to say so far has reinforced a lot of my own personal feelings. Firstly, your description of parents who consider their children to be geniuses because they are capable of doing things which they themselves find totally impossible. Both my wife and myself are musically incompetent. Now as far as I go that's no great surprise because music isn't in my genes, while as you yourself know it is in my wife's. But even so, Amelia here cannot even sing in tune. So of course when our beloved daughter picks up the violin and suddenly starts to play, she's the next whoever. The next Yehudi Menuhin.'

'Mr Fisher—' Lady Stourton said, as Richard paused to draw breath.

But Sir Iain shook his head at her. 'No no, my dear,' he said. 'Let the man have his say.'

'Thank you, Sir Iain,' Richard said with a smile and a nod. 'This really won't take long, but it will help us to make up our minds. You see and of course it's perfectly obvious – Fleur clearly does have some talent. But if she is not going to be the next whoever—'

'Yehudi Menuhin was your suggestion,' Sir Iain said.

'Precisely,' Richard agreed. 'Then if that is the case perhaps what we are doing is right. You see ever since people first heard Fleur play in public all sorts of things have been suggested, because obviously the child being still at school, and this being a small community—'

'You think matters have grown somewhat out of all perspective, I should imagine,' Sir Iain chipped in.

'Again, precisely. Now Fleur's greatest fear has always been that because of her talent she might be sent away from home.'

'Daddy—' Fleur said, only to be hushed by her mother.

'Fleur is our only child and we are a very close family,' Richard continued. 'And unless she is going to be the next Yehudi Menuhin – which apparently she is not – then rather than remove her arbitrarily from her home and subject her to the hothouse treatment to try and make her into the prodigy which she quite obviously is not—'

'No no, Mr Fisher, I must stop you here, I'm afraid,' Sir Iain said holding up his hand. 'You have lost me entirely.'

'Sir Iain, forgive me,' Richard said with a wise smile. 'But what we are looking at here is a child who can play the violin, because she has been taught to do so. *Very* well taught – fair enough, but that is all it is. Mr Stayner, her teacher, coached her in secret for months and months before anyone heard her. So it wasn't as if the child just picked up the violin and hey presto!'

'Daddy—' Fleur began again, but this time it was Lady Stourton who took her hand and indicated she was to keep quiet.

'You see I've been afraid of this all along,' Richard continued. 'That because she is a child who plays exceptionally well *for a child* – that things would get woefully out of proportion and the next thing we'd know would be that we'd have a child prodigy on our hands and that would be that. Which is why this meeting is so fortuitous and why I am so relieved, Sir Iain, to hear what you have to say.'

'Good,' Sir Iain said, carefully removing another length of ash from his cigar, 'because with the exception of your last remark I cannot agree with one single thing that you have said so far.'

'I beg your pardon.'

'I said, Mr Fisher, I cannot agree with one word you have said.'

'Excuse me, but you yourself said, did you not—'

'I cannot agree with you about her not being the next *Yehudi Menuhin* as you have it, about her not being brilliant, about her being very well taught, about her not just picking up the violin and playing – I can't agree with you about one of these things.'

Fleur's father stared at the great conductor as if he had taken leave of his senses, before looking at Amelia, Fleur, Lady Stourton and then finally back at Sir Iain Walcott.

'But you yourself said, Sir Iain, in as many words, that in all your time you yourself have never come face to face with what people call prodigy.'

'Neither had I, Mr Fisher,' the conductor replied. 'Not until today.'

'But,' Richard said, barely audibly, 'But I heard you myself. You said she was by no means even brilliant—'

'No I did not, Mr Fisher. I said that brilliant was not the word I would use to describe your daughter's talent. I do not know the word to describe your daughter's talent. I doubt if the word exists.'

'I see,' Richard said floundering. 'So now she is somewhat more than brilliant, yet now also, you don't consider she's been taught well.'

'She has been taught adequately, Mr Fisher. Which is all one would expect from an ordinary teacher in an ordinary school.'

'St Mary's isn't an ordinary school, Sir Iain,' Amelia offered. 'St Mary's has a tremendous reputation for music.'

'It is still an ordinary school, my dear lady,' Sir Iain replied. 'It is not a music school as such. You will not find extraordinary teaching in such a place, although you might find extraordinary teaching for such a place. Your daughter plays wonderfully in spite of the way she has been taught. Her wrist position, her fingering, her use of vibrato, her production of vibrato, her double stops, everything. Everything can be improved enormously with the best teaching. Which is what she must now have. In my opinion.'

'Thank you,' Richard finally said, after a long silence. 'Thank you very much, Sir Iain. It has been very interesting hearing what you have had to say. But of course the matter really rests in Fleur's hands, since it is her life and her career about which we are talking.'

'Just as long as it is, Mr Fisher, then of course she must be consulted,' Sir Iain replied. 'Well, Fleur? And what do you have to say?'

'I think I should do whatever you say, Sir Iain,' Fleur replied. 'Because as my father just said, if we have to listen to anyone else about this then it really ought to be you.'

What Sir Iain said before they all returned to the party was that Fleur would have to leave Lady Mary's and either go to a specialist music school, or else study the violin privately under one of the top teachers such as Isaac Kline or Walter Bernhard. This would mean her living away from home practically full time, coming home not for the normal school holidays but just at Christmas and in midsummer while continuing her scholastic education with the aid of tutors. Of the alternatives, Sir Iain had no hesitation in recommending the latter course because although it would be a far more rigorous and solitary existence, the benefit of a one-to-one teaching relationship would be inestimable in Fleur's case because of her exceptional gift.

It would also be the more expensive option, but Sir Iain pointed out that as soon as Fleur's career was properly initiated the investment would be recouped. Anyway as far as he understood it the costs would not be prohibitive to someone in Richard Fisher's profession, and any austerity would soon be forgotten when the income started coming in. Sir Iain pointed out that solo violinists of the top calibre earned a great deal of money, whilst a solo violinist of indefinable virtuosity such as Fleur would most surely prove to be worth, quite literally, millions.

'So there you are,' Richard said when the three of them, Amelia, Fleur and himself were halfway home across the park. Nothing much had been said for the first part of their midnight stroll other than small talk between Fleur and Amelia about how good the party had been while Richard had said nothing. Not until now. 'So there you are,' he said again. 'I hope you're pleased with yourself.'

'I don't see what I did that was so wrong,' Amelia said.

'I'm not talking about you just for once,' Richard said. 'I'm talking about madam here.'

'If you're worried about the money, Daddy, about what it's going to cost,' Fleur said, 'I promise I'll pay you back.'

'I'm not worried about the money. I'm worried about much more important matters,' her father replied. 'You don't seem to understand what this is going to do to our lives, neither of you! You don't seem to have an idea what this is going to do to our lives!'

And then he strode quickly ahead, leaving them, and disappearing into the enfolding dark.

26

It was the first time Leo had ever been late for one of their lessons. Normally when Fleur arrived in his music room he was there ready and waiting for her, but this afternoon there was no sign of him. In fact from the look of the room it appeared as if he hadn't given a lesson all day.

After waiting twenty-five minutes out of her double period of two hours, Fleur put away her violin and was just about to leave when her teacher finally arrived.

'Yes I'm sorry, I'm sorry,' he said before she could say anything. 'You were quite right to pack up, and I'm not sure that I was right to come. But anyway here I am, and here we both are.'

He collapsed on a bench and leaning on the wall behind him, stared up at the ceiling. He was sweating profusely but for once made no attempt to dry his forehead or upper lip, he just sat there breathing in and out very deeply as if he had run a very long race.

'Are you all right, Mr Stayner?' Fleur finally asked when he had said nothing more for three or four minutes.

'No, of course I am not all right, Fleur. Do I look all right?' her teacher replied. 'Of course I am not *all right*. Is that what you were expecting me to be? *All right*? No I am far from all right, Fleur, and we have your friend Lady Stourton, I would say, to thank for that. Who she thinks she is I have simply no idea. None at all. Some sort of benefactor, I suppose. Sees herself as some great patron of the arts, like so many of these silly old women do. These silly old women with nothing better to do than to interfere in other people's lives. Patron of the arts indeed! Why can't people just leave well alone? Eh? *Why cannot people just leave well alone*, Fleur?'

With that he suddenly bent himself forward and put his head in both hands, staying like that for another long period of silence punctuated only by an occasional deep exhalation of breath.

'Well?' he enquired, just as suddenly sitting back up and looking at Fleur. 'What are you doing here, anyway? I thought you were through with me. I thought it was Time We Moved On.'

'Mr Stayner,' Fleur began, only for her teacher to shoo her quiet with one hand.

'Apparently, at least according to your father it is,' Leo Stayner continued, leaning back once more against the wall. 'Apparently you have survived in spite of my teaching. Your Great Art mercifully has remained untrammelled by my lack of art. Of any Art.'

'I don't quite understand what you mean, but if you're referring to what Sir Iain said—'

'Sir Iain Walcott no less,' Leo interrupted, taking off his spectacles and twirling them round in a mock salute. 'That fagotty great *poseur*.'

Fleur frowned and tried again.

'I think what Sir Iain meant was that I should go to an *even* better teacher, not just another one.'

Leo Stayner eyed her, without the help of his glasses. His eyes looked much smaller unhidden by his lenses, smaller and intolerably sad.

'It's not your fault,' he said. 'Christ you're only a kid.'

'I think Lady Stourton was only trying to help.'

'Help who? She certainly wasn't thinking of helping me. And is this really just because I got a bit the worse for wear that night at your parents'? Because if it is—' Leo stopped and shook his head two or three times. 'If it is,' he said again. 'If it is, I mean Christ.'

'It really isn't that, Mr Stayner,' Fleur said. 'I think it's just – well.' Fleur stopped and shrugged, unable to think for a moment how to go on. She knew exactly what it was and why, but she simply had no way of putting it into words.

'I might as well not have bothered,' Leo said, beginning to bang the back of his head against the music-room wall. 'All these months and months of study that we've spent together. I might just as well not have bothered. No-one will know when they hear you playing that Paganini. The *Caprice* in E. How will they know it was me who taught you that? Or Elgar's *Salut d'amour*? Because whatever they say, Fleur, whatever else they teach you, whatever else they show you, you'll never play better than you do now – with such innocence and purity.' Mr Stayner stopped banging his head on the wall and instead ran his hands through his thick hair which was even more hopelessly knotted than usual. As he did so, Fleur suddenly realized how much she would miss him and all his peculiar mannerisms, the twirling of his glasses, the sudden exclamations in CAPITAL LETTERS followed by his eye-rolling trick, his multicoloured handkerchieves, his frightful bright knobbly socks, even his habit of suddenly sniffing long and deeply just as she was practising a particularly tricky piece of portamento.

'Had you any idea of what was going on?' Leo asked, putting his glasses back on uncleaned for once, their lenses all smudged with his fingerprints. 'You surely must have known something was afoot. That the old lady was brewing something up.' His voice sounded close to tears and even through his smudged lenses Fleur could see that his eyes were filling up, and as she did she knew what she must do to make the break. She had to make him hate her.

'It wasn't Lady Stourton,' she said. 'It wasn't anybody else. It was me.'

'You?' Leo looked at her eyes wide, then gave a guffaw of disbelieving laughter. 'Don't be so silly. Don't make me laugh. You indeed.'

'It was,' Fleur assured him. 'I've been very lucky, because you've been a very good first teacher—'

'First teacher?'

'Yes. But you're only able to take me so far along the way. I have a long journey to make, and you can only take me some of the way. You can't take me all of the way—'

Fleur stopped, trying to remember what else it was Lady Stourton had said to her as they had stood by the paddock gate.

'Yes?' Leo Stayner prompted her. 'I'm waiting to hear what else I can't do and why.'

'Because,' Fleur started, chewing her lip as she still tried to remember. And then it came back. 'Because I'm afraid I have already exhausted your resources,' she finished.

Her teacher stared at her, and then nodding slowly clapped his hands half a dozen times slowly.

'Very good,' he said leaning forward, and when he did Fleur noticed that for once he didn't smell of peppermints but of something much stronger and staler. 'Very good indeed,' he repeated. 'So why don't you go away now, little girl? Run away, go on. And save us both a lot of trouble.'

Deanie took her to the station in a taxi. She was to have gone up to London with her father the night before on the Sunday, but at the eleventh hour Richard had announced a change of plans. He said he had to go up to Birmingham instead so that Fleur would therefore have to take the train.

Her mother had a bad migraine on Monday morning, so it had been left to Deanie to organize the trip into Worcester and see Fleur onto the train.

'I don't mind going up with her,' the old woman had said. ' 'Cos I don't see that it's right sending a child all that way by herself.'

'She'll actually be safer by herself, Deanie,' Amelia had replied, standing at the sink and swallowing down some painkillers with a glass of water. 'If you remember the last time you took a train by yourself you ended up going in the wrong direction and Mr Fisher had to fetch you from somewhere in Wales.'

'That was night-time,' Deanie protested. 'This'll be broad daylight.'

'And you'll both probably end up the wrong side of the English Channel. As I've told you, Deanie, just find someone trustworthy looking and put Fleur in her charge. She'll be perfectly all right, I assure you. If she's big enough to go off to London to study, then she's big enough to travel on the train by herself.'

With that Fleur's mother took herself off back to bed.

Sir Iain sent Gregory Rogers to meet Fleur at Paddington, the arrangement being that Fleur was to live as a paying guest at Sir Iain's house in Hampstead while studying under Isaac Kline who lived the other side of Hampstead Heath. Sir Iain had explained that this would be the most convenient arrangement all round since Isaac Kline never took in his pupils as lodgers, believing that both parties needed plenty of time apart from each other when studying so intensely. On the other hand Sir Iain was only too happy to give her a roof, living as he did all alone except for the company of Gregory Rogers in his vast Hampstead mansion.

Gregory Rogers was a quarter of an hour late at Paddington, giving Fleur the most worrisome and lonely fifteen minutes of her life so far as she waited. Finally frightened sick by all the strange men who kept hovering around her, some of them coming up behind her to whisper things Fleur didn't understand, and the drunks and derelicts who shuffled round the station shouting senseless obscenities at the travellers who hurried past them on their way to work, she took refuge in the book stall on the main concourse. From here she could keep an eye out for Sir Iain's unmistakable old, but still magnificent, blue Rolls Royce.

At last she saw it pulling into the space reserved for picking up passengers and ran across to it as fast as her two heavy cases would allow, hopping into the front thankfully as Gregory Rogers leaned across from the driving seat to let her in.

'Sorry, duchess,' he said after he'd put her cases in the boot. 'There was a mega mishap in St John's Wood with stiffs everywhere, which wasn't very helpful really, hence the extreme tardiness.'

Fleur didn't quite know what the handsome, blond young man was talking about, but she was so glad to be safe and in the Rolls that she just smiled happily and told him everything was perfectly all right.

'Good-dee,' Gregory replied, brushing his hair from his eyes. 'Got to keep the customers satisfied.'

Sir Iain Walcott's house would have looked magnificent in a country location let alone an urban one, set as it was in a superb garden which was surrounded by an eight-foot wall made out of brick as old as the eighteenth-century house. Everything about it was immaculate, from the glossy black paintwork of the ornamented gates which opened automatically in response to a signal from the remote control Gregory Rogers allowed Fleur to press, to the verges and lawns which looked as though they were cut with an electric razor, the meticulously shaped hedges, shrubs, the rosebeds and ornamental box trees, and the lavish arrangements of exotic flowers which Fleur noticed everywhere she looked as soon as she went in the house. It was far more ornate and lavish than the traditionally furnished Stoke Park and her first impression of Sir Iain's home was that it had to be the most beautiful house in which she had ever been. In fact as Gregory Rogers showed her around, she felt guilty at the thought that she couldn't imagine missing her own home one bit, not while she was living somewhere which was like a palace under the guardianship of one of the most famous orchestral conductors in the world, and being taught by one of the most famous living teachers. At that moment it seemed that her life had become a fairy tale and as she was shown to her room which turned out not to be just a bedroom but a suite of three rooms – bedroom, living room and her very own bathroom – Fleur found herself grinning from ear to ear.

'I take it from the Cheshire Cat type grin that this is to madam's liking, then?' Gregory Rogers said as a maid arrived to unpack Fleur's cases.

'Yes thank you, Mr Rogers,' Fleur replied, watching owl-eyed as the maid put away her few belongings as if they were the silks and satins of a princess. 'This is absolutely lovely.'

'You're not really going to call me Mr Rogers, are you?' Gregory sighed. 'I mean not all the way through? Unless of course you're expecting me to call you Miss Fisher.'

'No, of course I'm not.'

'Then I'm not expecting you to call me Mr Rogers, Flower. You're to call me Gregory. But not – Greg, if you don't mind. "Greg" simply reeks of sport and corks on hats and cans of lager, and is just far too butch for words. So Gregory only, Flower, or I'll see to the spiders in your bath personally.'

Sir Iain and Gregory were out to dinner that night so Fleur ate in the kitchen with only Rita, the Filipino maid, for company. Rita, however, was either as shy as Fleur or else spoke very little English because the whole meal was taken in near silence, with Fleur sitting all alone at the large scrubbed pine table and Rita, when she wasn't serving or clearing away, polishing non-existent marks off her gleaming stove.

Neither Sir Iain nor Gregory had given Fleur any directions as to how she might spend the rest of the evening, other than telling her to make herself at home, so after she had finished her supper Fleur tried without success to find where the television set was kept. Finally she returned to the kitchen where Rita was now polishing the floor on her hands and knees, to see whether perhaps she knew where the set was.

'Teevee?' she said wide-eyed. 'Sir Yeen no have no teevee. Noway. No teevee nowhere nohow.'

'Oh,' Fleur said glumly, looking at her watch and seeing it was only just half past seven. 'I suppose I'd better go and read then.'

'You wanna see teevee?' Rita asked timidly. 'If you wanna see teevee, Rita got teevee.'

Rita lived in an annexe across the courtyard opposite the kitchen door. In the centre of the courtyard was a floodlit ornamental pond inhabited by several huge beautifully marked Koi carp which were lolling around just below the surface waiting, it transpired, for Rita to tickle them which she told Fleur she did every night and every morning.

'Now you try,' she said to Fleur. 'They love strokey. You try strokey and tickles.'

Fleur knelt down and stroked the beautiful fish, amazed at the texture of their skin which instead of being greasy and slimy as she had imagined, was silky smooth. She was also surprised at how tame and even affectionate the fish were, bending themselves round Fleur's fingers and rolling over onto their sides for more petting and attention.

'Sir Yeen love his feesh,' Rita explained as she led Fleur across to the annexe. 'He name them all. The feesh all name after someone world fame. That one called Kiri. Now we watch teevee.'

Fleur had never seen such brilliantly coloured television. The control button must have been set to the maximum so loud and vivid were the tones. In fact the colours were so shocking they bled into each other making the screen look more like some vat full of multicoloured dye. The brightness control must have been turned up full as well, so luminous was the picture. This was obviously the way Rita liked to view, however, so once she had tipped out the contents of a vast bag of pink and white marshmallows into a cooking basin, she and Fleur settled down to watch.

Or rather Fleur settled down to watch because Rita seemed to prefer to do her viewing standing up, more or less slap bang in the middle of the screen. Doing her best to look round her, Fleur noticed that whereas all the brightness, colour and contrast controls were turned up to the maximum, the sound on the other hand was turned to mute. After watching about ten minutes of this silent but near-blinding television and unable to make out quite what programme it was they were watching, Fleur tapped Rita on the back and politely enquired if they might have the sound up a bit.

'Oh!' Rita gasped, smiling suddenly while her eyes opened wide with what seemed to Fleur like terror. 'I so mad! I so mad! I so mad! I no hear the teevee for I no know what they say! Oh but you, miss! Oh but you, miss, you do yes? Oh my, I so mad!'

Whereupon she turned the set up so loud it made all the windows in the annexe living-room rattle.

'You don't have to have it quite that loud, Rita, honestly,' Fleur said, hurrying to turn it down before her eardrums burst. 'And you don't really have to have it quite so bright either. Or have quite so much colour.'

Fleur adjusted the picture until it resembled the way most people usually had their sets tuned, and then sat back on the sofa.

'Oh,' Rita said, still smiling in that peculiar way. 'I no like this, miss. Teevee not funny like this, miss. No. Teevee not funny no more.' Whereupon she turned all the controls back to the maximum before taking up her place once more, centre stage. 'That good now,' she said, nodding seriously. 'Teevee real funny again.'

As he was driving her to her first class with Isaac Kline, Gregory asked Fleur if she'd settled in all right the night before. When he found out what she'd done to pass the time, first of all he sighed deeply and closed his thickly lashed eyes before telling her that watching *teevee* with Rita was definitely not on the agenda. Fleur politely asked why, since once she had got Rita talking she had found her to be such a sweet-natured and good-hearted woman that she couldn't imagine her capable of doing wrong to anything or anyone.

'That wasn't what I meant,' Gregory replied as he turned the Rolls down a tree-lined avenue. 'But so what? It won't matter this once, and I won't tell. It's just that watching television is not on the agenda, full stop, Rita or no Rita. Sir will not have it. Sir does not watch television, even when he's on it, and he certainly does not allow his protégés any such luxury. You'll find you won't be allowed to listen to the radio either, at least not to the dreaded pop music.'

'Sounds just like home,' Fleur said with a wry smile.

'Out of the frying pan, eh?' Gregory asked, raising one eyebrow as he turned to her. 'Oh, Sir's not a bad old stick once you get to know her.'

'Her?' Fleur picked up. 'I don't understand, what do you mean by calling him "her"?'

'Just *une façon de parler*, Flower. Just a tiny example of Uncle Gregory's wicked sense of fun. We call Sir "Her" because she can be such an old woman. But not so Mr Kline.'

The car was approaching a line of modest detached houses set back from the road behind front gardens bounded by either low hedges or small brick walls, residences which starkly contrasted with the magnificence of Sir Iain's fine abode on the hill.

'Is this where Mr Kline lives?' Fleur asked, as Gregory brought the car to a stop outside a particularly gloomy looking bow-fronted house with a broken front gate and a garden which resembled a miniature jungle.

'Yes it is,' Gregory replied, turning off the engine. 'But do not be deceived. Mr Kline may look as if he lives like something out of a horror film—'

'He doesn't really?' Fleur asked quickly, her eyes gone to the size of saucers.

'This is the very house where they filmed *The Addams Family*,' Gregory replied in a graveyard voice. 'But, as I said, do not let appearances deceive you. The most successful violin teacher in this part of the hemisphere lives like this because only one thing matters to him. The violin.'

'Will I like him?' Fleur wondered anxiously as she followed Gregory through the broken front gate. 'I mean is he frightening?'

'Whether you like him or not, Flower, is up to you,' Gregory said knocking on the front door. 'But as for, "is he frightening?" Why do you think I'm off before he opens the door?' Gregory grinned and waved to Fleur from halfway down the garden path. 'I'll pick you up at lunch time in the Batmobile!' he called.

Gregory was in the Rolls and gone by the time the front door finally opened. Fleur could hardly make out who was admitting her, so dark was the house inside. All she heard was a voice from somewhere down the unlit hallway telling her to stop letting all the heat out and to come in and close the door behind her.

The shadowy shape ahead of her turned into a room on the left and Fleur made to follow it – in the process tripping over a cat which fled, screaming its outrage, to run the gauntlet through a whole crowd of cats which Fleur could now see in the half-light, sitting most of the way up the stairs.

'Come in – come in, please!' the voice ordered from the room on her left. 'And try not to kill any more of my cats as you do!'

When she entered the room in which she was to spend the best part of her life for the next nine months, Fleur couldn't see her new teacher anywhere. But she could take in the state of the room itself which had to be the untidiest she had ever seen. Up until this moment her best friend Lucy's bedroom at Stoke Park had been top of that list, but Isaac Kline's music room now went staightaway to Number One. It was as if he had originally moved in with all his possessions piled high on a cart, which he then simply tipped up so that everything spilled out all over the room. There was simply no order to anything anywhere, with music stands, instruments and instrument cases, metronomes, manuscripts, violin bows, pots of resin, as well as all the other usual musical accoutrements jostling for room with odd items of furniture which included a large stuffed brown bear, a small wooden statue of some three-headed Asian goddess, a church harmonium complete with a set of pipes in which sat yet another cat, several valetudinary plants standing in what looked like old floral chamber pots, a roll-top desk piled high with correspondence and bookshelves which were spilling over with a vast collection of magazines, books, records and tapes, while under the furniture and propped up in the corners of the room was an assortment of old sports equipment such as stringless tennis rackets, broken croquet mallets, as well as a set of rusted hickory-shafted golf clubs and one solitary oar with a dark blue blade.

Almost in the very middle of the room was a large open wardrobe packed not with clothes, but with sheet music, which was where Fleur came face to face with her teacher. Her first impression of him was that he wasn't a great deal bigger than she was, and that with his head of dark, cropped hair, his small almost-black eyes and what appeared to be a permanently wrinkled nose, he looked like a fierce bat-like rodent. Isaac Kline was far from blind, however, as Fleur was soon to discover. In fact he had absolutely perfect sight, a fact of which he was inordinately proud and of which he would perpetually boast, displaying his 20/20 vision by restringing violins, whenever necessary, in the darkest part of his half-lit music room, accompanied by much muttered self-congratulation at his remarkable vision.

All this was yet to come however, and for the moment all Isaac Kline did when Fleur found him at the far side of the wardrobe was ask her how many of his cats she had killed.

'I didn't kill any, Mr Kline,' Fleur said, taking him seriously. 'I think I just trod on one that I didn't see.'

'Don't you go killing any of my cats,' he said, unwrapping himself a boiled sweet. 'You do, and what am I going to use for strings?'

Fleur stared at him, trying her best not to look as appalled as she felt, while Isaac popped the sweet in his mouth and returned to sorting through his sheet music.

'You can look as well off as you like, young lady,' he said. 'But you ain't seen the price of catgut. Every violinist worth his salt keeps cats. Fritz Kreisler used to farm them. Now then, tell me what size instrument you've been playing, please? Quarter size? Half size? The whole shebang – what exactly?'

'I started off on a quarter size, but I'm playing a half size now,' Fleur replied. 'Although I can play on a full-size one if I have to.'

'And a cat can look at a king,' Isaac replied dismissively. 'You brought any of these famous violins with you?'

'I've brought my half size, Mr Kline,' Fleur said, holding up her case. 'It's all I have at the moment. The quarter size belonged to the school.'

'Okay,' Isaac nodded. 'Tune it and play me something. Here. Play me this.'

Fleur looked at the sheet and saw it was a Bach Partita which she didn't know. That didn't worry her, however, since she could sight-read fluently. What concerned her was finding somewhere in the room where there was enough light to see the music. Meanwhile she got her violin out of its case and began to tune up.

'The first thing you should know before we start, young lady,' Isaac said, sucking noisily on his sweet, 'is that I cannot abide children. I cannot abide them for lots of reasons, the main one being they find it such a big deal coming to terms with reality. You won't know what I am talking about and why should you, because you are too busy thinking up what to ask next – questions, questions, this is all children want to know, rather than actually just *thinking*. But make no mistake, until you learn to come to terms with things rather than to run away from them, you will always remain a child, even all your life. I know because I know a ton of people like this, so you pay attention. Children are always nosey-parkering and this is what I cannot stand. I don't mind questions. I welcome questions. But not waste-of-time questions which are nothing to do with reality. Like how long is a piece of string? Can you whistle with two fingers? Which King of Spain wore the largest shoes? What you have to do is learn to ask *why*. These are the only questions worth asking, young lady. What's your name?'

'Fleur, Mr Kline, and I'm nearly ready.'

'From now on the only questions you ask me, Miss Fleur, begin with the word why. You got that?'

320

'Yes, Mr Kline.'

'What sent the messengers to hell was asking what they knew darn well. "Why" is what we concern ourselves with. *Why* did Bach want to make it sound like this rather than that – not *how* do I play it. We understand why about Bach, we understand Bach. *Why* did the chicken cross the road, Fleur. Not *how* did it. Now play the Partita and when I tell you how I think you play it, you ask me why I think so.'

When Fleur had played her new teacher the selected piece, having set up her music stand to catch the light from the window, Isaac got up from the old horsehair sofa on which he had laid himself out at full stretch and returned to the wardrobe in which he spent the next few minutes rummaging around.

'Do you want me to play something else, Mr Kline? Is that it?' Fleur asked after nothing had been said.

'No, young lady, I want nothing of the sort. I have heard quite enough, I thank you,' Isaac replied. 'What I am looking for are my sweets. Ah!'

Finding them he offered the bag to Fleur, who took one, before selecting one himself.

'Here is a good Why-question for you,' he asked. 'Why is it the green sweets are always the worst and that they are always the most?'

'I don't know,' Fleur replied. 'I suppose because they must be the cheapest.'

'Good. Yes, that has to be the answer. Every time you buy a tube of gums, out of twenty sweets, eight are green. Almost half are always green. And this is what you remember when you are old enough to start playing in public. The world is full of people who cheat by putting in as many green sweets as they can. Good. Now the first thing we will work on today is your wrist position.'

Nothing was said about the way she had played the Bach. In fact nothing was said about the way Fleur played

321

at all, not for the whole of the first lesson. It wasn't until she was packing up her things to leave that Fleur dared ask her teacher.

'You told me to ask you how I played the Partita, Mr Kline, and I forgot,' she said. 'I'm sorry.'

'You didn't forget and you're not sorry, so let's start again,' Isaac replied, pouring himself a very small sherry out of a huge bottle. 'You were expecting my comment on the Bach, to which you might have asked me the question I told you to ask. But I didn't comment so that is that.'

'Why didn't you, Mr Kline? Don't you think I should know how I played it?'

'You know how you played it, Miss Fleur. You know you must have played it well because I was not occasioned to say anything about it. Not one thing. Until the same time tomorrow then, goodbye. I must now go and fatten up my catguts.'

'He doesn't really use his cats for strings does he?' Fleur asked Gregory Rogers as he drove her back to the house.

'Nobody knows quite what Isaac Kline does, Missie,' Gregory replied, affecting a Southern American accent. 'Why, some say he has a laboratory in the basement where he makes little geniuses – no of course he doesn't use his cats for catgut!' Gregory laughed, resuming his normal voice. 'He sells them to Sir for his *wigs*. What did you make of the house? Or rather the "Music Room"?'

'It's a bit of a muddle,' Fleur admitted before returning to the thing which really concerned her. 'And he doesn't really sell his cats as wigs, does he?'

'Fleur dear,' Gregory sighed, opening and closing his eyes very slowly. 'That was a jay oh kay ee. Isaac Kline is probably one of the kindest-hearted men you will ever meet – but just make sure you don't tell him I told you. In fact don't for a minute treat him as if he is. Pretend to be frightened. He loves that, and you'll get a lot of sweets that way. And no green ones.'

The longer Isaac taught Fleur the more she grew to adore him. Initially she had been terrified at the prospect of going to London to study under one of the great violin teachers, particularly since when he was at home her father seemed to spend the whole time telling her how temperamental and unnecessarily strict music teachers notoriously were, quoting horror stories in which would-be pupils were made to suffer the tortures of the damned in the cause of their art. Still, as her father invariably finished, *as I have said time and time again, you make your bed and then you have to lie in it.*

So it was small wonder that Fleur had been expecting the worst and that the first impression her new teacher had made on her only seemed to confirm her suspicions. Yet in no time at all she had forgotten her initial misgivings and forebodings as she came to realize both what a kind and brilliant man Isaac Kline actually was. As long as she was with him, she was happy and fulfilled. She came to love everything about him, the chaos in which he existed and the energy with which he lived, the way he refused ever to flatter or compliment her but apparently just took for granted the fact that she could play the violin, and most of all she loved the way he treated her as an equal, never patronizing her, never talking down to her, never simplifying issues or moderating his explanations, never indulging her and above all never trying to teach her by the-better-you-get-the-more-I-shall-reward-you method. From the moment Fleur had walked into the half-lit chaos of his music room and played for him, Isaac had put them both on a par. As he would explain, he was a musician and so was she, and his job was to organize her commitment and feed the obvious hunger she had to learn.

He would only ever play, not to demonstrate what

he meant or even how the music should sound, but in order to analyse his own playing of the piece which was in rehearsal so that he could then dissect it, and by so doing help Fleur to improve her own playing by showing how he himself could still improve.

'We none of us ever stop learning,' he would say as he walked round the cluttered room still playing, the only time it seemed he managed to do so without knocking anything over. 'Yes, I know this is a saying as old as the mountains but that is why it is old because it has been true for so long. As long as we keep looking we shall go on finding, do you not think? So when I play you can hear what I find just as I do when you play.'

Then another time he told her that when she played she was to think of it as if she was setting out across the ocean. 'This big vast ocean,' he said, 'but such a journey is no good unless you are sure of your direction. So this is what we are doing, you see? We are mapping out your journey, making sure you have both the direction and the savvy. Believe me, Miss Fleur, once you are fully in command you will sail this sea so well, because for this particular journey God has made a most wonderful vessel.'

Initially the plan was for Fleur to study with Isaac Kline for six months and then for all the interested parties to meet and examine the next set of options.

'Some will argue for you to go to the Academy for sure. The Academy, maybe the Juillard—'

'Where's the Juillard?'

'New York. And very good too, but a long way to go. Even so the options are The Academy, the Juillard or The Paris Conservatoire, but if I were them, me? I wouldn't send you no such place. Yes, a musical education is a good thing, who knows. No-one's saying it ain't.'

'Yes, but what more would I learn than I'm learning here, Mr Kline?' Fleur wondered. 'I mean I have my tutors at Sir Iain's for my school lessons, and no-one's going to teach me more than you can teach me.'

'That's a maybe,' Isaac said, frowning and searching his jacket pocket for his sweets. 'But if it was me and I was running these places you'd be the last person I'd have, that's for a certainty.'

'Why?' Fleur asked, caught as usual in one of Isaac's bear traps. 'They have people even younger than me at these places. I read about it.'

'Nothing to do with your age, Miss Know It All,' Isaac replied, finding a small bag of sweets. 'I wouldn't take you as a pupil because when all my other pupils hear you play they throw their instruments away, that's my why. Will you look at this?' He showed her the bag of sweets. 'Dolly Mixtures. I ain't had Dolly Mixtures in an age. Oh – and in case you were imagining that was a compliment what I just said, forget it. That was a fact.'

The rest of her teachers, the men and women who came to Sir Iain's house first thing in the afternoon in an attempt to further Fleur's general education, stood no chance against their unseen opponent. Most of them had taken the job of privately coaching a child prodigy hoping somehow to become a part of the legend themselves, but once they learned Fleur had one interest and one interest only they soon retired hurt, realizing they were never going to get much of a look in. Others of similar persuasion came for similar reasons and went for similar reasons, leaving only a small band of no-hopers who, unable to get a situation elsewhere, were prepared to take the money for just going through the motions.

Not that Fleur was in any way ignorant or illiterate. She had been too well schooled at Lady Mary's. Anyway, having a phenomenally high I.Q., she found she learned things far more quickly than her tutors could teach them – which was why all too soon it became clear that she was finding her general lessons a waste of time.

This fact worried Sir Iain and he told Fleur so. It wasn't that he worried about Fleur growing up into an ignoramus because he knew such was far from the case. His concern, as he explained to his protégée, was that if her father thought Fleur was neglecting her general studies, he might remove her from Sir Iain's supervision and send her to a formal London school to study with other children her own age when her schedule permitted.

'Parents are forever doing this when they have talented offspring,' Sir Iain explained one night over dinner. 'They call it the hothouse syndrome, arguing that an education which is concentrated mainly on just music is not what they want, but of course this is nonsense. If their child was good at French they would expect him or her to concentrate on French, and so on and so forth – but music? No no. Music is hothouse, so they must make sure their little darlings remain as normal as possible. And I am greatly afraid, young lady, that your dear father may well be one of this breed, which is why I urge you, indeed I beg you, to keep up with your general studies.'

'The trouble with this young lady here, master, isn't her keeping up with her general studies, but with her general studies keeping up with her,' Gregory explained.

'As long as she does all the written work expected of her, then that is all we can ask,' Sir Iain said. 'I am simply thinking of the future. Forgive me for saying so, dear child, but from my experience in running orchestras I know a little too much about human relationships and I fear your father is not a man with whom we should trifle. I have a feeling that he is single-minded almost to the point of obsession, a most determined fellow who would rather things went according not simply to plan, but according to his plan.'

'He does like Mummy and me to do well, whatever we're doing,' Fleur said. 'You know, even if it's just a game at home or something. We have to do it really well.'

'And he likes to do best of all?' Sir Iain wondered, arching his eyebrows. 'Daddy knows best and Daddy does best, I imagine.'

'Uh-huh,' Gregory said in a sing-song voice with a look at the maestro. 'And now for something completely different, because I have had a wonderful idea. Fleur. We are going to *changez votre nom*, sweetheart. Because Fleur Fisher is not quite wonderful enough.'

'Really?' Fleur asked. 'Why – what's wrong with it?'

'You haven't been listening, cloth ears. I said it wasn't quite wonderful *enough*. Fleur Fisher. It's just a little too Beatrix Potter, trinket. Not quite top-of-the-bill matter.'

'Any bright suggestions, Gregory?' Sir Iain wondered, as always rolling out the 'r' in his assistant's name.

'Needs to be something double-barrelled, I think, master,' Gregory replied. 'Either that or two first names. Although personally I go for the double barrel. What was Mummy's first name, treasure?'

'Her first name is Amelia.'

'No. Sorry – my mistake. What was Mummy's maiden name?'

'Oh. Um. Dilke,' Fleur replied. 'When she was a model she was Amelia Anne Dilke.'

'Excellent,' Gregory smiled, clapping his hands together once. 'Then how about you being Fleur Fisher-Dilke?'

Boredom was Fleur's biggest enemy, not at work but when she got home after class with Isaac. She found her general lessons more and more boring, particularly since she had no-one with whom she could share any jokes or pranks, and above all no-one with whom she could play. Sir Iain was very kind but he was old and not really interested in Fleur except as a musician. While once the evening came and dinner was finished, Gregory usually disappeared out somewhere, just as usually incurring his master's displeasure, with the result that Sir Iain retired early. Fleur was then left either to listen to music (classical only), or to sneak off when she was sure the coast was clear to watch what she and Gregory had dubbed Planet Zogovision with the ever-welcoming Rita.

'She's an odd one our Rita, don't you think?' Gregory once asked. 'I can never get used to it but apparently it's typical of Filipinos. They only laugh when they're unhappy and vice versa.'

'So that's what it is!' Fleur had replied. 'That's why whenever she says something isn't funny on the television she grins, and when she's really enjoying herself she looks as if she's about to cry!'

'They are here on earth among us,' Gregory intoned in his sepulchral voice. 'They have landed from the planet Zog and even now they are walking among us.'

But even the delights of Rita's multicoloured, brighter than bright *teevee* and her endless supply of popcorn and marshmallows soon palled, as did the equally endless games of gin rummy and canasta which Sir Iain, Gregory and Fleur played regularly when they were all in. The result was that Fleur finally found herself pining for the company of someone her own age.

As always, Isaac knew there was something wrong because he heard it in Fleur's playing.

'You might as well tell me,' he said, 'because for days now you even play music in major keys in the minor.'

'I don't, do I?' Fleur asked.

'That's how it's sounding, Fleur. As if life is one long funeral.'

'I'm sorry,' Fleur said looking up, genuinely shocked. 'I didn't realize – I mean I didn't think . . . I didn't realize I was playing badly.'

'No. No it's not that you play badly. I'd soon tell you when you do that. But you are playing poignant. So while this is fine when you play Massenet's *Meditation* like you played yesterday, it don't do for the Paganini

Caprices, or even the Ravel which you work on now. So. Out with it. Let us clear the air.'

At first Fleur felt foolish when she explained her feelings, but Isaac wouldn't allow her to feel that way for a moment longer than was necessary. Instead he applauded her as if she had just played a piece well, and then wandered round the room scratching his head with both hands while he thought about what to do.

'This happens all the time but then of course I imagined you had realized that long ago. Or else that Sir Iain had asked you what else you expect. Or that Gregory Rogers – who is a very kind young man despite all his affectations – Gregory will make plans to take you to the cinema, or the zoo, God forbid. Or some such. But of course *they* cannot do anything because what you want is what all kids want – you want friends of your own age. Now.'

He sat down beside her on the old sofa, sending up as always a plume of dust and horsehair.

'Now what we must ask ourself is this,' he said, producing an old tin lunch box full of chocolate Wagon Wheels. 'Why have you not been going home?'

Fleur explained that everyone had decided before she began her studies that it would be better for her to have as long away from home as possible at the beginning. They were afraid if she kept going home she might not see her course of lessons through.

'Because you love your home, I see,' Isaac nodded. 'Natural I suppose, but crazy thinking all the same. Either something works or it don't. You can lead a horse to water, eh? But a pencil can't be lead.'

'Sorry?' said Fleur, halfway through her chocolate treat. 'Why can't a pencil be lead? I don't understand.'

'Maybe because a pencil's made of carbon, you oaf,' Isaac sighed, finishing his own biscuit. 'A joke, you see, but even so I'm serious. What's a plan worth if it don't work? Zilch. I think it's time you went home, saw your friends, do whatever it is you do when you're at home. Get drunk. Get into a fight, beat up the town.'

'Perhaps if someone else asked,' Fleur said, carefully folding her silver paper into a square.

'Perhaps if someone else *said*,' Isaac corrected her. 'Perhaps if the Great Man himself spoke, eh?'

'Yes,' Fleur agreed. 'Perhaps.'

'Okay, and here—' Isaac said, handing Fleur his own bit of silver paper. 'I nearly was forgetting the guide dog.'

27

That Friday evening Richard called to pick Fleur up from Sir Iain's and drive her home with him. As Fleur discovered her father was not in the very best of moods.

'I hope this is all going to prove worthwhile, Fleur,' he said as they headed out of London. 'I don't mean financially, I mean morally worthwhile. Your mother worries about you, about how you're doing, about what you're getting up to, and of course some of that, a lot of that, rubs off on me. No, before you say anything let me finish, please.' Richard held up one hand briefly without looking at Fleur. 'Thank you,' he continued, 'because these things must be said and you're quite old enough to hear them being said now. You know how important my work is. I said you know how important my work is, Fleur?'

'You said I wasn't to interrupt, Daddy.'

'No, I won't have you being facetious. If this is the sort of thing you're learning . . . You're having the very best tuition money can buy, and if all it's teaching you is to be facetious—'

'I wasn't being facetious, whatever that means,' Fleur protested.

'You should know what words like "facetious" mean by now, young lady,' her father returned. 'If you are not neglecting your studies.'

'No I'm not. I've even brought my interim reports with me so that you can see.'

'Well I shall, make no mistake, Fleur, I shall see. Most

certainly I shall. Anyway, as I was saying, you know how important my work is.'

'Yes, Daddy.'

'Please don't interrupt. My work, unlike the work you are planning to do when and if the time comes, concerns other people's welfare. The state of their health. Coping with their diseases and disorders. Trying to make the world a better place to live in. It's extremely hard work, and very taxing work, Fleur, as well as being very important and it is not the sort of work you can do if you are burdened down with outside worries. Which is why I said to you at the beginning, this had better be worth it.'

'It will, Daddy, I promise you,' Fleur said. 'I'm sorry if Mummy is worried because she needn't be.'

'You can tell her that yourself. You make sure you tell her that yourself.'

'She can't be that worried, Daddy, because she's only written to me twice.'

'Because she didn't want you to be upset, knowing your mother,' her father replied, accelerating as they left the flyover to join the motorway. 'Your mother is a very unselfish woman and the last thing she would want to do would be to upset you as you were settling in to your new routine. But so far it hasn't been easy on her, and consequently not on me either. I do not like to go into the operating theatre with anything on my mind other than the job in hand. I am dealing with people's lives and sometimes their deaths, Fleur, while you are learning how to play the fiddle. Just remember that and possibly, just possibly we can keep everything in perspective. All right?'

'Yes, Daddy. If you say so.'

'Yes I say so, all right. And now this business of suddenly wanting to come home at a moment's notice. We've had to change all our plans to accommodate you, you realize. Your mother was perfectly willing to do so, but I have to say because your mother never would, I have to say we did as asked at a certain cost to ourselves.'

'You needn't have done,' Fleur said, biting her lip and frowning out of the window. 'If you didn't want me to come home, next weekend would have been fine.'

'Next weekend as it happens would have been even worse, Fleur,' her father replied. 'There is no way we could cry off what we are doing next weekend, while this weekend – well. We had to do a great deal of rearranging. It had just better all be worth it.'

Her father fell to silence, as did Fleur who had no intention of encouraging her father to talk when he was in such a difficult mood. Instead, after a good quarter of an hour's silence, she asked if they could listen to the radio, and when her father grunted his agreement Fleur turned it on to a concert to which she'd wanted to listen on Radio Three.

'Do we have to?' her father asked after listening to no more than a few bars of Bruch's Violin Concerto. 'Surely to God you can have too much of a good thing, yes?'

He reached a hand out and pushed in another of the preset station buttons, tuning in to *The World Tonight* on Radio Four. 'That's better,' he said. 'And if you listen, you might learn something useful for a change.'

Five minutes later Fleur was fast asleep, remaining so for the rest of the long journey.

No-one was up when they finally reached The Folly so after they had eaten the sandwiches which had been left out for them, and Fleur had drunk a glass of milk and her father a whisky, they both retired to their beds. Fleur sensed there was something different about the place, but exhausted both by a week of hard work and the long car journey, she was unable to put her finger on it before drifting off into a deep sleep.

Her mother was up before her and halfway through

breakfast when Fleur came downstairs wrapped in her quilted dressing gown. They kissed each other and in response to her mother's questions about London, Fleur began telling her all about her new life and its regime. Her mother listened, at the same time doing her best not to let her eyes stray too often to her copy of the *Daily Mail*.

'Where's Deanie?' Fleur asked, all at once realizing what was different about the house. 'Why isn't Deanie up? Isn't she well or something?'

'No,' Amelia replied slowly, having carefully folded her newspaper to the next page. 'No, sweetheart and I was going to write to you but then I thought it better to wait until I saw you. Deanie's gone back to Yorkshire.'

'But why? I don't understand. When she last wrote to me—'

'When was that?' Amelia asked sharply, looking up at Fleur over a pair of new reading spectacles.

'I don't know exactly,' Fleur replied. 'It was some weeks ago now, because funnily enough I was wondering why I hadn't heard back from her. But anyway when she last wrote she was saying how much she was looking forward to us all being together at Christmas, and most of all and even though as she said she'd probably have to get a new hearing aid she said how much she was looking forward to my first concert. Now she's gone back to Yorkshire, you say. Honestly, I don't quite understand.'

'When you've quite finished I'll tell you, sweetheart, then perhaps you will understand.' Her mother reached for her cigarettes and, lighting one up, took off her glasses and ran her fingers through her long glossy hair. 'Deanie's not been very well for some time now, as you may or may not have realized. But as you certainly will have realized, she's an old woman and really she should have retired long ago. But she wouldn't go. She said she'd been with the family for so long now she couldn't imagine life without us all, and that she'd prefer to die with her boots on.'

'She's not dead, is she?' Fleur asked, catching her breath.

'No of course she's not dead, Fleur, don't be so dramatic,' her mother replied before exhaling some smoke. 'But her health was deteriorating visibly and your father, once he'd had a good look at her, your father said the only thing for it, the kindest thing all round, was to send Deanie back up North, back home, to where her roots are. That it was much the kindest thing all round.'

'But where? She hasn't got any family left up there. She said so.'

'Yes of course she has, Fleur. That's all you know. Deanie's brother's wife is still going, and she also has a cousin who lives somewhere near Ripon. She'll be perfectly all right where she is. She's being very well looked after, I assure you.'

'But where is she, Mummy? I mean you do know where she is, don't you? Because I'd like to write to her.'

'Of course I know where she is, Fleur,' her mother replied, tapping her cigarette impatiently on the edge of her coffee-cup saucer. 'What sort of person do you think I am? I'm hardly going to send my own old nanny off somewhere and not know where that somewhere is, am I? I'll give you the address later. Now tell me some more about London, and how you've been getting on.'

Fleur told her only briefly about her own progress because her mind was quite elsewhere, as it seemed was her mother's. So after a short description of her new life and the people in it, Fleur soaked some stale bread in milk and went out to find her precious deer.

She was late for them but even so they were a long time in coming to her. When she had been living at home full time and had been late for them before, they were usually all waiting for her in the clearing at the edge of the woods, picking at any leaves which were still within their reach or truffling among the leaves for any fallen titbits. But this morning, as the winter mist began to clear, Fleur couldn't see any of them anywhere.

After a minute or so she gave the small soft whistle she used to let them know she was there, and then sat back on her favourite old tree stump to wait. At last she heard the sound of their feet in the woods and the inquisitive snorts of the older and more confident does, and then there they all were, eight, nine, ten of them, staring first to make sure it really was her before walking sedately right up to her, the first there helping themselves to the bread from her basket.

As she began to feed them by hand they seemed to remember the routine, and each waited their turn while Fleur looked beyond them to see if there was any sign of the white deer. But it was nowhere to be seen and there was no sign of it even when Fleur's basket of food was empty and the other deer had turned away to wander back towards the woods. So sadly, and still thinking of Deanie, Fleur turned to go back to the house, only to find the white deer standing stock still right behind her.

While Fleur had been out feeding the deer Lucy had telephoned to make sure that Fleur was coming over that evening for her birthday party.

'Ah,' said her father, up now and having his breakfast. 'So that was the reason for the return home! I thought there had to be an ulterior motive.'

'That wasn't the reason at all,' Fleur replied, earning a mock-surprised look from her father for her forthrightness. 'I wanted to come home and see you and Mummy, and I also thought you wouldn't mind me going to Lucy's birthday party. You said you were probably going out anyway, and Lucy is going to be thirteen.'

'Actually I don't see why not,' Amelia offered in the ensuing silence, giving a certain look to Richard. 'Barbara and David did say we could leave it open, just in case there was any change of plans.'

'Oh very well,' Richard replied, lightly buttering an oatcake. 'If that's the case go ahead, Fleur. If that's what you'd rather be doing.'

There were twenty of them at the party, ten boys, ten girls and no adults, at least not visibly. All parents who had driven any sort of distance were whisked away by Lady Stourton to have a fork dinner and drinks somewhere else in the house, leaving the dining and drawing rooms to the birthday party.

Fleur found herself next to Lucy's cousin Harry again, although only because Harry had switched several of the place names round so that this could be the case. Lucy was at the head of the table their end, with Fleur two places away on her right and Harry three.

'Luce says you're in training to be some sort of concert violinist, yes?' Harry asked her. Fleur nodded, trying not to stare at him since she found herself entranced once again not only by his strange medieval looks but by the habit he had of talking out of the left-hand side of his mouth, while hardly moving his upper lip at all. 'What's it like, this training then?' he continued. 'Are they fearfully strict? Bet they are.'

'It's very hard work,' Fleur replied, 'so it's strict that way. But my actual teacher, someone called Isaac Kline, he's tremendous. I mean he's brilliant, and although he's terrifically dedicated he still makes learning fun. We really do have fun.'

'Is that possible?' Harry shrugged once. 'Playing the sort of music you're playing. Bach, I don't know – Beethoven. All the Germans. Could you really call that fun? It's just not my scene at all.'

'I know. I remember you playing at Lady Stourton's birthday party.'

'I remember you playing too. But do you ever play anything else? Besides *Sturm und Drang*. I don't suppose you do, do you?'

'I play all sorts of things,' Fleur replied. 'We often finish a long session with all sorts of things. Isaac likes George Gershwin, for instance, so we quite often play some Gershwin.'

'Yes I see,' Harry said, nodding. 'Good. You're not rushing off home straightaway, are you? After?'

'I hope not,' Fleur replied. 'No I don't think so.'

'Fine,' Harry said, frowning. 'Good.'

Before Fleur could wonder why, Harry turned away to talk to the girl on his other side who'd been pulling at his sleeve and staring at Fleur most of the time Harry had been talking to her.

'You're elected,' Lucy said, leaning behind the boy between them. 'Cousin Harry's taken a shine, so you're elected. His family own most of Shropshire.'

When the party appeared finally to be breaking up and the parents who hadn't needed to stay for the evening began to arrive to pick up their offspring, Harry appeared from nowhere at Fleur's side holding a violin case.

'Here,' he said, thrusting it at Fleur. 'I've cleared it with Great-Aunt. Anyway, she said if you're going to play she's jolly well going to listen.'

'*Am* I going to play?' Fleur enquired.

'I am!' Harry replied, as if that answered everything.

'What are you going to play?' Lady Stourton asked as she joined them on their way to the drawing room.

'We're going to play some Gershwin, Great-Aunt,' Harry informed her, holding open the drawing-room door. 'I thought it better than me murdering the classics.'

'One really doesn't mind what you play, Harry,' Lady Stourton replied, preceding him into the fire-lit room, 'as long as it isn't that quite fearful rock and roll.'

Harry sat at the piano and gave Fleur an A.

'Know a tune called *Summertime?*' he asked, sketching the theme out as Fleur tuned up. Fleur nodded back at him over her violin. 'I play it slow, as a Blues,' Harry continued. 'Four in, two together, me two, you two, then two out. Okay?'

'It'll be okay if you tell me what on earth you mean,' Fleur laughed, tuning the last string on her violin.

'I'll take four bars intro, we play two choruses together, I solo for two, you solo for two, then we take two choruses out,' Harry explained, in a voice which suggested everyone knew what he was talking about, everyone but Fleur.

'What key?' Fleur asked.

'I don't know,' Harry replied. 'I don't read. This one all right?'

Harry again sketched out the theme to show Fleur which key he was intending to play the song, a key which Fleur immediately recognized as E flat minor.

'Fine,' she said. 'Ready when you are.'

Harry improvised his four-bar introduction then nodded Fleur in. He really was a very good pianist, Fleur thought the moment she heard him play again, very assured, almost ridiculously so for his age which from his rather senior manner she had already put at a possible fifteen, only to find out from Lucy after dinner that he was in fact over a whole year younger.

'Nice,' he called up to Fleur as she embellished the second chorus in. 'That's okay.'

Fleur then watched as Harry took his solo. His already tall frame half bent over the keyboard, he eyed the notes with a deeply perplexed expression as if not understanding from where the music was coming, as if his long slender hands had a life of their own, nodding to himself in apparent approval at his improvisation, with his tongue wedged firmly between his teeth and sticking well into one cheek.

Harry had taken it faster than Fleur was used to playing it with her teacher. Isaac liked to play it slow and moody as a ballad, but with Harry it was jazz, a slow blues with a firm laid-back beat. Fleur liked it more this way, and she particularly appreciated the way Harry filled in between her phrases and pointed them up, rather than just playing a straightforward accompaniment. She found she could respond to it, that Harry's playing prompted her into things, suggested ways she could go, places to take the tune. And they were most certainly swinging.

'Yes!' Harry said looking up and smiling for the first time. 'That's right!'

Everyone who was still there had crowded round the piano and when Fleur and Harry had finished at once demanded more, so they played I Got Rhythm so fast and furiously that Fleur collapsed in mock exhaustion as they both came off the last note perfectly and right on the button.

'I did like that,' Lady Stourton said. 'Do you think we could have one more?'

'I'm not sure what else I know,' Fleur said, trying to get her breath back. 'I mean that Harry and I could play.'

'You must know this one,' Harry said sketching out another melody. 'The Man I Love.'

Fleur said she didn't so Harry played it once through which was enough for Fleur.

'Right. Four in, two together, you two, me two, then two out as before?' she asked with a perfectly straight face.

'That'll do,' Harry agreed and then counted them in. 'One two three four.'

When they had finally been allowed a break by their audience, Fleur saw the time and hurriedly started to put away the violin.

'I really ought to go home,' she said. 'It's awfully late.'

Lucy and Harry fetched torches and walked Fleur back across the already freezing park.

'Welton said it's going to snow,' Lucy said idly.

'Too cold for snow,' Harry replied, and then whistled his way through *White Christmas* while Fleur and Lucy walked either side of him in silence. 'I've got Chris Barber playing that,' he told them when he'd finished. 'Pat Halcox cornet, Monty Sunshine clarinet, Lonnie Donnegan banjo, Jim Bray bass and Ron Bowden drums.'

'Fascinating,' Lucy remarked drily.

'Who's Chris Barber?' Fleur asked.

'God,' sighed Harry. 'Girls!'

'God,' Lucy laughed. 'Boys!'

By the time they reached the gate up to The Folly, Harry had long detached himself from them and disappeared somewhere in the darkness.

'Harry said something about you coming riding tomorrow,' Lucy said. 'And staying to lunch.'

'Harry asked me to come riding tomorrow—' Fleur began, only for Lucy to interrupt her.

'I thought you'd been made to give up riding?'

'I have,' Fleur replied, with a smile. 'But then who's to know unless someone tells them? Who's that? Is that Harry?'

Fleur pointed across to the nearest paddock where in the pale light of the November moon which had now risen they could just make out the long thin shape of Harry, hanging by both arms from the bottom branch of one of the huge horse chestnuts which graced the paddock lands.

'He's completely dotty, you know,' Lucy said. 'I mean he's brilliant, but he is completely dotty.'

'I think he's very nice,' Fleur said. 'I don't mind if he's dotty.'

'Oh God,' Lucy groaned. 'You're not serious, are you? I mean you're not getting a crush on him? You can't. He's got such dreadful hair.'

'What's wrong with his hair?'

'God, Fleur, it's such an *awful* colour! Imagine if you had children and they had Harry's hair . . . '

'All your cousin's done is ask me out riding. And to lunch.'

'At my house.' Lucy cupped her hands to her mouth and suddenly shouted at her cousin at the top of her voice. 'Harry!'

The figure hanging from the tree must have heard, but it paid no attention. It just went on hanging there.

'God, he really is completely mad,' Lucy said, her breath hanging in the freezing night air. 'Well?' she asked Fleur. 'Are you coming tomorrow or aren't you?'

'I'd like to, but I'll have to ask my parents,' Fleur replied.

Her father was obviously put out and said as much, complaining that if she went out again they would hardly have seen her all weekend. Fleur didn't argue, much as she wanted to go to Stoke Park, because she knew there was no way she would ever win direct arguments with her father. So she played her mother instead, having long been aware of what a snob her mother was, what snobs both her parents were as a matter of fact, but with her mother as the greater one.

'You've seen enough of Lucy surely, I mean for one weekend,' her mother said, carefully opening the *Mail on Sunday* magazine as if it were an antique manuscript. 'Christmas is coming up anyway, so you'll have plenty more time to spend together.'

'I know, Mamma,' Fleur said.

'What's this *Mamma* business for heaven's sake?' her father interrupted, looking up from his newspaper. 'We're not French for crying out loud.'

'You often speak French, you and Mamma,' Fleur replied.

'There is nothing wrong with Mummy, Fleur,' Richard continued, ignoring his daughter's remark. 'Mamma is so affected. Next thing we'll be having is you changing your name I should imagine.'

'I rather like being called Mamma, as a matter of fact,' Amelia said. 'I think it's less childish.'

Fleur was about to tell her mother that was precisely what Gregory Rogers had said, when she just managed to stop herself in time. She knew all too well her father would not appreciate being told what was preferable by someone like Gregory Rogers. Instead she continued her play for going to spend the day with Lucy and Harry.

'Lucy has a cousin staying, Mamma. His family is frightfully old and distinguished apparently and own most of Shropshire. You've probably heard of them. They're called the Grevils. Without an "e".'

'A Shropshire family, did you say?' her father asked, changing his tone and putting down his paper. 'Of course I know who you mean by the Grevils. Yes, they're a — they're a very old family.'

'Harry, that's Lucy's first cousin,' Fleur continued, pretending not to notice the look that was being exchanged between her parents. 'Harry's got some sort of title already I think. Even though he's only fourteen or so.'

'He would have,' her father announced. 'Because if my memory serves me right his father's an earl, isn't he? Or certainly a baron or some such. I must go and look them up in Who's Who.'

'And I'd better go and ring Lucy to say I can't go over to lunch.'

'Oh I don't think so, Fleur,' her father said, getting up from the table at the same time. 'I don't think your mother will mind this once. We're only having the Fanshawes and the Stallworthys, so it would probably all be a bit old for you anyway. Wouldn't you agree, Amelia?'

*   *   *

They didn't ride, the three of them that morning, because there was still too much frost in the ground right up until midday. Instead they sat on the floor of the drawing room at Stoke Park, around the huge log fire in the stone fireplace of the drawing room until their cheeks burned red, talking about what they were going to do in the future.

'Harry will have a jazz band,' Lucy announced. 'Won't you Harry?'

'Rather be a soloist I think, actually. Should imagine running a band's hell.'

'I'm going to breed exceedingly rare horses,' Lucy said, stretching upwards to ring the bell by the fireplace. 'Those terribly small ones. Fallabellas.'

'What – all your life?' Harry wondered idly, flicking through *The Field*.

'If I want to,' Lucy said.

'Weird,' said Harry.

'No points for guessing what Fleur's going to do,' Lucy said, glancing up as a maid arrived in answer to her summons. 'Anyone want a hot drink or anything?'

Nobody did, so Lucy sent the maid away again.

'That was pretty dim, Luce,' Harry remarked, lying down on his back and putting two large brown-shod feet up on the coffee table. 'You should have asked *before* summoning the maid.'

'I'll do what I like in my own house, thank you,' Lucy replied tartly, 'and I shouldn't let Grandmother catch you with your feet up there.' Harry ignored her, and began whistling *Tiger Rag* instead. 'As I was saying,' Lucy continued, turning back to Fleur after poking her tongue out at her cousin, 'there's no real point in asking *you* what you're going to do. Or be.'

'No – more a question of when,' Harry said, and then went on whistling.

'Grandmother was wondering at dinner last night when

344

you were going to start playing in public,' Lucy explained. 'I suppose once you do we shall never see you. Not that we see very much of you at the moment.'

'No-one's actually said anything yet, at least not about playing in public,' Fleur replied. 'There really aren't any definite plans. Only for my first recording.'

Harry stopped whistling again, but this time for longer, as he looked at Fleur sideways on from where he lay on the floor.

'Isn't that rather frightful?' he asked. 'People telling you when you're going to do things?'

'People do that all the time, Harry, don't be so stupid,' Lucy said. 'It's different when you're grown up, you can do as you like. But not when you're our age.'

'Fleur isn't "our age", coz,' Harry said, lifting his feet off the coffee table and stretching his legs back over his shoulders so that his feet touched the floor behind his head. 'Fleur is a peculiarity. Aren't you, Fleur? You're not our age at all. You're hundreds of thousands of years old.'

'Probably,' Fleur said, staring into the fire. 'Sometimes I think you might be right.'

'You're mad, both of you,' Lucy said. 'And there's the gong for lunch.'

By half past two the sun had defrosted the ground sufficiently to enable the three of them to ride. Lucy lent Fleur some breeches, boots and a couple of thick sweaters and they rode across the park and on to the foot of the Malverns. It was too cold and the tracks were still too frozen to ride up into the hills, so they hacked round the common land below before turning for home while it was still light. Nobody talked very much. It was far too cold to amble along in conversation as Fleur and Lucy often used to do, the temperature and the sudden chill wind forcing them to keep cantering in order to keep warm. Fleur was riding a small bay mare which Lady Stourton had bred and which like all the Stoke Park horses had perfect manners, while Harry, who was really very tall for his age, rode his Great-Aunt's big grey hunter gelding. Although nothing was said concerning each other's riding abilities, Fleur noticed Harry initially assessing everything she did once she was mounted while in turn she adjudged him likewise and just as readily.

'We'll go back through Ricketts!' Harry called over his shoulder after they'd turned for home. 'Jump some of the hunt fences!'

Then, without waiting to hear whether or not his companions were in agreement, he kicked the big grey on towards the distant copse. Lucy kicked on immediately after her cousin and feeling the little mare beneath her tugging at her bit in her anxiety to follow, Fleur tipped forward and gave her horse its head.

By the time they emerged from the twilight of the woods, Fleur was two or three lengths up on her companions, having cleared a line of good fences and several large fallen trees. They cantered on until the park gates became just visible in the growing darkness, when they all as one slowed their horses to a trot. Harry looked at his watch and said they'd better keep pushing on since his father was calling to run him back to school, so the three of them clattered down the back driveway to the house, still at the trot.

'Anything you can't do?' Harry suddenly asked Fleur out of the blue.

'Lots of things,' Fleur replied, thrown off balance by the unexpected one-off compliment.

'Right,' Harry said as he swung off his horse and handed over to Welton who had come out to greet them. 'Look, I really have to dash because that's most likely Pa now.'

Fleur shaded her eyes from the momentary dazzle of two big round headlights as a car semicircled in front of the house, and then she too slipped down from her horse.

'Goodbye,' Harry thrust a hand at her. 'I'll arrange for you to come and stay at home during the holidays.'

'You *are* elected,' Lucy laughed, once Harry strode out of earshot. 'Harry never talks to girls. All except me that is.'

'So what's this young man like?' her father asked as they were driving back to town.

'Daddy, he's not a young man,' Fleur replied with a sigh. 'He's a boy. He's not all that much older than me. He's not going to be fifteen until next month.'

'The way kids are today that makes him about eighteen compared to when I was growing up,' her father said, flicking the headlights to full beam and lighting up the frosted countryside. 'And you're way ahead of your years anyway. He comes from a good family, and I was right. His father is an earl.'

Her father shifted gears and glanced round at her. In the light of an oncoming car Fleur could see him smiling. 'Of course when and if people marry into families like that—'

'He's only fourteen, and I'm only twelve,' Fleur reminded him.

'I'm talking in the abstract,' her father informed her. 'And what I was about to say was that if you – if *one*. If *one* married into such a family, *one* does not need to have a career. Is he coming down to Stoke Park at Christmas?'

'I don't think so,' Fleur replied, deciding not to inform her father of her invitation up to Shropshire. 'Why?'

'I was simply thinking that if he does come down at Christmas you must ask him over, that was all. I know your mother would love to meet him.'

Stifling the irritation that was welling up inside her, Fleur put the radio on, this time without asking.

'Good,' her father said when he heard Albinoni's *Concerti a cinque* being played. 'Perfect for driving to. Excellent.'

Leaning her head back, Fleur closed her eyes and pretended to listen, but what she was really hearing was George Gershwin, Harry's improvisations and the way they had played together, and remembering what great fun it had all been.

28

'Danger first!' Isaac Kline shouted at Fleur from some-where behind the wardrobe in the middle of the music room. 'Not safety! Never safety! When you decide to play – remember! Always put danger first!'

Afterwards, when it was time to review the day's work, Fleur recalled what Isaac had said to her that morning as she prepared to play. In response she found her teacher frowning back at her even more intensely than was his norm, and waving one long index finger vaguely in the air while he circled around the room.

'You think I said it wrong but I didn't, Miss Fleur. When I said Danger First, I *meant* Danger First. I didn't mean what you might have thought I did, Safety First. I could see you thinking, *There he goes again, the daft old crow, getting everything front to back.* But if that's what I'd meant I should have said so. Then I hear you play and I say to myself, so what? Who needs telling, because listen to you. Already you are the adventurer. This is what excites people when you are playing, the way you play the spiccato passages just then, no? It ricochets. *Pheeew!*' He made a noise like bullets flying, making one hand into a pistol. 'Notes which are so like bullets we want to duck our heads! So bravo, Miss Fleur! Take the risks because you can, and you are prepared to do so – so take them! And remember every time you pick up your violin and bow – Danger First, *always* Danger First!'

Isaac plugged in his old electric kettle to make them both some tea, then sat down next to Fleur on the old leather sofa amidst the usual billow of dust and horsehair.

'You want to hear more?' he asked, drumming on his skull with both sets of fingers. 'Because I'm going to tell you anyway. Learning music isn't all playing and practice, music is understanding. It's a universal language so it is the way for us all to communicate. But to learn how best to play music we must learn, as I always say, not just the notes but what goes behind the notes. Except. Except that you cannot learn feelings, you can only have them. So learning about things won't make you play differently, it's only the feelings you have about things which will do this.'

'In that case I won't be able to play for years then, will I?' Fleur asked, pulling her knees up under her chin. 'At least not properly. Not like the way you play, because you're older and you've been through so much more than me.'

'No. What we don't make is comparisons. Hyperion to a satyr. That's where discontents come from. Odorous comparisons.'

'But it's true though, isn't it?' Fleur asked, as seeing the kettle boiling, Isaac jumped to his feet and reaching up for the tea caddy on the shelf above them hurried over to make the tea.

'You mean you won't be any good because you ain't been and seen what I been and seen, yes?' Isaac said, pouring tea leaves straight from the caddy into the teapot.

'Isn't that what you're saying, Isaac?'

'No. Most certainly not.'

'But what you have been through in your life—'

'No.'

'Sir Iain said that you had to play for your life. Practically every day he said—'

'No! No! No! No, Fleur! No! That is not what I am saying at all! Now have a cupcake. I brought them for us special when I went out yesterday afternoon.'

Isaac handed Fleur the box of cakes and then sat down beside her, stirring some sugar into his tea. For a minute or two both of them ate their fancies without talking, Isaac eating his slowly all the way round the edge until he was left with one last small circle of iced cake which he regarded studiously before swallowing whole, while Fleur removed the icing from hers to eat the cake part first, and then consumed the icing in triangles which she'd cut with a knife.

'Now let us straighten this thing out once and for all time,' Isaac said, wiping his hands carefully on a spotlessly clean handkerchief. 'The way I play is not because of what happen to me but because I learn how to make what happen work for me. I channel my feelings. I bet my socks that you're already doing the same, yes? You don't know it but everything that happens to you makes how you play sound different every time you pick up the violin. Because you are using your feelings. What I meant by what I say is that it is how you feel what matter, and how you use how you feel. That is all. Everyone's experience is different. For me maybe it was the war, for you maybe it is the countryside. But for you and I it is only ever good if it is love we feel, even if it is the pain of love, or the loss of it. That is what distinguish the artist from the soldier. Hatred is no good to us, because hatred makes people smaller than the people they hate. It finally leads to the whole extinction of any values at all, so where is our art then? Gone. Blown away by hatred. I have sadness in me, and you too, young as you are, I bet you have some in you even already. But to become great, you must take everything you feel and transpose it into your work in order to build understanding and compassion, to give people that hear you hope, to show them love. If you do not do this, if you cannot, then you might as well put away your violin and leave it locked up for ever till you die.'

'So Sir Iain is right then when we argue about what I should play,' Fleur wondered. 'There are certain pieces which I want to play very much – but Sir Iain says I shouldn't, at least not yet. Because he says my playing lacks depth, and that while I do my growing up I should stick to what he calls "young" music, the bright easy stuff.'

For once the perpetual frown vanished from Isaac Kline's seemingly permanently wrinkled face as he stared at Fleur. Then he muttered something to himself in German before standing up and grabbing one of his violins.

'Sir Iain is brilliant at beating time, but not talking sense,' he decided. 'Listen and I show you something.'

Isaac played, for once standing still and not walking round the room as he normally did. He simply stood by the side of the large wardrobe which was filled to bulging with his music and played. It wasn't anything Fleur had ever heard, so she just sat there and did as she was told and listened.

What she heard was utter anguish, a lament so purely painful that it made her want to cry out. As Isaac played the light changed, fading dramatically from sunlight to twilight as a winter storm suddenly brewed, so that by the time the last notes died away the heavily curtained room had been thrown into premature twilight and a quick gust of wind heralded a vicious shower of sleet.

'Okay,' Isaac said, putting down his violin. 'Now you play it.'

'I couldn't,' Fleur replied.

'Here's the music,' Isaac told her, pulling open a drawer in the bottom of the wardrobe and taking out an old faded folio. 'I have the music so all you have to do is read it.'

'Yes I know, but there's no point in me playing it,' Fleur insisted. 'You know what I mean, Isaac.'

'I know what you mean, Fleur. Because I've played it and in such a way you think you can't play it like I played it, and that's putting it simply. But when you hear Menuhin play the Elgar, do you see no point in playing that since he play it so well? No, of course not.

You know you can play it in your way. That is what the great composer does, he says here I am – play me. So why not this piece? I tell you why, because you think this piece is Isaac Kline. I say stuff! Listen again if you please.'

Once more Isaac picked up his violin and, after a moment while he stood there in the strange grey light with his eyes closed, he began to play one of Fleur's own compositions.

This time instead of the anguish of death and heartbreak in a frozen corner of some terrible place, Fleur could feel the warmth of an early summer morning and then see a girl catching her first sight of a white deer which was staring out at her from the shadows of a woodland. Now the girl holds her breath and freezes herself immobile in case the creature disappears back into the trees, or in case she has imagined it. Then suddenly a new rhythm shows the white deer walking out of the safety of the woods and across a dew-drenched lawn to stand in front of the girl who sits on a tree stump. It watches curiously as the girl holds out a basket full of bread to the other deer who feed from it undisturbed. Then a change of key recalls the moment of triumph as the white deer decides to join the feast, while the song of a morning lark hangs high in the air above them, then a rush and flurry of notes as the deer all jostle for new positions, followed by a passage of total tranquillity as all the deer now feed quietly from the girl's hand, their big wet noses pushing the bread to the ground while their stumps of tails flick up and down and up and down with the pleasure of it all, until a long minor chord shows something has startled them and their running feet are now a scatter of notes picked out across the strings pizzicato as they flee for the dark cover of the woodland once more, leaving a quiet garden at the start of a hot summer day with the lark still singing happily and undisturbed high above.

'Now, I play your piece with feelings of my own. But did I still make you think what you thought when you wrote it?'

'Yes,' Fleur agreed.

'Then do me the honour of playing my piece too. Not as I play it, but as you play it, with your feelings.'

At first Fleur hardly dared, not in case she made a fool of herself, but in case she betrayed Isaac's memories. So when she looked at the music she looked at it without seeing it. Then suddenly it became clear to her, just as if someone had taken a torch and shone it onto the manuscript she was holding. Setting the music on her stand in its usual place by the window, Fleur found her balance, cast her head slightly back and softly drew her bow down across the top string.

At first she saw nothing as she played, no images or landscapes, no people or places. She just felt a terrible pain and an inconsolable sadness for everything dreadful past and future, everything that had happened to love and everything which was about to happen to love. Then, as part of this, a strong curly-haired young man all at once becomes a bald and starving skeleton stretching out his arms to people who are forever gone from him and from the world, except in the memory of the music which flows from her violin.

'Good,' Isaac said as soon as the last note had died away, leaving not time or room for sentiment. 'Now, what I say is that you played that better than I and – no, don't interrupt me please to say this is not so because I am the judge here. I say you played that better than I, just as I played your piece better than you. I, who have never been a small girl in a garden seeing the wonder for the first time of a white deer . And you who know nothing of Treblinka. Maybe, maybe we each play these pieces best because we let them spring from ourselves. I cannot speak for you, but when I play I imagined nothing of your garden. I just allowed my feeling to speak through the music. Perhaps this is the same for you.'

'Yes,' Fleur nodded slowly. 'Yes I think it was. I'm sure it was.'

'Then I say good again.' Isaac smiled, but very differently. Usually when he smiled it was teasingly, or self-mockingly, or even childishly. But this time he smiled at Fleur with real love and genuine pride. 'So now you tell Sir Iain you are capable of playing anything, and if you don't I certainly will. Play the Beethoven Concerto now if you wish, and then play it again later. And then later still because you will always bring something to it, something new, now that you understand. Go with yourself and where you are. Play who you are and play when you are. Don't try and play the experience of others. Feel for your music, imagine what it says and what you want to say, but always play exactly who you are and no-one else. Above all things, follow your bliss.'

29

A week before Christmas Fleur was called in to see Sir Iain for the final review that year of her progress.

'Here we are, Master,' Gregory Rogers said when Fleur came into the study where the two men awaited her. 'The entire regiment, ready for your inspection.'

'Do you have to wear jeans?' Sir Iain asked. 'I do think little girls should look like little girls, and not something on a ranch.'

'Oh please don't be 'ard on the child, Sir H'iain!' Gregory said in his mock-Dickensian cockney. 'Why she's bin sweepin' chimneys all day long and in't 'ad time to change 'er poor togs!'

'Just as long as we don't appear like that on the concert platform,' Sir Iain replied, putting down his tumbler of whisky and picking up a sheaf of papers which he waved once or twice at Fleur. 'Talking of which, it seems we are fast approaching that point, faster than I would have dared hope.'

'Who's a clever girl then?' Gregory wondered, arching his eyebrows.

'First of all your teachers' assessments,' Sir Iain continued. 'Not that they count for much between the three of us here, but I should imagine they'll keep your father happy. They are positively adulatory. According to that load of over-paid parasites you're the next Brain of Britain.'

'Twice two?' Gregory asked her.

'Five,' Fleur replied with a grin.

'Much more to the point is what Isaac has told us this afternoon,' Sir Iain continued, ignoring the by-play.

'As you know I was most impressed with your, as it were, end-of-term recital which we attended yesterday. I thought that altogether your playing showed a near perfect blend of refinement and exuberance, and I have no doubt that with careful management and presentation you will make a profound impact when we let you loose upon the public. The question is of course, *when*. And this more than anything concerns the three of us this afternoon.'

'I don't think I'm quite ready yet, Sir Iain,' Fleur volunteered. 'I mean the plan was a year of tuition and then perhaps a talk about when I was to play my first concert.'

'Yes, yes,' Sir Iain said impatiently, holding his glass up to Gregory for a refill. 'But that was before Isaac had a chance to assess you and when I for my part considered you would need all of that time, if not indeed even more. This no longer appears to be the case. So if I may – and if you'll sit down and stop hopping from one leg to another – I will outline what we have in mind for you, always remembering that we have to put our proposals before your parents.'

Sir Iain sighed and looked glumly at Gregory who was busy refilling his drink and who looked even more glumly back at him.

'Why?' Fleur asked a little anxiously, imagining her mentor knew more than he was letting on. 'They haven't said anything, have they? I mean my parents?'

'No, no, at least not yet,' Sir Iain replied. 'But only because we've been holding our cards very close to our chests.'

'One peek is worth two finesses remember, Flower,' Gregory reminded Fleur, referring to the long winter evenings she had spent learning bridge with himself and Sir Iain.

'The point is, my dear child, that while I am convinced your father is a quite excellent surgeon—'

'He's just got a consultancy at long last,' Fleur said. 'At least not of his own, but a junior partnership I think it's called.'

'Yes so I gather,' Sir Iain said, breathing in deeply. 'I gathered at some length in fact when we last spoke. Anyway while your father is doubtless an excellent surgeon, it is my opinion that – as I understand the phrase has it – he knows chicken shit about music.'

Fleur didn't know what to do, whether to blush or laugh as she looked at the two serious faces watching her. Of them all, and most surprisingly, Sir Iain was the first to crack, giving a great hoot of laughter and slapping the top of his desk with one hand.

'Dear child – it was worth it just to see your face!' he cried, producing a red silk handkerchief to mop his eyes. 'I thought your eyes were going to pop out of your head, didn't you, Gregory?'

By now all three of them were helpless with laughter, with Gregory having to hold on to the back of his master's chair to stop himself sliding to the floor.

'Oh dear, sorry Flower,' he said as he regained control of himself. 'But it's as well you hear what he's really like now, because when he gets in front of the orchestra—'

Gregory pulled a terrible face and rolled his eyes upwards so that all that was left to see were the whites, which only set Fleur off again.

'All right, all right, children, that's quite enough,' Sir Iain ordered. 'Officially the Christmas party doesn't start until we get this young lady's reports out of the way. So. Where were we?'

'Discussing Mr Fisher's musical knowledge,' Gregory reminded him. 'I shall go no further.'

'Thank you, dear boy, where would I be without you,' Sir Iain mock-sighed before clasping his beautifully manicured hands together and turning his attention fully to Fleur. 'Now then, Miss Fisher.'

'Miss Fisher-Dilke, master,' Gregory corrected him.

'Indeed. Now then, Miss Fisher-Dilke. It is perfectly apparent the time has come to let your light shine before everyone. Isaac has confirmed my own belief that you are far in advance of any other pupils he has taught, and not just pupils of your age. Isaac says you have a truly unique and prodigious talent, and believing this to be indeed the case, Fleur, here is the plan. It is for you to make your first recording in the spring, with myself conducting obviously, and we are in the process of firming up the deal with Celestion. What we must decide now is what you shall play, and from what I have heard I would say the Elgar would seem to be the correct choice.'

'Not the Beethoven?'

'No. Isaac has explained to me your feelings about playing the Beethoven and I see your point as I see his. I may well be wrong in thinking you are not ready to play it. But I would prefer to be wrong privately than for you to be wrong publicly, while all of us know how well you are playing the Elgar. Make no mistakes about the Elgar either, young lady. It requires as much discipline as the Beethoven, particularly if we are to avoid any undue sentimentality.'

'I see,' Fleur replied, tossing back her mane of dark hair which was growing ever longer. 'I'm more than happy to play the Elgar because I so love it. Perhaps we can tackle the Beethoven next. So all we have to do then is ask my parents?'

'All we have to do is tell your parents, my dear. After all, I'm sure your father would hardly invite me to help him diagnose one of his patients. Although knowing doctors, I'm sure I'd come a lot closer to the truth than most of his profession. So if we are all met, Gregory, I think you can get out the paper hats and the crackers.'

*   *   *

True to his word, Harry had invited Fleur to stay with his family for Christmas, but her father would not hear of it. He reminded Fleur, when she rang to ask him if she might go, that Christmas was a time for families to be together so such a visit was quite out of the question. Harry seemed none too bothered by Fleur having to refuse, telling her he'd fully expected it and inviting her up in the New Year instead, an invitation Fleur accepted in advance of asking her parents.

There was one thing she did ask her parents before she came home and that was whether they could have Deanie down to stay for the holiday, and her mother promised her that they would do their best.

'And?' Fleur asked when she had finally got home. 'Is she going to be able to?'

'She's going to try her very best,' her mother answered. 'But it is a very long way, sweetie, so don't bank on it too much.'

Fleur asked if she could ring her old nanny but apparently according to her mother she wasn't on the telephone, so she asked for an address so that she could write to her as well as send a Christmas card. But her mother said she couldn't remember it offhand, promising instead that she would send Fleur's card off with her own when the time came. 'Where exactly is she?' Fleur asked, finally smelling a rat.

'I wasn't going to tell you, at least not before Christmas,' Amelia confessed, 'but poor Deanie isn't really herself so she's in a home, poor sweetie.'

'What sort of home, Mamma?'

'It's very nice, Fleur, so you don't have to look so worried. It's the sort of place designed specially to look after people in Deanie's condition.'

'What exactly is Deanie's condition?'

'Sort of senility really, sweetie. Although they call it something else nowadays according to your father. But as I said, she really isn't herself and just wouldn't be able to cope living alone. Now then, I really must get on with making the Christmas pudding. Are you going to come and help?'

Unable to bear the thought of Deanie being stuck in some old people's home so far away, and feeling guilty that she hadn't got round to writing to her before, Fleur vowed privately to herself that as soon as she had earned enough money she'd bring her old nanny down to live somewhere nearby. She wrote her a long letter telling her so, to which she received no reply. She didn't even get a Christmas card from her, but then as her mother kept saying that was hardly to be expected since Deanie simply wasn't herself any more.

As far as the family celebrations went Christmas would have seemed like any other weekend had it not been for the decorations and the visiting carol singers. The only event of real note was the arrival of a specially delivered parcel for Fleur, labelled 'Not to be opened until Christmas Day.'

Fleur left it till last, although it was not too long to wait because there were not very many presents since there were only the three of them. When she unwrapped the heavy duty brown paper she discovered a solid cardboard box on which was taped a large white envelope marked Fleur. Opening that first, she saw it was a Christmas card with a letter inside it, and that the card was from Leo Stayner. He wished her a very happy Christmas and an even better New Year but told her to open the present before she read the letter.

Inside the box, under a mound of special foam packing, was a violin.

'Who on earth's sent you an old violin?' her father said, looking up from trying to find out how the tie press Amelia had gifted him worked. 'I trust it's a halfway decent one.'

'It's Mr Stayner's,' Fleur replied, frowning deeply as she removed the instrument from the last of its packing. 'It's a Guarnerius.'

'Aren't Stradivariuses the only ones worth anything?' Richard continued without much interest.

'Not really,' Fleur replied. 'A lot of musicians prefer Guarneri. Isaac thinks a good one beats a Strad any day.'

'Must be worth a bit then.'

'It's worth more than a bit. It's worth everything to Mr Stayner.'

'Then what on earth's he doing giving it to you?'

'I'd better read his letter and I'll find out.'

My Dear Fleur,

I should have written to you weeks ago but I wasn't very well. The malaise was all of my own doing but I'm fine now and back in shape.

I wanted to write to apologize to you for my dreadful behaviour when you told me you were leaving. There was no excuse for it and even though I ask your forgiveness I won't blame you in the slightest if you refuse me. The point is I am lucky not just to have taught you but to have known you. It was ridiculous, greedy and selfish of me to have tried to lay any future claim to you, any claim other than to have been as you so rightly said your first teacher. How many people ever get the chance to teach someone a hundredth as talented as you, let alone you yourself? So now that I am back to my senses I thank God to have had the chance to be part of what I know is going to be your wonderful life and career.

I want you to have my violin. Not on loan but for ever. Do not listen to anyone who says you must send it back because of what it is worth and that I am a poor man, because I'm not. I have known and taught you, and therefore I am a rich man indeed. I want you to have it for two reasons. Firstly you will play it better than anyone has ever played it before and probably will ever play it again, and instruments such as this are meant to be played by people like you. Secondly I want you to have it for purely selfish reasons. Whenever I hear you play from now on, I shall know you are playing on the violin I gave you. This way I shall always continue to be part of your wonderful life whatever happens.

I hope you find it in your heart to forgive me and that one day when you are famous, as I know you will be, we will meet again. I wish you all the luck in the world, and send you my love.

Yours, Leo Stayner.

'So?' her father asked, holding out his hand. 'May I read what he has to say?'

'He says he's lending it to me, because he doesn't use it any more,' Fleur said, folding the letter up carefully and tucking it under the velvet-covered neck support in the violin's case.

'Lending it?' her father echoed. 'And what happens if anything happens to it while you have it?'

'It's all right,' Fleur said, remembering in time what Leo had said when they had once talked about such an eventuality. 'He says I'm not to worry because he has it insured.'

Neither of her parents were particularly interested in hearing what the instrument sounded like. Her father even joked that to hear one violin was to hear them all, although as far as he was concerned one violin was more than enough, so therefore Fleur waited to play it until Boxing Day when she had been asked over to tea and dinner by Lucy. She took the instrument with her because she knew there was every likelihood that Lady Stourton would have someone staying who played the piano, or failing that she knew she would be able to persuade Lady Stourton to accompany her.

As it happened her assumption had been right and one of Lady Stourton's house guests was the concert pianist Herbert Church, an affable man rumoured to have spent more time on the racecourse than in practice.

'We shall play a joke on him, you'll see,' Lady Stourton said when Fleur showed her Leo Stayner's gift. 'There is nothing Herbert enjoys more than a practical joke so you just leave this to me.'

After dinner when the distinguished guest had been coaxed into playing for Lady Stourton's house party, Lady Stourton went over to the famous pianist and explained for all to hear that her granddaughter's young friend had been given a violin for Christmas and was dying to have a go at playing it.

'But of course! Why not?' Herbert Church exclaimed, turning to Fleur as she approached the piano, violin in hand. 'What shall it be, little girl? What do you know? Do you know shall we say "Three Blind Mice"?'

'Yes, at least I think so,' Fleur said, entering fully into the spirit of the prank.

'Good,' Lady Stourton said poker-faced. 'Just as long as you don't play it too fast, Herbert.'

The pianist took the nursery rhyme at an almost funereal pace, followed at an equally funereal distance by the heavily frowning and grimacing Fleur, while Lucy had to stuff her hankie in her mouth and hide behind the sofa not to give the game away.

'Well done, little girl,' Herbert Church said when the excruciating piece of music finally came to an end. 'And for an encore?' he said with a wink to his hostess.

'What an excellent notion, Herbert!' Lady Stourton agreed. 'I was about to suggest the very same thing myself. Fleur dear, what would you like to play for us now?'

Fleur pulled the very worst I-wonder-what face she could imagine, before replying. 'How about *Dancing Doll*?' she asked very seriously. 'Do you know that?'

'Dancing Doll?' Herbert Church laughed, almost beside himself. 'You mean Poldini's Dancing Doll?'

'I think so,' Fleur nodded.

'Or even better, Poldini's Dancing Doll as arranged by Kreisler, I suppose.'

'Yes. Yes that's the one.'

'How about just doing "Three Blind Mice" once again, little girl, eh?' the pianist smiled and winked. 'And this time I'll try and keep up with you.'

'I'd rather do Dancing Doll if you don't mind,' Fleur replied. 'Unless of course you can't play it.'

'Oh I think I can just about manage it,' Herbert Church said with a smile. 'The point is to see how you fare, eh?'

He knew how Fleur was going to fare as soon as he heard the first notes sing out from the Guarneri and realizing he had been had, the great soloist at once slipped into the role of the perfect accompanist and together he and Fleur played what he later announced to be the definitive performance of Poldini's miniature.

'Bravo, young lady,' he said, bestowing a huge kiss on the back of one of her hands. 'If you were not going to be such a great violinist which you obviously are, I would say you would have an equally distinguished career as an actress. Now how about you and I really showing them what we can do by playing Wieniawski's Scherzo-Tarantella? Do you know it?'

'Oh yes!' Fleur agreed enthusiastically. 'And I just love playing it.'

By the time the evening was over Fleur and Herbert Church were the firmest of friends, and the pianist was seriously suggesting that they should do a recital together in the very near future.

'I can't say yes to anything without consulting Isaac and Sir Iain,' Fleur explained, 'but if they agreed I should love to.'

'Then we shall,' Herbert Church promised. 'Sir Iain is a very old friend of mine and so together we will make the arrangements. Obviously this will have to be after your concert debut, but it is something we certainly and simply must do. Now to cement our new friendship let us play everyone good night with Elgar's *Salut d'amour*. For after all it is love and nothing else that makes this funny old world of ours go round, do you not agree?'

The day before New Year's Eve Harry's mother rang to say she was very sorry but Fleur's visit to Brockeley would have to be postponed because Harry had been taken ill with severe tonsillitis, something it appeared he had been prone to since he was a child. Could Fleur possibly come and stay when he was up and about again? Lady Grevil enquired, perhaps around the second week in January? Unfortunately this wouldn't be possible, a deeply disappointed Fleur told Harry's mother, because by then she would have returned to resume her studies in London.

Harry wrote to Fleur several times before she left The Folly, and three times a week once she was back in London, which was how their friendship burgeoned. But once Harry was back at Eton there seemed no chance for them to meet until the following school holiday. Luckily Harry was a dedicated letter writer and even though he probably had less actual free time than Fleur, wrote at great length and in direct contrast to his somewhat clipped conversational style, while Fleur wrote almost as shyly as she behaved in Harry's presence, even though she felt more confident with him than she did with anyone other than Isaac and Gregory. Harry also embellished the margins of his letters with excellent caricatures of various of his teachers and his fellow pupils, characters whom he finally developed into a strip cartoon of his school life which he enclosed in his later letters on a separate sheet of paper, and which Fleur collected and pasted in a scrap book purchased solely for that purpose.

The thing Fleur liked most about Harry was that he made her laugh. At first she had mistaken his solemnity for just that, but very soon she'd realized that the face he wore was a poker face, and what was hiding behind it was someone very droll and very bright. Up until Harry there had been no-one in Fleur's life who had made her really laugh, not even Gregory Rogers whose humour was finally a little too dry and waspish for Fleur's taste and age.

But Harry was more than just someone Fleur found funny. Harry was a soulmate. Behind the long face he kept, and under the rather elderly clothes he wore, was a genuinely thoughtful and creative young man. Harry was also a nonconformist, not seditious or rebellious just for the sake of it like so many of the other teenagers with whom Fleur occasionally came into contact, he was just naturally iconoclastic. Fleur thought playing jazz had a lot to do with it, a theory which prompted a six-week cartoon strip from Harry depicting *The Jazz Rake's Progress*, in which after hearing his first blue note a young and bright-eyed Harry degenerates into a bearded and dark-bespectacled bopper dedicated to plotting the overthrow of Eton.

Most of all Harry got into her music.

'Okay,' Isaac asked one morning during their coffee break. 'Let's hear all about him.'

'About who, Isaac?' Fleur stuttered, quite thrown off her balance. 'Who do you want to hear about?'

'I want to hear about the young man who has got inside your violin, young lady. When you play the Beethoven sonata this morning, *O sole mio*.' Isaac slapped his forehead with the back of his hand mock-dramatically. 'I thought of nothing but Mantovani and his Silver Strings.'

'Don't be rotten, Isaac,' Fleur said with a grin, pretending to study the score on her lap.

'I'm awaiting,' Isaac sighed. 'So who is he?'

'He's called Harry, and he's just a friend, that's all.'

'Good. I'm glad, and I hope I'm not going to be sorry too,' Isaac said, finishing his coffee. 'If you're not careful, when the kissing start, the music often stop, you know.'

'No I don't,' Fleur said hotly. 'Anyway it's not that sort of thing. As I just said, he's just a friend.'

'Of course it can help, too, sometimes,' Isaac nodded, drumming on his head with both hands. 'I said to myself as I hear you play since you return, that there is a certain amount more *rapture*.'

'I've been practising a lot, that's all,' Fleur replied, still on the defensive. 'And this violin has made a lot of difference to my sound. You said so as soon as you heard me play it.'

'I am talking internals, Fleur. It goes back to what we are discussing before, about feelings. And I shouldn't say what I say about kissing and music, that was stupid of me in your case because even at your tender age I still say nothing can take you away from your music. It's just. Oh nothing.'

'What?' Fleur asked.

'Nothing,' Isaac said, suddenly standing up. 'It would just be – well what it would be would be indescribable, that's all.'

'Isaac, I am only twelve, you know,' Fleur said, 'and Harry's not quite fifteen. We're hardly going to run off and get married. And even if we did—'

'Oh it's not out of the question, young lady. Not when we remember Romeo and Juliet.'

'Honestly, Isaac,' Fleur laughed. 'I mean even just for fun, suppose we did. I'd never give up playing. Not for anything.'

'You promise me that, young lady?'

'Cross my heart, Isaac. Not for anything.'

Even so, Isaac still worried, because Harry started coming up to London during term time, at first just for the

Sundays when his parents were up in town, and then later for whole weekends when it appeared that for some reason either one or both of his parents had cause to be away from their seat in Shropshire. Initially he would just telephone Fleur and they would spend hours talking before Harry had to go back to school. Isaac found this out when Gregory Rogers rang him one Sunday evening to discuss Fleur's arrangements, complaining that he had meant to ring earlier but couldn't because as usual Madam had been on the phone all afternoon to her *jeune amour*.

Then came the request for a date, not from Harry but from Fleur.

'He wants to take me out to a concert,' she told Isaac.

'Isn't that a bit of whatever it's called? A busman's vacation?' Isaac wondered.

'He wants to take me to a jazz concert,' Fleur replied.

'Then there's no good asking me, young lady,' Isaac said. 'This is a matter for the committee.'

Fleur sat in the kitchen helping Rita bake while the triumvirate cloistered themselves in Sir Iain's study to deliberate on the matter of whether or not Fleur was to be allowed to go to hear the Humphrey Lyttleton Band in concert at the Royal Festival Hall.

'Your father said no boyfriends,' Sir Iain began, when Fleur had been called in to hear their decision. 'However I gather your father approves of this youngster—'

'Because as teach here says,' Gregory interrupted, nodding in Isaac's direction, 'the boy is rich and entitled. I should be so lucky!' Gregory laughed. 'Rich and entitled indeedy.'

'On the other hand, I have to say that all work and no play—' Sir Iain continued, only to be interrupted this time by Isaac.

'You have your first recording in six week,' Isaac said. 'All I'm saying is every minute counts, and anything other is distracting.'

'If I may be allowed to finish *one* sentence?' Sir Iain asked. 'Thank you. As far as your parents go, young lady, I consider it a matter of what the eye does not see. And as far as your proposed outing goes, my thinking on the matter is that it is much more likely to do harm than good were we to impose a ban on any, shall we say, social activities? Therefore we voted two to one in favour of you going to your concert.'

'I only have your good interests at heart, Fleur, that was all,' Isaac protested, in answer to Fleur's look.

'Believe that and see pigs fly, Flower,' Gregory sighed. 'Uncle Izzy voted no because Uncle Izzy is plain jealous.'

The Humphrey Lyttleton Band in concert was Fleur's first sight of a band in action and she was immediately captivated by the infectious enthusiasm and good humour of the music, although at first she had been quite unable to believe what was happening to the normally composed and sedate Harry once the band started playing. It was as if the whole of his body had become infected with an uncontrollable twitch. Both his knees jigged up and down with the beat, while with eyes closed and a heavenly smile on his face he rocked his head in half time from side to side, his fingers playing first the piano part on the top of his thighs and then the drum part. So that by the time the band was playing the last choruses, the whole of his body was twisting and turning and wriggling as if he was in thrall to some unappeasable itch.

Yet despite her initial amusement, in no time Fleur found that she too was quite unable to keep herself or her feet still, so infectious were the rhythms. The whole event enthralled her, the crisp, bitingly bright sound and the sheer drive and energy of the improvised music. She loved the theatricality of it as well, the way the lights danced in sparkles off the polished brass of the trumpet and trombone, and the drummer's sizzling cymbals, the expressions on the faces of the players, particularly the perpetually grumpy look on the face of the bandleader whenever he soloed, eyes shut, one foot tapping out the beat and one shoulder hunched up behind his shining trumpet, and the way the pensive and apparently puzzled alto saxophonist played his sax out of one side of his mouth. Most of all she loved the rapport between the players as they stood and listened to each other's solos, shouting out encouragement to each other, clapping appreciation at a high note or roaring with glee at a musical quote.

'That was fun,' Fleur told Harry afterwards as they walked back across Waterloo Bridge. 'I think all concerts should be like that, full of life and fun.'

'Some Proms are, yes?' Harry replied. 'Classical music doesn't have to be stuffy.'

'I'll make sure my concerts aren't,' Fleur said. 'At least I shall try. And when I give recitals I shall always include some George Gershwin.'

'Why not?' Harry said, sinking his hands in his overcoat pockets. 'Maybe some Bernstein as well. You know *Somewhere*? From *West Side Story*? It's not bad.'

Harry began to sing it as they went on walking across the bridge over the Thames, but had to stop halfway to clear his throat.

'Damn,' he swore. 'Think I'm getting another round of blasted tonsillitis. Mother says I'm going to have to have them out.'

'What, now?'

'Soon anyway. Took me to see a specialist and he said they should come out straightaway. Reason I'm thin, 'pparently. And why I take yonks to eat. Want to see?'

'Not much,' Fleur replied, as Harry stopped thoughtfully under a streetlight and opened his mouth wide.

'Quite interesting actually,' Harry continued, catching Fleur up. 'Specialist said they're prize ones.'

'So when are they thinking of taking them out?'

'I dunno. Spring hols some time. They only keep you in for three or four days. Right. Now I'm going to be blind,' Harry announced, taking a pair of dark glasses from his pocket. 'And you're going to be my eyes.'

'That wasn't funny, Harry,' Fleur said, pinching herself as hard as she could to stop herself from laughing as they got off the bus in Oxford Street. 'Particularly you sitting on that woman's lap.'

'That was your fault,' Harry said, still in his dark glasses. 'You should have helped me to an empty seat.'

'I don't care, it wasn't funny,' Fleur insisted, before giving in once more to an attack of helpless laughter. 'And then when you tried to get off the driver's end—'

'It wasn't that funny,' Harry said.

'No it wasn't!' Fleur shrieked, holding onto a lamppost for support. 'It wasn't in the slightest bit funny!'

'This person, some fan or something, asked George Shearing — know who I mean by George Shearing? He's this blind jazz pianist and anyway someone asked him if he'd been blind all his life and George Shearing said no, not yet.'

Fleur started to laugh all over again so Harry took her by the arm and walked her on to the next bus stop where she was to catch her bus back to Hampstead.

'Are you sure you don't want me to come with you? I don't mind,' Harry said.

'No honestly,' Fleur replied, wiping the corners of her eyes carefully with her hankie. 'The bus stops right outside the house. Anyway, it's so late you won't get home yourself.'

'I suppose so,' Harry agreed. 'I spent the money I was keeping for a taxi. As long as you'll be all right.'

'I'll be fine. Thanks for a terrific evening. It was the best time I've ever had, I think.'

'Me too,' Harry said. 'I'll write to you soon as I'm back at school. Goodbye.'

Seeing Fleur's bus coming, Harry put out a hand for Fleur to shake, but this time after a moment's hesitation Fleur reached up and putting her arms around his neck kissed him quickly on the lips.

'Goodbye, Harry,' she said. 'I'll never forget this evening. I promise.'

The next morning when she put down her violin having played through the Mozart sonata she was working on, Isaac nodded half a dozen or so times before speaking.

'Yes,' he said finally. 'I have to say that was perfect and that I was wrong. Today in your music I hear you rejoice and because of it I must apologize for being such a troll. Gregory was right, I was just being jealous, so please forgive me. Instead of adding I might have made you subtract. So. So don't say nothing, please. But to show you forgive a foolish old man, play me the Mozart once again and fill all this room again with the sunshine of your life.'

30

The time was now fast approaching the date fixed for Fleur's recording debut and as it did she found she had less and less time to write to Harry and finally even to talk to him on the telephone. Every one of her waking moments was taken up in a preparation so intense that some mornings when she awoke Fleur could hardly even remember going to bed the night before. But Harry understood entirely, with a maturity way beyond his years.

'People with two brains like me grasp these things much more clearly,' he wrote in one of his even more regular letters. 'Having two brains enables one to see both sides of any argument as well as being able to look both ways at the same time before crossing the road. So be of good faith. I dig.'

'And I have this brilliant idea,' Isaac told her one morning when they were only a week away from the recording date. 'I have discussed it with Sir, who at first of course thinks I am mad, but the more I tell him the more convincing I must be because now he says this is entirely up to you. Okay?'

'If you tell me what it is exactly, Isaac, I'd be able to tell you what I think as well,' Fleur replied, carefully unwrapping that morning's chocolate-cake ration. 'So go on, tell me.'

'I say you don't rehearse with the orchestra.'

Isaac sat back on the sofa amidst the usual dust cloud, while Fleur put her slice of cake back on her plate untouched and turned to her teacher.

'I'll tell you what I think, Isaac,' she said. 'I think for once Sir's right. I think perhaps you are dotty.'

'You just wait till you hear,' Isaac replied. 'Not only is it perfectly possible, but it has been done before! This nipper, this child, four, five years younger than you are now, at a day's notice she play the Paganini – in concert – *without rehearsal*! And everyone say, including the conductor who is a big friend of mine, they all say – critics, audience, orchestra, conductor – the whole bang shoot all say it was *fantastic*. No preconceptions, see? No ready-made contrivances, no tricks of the trade, no luggage brought and unpacked in advance – just a musician playing and the orchestra responding with total honesty to the moment. Now you see what I'm getting at? Now you understand? I even said to Sir maybe this is the way we do the concert as well, but of course such a thing is not possible in this instance because it will be the same orchestra, but no matter. If we can pull it off in the recording studio, it will be a sensation! And it will be a sensation and I tell you why, because of the way you have arrived at the Elgar. When the orchestra hear you, they will start to play as if they too are all this brilliant! So? So what do you say, partner? We go for broke, or we play for safe?'

Fleur thought long and hard while the two of them sat in silence, the only noise in the cluttered room being the purring of the cat in its usual place up the bass pipe of the harmonium.

'We go for broke, Isaac,' Fleur said. 'What was it you said about adventure?'

'It is the path to perpetuity of fame.'

'Then we definitely go for broke.'

The orchestra were not so sure, but then Fleur was not to know this, not until afterwards. Sir Iain had conducted rehearsals as if Fleur was to join them at the moment when the soloist normally came in to rehearse, before telling them at the eleventh hour that she was indisposed and would be unable to attend.

'The leader, Ivor, naturally enough wondered when you would be well enough to rehearse,' Sir Iain told his party over dinner, 'and of course since we have privately agreed that Miss Fisher-Dilke here will never be "well enough" to attend rehearsals, I simply said that we must take it day by day, hour by hour. But of course that I have every hope our soloist will be well enough to attend rehearsals tomorrow.'

'Which of course I won't,' Fleur said, still thoroughly enjoying the adventure.

'Of course you will not, my dear.'

'And it's still a badly infected finger, is it?'

'It is, which of course the good doctor − *cough cough*,' Sir Iain continued with a wink at Fleur, 'is going to lance tomorrow afternoon in a last-ditch effort to save the day.'

'Thank God for Doctor − what is his name exactly?' Gregory asked.

'Dr Zeus,' Sir Iain sighed, as if to ask how could Gregory be so foolish. 'Have you forgotten that if it hadn't been for Dr Zeus you would not be here, dear boy?'

'Do you know, maestro, I have?' Gregory replied equally straight-faced. 'What was it the good doctor did exactly?'

'He was the one who lifted the stone, Gregory,' Sir Iain replied, hooding his eyes. 'And let you slide out.'

Harry telephoned her from school the night before the recording.

'Are you nervous?' he wanted to know.

'Not really,' Fleur told him. 'Not any more. I seem to get worked up about things for days and weeks in advance, and then when they come round I feel sort of dead. It was just the same with the school concert.'

'That's right, because you shouldn't be nervous,' Harry replied. 'Read this thing once 'bout a musician who used to be really ill before concerts. Until this other guy in the band told him he was daft, because the audience were really much more worried that they weren't going to enjoy themselves. So if you're any good, you can't be nervous.'

'Okay, Harry,' Fleur laughed. 'I dig.'

'I shall be thinking of you,' Harry told her solemnly, and then rang off.

In the post next morning there was a parcel for Fleur, which Rita gave her at breakfast.

'Here's good luck from me too, Missie Floor,' Rita said, looking very serious. 'You play real nice and shiny now.'

Rita's card was very large with a silver horseshoe on the front and printed inside was every good wish for the recipient on her wedding day, while the parcel was from Harry and contained a small and extremely ancient Teddy bear dressed in a very loud tie, dark glasses, and a blue beret. The message tied round his neck simply read To the best in the band, Love Harry, followed by their favourite counting-in joke which went: One, two – one two three four five.

With the recording studios only a few blocks away from Sir Iain's house, Sir Ian left first and then a quarter of an hour before they were due to start sent Gregory back to fetch Fleur, who had spent the time practising with Isaac before going to get dressed in what she and Gregory decided would be the best and most comfortable outfit, her favourite black Snoopy tee shirt, a bright red corduroy skirt, matching red socks and old but clean white tennis shoes, with her dark hair collected and tied down her back in one long plait.

'How is the orchestra?' Isaac wanted to know of Gregory, as they headed for the studios. 'I am amazed they are not come out on strike.'

'Oh they're past the point of rebellion, Izzy,' Gregory replied. 'Now they are simply curious. How about you, Flower?' Gregory caught Fleur's eyes in his driving mirror and made a face at her when he saw her serious expression. 'Penny for them,' he said.

'It's nothing very interesting,' Fleur replied. 'I'm just thinking of someone.'

'Oh yes?' Gregory mock-sighed. 'And no prizes for guessing who.'

'Well you lose, Gregory,' Fleur replied, leaning back and shutting her eyes. 'Because as it happens that's not who I'm thinking of at all.'

She was thinking of morning, of just after dawn, thinking of herself as she made her way quietly down the garden as the sun began to shine through the faint blue haze, along the path and down the slope which ran towards the clearing in front of the woods, just by the old beech which had once been nearly pushed out of the ground by a gale, seeing herself stop now where she always stopped, by the old tree trunk where she stands with her basket of bread, stands without moving or calling until out of the faint blue mist, its shiny black nose twitching to catch her scent, large ears laid back in case of any danger from behind, out from the deep dark of the woods and of the faint blue mist of dawn the white deer comes to stand before her.

'Thank you, ladies and gentlemen,' Sir Iain says as the studio falls to utter quiet, the bray and the hee-haw of the orchestra's tuning finally over, the plick of each of Fleur's strings checked and double-checked, while the second hand of the clock on the wall jerks remorselessly on counting out the seconds in silence.

'Absolute quiet please, everyone,' the tall, immaculately dressed conductor reminds his players as he waits for the signal, as he watches for the light to go to red, and when it does he raises his baton in his right hand while every eye watches him past violins and cellos, over flutes, oboes and clarinets, by the necks of their basses, above the shiny surfaces of their drums until the baton flicks and the violins are in on the first beat, the tympanum and the basses on the second and the concerto begins, gathering pace and urgency with each sweep of Sir Iain's baton as the orchestra starts to explore the several different keys the composer has chosen to state his half-dozen themes, each theme so closely related that it seems to flow into the next one quite seamlessly until suddenly and as if out of nowhere the moment they have all awaited, that very moment finally comes, the moment Fleur Fisher-Dilke is born for evermore, the moment her life begins for real, the moment when her heart-stopping voice is to be heard in full flight for the first time by a waiting world, as after a half-second of silence which hangs in the air from her violin the first notes are slowly drawn, eight deeply expressive notes sing out, a sound so beautiful, so fully rounded and so deeply passionate that it seems to catch not only Isaac unprepared as he hears the sound through the studio speakers in the booth where he sits, but also Sir Iain, who turns back to look at the figure of the small girl standing beside him on her platform. It even catches the orchestra out as all eyes turn and look in wonder at the source of this simply wonderful sound that sings so rich and pure around them as the concerto unfolds, a sound sometimes so faint and plaintive that even Isaac, hard though he has tried to make his heart, can no longer bear it and his eyes haze with tears, and then the next moment so strong and passionate that as he watches he can see Sir Iain frown down at the little girl by his side to wonder from where within her this child has found a music which defies credulity and which sings the song of heaven itself.

It had been agreed that if Isaac's experiment seemed to be succeeding they should try and record the whole of the concerto as if it was being played in performance, so when the first movement ends, besides the odd quiet cough and repositioning of an instrument or a chair, there is complete verbal silence, just as if they were all in one of the world's great concert halls. No-one says one word, nor looks enquiringly at each other, nor even smiles at Fleur lest the spell is broken, until seeing his players ready once more, Sir Iain lets the second movement unfold. Above the wonderful music of the orchestra the violin sings of its longing and its tragedy, through from the tranquility of the opening passage to the breathtaking force of its conclusion, before once more after a short and again almost totally silent break the long finale starts, with the violin playing swift and dazzling ascending passages until the orchestra takes up the main march-like theme, before the soloist enters again, commanding the subject before recalling in variations the themes of the first and the second movements, her astounding virtuosity becoming ever more apparent and never more so when suddenly after the sound of a solo muted horn, she begins the long accompanied cadenza, summarizing the whole concerto, revisiting all the subjects, musing on them, embellishing them, and then finally revealing how they are all so well connected. At first behind her song the orchestral violins play *pizzicato tremolando*, a sort of rhythmic thrum joined gradually by other instruments while still the child plays, longingly, fervently, yearningly until it is almost done, until finally the vigorous tempo with which the finale opened is restored and with enormous brio and brilliance and power the concerto ends. And when it does those who have listened sit astounded as if they have heard great music for the very first time ever.

After an eternity of perhaps five, maybe six seconds every player and every person in the studio begins to applaud, standing up from behind their desks, putting down their instruments all protocol thrown to the winds as each and every musician and technician, some laughing, some crying, some just shaking their heads in wonder stands where they are to applaud this beautiful dark-haired, dark-eyed child who has just taken them into the fields of paradise, who has just let a new light shine in on a darkening world, who has just sung with the angels.

Sir Iain has tucked his baton under one arm and is clapping his hands as he comes across to Fleur to kiss her hand and then raise it above her head as if she was some lovely prize fighter, while from his booth Isaac has now fought his way out and through the ever-growing throng of people who surround the smiling Fleur until he is by her side. The moment that he is, the moment she sees him standing grinning foolishly at her Fleur puts her violin carefully down on her chair and then throws her arms around his neck as he throws his arms around her.

I knew you were good, he tries at first to whisper but finally has to shout to her, *I knew you'd do okay. But this. This* . . .

He can say no more, so Fleur hugs him happily once again and then still holding one of his hands she goes and shakes the hands of first the leader of the orchestra and then of every single member before she returns to where the still beaming Sir Iain stands. It's the first time Fleur has ever seen him smile this way, and when he sees her standing before him, he presses his thumb into the tops of the first two fingers of his right hand and kisses them in Italianate fashion to show all the things he cannot say before allowing Gregory to slip his jacket around his shoulders and lead him away for a rest.

When the congratulations finally finish and the members of the orchestra slipped away for a quiet smoke or some refreshment Fleur finds herself alone at last with Isaac, still standing by her side with the puzzled expression of someone who thinks they have just seen or in this case heard something miraculous.

'Was it really okay?' Fleur asks, as she searchs Isaac's pockets for the bar of chocolate she knows is there. 'You look as if you're going to be ill.'

'Was it really okay,' Isaac echoes. 'No, Fleur, no it was not okay. I don't think if someone paid you a million dollars you could ever play okay. What it was was sublime and no – no not even that. It was sublime one million times over. It was the most wonderful divine moment I have ever known and so no – no it was not okay, you loony. It was the very best. And most of all you got it. You said what had to be said in the only way it can be said. How don't ask me, but you did. You got it.'

'What, Isaac?' Fleur wonders, finally finding a warm bar of KitKat. 'What did I get don't ask you?'

'You got what it needs, what makes sense of this wonderful piece of music, that's what, but don't ask me how,' Isaac replies, putting one hand to her cheek. 'You got this sense of passionate regret. *Aqui está encerrada el alama de* . . . Elgar enscribed the head of the score, and you know what that means? *Here is enshrined the soul of dot dot dot dot dot.* The dots – there are five of them – and they are meant to be for this woman who inspired the composer. Someone he called *Windflower.* I think that is the perfect name for you too, because you are going to inspire so many people with your art and your beauty too. So if I may, I shall call you after those five dots but with a variation. I shall call you Windfleur.'

There was very little to do when they reassembled after lunch, most of the retakes being purely technical and not one of them artistic, at least not as far as Fleur was concerned. The risk Isaac had persuaded everyone to take by not allowing Fleur and the orchestra to meet and rehearse had paid off triumphantly according to all concerned, and when everyone had listened to the playback the only person with any dissatisfactions to express was Fleur. However, all her suggestions were overruled unanimously with everyone voting that such was the electricity of the entire performance any adjustments however minor could critically alter the balance.

'Good,' Sir Iain announced when the decision had been reached. 'It's a warts-and-all job then, and I must say, ladies and gentlemen, I agree with you all wholeheartedly. So if we can just wrap up these one or two technicalities, half a dozen cases of champagne await us.'

'So what now?' Isaac asked Fleur as the orchestra began to pack up. 'Your parents laid on some nice party?'

'If they have they haven't told me,' Fleur replied, collecting her violin case and her overcoat. 'No I think we're all just going straight home for the weekend to Worcester.'

Neither of Fleur's parents had attended the historic recording. Although there was some excuse for her father, being a working surgeon, Isaac could see no reason why her mother hadn't bothered to come up from the country to give her daughter moral support – and privately neither could Fleur. But since neither of them wanted anything to spoil the magic of the day they kept their disappointment to themselves, Isaac pretending that it would be all the more of a surprise for them when they finally heard the recording, and Fleur pretending that just going back home to The Folly for the weekend was a sufficient treat.

Unfortunately at the eleventh hour her father had to excuse himself from actually driving Fleur back down to the country that evening, because of a complication which had developed subsequent to the operation he had just helped to perform that very morning while Fleur had been recording the Elgar. He explained that he had to stay on call in case the patient had to be returned to the theatre and if such an emergency did arise, Richard said he might not even be able to get home for the weekend at all.

'This is going to be no sort of life for us really, is it, young lady?' he asked with a smile as he put Fleur in a taxi which he directed to take her to Paddington. 'If you're going to be famous and I'm going to be successful, we're just not going to see each other very much, are we?'

Fleur wondered about this fact all the way to the station, much as she often did when she was alone in Sir Iain's house, or endlessly practising by herself. She had known she was going to have to make certain sacrifices at the outset, but she didn't know well enough what those sacrifices were going to be. Now she was beginning to find out, even at this early stage in what Isaac and Sir Iain assured her would be a long and successful career. She pictured seeing less and less of her home, her parents and her friends, and it was at times like this that she wondered whether the sacrifice was worth it. What was the rest of her life going to be like? Was it going to be like this, travelling alone to railway stations in taxis and then waiting by herself on some busy and not altogether safe station forecourt before setting off for some destination where she wouldn't know anyone? Even now although she was at least travelling home to Worcester she'd only have her mother for company since all her friends would still be away at school.

This time, by good chance, the woman flautist from the orchestra was travelling west on the same train and seeing Fleur sitting all alone among the drunks and bagwomen on the forecourt came to her rescue, taking her under her wing for the whole journey. When her travelling companion expressed a muted dismay that somebody both of Fleur's age and importance should be travelling unaccompanied, Fleur shrugged it off with her usual and by now well-rehearsed bromide that her parents considered it to be a necessary part of her education. After all in the very foreseeable future no doubt she would be travelling unescorted to all parts of the world.

'I doubt that's the reason if you don't mind me saying,' the woman musician said. 'Personally speaking, my parents used to use precisely the same tactic. When they weren't too keen on me doing something or going somewhere, they'd just say fine – but you can do it by yourself. You soon find out, at least when you're that young, you soon find out what you really want to do and what you don't.'

'You think that's what my parents are doing?' Fleur asked.

'I don't know anything about your parents, Fleur,' her companion said. 'All I can say is that if I was a mother, firstly I'd have been there for you today, and secondly if I had somebody as precious and as pretty as you for a daughter I certainly wouldn't let her sit around main-line railway stations let alone travel by herself.'

'Maybe that is what my parents are doing then,' Fleur wondered. 'Seeing if I really am that dedicated.'

'Maybe they are. The Americans call it Tough Love. But then they don't usually apply it to kids your age. And with your unique gift. My guess is – and it's perfectly understandable, so don't get me wrong – my guess is that maybe it's easier said than done, having a *wunderkinder*. Maybe some parents aren't sure how to play it. Maybe some are just plain straightforward frightened. Or maybe they're just jealous.'

'Oh, not my parents,' Fleur assured her companion hastily. 'My mother ran away from being a musician, you see, because her father was a concert pianist and my mother always says it was the last thing she ever wanted to be. Anyway my father's a heart surgeon and so he's got nothing to be jealous about whatsoever.'

'No, of course not,' the flautist said after a moment. 'Come on, let's have another game of rummy.'

*   *   *

There was something wrong at home, however, something Fleur couldn't begin to identify but just something she could feel even before her father finally arrived down from London late on the Saturday night. While her mother seemed glad to see her and asked all about how the recording had gone, she only seemed to be half paying attention to her daughter's account as she sat on the opposite side of the kitchen table chainsmoking and drinking several glasses of white wine.

The recording engineer had presented Fleur with a tape of her performance to which Amelia promised to listen at breakfast the next morning, but Fleur slept in and when she finally got up she found her mother had already gone shopping without her. She offered to play it in the afternoon after lunch but, complaining of a bad headache, Amelia excused herself and went for a long rest, leaving Fleur to her own devices until dinner time. She countered Fleur's suggestion that they could play the tape while they were eating with her own, namely that by far the best idea would be to wait until Richard arrived when they could all listen to it together.

There was no time when her father finally surfaced on Sunday morning since at last they were to celebrate Fleur's recording debut by going out to lunch at The Elms in nearby Abberley, and they were already running late.

'We could listen to it in the car,' Fleur proposed, beginning to be embarrassed now at the amount of times she had suggested playing the tape, feeling that doing so made her sound conceited.

'There is plenty of time, young lady,' her father told her, handing her back the cassette as they got into the car. 'We can all sit down and listen to it quietly after lunch.'

'I'm sorry,' Fleur said, feeling herself going red. 'I just thought you might like to hear it, that's all.'

'As I have just said, Fleur,' her father repeated, 'we have all the time in the world.'

As it was, it seemed to Fleur that the drive to the hotel would have been the ideal occasion since it was a beautiful spring day and they were driving through some of the very same countryside which once had inspired Elgar. Moreover they passed the entire journey in silence since neither her father nor mother exchanged one word from the moment they left The Folly until the moment they arrived at the exceptionally beautiful and grand Queen Anne house which had for years been a famous country-house hotel on the outskirts of Great Witley.

'I suppose we really ought to have champagne, yes?' her father suggested once they had settled in the bar. 'After all it isn't every day one's only child – what is it they say? Yes. It isn't every day one's child cuts her first disc.'

Richard smiled briefly at Fleur and then, taking his half-moon glasses out of his top pocket, began to study the prices on the wine list.

'I don't want champagne, thank you, Richard,' Amelia said lighting up a fresh cigarette. 'I would like a large gin and tonic.'

'I can see you're smoking more than ever,' Richard replied, without looking up. 'Each one is another nail, you know that as well as I do.'

'You've no idea of how much or how little I smoke Richard,' Amelia replied, clipping her cigarette case back together. 'And I want a large gin and tonic in case you didn't hear me.'

'Oh I heard you all right, Amelia,' Richard replied, before glancing at Fleur. 'And I suppose you're old enough now to have a glass of champagne. How old are you exactly?'

'You know perfectly well how old your own daughter is, Richard. Don't be so absurd.'

'I had my first glass of champagne when I was nine,' Richard said, closing the wine list. 'I'd scored the winning try for my prep school Second XV and my father was so proud of me he let me have a glass on my exeat that Sunday. I'll never forget it. One of the best moments of my life. Wonderful! From that moment on all I ever dreamed of was playing for England.'

'But you didn't, did you?' Amelia reminded him curtly.

'No, alas, I didn't' Richard replied, managing to make it sound as if it was through no fault of his own.

'Alas, no,' Amelia echoed. 'Not because you didn't have the talent but because you didn't grow enough.'

Richard took a long look at his wife before turning to enquire of a waiter whether or not they served champagne by the glass. When he was assured this was the case, Richard ordered two, then stopping frowned at Amelia.

'I'm sorry,' he said. 'What was it? Oh yes of course. You want to go on drinking what you were drinking before we left. A large gin and tonic as well, thank you.'

Since both her parents then relapsed into silence, Fleur took it upon herself to try and make the conversation, asking her father if he would like her to tell him about the recording session. When he nodded and agreed that yes he supposed she might as well, Fleur did her best to recapture the excitement, but finally gave up the unequal struggle when she realized neither her father nor her mother were paying the slightest real attention.

'Jolly good,' Richard said at one point when Fleur fell silent, still a long way from the intended end of her account. 'I think we'll go in now, shall we?'

'Is something wrong?' Fleur asked sotto voce, after they'd settled at their table.

'Why should something be wrong?' her father smiled, while never taking his eyes off Amelia.

'Well. Because no-one seems to be in a very good mood, I suppose.'

389

'You're in a good mood aren't you?'

'Not really. I mean it's difficult to be in one when neither of you two are.'

'Your father's very tired,' Amelia said, without a trace of sympathy in her voice.

'Yes,' Richard cut in quickly, as if sensing danger. 'I didn't get down until very late last night.'

'I know, I heard you,' Fleur said. 'Then I heard you both talking. For ages.'

Her father looked at her briefly.

'We had a lot to say to each other,' he told her. 'Remember, we don't see each other all week.'

'And sometimes all weekend,' her mother chipped in.

'It sounded as if you were quarrelling.'

This time when Richard kept looking at Amelia, she looked just as steadily back at him.

'If we were, that's our business,' Richard said. 'Now take your elbows off the table, please. And sit up straight.'

'She's not a child any more, Richard, to be spoken to like that.' Amelia said tightly. 'And particularly not today of all days.'

'Ah,' Richard said, smiling sarcastically as he spread his linen napkin on his knee. 'Of course this comes well from someone who couldn't even be bothered to go to the recording.'

'I told Fleur why I couldn't go and she quite understood,' Amelia replied.

'No you didn't, Mamma,' Fleur said with a puzzled frown. 'You didn't actually say why you didn't come. Just that—'

'Anyway,' Amelia continued, scything through Fleur's objection. 'There was no reason why you couldn't have gone along, Richard. According to your secretary you had a completely free morning.'

Richard put down his glass of wine and for a moment stared over-deliberately at Amelia.

'I see,' he said finally. 'So you rang my secretary to check up on me, did you?'

'I just think that people in glass houses shouldn't chuck bricks, Richard, that's all.' Amelia lit another cigarette.

Leaning suddenly across the table, Richard whipped it out of her mouth before she could light it and broke it in two. 'Not – at the table, please, Amelia. Not – when people are eating.'

'Oh for Christ's sake, stop being such a damned goody-goody, Richard, will you!' Amelia exploded. 'Don't do this, don't do that. Sit up straight, take your elbows off the table, don't do your face in public, don't smoke when people are eating! Well do you know what I say to you, Richard?'

'Amelia,' Richard sighed, but Fleur could see from her father's eyes that he was frightened. 'Amelia – people are listening.'

'I don't give a tuppenny damn what they're doing, Richard,' Amelia replied evenly. 'What I say you shouldn't do is screw your partner's bloody wife!'

Before her husband could say anything Amelia had got up and gone, knocking over her gin and the slender vase of flowers in the middle of the table as she went.

Fleur sat there petrified, uncertain what to do and seeing this her father smiled somewhat bleakly at her and then summoned the waiter.

'What's happening?' she asked in a whisper. 'Why's Mamma gone?'

'Nothing is happening, young lady, nothing that need concern you,' her father assured her. 'Now we'll just clear up this mess and then you and I will get on with enjoying ourselves.'

Fleur saw her mother suddenly appear in the drive of the hotel and the moment she did, Fleur knew where she wanted to be. So while her father's attention was momentarily distracted by the waiter arriving to help tidy up, she slipped away from the table and ran out of the dining room.

'If you're coming with me you'd better be quick,' her mother told her when Fleur caught her up.

'Where are you going?' Fleur asked, looking back and seeing her father staring at them from the dining room.

'If you have to ask, don't come,' her mother said, unlocking the car door.

'How did you get the keys?' Fleur asked, as her mother got in.

'Silly bastard always gives me them to put in my bag,' Amelia replied as she opened the passenger door. 'And his wallet. Bet he's forgotten that.'

For a moment Fleur was torn as her mother fumbled to start the car and she saw her father still frowning at them from the window of the hotel dining room. Then remembering exactly what the quarrel had been about and seeing that she really had no option, she jumped into the passenger seat just as her mother engaged gear and began to drive off.

'Where are we going, Mamma?' she wondered as the car raced down the long drive away from the front of the hotel, where Fleur could now see her father standing helplessly in the drive looking after them.

'We're not going anywhere, Fleur,' her mother replied. 'Your father is the one who's going.'

By the time they had got back to the Folly where Amelia set about packing her husband's overnight belongings into his suitcase which she left with his briefcase and raincoat outside the locked front door, Fleur had learned about her father's apparent infidelity with the wife of the other consultant surgeon. She knew little of such things other than that the word 'infidelity' invariably seemed to precede separation, if not actual divorce, in the process certainly spelling misery to all concerned. So she had remained completely silent throughout her mother's long tirade other than finally to ask if her mother was sure.

'As sure as one can be without actually catching the two of them at it,' Amelia replied, without Fleur fully comprehending. 'In bed together, Fleur,' her mother said, seeing the blank look on her daughter's face. 'In flagrante, or whatever they call it.'

Having only the sketchiest notion as to what sexual intercourse actually entailed, Fleur preferred to leave the matter there in case her mother suddenly decided to go in for one of the long and detailed bouts of explanation which sometimes overtook her. Instead she asked what was going to happen.

'What's going to happen is this,' Amelia explained, once she had made sure the whole house was securely locked and shuttered up with the two of them safely inside. 'Your father is going to come back here and rant and rave for a bit, demand to be let in and maybe even ask to be forgiven, but he will not be allowed either.'

'Are you sure, Mamma?' Fleur asked, getting more and more frightened by the prospect of the disintegration of her family life by the minute.

'Yes, Fleur! I am totally bloody well sure!' Amelia shouted back at her as she finished checking the shutters in the dining room. 'The woman in question, Felicity Benson or whatever her stupid name is, rang me on Friday and said I couldn't have your father back this weekend until Saturday! How do you like that? And then on Saturday, just after your father had left I imagine, she rang to tell me he was on his way! Yes of course I'm bloody well sure!'

'No, sorry,' Fleur said, 'I meant are you sure about not letting Daddy back in at all? Even if he does want to be forgiven?'

'Fleur darling, I know you're still very young and this must all seem quite ghastly to you,' her mother said, taking her upstairs to her bedroom where she locked the two of them in. 'But this is not just a fling, a one-night stand, a quickie, or whatever else men like to call these things to pretend they don't matter. This has been going on for some time now, three, four months, maybe even longer. Nor do I think Felicity Benson is the first. I often really wondered, deep inside me, I often wondered, what was your father's real reason for burying us down in the country like this. And I got this feeling sometimes that all this stuff about giving you the best possible childhood, and the chance to do your growing up away from the rotten influences of city life, was maybe done just as much to suit him. And wasn't I right? He wanted us nicely tucked out of the way so that he could play around as he pleased. And fool that I was — even though I had my doubts — I let him do it! I only let him do it!'

'But what's going to happen, Mamma?' Fleur repeated, unable and even more significantly unwilling to come to terms with the reality facing her, that her parents seemed about to split up. 'We're not really going to sit in here and leave Daddy locked outside, are we?'

'You bet we are,' her mother replied, pocketing the keys to the locked bedroom door and lying on the bed. 'He can scream blue murder for all I care but it won't make one bloody bit of difference. What you are looking at, sweetie, is a woman scorned.'

Shortly afterwards father and husband returned from the hotel, obviously having somehow managed to sort out what he owed as well as persuading a taxi to bring him back to The Folly on credit. Finally, in response to his repeated ringing of the doorbell and vociferous demands to be admitted so that he could at least pay off the cab driver, Amelia threw him his wallet and car keys out of the bedroom window before telling him in no uncertain terms exactly where he could then go.

From Music Today, July 1986.
ELGAR violin concerto in B minor Opus 61. **Fleur Fisher-Dilke** (vln) **London Symphonia Orchestra/Sir Iain Walcott**. Celestion Masterworks. CM 6572 – 109.

The fact that this is arguably the very best recording of Elgar's sublime violin concerto made in the last thirty years should have music lovers everywhere running hotfoot to their record stores. Few recordings are made within one's lifetime which can be praised unconditionally and hailed without reservation as masterpieces. Yet quite remarkably such is the case with this truly inspirational recording by the musical debutante Fleur Fisher-Dilke with the London Symphonia under the baton of their mentor, the great Sir Iain Walcott.

What makes this recording unique and incredible is that Fleur Fisher-Dilke is not yet thirteen years of age. Certainly there have been younger prodigies, but few have shown the maturity and assurance of this young girl whose talent seems, at least on this showing, to be already fully formed artistically. There is an abundance of simply breathtaking technique to admire, but not once does it smack of precocity nor does it ever intrude between the listener and the music.

As for the interpretation, it can best be described as heartfelt and charged with emotion, but with exactly the sort of emotion one feels Elgar himself would have looked for in performance. It is full of honesty and warmth which again prompts the listener to wonder how a girl of such tender years could possibly find herself capable of expressing, with such accomplishment, feelings which even the most mature players often find great difficulty in depicting. But this has always been one of the great wonders of prodigy, and Miss Fisher-Dilke has to be one of the most wonderful prodigies yet heard. Certainly she must be the most well-rounded and technically talented violin virtuoso these islands have produced in living memory.

She seems happy at all speeds and with all emotions, whether dealing with the necessary fire and urgency and at speeds more in line than usual to the metronome markings in the score, yet these surges of energy never cloud Fisher-Dilke's natural understanding of Elgarian rubato, guided by the sensitive conducting of Sir Iain Walcott and the simply sumptuous playing of the London Symphonia. There is plenty in the first movement to hint at the wide-ranging expressiveness of the soloist, but nowhere is this shown to better effect than in the middle movement where her playing and most particularly in the heavenly writing above the stave is nothing less than ravishing, as indeed is all Fisher-Dilke's playing for the concerto's lyrical passages. As for the bravura sections, they seem to inspire her to capricious, thrilling fantasy, while the way she sustains her account of the long accompanied cadenza once again reveals a maturity way beyond her tender years.

The orchestra responds without fail to every call made on them by soloist and conductor, and great though this band of players is one cannot remember them in quite such sublime form. This is a landmark recording if not the one as far as the Elgar concerto goes and while final judgement on Miss Fisher-Dilke's astonishing gifts must need wait until she makes her concert debut as promised later this year, this recording will certainly be one of the discs of the year if not of the millennium.

RSF

31

By the time this and many other similarly ecstatic reviews had appeared, Fleur had long returned to her studies and her mother had set up home in a furnished flat in Maida Vale. It wasn't ideal but it was all Amelia could afford while she and Richard worked out a settlement. Since the flat was too small to accommodate both Fleur and her mother, and given the amount of practice and study Fleur needed to do in advance of her concert debut, it was considered more sensible for Fleur to stay where she was with Sir Iain, particularly since his house was no great distance from the one-bedroomed flat.

Her parents' separation had an unexpected consequence. Despite the fact that Fleur had naturally enough imagined the worst, one aspect of her life positively improved, namely her relationship with her mother. As pre-teenage children so often do, Fleur had been inclined to take the relationship with her mother for granted, imagining it to be as good as it could be. Her mother was elegant, slim and attractive, without being in any way outstandingly good-looking, although to Fleur, of course, she was beautiful, and she seemed kind and considerate enough when Fleur was very small for Fleur to consider her to be the perfect mother. It wasn't until she had reached the age she was now that she had begun to realize what an important part Deanie had played in her upbringing, particularly when she became aware of how fretful and – to use a word so often employed against herself – of how spoilt her mother appeared to be. So the very last thing she imagined when she and her mother were thrown together by this wretched change in circumstances, was that they would become such good and close friends.

It took time, naturally. At first Amelia seemed to blame Fleur as much as Richard for the break-up of her marriage, stating quite bluntly that if it hadn't been for her having to concentrate so much on having a budding genius for a daughter she might have been a better wife. Fleur gradually was able to make her mother realize that the very opposite was the case, and that her being up in London and away from home so much should have increased, rather than decreased, her mother's chances of being a good wife.

Her mother would try to argue this point, saying that it was her concern for Fleur that had obviously made her neglect her marriage – or take her eye off the ball as she liked to put it – until, once again, Fleur won the day by convincing Amelia that really she had shown very little concern for what she was up to both artistically and physically.

'Not that I minded, Mamma,' she reassured her, 'because I was so happy where I was, although of course I missed home like mad. I didn't actually want to be a nuisance to you as it happened, because I sort of knew how much you and Dad liked to be together, and as long as I was getting on okay I thought you were happy.'

'I thought I was too, Fleur,' her mother said sadly, uncorking another bottle of wine and unwrapping a fresh pack of cigarettes. 'But then you see I never really went into it. I don't know, perhaps I was afraid to. Afraid of what I might find.'

'The only thing I did mind was you not coming to the recording, I must admit,' Fleur said, 'but then you've explained that. And I'm sure when I'm older I'll understand even better.'

'I don't know, I think you've done a pretty good job for a kid of your age as far as understanding things goes,' her mother said with a smile and taking her hand. 'The thing was I knew by then, at least I was almost certain, and I suppose I wanted to take it out on you as well. In case when it came to the crunch your father took you off as well, and then I wouldn't miss you because I'd have stopped loving you.'

'So who knows?' Fleur smiled back. 'Maybe your not being there made me play even better. Just as Isaac is always saying. You know, about letting what I feel inside come out in my playing. Maybe if you had been there I wouldn't have been so determined.'

'Is that what you were? Determined?'

'Yes. I had something to prove to you, certainly,' Fleur replied. 'I hated you for not turning up.'

That was the first time her mother had hugged her, really hugged her so that Fleur could suddenly feel her mother's love for the very first time in her life. Amelia held her like that for ages while neither of them said anything, until letting Fleur go and backhanding a smudged tear from under one eye, she smiled at her and apologized.

'What for?' Fleur asked. 'You don't have anything to be sorry for, Mum, really.'

'I do, Fleur,' Amelia replied. 'I'm sorry for having been such a rotten mum. Which I was, so there's no point in arguing. Oh and by the way, and this is another surprise or at least it is for me. I think I actually prefer being called Mum to Mamma.'

'Fine,' Fleur said. 'Mum it is then, Mum.'

From then on things went on improving. Amelia stopped feeling sorry for herself and began calling up some of her old friends from her modelling days, most of whom, Fleur gathered, couldn't wait to see her again so by the time the summer was nearly over and Fleur's concert debut was less than a month away, Amelia was halfway into making a new life for herself. Divorce proceedings against Richard for his admitted adultery were well under way and while the final settlement was not exactly going to leave Amelia a rich woman, Fleur had signed such a lucrative contract with Celestion Records that Gregory Rogers thought the most sensible thing she could do would be to put some of the money towards buying a flat for herself and her mother.

'Are you sure that's a good thing, Gregory?' Fleur had wondered at the time. 'I mean won't my mother want a life of her own, particularly when she's single again?'

'And who's going to look after Babylegs?' Gregory asked her back. 'Or are you planning on setting up house by yourself aged all of thirteen?'

'I thought I was going to go on living here. With you and Sir Iain.'

'That's hardly going to be possible once you start touring. You're going to need somewhere of your own, a home, particularly a spoiled madam your age. So if I were you I'd ask Mummy and hope she says yes.'

At first Amelia felt guilty at the idea of helping herself to Fleur's money, as she put it. But once Fleur realized that was the only difficulty and that her mother would actually enjoy sharing somewhere with her and making a fresh home, she soon teased her out of her guilt and they set about looking for somewhere to live, finally deciding on a house in Parson's Green rather than a flat since Fleur needed a large soundproofed room in which to practice and the house they found, with which they both fell in love, offered three times the space of any of the apartments they had been shown. By October, with Fleur's concert debut over, the builders would be out and so that was when they planned to move in, the idea being for them to share the ground floor for family life, Amelia to have all of the second floor to herself, and Fleur to have the top floor – including a well-soundproofed attic. Until then the status quo would remain.

Meanwhile Richard had long since ceased his affair with Felicity Benson and according to some of Amelia's smarter friends was now to be seen around town with Lord Hurst's eldest and still unmarried daughter Delia, Lord Hurst having been awarded a life peerage for his services to cardiology.

Richard had also changed his name from Richard Fisher to Richard Fisher-Dilke.

Although Harry had kept in constant touch by letter all term, due to the pressure of both their work and activities Fleur and he had managed to see each other no more than half a dozen times by the time the end of July arrived and Harry was about to leave to summer abroad with his family — as was their annual custom. Fleur was invited to join them any time she so wished, either in the south of Italy where they would be for the first month, or in Provence where they planned to spend the second month. If the two youngsters had been allowed to have their way they would have spent the entire summer together but, with the preparations for the concert debut taking precedence, Fleur reckoned she would be lucky if she got a fortnight's holiday at the very most, a prediction which proved to be only too accurate.

She finally got away for the last two weeks in August, just when everyone's nerves were beginning to fray, trapped as they were in the baking heat in the city. She and her mother flew out together to Naples, her mother to go and stay with an old friend who had married a rich southern Italian and summered in a magnificent farm in the hills near Cassio, while Fleur went southwards to a small island off the coast near Positano where Harry's family had a villa. There in the company of Harry's father, mother, two older sisters and one younger brother, as well as a collection of friends who constantly drifted on to and off the island from the mainland, she and Harry swam and lazed, sailed, ate and slept for the most idyllic fourteen days of Fleur's life so far. Nothing spoiled it, the weather was the best Fleur had ever seen, hot and cloudless but with just enough sea breeze to make it comfortable, while the deep blue crystal-clear Mediterranean sea always seemed to be at the prefect temperature for bathing, whether first thing in the morning when long before breakfast and anyone else was up Harry and Fleur used to race each other out to a distant orange buoy, or at night when with the aid of diver's torches, snorkels and flippers, they would explore the waters in and around the rocky coastline and wonder at the myriad and colour of maritime life.

In the evenings the whole family would boat across to Positano and take a long leisurely meal in a large cheerful restaurant at beach level, where Fleur learned the difference between home-made and store-bought pasta, and became addicted to gigantic puddings of home-made ice cream soaked in grappa. Then around midnight everyone would boat slowly back to the island, where without much prompting Harry and Fleur would play requests which Harry's mother generally would sing in a surprisingly good nightclub voice before the household went to sleep by the light of a full Neopolitan moon, only for the whole intoxicatingly delightful circus to start up again next morning.

It was just what Fleur needed in advance of the rigours which lay ahead of her, and before she said goodbye to Harry at Naples airport she thanked him from the bottom of her heart. Then she made him promise by crossing his heart that he would be at the concert when she made her debut.

'Do you think anything could possibly stop me?' he asked her. 'I shall be there to count you in. One, two, one two three four five.'

Fleur laughed and then kissed Harry goodbye, sweetly and briefly, like they had been secretly kissing all fortnight.

'You will be there?' Fleur asked, suddenly anxious.

'Of course I will, Fleur,' Harry replied. 'If you want it in full. I'll always be there.'

Fleur could see him, right up to the last moment, right until the plane finally left the ground and climbed high above Naples into the cloudless sky, a tall red-haired figure in his baggy old tennis shorts, Greenpeace tee shirt and a pair of his mother's old sunglasses, one hand raised above his head and the other shielding his eyes against the evening sun until he and Fleur were both long gone out of each other's sight.

Because six months had been deliberately allowed to elapse between the recording of Elgar and the concert, Gregory Rogers had ample time to orchestrate an entirely new campaign for Fleur's debut. The musical world had been full of stories and rumours about the discovery of what everyone was calling the most sensational young violinist ever born in the country. But rumour is one thing and hard fact quite another, so the sceptics, of whom there were many, were already of the opinion that Fleur Fisher–Dilke was a morning glory and that the reason why the record had been issued in advance of any public appearance because much more could be done in the editing channels than on stage. In other words they were hinting at a deliberate legerdemain by Fleur's management, a case of hoping that because the public had both heard how good Fleur was on record and had been told so by the music critics, their minds would be made up well before this new musical wonderchild finally drew bow across gut in public performance. As these sceptical commentators were at pains to point out, all that so far had been heard of this budding genius was one carefully monitored studio recording. She had not as yet played even one professional recital, let alone concert.

'This is of course precisely what we want,' Gregory

informed the Fisher-Dilke camp when there was but one week to go before D day. 'You see they don't even know what Petal here looks like, because I have allowed not one unauthorized photograph to be issued, and absolutely no interviews – only information in the shape of carefully worded statements. If she'd been a pop star we'd never have got away with it. They'd have had this place staked out from the beginning. But of course because she's only a genius, it isn't of nearly so much interest – so we can, and have, got away with this low-profile bit.'

'You were smart about the record cover, Ge-regory,' Isaac said, still unable to pronounce Gregory's name properly, although Fleur was beginning to suspect it was an affectation. 'Showing just the painting of the Malvern Hills on the front, and only small two cameo pictures of Sir Iain and Windfleur on the back was good thinking. Not so at the time I must say, as I thought. But now I see what a clever boy you were.'

'The way I see it there is simply no sense, Izzy, none whatsoever, in feeding the press and the public dribs and drabs. What I have been banking on, in order to make maximum impact, is that really they'll all more or less have forgotten about Petal by now. So that when they hear her in person – and even more importantly – when they actually get to see her in the flesh it will be truly *sensational*.'

'Is there any guarantee of this, Gregory?' Sir Iain asked. 'The classical musical world is inclined to find its sensations aurally rather than visually. I trust you are not concocting some cheap and nasty gimmick.'

'Tsk, tsk, maestro, as if,' Gregory sighed unduly. 'What I'm saying, and I am saying it in the greatest confidence, mind, is that all that lot out there will be expecting to see is a child in her party frock. Playing the violin a lot better than anyone else admittedly, but that's all they'll be expecting. A pretty little girl in her party frock who can't half play the violin a bit. But that's not what her mum and I have in mind at all, is it, Amelia? I should cocoa.'

Gregory grinned at Amelia, who smiled back at him and the other members of the quintet.

'No, what Amelia Jane and I have in mind is something really very different indeed,' Gregory concluded. 'What we are going to give 'em is something they ain't ever been given before.'

Fleur and her mother found what they were looking for in a small shop half hidden at the top of the Fulham Road, something dramatic and unconventional without being in any way bizarre or too distracting, a stunningly beautiful and superbly cut three-piece black velvet knickerbocker suit which Amelia teamed with a large-collared white silk shirt ruffled on the front and at the sleeves, and a large black floppy velvet bow tie.

'Now. Black or white stockings, do you think, Fleur?' Amelia wondered as she stood back to appraise her daughter. 'Actually I think white really. You've certainly got good enough legs to wear white stockings – and then we'll need to find you a nice pair of black patent leather buckle shoes.'

'I look a bit like – you know, whoever,' Fleur said, turning herself round in front of the full-length mirror. 'Prince. That's who I look like.'

'Let's hope everyone else thinks so too,' her mother said. 'Because that's what Gregory and I are aiming for. To create the same sort of impact these pop stars get when they walk on stage. The oof factor, Gregory calls it. Theatrical enough to attract their attention, but not outrageous enough to upset the grannies.'

'I don't know, Mum,' Fleur grinned. 'Some of the grannies are the really far-out ones, you know.'

'I'm sure that's absolutely true,' Amelia agreed, 'but what I'm really saying is we don't want to go punk or black leather, or anything like that. We want you to look as beautifully different as you are.'

'That's nice, I like that,' Fleur said, putting her arms round her mother and kissing her. 'Thank you.'

'Thank you, sweetheart,' her mother returned. 'I'll tell you something. You're making me feel young again. I haven't had this much fun in an age. Now, are you sure you have enough freedom to play in that? That's the one thing Isaac made me sure to remember to ask.' Amelia turned to the assistant for her help, 'Particularly round the shoulders and under the arms,' she said. 'It doesn't have to be baggy or anything, but it mustn't restrict Fleur anywhere across the back.'

'It's fine, madam,' the assistant assured her, as Fleur flexed her arms and affected to play her violin. 'I think you've chosen brilliantly.'

'Thank you,' Amelia said, handing the girl an envelope full of cash. 'And this is for not saying anything to anybody.'

'I really don't need it, thanks all the same,' the freckle-faced girl said. 'My boyfriend gave me your daughter's record for my birthday. It's the first classical record I've ever had, and I think it's so fantastic I can't wait for her next one. We're going to the concert, too.'

'In that case that will help pay for the tickets,' Amelia insisted. 'It's also for all your help.'

'Bona,' Gregory said when he saw the whole outfit tried on. 'Ultra and utterly bona, Amelia dear. I couldn't have chosen more exquisitely myself.'

'What on earth does "bona" mean, Gregory?'

'It means really good, Mum,' Fleur laughed. 'Bona is the opposite of naff.'

'I wish your hair was, duck. We're going to have to get seriously inspired where the hair is concerned.'

'What about Renato at Twists?'

'Where you go, you mean?' Fleur asked her mother.

'I don't exactly go to Renato because I can't afford him. Toni does my hair. But Renato does all the top models, and a lot of pop singers as well. If that's what we're looking for.'

'Amelia, dear,' Gregory sighed. 'God sent you down on a special little cloud.'

A private appointment was made with Renato to come up to Hampstead to tackle the question of the right hairstyle for the big night. While he was closeted away with Gregory and Amelia discussing the problem, Fleur was called in to see Sir Iain to discuss anything that might still be worrying her about the concert.

'Of course it's far too late now for any turning back,' Sir Iain told her, 'yet sometimes I wonder if we were right in making the choice we finally did.'

'If I was right you mean, Sir,' Fleur corrected him. 'If anything goes wrong I only have myself to blame.'

'My job was and is to guide you, Fleur, and I shall have failed in my duty if I have allowed you to make the wrong choice, even if it was as you say you who finally made it.'

'The way I see it, if I can remind you—'

'Oh yes, please do. Go right ahead, child. When you're my age you need all the reminding you can get.'

'We worked so hard on the Elgar and it turned out so well I just felt in a way that I would just be repeating myself by playing it again at the concert, and within such a short space of time. I know you thought that people might be expecting me to play it, but then as Isaac has always taught me, I thought perhaps this really was a time when I should put Danger First.'

'Danger First indeed,' Sir Iain groaned. 'As if it wasn't difficult enough without having to make it more so. However, I know what both Isaac and you mean. This is probably simply because I'm an old man and I want guaranteed success at my great age, not potential failure.'

'I won't fail you, Sir, I promise,' Fleur replied. 'I mean you've been happy so far in rehearsals—'

'Yes, yes, of course I have, Fleur. You are playing superbly and I have no doubt that you will handle the Tchaikovsky every bit as brilliantly as you did the Elgar. I really only want to make sure of two things. I want to make sure you are always mindful of the pitfalls—'

'Sentiment never sentimentality—'

'Particularly in the central *Canzonetta* which we have decided to take at a flowing and easy songful speed. Good.'

'Beware of idiosyncrasies—'

'People stuff poor Tchaikovsky full of them, as if he is a Christmas goose.'

'And too many, especially too many tenutos and rallentandos, turn the emotion to syrup.'

'Just so. I shall be keeping an eye on you.'

'Finally, don't pull the melodic line out of true.'

'A very Russian fault, particularly in the concert hall. The Russian violinists love it because it lets them pull all sorts of faces, to try and cod their audiences how much they are suffering. The only people who end up suffering are the poor audiences. So — is that all?'

'That's all the major notes, I think,' Fleur said, with a frown. 'The motorway signs as you always call them.'

'Good. So what about you? Do you have any worries yourself? Any worries about the orchestra? Any worries about me?'

'Do you think we dare take the first movement just a little more slowly? Hardly even one mark. But I just feel I'm still missing something at the beginning. I just feel I need a little more room — what's the word? To expand.'

'Yes.' Sir Iain sat back in his chair, nodded and then nodded once again, this time more emphatically. 'It's a risk as I'm sure you appreciate, because we're sailing pretty close to the wind as it is. But if you feel you have something more to give us in that movement, then next rehearsal – which is our last rehearsal, might I remind you? Next rehearsal we shall take it down a whole mark and see what we find. Now I believe you have something much more important to attend to. Your hair.'

'Yes?' Renato asked, standing back for all to see.

'Oh yes,' said Gregory, suddenly very serious. 'Oh yes, most certainly yes. Yes. Amelia?'

'I think it's fantastic. Brilliant.'

'Can I see?' Fleur asked, unable to join in since they were not in a mirrored salon.

'Eh, *voilà!*' Gregory said, producing a large hand mirror which he held first to the front, then to either side. '*C'est sensas!*'

'Wow,' said Fleur, staring hard. 'You don't think it's a bit Tamla Motown?'

'I think it is truly sensational, Flower, and just try and imagine it with the whole cozzy,' Gregory assured her, leading her out to stand in front of the hall mirror. 'It is really very little short of a miracle.'

'Gregory's right,' Amelia said, standing to the side of Fleur and looking at her daughter's image in the mirror with her. 'Once you've got the whole outfit on, I mean I just think you'll look simply wonderful. You look wonderful anyway.'

'Listen she'll look such a knockout, Amelia,' Gregory said, 'she won't even need to take her fiddle.'

Gone was the schoolgirl look, the long straight dark hair trained into place by either a single plait or a large Victorian bow, and in its place was a brilliantly cut and arranged slew of trailing frizzes, covered with a mass of tiny glittering bows. It was wild but it was wonderful, Fleur finally decided as she stared at herself in the mirror, amazing but not weird.

'Look if you aren't happy, sweetheart, we can start again from basics,' Renato said.

'No I think it's wonderful,' Fleur assured him. 'Really. It's just – it's just so different. I'm only thinking about whether I can carry it off, that's all. I don't mean to criticize you, because I really love what you've done.'

'Of course you can carry it off, Fleur,' Amelia said. 'And you must remember most people are going to be seeing it from a long way off. It's not as if it's television, I mean we all talked about this and designed it to be seen from quite a distance, from where most of the audience will be sitting.'

'Yes I see,' Fleur said. 'Of course I'm looking at it from about a foot away.'

'While most of the audience will be ten, twenty, fifty, maybe a hundred feet away. We wanted to create this wonderful effect.'

'I think it's a triumph,' Gregory insisted, 'the real beauty of it being that although it gets away from the gauche schoolgirl bit, it still looks young in just the right way, without being in the slightest bit – you know this year's look.'

'Okay,' Fleur said. 'Sold. So why don't I go upstairs and change, and we'll see what it looks like with the – what do you call it, Gregory?'

'The full schmutter, heart.'

'Let's see what it looks like with the full schmutter, Mum.' Fleur grinned and started to go up to her room to get changed. As she went across the hall the telephone rang and out of force of habit Fleur picked it up to see who it was and found it was for Gregory.

'I have told you a million and three times not to answer it,' Gregory scolded her as he took the receiver from her. 'I have told you no newspapers, no radio or *teevee* and least of all no telephone calls.'

'Why not?' Amelia laughed, as Gregory stood waiting

with his hand cupped over the receiver. 'She's hardly going to learn anything dreadful over the telephone, surely?'

'It was Sir Iain's idea, not mine, Amelia, although I agree with it one hundred per cent,' Gregory replied. 'We were thinking of those wretched reporters and the last thing we want is something nasty getting into Madam's bonce. Now run *along*, Petal. Go on, vanish.'

With a grin Fleur did as she was told and disappeared upstairs with her mother to her bedroom, while Gregory took the call. She didn't hear who it was, although she did notice a sudden change in Gregory's tone as she heard him drop his voice and indicate that he was going to take the call in his office.

Half an hour later when she and Amelia returned downstairs to show everyone how well Fleur's concert ensemble went with her new hairstyle, the only person they could find was Renato who was having coffee with Rita in the kitchen. Immediately Renato fussed around, adjusting the cut and set of Fleur's hair, and Rita frowned deeply, sighed tragically and whispered conspiratorially as to how wonderful she looked. Fleur asked her where everyone had gone.

'Mr Roger say something come up, Miss Floor,' Rita replied. 'He, Sir Yan and Mr Kleen all must talk, and they say if Mister here happy with hair, you and Mrs Mum have afternoon to go to pictures.'

'It must be something quite serious to make them shut themselves away like this.'

'Mr Roger no say. He juss say make sure you take afternoon off.'

'I gather it was something to do with the concert arrangements,' Renato said, standing back to admire his work, having just executed his last buff to Fleur's hair. 'Someone crying off at the last moment or something boring. Now, what we are going to do before you disappear is wash all of this out so that no-one sees

411

it, since we're all so deliriously happy with it, then do it all again from new on the big day, okay?'

'Fine,' Fleur grinned. 'Anything to take my mind off it.'

Hannah and Her Sisters was showing at the Odeon Swiss Cottage, which both Amelia and Fleur were dying to see. So after lunch at the Chinese Green Cottage, they took themselves off to the cinema where they put all thoughts of the concert out of their minds as they immersed themselves in Woody Allen's affectionate and witty family portrait of three sisters, their loyalties and their affairs of the heart. To judge from their reception on their return whatever difficulties had arisen that midday had been overcome, and life in Sir Iain's house was back to normal. The Brat Pack, as Gregory had affectionately dubbed their number, all dined together, Sir Iain, Gregory, Isaac, Amelia and Fleur and when finally it was time for Fleur to go to bed, she kissed her mother *au revoir* and asked whether she would like her to call her a taxi as usual.

'Not tonight, Flower,' Gregory told her. 'There are just one or two things we need to run over with Mum, so you take yourself off to bed and I'll run her home when we're through.'

32

The debate had been long and keen as to which should be the venue for Fleur's debut, the final choice being between the Free Trade Hall, Manchester, the Royal Festival Hall or the Albert Hall, both in London. Isaac was all for Manchester, not because he was lacking in confidence, the opposite in fact being the case, but because he had always argued that moments as great as this one belonged just as much to the provinces as they did to the capital. No-one argued with this, particularly Sir Iain who was a Mancunian by birth, and right until the last moment it seemed that Manchester had won the day, only to lose out entirely due to an impassioned and serious plea by Gregory in favour of the Albert Hall, an appeal based not only on the aesthetics and theatricality of the great lyceum but also most convincingly of all, on the all important question of confidence.

'I agree with everything that has been said about Manchester,' he had argued, 'and being what they dub a "provincial" myself, Isaac has sung my very own song. But. But there is one all-important aspect which we are in danger of overlooking, and that is how important the choice of venue is for the as yet unconverted. No-one has seen Fleur play, no paying member of the music-going public, that is. So there is a danger that if we don't go for broke there will be those, and there will be quite a lot of "those" as there always are, who will prejudge us, saying that we don't dare take on the capital but are playing it safe in the sticks. Now we know that is nonsense but they don't, and the knockers will take it as a god-given sign that there's been a little bit too much puff in the pastry. However brilliantly Fleur plays, to these doubters it will not sound as brilliant as if she was standing there on the world-famous podium of one of the grandest venues of them all, namely the Albert Hall. Remember, one and all, the choice we have to make could in itself be a make-or-break one, and knowing that we have the goods, I say to you it is only he who dares wins.'

The vote when finally cast proved unanimously in favour of the Albert Hall and such was the word of mouth that within five days of opening the box office, every ticket for the concert was sold.

This time Fleur's nerves showed no sign of disappearing when the day of the concert dawned. Everyone in the household from Rita to Sir Iain did their best to joke their way through the seemingly endless morning and afternoon; but since they too were all suffering severely from the jitters, instead of easing the tension, by mid-afternoon the atmosphere was near hysterical.

Once again it was Gregory, supposed to be the most temperamental member of the household, who proved the most stable and managed to defuse the situation. He did so by persuading a friend of his who was a professional magician and an ardent concert-goer to come round after lunch and entertain the household in return for the last of the house seats that evening, thereby saving the day. As long as the conjurer entertained, all worries were forgotten and all fears allayed. In fact so bright was the idea, and so good was the timing, that once the cabaret finally ended the wagon had begun to roll in earnest so there simply was no more time left to sit round agonizing in corners, as Gregory liked to call it.

Half an hour later he was at the wheel of the Rolls, driving Fleur all by herself to the Albert Hall, it having been decided, again unanimously, that for the two-hour run-up period to the concert the only person who wouldn't unsettle Fleur would be not Amelia, not Isaac even, but Gregory.

'Let's go over your entrance once again shall we, Flower?' he asked as he swung the car off Exhibition Road into the turning behind the Albert Hall.

Fleur tried to swallow another army of butterflies which were trying to escape from her stomach. 'It's seeing the posters that's done it,' she said, breathing in deeply. 'Sort of rather brings it home really.'

'Je said – let's go over your entrance, shall we?' Gregory insisted.

'We've gone over it, Gregory. We've gone over and over and over it.'

'Then let's go over it one more time.'

'I don't just walk on.'

'No you most certainly don't.'

'I don't just walk on as if I've been standing in the wings waiting to come on. I arrive.'

'Wrong – you do not arrive. You *appear*.'

'And no-one must see me coming on.'

'Better,' Gregory agreed. 'Now they don't see you, now they do.'

'You will be there to tell me when,' Fleur said, turning to look at Gregory for assurance as he stopped the car.

'As soon as Sir tips me the wink,' he replied. 'I shall cue you *before* Sir raises his hand to beckon you on, remember. That way, because the audience won't be looking for you, because they won't yet be looking in your direction, you will already be onstage as the Master raises his hand and – *abracadabra*. You will appear to have arrived from nowhere, which will make you one up from the outset. The magic will have already started.'

'And it really works?'

'Believe me, Flower, it always works,' Gregory smiled.

'But with you it will work like it has *never* worked before.'

Because she had been deliberately kept out of the spotlight, as well as deprived of all media information about her debut, Fleur was genuinely astounded to see the mass of reporters and photographers on duty outside the artistes' entrance. Even Gregory, who had warned Fleur to prepare herself for a certain amount of attention, was a little taken aback. Telling Fleur he hadn't expected quite such a turnout, he suddenly swung the Rolls away from the back of the Hall to drive it round the front.

'What are you doing now, Gregory?' Fleur asked, looking through the rear window at the fruitlessly popping flashlights. 'I mean we've got to get inside somehow.'

'I don't want any piccies yet, Flower,' Gregory replied, looking for somewhere to park alongside the main entrance. 'So pull the hood of your cape up just in case there are any of them lurking round here, and then inside as quick as you can.'

The only people outside the Hall and in the foyer itself were concert-goers collecting their tickets, and such was the speed of Gregory and Fleur's entrance that they were up the stairs and in through a pass door without even being noticed. On their way to the dressing rooms Fleur did her best not to look down at the platform far below them. In less than two hours she would be standing there in front of the orchestra and a houseful of music lovers. Even so, as Gregory stopped to pull open a particularly stiff door, she found herself staring down hypnotized at the vast auditorium.

'If you must, you must,' Gregory said, holding the door open. 'But think of it this way. Far more people have already heard you play on record than will be sitting down there tonight. And none of them have asked for their money back, have they?'

'Not really,' Fleur agreed half-heartedly, taking one last

quick look at the empty hall below. 'Anyway I suppose it's a bit like going to the dentist's really. It's thinking about it that's the worst.'

'I don't know. Thinking back to some of the concerts I've had to attend, I'd have preferred being at the dentist's any day,' Gregory replied. 'Now come along, because we have a lot to do. You'd be amazed how quickly the time flies by when you're not enjoying yourself.'

Taking the arm that was then offered to her, Fleur walked off down the long corridor towards her ever-impending destiny.

With less than an hour to go and all her main warm-up exercises completed, Fleur had just stretched on the chaise-longue in her dressing room to read for a while, waiting for Renato and Amelia who were due to help her dress and put the finishing touches to her hair, when much to her surprise the telephone on the corner of her dressing table rang.

'Miss Fisher-Dilke?' A voice enquired. 'I know Mr Rogers said no calls but I have your father on the line, and he insists on speaking to you.'

Fleur hesitated. The last time she had seen her father had been some time back in July, when he had insisted on taking her out to a most discomfiting lunch during which he had proceeded to present his side of the marital dispute in full uncensored form. Fleur had managed to block out most of the detail by using the device she normally employed at such times, namely running some particularly complicated violin part through her mind from start to finish. Even so, some of her father's message had got through, and while she wasn't prepared to believe in his wildly overblown version, the memory of some of those half-heard stories lingered on somewhere in her head. Consequently on the couple of occasions when her father had tried to take her out again, she had pleaded her work as an excuse and had managed to stay free of him ever since.

Yet now he was on the other end of a telephone line waiting to speak to her before the most important moment of her life and she wondered why. She wondered why he hadn't rung her at Sir Iain's as he usually did, or even written to her, instead of ringing her at the actual concert hall within an hour of her debut.

'Ask him what he wants, if you wouldn't mind,' she instructed the girl on the switchboard. 'Tell him I'm meant to be resting.'

A moment later the telephone rang again.

'He says he just wants to wish you luck, because he can't manage to attend the concert itself,' the girl said. 'He really won't keep you from your rest for long, he says.'

'Very well,' Fleur said, pulling the telephone over to her and cradling it in her lap. 'Put him through.'

'Hello, young lady,' her father said. 'Did you get my flowers?'

'No I didn't actually,' Fleur said, looking at all the bouquets around her room, all of whose cards she had read.

'You didn't? That wretched florist. They promised they'd have them there by midday. They're probably still on their way. But you got my card.'

'No. No, I didn't get a card either. I got lots of cards, but there wasn't one from you.'

'This is ridiculous,' her father sighed deeply. 'I posted the thing myself, on Thursday, first class. Perhaps they haven't brought all the post up yet.'

'I think they have. The girl downstairs brought up the last lot only about ten minutes ago.'

'And mine wasn't with them?'

'No.'

'Isn't it unbelievable?'

Fleur was about to agree but her father gave her no time, pressing straight on.

'I'm sorry I can't be there tonight, I really am. It's just another wretched clash of interests, I'm afraid. We shouldn't both have careers in the ascendancy. I told you that. Goodness knows I've said that often enough to you.' Her father laughed shortly, and then sighed once more, while Fleur kept deliberately silent. 'The thing is it's business, you see. Although in one way I'm not sorry because it looks as though at long last I shall have a consultancy of my own. Isn't that good news? Not only that, but a Harley Street consultancy. Isn't that good news.'

'Yes, very,' Fleur said, glancing at her watch and thinking how much she still had to do. 'Look, Daddy—' she began.

'It's all a trifle complicated, but what it boils down to, my dear, is that once your mother and I are divorced I shall be getting married. To Lord Hurst's daughter, I don't know whether anyone's mentioned this to you?'

'No.' Fleur lied.

'Well I shall, you see, and Lord Hurst – I don't suppose you know who he is either?'

'No,' Fleur lied again. 'Daddy, I have a concert in less than an hour now—'

'Don't worry, I've nearly finished,' her father interrupted. 'Lord Hurst happens to be one of the top heart men in the country, and he's planning on retiring this year, giving me every indication that I shall succeed him in his consultancy. As you can imagine it's one of the very top consultancies in the land. So. What do you think of that, young lady?'

'I think it's terrific, Daddy, and I really am pleased for you,' Fleur replied, closing her eyes and trying to maintain what Isaac called her inner balance. 'But now I really must ring off because—'

'Yes I know, I know,' her father said, making no

attempt to conceal his lack of patience. 'I just wanted to share my good news with you. All right? That's all I wanted to do. Share my good news with you. And commiserate with you on your bad.'

'Sorry?'

'I think you're a very brave girl, but then that's what they say in your line of work, isn't it? The show must go on.'

'I don't know what you're talking about, Daddy,' Fleur said very slowly. *What bad news?*'

'Oh the sad news about that boy you knew,' her father replied. 'You know. The Grevil boy. Harry. Harry Grevil.'

'But I haven't had any bad news about Harry,' Fleur insisted, swallowing hard. 'There must be some mistake. The only thing I heard from Harry was good news—'

'Fleur, dear—'

'He wrote to me a couple of weeks ago saying how much he was looking forward to coming to the concert.'

'Fleur dear – how can he be at the concert, my dear? The poor boy is dead.'

'What?' Fleur said very faintly, hardly able even to hear herself. *What?*'

'I would have thought someone would have told you at least. He went to hospital to have a tonsillectomy, which is usually straightforward enough, God knows, these days, but the poor lad haemorrhaged a few days after the op and died within a matter of minutes.'

'This can't be true. I don't believe what you're saying,' Fleur whispered.

'Oh, I'm afraid it's true all right, my dear,' her father assured her with another deep sigh. 'I heard it first hand from his mother. But I really am surprised no-one told *you*.'

Fleur remembered nothing until she saw her mother sitting beside her on a chair drawn up alongside the chaise-longue.

'My God, what happened?' her mother whispered, clasping her hand. 'We thought you were dead.'

'Mum—' Fleur began, only for her mother to hush her.

'Don't say or do anything,' Amelia ordered. 'A doctor's on his way.'

'There's nothing wrong with me, Mummy, it's all right,' Fleur said, trying to hold on.

'Then what on earth were you doing collapsed on the middle of the floor?'

'Mummy – something dreadful has happened. At least I think it has,' Fleur said. 'Except maybe it isn't true. Tell me it isn't true. Please tell me it isn't true.'

'What darling? I'll tell you anything you want,' Amelia said, beginning to cry herself. 'But just tell me what on earth's the matter?'

'Mummy,' Fleur whispered. 'Daddy just rang and told me Harry's dead.'

After the doctor had finished examining her, he stroked her cheek and smiled at her and then ordered Fleur to remain lying down on the couch until he had spoken to Sir Iain and Isaac who were waiting outside. While the three men conferred, with only half an hour to go before the concert was due to begin, Amelia stayed with Fleur but could do nothing to stem the flood of her daughter's tears.

Every now and then between sobs Fleur would ask why she hadn't been told, why her mother hadn't told her, why nobody had, and hard though Amelia tried to explain she couldn't get Fleur to understand that everyone had thought that telling her in advance of the concert would make no difference to the fact of what had happened, so there seemed little point.

'But you all knew all this time!' Fleur cried. 'All the time we were going to the pictures! And playing stupid card games! And sitting having dinner and telling jokes and everything! And then watching that conjurer doing his tricks today, *you all knew!*'

'I didn't actually know until after we'd been to the cinema, until after dinner that night, sweetheart—' her mother tried to tell her, but Fleur wasn't having any of it.

'But you knew!' she shouted. 'You still knew and pretended you didn't! And you didn't tell me! I don't know how you could! I don't know how any of you could!'

'Because we were all thinking of you, that's why.'

'Because you were all thinking of the concert, you mean! That's all any of you lot were thinking!'

'That simply isn't true, darling. I promise you. We were only trying to do what we thought was best. All of us.'

Fleur turned her back then, turned and faced the wall, and cried so hard her mother feared for her – thinking that she would surely die of the grief, so terrible were her sobs. Minutes later the door opened and Sir Iain, Isaac and Gregory all came in, closing the door behind them.

'Is it all right for me to speak?' Sir Iain politely enquired. 'If it is, I would rather speak freely and in here, in front of the person it most concerns, and who concerns us most.'

'Yes of course, Sir Iain,' Amelia said. 'I'm afraid there's nothing I can say to comfort her.'

'No no, of course not, Amelia,' Sir Iain replied. 'Nothing anyone can say could possibly comfort this poor, dear child at a moment such as this. But we have a hall full of people out there and I am going to have to tell them that they are to be disappointed, for I fully agree with Dr Brewer that Fleur cannot possibly be expected to make her debut after such a terrible shock. Even though physically she is perfectly all right, she has received a desperate emotional blow and no-one in their right senses could expect a young woman of Fleur's tender age to make her first public appearance in such heart-rending circumstances. So with all your permissions I shall announce the cancellation of the Tchaikovsky violin concerto and once I have learned through Ivor whether the orchestra are willing to go along with my suggestion of playing Tchaikovsky's Symphony Number Three instead, I shall inform the audience that this will indeed be the substitution.'

'What will you say about Fleur?' Amelia asked. 'I mean what reason will you give for such a late cancellation?'

'I shall simply say she has been taken ill, my dear, which indeed the poor child has.'

'Perhaps if I might have a word?' Isaac said quietly from behind Sir Iain.

'I thought we had said everything we had to say outside, Isaac,' a puzzled Sir Iain replied.

'We said everything we had to say to each other outside, Iain, but not everything we have to say to young Fleur here. So if Fleur wouldn't mind? Maybe if she and I could have a small word together?'

'Yes,' Fleur whispered, without turning back. 'That would be fine, Isaac.'

'Good,' Isaac nodded. 'Then if you gentlemen would give us say five minutes? Before you go saying anything in public?'

Once the room had emptied and having selected a sweet from a bag bought specially for the concert, Isaac took a couple of turns around the room before sitting himself down back-to-front on the chair Amelia had vacated.

'We know each other enough not to beat about any bushes, eh? So here goes,' Isaac began. 'This without any question of possibility is the very worst thing that has ever happened to you and whoever doubts that loses my vote. Nothing is going to make this better. Nothing anyone says, nothing anyone can do. Nothing. Harry is dead. It is a tragedy, a terrible, terrible thing, it is the very literature of pain in black and white, it is the most

God awful thing. But it has happened, and your lovely friend is dead. You will ask *why* this is so, you will call on God and demand to know why such a terrible thing should be, but God can't tell you. He has given us life and he has given us death, and he has given us the right to choose our own path. And although Harry made no wrong decisions, someone else did, someone else took a wrong path maybe, accidentally I'm sure, but then this is the shape and the substance of life. So don't ask God why, because this will not help you. What maybe you should do is ask another why. And I'll tell you what and which why precisely. Ask why your father wanted you to know. Then ask why he wanted you to know right now.'

'What do you mean?' Fleur asked, staring up at Isaac through red and swollen eyes.

'Okay,' Isaac nodded. 'Now I'm no psychiatrist, but then I'm no dummy neither. When I heard all this, everything that had happened, finally − not the first thing, would to God I were that bright a boy − *finally* I ask myself but why? Why did this man do this? Even supposing he thought you knew already, it isn't the right thing to bring up again, right? Just before your only child goes on stage to make her world premiere? Don't tell me it is, I won't believe you. Your Poppa told you that for a damned good reason.'

'What do you think that reason was, Isaac?'

'What do *you* think that reason was, Windfleur?'

'I don't know.' Fleur shook her head uncertainly. 'I mean I'm not at all sure I can say.'

'Have a go. As soon as you do, you're halfway there.'

'Because he's − but it can't be, surely? Why should he be?'

'You've left out a word somewhere, cuckoo. Because he's *what*.'

'Because he's − he's jealous.'

'I think you got it. You know that? I really think you

got it! Now I have to go on, because we ain't got time for deep analysis here, not if we're going to sort this thing out. So suppose you and I are right, just suppose. What's the best thing he can do. He can stop you playing. He can spoil your moment of glory.'

'Yes,' Fleur agreed, but slowly. 'But first you see, Harry had to – Harry had to—'

'I know what Harry had to do,' Isaac said quickly, trying to stem another flood of tears. 'And sure, your father wasn't responsible for that. But you can bet your shoes that Harry's mother told him not to tell you, because that's what Gregory told her was the game plan. Yet he waits until an hour before you go on.'

Isaac shrugged and then nodded, before offering the bag of sweets to Fleur who shook her head.

'There aren't no green ones,' Isaac said. 'I made double damn sure.'

Fleur managed half a smile, and wiping the worst of her tears away with both hands, took and unwrapped a sweet.

'Now we have to come to the big question, and it has to be asked so I shall ask it, even though maybe I lose your love,' Isaac said, without any self-pity.

'No chance, Isaac,' Fleur said, putting the sweet in her mouth. 'That will never happen, whatever you say, or whatever you do.'

'Okay, so let's go for broke. Suppose your father – no. Start again. Suppose you don't play tonight, two things. Who wins?'

'My father, I suppose,' Fleur shrugged, sucking on her sweet.

'Two. Who loses?'

'I don't know. Not me certainly, because as far as this goes, I don't matter.'

'Everyone loses. Sure, you still get to make your debut and the world still gets to hear you, but the world will have turned a few more thousand times. Things will be different. You will be different, more than anything because you let Poppa win. What would Harry make of that? Ah – not much I say, not much at all. So now the million dollar questions, okay? One, suppose your father hadn't told you, right? You go out there and play and you are a sensation, which you will be, God knows. Then later you learn the tragedy and still you grieve. Still it makes no difference to your love or your loss. It doesn't. It really doesn't. You not knowing doesn't make no difference to Harry not being here no more. That is a fact, I'm sorry about it – but it is a fact and one I am sure you know. And two – before you tell me to go and mind it, two – imagine this all vice versa. Imagine you are Harry and Harry is you. What would your spirit tell Harry he must do?'

'I think you know the answer to that already, don't you?' Fleur said after a long moment.

'If I know you like I think I know you,' Isaac nodded; 'then sure as hens' eggs I know what you tell him.'

'Okay,' Fleur said, swinging her legs off the couch and biting her bottom lip as hard as she could. 'In that case you had better go and mind it, hadn't you?'

'Any particular reason, young lady?' Isaac enquired.

'Yes,' Fleur replied, taking a long, deep breath. 'Because I have to get dressed and ready to play.'

Remarkably, there is film of the concert. It exists not because it was televised (although it was broadcast), but because the BBC were already working on stereophonic sound for televised broadcasts and had quite by chance chosen this very concert to try out some new equipment, both visual and aural. So a complete record exists, although in the documentary this was probably the first time it had been shown publicly.

It is all there in the archives, for anyone who wishes to see it in toto, because of course the documentary only used excerpts from it — even so somehow managing to convey the atmosphere of that unique occasion.

What the viewer sees is this. A small figure dressed in velvet and silk appears as if by magic from the wings exactly as predicted by Gregory Rogers. Sir Iain Walcott seems hardly to have beckoned his soloist on and there she is, diminutive in long shot, almost but not quite lost against the orchestra. The lights catch whatever is in her tousled hair and, when the camera goes in close, this turns out to be a myriad of little reflective butterflies.

The camera, which knows nothing of the young girl's anguish, dwells for a moment on her face as she checks the tuning of her instrument with the orchestra, and while the camera can see her pallor and the sadness in her eyes, those in the auditorium naturally cannot. Perhaps those in the very front seats notice, but they ascribe it to nothing more than nerves, natural enough on an occasion as taxing as this.

Then there is a breathless quiet as both soloist and orchestra prepare to play. Sir Iain's baton moves only imperceptibly yet it is enough to engage the orchestra, which begins to play the first movement at what seems like an almost dangerously slow initial pace, courting disaster should the soloist not find the correct mood and tone. Even when the tympanum roll draws in the full orchestra there is still a sense that the full movement cannot catch fire, unless — unless—

Then there it is and in it comes for all to hear, a voice so pure and lyrical that even in that first long unaccompanied introductory phase, already the heart wants to break. The playing is so tenderly affecting and the pace so beautifully and carefully measured that the whole first movement, so often lost in a welter of over-romantic playing, is opened out into one of the most expansive, profound and exquisite readings ever heard. At least such was the consensus of critical opinion afterwards.

Nor does the profundity of the reading take away from any of the excitement, for as the first movement builds there is both tremendous energy as well as humanity, and more than anything a sense of discovery, as if both soloist and orchestra are finding something for the very first time which astounds those who had considered the concerto a tired old workhorse and thrills to the very marrow those who are either coming new to the work or at least relatively fresh. In fact so exhilarating and thrilling is the playing, so clean the soloist's annotation, so pure her sound, so heartfelt her emotion that when the first movement ends not one but dozens of those in the higher tiers broke into spontaneous applause, which they stoically continued despite the disapproving looks of the purists until almost the entire audience acknowledges they are witnessing the indescribable and joined in the unorthodox ovation.

Again, the camera shows what the audience cannot quite see, although some might have guessed from the sheer beauty and intensity of the playing, that the soloist, this young girl barely thirteen years of age, is not quite in control of her emotions. Indeed the conductor bends over to her, whispers something in her ear and then lends her his large immaculately white handkerchief which she uses with her back turned away from the audience.

When Sir Iain has calmed the house and there is quiet once more they play the Canzonetta absolutely as agreed, flowing and easily. It is as if the violin is singing it, refusing to sentimentalize the exquisite theme, with the result that there is more poetry and lyrical beauty than ever. When the flute sings its own brief song before the violin re-enters, the camera goes close on the violinist's face and catches a look in her eyes that speaks of something she has seen or is seeing even now before her instrument sings out its wistful lament once more, over orchestral playing so tender and understanding that again it seems as if the emotions cannot bear it. In fact the sensitive stereo microphones pick up from somewhere deep in the audience what sounds like a cried gasp of anguish, just before the tympanum thunders in the change of tempo and the violin starts to pick, then thread, and then dance its way through the subsequent scherzo.

As for the finale there is all the bravura you would want, even though taken at a speed deliberately chosen to avoid any danger of breathlessness. All the tiny cuts are opened out once more so that the entire movement may be heard and enjoyed as intended, brilliant, exhilarating, yet still deeply affecting. The soloist is unafraid to expose her emotions, yet without in any way turning in a subjective performance.

How could she have done? Remember how they applauded? They would never have applauded like that unless the soloist had made the music and the experience of it available to them all. If you were there you will never forget it to the day you die, just as you will never forget the astounding, dazzling, brilliant, breathtaking, fantastic and astonishing tour de force Fleur Fisher-Dilke produced for the finale, a cascade of glittering notes, a positive tumult of heartstopping music.

Listen to that applause if you have the record and you were not there, or even if you were there and need reminding of the ovation the entire audience gave to the child they had taken unequivocally to their hearts. Of course it isn't all on the record, because a five-minute ovation (or was it longer?) is too much to include at the end of a recording, so all you get is an idea of the uproar. While if you were there, you will remember exactly what it was like because you too must surely have been up on your feet and shouting just like everyone around you. Calling Bravo! Calling for an encore! Cheering and maybe even crying, as were so many of the audience, moved to helpless tears by the performance of that wonderful child in her velvet and silk suit, her tousled hair soaked with the sweat of her efforts, her big bow tie gone awry. That thirteen-year-old girl who just stood there with her violin hanging from one hand, her bow from the other, and her head bowed as the whole Albert Hall rose to her, the younger members of the audience stamping on the floor as well as shouting for more, shouting Bravo! as the whole orchestra rose and joined in the ovation while still the girl stood with her head bowed and her arms hanging down by her side, like a marionette whose strings have been cut until slowly she stood to face her audience and to bow again and then to stand again to bow to her orchestra, and then to stand again to bow to her conductor who held both his arms open to her as if she were his own child, while those near enough could see that Fleur was smiling, and the camera showed that there was not a tear in her eyes but just that smile, only that smile, a smile that for those who know has to be the bravest smile they have ever seen.

Sound Bytes

B AND B
Fleur Fisher-Dilke talks about Beethoven and Berg with Nick Sarjeant

There can be no serious lover of music alive today who has not heard of Fleur Fisher-Dilke, let alone has not heard her play. The most prodigious young violinist this country has so far produced, she would appear to be above criticism. So far nothing written or said about her concerning her musicality, professionalism and technique, has been anything other than laudatory, if not positively eulogistic.

So on meeting her for the first time in person I found myself trying to do two things, and most unfairly so. I looked for faults in her somewhere both as a person and a performer, and I'm happy to report (and to my shame) that I found none. Fleur Fisher-Dilke is as beautiful as she is painted, and musically she is as prodigiously gifted as universally acknowledged.

My real reason to seek her out, or rather the brief I'd been given, was to talk to her about her recording of the Berg Violin Concerto with the Chicago Philharmonic under Alfred Homer. The Berg is rarely the choice of young violinists, let alone those who are making their name as great lyrical or even romantic musicians. I suggested Fisher-Dilke might well belong to this category, only to be shot down in flames.

'I don't believe in categorization for starters,' she told me. 'Great music is there to be played, all of it, and you can't hide away from some of the great pieces by saying they're not your sort of stuff. Secondly if there were such things as categories, I wouldn't file myself under "R" for Romantic. I don't like schmaltz or syrup, not as a style of playing that is. I think it's very unfair that some composers are dismissed as being *overly romantic* simply because of the way they've generally been played – Paganini is "histrionic", Wieniawski's "too ardent", Sarasate is "just pyrotechnical gypsy fireside music", you know the sort of thing. And what about poor Tchaikovsky? As soon as you pick up your bow you can hear the highbrows groan – Oh no! Not that sentimental old *schmegegge* again!'

Schmegegge? One of her famous teacher Isaac Kline's favourite words for what Fisher-Dilke translates as a 'drippy old drone'. At least such a description could never be levelled at Berg, I say, bearing the purpose of our interview in mind. No, Fisher-Dilke agrees, but before leaving the question of repertoire, she just wants to make it clear that she believes in balance – neither too much of one or too little of the other.

'Isaac (Kline) still goes on at me about this, even though he knows I'm converted!' she says. 'Whenever he reckons I'm getting a bit heavy, he makes me play Kreisler's *La Gitana*, or maybe some George Gershwin. It's quite hard to go back to pomping on about whatever it was when you've just played *Fascinatin' Rhythm* as a duet with your foot flat to the boards.'

Back to Berg. Whatever the delightful Miss Fisher-Dilke has to say, the choice of the Berg is in direct contrast with the concerto which brought her instant acclaim, when she first recorded it at the age of 14, namely the Beethoven.

Again, she tells me, I'd be surprised. They are both enormously emotional pieces, both physically and emotionally draining when you play them properly. 'I know everyone thought I was too young to tackle the Beethoven,' Fisher-Dilke reminds me. 'But you see ever since I first heard it as a child, I knew I could play it, because I knew what I wanted it to say. And of course Isaac was a fantastic help since he made me keep the meaning of the work to the forefront all the time. He didn't tell me what the meaning was, because he trusted me when I said I could feel it. But what he did was he kept reminding me, and while of course the more I play it the more it evolves in me, the structure that I work from is still basically the same. I might just repaper a room here and there, or maybe move some of the furniture around, that's all.'

'It's an interesting thing with the Berg as well,' she continues. 'You hear about it being an intellectual exercise, that Berg was a "wrong-note Romantic" an abstract serialist, and all that jazz. But I think, and so do a lot of people, that Berg is about pain. I mean real pain. And while some audiences might find that a little too depressing, preferring their violin music to be lyrical and optimistic even when it is deeply felt, it isn't honest to play the Berg without trying to show what he was feeling. And he certainly wasn't in a party mood when he wrote it.'

Yet the ending of the concerto conveys serenity to a lot of people, as the violin wings ever higher to soar over an orchestra changing to the warmth of B flat major. Again, I meet with a firm rebuttal.

'What about that awful cymbal stroke?' says the soloist. 'I can never hear it, even when I'm playing it, without my hair practically standing on end.'

Yet a girl of Fisher-Dilke's age, what can she know of such things? Of the pain and torment behind works such as the Berg? This was a concerto written for and dedicated to 'the memory of an angel', Manon Gropius who died aged 18 only eight months before the composer himself died of blood poisoning in 1935.

At first Fisher-Dilke avoids the question, trying to sidetrack me into the old argument as to whether or not the concerto really does end in B flat major, but persistence wins the day and she finally

agrees to discuss how much of her young life so far has gone into shaping and affecting her musicianship and her interpretation.

'I hope nothing consciously has,' she says, for the first time not altogether anxious to look me straight on. 'I don't think, as Isaac always says, we should stand there with our wounds showing. It's not on really, to let one's own feelings get in front of the composer's – which can happen all too easily. You break up with someone and you say – "Great, now's the time to play Tchaikovsky." Or you have a bad case of unrequited love and you say, "Time to show 'em with the Elgar." *Wrong*. Don't you agree?'

Wholeheartedly, but if you aren't precisely what you play, you surely are how you play it?

'Up to a point,' Fisher-Dilke agrees. 'But Isaac says it must be osmotic.' What must be? 'Anything that happens to you. It must pass into you, then out into the music without diluting or altering the solution.' And so what had happened to her, to make her able, osmotically or not, to give such profound readings of the Beethoven Concerto and the Elgar? 'The Elgar is easier to explain I suppose,' she ponders. 'After all I lived for so long in his country, in the place where he wrote the work, right on the edge of the Malverns. I used to ride and walk the selfsame hills he did, look at the same views, hear the same birdsong.'

But not suffer the same private emotional agonies, I suppose? 'I had my own set of those,' she replied. 'I once made a list, you know, of the things that have affected me most so far, emotionally obviously. In order of their importance. I tried to be as honest as I could and I don't know really whether I should tell you this. Top of the list, of the things I've found truly unbearable, was the death of a childhood friend, someone I absolutely adored and who died tragically just before I made my debut at the Albert Hall.'

Having long heard the rumour but never known the whole truth, I wondered whether now was the time to find out more, so began by asking whether such a terrible occurrence had in any way altered her playing and interpretation of the Tchaikovsky – a performance which most critics now consider definitive. But Fleur was not to be drawn.

'I'd really rather not talk about it,' she said. 'This sort of thing is very private, while the music is there for all to hear and stands by itself. At least I hope it does.'

Even so I wondered what could have been going through her head during the performance if it was indeed true that she only learned the sad news just before she went on stage.

'Nothing went through my head but the music,' she replied. 'I knew that nothing else could. If I stopped and thought for one moment about what had happened, I could never have gone on playing. So I fixed my mind on the concerto, and my mind's eye on something else.'

'Can you say what that something else was?'

'Yes I can. Although it won't mean anything to you. It was a white deer.'

(The interview can be read in full in the October 1991 issue of Music Today)

THIRD MOVEMENT

Allegro molto vivace

33

Since it seemed that he'd found out everything he had wanted to know, Freddie switched the television set off before the end credits, thus missing the one vital piece of information which would have altered everything that was to happen afterwards. But such was his state of turmoil, it was hardly surprising that he chose not to bother with them. Perhaps if he had been watching the film in a cinema rather than a hotel room, he would have stayed slumped in his seat, using the darkness as an excuse to pull himself together before the house lights came up. But now, all alone in his room, he could do what he wanted, and what he wanted to do was to walk to the window and stare out across the darkened path opposite, while he tried to make sense of what he had just seen.

If, the only peacemaker, if the shortest of words with the biggest of implications. If Freddie had simply just left the set on while he walked to the window to stare without seeing out into the night he would still have learned the one more thing he needed to know because that information was transmitted not visually but by an announcement, one which he killed with the remote control just as a voice was saying *since this film was made*.

But then like everything else that had happened since Freddie had originally travelled to Worcester for his sabbatical, perhaps him missing the vital announcement was also ordained. Possibly the Three Sisters, out of compassion, had agreed this particular victim of theirs should turn his television off at that precise moment because they knew that he would be much better placed to understand and to act on the absolute truth when he did finally learn it. Perhaps.

So while several other million viewers who had not yet switched off their sets that Sunday night learned or were reminded of the end of the story of Fleur Fisher-Dilke, the man who now loved her was standing at his hotel window ignorant of the one fact he really needed to know. For it was this one piece of information which would have helped him understand why the woman he loved considered there to be absolutely no point in returning his love.

Next morning, before he had even had a cup of coffee, Freddie hurried downstairs to Reception to borrow the relevant telephone directory from one of the desk clerks. Not surprisingly there was only one Fisher-Dilke listed, and spelt exactly as he had imagined, Fisher-Dilke, R. FRCS, at an address in Harley Street, W1. He wrote down both the address and the telephone number although it was really only the address he was after, having decided during the night when planning his campaign that telephoning would be useless.

'FRCS,' he mused as he leaned on the desk. 'Remind me what that stands for, would you?'

'Fellow of the Royal College of Surgeons, sir,' the receptionist replied. 'You do know you can call direct from your room, of course.'

'Sure I do,' Freddie replied, turning away to go back upstairs. 'Thanks for your help anyway.'

Back in his room he ate a croissant and drank some black coffee while he sorted out what to wear. In his hurry to leave he'd only packed two changes of clothes, a pair of chinos and a crew-neck cashmere jumper plus his white linen suit with a dark blue cotton shirt. He finally chose the suit in case he bumped into Fleur's father, since it was much less casual. Then checking on the weather out of the window and seeing it was threatening rain, he grabbed his long blue raincoat and was about to hurry out when the telephone rang.

It was Stephen Noyes returning Freddie's call, delighted to hear that he was in London.

'But what the hell are you doing in the Hilton?' he asked. 'You hate big hotels. If you're planning on staying up in town for a few days I insist you come and bunk down here.'

'It was all very last minute, Steve,' Freddie explained. 'I rang you last night as you know—'

'Absolutely,' Stephen interrupted. 'But I got back so late I thought it best to wait till this morning to call you back. Is there something bothering you? You sound a mite *agitato*?'

'There might be. And there again there might not be,' Freddie replied. 'Look – I have to dash out right now. Can I catch you later? I need to talk to you.'

'Of course. I shall be in my practice all day and then I'm going straight home. Only condition is you check out of that place and come and put your head down here. We've got a lot of catching up to do.'

'Sure,' Freddie said with a sudden grin. 'I'll catch you later.'

By the time he was halfway up Park Lane, the rain which had formerly been just a slight drizzle turned to a violent downpour, suddenly teeming down from the skies and ricochetting off the pavements. Everywhere people hurried for cover and, as always when it suddenly starts to rain in cities, there wasn't a free taxicab in sight. So pulling his raincoat collar up around his neck, Freddie ran as fast as he could towards the nearest doorway in order to shelter from the downpour until he could get a cab or the rain had stopped. The rain however seemed to have no intention of stopping and in fact started coming down even harder, so that in the short space of time it took him to reach the sanctuary of a large car showroom, his hair was in rats' tails and his trousers were soaked practically up to the knee.

After ten long damp minutes, Freddie finally spotted a free cab making its way down the road towards him and, dashing out into the rain, managed just in time to attract the driver's attention. Hopping in, Freddie ordered the driver to take him to Harley Street, hoping that with the aid of the cab's heater most of him would have dried out by the time he'd reached his destination.

'Some day!' he called through to the driver.

'You bet!' the cabbie returned. 'No wonder the brolly's called the Englishman's third arm, mate!'

For once he had got himself a cab driver who seemed more content to listen to his car radio rather than put the world to rights conversationally, so Freddie sat back and watched London passing by through the rainstorm. He was in a fever of excitement now he knew who she was and where she lived. Yet a part of him also lived a little in dread, in case this turned out to be not just another cul de sac, but the final cul de sac.

When the cab turned into Wimpole Street it was still raining as hard as ever, the sort of summer rain which causes Test Matches to be abandoned and Wimbledon to go to a third week.

'Drop me as near the doorstep as possible, will you?' Freddie asked. 'This is just terrible!'

'Wish I could,' his driver called back. 'But there's some sort of diversion!'

Freddie stared out ahead of them and saw the traffic was jammed solid in the street ahead.

'Seems Wimpole Street's closed beyond this junction and I can't turn right even! We're all being diverted left!' the driver sounded frustrated. 'Sorry – but looks like I'm going to have to drop you here!'

Freddie found himself decanted on the corner of Queen Anne Street which, following the cabbie's instructions, he discovered joined Harley Street at right angles after about fifty metres. The problem was the number he wanted in Harley Street was right up the far end, the best part of half a mile away, so by the time he reached it, his feet, his trousers and his hair were once again soaking.

Even so, now that he found himself facing the doorway of the house where he knew she was, Freddie forgot his damp discomfort. Taking a long, slow and deep breath to try and calm his palpitating heart, he leaned forward and rang the brass doorbell.

'Yes?' a voice said to him sharply through an intercom grill which he hadn't seen. Freddie took one step back and looked up at the impregnable edifice of the tall house which towered above him. He hadn't thought of this one.

'Sorry?' he said into the intercom after a moment.

'What is your name please?' the voice asked.

'Oh. My name. Yes of course. The name's Jourdan. Frederick Jourdan.'

'Thank you. And who is your appointment with, Mr Jourdan?'

'I'm afraid I don't actually have an appointment,' Freddie replied. 'I'm here on a private matter.'

'I see. May I ask with whom?' the voice requested in a way that gave him the distinct impression that the drawbridge was being raised, not lowered. 'This is a medical practice, you understand. And admission is only to those with appointments. So who is it exactly you wish to see?'

Freddie took a deep breath.

'I'm here to see Miss Fisher-Dilke,' he said as naturally as he could. 'I'm sorry if I pressed the wrong bell—'

'That's perfectly all right,' the voice cut in, giving Freddie the idea that the drawbridge might be coming back down after all. 'If you wouldn't just mind waiting there a moment, Mr Jourdan.'

As it turned out, Freddie waited a great deal longer than a moment before the next announcement. While he did he huddled as close as he could against the door in an effort to keep as much rain off himself as possible, hoping in the interim that someone with a bona fide appointment might turn up so that he might slipstream in behind them. But no-one did, and the subsequent announcement soon scotched any such hopes Freddie had been nursing of alternative means of entry.

'I'm sorry to have kept you, Mr Jourdan,' the voice said, 'but I'm afraid there's no way I can let you in without an appointment. It's a matter of security. We have to have a very tight system here, as you may appreciate. So perhaps if you'd care to ring and speak to Mr Fisher-Dilke or Mr Halliwells' secretary, I'm sure they'll be able to fix you up with the necessary appointment. I'm sure you will understand. Good morning.'

The intercom went dead. Freddie pulled the collar of his raincoat even more tightly round his neck and stepped back onto the pavement to have a good look up at the house. As he did a woman arrived, rang the doorbell and was immediately admitted. Through the door when it was electronically opened, Freddie managed to catch sight of a small hallway and yet another solid-looking door, exactly the same sort of triple-entry system he imagined that had been employed in American medical practices for years. So even if he had been able to slip in behind the ingoing patient, he knew he wouldn't have got any further. Such systems were specifically designed to keep out intruders.

As for the house, when he crossed to the other pavement and looked up again, he saw it was on five floors and that didn't include a basement whose window was steel-barred for security, as indeed was the ground-floor window. Not that Freddie nursed any intention of trying to force an entry, far from it. All he wanted to do now, in fact all he could do now, was simply to see what sort of house Fleur lived in — and how it was placed in the street — before retiring somewhere to rethink out his game plan.

That she lived there he had no doubt at all, even though there was no actual proof since it was her father's name which was listed in the directory, not hers. Yet he knew she lived there the way he had known most things about her so far, by sheer instinct. He could sense her presence somewhere on one of those five floors above him, as he stood in the street below, and the thought of her being there filled him with a tremendous happiness. At the same time he also knew the real battle for her had only just begun.

Again, he knew of no real reason why this should be so other than because he felt it to be so, yet Freddie knew he was right because he also sensed a feeling of unease, or even animosity, as if something or someone first had to be conquered before he could reach Fleur and carry her away from a place he suddenly saw not as her home after all, but as her prison.

First, however, he had to regroup since he would do no good standing there in the street in full view of every window in the house. At least the rain had eased some minutes ago and by now had almost stopped, but Freddie was of course still soaked through to his skin. So having decided that his first and most sensible move would be to go some place where he could change, he recrossed the road and hurrying round the corner turned into Weymouth Mews where his friend Stephen had his practice and off which lived in a small mews house which — now Freddie came to think of it — ran right behind Fleur's particular block in Harley Street.

Dashing and splashing along the pavement, Freddie soon found the door of the practice. With none of the attendant fuss he had just encountered at his last port of call, he was admitted within moments into the presence of his good friend, his old friend, and now that he had announced the end of his engagement to Diane, perhaps pretty soon his only friend.

A great big shambling bear of a man who was much taken to standing in corners of rooms as if to try and minimize his bulk, Stephen was one of the most golden-hearted people Freddie had ever met. Nothing was ever too much trouble for this brilliant chaotic man, which was the reason he hadn't become anywhere near as rich as his colleagues, most of whom had only a fraction of his innate ability but a hundred times his money. For Stephen spent half of his working life administering to the poor and the homeless, often using his old and much loved classic Humber Super Snipe as a sort of mobile clinic.

Stephen welcomed him like a long-lost brother, and then seeing the drenched state Freddie was in invited him at once round to his mews house to dry himself out in comfort over a good drink. The house was as tidy as its owner was untidy, a fact which had always bemused Freddie until Stephen had explained to him that if he lived the way he thought, he'd never get out of the door.

'So what brings you to bandit country?' Stephen asked once they'd dispensed with the small talk. 'Nothing wrong with your health, I sincerely hope?'

'Nothing wrong with my physical health, Steve, thank God,' Freddie replied, 'least not as far as I know—'

'You'd know as well as most of the desperadoes round here would know,' Stephen growled, putting a large whisky into his guest's hand. 'Now we'd better get you out of those wet things and into something dry or else you will have something wrong with you.'

'I was about to add that although there's nothing wrong with me physically, I have my worries about up here!' Freddie tapped his head and called after Stephen who had begun to wander up the staircase, which led directly from the living room, to fetch a dressing gown. Freddie began to get undressed. 'I seriously thought I was losing my mind!'

'Yes?' Stephen stopped at the top of the stairs to peer back down at Freddie. 'You want to tell me why?'

'If you want to hear, sure,' Freddie said. 'Soon as I'm out of these soaking wet things.'

After Stephen had put Freddie's wet clothes in his spin dryer and Freddie was wrapped up in a thick blue towelling bathrobe, the two men sat with their drinks beside them while Freddie told all, right up to the events of that very morning.

'I can see why you thought you were losing it, chum,' Stephen nodded. 'It's quite a tale.'

'I'm glad you believe me anyway,' Freddie replied. 'Even when I tell it, it all still sounds a little crazy.'

'Who said I believed you?' Stephen asked him, widening his eyes. 'All I said was—'

'Okay, I know what all you said was, thanks,' Freddie interrupted with a grin. 'I'm just glad I've lost my heart not my voice. I don't think I could take being a patient of yours.'

'I'd rather deal with the voice any day, chum, than the heart. You know that's what her father does, don't you? You know that Fisher-Dilke's a heart surgeon?'

'I knew he was a surgeon. I got that from the documentary. I didn't know he was a cardiologist.'

'What's the big deal? Why the deep frown?'

'I guess because it's sort of ironic. That he specializes in the heart, that's all.'

'A heart is a heart, chum,' Stephen said, finishing his drink. 'It's an organ like any other organ. Like your liver, your kidneys, your spleen, what have you.'

'Funny they don't send cards with livers on them on St Valentine's Day, Steve,' Freddie replied. 'Or kidneys, or spleens, or what-have-yous, wouldn't you say?'

'No I wouldn't. The heart is a muscle, Fred. I know you've made a fortune writing soppy-date songs in shows for incurable romantics, but you know as well as I do that the heart is there to pump our blood round our bodies. It isn't there to form our emotions, to break when true love is gone. If that were the case, the health service would have had to pack up yonks ago. Imagine the doctors' surgeries. *Doctor — my girlfriend's just left me and my heart is failing—*'

'Okay,' Freddie said, putting up a hand to stop the pantomime being performed for his sake, as the large shambolic figure of his friend began to stagger around the room clutching his chest. 'Okay, I get the drift.'

'Cock and bull, Fred, and you know it,' Stephen said, collapsing in a chair. 'There's nothing wrong with your heart. You haven't lost it. The only thing love makes you lose is your senses.'

'It was a figure of speech, Steve. There was no need to go to town on it.'

Stephen looked across at him, half frowning, half glaring.

'I was only trying to lighten the atmosphere, Frederick,' he said with a sigh. 'I've never seen you so morose. If this is what love does for you, thank God when I got unmarried I stayed unmarried.'

Freddie knew this was the very opposite of the truth. Stephen had been married for fifteen years to his antithesis, a tiny delicate-looking ballerina with the unlikely name of Pansy, who dressed like a doll, lived like a pig and had the temper of a red donkey. Stephen had only survived her constant assaults because he was so large and she was so little, but he had adored her. When she suddenly ran off with an abundantly wealthy South American he was literally heartbroken, which was why whenever possible Stephen spent his time disparaging the notion of true love.

Freddie well knew this because the two men had become

firm friends shortly after Pansy had left, just as Freddie well knew that Stephen was the man to help him in his dilemma.

'I don't see exactly how,' Stephen replied when he realized what Freddie wanted. 'What can I do that you can't do?'

'You can think with clarity, Steve,' Freddie said. 'That's what you can do that I can't do. Not any more at least, not since that dream.'

For the first time since he'd turned up so bedraggled that day, Freddie felt that his friend was staring at him not as a friend but as a doctor, and he found himself looking away. Because he couldn't really blame him.

That evening over dinner taken in the panelled dining room of the Connaught, Stephen was able to paint in a few of the missing details. Although he had never met Fleur's father personally, he had heard all about him on the grapevine and from what Freddie could gather, as far as gossip went, Harley Street was little different from Broadway. Before his daughter's sudden fame Richard Fisher-Dilke had been plain Richard Fisher, struggling to make any sort of mark on the world of cardiology – until he divorced his first wife and married a top heart surgeon's daughter, inheriting the practice when the famous man retired.

'The house I was left standing outside this morning?' Freddie remarked.

'Lord Hurst's old practice,' Stephen confirmed. 'Fisher-Dilke runs it now, with two junior partners. A licence to print money really.'

'Is he any good as a surgeon?'

'He's probably better than he was, but he's no Dr Barnard. In fact he's no Lord Hurst even, and that's not saying much. In the wonderful world of medicine, practice certainly makes perfect. Or rather The practice does.'

'Okay,' Freddie nodded, 'but do you have any idea what sort of man he is, as opposed to what sort of surgeon?'

'Not really,' Stephen replied. 'He had a bit of a reputation as a ladies' man. When you get to meet him you might find that hard to believe, because he's certainly no Adonis. But then small men are a different breed, wouldn't you agree?'

'It's hard for either of us to say exactly,' Freddie replied, finishing the last of his wild duck and mangetout. 'I'm not exactly short, and look at you.'

'Well, Richard Fisher-Dilke is short and apparently he has most of the shorter man's foibles. Particularly as far as women go, and most particularly as far as other men's wives go. That's what broke up the marriage. He was having an affair with another consultant's wife.'

'So what of Fleur's mother?' Freddie asked, greedy for every detail he could get about Fleur now he knew who she was. 'Did she remarry or what?'

'Worse than that, I'm afraid,' Stephen replied, beckoning the waiter over. 'She died very suddenly.'

Freddie drank some claret and thought for a while, remaining silent while Stephen consulted the menu.

'Why should you remember that I wonder?' he asked when Stephen had indicated what he wanted for pudding. 'Opera's your thing, not orchestral music, so why should the death of a child virtuoso's mother stick in that great brain of yours?'

'Yes, I wonder why, too,' Stephen replied with a frown. 'Except that I do have a magpie mind, irrelevant facts a speciality.'

'I don't think so. I think that to make that sort of fact stick there must have been another aspect to all this. Something unusual about the mother's death that made you remember it.'

Stephen grunted and then shrugged, wiping his mouth on his crisp linen napkin.

'All I can say is that I remember seeing it in the paper.'

'But why? Why should Fleur's mother's death be in the paper? Unless it was an obituary. But then she'd have had to have done something notable or noteworthy herself.'

'Pass,' Stephen said. 'Anyway I never read obituaries. You don't at my age. Just in case you turn the page one day and find you're reading your own.'

Freddie smiled at Stephen's wisecrack, even though it was a chestnut, because Stephen had that god-given ability to make everything sound first-hand.

'So if it wasn't an obituary which it obviously wasn't,' Freddie continued as the waiter cleared away their plates, 'then it must have been a news story. And if it was a news story, then what could have happened to make it one? I take it she wasn't murdered?'

Freddie had chosen the same as his friend for dessert, a confection of meringue and fresh strawberry mousse which was now placed before them both, accompanied by two glasses of Muscat Beaumes de Venise.

'I don't want to put you off, Fred,' Stephen said, 'but you know crusades are more often than not likely to lead up gumtrees.'

'I think as far as this one goes, Steve, I've had my full share of disappointments, don't you?'

'Knowing this life, I don't think there is such a thing. Even so, if you think it'll be of any help we'll shuffle you off to the *Daily Mail* tomorrow. I know someone who can help you there. Nice kid. Helped her through a bit of voice trouble a couple of years ago. She's a promising young soprano who researches part time when she can't pay the rent.'

Next morning Freddie found himself sitting in a coffee shop on Kensington High Street studying a clutch of newspaper cuttings on the death of Amelia Fisher-Dilke.

He also found he had been perfectly right in his belief that, in order to make headlines, Amelia Fisher-Dilke's leaving of this world must have been something out of the ordinary. It was.

It had happened at the Salzburg Festival three years earlier and from what Freddie could gather as he skimmed through the file he'd been given, the news had made the front pages of The Times, the Daily Telegraph, the Independent and the Guardian, and feature stories in all the tabloids.

Out of habit, since it was the only newspaper he took when he came to England, Freddie selected the piece from The Times for the full story:

Tragedy at Music Festival
BY JAMES WYATH MUSIC CRITIC.

During last night's performance of Prokofiev's First Violin Concerto at the annual Salzburg Music Festival, the mother of soloist Fleur Fisher-Dilke collapsed and died in full view of her daughter.

Amelia Dilke, ex-wife of the heart surgeon Richard Fisher-Dilke, was seated in the second row when she suffered what was later confirmed to be a massive heart attack. She was pronounced dead on arrival at Salzburg Clinic. Her seventeen-year-old daughter Fleur, considered one of the world's violin virtuosos, was also taken to hospital suffering from shock, having witnessed her mother's collapse during what was apparently a definitive performance of the Prokofiev. The rest of the concert was cancelled, with Miss Fisher-Dilke obviously unable to continue.

Last night her father Richard Fisher-Dilke, who had been performing major heart surgery at Harefield Hospital, stated that the death of his former wife, aged forty-one, was a terrible shock, although as he understood it she had very recently been diagnosed as suffering from a chronic coronary misfunction for which she had been receiving treatment.

A spokesman for Salzburg Clinic told reporters that Miss Fisher-Dilke was too traumatized to comment, but refused to confirm rumours that because of concern for her own health the violinist had in fact been admitted to the intensive care unit.

Health, page 16

Freddie didn't bother with the in-depth article on *The Super-Stress of Prodigy* which was also included, but turned his attentions instead to flicking through the reports carried by the more popular press. Most of these included what looked like amateur photographs of a distressed Fleur being half carried from the stage by the conductor, Alfred Homer, and an unidentified member of the orchestra. There were also pictures of her collapsed mother. Most of the papers pegged their story on the same hook, namely the heartbreak of a heart surgeon's famous daughter during her definitive performance of Prokofiev's First Violin Concerto in front of a star-studded audience.

'I brought you these as well,' a voice said from behind Freddie, as a hand dropped another set of paperclipped cuttings on the café table. 'I didn't think you'd want to plough through her entire file because it's huge, but maybe this lot might help.'

Stephen's singing friend Lisa, a pretty short-haired girl who looked more like an athlete than most people's idea of a singer, sat down opposite Freddie with two fresh cups of coffee, one of which she pushed towards him.

'I thought you might need this as well,' she said. 'You look as if you need a bit of pulling together.'

Freddie thanked the handsome young woman and

sipped the coffee she'd rightly guessed he needed while he began to flick through the new set of cuttings.

'What are these?' he said. 'Or rather why do you think they might help?'

'I was just playing a hunch,' Lisa said. 'I'm more into your sort of music, you see. That's what I *really* love, musicals. I mean I like opera too, but not as well as I like your stuff. And Sondheim. And all the past greats – Rodgers and Hart, Oscar Hammerstein, Jules Styne, Lerner and Loewe. Last thing I did, last big thing that is, was a revival of *Carousel*.'

'Great show,' Freddie agreed. 'Rotten film but a great stage show, and I still don't see where this is getting us.'

'Sorry, I'm just being long-winded, as usual. All I wanted to say is that classical music isn't really my thing, although of course I knew Fleur Fisher-Dilke.'

'Wait a minute—' Freddie said quietly.

'I mean she was incredibly famous, a sort of female Nigel Kennedy in a way, although without the punk bit. But she was into cross-over music, you know – jazz, and blues, and a bit of rock. She even did an album with who was it? Yes, with Forever Green I think it was. It wasn't bad actually.'

'No no, wait a minute if you don't mind.' Freddie stopped her before she could go on. 'Why *knew*? Why *was*? Why the past tenses? What's wrong with *know*? *Is*?'

'Didn't you know she'd given up?'

'Given up?'

'Oh no, of course the piano's your thing really, isn't it?' Lisa reminded herself. 'And you're not into classical music.'

'Well I am actually, although you're right about the piano,' Freddie said, 'or rather it was just the piano, until recently. So no, I didn't follow the violin, and so of course I didn't know she'd given up. Any idea why?'

'All I know is and it's only from her cuttings, that

she's never played since her mother died,' Lisa said. 'She's never played again once. See here?' She pointed to a relevant cutting. 'Never even taken her violin out of her case apparently,' she said, tapping the newspaper item. 'Evidently when she announced she was giving up she meant it a hundred per cent.'

'But I wonder why?' Freddie asked, beginning to flick through the second batch of cuttings with a renewed urgency. 'It must say somewhere. It must say why a girl as brilliant as her should suddenly say she's giving her music up altogether. Okay, so her mother died and she died under her very eyes, which we'd all agree must be quite a terrible thing to happen, but surely with time—'

He stopped and looked across the table at Lisa who shrugged her agreement back at him.

'Stop playing for a year maybe,' Freddie continued thoughtfully. 'Or for how ever long it takes to get over something like that. God, I don't know how long it takes, but people get over these things. At least they do with parents, surely. We all have to. And particularly when people are unique, if they have some totally unique gift for the world then they have to get over it. But not Fleur Fisher-Dilke. Fleur Fisher-Dilke announced that she was never going to play again only three months after her mother died. That wouldn't be enough time for anybody. I lost my dog last year and I'm barely over it now, but to lose a mother – no, no way was she going to know whether she was coming or going after only three months. But here it is. It made headlines again.' He turned the cuttings back to Lisa even though she was already familiar with their content. 'You see?' he asked. '**Fleur Fisher-Dilke To Retire. Violin Virtuoso Bows Out. Last Chord for Former Child Prodigy.** But no-one says why. Least of all Fleur herself. There's just this statement issued through her press officer which says that, as from the date of this announcement Fleur Fisher-Dilke has decided never to play or perform in public or to record ever again for personal and private reasons. She thanks all her fans and friends all round the world and while she wishes them to know how much she enjoyed playing for them, she finds herself unable any longer to undertake the strain of public performance. Therefore it is with great regret that she announces this decision, but assures everyone that her decision is irreversible. And that's it.'

Lisa frowned into her coffee cup and then drank the remains.

'I suppose it has to have been her mother's death,' she said. 'Whatever you say.'

'That's what the papers thought,' Freddie replied. 'But I don't.'

'So what do you think? I mean what else could it be?'

'That's what I intend to find out,' Freddie replied. 'Can I keep these?' He indicated the file of photocopied cuts.

'Sure. I mean of course.'

Freddie put them all back in the document holder and, tipping some money into a saucer which held the bill, pushed his chair back and got up.

'Any particular off-the-cuff theories?' Lisa asked as he slipped his jacket back on.

'No.' Freddie shook his head and picked up his belongings. 'All I know, and I know it with absolute certainty, is that it wasn't because of her mother.'

'But how do you know?'

Freddie looked at her then smiled. 'Let's just say a little bird told me,' he replied. 'And I'll tell you something else I know. You just got yourself a part in my next musical when it comes to London. For all your help. And that's a deal.'

34

Their taxis passed within fifty yards of each other in Park Lane, Freddie's going north back towards Weymouth Street while Diane's was heading south towards Beaufort Gardens and the hotel where she knew Freddie always stayed when he came to London. In fact had they glanced across the central reservation as both their cabs pulled away from the traffic lights outside the Dorchester Hotel, they could very well have caught sight of each other. That was how close Freddie came to meeting Nemesis rather than Clotho, Lachesis and Atropos.

As it was Freddie was still reading through the cuttings concerning Fleur's sudden and extraordinary retirement, while Diane was busy catching up on fashion in the latest English copy of *Vogue* which she had bought on arrival at the airport early that morning. So within a matter of a few seconds Diane's last chance had gone, and Freddie was out of the reach of the goddess of Vengeance and safely back in the hands of the Three Sisters.

In the cab Freddie read a cutting from a Sunday colour magazine, headed *Relatively Speaking*. It was a two-page spread, most of it taken up with a three-quarter-page photograph of Fleur Fisher-Dilke and her mother Amelia. Freddie could see at once where Fleur got some of her wonderful looks. Although her mother hadn't been classically beautiful she had the sort of good looks which would breed on well, particularly in girls, in her eyes, the set of her facial bones, and the prettiness of her mouth.

The photograph was simply posed. Amelia was sitting

foreground, wearing a white silk shirt and what looked like black crepe trousers, while Fleur stood behind her, one hand on one of her mother's shoulders and the other holding her violin down by her side. Simple but effective, because like all good photographs it captured the essence not just of the two individuals but of their relationship, in the way that the camera can — when it is in the right hands — chart the landscapes of the face and explain man to man.

Amelia Dilke on her daughter Fleur.

It's pretty awful to say but I only ever got close to Fleur after I was divorced. Maybe this is often the case with the parents of only one child, I don't know, but it was certainly the case with me. It wasn't that I didn't want to have Fleur because I did. We both did, Richard (my husband), and I, so Fleur wasn't one of those early marriage 'accidents'. She was very planned and I think probably early on rather spoiled. Her grandparents certainly spoiled her. But she was always dreadfully shy. I mean cripplingly so and I don't think that helped establish a good early relationship. Not that I'm blaming Fleur for that or her shyness, I still could have tried a lot harder. But I became too caught up in my marriage, particularly after Richard moved us all (except himself)

lock, stock and barrel to the country. My old nanny Deanie Roberts came with us — to the most beautiful little house in Worcestershire — but even so I had hardly ever been out of London, so you can imagine!

Richard thought we'd 'improve' in the country. He was all into social 'improvement' and he probably still is, if that doesn't sound too bitchy. He wanted Fleur to be brought up as a young lady, maintaining that this was impossible in the city nowadays. Hence the move to the Shires and the concentration on Fleur, and to a certain extent myself, learning the social graces.

The last thing Richard ever wanted was for Fleur to be a professional musician, and I'm afraid I went along with that. My father was a concert pianist, you see, and his career wrecked his marriage. So somewhat illogically I thought that if Fleur was allowed to be a professional prodigy, because it was perfectly obvious from the moment she sat down at the piano she was extraordinarily gifted, then my marriage would fall apart just like my parents. I still think it must be horrendously difficult to keep a marriage together when you are trying to bring up an infant prodigy.

Anyway, that wasn't what happened. Our marriage fell apart for quite different reasons and it was only afterwards that I realized what a dreadful mother I had been. Fleur needn't have forgiven me. She was very well set up by then with a marvellous body of people, teachers, mentors, minders, you name it. They looked after her, and she'd just made her now famous first recording when I found out my husband had been unfaithful. But Fleur was quite wonderful and understood and forgave me right from the word go, which for a while made me feel even worse!

Now we are the very best of friends, which is the best that any parent can possibly hope for. I would prefer to go anywhere, or do anything, first and foremost with Fleur, over anyone else I know. She's still very shy in company, often painfully so, but privately we have a hoot. She's my best girlfriend. What more can a mother want?

Fleur Fisher-Dilke on her mother Amelia.

I always thought I was the failure because I was so shy. I was actually frightened more than anything, people I didn't know literally scared me rigid – they still do. So I thought I was a real no-hoper from the first day I started to clue these things together.

Mum didn't help, not because she didn't want to, but because she was always so poised and cool and confident-seeming. She says now this was just her model training, but to a child she seemed so sophisticated I thought hell – I'm never going to be like *her*. And she was so mad about my father and he was, or anyway seemed to be, so mad about her that I think I was jealous. I know I felt sort of out of it, but then don't all only children?

Anyway, I'm sure that's how the music started, or that was the reason for it. It was a world all of my own, something I could make myself and hide away inside, this fantastic world of sound and fantasy. Because that's what music is really, it's just fantasy. To a child particularly, it's a world of make-believe, another place to go and hide.

I didn't want to show off, but I did want my mother

and father to like what I was doing. So I suppose there were some disappointments early on when my father didn't show much interest, or Mum didn't come to a concert or a recording or something. And while I understand all that now, I didn't then. And rather than just finding it hurtful, I wasn't sure I was doing the right thing. If it hadn't been for Lady Stourton who lived in the big house nearby and who half adopted me, maybe I'd have stopped playing altogether. I came near to it once or twice, but it was she who kept me going, in fact it was she who sent me to Sir Iain and hence Izzy, Isaac Kline my teacher.

It's very different now. My mother and I go everywhere together, not because we have to because I could travel most places perfectly safely by myself, but because we want to. I can't imagine going to play a concert and Mum not coming. We have such a laugh all the time. It's marvellous whenever something goes wrong on tour, which it invariably does, because instead of agonizing in a corner all by myself I can let off steam by laughing about it with Mum.

She helps in all sorts of other ways of course, with my clothes and my hair, and my whole general look which is very important on the concert platform. She helps with any emotional wrangles I have as well, although with my itinerary I don't really have any time for boyfriends. One day, perhaps!

The only regrets I have about our relationship? Well actually there are three. I wish Mum would give up smoking. It's her only bad habit and she smokes far too much. Secondly I hope I'm not stopping her getting remarried by carting her all around the place with me all the time, and thirdly I wish she'd actually see me playing. Do you know, in all the time we've been travelling together, that's for over four years, she's never actually seen one of my concerts? She's always been so busy backstage helping me get ready, and then she says she's too nervous to go out front!

This year she's promised faithfully to make a special effort. I'm trying to arrange it so that she can be out front when I play the Salzburg Festival for the first time this year. I've nearly got a promise out of her, but I think I'm going to have to get my manager Gregory Rogers to draw up an actual contract!

35

'Your fiancée rang while you were out,' Stephen told Freddie as he walked through the front door of his house, stopping dead Freddie in his tracks.

'Yes,' Freddie said thoughtfully after he'd hung his mackintosh on a coathook by the door. 'I take it you didn't say?'

'No, I told her I'd seen you,' Stephen replied poker-faced before letting Freddie off the hook. 'I said I'd had lunch with you some weeks ago when you were last in town. And that was it. What's she doing ringing here?'

'It's okay. She's probably systematically going through all my London numbers, at least the likely ones that is. Where I might be staying, who I might be seeing.'

'My God, the last sort of woman you'd want to be shackled to,' Stephen replied. 'No wonder you're baling out. But the good news is that you're right: Miss Fleur Fisher-Dilke is at home.'

Immediately Freddie grabbed his friend's arm. 'How do you know?' he said. 'You mean you saw her?'

Detaching his arm from Freddie's grip, Stephen draped it round his shoulder instead and led him over to the spiral staircase which led upstairs.

'From my bedroom window, if you kneel down, you can just see the top floor of the house,' he said. 'And when I got dressed this morning I dropped a cuff link—'

'Why didn't you call me?' Freddie cried, turning round to his friend in desperation. 'For God's sake you should have come and woken me up!'

'All right, all right,' Stephen said, once more detaching

himself from Freddie's half-demented grip. 'If you'll hold your horses and listen. I was actually just going to come and call you, but at that very moment she looked down and she must have seen me—'

'So what? She doesn't know you! So what if she did see you?'

'Calm down, Freddie. And listen. It doesn't matter a damn whether or not she knows or doesn't know me. What would you think if you were her? If you saw what looked like some dirty old man kneeling at a window looking back up at you? You'd do what she did. You'd drop the blind.'

'Okay!' Freddie replied, now running up the staircase. 'But that was this morning, dammit!'

While he was waiting for Freddie to discover what he himself had discovered as soon as he had returned home for lunch, Stephen poured them a glass of wine each and sat down at the keyboard of his Broadwood upright piano. He had just begun to play a simplified Chopin Etude when Freddie came back down the spiral staircase.

'The blind's still down,' he said, collapsing on the sofa. 'Why in hell should it still be down at this time of day? Unless she's already seen me! Oh God of course she could have seen me—'

'Calm down, Fred, calm down.' Stephen stopped playing and half turned to Freddie. 'The chances of her seeing you are very remote. You arrived here in the middle of a rainstorm, we got straight into a taxi outside the door last night and straight back out of one when we came home, your bedroom is not visible from her house—'

'She could have seen me from the front, when I was trying to get in yesterday morning!'

'Well – if she *did*, which I doubt, and-or she saw you coming into this house, and-or she thinks you might just be in the neighbourhood, and she doesn't want you to know she's there, do you really think she's going to let herself be seen standing in full view at her bedroom window in her dressing gown? I mean *just-in-case*?'

'Okay,' Freddie groaned, leaning back on the sofa. 'So why is her blind still down?'

'Because,' Stephen said, beginning to play the Chopin Etude once more, 'she doesn't want to be clocked by some dirty old doctor on his hands and knees.'

'All right,' Freddie agreed grudgingly, sitting up to drink some wine. 'And that sounds dreadful in C. It was written to be played in E flat.'

Stephen ignored the remark and continued playing while Freddie sat staring into the bottom of his wine glass.

'I'm going to have to get in there, Steve,' he said finally. 'We're going to have to think up a way of getting me in there.'

'So I gather,' Stephen said. 'While I was out doing some shopping this morning I put what's left of my mind to work.'

'Yes? And?'

Stephen found Freddie was already looking up and staring hard by the time he swung round on the piano stool to face him.

'I couldn't come up with one damned thing,' he said.

Freddie was sure there was no point in telephoning her, and there was no point in writing to her either. There were good and obvious reasons why he couldn't do either one or both of those things, Freddie explained to Stephen for the third time. First of all he didn't know her private number, and even if he did, even if he did somehow manage to get hold of it, the chances were heavily odds-on that as soon as she heard who it was she'd simply put the phone down. After all, as Freddie explained, she'd been the one who had fled in the first place. She'd run away from him. She had reneged on the deal they had made

461

over him not reading her journal. It was all too obvious he wouldn't get anywhere by telephoning her.

As for writing, he'd tried that in the past as well, and what had been the result? She'd ignored his letters. And it was no good saying that it was high time he got the message, Freddie retorted, because Stephen didn't know what he was talking about, because Stephen hadn't seen the light that Freddie had seen in Fleur's eyes. Stephen hadn't seen the expression on Fleur's face when they met. Stephen hadn't felt the electricity in the air.

'You mean she's just playing hard to get?' Stephen suggested as the argument raged on that evening over dinner taken at Stephen's favourite local bistro.

'No she is not playing hard to get!' Freddie retorted. 'I don't know what she's playing, but that certainly isn't the name of her game.'

'She's certainly not making it easy for you.'

'For good reason, Steve. There's a lot more to this than meets the eye, you bet.'

'You spend too much time inside your head, Frederick. It's not good for you. You should get out of yourself more.'

'Very funny.'

'Actually I was being serious. People like you, the Hopelessly Artistic, as my father used to call them, your imaginations have been over-cultivated. Hasn't it occurred to you just once that this woman might not actually fancy you?'

'No it hasn't. Not once.'

'Oh I know such a thought is beyond the pale for an Adonis like you—'

'Lay off it, Steve,' Freddie warned his companion. 'This really isn't a laughing matter.'

'Oh dear now I know you're in love, Fred,' Stephen replied, with a sad shake of his shaggy head. 'Why? Because you've quite lost your sense of humour.'

*   *   *

As Stephen fell into a deep sleep Freddie remained
kneeling at his friend's bedroom window where he
had been more or less continuously since they had
returned from the restaurant. Stephen had long given
up the unequal struggle to get his friend to go to bed
himself, and instead had allowed Freddie to talk him to
sleep while he kept what showed every sign of being a
night watch on the still-drawn blind of the window on
the top floor of the house opposite.

A light had been showing in what they both supposed
to be Fleur's bedroom when they had returned, but as
he watched Freddie saw no sign of any life. Not until
exactly on the stroke of eleven o'clock, when a shadow
was suddenly thrown against the drawn blind. Freddie
narrowed his eyes, cupping both his hands above them as
if that would help distinguish the shape of the silhouette
which was enormously exaggerated by the position of the
bedroom light. Whoever it was seemed to be collecting
something from somewhere right beside the window,
something which they then held up to eye level as if to
check or read. Freddie couldn't even hazard a guess at
what was happening except that from the general shape
of the silhouette he was absolutely sure that the person
he was seeing wasn't Fleur. It was a woman certainly,
but apparently an older woman and, even allowing for
the distortion caused by the lighting, someone of large
proportions. As she turned sideways, this figure seemed to
be wearing a hat and a coat with some sort of exaggerated
lapels, leading Freddie to conclude that she was perhaps
the housekeeper returning from her evening off and was
looking in to make sure Fleur had everything she wanted
before retiring herself.

A few moments later the light was switched off and the
shadow play was over. Behind Freddie Stephen snored
once and then turned over in his bed, so realizing there was

nothing left for him to see or do, Freddie got up from his knees and tiptoed out of the room.

Lying in the dark in his own bedroom, Freddie tried to think of a way to get inside the house and finally to Fleur. He imagined the house would be laid out more or less exactly as Stephen had indicated such medical consultancies normally were, with the first reception area on the ground floor, while the main reception desk would be on the first floor together with either one or both of the consulting rooms. Certainly the first and second floors would be made over entirely to the practice, leaving the third and fourth – Freddie imagined – to be a duplex apartment inhabited by Fleur, and her father and her step-mother. Stephen had confirmed that Richard Fisher-Dilke did indeed list the Harley Street address as his only one in London, but had no idea at all whether or not he also maintained somewhere in the country besides of course The Folly, which in any case seemed to be rented purely for his daughter's benefit.

So if they were right in their summation then access to the flat could only be achieved via the elevator (which Stephen had assured him all such Harley Street practices now had), or through the back door which opened onto the mews and beyond which had to lie the service stairs. There would obviously also be a main staircase in the centre of the house, but that would run up through the consultancy and access to the duplex from the second floor undoubtedly would be only through an internal door. So even if somehow Freddie did manage to get inside the house at the back, which was the only feasibility, he would have to rely on two things, the service stairs running all the way up to the top floors quite separately from the main stairs, and being able to get into the house and up four flights of stairs without being seen, stopped and in all probability arraigned on a charge of breaking and entering.

But even for that unlikely plan to succeed, first Freddie would have to get into the house, so for the next couple of hours or so he tried coming at it in the way Hitchcock used to come at his audiences in his best film thrillers, playing How-Would-You-Do-It? By half past one Freddie had done it by disguising himself (quite unconvincingly in his own mind) as everything and everybody from the gas man come to read the meter, to a plain clothes policeman investigating a burglary which had just taken place in the top-floor apartment next to Fleur's. He knew perfectly well he was just wasting time as he ran through a series of scenarios with each one coming up more preposterous than the last because in order to succeed these sort of deceptions firstly required the perpetrator to have some sort of criminal mentality which Freddie most definitely did not possess. Secondly even if he had been of a criminal bent, his credibility would be shot to pieces the moment he opened his mouth. He doubted very much that there was one single gasman, let alone detective sergeant or telephone engineer, in the whole of London who spoke with an American accent.

By the time he finally fell asleep Freddie was in deep despair. To have come this far, and to have got so near to the woman of his dreams, and yet not to be able to reach her was almost too much to bear. In fact so bad was his attack of the mean reds, that by the time he was drifting off into unconsciousness Freddie was more than beginning to get the feeling he might be well and truly licked.

Stephen had long gone to work by the time Freddie surfaced, but he'd left a note on the breakfast table. *The mind has drawn another set of blanks. How about you? Am beginning to get the clear impression this is a job for Batman.*

Batman, Freddie pondered as he drank some strong black coffee — so how would *he* do it? Over the rooftops and then down a rope and in through her window.

Nothing to it! Or rubber suction pads on the hands and feet, and up the side of the building and in through her window that way. Easy! And if only, Freddie sighed to himself. If only life were anything like the movies.

The only event of any significance before eleven was the appearance at the back door of the house of the large woman Freddie had seen in the shadow play the night before. At least he presumed from her general physical disposition that this must be her, since her demeanour suggested she was someone employed in the house rather than a member of the family. She was also carrying on one arm a large heavy-duty plastic bag which suggested the purpose of her outing to be shopping, further underlining Freddie's deduction that she was indeed the housekeeper.

'Except I can't for a moment see where this is getting me,' he exclaimed out loud, standing up to go and make himself some more coffee just as the solution to his problem drove into the mews and parked directly opposite him.

Not that Freddie immediately saw it as his salvation. Far from it, all he saw when he glanced at the bright yellow truck was Ace Window Cleaning Services and he didn't give it another thought until he returned to his vigil with his freshly made cup of coffee. By this time the two operators employed by the window-cleaning service had got out of the cab and were preparing to start their next job of work. Again what they were doing seemed of such little interest to Freddie that he began to do The Times crossword while waiting for inspiration to strike or, failing that, for Fleur to appear at the back door in person, both of which things he now thought to be as unlikely as the other.

It was only when he saw the window-cleaning cradle being cranked up from the back of the truck that he began to pay serious attention to what was happening in the mews. He'd never previously given a lot of thought to window-cleaning procedures other than to appreciate the fact that ladders were used for small buildings and cradles for larger ones. So he was more than a little intrigued to see that from the back of the truck the cradle was being hydraulically raised on a hoist, rather like a smaller version of the outside broadcast camera towers which Freddie had often observed when watching golf on the television.

Fascinated, he watched as the cradle was raised higher and higher by the operator on the ground until the man in the cradle was level with the top-floor windows of the first house in the mews, which was the moment Freddie jumped to his feet and waved one tightly clenched fist in the air at shoulder height.

'Yes!' he shouted quietly but urgently. 'Of course – *eureka!*'

Grabbing his jacket he shot out into the mews, and then slowed himself down to what he hoped would appear to be a casual stroll as he made his way across to the truck.

'Hi there,' he said to the pony-tailed young man who was working the controls. 'Quite something, huh? Guess it makes life a little easier for you guys.'

'It's all right,' the young man replied, meaning it as a compliment. Then he grinned. 'Long as you've told 'em you're coming, know what I mean?'

'Hey,' Freddie said as if he'd just thought of it. 'You know that gives me an idea. I mean I take it you do all this block, right?' He gestured at the row of houses in front of which they were standing.

'We do now,' the operator replied, never taking his eyes off the cradle high above him. 'In fact we nearly do the whole damn street. Somethin' on your mind?'

'It's just that I have this idea.' Freddie laughed and then shook his head as if he wasn't quite sure. 'I don't know, but it was what you just said about as long as people know you're coming. You see my – my fiancée lives in this house here.' Freddie pointed to Fleur's house which was two away from the one on which the team were working. 'And it's her birthday today of all days. And then seeing you guys, and then when you said about people needing to know you're coming—'

'You want Kev to knock on the window and wish her all the best, that it?' the operator asked, still not taking his eyes off his mate for a second.

'Yeah well that would be great,' Freddie said, but without any real commitment. 'Something like that. Or even better—'

'Forget it. More than my job's worth.'

'I didn't mean by myself, pal. I wouldn't ask that of you for a minute. If anything happened and you had to carry the can – no I wasn't thinking of going up there by myself.'

'Don't bother thinking about going up there with Kev either, mate. It's just not on, right? Insurance, see.'

'Not even for a hundred pounds?'

'A hundred quid?'

A pair of bright blue eyes quickly took Freddie in before being refocused on what was happening above them.

'Each,' Freddie said. 'Hundred quid each, cash in hand.'

'Just once up and down?'

'Just once up and down. Or maybe just once up. Who knows?'

Freddie grinned his best boyish grin as the young man turned to glance at him once more.

'Okay. Cash up front, mind.'

'It's a deal.'

While they were finishing the first house before moving on to the second, Freddie dashed back into Stephen's house and up to his friend's bedroom where, kneeling down, he checked that Fleur's blind was still drawn. He didn't want her catching sight of him before the intended moment.

The blind was still down. Even so, he borrowed a large panama hat of Stephen's he found hanging on a peg and turned his jacket collar up before hurrying out of the mews in the immediate shadow of the buildings opposite. He told the man by the truck he had to do some shopping but he would be back well in time for his lift before hurrying off first to the bank, and next to find the nearest florists where he bought every red rose they had in the shop. Then, armed with ten bunches of perfect blood-red blooms, a vast and preposterously vulgar birthday card with a huge pink satin heart on the front, and a honey-coloured teddy bear he'd spotted in another shop on his way back, Freddie hurried home to the mews, taking care when he entered the little street to lose himself at once in the no man's land under the houses on Fleur's side. He had timed it perfectly as the crane was now level with the ground-floor window of the house immediately next door to the Fisher-Dilkes'. Freddie knew he was taking a huge risk, two in fact and both of them metaphysical rather than physical. Firstly and even though the blind was still down Fleur might not actually be in her room, and secondly even if she was she mightn't be the slightest bit taken with his enterprise and could well refuse even to speak to him, let alone let him into the house.

'Okay,' the pony-tailed operator said, swinging the cradle round towards Freddie. 'Put this harness on, over each shoulder, that's it. Then fix the belt round the front. Now we clip you on at the back and that'll stop you falling out 'cos that's fixed to the cradle. Now sit still, don't do anything heroic, and don't look down.'

'Okay,' Freddie said as the second operator closed the cradle in front of them both. 'Beam us up, Scotty.'

Freddie had a good head for heights so he enjoyed the trip up. The only vertigo he was suffering was from the heady thought of finally seeing Fleur again, which in fact made him feel quite dizzy with excitement. As the crane rose slowly upwards, he caught glimpses of activity in the building, someone in a white coat hanging X-rays up to dry in a room at the back of the ground floor, two receptionists chatting in a small office on the first floor, several people waiting in a comfortable reception room next door (none of whom took the slightest notice of the cradle in its ascent). But Freddie could see nothing on the next floor because all the windows were fitted with horizontally slatted blinds. On the third floor, however, he saw right into an elegantly furnished but empty drawing room. And then the next thing he knew he was suddenly face to face with the pale yellow blind, which together with a sheet of window glass, was all that now apparently separated him from Fleur.

There was no sound at all from within yet he knew she was there. He could sense her presence the moment the cradle came silently to rest outside her room, and when he did he felt his mouth go dry and his heart begin to pound. Yet he hesitated. With one hand raised ready to knock gently on the window, still he hesitated and while he did it really was as if all his life passed through his mind. So strong was the sensation and so vivid were his recollections that for a moment he thought he must have fallen from the cradle and was plunging to his death on the ground below until suddenly his mind jolted back from the last image he had of Fleur to the present moment, to him still sitting leaning forward in the cradle about to knock on her window.

There was no response to the first careful tap he made on the glass. So he knocked again but this time more strongly, although still not loud enough to give anyone a fright, just in case Fleur was still asleep. And then once more, firmly, three good taps, before sitting back with his arms full of roses, in front of which he had positioned the boxed birthday card and the toy bear.

A moment later the blind snapped up and there, at last, a couple of feet away and facing him was Fleur.

She was every bit as beautiful as he knew her to be, a pale-faced, doe-eyed seraph with her mane of long dark hair hanging loosely around her shoulders, emphasizing the fragility and delicacy of her features. Her enormous dark eyes were staring at him in a mixture of wonder, bewilderment and fear.

She was wearing a white cotton gown under a black silk robe, which she had probably pulled on, Freddie guessed, when she had first realized there was someone knocking at her window. Yet she made no move or gave any indication that she had been frightened. She just stood absolutely still with both her hands held as if in prayer to her lips. Freddie didn't know whether they had been in that position from the moment she had raised the blind and seen him or whether she had lifted them up to her face since, nor did it matter because somehow this was exactly how he had thought – no. Freddie frowned and shook his head a little as he corrected himself, because this was exactly as he had known she would be.

Then the next thing he knew – and if he hadn't remembered exactly where he was he would have jumped for joy – the next thing he saw was that she was laughing. She had now moved her hands away from her mouth and was holding them to both cheeks while she started to laugh and laugh, trying without success to stop herself from doing so by biting her bottom lip, until she was laughing so much her whole body began to shake.

'What-on-earth-do-you-*want*?' she finally mouthed at him, once she had more or less regained control of herself. 'What-on-earth-are-you-doing-here?'

'I've come to see you!' Freddie shouted back. 'So come on – open the window and let me in!'

Fleur hesitated, looking round over her shoulder before replying. 'I can't,' she said, shaking her head. 'I can't.'

'You're going to have to!' Freddie replied, undoing his safety harness. 'Because if you don't — I'll throw myself off!'

The man beside him immediately grabbed hold of Freddie, but Freddie shook him off and started to try and undo the front of the cradle.

'You wouldn't,' Fleur was mouthing at him. 'You wouldn't be so stupid!'

'Try me!' Freddie shouted. 'Believe me, Fleur — this is as far as I can go without you!'

Before he could unlatch the retaining bar at the front of the cradle, Fleur had opened the window and then stood back.

'What now?' Freddie asked the man who'd brought him this far. 'I can't reach the sill.'

'Give us another foot, Derek,' the window cleaner said into the microphone on his headset. 'It appears he's going in.'

There was a small jerk as the hydraulics started up, causing Freddie to grab the side of the cradle which was then raised the exact distance needed to enable Freddie to make it into the house.

'Don't undo the front, mate,' the cleaner advised him. 'I'll just hook on with me whatsit and then in you go.'

The window cleaner hooked an attachment on the end of a short pole over the ledge of the window, securing the cradle and giving it enough stability for Freddie to clamber safely out and slip in over the sill in a nose dive.

'Thanks, pal,' Freddie said to his helper when he was up on his feet. 'And thank your friend below as well.'

'That's okay. Not every day I get to play Cupid. Ta ra,' the window cleaner replied, and then easing himself into the centre of the cradle began to sing. '*Love is in the air*—' he sang, '*Oh yes — love is in the air*—'

Freddie shut the window and with one more wave the

window cleaner was gone, sinking slowly and silently out of sight.

'What do you think you're doing?' Fleur finally asked after she and Freddie had stood looking at each other for what seemed like an eternity.

'What does it look like I'm doing?' Freddie asked. 'You stood me up.'

'What are all the roses for?' she said, ignoring his remark.

'What do you think they're for?' he replied. 'They're for you.' He picked the ten bunches up from where he'd dropped them in at the window and handed them to her. She took them slowly from him and began to lay them carefully down on the bed.

'You do remember me, don't you?' he asked teasingly.

'How could I forget you?' she replied. 'Much as I've tried to.'

'Nice,' said Freddie with a nod. 'Good opening. I like that. Anyway it hasn't worked, because here I am.'

'So I see.'

By now, using the time she had allowed herself to put the flowers down, Fleur had recovered enough of her composure to walk away from where she'd been standing and position herself behind a button-back chair.

Here she stood and stared back at Freddie who for his part thought it best to stay exactly where he was, just for the moment, just in case she suddenly took exception to his presence and called out, which would mean Freddie having to make an impossibly quick exit from where he had first entered, namely the window.

'Anyway,' she said after a moment more spent studying Freddie. 'Anyway, now you're here you might as well tell me what you want.'

'Come on,' Freddie replied. 'Guess. You must be able to guess what I want. After all I kept my part of the bargain.'

Fleur looked at him and then closed her eyes, frowning as if she was suddenly in pain, before opening them again and replying.

'I couldn't help that,' she said, shaking her head. 'It wasn't my fault. There really was nothing I could do.'

'Yes there was,' Freddie insisted. 'For instance you could have called. You could have written. Even if it was just to say you'd got the book but you'd changed your mind and goodbye.'

'It wasn't as easy as that.'

'It never seems to be. But really a postcard would have done it. Just so I could have known where I stood.'

This time she covered her eyes briefly with one hand before coming round and sitting in the pale pink buttoned chair. 'I thought if I didn't keep my word, particularly since you had, I thought you'd finally have had enough. That you'd go away and leave me alone.'

She didn't look up, but sat with her hands in her lap and her head bowed.

'Christ – is that what you wanted?' Freddie asked after a moment, feeling suddenly insensitive and boorish.

'It wasn't a question of what I wanted. Really. What I want has nothing to do with it. You don't understand.'

She continued to look down, putting her hands together and slowly interlacing her fingers. As she did, remembering he still had two other gifts to give her, Freddie walked over to her chair.

'Anyway,' he said, clearing his throat to gain her attention. 'Here. This is for you as well.'

Fleur looked up and as soon as she did Freddie handed her the huge boxed birthday card.

'Freddie—' she said, making him frown at her suddenly because this was the first time she had called him by his name. By now she had opened the box and was looking at the huge card, with its enormous confection of a pink satin heart surrounded by smaller hearts and masses of sickly flowers. She was staring at it transfixed.

'No,' he said. 'Please don't tell me you like it or I'll go back to the window and jump out. It's meant to be a joke.'

'That's not why I'm staring,' she said. 'How did you know it was my birthday?'

Now the blood ran from his face, now it was Freddie who felt his legs go weak and his heart miss a beat. He took a good long deep breath but it was no good. Everything was still faint and distant and the room was spinning around him, so looking for somewhere to sit down, he collapsed on to Fleur's dressing-table stool behind him. He could feel the cold sweat beginning to break out on his forehead so he pulled out his handkerchief and began slowly to wipe it away.

'What on earth's wrong?' Fleur asked. 'You looked as if you were going to pass out.'

'I didn't know it was your birthday.'

'What?'

'I said – I didn't know it was your birthday.'

He was still holding the teddy bear in one hand, whose black-threaded mouth he saw smiling absurdly up at him, as if to cheer him up. 'I only bought the card as a joke,' he repeated. 'To try and make you laugh.'

'Do you mean you really didn't know it was my birthday?' Fleur asked, running a hand over the soft pink heart that was on the card she'd now removed from its box.

'How on earth could I have known?' Freddie returned, now wiping the palm of each of his hands carefully with his handkerchief. 'I couldn't possibly have done.'

'That depends on how much you know about me.'

'Look – I know who you are, Fleur. I know all that. Who you are and who you were. And when you stopped playing. And about your parents. And that's it.'

'You could have got it off a record sleeve or the notes

on a CD. *Fleur Fisher-Dilke was born in south-west London on 19th September 1974—*'

'Is that what you are? Twenty years old today?'

'Yes.'

'I promise you I had no idea. But would it matter if I had?'

'No,' Fleur replied. 'On the contrary, it matters much more that you didn't.'

Now Fleur sat down, on the edge of the bed, among all the bunches of red roses, one of which she picked up and looked at before looking over to him.

'All of this,' she suddenly said. 'This is all so – so odd. And I do wish it wasn't. I do so wish it hadn't happened. I wish *you* hadn't happened.'

Freddie was about to reply when all at once he saw her look up, the look in her eyes one of alarm, as if she must have sensed or heard something that he quite definitely hadn't.

'Oh God!' she whispered. 'He can't find you here! Oh God, what are we going to do?'

'Who is it?' Freddie whispered back. 'And why does it matter? We're not doing anything.'

'No – you don't understand!' Fleur urged. 'You've got to hide – quickly! Quickly – under the bed! Quickly!'

He heard the voice then as well, the voice that was calling up the stairs as Fleur began cramming the roses under her bed as well as the huge birthday card. Then it was Freddie's turn to follow as the voice called again, only this time from much nearer, as Freddie got down on his hands and knees and, still holding the teddy bear, rolled under the old brass bedstead to hide himself just in time, just as the door opened. From where Freddie was lying he saw a pair of feet in highly polished black brogue shoes come in.

'Ah, Fleur my dear,' the voice said. 'I'm sorry to disturb you. You weren't resting, were you?'

'No, Pappa,' Fleur replied. 'I was just sitting reading actually.'

'You know I wish you wouldn't call me that, Fleur,' the voice sighed. 'You know I hate *Pappa*.'

'I know how you hate Dad and Daddy just as much, Pappa,' Fleur returned, 'just as much as I hate *Father*.'

'Ah well,' the brogue shoes replied. 'You'll soon be old enough to call me by my first name, Deo volente of course. One more year and you can call me anything you wish.'

'I have been legally able to do that for the past two years, Pappa,' Fleur said. 'Anyway. What brings you up here? Is something the matter?'

Freddie saw her feet going round the bed until she was now round the same side as her father.

'No, no,' her father said. 'Delia and I have to leave a little earlier than planned because a patient has rung and asked if I could call in to see him before we fly out. So we shall in fact be leaving now, in about five minutes to be absolutely accurate.'

'That's all right, Pappa,' Fleur said, apparently edging towards the door. 'I don't need anything and if I do, all I have to do is ring for Mrs Eastman.'

'It just means we can't have lunch with you, my dear,' her father said. 'I thought I should at least come and tell you that in person.'

'You needn't have bothered,' Fleur replied. 'I thought you'd probably be too busy.'

'Awful, isn't it?' her father asked. 'We're still like railway trains even now. You going one way, me another.'

'I'm not going anywhere, Pappa. You're the only one who's going anywhere now.'

'You just make sure you don't,' her father said with a sudden change of tone, as if he were addressing a child and not a young woman. 'You're not to move out of your room.'

'Pappa,' Fleur sighed. 'You are going to be late.'

'Goodbye then, my dear,' her father said after a moment, and from where Freddie lay he could see Fleur's feet moving towards her father's so he guessed they were kissing each other goodbye, a presumption that seemed totally correct since the highly polished brogues then turned to make towards the door where all at once they stopped to turn back round.

'Now what's the matter, Pappa?' Fleur asked. 'You can't have forgotten anything because you didn't bring anything—'

'Whose hat is that, please?' her father's voice interrupted. 'That straw on the chair?'

Freddie clenched his teeth and screwed his eyes tight shut. He'd chucked Stephen's borrowed old panama into the room before he'd climbed in himself, and he'd left it lying on the floor.

'I thought it was yours,' he heard Fleur saying after only the slightest of pauses, cool as a cucumber. 'It was in The Folly and I was wearing it when I was down there. Isn't it yours?'

By now a hand had picked the straw hat up and the owner of the hand was obviously examining it.

'Since when have my initials been S.N.?' Fleur's father asked. 'Besides, it doesn't even fit me.'

'Must be an old one of Lady Stourton's then,' Fleur suggested. 'Or rather one of her guests.'

'Yes I suppose it must be,' her father finally agreed, although Freddie thought he wasn't sounding entirely convinced. 'You really should post it back to her.'

'All right, if you say so. I hadn't thought that much about it. Now you really are going to be late, Pappa.'

At last, after another brief silence, the brogue shoes left and Freddie saw the door being closed after them. A moment later Fleur's head appeared beside him, almost upside down.

'Don't come out yet,' she whispered. 'I'll tell you when.'

'When' was about ten minutes later during which time Fleur disappeared out of the room, leaving Freddie alone under the bed with his own and now somewhat crushed birthday offerings.

'I just had to make sure he'd left,' Fleur told him when she finally allowed him back out. 'My father that is.'

'I gathered that's who it was.'

'Clever you.'

'It took a bit of getting, but it was all the "Pappas" that finally clinched it.'

'He has the habit of sneaking up on you when you least expect it. He was actually meant to be operating at the clinic this morning. I'd never have allowed you in otherwise.'

'You're a big girl now, Fleur,' Freddie said, picking a couple of dust bunnies off his clothes. 'I can't believe you're not allowed men in your room, during the *day*.'

'You can believe what you like,' Fleur replied, her tartness taking Freddie by surprise. 'I just didn't want to have to do a lot of explaining, that's all.'

'Hmmm,' Freddie said, considering it. 'I'll allow that, but only because it's your birthday. Was Pappa going to take you out to lunch? Because since he can't—'

'We were going to have lunch here as it happens,' Fleur broke in.

'All I was going to suggest was that I took you out to lunch instead,' Freddie said calmly, seeing a look that had suddenly flashed into Fleur's dark eyes. 'There's a really charming small French restaurant around the corner where I thought I might take you, and then—'

'I'm sorry, but I can't,' Fleur broke in yet again, before Freddie was halfway through telling her what he had in mind.

'Oh come on,' he sighed good-naturedly. 'So what's

479

the excuse now? One minute you're all laughs and smiles and pleased to see me, and the next minute it's snowing again. What's up this time?'

Fleur looked at him, and her dark eyes seemed suddenly to have grown even darker. 'Nothing is up, as you like to put it,' she said. 'I just happen not to want to go out to lunch with you, that's all. Do you understand?'

'No, quite frankly, Fleur, I don't,' Freddie retorted, 'and just as frankly I've really had about as much as I can take of your so called fun and games. Now don't let's waste any more precious time in argument, when you know as well as I do that you and I were meant for each other. Okay?'

'No it is not okay!' Fleur shouted back at him. 'It is not in the slightest bit *okay*. Damn you anyway, Frederick Jourdan! Don't you ever think of anybody else? Don't you ever for one moment consider that perhaps there's a reason for the way things are! That things are not quite so cut and bloody dried the way you seem to imagine everything bloody well is!'

'Oh now come on, wait a moment—' Freddie said with a laugh which he didn't really quite mean, not when he saw the frightened look in those wonderful dark eyes, not when he saw what little blood there was in her cheeks fast running from them. 'Calm down and let's talk about it, shall we?'

'No we will not calm down and we will not talk about it, Mr Freddie Jourdan!' Fleur returned, still at fever pitch. 'I'm damned sure you're used to getting everything your own damned way all the time! That women just fall into a faint every time you walk into the room! That all you have to do is snap your fingers and the next moment they're jumping into your blasted bed! Well if that's what you're expecting here – if you think for one moment – if you imagine – if you think that because of the way things have happened between us—'

Freddie got to her just in time, as her knees seemed

suddenly to buckle and give way underneath her. He thought she might be about to collapse, not only from the way she had suddenly lost all her colour but also from the totally unexpected way she seemed all at once to lose her breath. It was as if she'd been running up the stairs far too fast or had suddenly been given a terrible fright.

She fell as limp as a rag doll into his arms, her own arms slack at her sides, her beautiful head heavy on his shoulder. Lifting her up carefully, one arm around her back, the other behind her knees while her head fell back with her eyes closed, he laid her down on her bed and sat down beside her, taking her wrist and feeling for her pulse. Her heart was beating regularly, albeit a little fast, but once he passed his hand close to her unblinking eyes he saw without a doubt she had lost consciousness.

For a moment he was completely at a loss what to do until he realized that with Fleur's father now gone, there was nothing to stop him from simply flying downstairs and soliciting the aid of one of the other members of the practice. With that as his firm intention he stood up and made towards the door, only to find himself stopped by a quiet voice behind him.

'Where are you going?'

'I was going downstairs to fetch help,' Freddie replied, turning back. 'I don't know whether you know it but—'

'There's no point,' Fleur said, closing her eyes slowly and opening them again to refocus on her surroundings. 'Just get me some water.'

There was a carafe and glass beside her bed, so Freddie came back to her bedside and poured her some water while Fleur sat up slowly and took a small bottle of pills from her bedside drawer.

'It's nothing,' she said, reading the all too obvious concern on his face. 'Really. It's nothing at all.'

'Sure it wasn't,' Freddie pretended to agree. 'You just passed clean out, that's all.'

'Women do that sort of thing all the time, I really shouldn't worry.' She managed a weak smile as she unscrewed the bottle top and tapped out a couple of grey and yellow pills.

'In that case why are you taking medication?'

'Because I've had a virus, that's all. That's why I'm stuck up here in my bedroom. Popping pills.'

Fleur shook the bottle of pills at him before slipping them into one of the pockets of her robe.

'That wouldn't explain why you passed out,' Freddie said. 'Unless you still have "the virus".'

'As a matter of fact, Mr Wiseguy, if you knew anything about medicine and certain medicines, particularly very strong ones, you'd know that people often get really bad dizzy spells when they're on them, i.e. me. Okay?' Fleur popped the two pills into her mouth, washing them down with a good mouthful of water. 'So you don't have to look so worried,' she continued, 'unless you think it was your wonderful looks that had me swooning.'

Fleur suddenly smiled at him and when she did every worried thought left Freddie's head.

'Sure,' he said finally, taking one of her hands in his. 'But I don't know. I still don't get it. I don't get you. As they say in all the old movies, you have the advantage of me. It's not that I want everything to be predictable, because if I did I certainly wouldn't be here—'

'No you most certainly wouldn't,' Fleur agreed.

'But on the other hand there seems to be no rhyme or reason sometimes for the way you behave. Take just now. One minute you're reading me the Riot Act, the next you're out cold in my arms, the next you're smiling at me as if we've been friends all along and like I said—'

'I was reading the Riot Act at you?' she asked. 'I don't remember that. All I remember is—'

'You were reading the Riot Act all right, sister,' Freddie grinned. 'Good and proper.'

'I don't remember that at all. All I remember is—' She stopped again and looked up at him, this time without a smile, only with longing.

'What do you remember, Fleur?' Freddie asked, as his heart began to melt all over again.

'I just remember wanting you to kiss me.'

What Freddie couldn't remember was how they came to be in each other's arms, but at last there she was in his, and there he was with his strong arms about her and they were kissing. They were kissing as he'd dreamed of kissing her and she of kissing him, and as they kissed heaven opened its very gates for them. So long did they kiss it seemed they must surely die from suffocation yet neither cared, for at last the Fates had allowed them into the place where they both belonged.

'Freddie.'

'No,' he said, holding her tighter than before in his arms. 'Don't say one thing, not a thing.'

'It's all right, Freddie, I won't fight you any more,' Fleur whispered. 'How can I? Anyway, I've fought you too long and it's just been a waste.'

'No, Fleur, no nothing has been wasted, not one moment,' Freddie whispered back. 'Not when a kiss tastes like that. Now you must do as I say.'

'I will. I shall do whatever you say,' Fleur promised. 'I swear I shall.'

'You knew, didn't you, Fleur? You knew that very first moment. Tell me you did because I know it's true.'

'Yes, Freddie. I knew it the moment I saw you in the garden. I knew that you'd come to claim me.'

'I had,' Freddie whispered. 'I had been waiting for that moment all my life. I knew that then, and I know it more than ever now.'

'So do I. I've never felt so certain of anything. Not even of my music.'

'But how, Fleur?' Freddie wondered, his arms still

around her tight. 'How is it we both know each other? How is it that we know this is meant?'

'I don't think we'll ever know the answer to that, Freddie,' Fleur replied with a gentle shake of her head. 'I don't even think there's any point in asking.'

'No,' Freddie agreed. 'No there's absolutely no point at all.'

'So what are we going to do?' Fleur lay her head on his chest and sighed. 'Please tell me what we're going to do?'

'No. No you tell me what we're going to do, Fleur. I want you to choose. You say exactly what you want to do because I want the choice to be yours.'

'In that case it's easy, and it's very traditional,' Fleur said, smiling up at him. 'I want you to take me away somewhere, anywhere, somewhere very beautiful, where I want you to make love to me.'

36

Freddie had wanted to leave there and then, just take to the road and busk it, as he put it. But much as Fleur had been tempted she needed time to organize herself, to make sure she had everything vital she needed for the time they were going to be away together, and she knew she couldn't organize all that in less than half a day. So she asked for time, just a little, making her femininity an excuse, teasing Freddie that surely he knew what women were like by now? To surprise a woman you had to give her at least one day's notice of intention.

'To shop and get their hair done,' Freddie had grinned.

'To shop and get their hair done *exactly*, Mr Clever-Clogs,' Fleur had replied, kissing him and easing him out towards the bedroom door. 'And you had better be out of here before the Terminator returns.'

'The big woman I see silhouetted on your blind? The storm-trooper I saw leaving out back this morning? Who is she anyway?'

'She's called Mrs Eastman and she's the housekeeper,' Fleur had lied, before assuming a cod German accent. 'But she iz in ze pay of mein pappa.'

'The voice of The Folly,' Freddie'd remembered. 'The woman on the entryphone.'

'That's her,' Fleur had said, still easing Freddie out of the door. 'And she's a first dan in Judo, so on your bike, Mr Jourdan, if you want to make wherever we're going in one piece.'

After Freddie had kissed her sweetly but briefly and hurried downstairs to let himself out the back way before Mrs Eastman returned, Fleur sat down on her bed and wondered what she was doing, only to wonder immediately why she was wondering such a thing in the first place. If the only hope her father had offered her didn't materialize and materialize soon, then this might be not only her one chance to be with the man she loved but also her last one.

It wasn't that she was feeling any worse or any weaker, she just wasn't feeling any better or any stronger. Her father said her condition was stable, but that it was only so due to the careful administration of certain new heart drugs and the constant monitoring of her condition. In the meantime, Fleur must have total rest. She must lead the life of an invalid, she must have absolutely no excitement, otherwise just as her mother had done before her, Fleur could suddenly drop dead.

But Fleur knew there was something else that she must have regardless of the mortal danger it might put her in, and that was Freddie's love. As it was she had almost died through having to deny him time and time again, through having to hide from him and lie to him, through having to be so hard-hearted when all she wanted was to be in his arms and have him make love to her. Now that they had finally met again, from the moment she had seen his beautiful face staring back at her through the window, she knew there was no argument. He had come to her out of the everywhere and into the here. Come what may she would go away with him for as long as he wanted her. She would stay with him for as long as she lived.

So when Nurse Eastman returned from John Bell and Croyden with a complement of renewed prescriptions and medications, even though Fleur knew her dosages by heart she made doubly sure by casually talking her nurse through them all.

'Gracious, Fleur, you should know these like your catechism,' Nurse Eastman said when Fleur was quizzing her that evening. 'You've been on these drugs long enough.'

'Yes but my father's always updating them as you know,' Fleur argued, 'and one or two of these are new.'

'There are none that need give you any concern,' her nurse replied. 'None that will give you any side effects, except this johnny here.' Nurse Eastman held up a phial of bright yellow tablets. 'You might find these give you the odd headache, but then what's the odd headache when you consider the alternative? The good news is that because your father has prescribed them, it means an end to your daily injection. So if you'd like to roll up your sleeve, young lady, you can say goodbye to Mr Needle. For the time being, anyway.'

Fleur had been hoping to have got everything done before this moment, because the injection of whatever it was always made her sleepy and she had still to pack her suitcases, something she couldn't do while Nurse Eastman was still on the prowl. She had left that task to last, although she had already put all the clothes she wanted to take with her to one side, so that even if she was feeling bleary, all she had to do was put them in her suitcases before collapsing into bed.

'Good,' said Nurse Eastman, dropping the disposable syringe back into the kidney tray before rubbing the point of injection with a fragment of disinfected cotton wool. 'And I must say these roses look and smell like a dream. It must be wonderful to have fans as loyal as that. Fans who still remember your birthday, even though you're not playing any more. Even though you'll probably never play again.'

As the large Scotswoman departed, Fleur mimed shooting her in the back with a machine gun before rolling over on her bed to pick up a pad and pencil on which she began to make a final list of everything she needed to take with her. The one thing she couldn't take, because there was no way of disguising it, was the small and as yet thankfully unused oxygen bottle and mask which stood at the back of her wardrobe.

Freddie's arrangements had all gone exactly to plan. By ten o'clock in the evening he had everything organized and as soon as the last piece of the jigsaw was in place, he telephoned Fleur.

She sounded a little drowsy so he asked if he'd woken her and she said no he hadn't, that she had gone to bed early so that there was no danger of her sleeping in the next morning.

'Everything is fine,' she whispered back to reassure him. 'There was nearly a sticky one when the Terminator saw the roses, but I told her they were from an ardent fan who never forgot my birthday and she swallowed it.'

'Well, so what if she didn't?' Freddie asked blithely. 'It's your life.'

'Yes,' Fleur replied, not knowing what else to say to Freddie's coincidental observation. 'It's just that I don't want her telling my father. He'll only say I'm not well enough yet to travel, you bet.'

'Are you?' Freddie asked. 'I mean what exactly *has* been wrong with you?'

'I *told* you,' Fleur sighed. 'I've had this virus.'

'You mean you've had one of these things they all call viruses nowadays.'

'They actually identified this one. I picked it up in Italy, apparently. It's called Harbour Virus.'

'Pass.'

'So has the virus, don't worry. I just still get a little wobbly now and then, that's all.'

'I noticed,' Freddie said.

'That wasn't the virus,' Fleur replied. 'That was you.'

'But you're sure you're well enough to come away?'

'Even if I wasn't,' Fleur replied with perfect truth,

'do you think I'd tell you? Till six o'clock tomorrow morning.'

'Make it five to. I love you, Fleur.'

'I love you, Freddie.'

She was packed and ready to leave an hour before the agreed time. To travel she'd chosen an old favourite of hers, a long grey-blue suede skirt with a cowl-necked cashmere jumper and matching boots. Lots more of her favourite cashmeres went into the soft leather luggage which was still festooned with labels from her former life, Salzburg, Chicago, New York, Moscow, Paris, Sydney, Tokyo, Berlin, there seemed to be hardly a capital in the world where she hadn't played, and all in the space of just six years. When she had been forced to stop playing she'd thought she would not be able to live without her music for a day, yet here she was now, over two years later, still alive and thinking that she wouldn't be able to live another day without Freddie, never mind her violin.

She unhooked her old favourite black velvet jacket from its quilted hanger and folded it carefully into her case, packing with it all the memories of the various concert platforms all around the world. Along with it went her favourite large-collared silk shirt which she invariably wore with the jacket, its cuffs fastened with a pair of beautiful gold links presented to her by the great conductor Marc Antonio Bennini after a heroic performance of the Beethoven Concerto in Chicago. She made room, too, for her black velvet trousers, an embroidered waistcoat, in fact all the romantic clothes that she loved and associated with happiness, including a long black silk evening skirt and a pale blue serape. Besides these more formal clothes, along with her cashmeres she put in some warm leggings and a dark blue-black fine wool coat by St Laurent in case they went walking.

*　　*　　*

Freddie was also packed and ready to go early. In fact he had packed then unpacked and packed again the night before, not because he was unhappy with his choice of clothes (which would be difficult seeing he had only brought the two outfits up from the country with him), but because he'd been too excited to sleep. He had told Stephen all his plans of course, as soon as he'd walked in the door in fact. Freddie had told him everything that had happened from the moment he had seen the window cleaner's truck in the mews. They had celebrated with a large glass of whisky each before Stephen, sworn to secrecy, had retired to bed leaving the lunatic, as he called Freddie, to pack and to unpack over and over again until he finally made it to bed just before crashing out to sleep.

He was up again four hours later and the first thing he did was to creep into Stephen's bedroom to look and see if Fleur's light was on. Seeing that it was, he hurriedly bathed, shaved, washed his hair, and was dressed and ready to leave by ten to six. It was fully light so he tiptoed once more into Stephen's bedroom to see if he could catch a glimpse of Fleur at her window, but her blind was still drawn.

A moment later the curtains were suddenly drawn in the room next door to Fleur's and to his horror Freddie saw a large figure appear briefly at the window. The housekeeper? Fleur had assured him the woman didn't usually rise until seven o'clock but what if she chose this morning of all mornings, Freddie wondered in dismay, to get up early and to stay up? She would surely hear or see Fleur trying to leave and as far as Fleur was concerned the game would be up. Not that the woman could physically prevent Fleur from doing what she wanted, but she would know what was happening. At least she would know that Fleur was going away somewhere which, according to Fleur, was the very thing that had to be kept secret. And the very reason why they had planned to leave so early in the morning was so that the housekeeper wouldn't be able to find out that Fleur was gone until it was too late.

There was nothing Freddie could do now but wait. He moved himself back from the window just in case the housekeeper should look down and see a face watching her, but apparently she had left her room for there was no sign of life. Not until one moment later when the back door of the house opposite was flung open and Fleur appeared with her luggage. Freddie was down the stairs and out of Stephen's house in a trice, grabbing his things as he went and meeting Fleur halfway across the mews.

'What is it?' he asked. 'Have you been seen?'

'I don't know,' she replied. 'Which is the car? Just get in the car. Get in the car quickly.'

Freddie took her case and threw it along with his own luggage in the boot of his rented Toyota which he had left overnight right outside Stephen's house. Fleur had got in the front passenger seat and shut the door. For once Freddie had parked pointing in the right direction for a direct exit, so with one more glance up at the house to see if they were being observed and swearing he could see the large figure of the housekeeper looking out of her window, he jumped in, fired the ignition and with a noisy engagement of the gears accelerated out of the deserted mews and into an almost empty Weymouth Street.

'What happened?'

'I don't know. I don't know whether she heard me or what. But I very nearly ran into her. Just as I was about to go downstairs. It's all right,' Fleur added, as Freddie glanced anxiously at her. 'She didn't see me.'

'How can you be sure?'

'Freddie, you just shot a red light.'

'Never mind that, how can you be sure?'

'She'd have said so, don't you worry. You don't think she'd want to know where I was going this time of the day? No of course she didn't see me. She went to the bathroom which was obviously why she'd got up, and the moment she was in there I flew.'

'It doesn't really matter if she's found out since,' Freddie said reflectively. 'Because it's too late. There's nothing she can do. She might know you've gone, but she won't know where.'

'She's not the only one,' Fleur said with her first smile of the day as she turned to Freddie. 'This is exciting! I haven't been up this early in ages. There's never been any point. Now tell me where we're going exactly.'

'Away!' Freddie replied. 'Away from all this. And all that. Away from everything. And by going away we're going to arrive somewhere at last, the two of us. You and I. Remember, every exit is an entrance somewhere else.'

'That's clever,' Fleur said. 'I never thought of that. So when somebody goes out of the room, they're actually arriving in another room somewhere else.'

'Right,' Freddie agreed. 'Which is what we're doing. We're both leaving one room in each of our lives to go into another. But whereas we're exiting from separate rooms, we're going to arrive in the same one, from where, when it's time to leave, we shall go out the same door.'

Freddie glanced at her, but when he did he saw Fleur had looked away out of the window and had fallen to silence. Just in time Freddie returned to watching where he was going, to see more traffic lights ahead of him, again turning to red.

Fleur put a hand against the dashboard and braced herself as the car braked.

'Interesting,' she said.

'I really should mention my driving here,' Freddie said. 'And what I should mention is it's terrible.'

'Mine's even worse,' Fleur said. 'Because it's non-existent. I wanted to learn but first of all my father wouldn't let me—'

'Why ever not?' Freddie looked round at her.

Fleur ignored him, pointing ahead of them instead, 'The lights have been green for about half an hour,' she said.

Freddie accelerated but the car remained stationary.

'Try putting it in gear,' Fleur suggested.

'This is all your fault,' Freddie replied. 'I'm usually bad but not this bad.' He put the car into gear and accelerated away from the lights which were turning back to red. A taxi sounded its horn at them as it had to brake, but Freddie seemed unperturbed.

'What are the chances of us making it in one piece?' Fleur wondered.

'Listen, it's only good drivers who have accidents,' Freddie told her. 'Everyone keeps the hell away from us bad ones. So anyway, tell me. Why didn't your father want you to drive?'

'Oh I don't know,' Fleur said dismissively. 'Does it matter? I suppose he never saw the need. Once I started playing I was always taken everywhere. A car would have just been one more thing. So who didn't teach you?'

'For the journey you are about to experience you can thank my darling mother,' Freddie said with a grin. 'No-one taught her, you see, because my mother didn't like being taught things. She still doesn't. She has turned impatience into an art form, and when the time came for me to learn how to drive she just said, *C'est rien. It is nussing! It is so much easier zan 'orse riding because ze car do everysing while ze 'orse do nussing! Bang into gear — forward! Turn on ze wheel — steer! Bang on ze brake — stop! And when anyone get in your way! Bang on ze horn — parp!*'

'Your mother is Australian?'

'Oh very funny. My mother is French—'

'Yes, I think I just about got that.'

'Very French. Down to her St Laurent wardrobe and up to her incredible self-mixed perfume. She was a famous opera singer. Self-taught, needless to say. She gave up singing when I was born.'

'The first born?'

'God, no! I was the last. My father used to say she gave up because she'd had a boy at last. I have five sisters, you see. And as far as girls go, Maman says they can look after themselves. While boys can't.'

'Did you feel – or do you feel – you know – any guilt about that?'

'Guilt?' Freddie glanced round at her. 'No. No, should I have done? I was only nought at the time. I didn't say to her – hey Momma, I want you home, you dig?'

'What about your father? And please don't look round at me Freddie, while you're driving. Keep your eyes on the road at least while we're moving anyway. Please. And I think this is a one-way street. And don't say it's all right because you're only going one way. Just turn off here. Turn left here.'

Freddie followed Fleur's directions just in time to escape the full wrath of a van driver who had come to a standstill in the middle of the road, and who was leaning out of his cab ready to berate Freddie to oblivion.

'You were asking about my father,' Freddie said, still following the directions Fleur was giving him with her finger. 'Or rather my late father. He died six years ago.'

'I'm sorry.'

'Sure. Everyone was.'

'But he wasn't French.'

'No, my father was all American,' he replied. 'From the bottom of his cashmere socks to the top of his distinguished grey head. Would rather have played tennis and golf all his life, but instead he ended up as Senator for Maine.'

Fleur stole a sideways look at Freddie now they were safely on the long extension of the Cromwell Road which led out of town to the motorway. While he drove he talked of his five sisters, his totally happy but extremely cosseted childhood, his beloved and now dead father and his 'conversion' at his first visit to a Broadway musical aged six. The rest of his early family life sounded to Fleur as if it came straight out of a Frank Capra movie. Without him noticing she looked at him longer and longer the more he talked. As she did she became all the more convinced that she had always known him, that this conversation was just yet another in the long line of conversations they had always been having.

How she loved him, she thought as she watched him, how she loved the look of him, with his fine long slightly curving nose, his straight eyebrows and his long brown curling hair. He reminded her of a young medieval Florentine nobleman, of a portrait she used to stand in front of in the Uffizzi. Looking at him reminded her he was the most beautiful man she had ever seen. Yet he could defuse those wonderfully good looks, just as he was doing now, by saying something funny, usually against himself. By pulling a face or grinning or frowning, or merely just sighing a little, he made people forget all about those looks and remember the wonderful person that he was.

'Freddie,' she suddenly said, interrupting him mid-flow. 'Freddie I don't want to waste one minute of this. Not one. I want to live out these days with you as if they were my last, not my first. Do you understand?'

'Nope,' he said, glancing round at her and putting one hand on hers. 'It sounds too kind of doomy for me, but if that's the way you want to look at it, as I said . . . Your wish is my command.'

They drove on for a while in silence, both lost in their own thoughts. What Fleur was thinking was that no road had ever seemed so important as the road that lay ahead of them now. All at once she was alive again, more alive than she had been since she had stopped playing, even though according to her father she could die at any time. She felt so much part of everything again, part of the life she had been forced to sacrifice when they had found out what was wrong with her. And even though her new life might only be months, weeks or even days long, she felt an exhilaration she had never felt before – not even when she had stood to take her bows in front of rapturous audiences all around the world. It was like a rebirth, not just of herself but of the whole world, such was the strength of her love for the man beside her.

The road ahead now became a flyover, across which in the opposite direction the early morning traffic was beginning to pour into London, and then it turned into a ribbon of motorway heading due west.

'Do you want some music on?' Freddie suddenly asked. 'Here have I been jamming away, and you'd probably prefer to listen to some music.'

'At this point in time, Freddie,' Fleur replied, 'I can honestly say I've heard enough music. I want you to talk. I want to know everything there is to know about you.'

'You want to know why this finger's such a funny shape?' he asked, showing her one hand. 'You want to know why I don't like wasps, how my nose got broken, what sort of dogs I like, how I can't do math, what I plan to do to stop from getting hair in my ears, and why I nurse a quite irrational hatred for organ solos?'

'Yes, please. That's exactly what I want to hear. I want to know exactly what makes you run,' Fleur said, pulling her cashmere cardigan round her shoulders.

Freddie had forgotten what made him run until he began to think about it, or if he hadn't exactly forgotten he'd certainly put it out of his mind. For a long time, as he explained, he'd thought it had been the need to live up to his father. First of all to live up to what he thought his father expected of him, and then actually to live up to the old man himself. His father had been such a vivid character, good at everything he did, from fly fishing to public oratory. He had been such a good man too, such a humane and compassionate one, admired as much by his political adversaries as he was loved by his confederates. And he was a wonderfully good-humoured father as well as the perfect husband, according to his mother. He'd been a hard act to follow.

Of course he still missed his dad, but he didn't miss the effect he'd had on him, not at all. There was no denying that in most ways it was quite a relief not to have to measure up to him. Freddie could do his thing without wondering all the time what his father would think, or what his father would hear from other people.

'He didn't mind me going into music at all,' Freddie said. 'At least I know that now and that helps. He said so at the time of course, but I kind of didn't quite believe it, probably because friends and relatives were always making remarks, not to me, to the old man. He had a kind of Kennedy aura and following in a way, although he never got that far of course. He might have done if he hadn't died so young, who knows? But I always had this feeling his own father and the rest of his family were all expecting some kind of dynasty, and that being the only son I blew it by going into the theatre.'

Freddie knew he had blown it for his father's family because he'd been told as much by his Uncle Dan, the older brother who was as different from his father as a sigh from the south-west is to a breeze from the north. Uncle Dan had taken him into his study the Christmas Freddie was fifteen and told him what a disappointment he would be to his father if he didn't follow directly in his footsteps.

'Your father's too much of a saint to say it, Frederick,' his uncle had told him, as he stood by the fireplace lighting a fat Havana. 'But he really believes you're destined for great things once you grow out of all this arty-farty nonsense. He says they're beyond him which I don't believe for one moment, but you could do it, boy. There's no doubt in any of the family's minds that with your ability and determination you could make the White House.'

'Can you imagine,' Freddie laughed and gave Fleur a forbidden glance. 'Frederick Jourdan – Senator? I'd never even find Washington! And if I did I'd lose the bill I was trying to get through the Senate. And if I didn't lose the bill, I'd certainly lose the electorate. Hey, I'd probably end up turning the Constitution into a musical!'

'And so far that's what's made you run?' Fleur asked. 'The need to prove yourself to your father? And that bus is just about to pull out.'

'I got it,' Freddie replied, braking and keeping a good safe distance from the errant vehicle. 'He could have signalled, but then I guess he's bigger than me.'

'Gregory Rogers, who was my manager, he always said you had to do it for someone, whatever you were trying to achieve. Your teacher, your parents, your best friend, you had to do it for someone else, or you just didn't do it. So for you it's your father?'

'It *was*,' Freddie corrected. 'It sure as hell isn't any more.'

Fleur rested her hand on his which was on top of the gear shift and interlaced her fingers through his.

'How about you? I suppose you were doing it for Daddy too, right?'

'I don't want to talk about me,' Fleur replied. 'Not that way anyway. You know far more about me than I do about you, because you've read my press cuttings.'

'I read a great interview with you and your mother talking about each other,' Freddie agreed. 'So maybe that question doesn't need answering, because you answered it pretty good there. So what would you rather talk about?'

Fleur changed her position slightly in her seat and for a moment leaned her head back and watched the darts of sunshine glint off the car's bonnet and the windscreen. It was strange how completely at ease she felt with Freddie, even when they both fell to silence. She had never felt this way with anybody, or not since Harry she suddenly realized with a jolt, and she had been still only a child when she had known Harry. Ever since then most of the young men with whom she had gone out, or spent her off hours, had been acquaintances, people whose job it was to talk to her or look after her, so called friends, many of them there simply because it was useful to their own careers.

'Let's talk about this,' Fleur said after a silence. 'Let's talk about you and I, and how to explain this. About how easy this all is, how seamless and perfect.'

'You know, I think there's only one way to explain this, Fleur. I tried to tell you that morning in your garden. When we first met.'

'All that stuff about the Greeks.'

'Sure. What did you feel at that moment? Tell me.'

'It sounds ridiculous, but then I can't get away from it, from this particular feeling, however hard I try.'

'Which is?'

'That — I don't know. That I've known you before. That's what I felt that morning, as soon as I saw you. That I knew you.'

'Do things keep coming back to you?' Freddie asked, this time managing to keep his eyes on the road ahead.

'Coming back to me?' Fleur wondered. 'I've never thought of it that way before, but yes. Yes, they do.'

'As if they knew the way.'

'As if they knew the way.'

They crossed the Severn Bridge and turned off to head for Hereford before they picked their conversation up again.

'Don't you want to know why I stopped playing?' Fleur asked.

'Of course I do,' Freddie said. 'But then I know you'll tell me when you're ready. I'm trying my damnedest not to play the inquisitor. People always tell me I ask too many questions.'

'By people you mean your friends?'

'I don't have many friends, as a matter of fact,' Freddie said, offering Fleur a travel sweet, the same brand Izzy used to offer her when they were travelling together. 'How about you? Have you got a full address book?'

'I did have, once upon that famous time. But I don't know what happened. One minute I had a mass of friends, the next minute none. Not to talk of.'

'Sure you know what happened,' Freddie said. 'Same as what happened to me. You got too successful.'

'Is that what happened to you?'

'You bet.'

'It's awfully depressing, but I suppose you're right.'

They were in the Wye Valley, driving along a long winding road cut through a heavily wooded valley where a sparkling umber river meandered through lush meadows below.

'I had one girlfriend I really liked,' Fleur went on, looking out at the beautiful view which was unfolding alongside her. 'Lucy Stourton, the granddaughter of the woman who owned Stoke Park actually. Lucy and I were best friends, yet I don't even know where she is now.'

'She's in New Zealand,' Freddie said. 'She's married and breeding racehorses.'

'How do you know?' Fleur had turned to look at him, wide-eyed.

'No there's no magic here, I promise,' Freddie laughed. 'Not this time. Someone I know turned out to be a distant cousin of your friend Lucy, that's all. A guy called Theo de Burgh who I've known for years.'

'New Zealand,' Fleur said with a frown. 'I can't imagine Lucy in New Zealand. Lucy was – Lucy is – so utterly and completely English.'

'Tell me about her,' Freddie said, so Fleur did.

The last time she had seen Lucy had been at the Albert Hall when she was sixteen. Lucy had come round backstage with some boyfriend who had brought her to hear Fleur play the Mendelssohn Concerto, a small shy young man in glasses who had been so overcome by meeting Fleur that at first he'd managed to say nothing at all, not even how-do-you-do. While Lucy, who had grown even taller since the last time Fleur had seen her, had just stood smiling shyly at Fleur as if she hardly knew her, as if they were two girls who had only just met rather than inseparable friends who'd spent so many childhood hours together riding ponies, fishing Stoke Park lake with worms on bent pins, stuffing snowballs down each other's backs and tobogganing through the woods round The Folly on Deanie's best tin trays.

Lucy had said hardly anything at all she was so tongue-tied, and in fact it had been the shy young man with her who finally had told Fleur how much Lucy had loved the concert, how she had all Fleur's records at home, her favourite being the Elgar Violin concerto because it reminded her so much of Stoke Park. Fleur had been pleased and, trying to bring Lucy into the conversation, had said that whenever she played it one of the pictures she always conjured up in her mind's eye was of the two of them riding through the Malverns. But still Lucy said nothing. At least nothing other than 'Really?' Or a 'Yes', or a 'No'.

Fleur thought the trouble was that there had been too many other people in her dressing room. In fact there had been a stream of visitors pouring continually in and out to congratulate the child prodigy on her sensational performance, famous people from every sort of profession, stars and politicians, musicians and jetsetters. Fleur had religiously spent as much time as she could talking with her best friend, but it had all been in vain. The real Lucy never surfaced although Fleur could see her there behind her eyes, but already they were talking the polite talk of people who had become distanced.

Finally Gregory Rogers had brought in the massive and grandiose figure of the great Italian tenor Paulo Bellini to tender his especial congratulations and when Fleur looked again Lucy had gone, leaving a message with Fleur's mother saying that she would ring Fleur soon and ask her down for a weekend in Worcester. That message had been the last time Fleur had ever heard from her.

'No that is just a fact of life, a fact of our sort of life,' Freddie said. 'So there's no good in blaming yourself. We may want to run with the pack, more than anything else maybe, because we see ourselves as being as ordinary as the next person which in most ways we are. But it's no good. It just doesn't happen. The pack can't keep up with the pace and so you suddenly find yourself stopping and looking round and saying hey – where is everybody? We can't even be friends with our own sort dammit, because who wants to talk nothing but shop all day? And anyway, people in our line of country don't have friends, we only have rivals. So what happens? You end up like some big film star I was just reading about whose best friend is the guy who tunes his race-car. Or like me, whose best friend is a Good Samaritan doctor.'

'Haven't you made any new friends?' Fleur asked. 'Since you became successful?'

'After you on this one,' Freddie said wryly.

Fleur hesitated. Friends. She knew so many people, had known so many people, but how many of them could she count as friends?

'I don't know, it was different for me,' she began. 'First of all, when I was studying that is, I was surrounded by adults. I hardly ever saw anyone my own age and when I did they were kids like me, brought to Izzy's just for their music lesson and then whipped away back home in case anything happened to them and their precious hands. Then when I started playing in public it was always with different orchestras, which meant I never had time to get to know anybody. Even the year I had under Wilhelm Hertzhog with the Mannheim Philharmonic – for a start I didn't speak any German, and even if I had it wouldn't have made any difference because Hertzhog never let me out of his sight. He wouldn't even let me make friends with his dog.'

'Is his temper really as bad as they say?'

'Oh – worse!' Fleur laughed. 'Much, much worse.'

'I love your laugh,' Freddie said, with a sigh. 'Like beech leaves ringing in the light.'

'He once lost his temper completely with a replacement clarinettist who'd been forced upon him at the last moment,' Fleur continued, 'and stopping rehearsals yelled at him, "Your bloody nonsenses can I stand twice or once, but sometimes always, by God, never!"'

Freddie laughed so much Fleur thought they were going to leave the road and end up in the river far below.

'Right,' Freddie said, wiping the tears of laughter away from his eyes. 'Next question. What about boyfriends?'

'If I didn't have any friends, Freddie Jourdan, how on earth could I have had boyfriends?'

'You must have had!' Freddie stared round at her. 'You must have. Someone as beautiful as you.'

'Once upon a time in a land faraway there was a princess locked up in a tower,' Fleur replied. 'And you're on the wrong side of the road.'

Freddie corrected the path of the car which had been just about to cross the white line in the middle of the road, slowing down as he did.

'But you must have had someone,' he persisted. 'I mean you must have been in love.'

'Oh God, I've been in love masses of times,' Fleur said, looking at her watch. 'And I don't know about you, but I'm hungry.'

'Who have you been in love with?'

'I'll tell you over lunch.'

'The list's that long?'

'I was in love with André Previn, Al Pacino in *The Godfather*, the second trombone in the London Philharmonic, the man who used to cox the Oxford Rowing Crew, Billy Crystal, one of the *Blue Peter* presenters but I can't remember which one, Sir Kenneth Clark, Dustin Hoffman in *The Graduate*, a certain British conductor who shall be nameless, you want me to go on?'

'I meant in love with somebody as in in love with somebody.'

'There's you.'

'Okay,' Freddie said, his smile suddenly gone shy on him. 'Besides me.'

'There was one boy,' Fleur admitted. 'The first boy I ever really knew. I'll tell you over lunch.'

They stopped in Ludlow and looked around to find somewhere to buy a picnic. Freddie insisted on eating out of doors because it was such a beautiful day. And even though Fleur knew she would certainly be cold, such was Freddie's enthusiasm she knew equally certainly she wouldn't be miserable so she agreed with his proposal. All heads turned when they entered the delicatessen they found down a side street, a fact which neither found surprising since they both considered it was the other one of them who was attracting all the attention, Freddie imagining everyone to be staring at the delicate Pre-Raphaelite beauty of Fleur while Fleur was equally convinced everyone had been rendered speechless by the aquiline looks of the tall, long-haired man whose arm she was holding. In fact the inhabitants of the little black-and-white timbered shop were struck equally by them both and although they had no idea who the couple were, they were of the united opinion that they were undoubtedly famous if just for their looks alone.

Unlike his performance behind the wheel Freddie was obviously an expert shopper, taking infinite care with the cutting of the ham, the choice of olives which he insisted on tasting first before deciding on the black Spanish ones rather than the slightly too oily Greek ones, and the absolutely right wine for the occasion. Naturally he consulted Fleur first as to her particular preferences but she said she was only too happy to trust his judgement because, such was their mutuality, she knew they would both like the same things. They discovered indeed they did, right down to the choice of cheeses, fruit and even the type of chocolate cake.

'I've had a passion for chocolate cake since I was small,' Fleur said. 'It was so bad everyone got to know about it, the people with whom I was working . . . everyone. I remember once when I was thirteen and I was playing the Sibelius in Birmingham, I suddenly felt absolutely whacked after the first movement. I'd just come back from eight concerts in a ten-day tour of Scandinavia so it was hardly surprising I was fit to drop. Anyway I felt as if I could go to sleep right there and then and the famous British conductor who-shall-be-nameless must have seen what I looked like, because he leaned forward and whispered to me *Chocolate cake. Think only of the chocolate cake.* And in a second I was fine. We went out to dinner afterwards and he who-shall-be-nameless ordered chocolate cake for my main course.'

'No wonder you fell in love with him,' Freddie said as they got back in the car. 'Now. One of these nice ladies in the shop said on a day like this we should go and eat our lunch up on the Stiperstones. You ever heard of them? They're legendary rocks apparently, haunted by some guy called Wild Edric who they say rides forth in warning when England's safety is threatened. I'm a sucker for that sort of thing, so if it's okay with you—'

'I love legends too,' Fleur said, taking the map from Freddie and the pamphlet on the area which one of the shop ladies had donated to him. 'When I first came down to The Folly for the summer I read up all about the myths in this part of the country. For instance there's a peculiar hill somewhere round here which is set apart from all the other hills and composed of different materials as well. Folklore has it that it was made by a Welsh giant dumping this huge load of earth he was carrying to dam the River Severn and drown out Shrewsbury. But some quick-witted local told him he was still miles away from the town and because he was so fed up he dropped his vast load of earth where he was standing, and formed and here it is— the Wrekin.' Fleur pointed out where she meant. 'And this,' she said, 'this little hill next to it, the Ercall, that's where the giant scraped the mud from his boots before tramping all the way back to Wales.'

'I must compose an opera based on this story straight-away,' Freddie told her with mock solemnity. 'I can hear the overture already. *Doom, doom, doom!* '

'I don't think you should be standing up, not if you're meant to be driving,' Fleur cautioned him, 'and you want to turn left quite soon, on to the A489.'

'Come on, Miss Fisher-Dilke, let's make with some more of those British legends of yours. Do you know anything about these rocks where we're having lunch?'

'If it's the rocks I remember reading about, I seem to remember one of the stones was meant to be a witch who was turned to stone for milking a fairy cow dry.'

'That doesn't seem to be such a big number.'

'Oh yes it was. The cow happened to be the only source of milk for the locals whenever there was a famine, right?'

'Got it. So lucky I bought us some wine, fair lady,' Freddie said. 'Because I for one don't fancy spending the rest of my days as a lump of sodium chloride.'

Being such a tourist feature, the Stiperstones were easy to find and when they'd parked Freddie set out their picnic on a sheltered spot well below the summit. He'd been keen to climb to the top but something told him not to suggest it, just as something had told him not to press Fleur for the information he was dying to hear, namely what had happened to her in the intervening years since she'd stopped playing. So far she had said nothing about it, not one word. He had thought she was about to open that particular chapter up just after they had crossed the huge suspension bridge over the River Severn, and had begun to thread their way through Herefordshire. But somehow they'd switched subjects, and now he was left wondering and waiting for the right time to ask.

Instead he made sure she was comfortable and sheltered from the breeze before setting out their lunch. He knew whatever she wanted to tell him she would, and besides, they had plenty of time to talk and the subject was bound to recur sooner or later. What was truly concerning him now was that even though the day was still warm and they were well sheltered from any wind by the huge rocks to their back, Fleur was very obviously cold.

'I'm just a cold person,' she said, shrugging it off with a smile. 'Don't worry, really. It's just a side effect of this stupid virus. I feel the cold, that's all.'

'I'll get you my coat from the car as well,' Freddie said, hopping back up. 'You can put it over your knees, or round your shoulders. I won't be a moment.'

While he was gone Fleur poured herself a glass of water and quickly tapped out the handful of pills she should have taken an hour earlier, ever since when she had in fact been trying to work out how to take her dosage without Freddie seeing. It was just that she didn't want him to see quite how heavy the medication she was on actually was. At the outset of the journey she'd banked on the fact that they would stop for lunch in a hotel or a restaurant where she could have disappeared to the Ladies, but Freddie's insistence on a picnic had put paid to that idea.

She would of course have found a pretext or managed somehow to distract Freddie, that she knew, but the problem was she couldn't rely on when. It had begun to worry her, just as she had been worried by the venue Freddie had chosen for their intended picnic. Luckily for some reason he hadn't insisted on climbing any higher than they had, but even so Fleur had been worried when they'd stopped and she'd seen how steep the paths and climbs ahead of them were. Most men Freddie's age and of his physical disposition would have insisted on climbing to the top, particularly on such a beautiful autumn day, but there was no way Fleur could climb those steep slopes and rocks without becoming exhausted. In case Freddie should insist on doing so after lunch, which she felt sure he would, she decided to excuse herself on the grounds that she suffered from vertigo.

Once Freddie returned and wrapped his mackintosh around her, with her pills safely taken, half a glass of red wine inside her and snuggled up against the huge rock well out of the wind, Fleur felt infinitely warmer and began again to relax. The food helped warm her up even more as the long French loaf was still warm and Freddie made baguettes filled with ham, cheese and sliced olives, which they washed down with a delicious smoky Rioja.

'Okay,' Freddie said when they had finished their picnic. 'I thought we might hack on up to the top to look at the view. Okay with you?'

Fleur shook her head.

'You go,' she said, 'I can't. I really have no head at all for heights.'

'Come on,' Freddie laughed. 'It's not that high.'

'No I mean it, Freddie. You make me go up there and that's it. I can't even stand on a chair. Anyway, I've only just got warm.'

'Okay,' Freddie agreed. 'As long as you're sure you'll be all right by yourself.'

'I'll be fine,' she assured him. 'You're not going to be that far away, so if Wild Edric suddenly leaps out and ravishes me you'll hear my screams. Or who knows? Maybe he'll be so handsome they'll be different sorts of screams.'

Once he was sure she was warm and comfortable, Freddie began his climb. The tumbled mass of rock wasn't far away but the climb was steep and it took him a good twenty minutes to reach the top. When he looked down he could still see Fleur sitting where he'd left her against the rock, and she could obviously see him because she responded at once to his wave. The view from where he stood was wonderful but Freddie imagined it was not any place to be in inclement weather. He'd been up seemingly innocuous-looking hills and small mountains like this back home when the weather turned, and the speed at which the change came about could be frightening. This rock-strewn hilltop, regardless of the green valleys nestling apparently so close below, would definitely not be the place to be caught in a sudden storm he decided.

Over lunch Fleur had told him that these Shropshire hills had been a battleground for the Welsh and the English until early in the fifteenth century and indeed the whole area seemed to resound with history and speak of a turbulent past. Freddie stared around him at the wonderful landscape, the artist in him unable to stop imagining what it had been like way back when the local tribesmen had fought the invading Romans in and around these very hills, and in the years before that, before the Saxons and the Celts. What rough men and wild creatures he wondered had lived and stalked these very mountains and verdant valleys then?

Turning around to look at the view behind him, Freddie

noticed that the tumbled mass of rock on the crest was like a huge chair, a perfect set for something or other, or so it seemed to him. Understandably leg-weary after his climb he sat himself down in it to survey the countryside, and he was at once a Roman warrior, a conquering Celtic king, not to mention a musical poet. Then as if designed by some unseen hand, the lighting plot changed, and the next moment a dark and heavy grey cloud blocked out the sun. Looking out across the valleys to the distant horizon, Freddie could see what looked like storm clouds suddenly gathering. The cloud obscuring the sun was ominous as well, not a passing fleecy one but a bringer of rain, and perhaps even thunder judging from its size and colour. It had suddenly got colder as well, with a wind whipping up from nowhere at all.

Concerned in case Fleur got caught in a sudden downpour, Freddie jumped down from his rock throne and made his way quickly back to the picnic spot. As he did he thought he heard a distant rumble and he certainly felt large drops of rain on his face.

'Come on or we're going to get soaked,' he said when he reached Fleur, but she was ahead of him and already had everything packed up and ready to go. Grabbing the cardboard box full of what was left of the picnic, and with the rug they'd bought specially for the occasion when they'd shopped for lunch under his other arm, Freddie led the way to the car with Fleur picking her way carefully down the stony path behind him.

'I'd say we're just in time,' Freddie said looking up at the sky above, and in fact the heavens opened the very moment they shut the car doors on themselves. Sudden rain that like the wind seemed to have come from nowhere. In another moment it had turned to hail, bouncing like shotgun pellets off the bonnet of the car.

'Wow,' Freddie said, backhanding the condensation off the windscreen as they drove off. 'I guess I'll never get used to this climate of yours. Where in hell did all that come from?'

'I don't know,' Fleur replied quietly. 'One moment there wasn't a cloud in the sky and then suddenly – and look at that lightning!'

A second later it was as if an ocean wave had crashed on the roof of their car as a clap of thunder cannoned across the sky.

'My God,' said Freddie, 'I haven't seen a storm like this in years. That was a Jove-is-angry sort of thunder.'

Another brilliant fork of lightning zigzagged in the sky right in front of them, followed immediately by another deafening thunderclap.

'You're not going to believe this, but here goes,' Fleur said. 'I've just been reading the pamphlet you were given in the delicatessen, and that rock you were sitting on is known as the Devil's Chair because it looks like a very large sort of throne.'

'It certainly does,' Freddie said, having another go at clearing the windscreen. 'Feels like one, too.'

'Well you're not meant to sit on it,' Fleur told him. 'Because legend has it that if any mere mortal sits on it, frightful storms begin to rage and all manner of hell breaks loose.'

Freddie looked at Fleur and Fleur looked back at him, while above them the storm broke in good and earnest.

'Holy cow,' Freddie said finally. 'And there was I thinking I was no mere mortal.'

'I just hope we haven't really brought down the wrath of the gods,' Fleur said, shivering as she turned up the car heater.

'You don't really believe in all that stuff, do you?' Freddie called above another peal of thunder.

'I thought we both did,' Fleur said, looking at him steadily.

'Touché! ' a sheepish-looking Freddie shouted back as the

noise of the hail became too loud to talk over. 'We'll talk about this later! In the meantime I'd advise us to get the hell out of here!'

Fleur wiped her side of the windscreen clean as well, while Freddie battled with the heating controls as he tried to find the demister. Finally a blast of warm air indicated he'd won the battle as the screen began to clear itself.

'Turn right when you get to the main road!' Fleur shouted back. 'And look for the signs to Dolgellau!'

They left the storm behind them within minutes of leaving the hills.

'Seems to have been a local disturbance,' Freddie said when as suddenly as it had begun, the rain ceased and the sun again broke through.

'Next time I vote we read the Information for Tourists before we go sitting on anything,' Fleur said, 'Provided it's not too late.'

'It's never too late,' Freddie told her in return, 'and I think we were still on the subject of boyfriends.'

'Do you want to hear about Harry?' Fleur asked after a moment. 'He was the only person I ever loved besides you.'

'Do I want to hear about him? You tell me,' Freddie said. 'Were you just wild about Harry?'

'Harry was a soul,' Fleur said, turning away from her window to lean back in her seat and stare straight ahead. 'He was like a fifteen-year-old you. Harry and I had one of those friendships that can only be born, not made. I mean I realize that now. Then he was just Harry and I was just me. You'd have loved Harry.'

'I'm sure I would if he was just like me,' Freddie returned.

'Seriously,' Fleur looked at Freddie before continuing. 'You'd have been soul mates. That's what we were. We felt we'd always been friends, we felt it without even saying it. It was something we just accepted as being there, in exactly the same way you and I accept that we were meant for each other. I know we were only kids. I mean I was twelve and Harry was fourteen when we met, but straightaway we had this bond. He played jazz piano, I mean really good jazz piano particularly for someone his age, and we used to play together. Most of all he could make me laugh, and I suddenly realized last night that until I met you, since Harry I've never really laughed. Not really, you know, not until you ache. First time I saw Harry doing his gibbon act on a tree, I thought I'd die. He used to just hang from these trees in Stoke Park. I know it doesn't seem particularly funny now, at least not to describe it, but you'd be walking around the park, or other people would and they'd suddenly see this tall thin person hanging by his arms from the branch of some tree. And if you knew Harry, you'd just laugh. Some people are just − just funny, don't you think? Harry was. He used to do this terrible blind musician act which I would keep telling him wasn't funny, but it wasn't any good because he just had to do it and everyone started to die with laughter.'

'So what happened to him? Did you just grow out of each other?'

'No,' Fleur said. 'He died. He went into hospital to have his tonsils out, he was perfectly all right, and then suddenly he haemorrhaged and it was too late. He died in minutes.'

'Jesus Christ,' Freddie said slowly. 'I know. I mean I remember. The childhood friend. The one who died just before your debut concert.'

'You did do your research, didn't you?' Fleur looked round at him.

'It's the only study I've done which has ever really led me to anything,' Freddie replied.

A few miles further on the road crossed a river and high hills grew up either side of the car. Fleur hadn't wanted to talk any more for a while, in fact neither of them had so she had chosen a tape from Freddie's bag. They listened enthralled to Bergonzi singing I *Pagliacci* as the countryside became as glorious and grand as the music, the road suddenly dropping down into a tiny village before sidestepping the southern foothills of the Arans, magnificent peaks higher than anything south of Snowdon, and then climbing up and up to about a thousand or more feet prior to plunging down to Dolgellau with the mighty Cader Idris clearly visible ahead of them to the left.

Past the town they headed due north along purely sensational valleys sliced out of the landscape by the mighty Mawddach river and its teeming tributary, the Eden; past forests through which sparkling waterfalls raced until all at once the road emerged from the shade of thousands of trees into a savage landscape of scattered rocks and runty trees backed by the peaks of more great mountains to the left. Then on past a beautiful lake marred only by the sight of a nuclear power station on its shores, and down into the lovely Vale of Ffestiniog. They were heading north-west now, until Freddie found the sign for which he had been watching and turned the car off the long straight main road into a quiet estate of pines and rhododendron bushes, which finally led to an estuary warmed by the glow of the early evening sun.

At the water's edge stood a pink-washed house set in an exquisite terraced garden.

'What is this?' Fleur asked, leaning forward in her seat to take in the magic surroundings. 'Where are we?'

'Don't ask me to pronounce the name of the place, it looks like parallelogram spelt backwards,' Freddie replied with a boyish grin. 'The house belongs to a friend of mine. It's his bolt hole. He is one of the biggest producers of lyrics in the world, but that doesn't stop him from being *hombre.*'

'Really?'

As he swung the car round to park it outside the front door of the house, Freddie glanced at Fleur and saw what he'd hoped he would see in her eyes, a look of slight disappointment at the thought that they might be coming to stay with someone rather than being on their own, or even in a hotel.

'Lovely. So that's what we're going to do, is it?' she said, for her own part doing her best to hide her concern. 'We're going to stay with this friend of yours? Is that the plan?'

'No,' Freddie said, swinging open his door. 'No that isn't the plan at all, Miss Fisher-Dilke. What we are not going to be doing, is we are going not to be staying with an old buddy of mine, but we *are* going to be staying at his house.'

Before she could ask further Freddie was round her side of the car and opening her door. Fleur got out and as Freddie went round to the back of the car to fetch their luggage, she stretched and breathed in the beautiful fresh breeze blowing in from the sea.

'As for you, Miss Fisher-Dilke,' Freddie continued, leading the way to the front door, 'you will be doing absolutely nothing at all. I am even going to be cooking for you, Miss Fisher-Dilke. I may be the world's worst driver but hell, can I cook. Seriously. And what you are going to find out, which is even more to your advantage, is that great cooks besides making great food make great love. So follow me please.'

Fleur smiled happily. If Freddie's cooking was anything like his kissing, then she was going to be in for the most wonderful time.

The house was cold inside, as all houses which are only occasionally occupied during the year usually are. Freddie automatically checked the radiator but it was cold and already he could see Fleur pulling her clothes around her as she noticed the drop in temperature.

'I'll light some fires at once,' he said. 'I asked the couple who look after this place to make sure the heating was up full, but it being still summer to them they probably thought *another crazy American.* But first, here — let's show you upstairs.'

He took hold of all the bags again and went up the stairs in front of Fleur, with her following on a few steps behind. She hadn't really thought anything through, not the particulars of what was going to happen once they'd arrived at their destination, only how to run away from home and be with Freddie for these few days. But now she remembered details such as how much she needed to have, if not a room of her own, at least sufficient privacy to be able to take her medications without Freddie seeing.

'Obviously you've been here before, Freddie,' Fleur said as she followed him upstairs to a bedroom with old Chinese wallpaper, oak furniture, and a four-poster overlooking the estuary.

'I always bring my women here,' Freddie replied, switching on an electric fire for her after he'd put down her cases. 'I bring a string of broads for weekend orgies, and then to stop 'em kissing and telling I give them walk-ons in my shows in true show-business tradition. I got Walter Matthau rather well then, don't you think?' Freddie grinned at her before kissing her on the cheek. 'Actually, I've never been here before, Fleur,' he said, 'not once. I happen to know the layout because I asked the owner, and also they did a feature on it recently in some magazine or other. Now if there's any hot water, which I will go and check—' He disappeared into the bathroom which was next door and came back a moment later wiping his hand dry on a hand towel. 'There is plenty of hot water so I'll go and turn the heating up as well, while you take a bath and put your feet up.

I've got to go down to the kitchen to make sure they got all the shopping I ordered, and by all the shopping I mean all the shopping. Hey – that was good. I got old Walter again there, spot on!'

Freddie disappeared leaving Fleur all alone in the beautiful bedroom, but rather than admire the wonderful view, or run a bath, or collapse on the bed, she went to the door instead and called out after him.

'Freddie? I'm not going to rest, if you don't mind.'

'On the contrary,' Freddie replied with a smile. 'I just thought that after such a long journey, and since you were—'

'That's the whole point,' Fleur stopped him. 'I've spent over the last two years just resting, and I'd really rather be with you.'

Freddie came back into her room and took her in his arms, looking straight in her eyes.

'I want you with me every waking moment,' he said. 'And every sleeping one, come to that. But first I must go and check the shopping in case they've left anything out.'

'Of course,' Fleur demurred. 'I'll just have a quick bath and follow you down. A bath will warm me up.'

Once Freddie had gone, she went quickly to her suitcase for her pills, counting up the hours in her head since she'd taken her last quota. She was almost an hour late for this dose and had just begun to feel that odd brightness coming upon her which her father had warned her would come about on the rare occasions when, left to herself, she forgot to take her pills, particularly if she'd had a drink. She had in fact a special watch with a chime she could set to remind her, but had deliberately left it off for this occasion.

After she'd soaked for a quarter of an hour in the bath, the medication took effect and her normal feeling of calm returned. She dried herself slowly and carefully before easing herself into her favourite velvet suit, white silk shirt and a pair of brocade slippers, then she went back downstairs and into the drawing room where Freddie had lit a large log fire.

It was a lovely room, furnished in classic English country house style, elegant but thoroughly comfortable with its fine mixture of antiques and chintz sofas and easy chairs. Someone of great taste had obviously arranged its mixture of carefully faded colours, old pieces, and fine paintings.

'I thought I heard you,' Freddie said, reappearing dressed in a striped cook's apron. 'How was the bath?'

'The bath was just what I needed,' Fleur replied. 'And this house is simply beautiful. Have you really never been here before?'

'On my honour,' Freddie confirmed, struggling with the cork of the bottle of champagne he had with him. 'In fact if you pick up that magazine—' He nodded at a glossy journal on top of the pile on the stool in front of the fireplace. 'You'll see the article on it in there. I've been asked down several times, but never managed to make it, much as I wanted to. I'd always heard it was one of the most romantic houses in the country.'

'So what did you do?' Fleur asked, flicking through the magazine until she came to the piece. 'You mean you just rang and asked if you could borrow it?'

'Sure,' Freddie said. 'I told you, the guy who owns it is a buddy of mine. I did him a favour once, and he said – any time.' Freddie popped open the champagne cork and grinned at Fleur, holding the bottle up in offer.

'No, I don't think I should,' she said quickly. 'I mean I love champagne, but it usually gives me a terrible headache.'

'This is vintage,' Freddie protested. 'This won't give you a headache.'

'Okay,' Fleur relented, sensing Freddie's disappointment. 'But only half a glass. Really.'

518

'Half a glass,' Freddie groaned, pouring the wine. 'This is going to be some party on half a glass of champagne.'

'Don't worry. You're all the intoxication I need,' Fleur replied, taking the half-filled glass from him. 'Now tell me more about your famous buddy. What did you do for him? Write him a song, or something?'

'Something,' Freddie grinned again, boyishly. 'I wrote him a show, actually. The guy who owns this place among many other places now, put on a show I wrote called *Perfect Strangers* here. Got him started. Now he produces all my stuff over here.'

As they drank their champagne they sat for a while away from the now brightly burning fire on the window seats, while Freddie told Fleur of how his friend had made his fortune from musicals, before turning the talk round to the colours of the evening and the shape of the distant mountains which could be seen the other side of the broad estuary. In fact they talked of this and that, and everything except what they really wanted to talk about – which was each other. Simply because now they had arrived at their destination neither of them knew quite where to begin.

'Listen – I have to go and cook, if you'll excuse me,' Freddie said when they fell silent for a moment. 'Would you rather stay here by the fire or—'

'You know what I'd rather do, Mr Jourdan, I told you,' Fleur said, getting up and following him out of the drawing room and across the hall into a large and beautifully equipped country kitchen.

'Now this is just the sort of kitchen I've always dreamed about,' Fleur sighed as she looked round the room. 'I mean this is a room for serious cooks and serious cooking, which you obviously are and which is what we're going to have, if you see what I mean.'

'I'm making us *Pissenlit aux lardons* which might sound very rude but in fact is a delicious warm spinach and endive salad with bacon,' Freddie told her as he lifted

Fleur up to sit on a high kitchen stool near him, 'and then a poached beef dish called *Boeuf à la Ficelle*. They're two of my mother's recipes, they are quite fantastic, and we shall wash them down with probably the best Pomerol you have ever drunk.' He swung the uncorked bottle on the central table round to show Fleur the label and then began preparing the meal, passing a long piece of string through a series of perforated slices of beef before tying them to the ends of a carving fork. That way, he explained, they wouldn't touch the bottom of the saucepan when the time came. Fleur stared out at the wonderful view from the huge kitchen window as Freddie prattled on. The weather was now perfect with only the faintest breeze coming in off the sea, ruffling the waters of the pinkening estuary as the sun began to set. A fishing smack was setting out for its night's work, bobbing cheerfully against the stream, followed already by a swirling halo of expectant gulls, while not more than a hundred yards downriver from the house, Fleur suddenly spotted a family of seals basking on the rocks.

'Isn't this just the most heavenly place?' Freddie asked, as he paused for a moment to look out at the view with her. 'You know, this has to be the place to come and die. And what in hell was that?' he asked at the sound of breaking glass.

'Just me knocking over my champagne,' Fleur whispered, biting her lip and staring at the pool of wine which was making its way across the table remorselessly towards her. She had just been reaching out for her glass when Freddie had spoken and now it lay broken on the floor.

'I'm terribly sorry,' Fleur said, staring down at the damage. 'I don't know what I can have been thinking. Or doing. I'm so sorry.'

'It really doesn't matter,' Freddie said, effortlessly lifting her out of the way of the approaching flood. 'But it would be terrible to get it on that wonderful outfit.'

'I don't know what I can have been thinking,' Fleur repeated quietly. 'I'm not usually that clumsy.'

'Come on,' Freddie said cheerfully. 'It's only a glass and not a very good one and there is plenty more champagne.'

He fetched her another glass and refilled it but try as she might Fleur couldn't get his words out of her head. *This has to be the place to come and die.* Suppose it was, she wondered, while Freddie returned to his cooking and chatting, suppose it really was? What would happen if she did die here? Would he hate her forever more, or would it break his heart?

She looked at his lovely funny face as he hurried about the kitchen keeping up a running commentary as he put the herbs and peppercorns, the carrots and celery, the potatoes and cabbage, in a saucepan of boiling water before preparing the mustard croquettes. And she wondered if she wasn't just being purely selfish, grabbing what she considered to be her one true and possibly last chance of happiness with the man she loved — without considering what it might do to him if the worst should happen. But she found she couldn't answer her question. It had suddenly seemed so easy on the day of her birthday, the morning he had surprised her at the window like some wonderful god risen from the ground below to capture her heart all over again. Just as he had done the morning he'd appeared through the mists at the garden of The Folly. There had been no problem in saying yes to herself then, in persuading herself to go for broke as Freddie would call it, to cry to hell with everything and run off with her lover. Yet now she was here with him, alone in one of the most beautiful places she had ever been and on one of the most lovely evenings, she tried to imagine herself dead in his arms. Not out of self-pity but in order to try and feel somewhere near coming to terms with what that might do to this wonderfully warm and funny man she loved.

'Freddie,' she said, as he threw down his spectacles on the table and ran a hand through his long, luxuriant hair.

'Plates,' Freddie said. 'Plates in the oven, croutons, and red wine vinegar.'

'Freddie, I want to talk to you,' Fleur began again, but Freddie was in full culinary flight.

'Not now, angel, not when I'm in the middle of cooking.'

'I have to. Seriously.'

'I have to cook. Seriously.' He looked up at her, mock-cross, dropping his thick straight eyebrows even lower and pouting in traditional French-chef style. 'My muzzer she always say cook in ze kitchen, eat at ze table and talk in ze bedroom.'

'You mean we can't talk over dinner?' Fleur asked, finding the weight of the problem seeming to lighten as soon as Freddie began to fool around.

'If you want to talk over dinner, Miss Fisher-Dilke,' Freddie warned her, 'then I shall want to sleep when we go to bed. Now. We should be ready in about five minutes, so in the meantime you may entertain me with gossip from the concert halls while I bake the croutons for the pissenlit.'

'Why's it called that?' Fleur wondered. 'Pissenlit. Doesn't that mean wet-the-bed?'

'I guess because in France it's usually made with dandelions,' Freddie replied, 'and isn't that meant to be the end result when you pick dandelions?'

'I'm glad you're using spinach.'

'I'm using spinach because spinach gives you strength.'

They ate where they were in the kitchen, neither of them wanting to break the moment, nor leave the view which grew more like a Turner landscape with each passing moment. Fleur brought the candlesticks from the dining room and laid two places at the end of the scrubbed pine table facing the window, while Freddie tidied away his debris and prepared to serve dinner. The room was wonderfully warm from the Aga and the heat of the cooking, so Fleur was both happy and comfortable as Freddie presented her with her first course and then poured them both some wine.

'Oh wow,' Fleur said when she tasted the dish. 'I just love warm salads, and this *dressing.*'

'Isn't it out of this world? It's really pungent, right? Without being too tart.'

'Oh yum,' Fleur said. 'You are a genius.'

'No. Mamma is a genius, like all the French with food.'

'Okay,' Freddie said, after he had cleared away the first course and served them with the poached beef, 'I shall break one of my golden rules specially for you. After you have once again told me how brilliant I am and after I have once more modestly denied it and attributed my great art as a chef to my mother and her mother country, I shall allow you to talk. Not just because I love the sound of your voice which I do, but because there are still about nine million and two things I don't know about you.'

'The beef is fantastic,' Fleur said. 'So tender and the *taste.*'

'It's very simple,' Freddie said. 'Like so much great cooking.'

'Like so many great things.'

'Like love.'

'Love isn't simple, Freddie.'

'Falling in love with you was the simplest thing imaginable.'

'Think of the terrible time you have had since,' Fleur reminded him, at which Freddie held up his fork in mock warning.

'That is *being* in love,' he said. 'I only said falling in love was simple.'

He smiled at her through the candlelight and when he did she thought her heart would burst with the sudden happiness she felt, so much so that she decided not to bring up, let alone pursue, the subject she had been intending to raise just before dinner.

Freddie, however, had different ideas.

'I have to know why you stopped playing,' he announced. 'I know when you did, everyone knows that, but no-one knows why you did. Not according to your press files, anyway.'

'Can't we talk about this some other time?' Fleur asked.

'Sure,' Freddie shrugged. 'I just thought you wanted to tell me, that's all. You almost told me in the car. I think.'

'Yes I did,' Fleur agreed, and then fell back to silence as she ate some more of the mouthwatering *Boeuf à la ficelle*. 'Are you sure you want to hear?' she asked finally.

'If you want to tell me.'

'As you know, it was when my mother died. No-one told me she was ill. I mean she certainly never mentioned it, although I remember she went to a doctor, a specialist rather, for a check-up because she'd been feeling tired. Anyway. I had no idea she had something wrong with her heart, although she must have done because of what they said about her having started having treatment. Then, of course, there was the fact that it happened at the one and only concert at which she'd ever actually been out front.'

'I know,' Freddie said quietly. 'I read all that, but you surely didn't attach any blame to yourself about that?'

'Who said anything about blame?'

'You have a blame voice on, and a blame look. I know it. I used to get bad attacks of the blames myself. You're looking at a fellow sufferer. By name of Frederick Jourdan; I'm a blame-aholic.'

'Are you really?'

'I was, and in spades. Go on.'

524

Fleur shrugged and ate another mouthful of beef. 'After it happened—'

'After your mother died.'

'Yes, Freddie, after my mother died, thank you.'

'We have to say these things, Fleur. I'm not being all American about it, sweetheart. I just happen to know it helps.'

'After my mother died, right there in front of me, will that do you?'

'If it does you, yes.'

Freddie smiled so sympathetically Fleur immediately apologized, only to be reprimanded for doing so and told to carry on.

'Well my health just went to pieces,' Fleur shrugged. 'You know I really hate talking about my health, it makes me sound so self-centred.'

'We're actually talking about how you came to stop playing, remember?'

'Yes, that's true. Anyway. At first the doctors just thought it was simply a bad case of grief and shock, and given the circumstances who could blame them? But then, and I won't bore you with all the symptoms – but then this so-called grief-stroke-shock not only wouldn't go away, but manifested itself in what they like to call a virus. One which all but wiped me out—'

'This was the famous Harbour Virus?'

'Yes. Before I played Salzburg I'd played concerts in Florence and Rome, and then took a short holiday in the South of Italy where they think I contracted this particular virus. Anyway it got bad enough to put me into intensive care for a while, but when I was well enough to come home to convalesce – some hope – I didn't. I started getting worse.'

'Viz? Worse as in?'

This is the moment of truth, then, Fleur thought. This is the moment when I have to tell him what they told me then, to test his love more than anything, to prepare him for what might happen. But if I do, if I tell him the real story, of what they finally diagnosed and what will happen if I don't get what I need— She looked at him through the flickering candleglow, head slightly down while he finished his food, now looking back up at her and smiling with shining eyes as he raised his glass of wine to her, as he mouthed a small sweet kiss. If I tell him he'll be gone, she knew it. Not from me, but taken away by the fact of my impending death. He won't dare take me in his arms, he won't dare make love to me, he won't dare even tell me any more that he loves me. Because he'll be too frightened, just like I was. He'll be so frightened he'll just simply stop and seize up inside, and think poor kid. Poor girl. Poor Fleur. He'll think he's taking death into his very arms. So I'll tell him the B version, the family version, the one with here comes the happy ending written all over it. Because I love him too much to tell him, and I don't yet know whether or not he loves me enough to know.

'Sorry? What did you say?' she asked.

'I said viz? Worse as in?'

'Oh yes, of course. As in terrible headaches and pains, mostly in my arms and chest. And I was so exhausted I couldn't even get out of bed, literally. The doctors were all still saying virus, except that it was now a persistent viral infection which they finally thought had damaged the immune system. And that's when they called it what they called it. Harbour Virus.'

'But they call it something different now, right?' Freddie said. 'Something like Post Viral Fatigue Syndrome, isn't that the one?'

'They prefer Yuppie Flu, at least most doctors do,' Fleur said. 'As if it's something you get from buying a Porsche. Anyway, my father sent me to this specialist who took the thing seriously—'

'Sorry to interrupt, but you can't test for it, can you? At least not specifically?'

'Yes,' Fleur replied, a little too quickly, thrown by Freddie's apparent knowledge of something she thought she could just run by him. 'At least this doctor could.'

'What did he do?'

'What did he do?' Fleur thought quickly, trying to remember what she had read and learned up about the disease when, initially, it had been thought that was all she had. 'He used the Exclusion Theory,' she remembered in time. 'You reach a diagnosis by excluding all the other symptoms which could account for what you're suffering from. And in my case it came up quite positively as ME.'

'Which was what?' Freddie asked. 'Where are we now? You've just had your twentieth birthday so that would make it—'

'Just over two years ago.'

'I see,' Freddie said, sitting back. 'And you had it badly enough to stop you playing altogether.'

'It's much worse than people imagine, you know.'

'No I know it is. Someone I know over here, a girl who used to dance in all my shows, she had it so badly when she had an attack she couldn't get out of bed.'

'I couldn't even stand up for more than five minutes, Freddie, let alone play a twenty-minute concerto.'

'Yes, but what I don't understand – well there are two things, actually. Firstly why announce your retirement for good? And secondly why not give the reason? Or rather the other way round. Because from what, admittedly little, I know of the condition, although it's not precisely curable, you can have long periods of remission and generally it finally clears up altogether.'

'There are some cases much, much worse than others,' Fleur replied. 'And some that simply don't clear up.'

'Yes but even so, sweetheart,' Freddie persisted, 'when you made your announcement, you didn't know that then, Fleur. You didn't know what sort of case you were going to be, and it is only two years ago.'

'Can't we talk about something else, please?' Fleur asked. 'This is really rather boring. And not very romantic.'

'No of course it isn't,' Freddie agreed, but still refused to let go. 'It's just that it doesn't make sense. Not for someone quite as popular and famous as you.'

'All right,' Fleur said carefully, regretting she hadn't thought this one through properly in advance, while realizing the only possible way out was a variation of the truth rather than a full-blown fantasy. 'If you must know it was my father's decision.'

'Your *father's* decision?'

'If you'd just let me finish, Freddie, before you start exploding all over the place,' Fleur insisted. 'Yes, it was my father's decision because at that time I was so ill he thought I might – he thought it best to announce an unqualified and unconditional retirement then. And if you want to know why, it was because he said – and I agreed with him – that when and if I did get better and felt well enough to start playing again, there wouldn't be anything to stop me. But if we hadn't said anything definite then—'

'No it's okay,' Freddie stopped her. 'I get the picture now. Otherwise they'd never have left you alone. Is-she isn't-she, will-she won't-she – sure, it was by far the most sensible thing to say. Particularly when you were that ill for – well, how long?'

'I'm still not exactly a hundred per cent even now. I couldn't make it through the first movement of a concerto let alone three.'

'No you certainly couldn't,' Freddie said, putting a hand out to take one of hers. 'I'm sorry, but I had to know, Fleur. I mean I knew you weren't well, that was pretty damn obvious, but somehow something wasn't quite making sense—'

'I hope it's making sense now,' Fleur said hastily. 'I am a lot better than I was two years ago. It's just that I'm still a bit of a way from being match fit. I couldn't have climbed up to those rocks with you today, for instance. And I get tired quickly. And I feel the cold.'

'Hence the summertime fires at The Folly.'

'Yes. I go back to The Folly for summer because I can't stand being cooped up in London all year. The Folly's where I was brought up, as you probably gathered when you were doing your research, you see. We were the family who used to rent it – and do stop looking so anxious.'

'I love you, Fleur. I can't help looking anxious knowing you're not well.'

Fleur smiled at him gently. 'I'm fine. I'm getting the very best treatment possible. My father keeps updating my medication—'

'But your father is a heart man, right?'

'He's also a general diagnostician,' Fleur added quickly. 'He works hand in glove with this specialist and they make sure I get the very latest drugs. But best of all, I'm on something now which is doing me more good than anything else I've ever had.'

'Namely?' Freddie asked.

'You,' Fleur replied.

After dinner, Fleur asked Freddie to play to her which Freddie was only too delighted to do. He also sang to her surprisingly well in a good baritone. He sang her songs of his but only ones which Fleur requested because he was not one to show off his talent. Mostly he chose standards, Gershwin, Kern, Rogers and Hart, Sammy Kahn and Harold Arlen.

'Only love songs,' she had insisted. 'And no sad ones. I don't want to hear any sad ones, any regretful ones, no *One for my baby and one for the road* ones. I just want happy love songs, the ones which celebrate love and people who are in it. *Violets for Your Furs* songs rather than *Mean to Me* ones.'

When he'd finished playing, even though Fleur was wanting more, Freddie came and sat down beside her by the fire because that was what *he* wanted.

'Do you really think all this, I mean everything that's happened to us, Freddie,' Fleur asked after a time when they had just sat staring into the fire, 'do you really think it was all meant?'

'I don't know what it was, Fleur,' Freddie replied. 'For a start I don't know what *meant* means. I just have this feeling, as I keep saying, that we've always known each other, and that it was only a matter of time before we met. And that once we did, we'd know it. We'd know that we'd found each other.'

'So the reason you were at the window that night—'

'And the reason you were at your window that night—'

'I don't know why I was,' Fleur whispered.

'Neither do I,' Freddie replied. 'That's what I mean about this whole thing. It's so weird. But you see if you were feeling the same right from the start, the same as I was feeling—'

He sat back slightly as he realized she hadn't been telling him the truth, and as he did she turned round to look at him anxiously.

'What is it?' she asked, taking both of his hands. 'Now what's the matter, Freddie?'

'It's just that if everything you say is true—'

'Of course it's true, Freddie.'

'Then why wouldn't you see me? Why if you fell in love with me that morning like I did with you, as if I'd been hit by a bolt of lightning out of the blue, then why in hell did you run away?'

'I've just explained all that, Freddie.'

'No. No you haven't. You haven't explained why you told me *there was no point*. Why you kept telling me. Why you ran away from me in London after I'd sent you back your precious book. After you'd promised to meet me. You haven't really explained to me why you fought me, Fleur, right up to the eleventh hour, have you? Only giving in to me when it was almost too late. When one more refusal or rebuttal would have meant we never saw each other again.'

'No I haven't, have I,' Fleur agreed, looking away into the fire so that he mightn't see her eyes. 'It's because I didn't think it would be fair.'

'While you thought not seeing me was?' Freddie asked, wide-eyed.

'I don't think you understand what it's like when you're really ill, Freddie. How paranoiac you get. And I was paranoiac, believe me. I really and truly didn't think there was any point because I thought I was chronically ill, which for God's sake I still might be! And because it was obvious that unless I got better I wasn't going to be able to do anything normal, like play a game of tennis, go dancing, go to parties, swim, just walk up the stairs for heaven's sake, let alone fall in love, and maybe – maybe get married and have a baby—'

'You took the words right out of my mouth,' Freddie whispered.

'No, Freddie, listen,' Fleur insisted. 'It wasn't that I thought there wouldn't be any point, that's just the way I said it. What I meant was I didn't want you to be shackled by an invalid. Don't you see? Someone like you, with such an active and creative and important life? Can you imagine what it would be like being lumbered with somebody who can't even get out of bed and get herself dressed in the morning?'

'Oh Fleur,' Freddie sighed, taking her in his arms. 'Now I see what you meant by what you were doing, I just love you even more. I don't care if you can't lead the sort of life other people lead—'

'I do. I care like crazy.'

'But you will. In time, you bet you will. Now we have each other, we'll beat this thing together.'

But Fleur said nothing. She just put her head on his shoulder and began to cry inconsolably.

'Fleur, sweetheart, don't cry,' Freddie said aghast. 'There's nothing to cry about now. Not now we've found each other.'

'Oh Freddie,' Fleur sobbed. 'Freddie you just don't understand.'

'Now what don't I understand, you moonhead?' Freddie laughed, tilting her chin up to him.

'Oh—' Fleur cried hopelessly. 'Oh just how much I love you, Freddie!'

'And you don't understand just how much I love you, Fleur,' Freddie said. 'We are going to have such a wonderful life together.'

Fleur looked up at him, straight into his eyes. She really hadn't got that far. She hadn't got as far as Freddie asking to marry her, or spending his life with her. She'd only got as far as Freddie taking her away somewhere and making love to her before she died, but as she looked into his large, gentle eyes she knew there were no more protests, no more excuses, no more half-baked reasons, or no more prevarications to be made. Nor did it matter. All that mattered was that they were alone and together and that she knew he was going to make love to her, and anyway even if she said yes to him, yes that she would spend the rest of her life with him, it was true because that is what she meant to do. The only thing she couldn't tell him was how short that life might be.

And so she said yes, yes that she would spend the rest of her life with him, yes that she loved him with all her heart. And when she did Freddie kissed her, and as he did, even as he held her so tightly to him and kissed her, Fleur thought then she might die. How long he kissed her she had no idea, nor how many times. All she knew was that she felt as if her whole being was swimming, as if she was being engulfed in a whirlpool somewhere in a deep dark corner in space, while for Freddie the kiss Fleur was giving him back made him feel as if he had finally arrived out of the infinite to land in the fields of heaven.

He took her hand to lead her out of the room and upstairs but she held back and whispered no, here, by the fireside, by the warm red glow of the fire so that nothing should break the spell or the moment. So he turned off the lamps and, pulling the curtains back, let the full moonlight spill in on them from over the mountains and across the estuary before taking her back in his arms and kissing her tenderly once more as she kissed him tenderly back, while he slipped her velvet jacket off and undid the buttons on her silk blouse to run his hands around her back and then on to the softness of her sweet firm bare breasts as she gasped a little, throwing her head back and letting him kiss her on the neck as she did so, and then on her breasts as he eased her silk blouse down from her shoulders while she searched for the buttons on his shirt. She had to fumble to undo them unseeingly because he was kissing her on her mouth again now, taking her breath, drawing out her very soul before whispering to her as he held her to him. *If we love in the other world as we do in this, I shall love thee to eternity.*

'No don't,' she whispered. 'Don't, no please don't answer it.'

He hadn't heard it at first, at least not clearly. He had heard it ring, but it had seemed so far away until she spoke and told him not to answer it, not to answer the telephone which he realized was ringing there on the table beside them.

'It's okay,' he whispered. 'It's an answerphone. So I'll just make sure it's on answer.'

'Can't you just turn it off?' Fleur whispered back. 'I mean it's not going to be for us. For a start no-one knows we're even here. Do they?'

'Only Stephen,' Freddie answered, having found and

pressed the right button. After another ring, the machine switched itself on and they heard a recorded voice, short and to the point.

'*There's no-one here so please leave a message after the bleep. Thanks,*' it intoned.

'Not very romantic, is it?' Fleur smiled. 'You never see this sort of thing in films.'

'Hang on and I'll try and find the volume control and turn the damn thing down,' Freddie hissed, as if the machine had ears. 'Either that or rip it out of the wall.'

But before he could do either whoever was calling in started to speak. Even before he gave his name Freddie recognized the voice.

'Hello, Freddie? Freddie are you there?'

'It's Steve,' Freddie whispered, frowning. 'What in hell can he want?'

'Can't you just turn it down and find out later?' Fleur beseeched, pulling her silk shirt back around her shoulders and shivering.

'Freddie are you there?' the voice repeated. 'Because if you are, pick up the phone. This is urgent.'

'Well it had better be,' Freddie grumbled, 'because for the life of me I can't find how to turn this damn thing down.'

'Freddie?' the voice asked again. 'Freddie are you there? This really is something I can't leave on a blasted machine.'

'Hang on, Stephen, I'm here,' Freddie said, picking up the phone, while Fleur groaned and sat back on the sofa. 'This really had better be urgent.'

'Yes it is, old friend, believe me,' Stephen assured him, his voice now only audible to Freddie. 'Are you alone?'

'No. No what do you think?'

'No, I didn't think you would be. But what I have to say to you I have to say to you alone. I mean it.'

Freddie looked round at Fleur lit only by the glow of the firelight, lying back on the sofa with her velvet jacket held back to front over her. 'Hang on, Steve,' he said. 'Give me a moment.'

Putting the receiver on the table, Freddie went and sat by Fleur. 'Sweetheart I'm sorry—' he began.

'It's not your fault,' Fleur smiled. 'It doesn't matter.'

'It does. It's broken the moment.'

'We'll get it back again.'

'Too right we will. But I have to speak to Stephen because as he says, it's urgent, obviously.'

'Obviously.'

'So since the fire's nearly done, why don't you go on upstairs and I'll be up in one sec, okay?'

'Good idea,' Fleur agreed with a shy smile. 'I was beginning to get a little cold.'

'I really won't be a minute. Just don't you dare go to sleep.'

'Don't you dare be more than a minute,' Fleur replied, getting up and kissing him. 'And stop frowning like that. I still love you.'

'I love you too, sweetheart.'

When she was gone with the door closed behind her, Freddie picked the phone back up. 'As I said, Steve old buddy,' he sighed, 'this had better be Stop Press stuff. Talk about opportune moments.'

'That's what I was hoping,' Stephen replied. 'Because I've just had Richard Fisher-Dilke on the line. I'd have rung earlier but he only just got me because I only just got back in town and—'

'Her father?' Freddie chipped in. 'But how in hell?'

'Fleur was spotted leaving this morning with you, and you were seen coming out of my house. So putting two and two together, there you go.'

'Okay so what? The lady in question is over eighteen.'

'The lady in question, chum, is mortally ill.'

'The lady in question may be ill, buddy, as indeed she's told me, but—'

'I don't know what she's told you, nor in a way do I care, Freddie. Because I have it from her father, who is a specialist in this particular field, that this is a matter of life or death. Fisher-Dilke wanted to ring you himself but I said that was not a good idea because Fleur might get to hear he'd rung. While if I rang you I could tell you possibly without her suspecting anything.'

'Tell me *what*, Steve!'

'Fleur has a chronic *heart* condition.'

'Jesus Christ,' Freddie whispered, sitting suddenly on the chair beside him. 'A chronic heart condition?'

'Probably terminal. Listen. I can't go into all the details now, Fred, not that her father gave me them anyway. But what he did say — and stressed — and I believe him, was that any undue strain, or excitement, either sudden or prolonged—'

Freddie said nothing as Stephen left his sentence significantly unfinished. He heard what his friend was saying and glanced upstairs. *Any sudden or prolonged excitement.*

'She told me she was ill,' Freddie said, 'but what she said was—'

'She doesn't know quite how ill she is, Fred. She knows there's something wrong, of course she does, because her father is treating her. But he said she doesn't know just how bad it is. She's been in the queue for a transplant these past eighteen months.'

'A transplant?' Freddie could hardly believe his ears.

'That's right. It's difficult enough getting the spare parts as you well know, but on top of that the patient's a rare blood group as well. So when all's said and done, and whatever you may be feeling — it's just as well I got you when I did.'

'Jesus Christ, what am I going to *say*, Steve?' Freddie wondered next, staring down at the floor between his feet. 'Like I said, you rang at an opportune moment, or rather the very opposite.'

'I don't know, Fred,' Stephen said in return. 'I don't know, Fred. But you're going to have to think of something, make some excuse.'

'Any ideas?'

'No damnit. I don't have one. All I know is Fisher-Dilke says you're going to have to bring her back to London ASAP, Fred. And he means it. He says you've got to bring her back – or he'll hold you responsible.'

With this Stephen fell to silence and let Freddie fill in the implication.

'Meanwhile?' Freddie asked.

'Meanwhile,' Stephen replied slowly. 'Look – couldn't you say someone in your family was ill? One of your sisters maybe? Or even your mother? I'm sure under the circumstances God will forgive you.'

'No!' Freddie almost shouted down the line. 'No I will not say anything of the sort! That's just asking for trouble, Steve!'

'You're going to have to come up with something, Fred. And fast. And I really think your family's your best excuse.'

'And if you weren't my best buddy I'd tell you to go to hell,' Freddie said, putting down the phone.

After he'd done so, Freddie remained where he was, sitting on the sofa and staring into the fire while he tried to make some sense of what he had just heard, let alone think of what he might or could do. He didn't hear her come back but without even looking round he knew she was there.

'Freddie?'

He couldn't even bear to turn and look at her so he just sat with his head in both hands, staring into the embers of the fire.

'Freddie darling?' She was in front of him now, kneeling down, staring up into his eyes, her face death-white against her shock of dark hair. 'Darling, what is it?

You look awful, darling – what is it? Please tell me. Please.'

'There's been an accident,' he heard himself saying way out in a void somewhere. 'There's been a terrible accident.'

'What sort of accident, Freddie?' She had her hands round both of his. 'Who? What sort of accident and who's had it, darling?'

'It's one of my sisters,' he said quietly, before finding himself adding and without quite knowing why – 'She's had an accident with one of her horses.'

'Oh my God, you poor darling,' Fleur said, sitting up beside him and putting an arm around him. 'Oh God she's not dead, is she?'

'No,' Freddie said, trying hard to control the tears he felt beginning to smart his eyes. 'No Fleur, she's not dead – but it was very bad. And – and—'

'It's all right, Freddie, it's all right,' Fleur said, cradling him in her arms, as he put his head against her breast. 'You don't have to talk, it's all right. You don't have to say anything. Don't say anything at all, darling Freddie, my love. You'll want to go back home obviously, so we'll leave for London just as soon as you say.'

Freddie wanted so much to cry. Every time he looked at Fleur, at her big sad dark eyes and her snow-white skin, he saw her dead, dead because of him, and the thought of it almost wrenched his heart from his chest until he thought that he would die himself. But he held out, because he knew that if he gave in everything would come out which would be a terrible thing even if Fleur knew the whole truth, but since she didn't it would be beyond forgiveness. So he said nothing. He just sat holding Fleur in his arms until they both finally slept, until the gulls started to wheel and cry in the lightening sky as dawn crept up over the tops of the mountains the far side of the estuary.

They were back in London mid-morning with Freddie apparently unsure of what he was going to do until he had telephoned America.

'I'd better drop you off at your house first,' he said as they neared the turn into Wimpole Street.

'You don't have to, Freddie,' Fleur said, suddenly disconcerted by this suggestion since she'd assumed from now on they would be doing everything together. 'You can call from the flat, there's no problem.'

'It's not that, Fleur,' Freddie said, seeing the turn just in time. 'It's just that I want to sort a few things out and I think I need to be by myself. I'll come round as soon as I know what the position is.'

Supposing Freddie's need for privacy to be in case his sister's condition had deteriorated or, worse, in case she might have died, Fleur concurred without any further argument. Seeing how bad the early morning traffic was, she directed Freddie to drop her off at the corner of her block to save him going all the way round the one-way system, a suggestion with which Freddie finally agreed when after five minutes the traffic had barely moved. He told her he'd bring her bags and the rest of her stuff round when he called.

Fleur kissed him sweetly and then with one last wave was gone away down the street and in through the front door of her house where, in the third-floor drawing room drinking a cup of coffee and reading the newspaper, she found her father waiting for her.

37

'What on earth are you doing here?' she asked him as he got up to greet her. 'You're not meant to be back until the beginning of next week.'

'The trip was cancelled,' her father said, folding his newspaper and putting it on his lap. 'There's an outbreak of Legionnaire's Disease in the hotel, so in the words of the old magician, we go, we come back. Where have you been at this hour of the morning?'

'Me?' Fleur asked hopelessly. 'Nowhere.'

'Nurse Eastman said you weren't in your room when she went to call you.'

'I know. I – I went for a walk.'

'A walk?' her father wondered slowly. 'Why would you want to do that?'

'Why would anyone, Pappa?' Fleur replied more than a little tartly. 'Surely I can go for a walk without Nurse Eastman's permission?'

'Of course you can,' her father replied with a smile. 'It's just so unlike you. And without your medication.'

'That's not due until nine. And it's only quarter past nine now.'

'True,' her father said, getting up and going to pour himself some coffee. 'True. Would you like a cup of coffee? It's only just been made.'

'Yes,' Fleur said. 'Yes I could do with one actually.'

'You don't look very pleased to see me, my dear.'

'I'm just a little surprised, Pappa. You might have called to say you were coming back.'

'I did,' her father replied, handing her a cup of coffee. 'I rang last night.'

'It must have been after I'd gone to bed.'

'Yes it must have been. I left word with Nurse Eastman. She said you'd gone to bed early. Talk of the devil—' Her father looked towards the door as he heard the main door of the apartment close. 'That was quick. The dispensary can't have been very busy.'

'The dispensary?'

'I sent Nurse out for a prescription. For you actually.'

'I'm not running short of anything. We had a top-up only yesterday if you remember.'

'This is something new, my dear,' her father replied. 'Something that's been highly recommended which they've been using with great success across the water. If it's as good as they say it is, we can take you off half the stuff you're on at present. You know, I'm not at all sure you should have got up, are you?' He came towards her and taking hold of both her arms scanned her face for a moment, before checking her pulse. 'You look absolutely washed out, Fleur. I don't really think you should have gone walkabout, do you?'

'I felt perfectly all right when I woke up,' Fleur replied, uncertain as to just how much her father knew. He had various ways of asking questions, and the last had been phrased in his you-think-I-don't-know style, one which he used to employ with great effect when Fleur had been a little girl.

'You have just had rather a nasty setback, you know. That infection you picked up was no laughing matter.'

'It didn't develop into anything, did it? Besides an extremely slight cold. I'm still alive, aren't I?' Fleur replied tit for tat, challenging him just the way she always had when they'd been in this mode.

'Because something didn't happen doesn't mean it wouldn't have happened,' her father said. 'I have to tell so many of my patients that. And don't make facetious remarks about still being alive, you know how much I hate it. And good, here's Nurse Eastman.'

Fleur looked round and saw her uniformed nurse arriving in the drawing room with the tray on which she carried all her medications, which when she later came to think of it Fleur realized was the last thing she remembered.

Not having been able to find anywhere to park in the mews, Freddie had luckily found a meter on the corner of the street, but in his hurry to make it to Stephen's consultancy he forgot to put any money in.

Stephen was in a consultation but broke off when he heard it was Freddie.

'Her father just called again,' he said, taking a memo sheet from his secretary. 'Here. He left this message.'

It was a request for Freddie to call on Richard Fisher-Dilke as soon as possible that morning, so that they might discuss a matter of the utmost urgency. Freddie asked the secretary if she'd be so kind as to ring Mr Fisher-Dilke to say he'd be round in half an hour, giving himself time to go back to Stephen's house to freshen up.

As he hurried back to the mews he almost knocked over a traffic warden who was about to cross the road to book the red Toyota on the long-expired meter opposite.

Twenty-five minutes later he was admitted to the third-floor drawing room of the Fisher-Dilke Harley Street house by a small woman in a housecoat who surprised Freddie by announcing herself as Miss Cook, Mr and Mrs Fisher-Dilke's housekeeper.

'I'm sorry,' he said as he followed her in. 'I thought your name was Eastman.'

'No, sir,' the housekeeper corrected him. 'Mrs Eastman is Miss Fisher-Dilke's nurse.'

Richard Fisher-Dilke kept him waiting for ten minutes

during which time Freddie hoped Fleur might put in an appearance, which she failed to do. In fact no-one came near him while he sat in the elegant and expensively furnished room so he was unable to find out where Fleur was. Then remembering what a long and tiring journey they had undertaken that morning, Freddie assumed that in light of her condition she must be resting up.

'Mr Jourdan,' Richard Fisher-Dilke said as he entered, extending a hand to Freddie. 'How do you do? Please forgive all the high drama but I think you'll understand when I explain. Can I get you anything? A drink? A cup of coffee? A Perrier?' He asked the last question with almost a smile, as if to say I-know-you-Americans, and out of bloody mindedness more than anything else Freddie said he'd like a whisky.

'What an excellent idea,' Richard agreed. 'I'm not working today and even though I don't normally drink before midday, I think this occasion merits something stronger than just caffeine.'

Richard indicated where Freddie was to sit and then poured them both large whiskies.

He was a smaller man than Freddie had imagined, even though he had gathered both from the documentary and from Fleur's description of her father that he wasn't precisely a tall man. But he had become much balder since the film had been made, now with only a small amount of greying hair left over his ears. He was so plain and unprepossessing it was impossible for Freddie to imagine him as the father of his beautiful Fleur. He had absolutely none of her physical qualities nor apparently, as Freddie was soon to learn, any of the intensity and wonderful sincerity that made his daughter stand out from everyone else.

'I must say you've been very persistent, Mr Jourdan. And I admire you for it.' Richard nodded in acknowledgement after he had sat down opposite Freddie.

'I happen to be in love with your daughter, Mr Fisher-Dilke,' Freddie replied. 'I'd like to get that clear from the start in case you think otherwise.'

'Why should I think otherwise? As I said, you've been most persistent. But then I too like to keep my eye on the ball, not because I'm meddlesome, but because I too love my daughter. The difference being that I know what your love would do to her whereas you do not. Of course you'll want to know all sorts of things,' he said quickly, putting a hand up to fend off Freddie's stillborn interruption. 'This whole thing must seem more than a little bizarre, although because you are a man of great imagination I am sure you will quickly appreciate the niceties involved. Most importantly, you know Fleur. Not very well, although I'm sure you feel you know her a lot better than you actually do. This is the way with people when they fall in love, particularly under such dramatic circumstances. Even so from what you know, and from what you can only guess, you will realize that Fleur is a very highly tuned person, a very sensitive one, and sadly also a very sick one – although as I trust your acquaintance made it clear to you last night, she does not know quite how sick she is. I am not one of those doctors who insist on telling their patients the whole truth, regardless of whether they themselves wish to know or not. I see no point in it.'

'I agree,' Freddie said.

'Good,' Richard replied, without sounding for one moment as if he meant it. 'While there is life there is hope, and in cases such as Fleur's while it would not be exactly fair to say hope is plentiful, medicine is at least wearing seven-league boots these days. Particularly in the world of cardiology. So we are much better placed nowadays to control and contain conditions such as Fleur's with drugs, and careful monitoring to keep her out of any immediate mortal danger, while we wait for the right organ.'

'Then it really is so that a transplant is Fleur's best hope?'

'Her only hope, I'm afraid, Mr Jourdan.'

'Is this the same thing as her mother had?'

'Oddly enough, no, Mr Jourdan, although this particular condition often is inherited. My ex-wife technically killed herself through excessive cigarette smoking, but Fleur's case history, if you're interested—'

'Of course I'm interested, Mr Fisher-Dilke. I love your daughter, remember?'

'Yes indeed, Mr Jourdan, I am all too conscious of the fact. Briefly then, this is my daughter's case history. At eleven she had a bad case of what was thought to be flu but was in fact, as I suspected all along, not flu but rheumatic fever. Now I don't know whether you're aware of the fact—'

'Rheumatic fever can result in heart damage, yes I'm aware of the fact. The valves in particular I seem to recall.'

'The mitral valve in particular, Mr Jourdan.' Richard finished his whisky before continuing. 'It can lead to either mitral stenosis or mitral incompetence, both defects increasing the work to be done by the heart, sometimes to the point where the heart muscle – which is often itself seriously weakened by the fever – can no longer meet all the demands normally made on it and we get heart failure. It depends very much on when the damage is first noticed and on exactly how much damage has been done. The longer it goes unnoticed, the greater the damage.'

'You said you suspected it straightaway?'

'Yes I did. But I was talked out of it. I was only a young surgeon then, and since there are no reliable tests which one can run to establish rheumatic fever—' Richard shrugged to show the hopelessness of his position at the time.

'There are tests which establish heart damage.'

'You only look for heart damage in these instances if rheumatic fever has been diagnosed. It's one of those round-the-house dilemmas, do you see? And the doctor who attended Fleur, a very good GP who'd seen an awful lot more action than I had then, believe me, he was one hundred per cent certain it was the flu. Since Fleur recovered without any apparent after-effects who was I to disagree with him?'

'So what made you change your mind?'

'When Fleur fell so desperately ill after her mother died, I insisted on running tests on her heart which showed me not only evidence of mitral stenosis but tricuspid stenosis as well, a much more serious and damaging after-effect.'

'Yet nothing had been noticed up to this time?'

'After the divorce I saw very little of my daughter. Apparently she used to tire easily, but I knew nothing of this. Her mother allowed me practically no access. But once I was called to attend her and brought her back here, I ran my tests and it became perfectly and tragically clear that Fleur had developed a Restrictive Cardiomyopathy which I'm afraid finally proves fatal if left untreated.'

'But you have been treating it,' Freddie said, finishing his whisky which he realized he'd drunk too fast. 'You must have it under some sort of control now for Fleur to be able to lead the sort of life she's been leading.'

'What sort of life do you think she's been leading, Mr Jourdan? Until you burst on the scene like a volcano my daughter spent half her year semi-bedridden up here and the other half semi-bedridden in the country. Yesterday was the first day she broke bounds, the first time she went out freely, with someone other than myself or her trained nurse that is. It was the first time she has been out by herself for over two years. Thank God you were found in time, that's all I can say.'

'Are you really saying that if I had made love to your

daughter it would have killed her? Because if so I don't believe it.'

'You won't believe it, you mean,' Richard suggested. 'And I'm not saying it would, I'm saying might or even might well. I can't say with any certainty how, when or where. All I can do is try and minimize the risk factors.'

'What about all the drugs she takes? They must afford her some sort of protection?'

'Some sort. They're immuno-suppressants mainly. Some anti-arrhythmics, some peripheral vasolidators—'

'Even so,' Freddie insisted, clutching wildly at any passing straw.

'All they do is keep it under control, Mr Jourdan,' Richard replied. 'We call it Disease Management. It has nothing to do with remedy. There is only one treatment for this sort of cardiomyopathy as I have told you. And that is a new heart.'

'And that is perfectly possible nowadays, given the state of your art, and compared with how risky it used to be,' Freddie said. 'People have heart transplants practically every week.'

'Practically every day of the week to be precise, Mr Jourdan. But we have to have the right heart, and by the right heart I mean with a tissue typing as near the patient's HLA as possible. HLA's your tissue type and the nearer you get to your own, the less the chance of your body rejecting the donor organ. The nearest you can get is from a blood relative, so as far as heart transplanting goes you are not likely to get that close. Hence the still far too high percentage of rejection, although the huge improvement in drugs has helped deal with that major problem. Anyway, the point is that as far as my daughter goes we have not yet been offered a suitable heart. We haven't even come *near* to matching Fleur's HLA so far, and of course I simply won't operate unless I have as near a match as possible. And I must be offered a brain-dead heart, that is one that's still beating when the donor is pronounced clinically dead. It must come from that sort of source to give the patient the best chance, you see. It has to come from someone whose brain has been irreversibly destroyed by disease or accident. The heart has still to be beating when it's removed.'

'In California—' Freddie began.

'I know all about the Stamford Heart Transplant programme, thank you. But we are not in California.'

'You could go there.'

'They have their own over-extended waiting list, Mr Jourdan. We have to take what comes, and we are right on the top of the list now. So hopes are high, higher than they have ever been.'

'Suppose you do get the right heart? What are the chances then?'

'You mean how long would Fleur survive?' Richard was looking at Freddie hard now, as if to try and disconcert him, but Freddie wasn't going to be put off that easily.

'I mean how long would Fleur survive, yes,' he returned, matching the surgeon's stare with as even a look as he could manage.

'With everything in her favour, with today's wonder drugs, with no undue strain. Or emotion.' Richard was still staring at Freddie and Freddie knew exactly why. Yet still he didn't drop his own eyes. 'Who knows? Five years. Maybe more. The longer she survived the better, strangely enough, would be her chances, since we're learning how to deal with all the side-effects and difficulties more effectively each day. But if the conditions were not exemplary, if her environment was not precisely how it should be ordained, then probably Fleur would live no more than a year, two years at most.'

Freddie got up and walked to the window and stood looking out and down on the busy street below.

'You understand what I'm saying, Mr Jourdan?' Richard asked from behind him.

'Yes I hear what you're saying, Mr Fisher-Dilke. You want me to get the hell out of Fleur's life.'

'You said you loved my daughter, Mr Jourdan.'

'I love your daughter more than life itself, Mr Fisher-Dilke.'

'In that case there really is only one thing you can do.'

'No, there isn't. There's something else I can do,' Freddie said, still staring down at the street below. 'Fleur can have my heart.'

'I find that quite touching, Mr Jourdan,' Richard said after a moment. 'I really believe you would make the sacrifice. But before you assure me this is indeed the case, I have to tell you there would be no point, not even in discussing it. Even if your heart was the right heart it wouldn't work, you see, because in order for me to use your heart you would have to die from brain damage, and for the life of me I don't see how you could arrange to kill yourself in such a way. So much as I applaud your generous offer, alas – we can't even begin to entertain such a notion. Besides, Mr Jourdan, think of Fleur. If she loves you as much as you love her, what is life going to mean without you? I should imagine that Fleur would only want to live if she was going to be able to live with you.'

'So what am I going to do?' Freddie asked. 'I'm in an emotional cul de sac here, don't you see? If I can't have Fleur then my life's not worth living, yet if I do have her she'll die.'

'I take it you mean by "having" my daughter as in to have and to hold, rather than purely in the carnal sense?' Richard enquired with an edge of distaste in his voice. 'You Americans do have such very odd ways of saying some things. It goes without saying that for both of you, being young and passionate, it would be all but impossible to love each other in just a platonic fashion. Even if it meant saving her life.'

'Why don't we ask Fleur?' Freddie suddenly suggested, turning to his adversary. 'Why don't you tell her the truth and see what she says – because after all it's her life we're talking here, not yours or mine! So go on, Mr Fisher-Dilke – I suggest you call Fleur down here and let her decide this thing for herself. Because if you don't, then sure as hell I will!'

'I don't think so, Mr Jourdan,' Richard said, lazily from behind him. 'Because even were we agreed to do so, it wouldn't be possible to bring Fleur in on this for the very simple reason that she isn't here. She collapsed just after she returned. She was utterly exhausted, began to hyperventilate and finally she passed out. So naturally she had to be transferred at once to my clinic.'

'Can I see her?'

'No not at the moment, Mr Jourdan. She is far too unwell. Once she is sufficiently recovered, of course. But as things are at the moment I would very much doubt if this would be the very best time to ask her to make a choice as to what she would like to do, don't you agree? Now from the look of you I would say another whisky is called for. In fact let me get us both another drink.'

Suddenly feeling exhausted, not so much from the shock of the revelations but from all the emotion – not just of the last twenty-four hours, but of every day since he had first set eyes on Fleur in her enchanted garden, Freddie collapsed into a large chintz-covered armchair and ran a hand through his now dishevelled hair.

'Come on,' he said wearily as Richard took the stopper out of the whisky decanter. 'You must have thought this thing through all the way. And when you did, you surely must have realized that I can't just vanish out of your daughter's life.'

'No I didn't, Mr Jourdan,' Richard said, pouring the drinks. 'I didn't think everything through. Not for one moment did I think that someone would fall in love with Fleur the way you did. And that she would reciprocate. Of course you can't disappear from her life just like that, I'm beginning to see that now.' Richard smiled slightly and offered Freddie his refreshed glass. 'I don't think Fleur could or indeed *would* live with that. In fact on reflection I think expecting you to make the sacrifice of leaving, and thereby causing my daughter God knows what sort of heartbreak, would be the very last thing she needs. So in that case, and reviewing the circumstances, perhaps we should talk this over further? Like gentlemen? And see if we can't come up with the best solution all round?'

Helped by the whisky, the exhausted Freddie slept from the moment he let himself into Stephen's house, crashed out on the spare bed where he lay until the alarm woke him at half past four in the afternoon precisely. Since he still had half an hour before he had to be back round at the house for his rendezvous with Fleur's father, Freddie washed, shaved and made himself a cup of strong coffee before letting himself out of the house.

When he rang the private bell he got Miss Cook, the housekeeper, on the entryphone who told him her employer had left word that he would be out of town for the next few days.

'Where's he gone?' Freddie asked, a now all too familiar icy hand grabbing at his entrails. 'What does he mean *out of town*?'

'I'm very sorry, Mr Jourdan, but I'm under strict instructions not to say,' the housekeeper replied. 'Not to anyone.'

'Well, perhaps you'd be kind enough to tell me where Mr Fisher-Dilke's clinic is situated?'

'I'm afraid not, Mr Jourdan. Mr Fisher-Dilke's strict instructions were that I was to pass on absolutely no information whatsoever.'

'My guess is you've been outflanked, chum,' Stephen concluded once he'd heard Freddie out. 'Fisher-Dilke sounds like a man who gets up *very* early in the morning. Or maybe doesn't go to bed at all.'

'He never meant a word he said, did he?' Freddie perceived. 'All that bull about him coming to the best decision, and having Fleur's best interests at heart. He was just buying time, wasn't he? He just wanted me out of the way for a while so as − so as what, Steve?'

'So as he could take Fleur somewhere, I imagine,' Steve replied, topping up their glasses. 'My bet is she was still in the house when you were there. Fast asleep thanks to some nice sleeping draught.'

'You mean he moved her to his clinic after that? After he'd sent me home promising that when Fleur was up to it I could go and talk it over with her?'

'That'd be the way I'd read it, yes.'

'Lying bastard.'

'I'd drink to that as well, Fred. From what I've been gathering he's not one of Harley Street's most popular rabbits.'

'Oh God,' Freddie groaned. 'Oh no oh God!'

'Now what new anguish?'

'I've just remembered I forgot all about my car!'

An hour later and a hundred and twenty pounds poorer, Freddie and Stephen got back from the pound with Freddie's rented Toyota.

'Is that everything?' Stephen asked as Freddie brought the last lot of cases and bags into the house.

'I think so,' Freddie replied, putting down Fleur's case on the floor, and her half-open shoulder bag on the table, where it immediately spilled most of its contents.

'Mmmmm,' Stephen mused, collecting up some of the many phials of medicine which were rolling their way towards the table's edge. 'There's some big stuff here right enough. Atenolol, disopyramide, and a generic digitalis, digitoxin, all of which makes sense. No luck?'

Freddie had been trying to make a telephone call but had just slammed the receiver down in anger.

'Damn answering machine again,' Freddie said, crashing down the receiver. 'To hell with the man who invented them anyway.'

'You don't think F-D's the sort of man to leave any lines open, do you?' Stephen asked. 'Come and look at this little lot instead. I mean this is serious stuff here, chum. He's even put her on quite a heavyweight anxiolytic, which is a little surprising,' Stephen continued. 'Certainly if it's a long-term prescription. This stuff, Solis, is a benzodiazepine and has a very sustained action. Except – that's funny.'

Stephen stopped and at once had Freddie's full attention.

'What is, Steve?' Freddie asked. 'What exactly is funny?'

'Hang on, chum, just a tick,' Steve said, going to the bookshelves and taking down a red paperback book. 'Let's just see what the BNF has to say about this.'

'The BNF?'

'British National Formulary. All you need to know but never asked about what us quacks shove down your throat. Here we are,' he said as he found the right page. 'Two milligram – violet and what is it? I'm a bit colour-blind, Fred, so what colour would you say these are?'

Stephen held a pill up for Freddie to inspect.

'Almost a uniform colour, almost,' Freddie said, taking the pill and looking at it in the light. 'Not quite though. I suppose you'd call it two tone in violet and well – mauve really.'

'Violet and mauve are five milligram,' Steve replied, taking up the pill bottle. 'These are labelled two mg.

If they're two mg according to the BNF they should be violet and turquoise.'

'Turquoise they are not.'

'Then two milligram they are not.' Stephen opened another phial of pills and spilled some out on the table. 'These berkolol should be scored – and all pink. But they're white, and not scored. It doesn't say what digitoxin should be, but I have a feeling they should be a tablet and not a capsule, certainly not a black-and-grey capsule.'

'You know about these drugs, then?' Freddie enquired. 'I'd have thought they were a little out of your field.'

'I cover the waterfront, Fred, medically speaking,' Stephen said, sorting through all the pills once again. 'I'm a general practitioner as well. So I have to keep up with what's available and for what. And somehow—'

'Yes?'

'I don't know. Somehow this doesn't feel quite right.'

'You think Fleur's not getting the right drugs, is that it?'

'Nominally she is, certainly. It's just – look.' Stopping in mid-tracks, Stephen carefully began to brush all the pills back into their correct bottles. 'Leave this one with me, Fred. I'm just playing a hunch, that's all, and if it's a wrong 'un there'll be no harm done because I'll have kept it to myself. All right?'

'Sure. This is your sort of thing, not mine. My thing is finding a way, somehow, to smoke out that bastard Fisher-Dilke.'

He had no need. The telephone in Stephen's house rang at seven o'clock the next morning, and when Freddie grabbed the extension by his bed he heard Richard's smooth voice the other end of the line.

'Forgive me for ringing you so early,' he said. 'I thought we might have lunch.'

'What's wrong with breakfast?'

'I'm busy all morning, I'm afraid, so lunch would be more convenient.'

'So what happened yesterday?'

'That's what I want to talk about at lunch. Think you can find your way to a restaurant called Rules in Maiden Lane at one o'clock?'

'I wouldn't put it past me,' Freddie said, thankful at least that contact had been restored.

'Till then,' Fleur's father said. 'Goodbye.'

Richard hung up before Freddie had time to ask anything more about Fleur.

Halfway through the first course of lunch in the splendidly amiable old-fashioned restaurant in Covent Garden, having listened to his host's digression on the future of virtual reality in surgery, Freddie had done with good manners and came to the point.

'I want to know what happened yesterday,' he asked.

'Naturally,' Richard answered. 'I'm sorry we couldn't keep our appointment, but I was called out to the clinic to see Fleur.'

'Is she all right?' Freddie asked quickly, forgetting his own indignation.

'She would hardly be all right, Mr Jourdan, if I had to be called out to see her,' Richard replied. 'No I'm afraid her condition gave us some immediate cause for concern, but happily she is out of those particular woods for the moment. Obviously. Otherwise I would hardly be sitting here having lunch with you. Would I? In fact when I left her a short while ago she was sitting up in bed watching television. Anyway, before that, I explained the situation in its entirety to her. Oddly enough she asked me to do so, prompted I think by her sudden collapse on her return from your little jaunt.'

'Yes?' Freddie prompted. 'And? So what was her response?'

'Yes,' Richard said reflectively. 'She asked me to leave her alone, not unnaturally, and then about an hour or so later when I had finished my rounds she called me back to her room. She was very calm, almost as if she had been expecting such a thing, very calm and very rational. We talked, not a great deal, just about matters immediately in hand and what was going to happen to her while she was still on the waiting list for a transplant—'

'And what is going to happen to her?' Freddie cut in. 'And what did she say about – about us?'

'About you and her, you mean? Let's take first things first. First of all until she recovers sufficiently to be nursed at home, which at this moment I very much doubt she will, she must remain where she is at the clinic – where of course she will receive the very best care possible.'

'What is this clinic exactly?' Freddie asked. 'I mean where is it?'

'It belongs to the practice,' Richard replied. 'It's out in Buckinghamshire. Are you all right, Mr Jourdan? You have gone a very pale shade. Very pale indeed.'

'I'm okay,' Freddie said, knowing that he was not, beginning to feel the anxiety pressure-cooking inside him, the first time he had felt like this since leaving America. 'It's just I haven't been sleeping, and when I don't sleep—' He took out his small silver pillbox from his pocket and tapped out one lozenge into his hand. 'So if you'll excuse me—' he said, swallowing it with some water.

'I imagine that's some sort of anxiolytic, correct?' Richard asked, looking at Freddie over his gold half-moon glasses. 'What you probably like to call a tranquillizer?'

'That's right. It's something called Zanad or some such,' Freddie replied. 'I haven't taken one of these in an age. But as you can no doubt imagine—'

'Quite,' Richard agreed, reaching for Freddie's pillbox and tapping out a couple of tablets into the palm of one hand. 'Quite,' he repeated as he examined the pills. 'Why exactly were you put on these, if you don't mind me asking?'

'I had something you fellows like to call an anxiety crisis at the beginning of the year,' Freddie admitted as the waiter cleared away their first course. 'Actually all I'd been doing was overworking, that's all it was, which is why I took a sabbatical.'

'You say you haven't been taking any medication since you got here, am I correct?'

'Look – what is this?' Freddie wondered. 'I came to have lunch with you and discuss your daughter, not run through my own case history.'

Richard smiled, leaning back as his second course was put before him. 'I do hope you like it here,' he said. 'It went a little off the rails for a while but now it's back to its old high standard.'

Freddie waited until he too had been served and the waiter had poured them some wine, before asking why whether or not he had been taking any medication should have the slightest relevance on the matter in hand.

'You'd be surprised what these little fellows can do,' Richard replied, carefully replacing the tablets in the pillbox. 'Particularly if taken over any length of time. And whether or not one drinks with them, for instance.'

'I really don't drink that much,' Freddie countered. 'Anyway, since I more or less stopped taking them as soon as I got to Stoke Park—'

'More or less,' Richard mused. 'But not entirely?'

'Like I just said, I haven't taken one of these in an age,' Freddie said, taking back his pillbox.

'Those are fairly big boys, Mr Jourdan,' Richard told him. 'Those are five hundred microgram a go, so if you were taking them three times a day as prescribed, hmmm.' Richard smiled at Freddie politely. 'You most certainly shouldn't have drunk any alcohol, not only while you were taking them but for quite some time afterwards. Those chaps have known side-effects which affect some people to a far greater extent than others, side-effects which are greatly exacerbated by continued use of alcohol.'

'Such as?' Freddie challenged. 'For instance?'

'Oh delusion, for instance,' Richard replied smoothly. 'As in false impression. As in fantasy. As in misconception. Particularly emotional misconception.'

Richard looked up from his forkful of food and smiled, before popping it in his mouth.

'Bullshit,' Freddie said after a moment. 'That's just too neat and tidy.'

'To you maybe,' Richard said, wiping one corner of his mouth on his napkin. 'But if I was your psychiatrist I'd want you back in for a road test as soon as was possible.'

Freddie stared at him, fighting the almost ungovernable urge to tip the table up and spill its dishes all over the smug-looking surgeon sitting opposite him. But he knew all too well that would only be playing right into his adversary's hands, particularly in light of the theory he was developing. So he just took a deep breath instead and switched tacks back to the only thing which really mattered to him.

'Do you mind if we just talk about Fleur?' he said. 'After all, that was the reason for our meeting.'

'Of course,' Richard agreed. 'Except I don't think you'll like what I finally have to relate to you. I don't think you'll like it one bit.'

'I don't follow,' Freddie said. 'Why shouldn't I like it? What did she have to say?'

'About you, you mean?'

'That's right, Mr Fisher-Dilke, about me. About me and about her. About the both of us.'

'She had absolutely nothing to say whatsoever, Mr Jourdan,' Richard replied. 'Nothing whatsoever.'

'She must have done. She must have said something,' Freddie insisted, somehow managing to control his new urge to lean across the table and strangle his host. 'She can't just have said damn all.'

'I'm afraid so, Mr Jourdan,' Richard replied, putting a hand to his inside pocket. 'Instead what she did do was ask me to give you this.'

The pale yellow envelope with just the four words FREDERICK JOURDAN, By Hand scribbled on it remained unopened until Freddie was back in Stephen's sitting room with a large whisky by his side, despite Richard Fisher-Dilke's warning. He had excused himself and left the restaurant almost immediately after Richard had handed him the envelope, uninterested in finishing his lunch and in hearing anything else that his host had to say. All he wanted to do was get somewhere private as soon as was possible and read what his beloved Fleur had to say to him.

Fleur's handwriting was larger and slightly less tidy than he remembered it, although in fairness he recalled only ever seeing it once and then only fleetingly, the time he had found her precious Dante stuffed full of her notes and jottings in the piano. But then the circumstances were so different. Whereas before she had been carefully annotating her personal recollections and comments, now she was writing a letter to someone she loved while desperately ill, so it would be small wonder if her writing was less neat and tidy.

He sat and stared at the letter for a long time before plucking up the courage to open it and when at last he did, he found there was only one sheet of carefully folded matching pale yellow notepaper inside.

That was the first thing that bothered him, namely the matching envelope and paper, expensive paper too, with her name 'Fleur Fisher-Dilke' printed across the top of it. How come she would have her own paper with her in the clinic, in a clinic to which she had been taken in an emergency? He couldn't for a moment imagine that as she was being transferred from house to ambulance, the one thing she determined to take was her headed notepaper. The only explanation could be that she had requested her father that morning to bring her in some items which included her writing things, but then again that presupposed that she knew she would be writing letters.

Then there was the spelling.

Dearest Freddy.

That was how the letter opened, and at once Freddie put it down without reading on any further for a moment. He could have sworn Fleur knew how he spelt the abbreviation of his name because he remembered talking about it. In fact she'd teased him about it and he'd told her it was just one of the things he had, that it just got under his skin – for no good reason whatsoever he recalled admitting – seeing his name spelled with a 'Y' instead of an 'IE'. But then again, he argued as he stared at the opening of the letter, people forget things, people get things wrong, particularly people who are seriously ill and taking medication. So maybe Fleur simply got it wrong in her anxiety to communicate.

Even so, Freddie was already frowning deeply and feeling unhappy before he even got to the contents of the letter.

Dearest Freddy,

I have to write you this because there is no other way. I couldn't tell you face to face because I'm not strong enough and you'd try to make me change my mind and I probably would. But I mustn't, not now I know the whole truth. You see I knew most of it before, as Daddy has obviously told you, but not quite how bad it was. Or rather might be, because of course there still is hope, and very positive hope. Even so, my darling, I know the decision I've arrived at is the right one.

Daddy has explained that you have both agreed to stand by what I decide is best. So when you hear what I have to say please remember that, darling, and remember that what I have decided is in your best interest, not in mine.

It's because I love you so very much that I know we mustn't ever see each other again. There is no way we could go on seeing each other because if we did there is only one place I would want to be and that is in your arms. There is no way we wouldn't want to make love, you know that as well as I do. But now you know, and so do I, what the consequence might be — maybe not at once, but some time, some time sooner or later, some time maybe sooner rather than later. Don't misunderstand me, I'm not afraid to die, and there is nowhere I would rather die than in your arms so this isn't for my sake, you see darling, it's for yours.

I couldn't bear you to think you were the cause of my death. I know you, and I know you would blame yourself even though you would be entirely blameless. And there is no point in waiting, because even if I do finally have the operation I need then, as Daddy says, I would have to take things carefully for goodness knows how long. If we were together how could we do this? God knows it would be hard enough if we were older but at our age and given how we love each other, it would be impossible.

So since we cannot be together in the way we both want, we have to say goodbye. More than anything I am doing this for you. You have your whole life and your career ahead of you, and I don't want you to jeopardize your work which you would do if we don't stop seeing each other now. The outcome might be disastrous, darling, to your wonderful talent that belongs not to me but to the world.

You will get over me, I know you will. I don't want you ever to forget me but you will get over me. The heart is a strange and wonderful thing, but it is also as my father always says a muscle, and a resilient one at that. So your heart will recover in time whereas mine may not. But at least I met you and loved you for however brief a time, and while I am still alive and on this earth I will always, always think of you.

Fleur.

'She didn't write this,' Freddie said aloud but very quietly, staring at the letter in his hand. 'She didn't write one single word of this, because not one word of this makes any sense. If she knew she was that ill before we went away, she must have thought she could die then — so why this sudden change of heart! No! No! Fleur Fisher-Dilke! You didn't write one single bloody word of this!'

Freddie was convinced of it. Picking up the letter from where he had thrown it aside on the table, he read it again and then reread it. And the more he read the letter the more he became certain that somehow either Fleur had been forced into writing it, or more likely someone had written it for her. It wasn't just the notepaper, it wasn't just the misspelling of his name, it was the whole tone. It didn't read like Fleur would talk, it didn't sound like Fleur's voice, it wasn't thought out the way Fleur would think it out, and it wasn't put the way Fleur would put it. There were no inner references either, no allusions or intimations to things only the two of them could know, there was no sound or sense of their passion. In no time at all Freddie was utterly sure she had written not even one word of the letter.

And yet. Yet the more he sat there thinking of what the letter said, the more the reasoning behind it seemed perfectly good and sensible. If she died when they were together or because they were together, he would blame himself, whenever or however it happened, no matter what she said to reassure him in advance, no matter how much she promised him that it was what she wanted and

563

the way she wanted it. Were she to die in or out of his arms Freddie would find himself guilty, and when he did he would then start to die himself, if he didn't in fact take his own life there and then. There could be no other conclusion. That was how much he loved her.

But this way, whether it was the sick Fleur dictating it or whether it was her father suggesting it to her, the proposal did at least offer them both some sort of survival. Freddie saw that now, and while one part of him railed against it, the other part saw the sense. If he never saw Fleur again and even if he never got over the heartbreak of it, he would still have his music and into his music he could put Fleur and his undying love for her so that not only would she never be forgotten but also the love they had for each other would be known and celebrated by millions. While for Fleur, by denying herself Freddie she might prolong her life long enough to have the transplant she needed, an operation her father said she might survive thanks not only to the huge and swift advances being made by cardiology, but also to the fact that living peacefully alone rather than passionately with Freddie, she could recuperate safely and perhaps even live a normal life span.

It all made perfectly good sense.

And yet, Freddie thought. Yet what is life without love? What is life without the one you love? Particularly if you are both still alive and cannot be together? It might be the most sensible thing in the world not to see each other any more so that they both could survive, but what is survival if there is no point in surviving? It simply becomes subsisting and Freddie had no intention of living just to subsist. As his own father had always said there is victory in dying well and for a purpose, and since both Fleur and Freddie truly believed they had met before in another time then what was to say they would not meet again in the future?

'So no, Mr Fisher-Dilke!' Freddie announced to the

room. 'Sorry but there is no taste in nothing! And who knows? Love may yet conquer everything!'

He started for the telephone, intending to ring Fleur's father not only to find out the precise location of the clinic where Fleur had been admitted so that he could either write to her there or get permission to visit her but because he no longer gave a damn what he and Fisher-Dilke had agreed between them because he didn't believe for one moment that Fisher-Dilke had kept his part of the bargain, a fact which he intended telling Fleur's father just as soon as he could get hold of him. But the telephone rang before he could make his call. Freddie grabbed the receiver and found it was his answering service who had just been called by Kitty, his youngest sister, with a message for him to ring home urgently.

'No-one seems to know where the hell you are,' Kitty said frantically when he got through to America a few minutes later. 'No-one at the house you've rented knew where you'd gone and if you hadn't given your service your number—'

'Yes all right, Kitty,' Freddie interrupted. 'I'm sorry, honey, something came up but you got me. Now what's the big deal?'

'It's Bette, Freddie,' his sister replied and suddenly Freddie became aware of the tone in her voice. 'Do you think you can come home? Bette's had an accident with one of her stallions. You know her favourite? Swinging Peach – the big black fellow you could put your kids on? All of a sudden—'

'*What did you say?*' Freddie interrupted, grabbing hold of the edge of the desk. '*Did you say an accident with one of her horses?*'

'Yes. Swinging Peach. He suddenly went berserk yesterday and savaged her. It's kind of touch and go, so—'

'An accident with one of her *horses?*' Freddie repeated. 'You can't be serious. You can't mean this.'

'I know,' Kitty replied. 'We all feel just the same. It's so unreal. And of all her horses I mean Swinging Peach – it just doesn't make sense. But can you come over, Freddie? Please come over if you can, because she's asking for you.'

'When did this happen, Kitty?' Freddie asked, still holding on for dear life to the edge of the desk. 'I have to know when this happened. Tell me when it happened.'

'It happened the day before yesterday, Fred,' his sister replied. 'The day before yesterday and somewhere around midnight your time, I guess.'

'I'll be over on the first flight I can get on,' Freddie said, before dropping the receiver and only just making it to the bathroom where he was violently sick.

38

When she awoke Fleur had no idea where she was, other than in an all-white room with the blinds down. There was absolutely no sound from outside, and it seemed no sound inside either. In the middle of the ceiling above her there was a flat round light fitting she'd never seen before, and on the wall opposite the end of her bed hung an abstract pastel-coloured print behind glass but without a frame.

She was lying on her back which she found unusual too, because normally when she woke up she was on her right-hand side under a pile of tousled bedclothes. But now she was definitely lying on her back and apparently held in place by a set of very firmly tucked-in blankets and sheets. There was something in her arm as well, the one lying outside the top sheet, something held in place by a light adhesive plaster and a transparent sleeve of plastic, a tube which ran from under the adhesive plaster and up to a bottle hooked high on a stand beside her.

A drip, Fleur thought. Why am I on a drip? I must have been in an accident. I'm in a hospital obviously and I must have been in some sort of accident.

She closed her eyes and tried to remember the last thing she could. Freddie. She remembered being with Freddie and then she remembered being in his car. They'd been driving back to London from somewhere in a red car and they must have had an accident, but then she knew that wasn't so because she remembered walking in through the front door of her house and up to the drawing room where who was it who had been waiting? Yes. Yes her father had been waiting. She remembered her father sitting reading the newspaper when he should have been somewhere else. All that was clear in her mind now. She had been in the drawing room of the house with her father who shouldn't have been there, and now she was obviously in hospital.

Hospital. That could only mean one thing. Particularly if she was on a drip and all wired up to a bank of machines. It must have been just as her father had warned. She must have had a heart attack.

Fleur looked round for the bell and found it right by her hand. She pressed it once and then lay back deep into her pillows. Freddie, she thought. Why did she keep remembering being with Freddie? *Because she had.* There it all was now, clear as light in her mind's eye, the whole picture. Escaping from London, going to Wales, the lovely house, the dinner, and then – then they had been just about to make love, hadn't they? Yes. Yes they had been making love in the moonglow and the telephone had suddenly rung. Oh God yes, Fleur groaned softly. The phone had rung and Freddie had got some terrible news. About – about one of his sisters, which explained how she had come to be back in London and in the flat with her father. But not this. One minute she had been talking to her father, about what she couldn't for the life of her remember, and that was all. Now this. Now hospital. A drip. A bank of life-support machines. She can only have nearly died.

'Good,' a voice from beside her said, a pretty voice, a voice with a soft Southern Irish accent. 'Great you're awake now, so that's marvellous. Hello, I'm Marie.'

'Hello,' Fleur whispered. 'I'm Fleur.'

'Ssshhh,' the nurse said kindly, taking hold of Fleur's wrist. 'Sure I know who you are well enough. My dad used to take me to all of your concerts.'

'Hard luck.'

'Hard luck? I was addicted from the first moment I heard you play.'

The nurse was very pretty, with bright hazel eyes and short dark hair, and she smiled at Fleur as she took her pulse.

'Where am I exactly?' Fleur asked, trying to look round the rest of the room as if that would give her some clue.

'You're in your father's clinic,' the nurse replied, letting go of Fleur's wrist and going to check the drip. 'You were brought here yesterday.'

'What was yesterday?'

'Tuesday all day.'

'And what time is it now?'

'It's now four o'clock Wednesday afternoon. And don't ask me what happened because I have to leave all that to your father. But just don't worry. You're fine now. Your condition is a hundred per cent stable.'

'Did I – did I have a heart attack?' Fleur asked quietly.

'Like I said, I've been told to leave everything to your father. No-one else is even allowed a look at you.' The nurse smiled and re-tucked Fleur's bedding in, even though there was absolutely no need since as it was Fleur could barely move. 'Now is there something you want? Do you want a drink perhaps?'

'Yes,' Fleur agreed, suddenly realizing how dry her mouth was. 'Yes I'd love a drink, and do you have any idea when my father's going to be here?'

'He'll be back for his evening rounds,' the nurse replied. 'And now here—' Marie slipped an arm behind Fleur to ease her up in the bed and higher onto her pillows. 'Here's your water, and you're to take these pills like a good girl.'

Fleur drank a whole tumbler of water first and then swallowed the two lozenges and the two small white pills the nurse was holding out. Then she settled back onto her pillows again, feeling suddenly as if she had absolutely no strength left anywhere in her body. Five minutes later she was fast and deeply asleep.

She only very vaguely registered her father standing by her bed some time that evening. She had this image of him looking down at her, with a smile on his face which seemed to get broader like the Cheshire Cat's, before falling back into a deep and untroubled sleep until the next morning.

This time when the nurse showed her father into her room Fleur was awake and propped up in bed on a pile of freshly cased pillows.

'Hello, my dear,' he said as he put his case down on the floor. 'You look like Snow White.'

'I thought you were due in last night,' Fleur replied, as her father first checked her pulse.

'I *was* here last night, but you were so fast out I hadn't the heart to wake you right up,' her father replied. 'Besides your condition had stabilized, and after what you had just gone through you needed to sleep, and you still do.'

'What have I been through exactly?'

Her father frowned and grunted quietly to himself, before pulling up the chair beside her bed.

'I hate to say this to you, Fleur, but you can't say I didn't warn you,' he said. 'You suffered a myocardial infarction.'

'As in heart attack?'

'If you like. Not a major one, not one that required emergency surgery, but one serious enough to have you admitted here double-quick.'

'But why was I unconscious? I don't remember anything about it? I always understood when people were having heart attacks they felt it. I mean really felt it.'

'This is perfectly true, in most cases,' her father replied cautiously. 'But there's this new wonder-drug on the market which instantly re-regulates the disturbances to the heart rhythm but may also induce coma, and I used this on you the moment it became obvious you were undergoing an attack. And I'll bet you don't remember one thing about it now.'

'No I don't actually.'

'Good. That's one of its blessings. On the downside it's inclined to keep you semi-comatose longer than one would like sometimes, although I stress without any danger to the patient.'

'What's the prognosis?'

'Well. Let's say this is a setback. I can't pretend about that. But then you would go and stick your neck out.'

'What do you mean? All I did was go for a walk.'

'All you did was go off with some young man to Wales. It's no good looking like that, my dear. I had lunch with Mr Jourdan yesterday and we had a long talk.'

Fleur stared at her father who smiled back at her, just the way he used to when she was little. Then she looked away and up at the ceiling for a long while, as her father sat whistling almost inaudibly to himself.

'Did you tell him what was wrong with me?' she finally asked. 'Did you tell him all about my heart condition?'

'It seemed only fair, my dear,' her father replied. 'The poor young man was labouring under the illusion that you were suffering from ME or some such nonsense. He could have killed you. You could have killed yourself.'

'Where is he now? And I don't understand—' Fleur struggled to sit up but her father eased her back down with a warning shake of his head. 'I don't understand how you could have had lunch with him, what was it – yesterday? He had to fly back to the States. One of his sisters has had a really serious accident.'

'He never mentioned such a thing over lunch,' her father replied. 'Not a word.'

'You're sure you didn't have lunch on Tuesday?'

'Dear girl, I was out here with you on Tuesday. You collapsed in the drawing room early morning, and at lunch

571

time on Tuesday I was standing right here monitoring your condition.'

'Perhaps he couldn't get a plane until Wednesday.'

'You can think what you like. I'm just surprised he didn't mention his sister's accident over lunch. He talked about all the rest of his family.'

Fleur stared at her father again, but he just smiled briefly back and then got up to check the readings from all the machines fixed above and behind Fleur's bed.

'Did you tell him where I was?' Fleur asked. 'Obviously when you told him what had happened, he must have asked where I was.'

'Of course I told him where you were. What sort of a father do you think I am? I told him exactly where he could find you, but that he would have to check with me first as to when you would be fit enough to have visitors.'

'And when will that be?'

'I don't see anything against a brief – and I mean brief – visit now, do you?'

'So is that what you told Freddie?'

'Who?' Her father stopped and frowned. 'I see – that's Jourdan's first name is it? I hadn't realized. No, no, no I said nothing of the sort, my dear. For the simple reason I haven't heard another word from him.'

The next morning Fleur's nurse brought her a letter postmarked London and posted the day before. It read:

Dearest Fleur,

I have to write you this because there is no other way. I couldn't tell you face to face because I'm not strong enough and you'd try to make me change my mind and I probably would, which I mustn't, not now I know the whole truth. I guessed it might be something like this but not as your father has since told me anything quite as bad as it is, or might be because of course there still is hope, and very positive hope. Even so, my darling, I know the decision I've arrived at is the right one.

Your father and I have had a long talk about you and about you and I, and while he has been as helpful and fair-minded as any father could be under such difficult conditions, it is perfectly obvious that while he can help you to get better I can't. In fact what I am afraid of is that I may do the very opposite. You'll understand, darling, if you read on, because it is your best interests I have at heart, not mine.

The decision I have reached has been the hardest one I have ever had to make, but it's because I love you so much that I have decided what I have. It's because I want you to get better that I have taken this decision, darling, and with your health still so very delicate — your father told me what happened after I left you back home — the point is it would be my fault if anything happened to you. I see that quite clearly. We mustn't see each other again, not if you are to get better and that is the issue which overrides all others.

I hope you see what I mean, darling. I love you so much I am prepared to give you up so you have the best chance to get better. I want only the best for you, and a passionate love affair doesn't represent that best chance apparently, not compared with proper medical care, treatment and convalescence. If we were together then it would have to be as one, and since this would be the very worst thing for you now and even in the foreseeable future, then I know we must say goodbye. I love you so much I want you to live, not die, even if you have to live without me and I without you.

I shall never forget I met you and that I loved you, and that while I live you will be somewhere in my heart always.

Freddy.

Unlike Freddie on receipt of his letter, the drowsy and drugged Fleur had no other reaction than to let the letter slip out of her hand to the floor while she turned her head away on her pillow and stared sightlessly at the blinded window where somewhere beyond shone the pale September sun.

She didn't wonder as to whether or not he had written it, even though she had seen more of his handwriting than he had of hers. In fact she didn't doubt that he had, not for a moment. Nor did she wonder why he had spelled his name with a 'Y' rather than with an 'IE' as she knew he preferred, nor why the paper he had written his letter on was identical to the follow-on writing paper she had at home. She wondered none of these things because she no longer cared because she believed what Freddie had said was utterly true. If she died he would blame himself, and she could never allow that. She loved him too much to be the cause of that much pain. Just as she had told him on the way to Wales, and just as she had been about to tell him in even greater detail at their fairy-tale house on the water's edge, she had tried to run away from him precisely because she didn't consider it fair for an invalid to inflict themselves on an utterly healthy and happy person. So how could she argue otherwise now, she asked herself as she stared at the window? Freddie might be leaving her for the most altruistic reasons, but whatever – in the end they were the right ones. She would probably be dead in a matter of months or maybe a year, and he would probably get over her in a matter of months or maybe a year. They had hardly begun their journey together, so much better that they curtail it now.

Whereas if she called him back and said no, no she wouldn't accept anything that he said and that she was happy to die in his arms, what then? It would be two lives gone for the price of one. Better for her to slip away from the moorings and into the quiet depths of the lake, while he could live on and live up to his fame.

But there was no way Fleur was going to live, that she knew. Whatever they did to her, whatever they put in her, Fleur now knew she would die, because without her love, what was her life?

As soon as she was asleep she saw the deer. It was in her woods, in the beech woods which lie around the boundary of The Folly. But this time it was as if she was the creature herself. She had to be because she could feel her breath shortening as she ran. She could see the undergrowth flying by, and she could hear the men closing behind her in the faint sunlight, the crunch of their boots on the sticks underfoot and the cocking of the bolts of their rifles. She could see the beam of sunlight ahead of her just where she knew it would be, just as she knew that beyond it lay safety, that somewhere there was the gate and that someone was there to open it for her.

Or that someone should be there to open it for her. Which there was, except as she ran into the light and then through it she saw the person wasn't him, that it was someone else, a man with small black eyes and a loose-lipped mouth who grinned now that he saw her, grinned as she stopped running, grinned as he slowly raised his rifle and shot her where she stood, and then twice more where she lay.

The voices were as faint as the last of the summer light. 'Not much of a size,' one voice was saying, 'hardly worth the bother really.' Another voice said he hadn't shot her for the meat. He'd shot her because of what she was. He'd shot her as a trophy because look, hadn't they seen? She was no ordinary deer. This one was pure white.

39

As soon as Richard saw Fleur he knew she was dying. He knew the signs too well, he'd seen them all too often to mistake them. The moment he entered her room and stood alone by her bed, he knew she couldn't have long to live, probably no more than a matter of weeks. She was almost as pale as death itself, and her flawless skin was beginning to stretch itself so tightly over her cheekbones and her forehead that he could see the shape of her skull beneath, while her huge and beautiful eyes, which everyone always said were her best feature, were now sunk deep in their sockets and there seemed to be no blood in her lips at all.

'Fleur?' he said, quietly but firmly. 'Fleur look at me. It's your father.'

Fleur looked at him but that was all she did. She just turned slowly once and looked at him then turned away again.

'Fleur, what is the matter with you? What's happened?' Richard demanded.

'What do you think?' she whispered, still looking away from him. 'What's happened is what you always said would happen.'

'But it can't!' Richard hissed furiously. 'You can't die, Fleur! It just isn't possible!'

'All things must pass, Pappa,' Fleur whispered. 'As a doctor you know that more than anyone.'

Richard picked up his daughter's wrist to check her pulse and for one heart-stopping moment was unable to find one.

'You were perfectly all right when I left you to go to

Zurich,' he said, privately appalled at how weak her pulse was. 'I mean what have I been gone – three weeks?'

'I wasn't all right,' Fleur whispered. 'I'd just had a heart attack, remember?'

'You had not had a heart attack, Fleur.'

'What do you mean?' Now she looked round at him, a frown on her forehead, her eyes half closing as she tried to comprehend.

'I mean you had suffered a suspected heart attack,' her father corrected himself. 'But when I left to go abroad you were well on the way to recovery.'

'That was before they shot the deer,' Fleur whispered.

'What did you say?'

'I said. That was before they shot the deer.'

Fleur closed her eyes fully and lay facing upwards on her pillow. Her breathing was still regular but it was shallow, and her pulse was weak and occasionally irregular.

'You can't be dying,' Richard said again, having checked all the machines banked above her bed which seemed to be telling him otherwise. 'It simply isn't possible. At least you cannot be dying from what I told you that you were dying of.'

'What do you mean then, Mr Fisher-Dilke?'

Richard wheeled round. He hadn't heard Christian Fadiman, his newly arrived partner, come in.

'If your daughter isn't suffering from heart failure, then what? Everything indicates irreversible heart damage, including your original diagnosis.'

'No!' Richard almost shouted as he contradicted his junior before taking him aside and dropping his voice. 'It has to be something else. It has to be a virus, a cancer, a brain tumour, a blood disorder, anything but what I said, what I thought! Anything! It has to be something virulent and malignant, it would have to be, wouldn't it? Because what else could explain the rapidity of my daughter's decline?'

'But according to your daughter's records and her file, Mr Fisher-Dilke, in the blood tests you've run regularly there has never been the slightest sign of any abnormality whatsoever. Right up to the last ones you took before you went to Zurich. In *all* the tests you've run—'

'I know what the tests showed, Mr Fadiman! But what I'm saying is I've missed something! Because it cannot possibly be her heart, dammit! Not for her to decline as quickly as this!'

Christian Fadiman looked at Richard and then drew him aside from Fleur's bed.

'I think perhaps we should continue this outside, Mr Fisher-Dilke, for fear of upsetting the patient even more.'

'I am telling you it cannot be her heart that is killing her, Mr Fadiman. Not like this. It isn't medically possible.'

'And I'm sorry to disagree with you, but I feel perhaps because of who the patient is you aren't quite seeing this as clearly as you should. Perhaps if you'd like to show me her X-rays? And the results of the electrocardiograms and the echo-cardiographs? And the scans?'

'No!' Richard wheeled round on him, his eyes blazing. 'No because this is my patient, and as I told you when you arrived here I have always insisted that only I treat her! So since there is some confusion, if anyone is going to run a new set of tests on my daughter it is myself! I shall go and make the necessary arrangements now!'

Richard stormed out of the room, leaving his bemused partner to wander over to inspect the readings on the bank of machines, and then to check on the patient herself.

'Fleur, you're awake, are you?' he asked her, seeing her eyelids open once and then twice. 'How are you feeling?'

'I'm all right,' she whispered, 'but I don't want any more tests.'

'Why not, Fleur?' Christian Fadiman asked, bending over her.

'Because there isn't any point.'

'Your father seems to think there might be something else wrong with you,' the doctor replied.

'There is. But it won't show up on any tests.'

'I don't understand.'

The beautiful ashen-faced young woman in the bed smiled faintly up at him.

'It's all right,' she whispered. 'I wouldn't expect you to.'

Freddie had just received good news. The hospital had just rung his mother and confirmed that his sister Bette was finally well and truly out of any danger. The wounds she had suffered had been grievous, but the family were all assured that there was nothing which couldn't be repaired with cosmetic surgery and skin grafting, all except Bette's right bicep which had been so badly mutilated it was beyond surgery. Fortunately the second-worst bite the horse had inflicted on its mistress, the point where it had sunk its twelve incisors into her shoulder and neck, had missed the jugular vein by a matter of millimetres. Had it not, Freddie's beloved youngest sister would have been dead within minutes.

As for news from the other hospital, the clinic somewhere in Buckinghamshire, England, what little news there was from there wasn't so good. Once Stephen had procured the telephone number for him, and despite the decisions couched in Fleur's letter to him, Freddie had rung on several occasions for a progress report only to be told that the patient was as well as could be expected. When he asked for a definition as to what that precisely meant, he was told that the patient was as well as could be expected given the circumstances, and that was all the information the clinic was allowed to give to non-relatives. As for speaking to the patient person-to-person, Freddie learned on his first enquiry that such a notion was completely out of the question.

'So what do you plan to do now, Frederick?' his mother enquired of him as he stood pouring them both a drink in her Manhattan apartment. 'There's always the dreadful Diane, I suppose.'

'Wild horses, Maman,' Freddie replied. 'Not just a team of them but it'd take practically every goddamn wild horse in the world to drag me even within hailing distance.'

'You can't say she isn't a trier, Frederick. She most certainly gave you a good run for your money,' his mother laughed in reply. 'Or rather you did for hers. When did the penny finally drop?'

'I guess when I took the billboard out on the freeway,' Freddie replied. 'Frederick Jourdan Says No to Diane Smith-Werner.'

'Tu parles sérieusement, mon cher?'

'Seriously, Maman, I really don't think she's got the message yet,' Freddie sighed. 'I've even had the dreaded Dr Klein after me on the phone. Saying by all the sounds of it, I really should stop by for a consultation. Diane still thinks it's a simple case of the wheels coming off and that's it.'

'Ah well if nothing else,' his mother sighed, 'the very least all this has done is save you from death by boredom. So what now? What do you plan to do now Bette is no longer in any danger? Return to England and complete your sabbatical?'

Handing her a perfectly mixed dry martini, Freddie told his mother he thought he'd finished with England for the time being. Instead he was planning to arrange the shipment of the items he had left behind at Stoke Park back to him in New York. He thought he'd stay around the city until Bette was well enough to go home, when he planned to drive his as yet unmarried sister back down to Virginia and look after her until she was completely mended.

His mother agreed that this was an excellent notion.

Freddie had said little of his own unhappiness during the family crisis but now he needed some time to recover, and he knew of no better place to convalesce than his sister Bette's beautiful farm set in the famous blue grass country. Not that he was to get within a thousand miles of it as it happened, because just as he thought he had finalized his plans the telephone rang again.

This time it was Stephen calling from London.

'I should have rung you before, or rather I would have had I been in London,' Stephen said, 'because the letter's been lying here all the time I've been away. But I only just got back.'

'You care to translate, Steve?' Freddie asked. 'So far I haven't got one thing you've said.'

'Is this a bad line?'

'No just an incomprehensible conversation.'

'Sorry,' Stephen replied, 'I'll start again from the beginning. You remember Fleur's pills? All those pills we found in her bag and I thought there was something odd about them?'

'Sure I do,' Freddie said, pulling up a chair by the phone and sitting down. 'Go on.'

'I was right, Fred. All the heavy stuff, the drugs Fleur told you she was taking for Post Viral Fatigue or ME or whatever they like to call it now— the ones which you then, having talked to Pappa, realized he was prescribing for a heart condition? Which seemed to make sense when we looked at the labels? You *savez*?'

'I do, Steve. What about them?'

'They're placebos. And I'm sure a boy of your education knows what placebos are.'

'They're dummy drugs.'

'That's it. Or more correctly they're chemically inert substances given in *place* of drugs – either to hypo-chondriacs who are driving doctors even more to drink, or as in this case to fool someone the docs are treating

582

when their condition – or rather the patient's lack of any condition – doesn't merit any real medication.'

'Are you saying there's nothing wrong with Fleur?'

'If there's anything wrong with Fleur it certainly isn't what her father told you it is. Or even more importantly, what her father told her it was. If she really did have a serious heart condition he would hardly be prescribing her a set of dummy drugs, would he?'

'Okay. Okay but what about the tranquillizers? You seemed to think they were real enough.'

'They are, Frederick, my boy. In fact just as I suspected, they were more real than they said, inasmuch as they were labelled five-milligram doses when in fact they were double the dosage. For some reason best known to himself her father has been keeping her in an almost semi-hypnotic state.'

'A semi-hypnotic state?' Freddie said. 'Jesus Christ, Steve, if this is true—'

'It's true all right, Fred. I have the report from the lab right here in my hand. I don't know how long he's had her on this dosage, or whether he manipulates it or what. But if you or I were taking the amount of benzodiazepine Fleur was taking—'

'Benzodiazepine?' Freddie echoed, not meaning it as a question.

'Anxiolytics,' Steve continued. 'Tranquillizers, sleepers, downers, call them what you will. Tools of the trade to treat severe anxiety, but which can also be used as stoppers, like on a racehorse if you get my drift.'

'You bet I get it, Steve. I know exactly where you're coming from.'

'Right. Then as I was saying if you or I were taking this kind of dosage we wouldn't be altogether rational. We'd certainly be subdued to say the very least. We certainly wouldn't be at our brightest and most positive, shall we say.'

There was a long silence from Freddie as he drew the deepest breath he could in order to try and stem his rage.

'Fred?' Steve asked after a minute. 'Fred are you still there?'

'Not for long, Steve,' Freddie replied. 'I'll be over with you as soon as I can get a flight.'

Once he had his delirium under control, a delirium induced by the sudden realization that there was nothing wrong with Fleur at all, at least nothing bad or wrong enough to kill her, Freddie almost became delirious again. For this meant there was no cause or impediment just or good enough to say why Freddie and she shouldn't spend the rest of their lives together.

On the long flight over he got to thinking about what he and his mother had discussed at great length, as to why any father should do anything so appalling to one of his children, particularly his only child, particularly a child as beautiful, as sweet and as loving as Fleur. They had come to the conclusion that there was only one explanation, that Richard Fisher-Dilke was seriously paranoid.

'He has to be,' his mother had assured him. 'It has to be a power thing, a possession thing, something quite as crazy as that. Some men are like that about their daughters. Your father no, thank God. Your father was perfectly able to treat them all with great equanimity and fairness. Maybe because he had so many. Who knows? But I don't think so, because your father was a very fair man. Maybe it would have been different if we had only had the one child, and this child had become more famous, more successful than him. This happens certainly with many parents. I hear about it all the time.'

'You're right, *Maman*,' Freddie had agreed. 'I mean I think the man is sick, but there it is. Stephen has the proof and I have to go over there and face FD with it. And see what he has to say. He's bound to have some defence ready, because any guy as clever as this, as devious as this, he isn't just going to leave all the doors and windows open, is he? No way. He'll probably say that Fleur has another condition, because it's there right enough on record how seriously ill she was after her mother died . . . and that because Fleur was such a lively young woman the only way to control her reaction and make her rest up, so that she'd fully recover, was to put her on placebos and – and . . . '

'What?' his mother asked as she was driving Freddie to the airport. 'You've gone a very strange colour, Frederick.'

'I was going to say and make her give up her concert career—'

'But of course!' His mother took both hands off the wheel and clapped them together, nearly swerving into a Yellow Cab next to her as she did so. 'Yes! We are forgetting the world-famous concert career!'

'Jesus, you bet we are!' Freddie agreed. 'First out he was plain Mr Richard Fisher not getting anywhere fast, then Fleur gets famous, then he gets position and power by changing his name to Fisher-Dilke, then hey presto! He wipes her out. He takes out the thing he has never been able to stand but has had to, the thing he's had to grit his goddamn teeth about—'

'The daughter who become more famous than her father!' his mother cried.

'Too right! It must have nearly killed the bastard.'

'Ooohh,' his mother said, wide-eyed and pouting, suddenly very French. 'Ooooh and what a bastard, huh?'

'The daughter who became more famous than the father,' Freddie mused, tapping out a rhythm on the dashboard. 'Bad enough for unknown Daddy if that should happen with his son, but a daughter? I mean it has to be the one sin that must not be committed by a female offspring. Thou shalt not grow up to be more famous than thy father.'

'So what a revenge lie in wait for him, yes?' his mother picked up. 'At last to have it in his power, when she become ill, when her poor Mamma die – to haul her off the concert platform! The great God medicine has had to take the back seat, yes? To the Greater God of Music. But now for his revenge!'

'Fleur is ill, maybe just as she said – with some virus she picked up abroad—'

'Why not? You remember how ill your sister Kitty get in France? When she stay with my sister in Brittany? She had what they call Harbour Virus.'

'That's just what Fleur said she got, Maman!'

'Then how easy to turn it into something more serious, because it attack the heart muscle! Et voilà! Everything it play into the doctor's hands, yes? My, my, Freddie darling, this is just like the plot of an opera!'

'So he turns the virus into a deteriorating heart condition, he runs all the tests himself, his daughter would know no better—'

'And which of us would, may I ask? At eighteen do we say to our Pappa, who we believe to be this famous heart-surgeon, I demand a second opinion! No, no! The poor child – she was lost before she begin.'

'Can you believe it?' Freddie asked as the car pulled into Kennedy airport.

'Can I believe it?' his mother echoed. 'Of course I believe it! What else can you believe? So – and which is after all the most important thing, darling boy – do you believe it?'

'Right on,' Freddie nodded slowly. 'Every comma, every word, every goddamn sentence. You bet I believe it.'

The very moment Concorde took off from Kennedy with Freddie on board, Fleur's condition stabilized. The change went almost unremarked by the nursing staff simply because only twenty-four hours earlier Fleur had begun to deteriorate so quickly that, in the absence of her father, Dr Fadiman had taken it upon himself to transfer her to the intensive-care unit so that her condition could be monitored constantly at the central control station. Her blood pressure which had plummetted dangerously low had now levelled out and was slowly, albeit almost imperceptibly, beginning to rise and the rhythm of her heart was becoming gradually more regular and effective, but the staff ascribed this simply to the fact that Fleur was now safely on a life-support system, and to no other reason.

When all the time, the reason for the end of what had already been considered as her terminal deterioration was now sitting on board an aircraft which was flying him back to her at one and a half times the speed of sound across the vast Atlantic Ocean.

Freddie found Stephen waiting for him at Heathrow.

'I was going to take you straight to the clinic,' Stephen said. 'I found where it is from the BMA, that was no problem. It's about thirty minutes north-west of London, out near somewhere called Gerrards Cross. Unfortunately I've got a visiting diva who's lost her voice – she loses her voice every time she comes to London – and I'm going to have to see her. You can borrow the car and go straight out yourself. It's easy to find, don't worry. Even for you.'

'Suppose the son of a bitch won't see me, Steve? Suppose when I get out there he doesn't let me near him? Or more importantly Fleur?'

'He will. First of all he's at the clinic today because he's operating there, and secondly as long as you behave yourself there's no way they're going to keep you out. If he knew you were coming it might be a different story, but not this way. Anyway if he does try and make it difficult for you, just make sure he knows you know about the pills. That'll soon bring him to heel.'

'Reckon, do you?'

'It'll be like shooting fish in a barrel, old chum.'

On the rest of the journey into London Freddie explained the theory he and his mother had worked out. Stephen agreed whole-heartedly, saying that he'd more or less arrived at the same conclusions himself.

'I also ran it past a shrink I know,' Stephen added, 'and he gave it nine out of ten as well.'

'Why only nine out of ten?'

'Because he's a shrink. Ten out of ten would put him out of work.'

It just doesn't make sense, Richard hissed to himself as he stood alone in Fleur's room in the clinic examining the results of the last set of tests he'd run on her early that morning. It has to be something else, he reasoned. Because none of this makes sense.

He started from the top again, from the first page of Fleur's confidential file, right up to the latest readout he'd just had his computer print from the ECG and the echocardiograph. He also looked at the MRI scan and every result was the same. Every result showed Fleur's heart was failing but from no visible or diagnosable cause.

When he'd finished his reading Richard closed the file, tucked it under his arm and then walked over to where his now comatose daughter lay. Pulling out the chair that was by her bedhead, he sat down beside her and stared at her for a long silent time.

Either I have missed something or else I must be going mad, he finally whispered to her, as if she were awake. Since your sudden collapse and they admitted you here to IC you've shown every symptom of cardiomyopathy, so patently obviously that even a houseman could diagnose the condition just by listening and looking. And these machines above you here. They've shown exactly what they would be expected to show wired up to someone dying from heart failure, weakness and irregularity of the P, Q, R, S and T waves produced by your heart. Then there's the evidence of serious heart-muscle disorder shown on the echocardiogram. Yet the result of the MRI scan I just ran on you, and I have it right here – Richard opened the file again and took out a computer-imaged photograph of Fleur's heart which he examined again carefully. *Here it is, my dear. Here is your heart in two dimension, just as I saw it on the computer, just as I saw it on the video I made over and over again this morning. And there is nothing there, no damage whatsoever, not one trace. And yet.* Richard took a deep breath. *And yet the readout from the echocardiograph and from the ECG show that your heart is failing. So what in hell are you up to? Because as I know and as the scan proves there is absolutely nothing wrong with your heart.*

A knock on the door brought Richard back to his senses and closing the file for a final time, he got up as if he was checking the readings on the bank of machines while Nurse Moore let herself in.

'Excuse me for the interruption, but I need to check the sphygmomanometer in here,' the nurse said. 'I was wondering whether there's some fault in the link between the AS in here and our screen on the desk because the reading – but no – no the reading's exactly the same.'

'What is the precise nature of your concern, nurse?' Richard asked. 'Is the patient's blood pressure dropping more, because if this is the case—'

'No on the contrary, Mr Fisher-Dilke,' the nurse interrupted. 'It's levelled out, and if anything it's showing a very slight rise.'

Richard stared at the nurse and then looked at the AS for himself. Sure enough Fleur's blood pressure had climbed up a good point from its previously dangerously low mark.

'Nurse Askey and myself both noticed it,' Nurse Moore continued. 'It's only very small but it could well be significant.'

'Indeed, nurse,' Richard replied coldly. 'The significance being that the patient is now being helped by this array of life-support machinery. So we would be looking for some sort of stabilization at the very least.'

'But not an improvement surely?' Nurse Moore argued.

'Not with this sort of prognosis. Not with the sort of prognosis you've given the poor child.'

'Thank you, nurse,' Richard said curtly. 'I do not need you to remind me of my findings.'

'Of course you don't, Mr Fisher-Dilke,' Nurse Moore replied. 'After all you're the doctor and I'm only the nurse, and an Irish one at that.'

'Meaning?'

'It really doesn't matter. You'll only say it's blarney.'

'Then blarney away. Say what's on your mind but for heaven's sake just don't take all morning.'

'Fair enough,' Nurse Moore agreed. 'For there's no law against having a theory now, is there? It's just that what with one thing and another—'

'Do at least try and be specific, nurse.'

'That's very difficult, Mr Fisher-Dilke,' Nurse Moore smiled. 'As my mother always used to say there's no point in being a woman if you have to be specific as well. And this isn't a case for specifics. This is only a woman's intuition at work.'

'And?'

'Well. Even being a nurse and even having been a nurse for so long now, Mr Fisher-Dilke, and having got to know your daughter so well, so very well in fact over these last weeks, I wouldn't say it was a cardiomyopathy that we're looking at here at all,' the nurse said straightening up and looking Richard in the eyes. 'I'd say this was an open and shut case of someone dying from a broken heart.'

40

Exactly as Stephen had predicted, finally Richard Fisher-Dilke had no option but to see Freddie. Freddie had simply asked the white-coated receptionist to pass a message on to the surgeon in advance of his even requesting an interview. When Richard understood the position, in turn he directed his visitor to be sent up immediately.

Refusing all offers of refreshment, Freddie sat down opposite Fleur's father and came straight to the point. He didn't concern himself with theory or speculation but instead simply concentrated on the facts at his disposal, namely the constitution of the drugs which Richard had been prescribing his own daughter. When his visitor finished, Richard said nothing at all. He merely got up from his antique desk and stood at the huge picture window which commanded a view across the grounds of the clinic's gardens. He stood there for fully five minutes before speaking, his hands clasped behind his back and his head tilted slightly back as if he was studying the sky rather than the view. Then finally he came and sat back down at his desk, placing both hands on top of it and looking Freddie straight in the eye.

'We are going to have to leave such matters to one side for the moment I'm afraid, Mr Jourdan,' he said, 'because we have been outrun. The both of us.'

'No I don't think so, Mr Fisher-Dilke,' Freddie replied. 'If you don't release Fleur into my charge at once, so that I may get a totally independent and fresh opinion on what, if anything, is wrong with her—'

'But there is something wrong with her, Mr Jourdan,

591

this is where Fate has dealt us both such a cruel blow,' Richard broke in, slipping the file across the desk towards Freddie. 'Have a look in there. Even though you won't understand all the medical jargon you will see from the summary at the bottom of the last page that, for whatever reason God alone knows, my daughter is in fact only a step or so away from death.'

'Bullshit,' Freddie said without even opening the file. 'There's nothing seriously wrong with her. And if you can cook her medicines there's sure as hell nothing to stop you cooking the books.'

Richard leaned over and flicked the file open at the relevant page.

'I didn't draw up this report,' he said. 'I was away on holiday with my wife when this happened, and one of my partners had to admit Fleur to Intensive Care. Read for yourself! Over the past weeks my daughter's life has been hanging by a thread. Read what it says there and you'll find out for yourself.'

Freddie read the laser-printed summary at the end of the report. It was signed by two doctors, a Dr Fadiman and a Dr Alderman, both of whom were of the opinion that the patient admitted to Intensive Care on the given date was suffering from major heart failure which was likely to prove irreversible.

'This can't be so,' Freddie said after a moment. 'This just isn't possible.'

'My thoughts precisely, Mr Jourdan,' Richard agreed. 'I have been trying to make sense of this all morning.'

'All morning? But this happened weeks ago—'

'I ran a fresh set of tests early today and—' Richard stopped. He had been about to reveal the paradox of the case when he suddenly decided better. 'And the results confirm the findings of my partners,' he finished instead. 'We have lost the final play, alas. Fleur is an innocent in all this and so I would not have thought that

592

this was a case of nemesis – you know what nemesis is?'

Freddie nodded. 'Sure,' he said. 'Nemesis was the goddess of vengeance in both Greek and Latin myth, and personified the gods' resentment of anyone who crossed their path.'

'Perfectly correct, Mr Jourdan,' Richard agreed. 'Which is why I could understand if I was the victim of their retributive justice, because I am the guilty one. But not Fleur. Why Fleur? Fleur has done nothing to bring down vengeance on herself. Except fall in love with you.'

Freddie suddenly found himself fixed with a look of hatred he had never before seen in the eyes of anyone.

'I don't believe Fleur is dying,' Freddie said, determined not to be bested by the look of sheer malevolence. 'I still believe that this is another of your deceits. You're full of them, Mr Fisher-Dilke, from the moment you got your daughter to stop playing the piano by lying to her, to keeping her doped up so she couldn't continue with her wonderful career, to this moment now, when you seriously think you're going to get rid of me by your ridiculous charade! You are mad, Mr Fisher-Dilke. I tell you that you are certifiably insane.'

'Then come and see for yourself, Mr Jourdan,' Richard replied. 'Your beloved Fleur really is dying. She is dying from a major cardiomyopathy. Which to the layman means she is dying from heart failure.'

'But there is nothing wrong with her heart, you bastard!' Freddie returned. 'You have already admitted as much!'

'I said there *was* nothing wrong with her heart, Mr Jourdan,' Richard contradicted, again looking up at him with steely eyes. 'But there is now, and I am as much in the dark as you are. Because for the very life of me, I can't think of one good reason why an otherwise perfectly good and healthy heart should suddenly fail anyone.'

'But I can,' Freddie said after a moment, getting up and beginning to make for the door. 'I can! I can think of a very good reason why!'

He found the room easily because the IC unit was posted with wall signs like all the other departments. When he reached the central control unit, beyond which he could see the row of single rooms for critically ill patients, a nurse called to him to ask if she could help.

'I have to see Miss Fisher-Dilke,' he explained breathlessly, looking round to see if her father was anywhere near catching him up.

'I'm afraid she's not allowed any visitors at the moment,' the duty nurse said. 'Not without her father's specific permission.'

'No,' Nurse Moore suddenly interrupted, getting up from her station. 'That's not particularly true, Deb. Not if this man is who I think he is. You're Freddie, aren't you?'

'Yes,' Freddie agreed. 'I am. Why?'

'Don't think me rude but I don't remember your last name,' Nurse Moore replied, grabbing him by the hand. 'But quickly, before Mr Fisher-Dilke can stop you.'

Nurse Moore hurried him through a pass door and then into a room where Freddie saw Fleur lying on the red blanketed bed, attached by a mass of wires to a bevy of life-support machines. Her head was turned away from him so Freddie hurried quickly around the bed, carefully avoiding all the machinery until he found a place between the ventilator and the bed where he could kneel down in order to be at Fleur's eye level. There was a tube running into her nose, her right arm was wired up to a machine on a shelf above her, and the breathing tube from the ventilator was fixed on a band round her head to prevent it from slipping out of her mouth.

Yet the moment Freddie knelt down her eyes opened,

and when they focused on who was kneeling beside her they opened even wider, and even with the breathing tube in her mouth Freddie could see she was smiling.

'Fleur,' he whispered, putting his hand gently on her left one which was folded across her stomach. 'Fleur darling, I'm here. I'm here and I won't ever go away from you again, I promise, not ever.'

He didn't move from her side for forty-eight hours. Except to go to the bathroom he never left her room, not even to sleep. With the doctors' permission Nurse Moore wheeled in a second bed, so that when fatigue finally overcame him Freddie could lie down and nap at least. But for the first day he ignored the luxury, sitting instead at Fleur's bedside where he watched and waited while Fleur slowly and surely came back to life.

Once his fellow doctors had indicated the effect Freddie Jourdan was having on his daughter, Richard Fisher-Dilke could do nothing but sanction Freddie's vigil. Unable to give a textbook medical reason for what was happening, he could only stand by silently and wonder like the rest of his staff at the transformation in Fleur's condition. Every hour she seemed to improve and strengthen. Within twenty-four hours her blood pressure was back to normal and her body fluids and blood-sugar levels were within their optimum limits while another twenty-four hours later Fleur's heart rate had recovered to a strong and steady seventy-six beats per minute.

Even so, for two days Fleur barely spoke. She just lay in her bed and looked at Freddie who sat holding her hand in his and looking back at her. As she grew visibly stronger, and as the team of doctors and nurses confirmed that this was indeed the case, Freddie began to talk very quietly to her now and then. But never in the presence of anyone else, so no-one ever knew what he said.

On the third day when Fleur was sleeping soundly,

unaided by any medication, Richard asked Freddie to come and see him in his private office.

'I have to know what you have been saying to my daughter,' he said as he shut them both into his office. 'I cannot bear it any longer.'

Freddie smiled. 'You're afraid I might be blowing the whistle on you, right?' he asked. 'You're frightened sick in case I'm telling Fleur exactly what sort of sick bastard her father really is.'

'You're only here on sufferance, you understand. You're only here because I have allowed it,' Richard replied, but with none of his previous conviction.

'No. I'm here because if I wasn't your daughter would be dead and you know it,' Freddie replied. 'And you're the one who's here on sufferance, pal.'

'There's no proof that what you just said about my daughter is the case, Mr Jourdan,' Richard argued, ignoring the threat.

'No, but there's plenty of proof of what you've been doing, Fisher-Dilke.'

'The point I was about to make is that your being here and Fleur's apparent recovery could be entirely coincidental,' Richard said, doing his best to ignore the implied threat.

'That's good,' Freddie smiled. 'You mean not only didn't you know what was wrong with your daughter, now you don't know what's making her better. Nice work, doc.'

'You're not seriously going to suggest this is an affair of the heart rather than a medical matter, I trust?'

'You're the diagnostician, Fisher-Dilke,' Freddie replied. 'My only concern is to see Fleur get better. Which I'd say she is. Wouldn't you? Now if you'll excuse me—'

Freddie made a move for the door but Fleur's father intercepted him.

'I just want you to tell me what you have been saying to my daughter, Mr Jourdan. Surely that is not unreasonable?'

'I think it's totally unreasonable, as a matter of fact,' Freddie replied. 'I don't owe you one damned thing and neither does your daughter. Least of all your daughter. But for her sake, and only for her sake, and to stop you calling me to your office like some goddamn headmaster, I haven't said one damned thing to Fleur about you. That's because the most important thing as far as I'm concerned is to see Fleur well again and the hell out of here. Telling her what you've been up to might set her right back and then some. Now if you don't mind I have to get back to where I'm really needed.'

Freddie stared at Richard, who realizing that he was no match either physically or mentally, finally stepped aside and let Freddie out of the room.

'Where was I?' he asked Fleur when he got back to her room and found her awake once more.

'You'd just sung "Funny Valentine",' Fleur smiled back at him, 'and you were about to sing "A Foggy Day".'

'With the gestures?' Freddie teased. 'Because it's more expensive with the gestures.'

'With the gestures,' Fleur grinned back at him. 'What the hell, I'm on BUPA.'

This time Freddie went in search of Richard. He caught him as he arrived at the clinic, and taking him by the arm marched him past his secretary and into the sanctum of his office.

'I think it's safe to say Fleur's out of the woods now, don't you? It is a fortnight now since I arrived here, and according to your partners your daughter's improvement continues to astonish everyone.'

'Even you, Mr Jourdan?' Richard asked, looking at him over his gold-rimmed half-moons. 'Surely miracle-makers become somewhat inured to their own miracles?'

'What I think is that you should know what is going on,' Freddie continued, ignoring the sarcasm.

'How very thoughtful of you, Mr Jourdan, seeing that this is my clinic.'

'And a rose is a rose is a rose. Just as your daughter is no longer just your daughter, Fisher-Dilke. Because the moment she is pronounced one hundred per cent recovered – by an independent third party – Fleur is going to become my wife.'

Richard put down his file of letters on the desk and took off his spectacles.

'On the understanding, Mr Jourdan,' he said slowly, 'that you have my consent.'

'Not so,' Freddie corrected him. 'We're going to get married and you can stick your consent.'

'Then what exactly is the purpose of this visit, Mr Jourdan? I do have my rounds to do, you know.'

'It's to put a deal to you, sport. Fleur has been hurt quite enough in her life, more than enough I'd say, and I don't want to see her hurt any more. So what I propose is this. I don't know whether or not Fleur still loves you, but you are still her father, and whether we love them or loathe them parents rank in our lives. But I wonder how she'd feel about you were she to know the whole truth? Somehow, even given the remarkable person she is, somehow I think even Fleur might in the end find it impossible to forgive you, to forgive somebody who deliberately tried to wreck her life at every given opportunity, killed her wonderful career, and finally by his lies, deceptions and criminal activities almost ended up killing her. No, no somehow I don't think even your wonderful and loving daughter would be able to see you in quite the same untarnished light again. The man who frightened his daughter sick out of playing the piano, who let the fox kill her rabbit so that she'd have to go hunting, who despatched her old nanny

598

off unannounced and without explanation, off to die in some far distant old people's home—'

'My word,' Richard cut in, 'we have been doing our detective work.'

'It wasn't very difficult,' Freddie returned. 'You obviously worked on the principle of blatancy. The more obvious the move, the less it's noticed. Would you like to hear some more?'

'I don't think so,' Richard said. 'Memory Lane's never been one of my favourite venues. So. So what precisely do you have in mind, Mr Jourdan? Or as you would probably prefer, what's the game plan? It surely can't be money.'

'First of all I want your approval. Not for me, but for Fleur. You can start making amends that way, because despite all that's happened to her, Fleur would really like it if you gave her your blessing. Because that way she'll be free, do you understand? No guilt, no hang ups, not if you could for once sanction something that she does, in this case the most important thing in her life so far. Then she won't have to spend the rest of her life looking to you to make sure everything's all right. She needs your approval for once, something you've always deliberately held back from her. I don't think that's asking too much, do you? Not given the circumstances.'

'And if I don't?'

'For starters she finds out what a bastard you really are.'

'For starters? You mean there's more?'

'You bet your life there is. You don't think you're going to be left loose on the streets, do you? No, pal, no what you're going to do once you've given your daughter your blessing is you're going to hand in your badge. And for good.'

'Oh I don't think so, Mr Jourdan,' Richard replied. 'For a start I'm doing rather well in this job, and secondly my wife wouldn't like it. She has rather high expectations of me, particularly following as I am in her own beloved father's footsteps. A knighthood, for instance. Which I have to say I find rather attractive too. Maybe one day even a life peerage, so no. No no, I've come too far now, and after far too much graft I'm not going to throw in the towel at this stage. Sorry, but there it is.'

Freddie looked at his adversary and saw at once the bluff in his eyes.

'I bet you're the sort of poker player who always draws to a straight,' he said.

'I'm afraid I don't play poker, Mr Jourdan,' Richard replied.

'And I'm afraid that's your loss not mine, because I do,' Freddie said. 'So let me tell you what I have in my hand, because I'm not bluffing. You do as I say when I say, or else I report the case chapter and verse to the General Medical Council.'

'I don't think so,' Richard said, but without any real assurance. 'I don't think you'd go as far as that. Think what it might do to Fleur.'

'Think what you've already done to Fleur,' Freddie replied. 'So you'd better believe it, believe me.'

Richard thought for a moment, going to his window again to look out across the lake, before turning back to Freddie and smiling.

'Allow me to think about it, Mr Jourdan,' he said. 'Not that I can foresee any difficulty with your proposal, but whereas you have had the time to consider it, I now would like time to do the same. Could you give me until say after the weekend?'

'I don't see why not,' Freddie agreed. 'Although you know as well as I do that there really is only one answer.'

For the whole of the past week and for longer each day, Fleur had been allowed up and about. She was also allowed out for short walks with Freddie so since it was such a fine warm October day that afternoon, they strolled around the grounds of the clinic discussing their future together. They got as far away from the building as possible, because a team of workmen were busy erecting scaffolding around the house prior to repainting it.

'You want the good news or the good news?' Freddie asked as they crossed a lawn in the direction of a large ornamental pond. 'We found Deanie.'

'You're joking?' Fleur stopped and turned to Freddie in delight. 'Where? Where did you find her? I mean how? And how is she?'

'One thing at a time, please, Miss Fisher-Dilke,' Freddie laughed. 'And remember, not too much excitement in one day.'

'Fat chance of that when I'm with you,' Fleur retorted. 'I only have to hear your voice, or your footsteps coming down the corridor. Now tell me about Deanie.'

Freddie did so, explaining how using his contacts Stephen had easily been able to trace the home to which Fleur's old nanny had been summarily despatched up in North Yorkshire. And how he had learned that although she was in good health how much she hated the home, as much as she hated being away from everyone she knew and loved who were all down south now, most of all a certain young lady she'd help raise since she was one minute old.

'So I thought what we'd do, all things being equal,' Freddie explained, 'was when you and I are organized we'd bring her down here and put her in some sheltered housing. That's what Stephen suggested. Apparently she's still perfectly able to look after herself and should never have been shut up in a home in the first place.'

'Freddie,' Fleur said seriously. 'Do you know something? I thought it simply wasn't possible to love you any more than I do already. But you want to know something else? I was wrong.'

Taking his arm again Fleur walked on across the lawn until they came to the edge of the pond.

'Now there's something I have to ask you, something I've been meaning to ask you for ages in fact,' she said as they stood at the water's edge looking for the fish. 'How do you spell your name? The abbreviation, that is.'

Freddie looked round at her.

'Why do you want to know that now?' he asked. 'Anyway, you know how I spell it. I told you.'

'I just want to make sure, do you mind?' Fleur said with a frown. 'It is F–R–E–D–D–I–E, isn't it?'

'That's right,' Freddie said. 'And you didn't forget, did you?'

'No.'

'I didn't think you had.'

'How could I? Freddie with an "I.E."? You made such a song and dance about it.'

'Essentially I'm a very trivial person, Fleur.'

'No you're not, Freddie, I.E. I think you're an utterly wonderful person, and I love you.'

'I love you too, Fleur Fisher hyphen Dilke.'

'I know. Otherwise I wouldn't be here, would I? I wouldn't still be alive.'

'If it wasn't for me you wouldn't have been nearly dead in the first place,' Freddie countered. 'If you hadn't fallen in love with me, you wouldn't have had your heart broken.'

'I think we're already agreed, aren't we? That there aren't any ifs and buts in our relationship. Just the plain fact of it. It was inevitable.'

'Agreed,' Freddie said. 'But just tell me why you wanted to check up on how I spell my name.'

'Because I knew you hadn't written that letter.'

'What letter?'

'The letter you wrote me saying why you thought we had to stop seeing each other.'

'The letter I wrote you? What about the letter you wrote me?'

'What letter?'

'The letter you wrote me saying why we had to stop seeing each other.'

'I never wrote you a letter, Freddie.'

'I never wrote you a letter either, Fleur.'

'Then who did, Freddie? Who wrote the letters?'

'I think that's pretty obvious,' Freddie replied. 'Don't you?'

'Yes,' Fleur agreed. 'Not that it matters now. And look – there's a fish.'

As they were going back into the clinic, the girl on duty on the main reception desk advised Freddie to move his car because the scaffolders were about to start work round the front of the house. Freddie saw Fleur up to her floor and then, kissing her quickly, told her he'd be back up as soon as he'd done what he'd been asked before hurrying back downstairs, not bothering to wait for the elevator.

Perhaps because he was still turning over the matter of the phoney letters in his mind or perhaps because Freddie simply was not the most diligent of drivers, he was paying even less attention to what he was doing than usual when he got into his car to repark it. Not that what happened was in any way his fault, but even so had he parked in the space marked *Visitors* rather than in a clearing in the car park which had been marked out of bounds with traffic cones by the scaffolders, he most certainly would have avoided the calamity. As it was, with a long look over his shoulder to make sure the park was clear behind him he reversed his hired car away from the front of the clinic to the side of the parking lot without seeing the line of cones, his head turned away from the building but his chest fully exposed to it, so that the twenty-foot-long scaffolding pole which then slipped from the grasp of the men who were working above him fell at an angle of forty-five degrees straight through the car windscreen, crushing Freddie so hard that the driver's seat was torn off its mountings by the impact.

He was barely conscious as they struggled to free him, but he was aware of what was going on and of the terrible pain. He heard voices far away thank the Almighty that the car had been travelling backwards at the time of impact. Had it not been, another voice said, to judge from the look of his injuries the poor man would undoubtedly have been killed outright. But I wasn't, he heard himself whisper, I'm alive, aren't I? Look, listen can you hear me? I'm not dead and I'm not dying, am I? But whatever happens, don't tell Fleur. For Chrissake don't tell Fleur. Don't worry, someone was saying, someone he could see, pretty green eyes and dark hair. Don't worry Freddie, this voice was saying, we won't say a thing to Fleur. Don't worry don't worry you really don't have to worry now . . .

Then it is another voice and another nurse someone who is asking what his chances are but he can see her as well which he can't understand because that is him on the table there below although it's difficult to see at first because there is this shimmering haze in front of his eyes.

'The chances are not good,' someone says, the man at the head of the table, the anaesthetist. 'We have only a very weak pulse and his blood pressure is falling all the time.'

That is certainly him down there yet he feels very calm no sense of panic just peace as he sees himself beneath the green gowns his face under the oxygen mask as the anaesthetist watches a green line on what looks like a television screen hardly moving up or down while everyone gathers round the table past which a nurse hurries with a tray of instruments and another man a doctor another surgeon perhaps? He's also wearing green too and a mask so how can Freddie tell but this man speaks he says

'Who's operating?' he asks.

'The man himself,' the anaesthetist says back. 'He insisted.'

'Then good luck, Mr Jourdan,' the surgeon says, the man Freddie now realizes is Dr Alderman, 'because you're certainly going to need it.'

'Not only that, the sooner we get him on a heart-lung machine the better,' the anaesthetist continues, checking his gauges. 'Although I doubt if soon will be soon enough.'

Through the swing doors Freddie can see the robed but as yet unmasked figure of Fleur's father scrubbing up and he wonders without any sense of fear what sort of job he's going to make of trying to save the life of the man who can ruin his this will be interesting he thinks from his corner of the ceiling high above the table what a god-given opportunity for Fisher-Dilke with no suspicion whatsoever of foul play he can just fail to save his life a life that is hanging in the balance and then walk away scot-free without the slightest suspicion and here he is now masked up by the table sawing open Freddie's chest what is that he is saying?

'Damage to the superior vena cava and to the right atrium,' Richard says as he examines Freddie's heart. 'Apparently no rupture of the main organ as such. Another half an inch and it would have been a different story.'

'It would have been an end of story,' Dr Alderman says as he also examines the damage. 'As it stands, is it repairable?'

'Possibly. Outside chance. If I can stitch the vena cava and relieve the pressure on the atrium—' Fisher-Dilke glances at the anaesthetist. 'A lot depends on you, John.'

'We're stable,' the anaesthetist replies, checking the digital readout on the heart-lung machine. 'But you're going to have to extract the old digit.'

'At least we can see what we're doing now,' Fisher-Dilke says. 'The great thing about these machines is they keep the site clean. So we've got a much better view of what exactly the damage is. If we can just get the rest of that rib out of the way—'

Even though he hangs high over the table Freddie can see everything clearly he can see the two surgeons working in silence as they ease back one of Freddie's three broken ribs in an effort not only to give a clear sight of the heart but also to reduce any further pressure on it

'Good,' Fisher-Dilke says, turning to Dr Alderman once that phase is completed. 'The area around the right atrium appears to be unpunctured, if actually damaged at all.'

'Suppose we ease that side of the heart back into shape?' Dr Alderman suggests.

'Hmmm. Worth a try,' Fisher-Dilke grunts.

This time when he falls to silence Freddie sees with interest that he is using one of his hands to massage and remould the right side of Freddie's heart

'From the look of things now,' he begins, 'perhaps all we have to repair is the vena cava, before taking a look round the rest of his bits and bobs. To make sure everything's still functioning. Except—'

Now he stops and looks closely again at the apparent damage.

'Except, looking at the entry wound, or rather where the maximum compression was, I wouldn't be at all surprised if there weren't one or two nasties actually inside the heart. So I'm going to cut the heart open and go in. It's a big risk, of course it's a risk, because any invasion of the heart itself is always fraught with all sorts of dangers but we have no choice.'

Everyone round the table agrees.

'The patient's pre-operative condition was critical enough to lead one to expect to find a rupture of the heart. And since we haven't, I have more than the faintest feeling that with the blood pressure running so low and the faintness of the heart beat, there has to be serious damage somewhere or other. So I'm going in.'

Everyone round the table bends forward as Fisher-Dilke goes to make the incision and for a moment Freddie thinks he is going to miss it going to miss the moment when his heart is cut open but by moving round the ceiling slightly he manages to see and there it is there is his heart cut open inside him which doesn't disturb his tranquillity in the least particularly since Fisher-Dilke is now calling loudly as he examines his work

'It seems that due to the impact, the mitral valve is all but closed – which would explain the rapidly failing heart function. Looking at the damage and given the circumstances, I really don't think this is repairable. Not with the shock the system has suffered and the amount of physical damage here.'

Now the whole team glances round at each other all except Fisher-Dilke who as Freddie watches keeps his eyes fixed firmly on Freddie's non-beating heart

'Suppose,' Dr Alderman says suddenly, jolting the team back to action. 'Suppose we went for this as if we were doing a straightforward valvotomy, in the hope that we've got to it in time. There's a chance of course we might not get a restart, that the heart has already suffered too great a blow, but then that is a chance we'd have to take because there is no other option.'

Fisher-Dilke looks at him over his mask a pair of dark brooding eyes staring at his second in command

'Not a chance,' he says. 'Not an ice cream's chance in hell, Peter.'

'We don't have any choice, do we?'

Silence

'No we don't,' Fisher-Dilke says suddenly. 'Nurse – a prosthesis, please, in case I can't repair the damage manually, which is the first thing I'm going to attempt.'

Away goes the nurse to fetch an artificial heart valve while Fisher-Dilke continues talking aloud easing his little finger into what he describes as the damaged valve

'Technically if we're going to have to insert a prosthesis we should use a homograft but time is against us,' he says as he bends lower to examine the damage. 'Not having had the chance to prepare the patient for such an exigency militates against a biological implant or homograft—'

'But if we do have to use a mechanical valve we can always replace it with a homograft at a later date, surely?' Alderman asks as a statement of fact.

'Always provided we can kick-start the heart back into life, Alderman. Except—' Fisher-Dilke stops and straightens up, having removed his finger from the damaged valve.

'Now what?' the second surgeon enquires.

'I'm afraid it's beyond repair,' Fisher-Dilke says. 'Time's against us. There just isn't time.'

I'm going to die Freddie says

'Take a chance!' Alderman is urging. 'The quicker we try to get a restart, the greater the patient's chances! Look – if we use the principle of ballooning as we would in a valvuloplasty, except that instead of using a catheter we force the damaged flaps apart thus—'

All the time he is speaking Alderman is working on the heart exactly as he is describing putting his fingers in the damaged valve of the heart

'And then by pumping air through the channel here – with a bulb pump and a smaller catheter – and here's hoping the flaps of the valve stay back until we've got the heart running again—'

'Needle and thread, nurse,' Fisher-Dilke says, holding a hand out. 'We'll need to suture the entry I've made into the heart as quickly as humanly possible.'

Practically silent now and Freddie wonders curiously whether or not he's going to make it

'Then by taking the pressure off the upper chamber where the ribcage collapsed here—' Dr Alderman.

Cutting around the damaged muscles above the heart itself

'And by clearing away any bits of debris here which might also not only interfere with the heart function, but more likely set up some sort of nasty secondary infection – we might be in with a shot.' Fisher-Dilke.

Then silence again as he sets about doing what he has just depicted before finally standing up and to one side

'Good,' he said. 'So Peter, if you wouldn't mind checking the repair on the vena cava, and nurse do a swab count. And a visual. Then we'll go for a restart.'

The surgeon stands aside for a moment to allow his team to obey his instructions, and raises a questioning eyebrow to his anaesthetist who nods back as Freddie thinks so this is it this is it now or never now it's just wait and see

'Ready when you are,' the anaesthetist replies, 'but you're only just within the time limit – even so while there's life—'

'If there's life,' Fisher-Dilke says, stepping back up to the table to resume his position now the final checks had been run.

'Good,' he said. 'So let's go for it, please.'

Alderman hands Fisher-Dilke something that looks like a set of electrodes which the surgeon places on the watching Freddie's unbeating heart before nodding once for power

'Zero,' John the anaesthetist said. 'Sweet damn all.'

So I am dead after all no heartbeat no nothing which obviously explains why I can see all this because it's all already happened Freddie thinks while below him Fisher-Dilke draws a long slow breath and nods once again sending yet another pulse of electricity through Freddie's heart

'Still reading zero,' the anaesthetist's voice told him. 'Still as flat as a pancake.'

'No good,' Fisher-Dilke says. 'Lost him, I'm afraid.'

Fisher-Dilke looks up seemingly directly at Freddie as if he knew where he was before they make another effort to restart his heart but he can see it's in vain because the green line on the television screen is still reading as flat and straight as a ruled line

'He's gone all right. Damn. Damn damn damn.'

Fisher-Dilke's voice again, bending over Freddie's chest

'In that case we're going to have to give him an old-fashioned crank start, and see if that won't do the trick,' Alderman says and as he does Fisher-Dilke whips round to him.

'Not a chance, Peter!' he shouts. 'We've lost him! He's dead! Don't try and play God!'

'Never say die,' his assistant answers. 'Never say die.'

'The patient is dead, Peter! Isn't that right, John?'

'Can't say, Richard,' the anaesthetist answers. 'Not at this stage while he's still plugged in.'

'Never say die,' Alderman insists, digging into Freddie's chest. 'Do I have your permission, Richard?'

A look between the two men, one of whom is holding Freddie by the heart

'Richard we have to give it a go!'

'Yes all right! All right! What have we got to lose?'

This is wonderful this is purely amazing because Peter Alderman actually takes Freddie's heart into his hands Freddie can see him doing it and then slowly but rhythmically he begins to massage it everyone else is looking at the various monitors beside the table to see if there is any visible return of life everyone except Fisher-Dilke who keeps staring up at the ceiling, while Alderman massages the heart which is in his hands, slowly and in a steady rhythm which he is counting out aloud Freddie reckons much as a coxswain would do in a rowing eight

'One, two,' he urges. 'One. Two. And one, and two, and one and two, and—'

'We have two heart beats!'

The anaesthetist

'We have two beats! Well done, Peter! We have a restart!'

And there yes sure enough yes there it is the line on the monitor is bleeping now faintly softly softly faintly as Freddie sees his heart come back to life, and then more and more insistently until at last there is a steady rhythmic pulse while

'Thank God,' Peter Alderman is saying, carefully withdrawing his hands. 'That was a little too close.'

'I'll drink to that,' the anaesthetist replied. 'And to this nice steady rhythm we've now got going.'

'Well then let's keep it going, shall we?' Alderman says. 'While we get this poor chap sewn together again.'

'Well done, Richard,' the anaesthetist says. 'Well done everyone. A seriously major piece of surgery, if I may say so. Absolutely brilliant. You brought the bugger back from the dead.'

'Yes indeed,' Fisher-Dilke says slowly, as he takes needle and gut from his nurse. 'We brought him back from the dead. Thank God. I'd hate to have gone out on a failure.'

'Gone out?' Peter Alderman enquires. 'What are you talking about, Richard? Not off on yet another holiday, are you?'

'No, Peter,' Fisher-Dilke replies, bending over Freddie's chest. 'This is my last operation. I'm retiring.'

'Retiring? What on earth are you talking about?' Alderman says. 'You can't possibly retire now! Not when you've got it all ahead of you!'

'I'm afraid I have to,' Fisher-Dilke insists. 'Let's put it this way. I have something wrong with me, you see.'

'Christ,' Alderman whispers. 'Christ what, Richard? What on earth do you have wrong with you?'

'Something alas which can't be cured, Peter,' Fisher-Dilke replies, staring down at the heart he's stitching back up. 'Something which I have no hope of surviving – unless I stop work at once.'

'Will you two old women stop rabbiting on?' the anaesthetist says, looking at his gauges and screens. 'Charlie boy here is out of the woods now, and up and running all by himself – so stand by because I'm switching him over now. Off the heart-lung . . . '

Which is when it all suddenly goes black

41

The first thing Freddie saw when he woke up was Diane.

'Hi there,' she said. 'Boy, I'll bet that was good.'

Freddie stared at her blankly. He knew who she was all right, that wasn't why he was staring so hard. It was because his head was full of so much stuff, so many things, images, memories, sounds, shapes, so much stuff he couldn't begin to think where he was.

'Diane?' he said.

'Good,' she replied. 'Well that's a start.'

'Diane?' he repeated.

'It's okay, they said this would happen,' Diane said, getting up from the armchair in which she was sitting and smoothing out the creases in her white linen skirt edged with blue. 'Take your time, Freddie. You have all the time in the world to make everything out. Or do you want me to help you?'

Freddie said nothing at first. Instead he looked around the room. It wasn't a room he knew. It was a plain room, with a couple of nondescript pictures on the walls, carpeted wall-to-wall and furnished with the sort of mock-antique furniture found in would-be upmarket hotels. And nursing clinics.

'This isn't my room, Diane,' he said.

'No, that's right, it isn't,' Diane affirmed, tossing her perfectly styled hair back a little and smiling at him with white even teeth.

'So if it isn't my room, then where am I? And what am I doing here?'

'All in good time, Freddie. They told me we have to take it little by little, step by step.'

'Who's they? Who's this "they" you keep talking about?'

'Your doctors. In fact here they are now. We'll let them do the explaining,' Diane said as the door opened and a man in a white coat, followed by another man similarly dressed, came into the room with a nurse.

'Good,' the doctor said. 'So you're fully awake now, Mr Jourdan, just as you should be. So this is good.'

Freddie looked up at the doctor blankly. He knew the face vaguely, he knew he'd seen the doctor before somewhere or other but he couldn't put a name to the face to save his life.

'In case you're having trouble remembering,' the doctor said. 'I'm Dr Klein. I'm the man who's been in charge of you these last few weeks.' He paused and looked at Freddie, waiting for a reaction. When none was forthcoming he continued.

'I see you don't remember who I am, but no matter. This often happens. This is a common occurrence after this particular therapy.'

'He remembered me I'm happy to tell you,' Diane said. 'You recognized me the moment you opened your eyes, didn't you, Freddie?'

'Sure,' Freddie said before turning his attention back to the doctor. 'Did you say therapy, doctor? And if so, would you mind explaining? Because I don't remember one thing.'

'No you wouldn't, and I shall be more than happy to explain,' the doctor replied, pulling up a chair. 'In fact that is the nature of my visit. When the treatment is finished and my patients regain their full awareness shall we say? None of them can remember why they are here, how they came to be here, or indeed what they have been through. But then of course, that is the beauty of this particular treatment. My particular treatment.'

'So pitch it to me, doctor,' Freddie said suddenly yawning, before easing himself up on his pillows. 'Because believe me, I'm all ears.'

'You feel, do you not? As if you have been asleep, Mr Jourdan,' the doctor said.

'You bet,' Freddie replied. 'I feel, I guess, how old Rip Van Winkle felt when he woke up in the Catskill mountains. I feel as if I've been asleep for twenty years.'

'Yes well you have not, Mr Jourdan, I assure you. Just in case you think you have and now you're thinking – good. Now I can sue this quack for doing something which is no longer allowed.'

'You just lost me again,' Freddie said.

'A lot of doctors used to believe and indeed employ something called Sleep Therapy, but not any more,' the doctor smiled. 'At least not in the recognized medical establishments. It was found to be highly dangerous, as well as using addictive and very dangerous drugs. However, the basic premise of the treatment, giving the mind time to heal itself you understand? To purge itself if you like, to be cleansed – this was not bad thinking at all. In fact to a lot of us, and to me in particular it was very good thinking. Which is how I came to arrive at my own particular treatment. The treatment you have just undergone. In layman's language—'

'That's how I like to hear it, Doc,' Freddie interrupted.

'Of course,' the doctor agreed. 'Then let us say that by the skilful use of certain new semi-hypnotic drugs you have indeed been asleep for three weeks without in fact being so. What you have been in is more a state of suspended animation.'

'I see.' Freddie said nothing more at this time. He just lay back and thought about it because something somewhere was beginning to come back to him.

'Good. So basically, so as not to crowd your memory which will still be hyperactive from three weeks of nonstop dreaming as it were—' the doctor began, only for Diane to cut in.

'My heavens,' she laughed. 'I never thought of that. Three weeks of nonstop dreaming, Freddie. I do hope you behaved yourself.'

'If I dreamed, Diane,' Freddie said, doing his best to ignore the playful finger she was wagging at him, 'I don't remember a thing. Not one thing.'

'No,' Dr Klein agreed. 'That is how it should be. Patients rarely if ever remember anything they have dreamed after this treatment. Because as I said, it is as if you have in fact been asleep for all this time. And it is hard enough, is it not, to recapture the dreams of one night? Let alone twenty-one nights? No, no, you shouldn't have one clear memory anywhere in your head, but nonetheless your brain will have been busy, so we must take things easy. It will all come back to you in time, Mr Jourdan, what I am about to say to you that is. All I'm going to tell you, I assure you that you will remember in your own good time. You were overworking yourself, this is how it began you see. You were working yourself far too hard and Miss Smith-Werner here, concerned about your general wellbeing, asked if you would come and see me for a consultation, to which suggestion I am happy to say you agreed. Had you not—' Dr Klein shrugged. 'I'm not saying things would have been a lot worse,' he continued, 'but what I am saying is that things would not have got better. So. You came to see me three or was it four times I think, and finally I advised this particular therapy which I am most happy to assure you has already met with quite remarkable success. And with absolutely no side or unpleasant after effects. In such cases, such as your kind of case I am convinced this is the way ahead. So we put you on hold, if you like, for what we think is the correct amount of time, all the while monitoring your physical and mental conditions, as well as feeding you of course, and watering you naturally, and attending to all your other necessary functions, none of which things you will have the slightest recollection of because of the types of drugs we are using. You understand?'

Freddie nodded. He remembered nothing at all of the last three weeks. The last thing he remembered was sitting in this man's surgery, an occasion which he could now vividly recollect because he remembered the doctor somehow managing to talk him into letting him treat him. That was the only thing which was still stuck in his memory.

'So now,' Dr Klein was continuing, 'now we take it little by little and day by day. You will be weak at first, naturally, because although the nurses walked you round your room twice every day, you have not had proper use of your limbs for three whole weeks. And we must fill in the gaps in your mind gradually too, so that you will have a complete picture of yourself by the time you come to leave here. Good. So the first thing I must ask is what questions you have at this moment.'

'Only one,' Freddie replied. 'What is the exact date?'

'That's easy,' Diane said. 'I'll answer that one. It's Friday, April the thirteenth, nineteen ninety-four.'

The plan was perfectly straightforward. Now that Freddie was debriefed and out of the clinic he was to take a holiday, but by 'holiday' Diane didn't mean two weeks in the sun somewhere and then back to work. She told Freddie she'd watched him nearly kill himself and if they were going to live a full and happy life together, then he was going to take a holiday as in sabbatical.

Freddie agreed. Now he realized the damage he had done to himself and the trouble everyone had taken to repair that damage, then he knew it would be churlish to disagree. But he wanted to be alone. He didn't know quite how to say this to Diane who seemed to have completely taken over his life. But he knew that it was going to have to be said, because at this stage of his recovery six months off with Diane round his neck and he would be back in the clutches of Dr Klein. Luckily he didn't have to mention it because the suggestion came from Diane.

'I would love to be with you, Freddie,' she said, 'but as you know I too have work to do, and some pretty important stuff's coming my way, I *have* to tell you. So what I suggest is that you choose where you want to go and we make all the necessary arrangements this end, then whenever possible I come and join you. How does that sound?'

'That sounds good, Diane,' Freddie replied. 'And how does England sound to you?'

'England sounds a little too far away, Freddie.'

'I'd say that was the whole point, Diane. Not to be far away from you, honey, but to be a distance from here. If I stay here, anywhere in America, I'll find my way back to New York sooner or later and that'll be that. If I'm to take a real sabbatical then I think I should get out of the country, period. I love England. I've always loved my trips there. So what better than to find somewhere deep in the countryside where I really can turn off and drop out? And what's to stop you coming over and joining me there whenever possible? By Concorde it's half the time it is from here to Los Angeles.'

'Okay,' Diane finally agreed, after much thought. 'I don't see why not. Have you given it any thought already?'

'Yes I have as it happens. And a couple of very old buddies of mine, who know exactly what the best bits of England are, reckon they know just the place. It's in Worcestershire. It's a beautiful house in wonderful gardens with a trout stream and a lake, there's no-one living there at present. And it's called Stoke Park.'

Cadenza

42

Freddie was still trying to find out which button to press for recording from the radio when Mrs Davies came in to tell him he was wanted on the telephone.

'Hell,' he muttered, getting up from the floor with a tangle of hi-fi wires around one foot. 'Darn it, is it urgent?'

'It seems so, Mr Jourdan,' his new housekeeper replied. 'It's a Miss Smith-Werner calling from Washington.'

Freddie went and answered the telephone, pulling the wires from round his foot as he did. Diane only ever called him when he was in the middle of something, and knowing how she talked now not only wouldn't he be able to record the violin concerto to which he was listening, because he had tuned in late he wouldn't even know what the music was or who was playing it.

He talked to her for over half an hour, stretched out in one of the pair of fine Chippendale carvers which stood either side of the telephone table, during which time he told her all about the handsome Queen Anne house which he had rented for his sabbatical and about how it stood in fine parkland originally designed and laid out – so he had already been told – by a pupil of the enchantingly nicknamed 'Capability' Brown, while managing to deflect his fiancée from making any plans to come over and join him in the foreseeable future.

What he hadn't told her, he realized when he put down the phone, was anything about the pretty little white house which stood in its own grounds on a hill to the north end of the park, known apparently as 'The Folly'.

He hadn't told Diane about it because even after only two days at Stoke Park, he found that for some unknown reason he was already intrigued by it and he determined that for as long as possible it should remain his secret.

Later that day, when he was exploring the house more fully he found himself up in the attics on the fourth floor. From the largest of the rooms he saw there was a perfect view to be had of the little white house which today, in the summer haze, looked as if it were something out of a fairy tale. Sitting on the window seat he gazed out at the little house only to discover later and with a start that he must have fallen asleep.

Fully awake and still intrigued by the enchanting house on the distant hill, Freddie went and fetched a pair of powerful field glasses from a downstairs cloakroom and returned upstairs to get a closer look. He could see no visible sign of life, although the place was quite obviously immaculately maintained, with its lawns freshly mown and the earth in its full-flowering rose borders recently turned over. But nowhere was there any sign of human life, neither at any of the windows nor anywhere in the gardens.

Then he saw something. Behind some shrubs he caught sight of a slowly moving shadowy form and training his glasses exactly on that spot, he could see the branches of a bush moving quite vigorously as if someone was tugging at them.

Seconds later the culprit came into view, and the moment Freddie saw it the back of his neck prickled and his hands began to shake, for there standing looking out across the lawn chewing the leaves it had just plucked from the branches of the shrub it was attacking was a deer.

But that wasn't what took Freddie's breath away. What made him look so hard and look again was the fact that the deer was white. It was the very first albino deer Freddie had ever seen. Except for the one in his dream.

And more than that, the more he stared at it the more something stirred deep in his mind and began to come back to him, only very vaguely at first but even so back it began to come, exactly as if it knew the way.

Finale

**From The Sunday Times
May 12th 1996**

Last night in front of a capacity audience at the Albert Hall, four and a half years after her apparently unconditional retirement from the music scene, Fleur Fisher-Dilke made her comeback.

For her return to the concert platform in typical style the violinist bravely chose to play a brand-new and previously unperformed work, a violin concerto composed especially for her by the man she married just over twelve months ago, the brilliant American musical composer hailed as the man most likely to succeed Leonard Bernstein – Frederick Jourdan.

After the London Symphonia Orchestra had played Edward Elgar's Introduction and Allegro for Strings under the baton of Sir Iain Walcott, who himself had come out of retirement for the occasion, near pandemonium broke out as Fleur Fisher-Dilke at last took the stage, dressed in an off-the-shoulder full-length burgundy silk gown and with her famous long dark hair in a variation of her equally famous 'butterfly' style. The whole of the star-studded audience rose to its feet to give the virtuoso a near five-minute ovation before allowing her to play.

Whereupon almost ankle-deep in the flowers thrown to her by her admirers Fleur Fisher-Dilke produced a performance of such brio and bravura that eighteen and a half minutes later the concert hall once again erupted into frenzy, the audience rising to give Fisher-Dilke an ovation seemingly twice the length of their welcoming one.

Even long after the violinist had finally persuaded her composer husband to come out to take his own bows, still the audience refused to let the pair go, showering them with flowers and confetti made from their torn-up programmes. In response to the demands not only of the audience but also of the entire orchestra, Sir Iain Walcott handed the baton to Frederick Jourdan for him to conduct the Symphonia Orchestra as his wife played a series of encores, concluding with Elgar's famous and enchanting romance *Salut d'amour*.

For more pictures and a review of the Concerto see Alexander Davis on p.12 of Section 6.

THE END

Author's Note

Here is a list of recommended recordings of the music as played by Fleur Fisher-Dilke in *Change of Heart*.

Brahms

Violin Concerto in D, Opus 77
Yehudi Menuhin/Berlin
Philharmonic Orchestra/Kempe

EMI CDZ7 62608–2
HMV TC–A5D 3385

_____

Debussy

Violin Sonata in G minor
Kyung Wha Chung, Radu
Lupu

Decca 421 154–2

_____

Schubert

Violin Sonatina in D, D.385

Decca 425 539–2

_____

Bach

Unaccompanied Partita No. 2
Itzhak Perlman

EMI Dig CD5749483–2

Sarasate	Concert Fantasie on Carmen Sarah Chang
Kreisler	Liebeslied
Wieniawski	Scherzo-tarantelle
Poldini/Kreisler	Dancing Doll
Paganini	Caprices including Caprice in E
Elgar	Salut d'amour

Kyung Wha Chung 'Con Amore'
EMI Classics CDC 0777 7 54352 21

Mendelssohn	On Wings of Song Ida Haendel (violin) Geoffrey Parsons (piano)
Massenet	'Meditation' from Thais Anne-Sophie Mutter/Berlin Philharmonic Orchestra/Karajan

both on The Ultimate Violin
Collection
EMI Classics CD 0777 7 64894 21

Bruch	Violin Concerto No.1 in G minor, Opus 26 coupled with the Mendelssohn Violin

Concerto in E minor, Opus 64
Cho-Liang Lin/Chicago Symphony
Orchestra/Slatkin

CBS Dig MDK 44902

Beethoven

Violin Concerto in D, Opus 61
Itzhak Perlman/Berlin Philharmonic
Orchestra/Barenboim

EMI Dig CD C7 49567–2

Tchaikovsky

Violin Concerto in D, Opus 35
Kyung Wha Chung/Montreal
Symphony Orchestra/Dutoit
(coupled with Mendelssohn)

Decca Dig 410 011–2

Prokofiev

Violin Concerto No. 1 in D, Opus 19
Mintz/Chicago Symphony
Orchestra/Abbado

DG Dig 410 524 2

Elgar

Violin Concerto in B minor, Opus 61
Nigel Kennedy/London
Philharmonic Orchestra/Handley

EMI Dig EMX 2058

Berg	*Violin Concerto* Anne-Sophie Mutter/Chicago Symphony Orchestra/Levine (coupled with Rihm) DG Dig 437 093–2

Mozart	*Sonata for Violin and Piano No. 17 in C Major* Itzhak Perlman, Daniel Barenboim (*Violin Sonatas 17–28; 32–4; Sonatina in F, K.547*) DG Dig 431 784–2

DEBUTANTES
by Charlotte Bingham

A century ago marriage, and marriage alone, offered a nicely brought-up girl escape from the domination of her parents. Indeed it was the only path to freedom. That path led her to a Season in London and, the ultimate goal, Coming Out as a debutante. But along the way she had to survive a terrifying few months, a make-or-break time in which her family's hopes for her could only be fulfilled through a proposal of marriage.

For Lady Emily Persse, Coming Out means leaving her beloved Ireland, and its informalities, for England its stricter codes. For Portia Tradescant, released from the boredom of life in the English countryside, it means trying to get through the Season despite the best efforts of her eccentric Aunt Tattie. For beautiful May Danby the Season is an entree to a whole other life, worlds away from her strict convent upbringing in Yorkshire.

Debutantes, Charlotte Binghams's delightful and stylish new saga, centres around a single London Season in the eighteen-nineties. But it is not just about the debutantes themselves. It is as much about the women who launch them, and the Society which supports their way of life. It is also about the battle for power, privilege and money, fought, not in the male tradition upon the battlefield, but in the female tradition...in the ballroom.

Now available in Doubleday hardcover
0 385 40605 3

NANNY
by Charlotte Bingham

Grace Merrill is born into the middle-class life of provincial Edwardian England, the world of long golden afternoons, and tea on the lawn. In any other society Grace's talent for painting would be a cause for celebration but, in Keston, Art is simply not the done thing. Despite this, Grace is encouraged in her painting, ironically by the very woman who brings about the destruction of her comfortable world.

Grace is forced to enter service as a lower housemaid at the Great House, Keston Hall. That she rises rapidly through the ranks from housemaid to under-nanny, and eventually nanny, is a source of surprise more to herself than it is to those who know her; least of all her employers, the fascinating and idiosyncratic Lord and Lady Lydiard.

Serena Lydiard and Grace become friends and allies, and Grace becomes devoted to the Lydiard children, Henry and Harriet. But it isn't until the favoured visitor, Society painter Brake Merrowby, falls in love with Grace that she begins to understand the kind of commitment that she has been asked to make to children who, while demanding and securing her love, are not actually hers.

In Grace, **Charlotte Bingham** has created an unforgettable character, a loving soul who cannot bring herself to abandon those who have come to depend on her for that most powerful of emotions, mother love.

Available in Bantam Paperback
0 553 40496 2

IN SUNSHINE OR IN SHADOW

'Superbly written... a romantic novel that is romantic in the true sense of the word' *Daily Mail*

Brougham is the stateliest of stately homes, but for Lady Artemis Deverill it proves a lonely, loveless place. Eleanor Milligan, born in downtown Boston, knows only poverty and a continuing battle against bullying brothers and a sadistic father.

When Artemis and Ellie meet on a liner sailing to Ireland, they become friends, and spend an idyllic time in County Cork. But with the arrival of handsome artist, Hugo Tanner, it seems as though nothing will be quite the same. For in the sunlit prewar summer, all three become emotionally entwined, with startling consequences that threaten to haunt them for the rest of their lives.

Charlotte Bingham

Available in Bantam paperback
0553 40296 x

STARDUST

Elizabeth Laurence is astoundingly beautiful. So beautiful she has never known what it is to have even a plain day. Used to the admiration of all, it seems that she will always be in charge of her own destiny. A star from the first minute she appears on celluloid, her future is certain, until she is cast opposite Jerome Didier in a hit play. Staggeringly handsome and tipped to become the leading actor of his generation, Jerome would appear to be made for Elizabeth.

But Jerome has fallen in love with the tousle-haired and carefree Pippa Nicholls, who is neither conventionally beautiful nor an actress and, much to Elizabeth's fury, he marries her. All is set for them to live happily ever after until the playwright, Oscar Greene, creates a part for Elizabeth which she intuitively recognizes is based on the character of Pippa - and Jerome is tragically deceived by the duplicity of his art.

Set against the glamorous world of theatre in the 1950s, *Stardust* is full of sharp insight into the destructive power of beauty: the stars who possess it, and those who live in their starlight. In Elizabeth, Jerome and Pippa, Charlotte Bingham has created three unforgettable characters, and *Stardust* is the triumphant achievement of a novelist at the height of her storytelling powers.

Charlotte Bingham

Available in Bantam Paperback
0 553 40171 8

TO HEAR A NIGHTINGALE

'A delightful novel pulsating with vitality and deeply felt emotions' *Sunday Express*

Brought up in smalltown America, Cassie McGann's childhood is one of misery and rejection. Fleeing to New York she falls in love with handsome Irish racehorse trainer, Tyrone Rosse, and when he marries her and takes her back to his tumbledown mansion in Ireland, it looks as if she has found happiness at last.

Passionately in love as she is, Cassie finds the all-male world of horses and racing rather lonely. There is much for her to learn, not least about the man she has married. And when tragedy strikes, it seems that Cassie must once again face rejection and lose her hard-won security.

THE BUSINESS

'The ideal beach read' *Homes and Gardens*

Meredith Browne came up the hard way, starting at the bottom as a child actress. Max Kassov has always had everything. Despite their different backgrounds the two are very alike, and a mutual attraction deepens into a passionate love affair. But Max betrays Meredith; a vicious betrayal that leaves her humiliated and determined to rise to even greater heights than he - if only to exact retribution ...

Set in the glittering world of showbusiness, *The Business* is a powerful tale of romance and sex, of money and corruption, and of brilliant talent used and abused.

Charlotte Bingham
Available in Bantam paperback

Meet Georgiana, poor, posh and very beautiful, and Jennifer, rich, middle-class and very fat. Both girls share a common purpose; to find a suitable husband that will enrich or ennoble them.

Follow the changing fortunes of these two wonderful characters and their eccentric contemporaries in **Charlotte Bingham's** sparkling romantic comedy series.

BELGRAVIA

COUNTRY LIFE

AT HOME

BY INVITATION

Published by Bantam Books

A SELECTION OF FINE NOVELS
AVAILABLE FROM BANTAM BOOKS

THE PRICES SHOWN BELOW WERE CORRECT AT THE TIME OF GOING TO PRESS. HOWEVER TRANSWORLD PUBLISHERS RESERVE THE RIGHT TO SHOW NEW RETAIL PRICES ON COVERS WHICH MAY DIFFER FROM THOSE PREVIOUSLY ADVERTISED IN THE TEXT OR ELSEWHERE.

☐	40727 9	**LOVERS AND LIARS**	*Sally Beauman*	£5.99
☐	17632 2	**DARK ANGEL**	*Sally Beauman*	£4.99
☐	17352 9	**DESTINY**	*Sally Beauman*	£4.99
☐	40429 6	**AT HOME**	*Charlotte Bingham*	£3.99
☐	40497 0	**CHANGE OF HEART**	*Charlotte Bingham*	£4.99
☐	40427 X	**BELGRAVIA**	*Charlotte Bingham*	£3.99
☐	41063 7	**THE BUSINESS**	*Charlotte Bingham*	£4.99
☐	40428 8	**COUNTRY LIFE**	*Charlotte Bingham*	£3.99
☐	40296 X	**IN SUNSHINE OR IN SHADOW**	*Charlotte Bingham*	£4.99
☐	40496 2	**NANNY**	*Charlotte Bingham*	£4.99
☐	40171 8	**STARDUST**	*Charlotte Bingham*	£4.99
☐	17635 8	**TO HEAR A NIGHTINGALE**	*Charlotte Bingham*	£4.99
☐	40072 X	**MAGGIE JORDAN**	*Emma Blair*	£4.99
☐	40298 6	**SCARLET RIBBONS**	*Emma Blair*	£4.99
☐	40372 9	**THE WATER MEADOWS**	*Emma Blair*	£4.99
☐	40373 7	**THE SWEETEST THING**	*Emma Blair*	£4.99
☐	40614 0	**THE DAFFODIL SEA**	*Emma Blair*	£4.99
☐	40504 7	**FLOWERS ON THE MERSEY**	*June Francis*	£3.99
☐	40719 8	**FRIENDS AND LOVERS**	*June Francis*	£4.99
☐	40820 8	**LILY'S WAR**	*June Francis*	£4.99
☐	40400 8	**A SEASON IN PURGATORY**	*Dominick Dunne*	£4.99
☐	40321 4	**AN INCONVENIENT WOMAN**	*Dominick Dunne*	£4.99
☐	17676 5	**PEOPLE LIKE US**	*Dominick Dunne*	£3.99
☐	17189 5	**THE TWO MRS GRENVILLES**	*Dominick Dunne*	£3.50
☐	40730 9	**LOVERS**	*Judith Krantz*	£4.99
☐	17504 1	**DAZZLE**	*Judith Krantz*	£4.99
☐	17242 5	**I'LL TAKE MANHATTAN**	*Judith Krantz*	£4.99
☐	17174 7	**MISTRAL'S DAUGHTER**	*Judith Krantz*	£2.95
☐	17389 8	**PRINCESS DAISY**	*Judith Krantz*	£4.99
☐	17505 X	**SCRUPLES TWO**	*Judith Krantz*	£4.99
☐	17503 3	**TILL WE MEET AGAIN**	*Judith Krantz*	£4.99
☐	40206 4	**FAST FRIENDS**	*Jill Mansell*	£3.99
☐	40361 3	**KISS**	*Jill Mansell*	£4.99
☐	40360 5	**SOLO**	*Jill Mansell*	£3.99
☐	40612 4	**OPEN HOUSE**	*Jill Mansell*	£4.99
☐	40682 5	**THE GOOD MOTHER**	*Sue Miller*	£5.99
☐	40642 6	**FOR LOVE**	*Sue Miller*	£5.99
☐	40816 X	**IF WISHES WERE HORSES**	*Francine Pascal*	£5.99
☐	40720 1	**MALINA**	*Penny Perrick*	£4.99
☐	17630 7	**DOCTORS**	*Erich Segal*	£5.99
☐	17209 3	**THE CLASS**	*Erich Segal*	£5.99